GOLDHEART

FOXGLOVE & FEUD
BOOK 1

TESS CARLETTA

ISBN 9798988101567 (paperback), ISBN 9798988101574 (eBook)

Cover illustration by Jan Falk of Thistle Arts
Cover layout by Sleepy Fox Studio
Interior formatting by Tess Carletta
Developmental editing by Rhiannon Martinucci
Copy editing by Sam Willow of Scrollwork Edits
Accuracy reading by Jaida McDonald (@jaysbookiverse)
Map Art by Melissa Nash

First edition 2025

CONTENTS

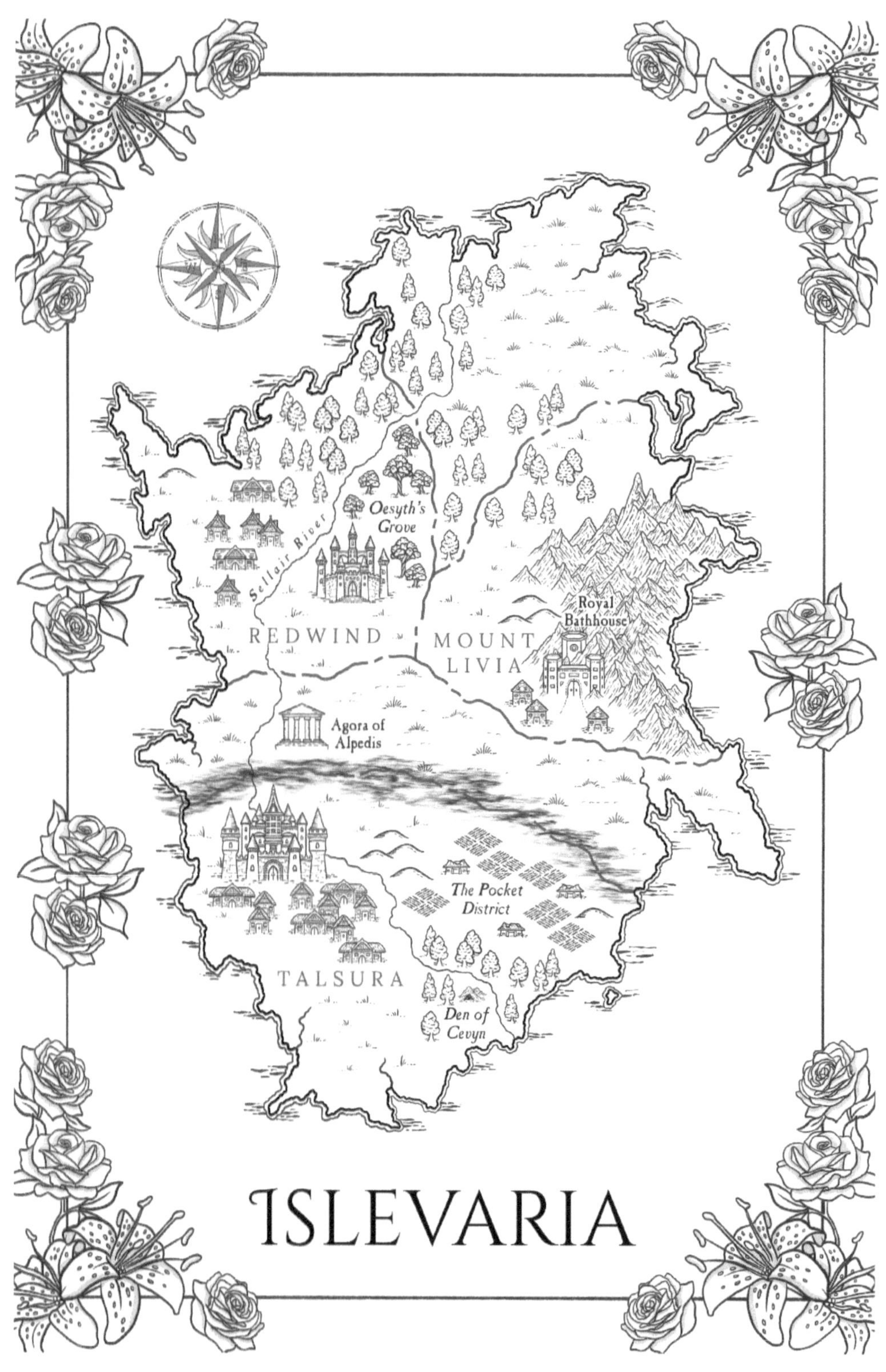

Oesyth's Grove
Sellair River
REDWIND
MOUNT LIVIA
Royal Bathhouse
Agora of Alpedis
The Pocket District
TALSURA
Den of Cevyn
ISLEVARIA

Content Warnings

Body horror (humanoid monsters)

Brief binge eating episode

Major character death

Mentions of child abuse

Dissociation

Emotional manipulation

Grief

Physical and emotional religious abuse

Past parent loss

Minor self-harm

Graphic depictions of starvation

Trypophobia (plants coming out of skin)

Brief instances of vomiting

Lastly, this book contains consensual cannibalism, in which characters grow fruit from their bodies in a sexual setting and partake. All participants remain unharmed.

Pronunciation Guide

Alpedis: ahl-pay-dis

Acathea: ah-kay-thee-ah

Caenia: kay-nia

Canon: kay-non

Ceday: sih-day

Cevyn: like "seven"

Hedela: hee-day-la

Ilias: like "Elias"

Islevaria: aisle-vah-ria

Nare: nah-rah

THE ASSEMBLY OF CANONS

Alpedis - canon of sky and sun

Cevyn - canon of lost things

Hedela - canon of healing

Jasrath - canon of thieves

Oesyth - canon of favors

Rira - canon of destruction

Varyan - canon of inflorescence

Part One

O N THE DAY HE became the goldheart, nine-year-old Senna Kane fell asleep in his cot with his only friend and woke tangled up in a corpse.

A bone-deep sting wrenched Senna from the refuge of his dreams. He lurched awake, pawing at his legs like an injured animal, finding the burning wound wet with blood. He was used to his scratchy sheets, but they'd never hurt him. Not like this.

Pulling back his yellowing sheets, Senna found woody, claw-like barbs half-stuck in the gashes tearing through his thin skin. He hissed, trying to scramble backward, only to find that the thorns leached through the entire mattress. There was nowhere he could put his hands or feet that would not bite.

Yet, the scariest thing was not that thorns had somehow beset his bed, but that Orphan Mother Mabel would come when the sun rose and punish him for the mess his bloody limbs left behind.

Senna bit his lip to keep from crying out as he felt through the dark, over the thorns, in search of smooth blankets. He froze when something cold and damp smeared over his fingers. Listening to make sure no one else in the orphanage was stirring, Senna held his breath and snapped his fingers nearly silently. A tear of fire no bigger than a match lit on Senna's thumb. Breath shaking, he moved the tiny light over the bed, only to stop when he realized where the thorns had stemmed from.

Conall Gray. Senna's best—and only—friend at the orphanage.

Conall's throat was torn wide open by thorns as big and as sharp as wooden stakes. They protruded out of his mouth, dislodging his jaw and spilling blood from his tear ducts. The massive thorns had grown tendrils, which had spread about the bed, over Conall's body, and through the hay of the mattress to claw at Senna's body.

"Conall," Senna mouthed. He couldn't speak. His voice had been stolen by misery and fear long ago. But it didn't matter. He knew Conall would not wake.

But how could such a thing have happened? Only a few hours ago, Conall had been crawling into his bed, saying *"I don't feel quite right"* and *"Could I sleep with you, Senna?"* Hadn't he just been breathing beside Senna minutes ago?

Was this the sun sickness he'd heard the Orphan Mother and Mister MacBennal whispering about in the kitchen? Senna squirmed, nausea churning in his stomach. Was it contagious? Would this happen to him too?

Downstairs, someone banged on the orphanage's front door. None of the other children stirred at the sound, so Senna crept out of bed and peered out the window. Perhaps it was a healer come to help?

A carriage like from a storybook was parked in the street. From it emerged a woman wearing a black gown and a spiderweb veil. Senna knew this type of lady. So many of them came in their mourning clothes when they'd lost a baby and wanted another.

The walls muffled the conversation downstairs, leaving only the sound of two stringent women exchanging muddied words. But Senna heard when the voices died away and the Orphan Mother began to climb the stairs toward the sleeping quarters.

It was with all the bravery he could muster that Senna lay back into the bed of thorns, covered his bleeding legs with the stained sheet, and forced his face to fall lax. Through the crack in his eyelids, he could not look away from Conall's ruptured form.

Mother Mabel did not knock when entering the room. She bounded in like a storm, a flash of terror before the thunder of her movement. Through cracked eyes, Senna watched her tear the blankets off the other boys, appraising their arms and legs. She tsked with each one, plucking little clovers off of elbows and yanking tiny wildflowers that wound up around knees.

It'd been happening so much lately—the other children growing strange plants from their skin. None so bad as Conall, but then, Senna wondered if maybe it was the same thing, only worse. Senna had been checking his own body for days, just shy of obsession. Each time he looked, his skin was perfectly smooth—no plants in sight.

The same could not be said of Logan, the oldest of the boys, who had been coughing up prickly ivy. Nor Diro, a boy who had been made as quiet as Senna by roots sewing his lips shut. Mother Mabel approached them all, becoming more frenzied with each boy she passed.

When she made it to his bed, Senna waited through the silence for Mother Mabel to observe that Conall had been devoured in the night. He prepared himself for whatever would come next. A shriek of horror. A bout of sobs. Maybe she'd even be sick, like Senna felt he would be.

Instead, she sighed, as if inconvenienced.

"Even a cockroach's death is foul," she muttered bitterly.

Senna's heart sank further than he knew it could go. His own horror and devastation began to swell in his stomach, mixed with the onslaught of a single thought: *I hate Mother Mabel. I hate Mother Mabel. I _hate_ Mother Mabel.*

A chill ran down his spine when the same wretched object of his ire turned her gaze to him.

"Senna, dear," she said, as if getting an idea. "You never go outside. You're an obedient little rat."

Senna fought to keep his eyes closed, but it was in vain. What was she talking about?

Like the life-sucking teeth of a viper, Mother Mabel's hand clawed into Senna's hair, pulling him up and away from the bed. Senna's body dragged painfully across the thorns into the air. Tears trickled down his face now, ebbed on by his fear.

The lines of Mother Mabel's frown were blade-sharp as she assessed him.

"Are you dying?" she asked him.

"W-what?" Senna whispered. His ability to speak at full volume had been gone so long, he couldn't remember what his voice sounded like above these terrified murmurs.

"Are you stupid?" Mother Mabel pressed. "Do you have the plant disease? The sun sickness?"

Senna dropped his gaze down to Conall. That *was* the sun sickness, wasn't it? If Conall became like—like *this* from the sun, then Senna didn't have it. He hadn't played outside with the other children in . . . he couldn't remember how long.

Clenching his teeth together, Senna shook his head, assured.

"Good. Change out of those filthy clothes this instant."

With that, she dropped him with as much care as a dirty sock. The crash of his body against the floor woke the rest of the boys, but Senna didn't dare look up at them. He found his singular set of clothes from the decrepit chest all the boys kept their sour-smelling belongings in and changed. Mother Mabel only snapped at him twice to hurry up.

Leaving the bloodied clothes beside his bed in a heap, Senna spared one last glance at Conall, and followed Mabel downstairs.

The woman from the carriage sat alone on the only nice chair the parlor had. Her overflowing black skirts spilled onto the dusty floor. She folded her hands together, the dainty gloves the same midnight color as her dress. Her veil might not have hidden her features so well in the daylight, but in the dawnless orphanage parlor, Senna might as well have been trying to recognize a ghost.

Up close, Senna could smell the sickly sweetness of her perfume. It reminded him of a time he'd watched a funeral procession march up the street past his cracked window. The perfume they'd drenched the coffin in, mixed with the awful scent of rot, had been so strong, he'd smelled it from his bed and gagged. Senna didn't think Mother Mabel would appreciate it if he gagged in front of a noble lady, so he breathed through his mouth.

"Answer 'yes' to all of her questions," Mother Mabel hissed into his ear. "And let her *hear* you, damn it."

She turned to the woman.

"He's the only boy who isn't sick with weeds," Mabel said, taking on her best high society tone. It sounded forced and unfamiliar, even to Senna's young ears.

"Yes," the woman agreed smoothly. "But is he immune?"

Mabel turned to Senna, nudging him to answer and he remembered what he'd been told.

"Yes," he mouthed. The woman lifted a brow.

"Can you *speak*, boy?"

Senna hesitated, but the woman waved her hand dismissively.

"Just as well. I prefer it when they don't talk. Ilias had so many *opinions*," she noted to Mabel. It reminded Senna of one of the rare times he'd been in the market watching a farmer sell a lame cow for meat.

Without warning, the woman cycled through more questions than Senna could keep track of. Was he strong? Could he read? Was he a hard worker and a fast learner? If given the chance to prove to the royal family that he was the most loyal boy in Talsura, would he?

"Yes," he answered, this time managing with his voice. Yes, Yes, yes, yes, until it stopped sounding like a word.

It was the first time Senna could remember lying to anyone. In fact, it was the first conversation Senna had found himself a member of in quite some time. He had questions of his own, but he suspected a woman in fine clothes like these had better things to do than subdue his confusion.

"There's blood trailing down his arms and legs. Why is that?" This question was directed at the Orphan Mother.

"Sometimes the youngest boys find comfort in each other's company when they miss their parents," Mabel explained. Though she made it sound like a pitiful symptom of their orphanhood, and not the grave transgression she usually spanked the boys for. "The boy who shared Senna's pillow last night unfortunately succumbed to the sickness. There were thorns all over the poor boy's bed, Your Majesty."

Senna's frightened gaze snapped to the woman. *Your Majesty?*

Queen Phaedra lifted her veil, revealing her pallid skin and face of sunken features. She'd applied some sort of rouge powder over the colorless apples of her cheeks, but it was like trying to give a corpse life. She seemed like the sort of woman who had let heartache take over her entire countenance. Senna bore a small hope that if the queen saw what he had endured, she would force Mother Mabel to stop.

Instead, she curled her fingers around each other and said, "You slept on thorns and did not complain?"

Senna shifted his weight.

"As you have observed, the boy does not speak," Mother Mabel said through her teeth.

"Then I believe he shall suit my purposes quite nicely." The queen knelt before Senna so they stood eye to eye. "What is your name?"

"Senna," he rasped. "Senna Kane."

The queen smiled, a thing made of dark edges instead of actual pleasure.

"Long live Senna Kane," the queen said. "Goldheart of Talsura."

SENNA

EIGHTEEN YEARS LATER

Today was the day Senna Kane discovered the rumors were true: the queen of Talsura *did* keep the last polluted dredges of sunshine all for herself in a jar.

He had to crane his neck to get a good look at the empty poison bottle on her shelf, but the bead of bright light swirling around inside was unmistakable.

How like the queen to hoard for herself the one thing she forbade her kingdom from having. Judging by the size of the bottle, there wasn't any to share. Just a single sun drop trapped in a cage, unable to help—or hurt—anyone. Senna remained transfixed by the solar tear, unblinking as the pearl of fiery light churned on itself in an endless cycle. *Flicker, grow grow grow, die down. Spin. Flicker.*

"I see my prized possession has caught your attention."

Senna felt all of his nerves jolt. Among all of the queen's detestable qualities, Senna's least favorite was her tendency to move about like her feet need not touch the floor. He strongly suspected she had her office door oiled regularly to keep it from moaning, always keeping her visitors on edge. Senna was not immune to surprise, but he had trained his body to contain his reactions. She might've snuck in with the intention of rattling him, but he refused to give her the satisfaction. Instead, he clenched his fists, shot out of his chair, and stood at attention.

Senna was careful to keep his head bowed, letting his eyes slip up just enough to track her narrow slippers and silken skirts as they crossed the floor. To his surprise, she didn't take the seat at her pristine desk. Instead, she plucked the jar of sunlight off the shelf and gave it a shake.

If she had been anyone else, Senna would've had the authority to snatch the bottle out of her hands and refuse to hand it back. The bottle contained the only brightness Talsura had to offer, and the queen was rattling it like a child tormenting a pixie.

"You know, I've never had a bigger thrill than the day I made the decree to the mages to raise the Dam and block out the sun," she mused. "A bit risky in the moment, but fear gives way to exhilaration, given time."

Senna's gaze drifted to the window behind her desk. The Dam's black swirling veil covered the kingdom, stretching far into the horizon, blanketing every inch of the sky in black. He'd lived under its inky darkness for eighteen years now and he hadn't felt the exhilaration yet.

"One of the apprentice mages went wild with grief," Phaedra continued. "He was so angry that all of his magic had to go toward raising the Dam, that he used the very last of his power to bottle up this sunlight to keep. I apprehended the jar and now it sits on my shelf as a reminder."

She peered at him through the jar. His own reflection met him on the other side, his face nearly the same color as the warm brown amber of the glass. The rest of him, his round gold eyes and full mouth, were perfectly neutral.

"Do you remember sunlight, Goldheart?" Phaedra wondered.

It wasn't the first time Senna had been asked to recall a time before the sun sickness and the Dam. Only—it was the first time the question had come from Queen Phaedra. He had lived inside the walls of her candlelit castle long enough to detect traces of suspicion and ulterior motives in everything the queen said. That was her lifework, in his estimation. To manipulate words, to twist them and disguise them, until their true purpose was barely a wisp of memory.

Senna was not thusly blessed. Sometimes it felt like his mind and his throat worked together as an ancient machine, chugging words into phrases and phrases into sentences. The gears of the mechanism were clunky and unoiled, only allowing him words in short supply, and only to those he trusted. When his voice finally managed to spill out over his lips, it usually sounded like snipped up sandpaper.

That she had asked this *today* of all times made Senna's stomach churn with wary suspicion. Did she *know?*

It took all of Senna's concentration to remain neutral. His body would not allow him to answer. After eighteen years, Phaedra was accustomed to his silence. She continued as if her question had merely been rhetorical.

"I admit, my memory of it is so wholly underwhelming. I don't understand those who prefer it." She shoved the jar in his direction. "Hold it. See if it sparks any recollection."

Senna did not take the captured sunlight. If he held the jar with the reverence it deserved, she could accuse him of treason—of going against the decree she'd made right after he became goldheart: *"To desire for the days of sunlight is to dishonor the harrowing deaths of your own people. It is poison. It is corruption. But I swear I will rid this kingdom of its unholy curse."*

It was a disgraceful contradiction. Phaedra had caused nearly all of the *harrowing deaths* by exiling all the sick Talsurans to the open moorlands beyond the kingdom's boundaries—damning them to endure miles of pure sunlight. Only a third of them had survived the exile. Maybe that was why she kept sunshine in her office. Not to remember it, but to abuse it. To trap it in a bottle of poisonous vapors and set her wrath upon it, just as she had done with the exiles.

"Well?" Phaedra asked, still holding out the bottle. "Anything?"

Senna shook his head.

"Very well. Sit."

Dread brewed like a potion of expired ingredients in Senna's stomach, thick and vile. He'd been so distracted by keeping Phaedra off his scent, he'd forgotten the real purpose of this meeting.

Queen Phaedra sat at her desk with the same regal terror with which she sat on her throne. Using the same withering command that brought her subjects to their knees, Phaedra folded her hands and said, "What is your report, Goldheart?"

"I . . ." *You command your voice, Senna Kane,* he thought. *Command it!* "I . . ."

They did this every half year and it was always the bloody same.

"Were you able to complete the inspection or not?" Phaedra demanded.

Senna's hand clutched the hilt of his blade. They both already knew the answer.

"A loud silence, and yet, one that does not signify," she mused, opening her ledgers. "What do you suggest I mark in the written record for the Gray House Orphanage inspection? Your report is . . ."

He might as well let his report speak for itself. He reached into his satchel and slid the parchment across her desk. From his chair, he could see the word *INCONCLUSIVE* scrawled into the results section at the bottom.

Phaedra didn't even bother writing the word down before slamming the book closed.

"Inconclusive *again*. Tell me, Goldheart. How can a man be the highest ranking knight in his kingdom and get shaky knees doing a simple inspection of his own home?"

Senna wanted to scoff. That dank, musty rathole could barely be deemed a *building*, much less anyone's home.

"Tell me, did you even make it past the front door?"

Senna looked down. He had not.

"A report cannot be classified as inconclusive if it is not even *started*. It baffles me that time after time, you always return with an empty sheet of paper. I thought that it was only right that you were the one to do rounds on the orphanage. Those children are practically your siblings. Don't you want to help keep them safe?" continued the queen.

He did. That was why it was even worse when he couldn't. He'd knocked on the orphanage's door, taken one look at Orphan Mother Mabel, and felt for a disorienting moment that he'd been peeled out of his own skin. He hadn't had to announce what he was there for, which was fortunate, since he didn't believe he would've been able to.

"Oh, Senna, how you've grown into such an obedient young man! I know you're here for the inspection, but the children are all sleeping and they ought not be

disturbed. But you trust us, right? You know we would never *hurt a child,"* Orphan Mother Mabel had said.

Senna had opened his mouth to try to speak, but Mabel's expression had dropped in a heartbeat, turning dire and callous. It was as if the breath had been stolen from him. He couldn't have uttered a word if he'd tried.

Her voice had been all frozen acid when she'd snapped, *"Listen to your mother, Senna."*

To his own disgust, he'd obeyed. His body had been numb as he'd stomped away, save for his racing pulse, which still hadn't quieted.

What Senna really wanted to know was why the highest ranking knight in Talsura had been burdened with the responsibility of performing inspections at all when there had been a perfectly qualified auditor before him—one who didn't get *shaky knees*. Deep down, though, he had a guess.

In giving Senna an impossible task, Phaedra could keep him chained down on the tight leash she had him on. It kept him permanently in her displeasure, in hopes that he'd be quick to fear and obey—and it had worked.

Across the desk, the queen sighed. In the dim candlelight of the royal office, Senna noted the disappointed lines of her mouth were curled deeper than they usually were. But when he finally mustered enough defiance to meet Phaedra's eyes, he found them *eager*.

"There are many individuals of your same training, you know," she said finally. "Those who would be able to complete all of the things their queen asks them to do. I've kept you on as my son's goldheart because of his attachment to you. Lately though, I've wondered if your shortcomings are proving too insurmountable. How can you possibly uphold protection of your prince in this condition? Perhaps it is time to pursue a replacement."

"No."

This time, the word tumbled out of Senna's mouth without a moment's hesitation. Pain tore up his arm as he clenched his fingernails into his palm. She couldn't actually be considering . . . She *wouldn't*.

"I have oft given you the benefit of my endless fount of mercy, but even wells grow dry. Provide me one good reason why I shouldn't assign Percy a more qualified goldheart."

Senna didn't have to search his mind: the reason wasn't one Phaedra would accept. He was the only person who could keep Percy safe. Hells, Percy was the only person Senna could *talk* to. Neither of them had anyone else. If Senna was reassigned, he would be plagued with dragging around his wasted failure—worthless and utterly alone.

He couldn't tell Phaedra any of that and—thank the canons—he didn't have to. Because as soon as he opened his mouth to utter the first acceptable excuse that came to his mind, the study door slammed open, hitting the wall so hard the floor shook. An iron-breasted silverheart poured in through the opening, clasping his hand over his chest with a slight bow. Senna rose to his feet and returned the gesture.

"Your Majesty, I'm afraid there's been a breach in one of the northern trade channels. Sentries report sighting at least a dozen Grit Fingers throughout the network. Exact numbers are unclear, but it seems the Grits have roped in the support of non-guilded thieves. Maybe an initiation of sorts?"

On instinct, Senna snuck a hand under his cloak and squeezed his knuckles against his gilded sword. He had known it would only be a matter of time before this happened. Talsura had been no stranger to theft in the days before the sun had been blocked away, but now that the kingdom existed under a pool of darkness, instances of stealing and heists had catapulted. The Grit Fingers were the most skilled of the recent thieving guilds, known for leaving no evidence behind except their sooty fingerprints. They were said to live in the abandoned houses in the east Pocket District, spread as plentiful and difficult to catch as sewer rats.

"We require permission to initiate a blockade," concluded the silverheart.

Careful to stand perfectly still, Senna thumbed the embedded gem at the heart of his sword's hilt, a nervous habit he'd picked up as a child during knightheart training. Of all the days to plan their first escape.

Senna had never believed Percy when he'd said that their first trip out of Talsura would be easy. It'd taken months for Percy to convince Senna to allow it, then even *more* months for Senna to craft the perfect escape plan. But even he couldn't have expected this.

Worse, Percy was meant to be waiting in the northwestern channels right this second. If Senna was lucky, Percy would've had the wisdom to retreat back to the castle. But Senna was generally not a very lucky individual, and Percy's judgment was rarely sound when tempted with any notions of *freedom*. If Senna was going to do something, it needed to happen right now.

Senna nearly made it all the way over the office's threshold when Phaedra called out his name.

"Where do you think you're going?" she demanded.

"To Percy," he answered, as if it were simple. And it was. Because even if the queen wanted to demand that Senna be confined to his seat until he resigned, she had an image to maintain. One that included pretending to care for her son's protection.

Jaw tightening, Phaedra waved him away. Senna didn't wait around for her to change her mind.

S ENNA MADE IT UNDERGROUND without anyone being any wiser. He imagined that was part of the reason the Grits had managed to slither inside in the first place.

There were entrances to the trade channels all over the kingdom—you only needed to know where to look to find them. The castle had access to channel entrances with actual latching doors and stairs, but today's plan involved the hatch in one of the forgotten linen closets. Like the rest of the underground trade channels, it'd been created to allow traders from outside Talsura—merchants who didn't fear the sun—to deliver their goods to those living inside the Dam. Now, with animosity festering on both sides of the Dam and strict trade rulings from the queen, outside traders ventured in less and less.

This was all so foolish, Senna thought, trying to follow his mental map of the trade channels. He'd only gone along with it because Percy—with his adventurous heart—had gotten himself too involved by the time Senna had learned enough to stop him.

It began two years ago with a letter Percy had magically, secretly sent to the princess of the nearby rival kingdom.

Redwind.

It was home to the Talsuran exiles who had survived the sun sickness—people who had not only recovered, but thrived from the sun's magic and made it their own. They refused to hide from the sun, instead harnessing the magic that had been so cruelly bestowed upon them. Courageously and purposefully, they grew plant life from their bodies and cast magic with the power the growths gave them. It was the ultimate spit in the face to Queen Phaedra.

They called it inflorescence. Quietly, Senna admired it, even if he didn't understand how it was possible.

By fate or by miracle, the princess had responded. Percy had burst into Senna's quarters, exclaiming that, *"The princess was moved by my honesty and humor, and has offered to be my friend!"* It was only when he caught his breath that he remembered he was meant to be keeping a secret. Senna had merely laughed. The damage had already been done.

After, Percy insisted on reading all of Princess Thea's letters aloud to Senna. Senna had done his best to remain wary, but it was hard not to be drawn in by her eloquent descriptions of all that they lacked. The wonders of the dawn and dusk. The joy of eating food fresh from a garden. The comfort of sunbathing. In turn, Percy offered what he could in return: palace gossip and his thoughts on her favorite book.

Things shifted the day Percy told Thea the truth of the dreary lives the Talsurans lived. Once he'd begun writing, he couldn't stop. He'd sent page after page after page expounding on his frustration with the sunless sky, the flavorless, magically enhanced food, and the headaches he got from artificial light sources. Instead of showering Percy with pity, the princess offered a solution: Percy should come to Redwind himself, and together, they would find a way to repair the relations between their kingdoms and give Talsurans back their sunlight.

That visit was today.

That left Senna where he was now—sprinting through the underground trade channels in hopes he could reach Percy before the Grit Fingers did. Every groove on the stone walls and every flame torch would've seemed dizzyingly repetitive to anyone else, but Senna navigated the tunnels with ease. He hoped beyond all hope that he'd make it in time, but it was tight. Without the luxury of a map, he had to trust his instincts and memory. But if he was right, he only had to turn one more corner before he'd arrive at the prearranged meeting place—a checkpoint room where traders used to eat their meals while traveling.

Voices echoed around the corner, cheering in a jaunty accent all the royal knighthearts were forced to lose in their training. That could only mean one thing—he was too late.

Ignoring the sinking dread of his heart, Senna stepped into the room's doorway. The sight before him almost made him drop his arm to his sides in surprise.

Prince Percy Laurent of Talsura was in the side room, sitting at a wooden table with three masked thieves *playing cards*.

Percy was at the northernmost chair, five cards pulled so closely to his face, they almost blocked out his look of growing satisfaction. He was dressed in his traveling clothes that gave no hint of his royal station. His brown hair was combed, but loose on his face, kept out of his brown eyes only by his round glasses. The rest of his face was softer than many thought a prince's ought to be, but Senna had promised Percy that age would strengthen his jaw and brow.

In the remaining seats, the thieves appraised their own cards and eyed the prince with reluctant scowls.

"Sun slay me," one of them murmured at their hand. Senna was inclined to agree.

He'd been so taken aback by the strange sight, that when the shadows at either side of him dissolved into human beings with rusty daggers, he barely had any time to react. He reached for his sword, but before he could produce it from its sheath, one of the pointed daggers pressed beneath his bottom rib. Somehow, they'd slinked behind him.

"I'd think very carefully about your next move if I was you, baneheart," seethed one of the bandits from under their stained mask. It'd been some time since Senna had heard that word. *Baneheart.* It didn't offend him so much as the thief's rotten breath spilling over his face.

Setting his jaw, Senna lifted his hands from his blade and held them up in the air. He had no doubt that he could overpower a group of this size, but with Percy in such tight quarters, it wasn't worth taking any risks.

"I'll just be takin' that," said the thief closest to the sword. She had her filthy hold on it in a second, drawing it from its scabbard and tossing it to the ground by the table. "No funny movements now." She twisted her own rusty blade, the blunt tip nearly slicing a tear in Senna's leather jacket. "I really hate laughing."

Senna glanced up at Percy—who was not bothered, nor paying attention—and cleared his throat.

Percy looked up at the sight, threatening blades and all, and grinned in delight.

"Oh, hullo, Sen! Is it that time already?" In his excitement, he dipped his cards, revealing them to a man beside him. The bandit had tattooed black lines like snake pupils over his eyelids, a threat with every blink.

"I fold," Snake-Eyes groaned, tossing his cards on the table. "Buggering git's got a royal flush."

"Hey! Bad form, old fellow," protested Percy. "I saw your cards two times this round and you didn't see me announce it to the table. But now I think I might. Eat him alive, boys. This man only has a pair of twos!" Then to the bandits surrounding Senna: "For the love of Alpedis, you don't need *two* blades turned on him. One is quite sufficient. As you might've *rudely* heard, I will be ending this shortly."

"*Percy,*" Senna said lowly as the daggers inched closer to him.

Over the course of their twelve years paired together, Percy's name had come to mean an abundance of things when uttered from Senna's careful lips: *Sorry, I will not help you sneak chocolates into your bedroom. They have not yet been tested for poison.* Or *Please do not go searching for "pretty stones" in the riverbank; the water is filthy and you have a whole closet of jewels in the castle.* Or simply *No, no, absolutely not.*

In this case, it meant *Why the dark hells are you playing cards with a gaggle of thieves?*

Percy chuckled nervously. "Well . . . where does one begin?" He folded his hands together on top of his cards and pursed his lips. "It appears I've been captured. Or, perhaps more accurately, taken hostage."

"It was more of a snatching," suggested one of the thieves, barely looking up from over his hand of cards.

"Right you are, good fellow," Percy agreed. He turned to Senna resolutely and amended, "I've been snatched."

Senna's eyes passed over the thieves at the table, who watched him in return with lazy disinterest. He was proud to state that Percy had never come to any harm under his protection. But that wasn't to say that he hadn't been kept up at night wondering what it *would* be like if it finally did happen. The scenarios plaguing his mind involved filth-ridden scoundrels. Blades pressed too tightly against Percy's throat, drawing beads of scarlet blood. Goads and jeers of *Come on, Goldheart. Show us how low your balls hang and save your dearest prince.* He'd imagined spilling blood and nearly collapsing from relief after a very close call.

He'd imagined . . . well, *not* whatever was happening here.

"Your hands aren't tied," Senna observed.

"Well, I very well couldn't expect to play cards with them bound up, could I?"

Senna felt a bit as though he'd gone to sleep and never truly stopped dreaming. He peered down the long corridor, toward where the cave would open its mouth wide into open air and away from Talsura. Next, he turned his ear to the corridor he'd come from. No echoing sound of fellow guards approaching—they were completely on their own.

"Lower your blades," he ordered impatiently.

The hands holding the daggers wavered. Senna did not often give commands, but when he did, he knew how to lace them with poison that could make even a grown giant tremble. He found orders like these were not as difficult as regular speech, having practiced them so much during his goldheart training as a boy.

"We're going," continued Senna.

"Wish I could, but uh . . ." Percy shrugged. "The trouble is, my *feet* are tied."

To prove his point, Percy kicked his legs out from under the table. Sure enough, his ankles were bound four times over with hemp rope. The knot was such a pitiful thing, Percy probably could have wriggled his feet free if he hadn't minded the bite from the scratchy twine.

Senna turned to the rest of the table.

"Unbind him."

"No no no," Snake-Eyes chirped amiably. "Now that we caught one rat, I think we want another!" He slammed his cards on the table hard enough to send them flying over the edge.

He did not match Senna's notion of what a thief ought to look like, all stout legs and arms so strong they did not lie flat against his sides. A man of such musculature could not be expected to possess the stealth required for even a novice pickpocket. When he rose to his feet, though, he fixed Senna with a stare that revealed another skill entirely: intimidation.

Snake-Eyes rounded the table, tossing a cord of rope in his hand like a child's ball. Senna inched back a step, only to be met by a third dagger pointed into his side. Its wielder stared up at him from beneath her long fringed hair.

"Move and your innards will taste rust," she rasped.

"You're wasting your energy on the wrong people," Percy said exasperatedly. "If you desire the castle's jewels, then your efforts are better suited in the vaults and not in our caves. We won't stop you."

"This is strange. Strange indeed. Must concede," Snake-Eyes hummed. "The generous rats welcome us to the crown jewels? What pitiful protection! What failure of arms!"

If they wanted to see Senna protect the crown, then who was he to withhold a demonstration?

With barely a gasp of warning, Senna spun to the first bandit, ramming both fists into the hand bearing the knife. The blade went flying out of his hold, skittering at Percy's feet. The second attacker jabbed Senna with an off-balanced grip. Senna lurched to the side, leaving a window open for the blade to lodge deep into the arm of the bandit behind him. She yelped, dropping her blade, blood dying her dark clothes midnight black. The last armed bandit stood frozen, wide-eyed at what he'd done. Senna kneed him and seized his short sword deftly.

The color drained from Snake-Eyes' already pale face. He dove to grab Senna's forgotten sword, but Senna was quicker. He turned both his gemmed blade and the bloody short sword on to him.

Behind Snake-Eyes, Percy grabbed the knife and sliced through the bindings at his feet. They really should've tied his hands up.

"I see the mistake," Percy chimed in, as if he were clarifying someone's slip of the tongue. When the bandits spun to him, he was unbound and steady on his feet. "I'm not a guard at all. I'm the prince. Here I had been wondering why you didn't go straight for my signet ring." He held it up like a bride boasting of her betrothal ring. "Now, I suggest you reconsider this whole snatching business."

Face red with some strange mix of anger and humiliation, Snake-Eyes turned a snarling lip at Percy.

"You're a whoreson," he spat.

Percy only shrugged. "I count my cards too."

Snake-Eyes drew a small moon-edged dagger from his belt and tried to cleave it into Percy's space. Senna was faster. Expelling an ounce of his pent-up frustration, he punted his boot into Snake-Eyes' chest, sending him flying backward. The bandit hit the jagged cave wall so hard it knocked the air from his lungs and dislodged the mask covering his lower face. He pushed onto his elbows to fight back, but a call from down the corridor stopped them in their tracks.

Senna tossed a look at Percy. *Better late than never.*

Filling the length of the cave came copperhearts and silverhearts, swords drawn and shields raised. They spilled forward with a thunderous fury, their roars only amplified by the hollow stone walls.

"That's our cue," Percy murmured, coming up behind Senna. "Now come, before the guards see us."

An escape artist in his own right, Percy dashed through the door and off down the empty corridor in the direction of freedom and clean, open air. Senna followed close behind, but not before dragging the wooden table in the way of the bandit who had tried to stop them. It hit their gut, forcing out an impressive wheeze.

A second later, the knighthearts descended upon the bandits.

Senna and Percy were long gone.

THERE WAS A CHANCE that if Senna took one more step, he would die.

A few seconds in the sunlight wasn't enough to kill most people, but it wasn't impossible. He'd seen the sun sickness in person often enough to know that sometimes, it came without warning. Just a brush against a warm sunbeam and he might begin to feel the telltale burning itch of thorns and leaves breaking through his skin. If he didn't retreat back into the shadows immediately, they would plug his throat and wrap around his heart. Every empty space inside of him would fill with snarled roots until there was no room left, forcing the sickness to break through the surface.

When the sun was done with him, there'd be nothing remaining but a killed trophy Mother Nature could claim for herself.

Of course, there was always a chance that the inflorescence would be slow. That the itch wouldn't burn, that he'd make it through the day with only a few clover leaves on his arms.

It all depended on his ability to withstand it. Some said it depended on the favor with the canons, the pathetic gods who had cursed Talsura in the first place. Senna had long given up on trying to get them to listen. If this was going to work, he had to do it himself.

He and Percy now stood at the end of the trade channel, the open world of sunlight just an arm's reach away. Senna had half a mind to grab Percy by his royal belt and drag him back to the palace. Anywhere under the doming misty black veil that blocked out the sun was safer than out among the sunbeams.

"Don't even think about changing your mind now," Percy said, eyeing the reluctant expression on Senna's face. "It took months of convincing you to go along with this. I still don't know how I managed it."

Senna sighed. It was no secret that he had a soft spot for Percy, having practically raised him as a baby to the eighteen-year-old prince he was now. He'd never seen anything give Percy joy like the letters they received almost daily from their friends in Redwind. Percy kept impeccable care of each missive that magically appeared before him, tucking them safely in a locked box at the bottom of his dresser. If the letters brought this much happiness, Senna could only imagine what it would be like once they all met in person.

There was also the selfish nudging that made Senna honored that the prince would share such precious secrets with him.

"I trust you with my life already, Sen," Percy had told him once. *"I can certainly trust you with my secrets. They're tawdry little things, anyway."*

To Senna, they were gifts—ones that he would repay today by protecting Percy with his life.

"Well, no time like the present," Percy announced. "Do you think maybe I should go about it pinky first? The pinky is easiest to remove if it starts to sprout.

I believe it's the only finger I could lose that wouldn't affect my handwriting and I doubt my mother would notice it missing."

"Just take a step out," Senna replied, more evenly than he felt. "If either of us notices any inflorescence, I'll pull you back in."

Percy's terrified eyes drifted to the world before them both. Blinking against the shocking light, Senna thought they might be looking at a field of green wild grass, but it was too bright to tell. Had the world outside Talsura's inky Dam always been so blinding?

"You want me to go out there—" He pointed at the blur of blazing green. "*By myself?*"

Senna decided not to mention that this whole ordeal had been Percy's idea to begin with—one that he'd begged and pleaded for.

"I don't want us to get sick at the same time," Senna urged. "My top priority is—"

"Keeping me safe, *I know*. But—"

"Who's changing his mind now?"

"I haven't changed my mind," Percy cried unconvincingly. "Seeing it has only made my need to experience the sun all the more dire, but you'll forgive me if I'm a little apprehensive." He clenched his fists at his side. "Sun slay me, here I go."

It was perhaps not the smartest curse to use before taking his first steps into the open. Senna held his breath as Percy strode into the open air. He inched closer, trying to get a better look at Percy's appearance in the blinding rays. Percy's pale skin was practically translucent and his eyes, which were usually as dark as cognac leather, were bright auburn. He held out his arms, twisting them around to check them for plant growth, but he was fine. Completely fine.

Then, Percy was grinning. A euphoric, blissful grin that cracked his face wide open. He tilted his head back, drinking in more, more, more of the sun. The brightness revealed facets of Percy's face that were usually imperceivable in the constant magical candles the castle used for lighting. The prince had *birthmarks*. Tiny little flecks of tan sprinkled along his nose, and Senna had never seen them before.

Senna couldn't help it. A short burst of laughter bubbled out of him. Had he ever been so delighted?

Percy turned toward the sound, smile stretching even further. His eyes were still scrunched together, but he blinked forcefully until he could see clearly, then held his hand out to Senna.

"Your turn," he said bravely.

A long-forgotten soreness surfaced in Senna, the pieces of himself that had lost the memory of the sun and were bitter with a life plunged in darkness. If he took Percy's hand now, maybe all of that unrest would quiet.

Senna took a step further and let himself take a deep breath of the fresh air.

Then, he was drenched in sunlight.

He felt the world outside the Dam before he saw it. Tall grass catching a breeze and grazing against his hands. A breath of warmth on his cheeks. Then his eyes adjusted and the world was full and beautiful and *green*. Senna held his hands over his face, finding his skin brown amber, richer and fuller than he'd ever seen it. Bright rays reflected off his steel gauntlets, forcing him to look away.

"You're positively glowing, Sen! Why, you've got the faintest little freckles!"

Senna turned to Percy. He opened his mouth to say something unbearably selfish like *What would happen if we never went back?* But before the words could fall out, Senna caught a hint of a small yellow flower under Percy's elbow.

Without thinking, Senna yanked Percy's sleeve further back. When he did, the tall, yellow wildflower bounced away, revealing the stem that was planted in the ground and decidedly *not* in Percy's skin.

"I'm fine," Percy insisted. "Really, I haven't even got an itch!"

Senna looked down intently for any sign of green sprouts or colorful petals poking through the prince's skin.

"Your chest doesn't feel full? No stabbing pains anywhere, like—like needles?" Senna prodded.

Percy shook his head, but Senna stopped him mid-shake to tilt his face and look up his nose.

"Do you smell pollen?"

"For the love of—" Percy swatted Senna away. "I said I'm *fine*! And so are you!"

To prove it, Percy nudged Senna aside, stripped off his vest and the cotton shirt underneath, and sprawled into the flowery grass. His round glasses fell crooked on his face, so he tossed them aside and let the warm sun ignite his dark hair. Senna hadn't known until that moment there were strands of gold mixed in Percy's chestnut hair.

It took all of Senna's trust to believe Percy when he said he felt fine. Everyone who suffered sun sickness always felt perfectly healthy at first. Then, there'd be an itch, just on the surface of the skin. If one scratched at it, they'd find some small growth—a root or a thin clover. By then, whatever deadly plant was bursting forth from the skin would have begun to puncture the organs, including the lungs and heart, climbing up the throat, coming out in a bloody cough. The end was never far behind once the sufferer coughed out petals and leaves and thorns.

Percy didn't cough thorns. He didn't so much as scratch an itch. With no signs of inflorescence, by all accounts, he was safe—maybe even completely immune. Once Senna let himself feel the dregs of relief, he realized he was safe too.

Percy spread his arms out at his sides. He combed the wildflowers, pausing over leaves and smoothing them between his fingers. Senna sat beside him.

"We're *immune*," Percy said.

"Maybe."

As if he'd been holding it for hours, Percy heaved a mammoth sigh and tilted his head backward to set a strange look on the wall of inky magic shimmering around the cave's opening. He groaned.

"Now I've done it. I've gone and looked at that nasty eyesore. Gets uglier every time I see it, and somehow it's *worse* from the outside. I didn't understand why they called it the Dam until just now, but it truly is a thing of hellish machinations. Being near it does nothing for my tremors."

Senna turned his own reluctant gaze to the Dam.

To some, the Dam was the most impressive thing Talsura had ever accomplished. Its walls of tangible magic scraped across the sky, black as death and hot to the touch. Up close, it looked only of compressed smoke, like a candle in a jar snuffed out by a lid. But the puffing whisks of magic could not be penetrated by any person, spell, rain, wind—or indeed, any sunlight.

The Dam had a single job—keep the sunlight out of Talsura. Absorb it. Draw it away from the city. Keep it off the people, lest they become inflorescent and begin to grow plant life from the very pores of their skin.

Senna had been nine years old when the mages had pulled their strength together and raised the Dam. What had they been left with? For the mages, drained power that made them as useful as empty potion bottles. For Senna, a nightmarish memory of the sun being snuffed right out of the sky, never to return. For them all, a home that suffered under a blanket of black that ate alive any natural light it saw.

"Can I tell you a secret?" murmured Percy, weaving his fingers in and out of a patch of wildflowers.

"Always."

"If I wasn't prince of Talsura, I would've left with the Redwindans."

"No, you wouldn't have. You're immune to the sun sickness."

"I would've pretended I wasn't. Faked a pressure in the lungs. Coughed a little. Itched my arms until they bled. I wouldn't have stayed."

"Don't say that in front of Princess Thea. Or any of the Redwindans. You know what they suffered."

Percy frowned and turned his head away. He did know—Princess Thea had told him at length in her letters. It plagued Percy to know that his own mother had decreed the suffering and slaughter of so many people. When he'd finally been old enough to learn the truth, he had paced around his bedroom, tears pouring over agonized eyes, begging, *"Why would she do that? Why would she exile her own people just because they were* sick?"

Because she was afraid. Because she'd just lost his father days after he was born. Because she was a cruel woman who was inclined to suffering before logic.

"Because she did not yet know how sun sickness came to be," Senna had explained instead, trying to sound as steady as he could. *"Her advisors warned her it spread like any other illness. Through sickened breath, coughs, touch."*

"Why not a seclusion? Quarantine them all in a place where we could have provided for them?" Percy had shrieked. *"Why shun them like lame dogs? If she had just given them a chance, they never would've had to leave! We would still have the sun and all those people who died in exile would still have their lives!"*

Senna kept his lips closed. Percy had likely sensed his agreement regardless.

After that night, Senna watched the weight of the queen's crimes rest on Percy, forcing him down into a bitter place not even Senna could reach. It was only when Percy convinced Senna to sneak out of Talsura and see Redwind for himself that his old self seemed to return again.

"Do you want to keep moving?" Senna asked in an attempt to draw Percy's attention back to their task.

"No, I think not," replied Percy. "Not just yet. My hands are still shaking. Between our run-in with the Grits and seeing the sun for the first time, my knees are feeling a little weak."

"Then can I have another look at that letter?"

Percy hummed. He retrieved a square folded piece of paper from his pocket and gave it to Senna. Senna unfurled it and held it above his face, blocking out the bright sun. It shone through the pages, but he could still make out the words.

The letter was a mess to behold. Princess Thea's initial missives had been written primly on royal stationery. Now, they arrived on her favorite scrap paper in much messier handwriting. In the last year, they'd arrived bearing notes in the margins written by a different hand—that of her guard, Emrys Calloway, Captain of the Princess' Guard.

Senna would be lying if he didn't say he looked forward to Captain Calloway's notes on the letters. They often took him by surprise, pulling a laugh out of his mouth before he even felt it coming. Senna knew all one hundred of the silverheart knights under his command, but none of them were as charming as the man on the letter's edges. Once, Captain Calloway had written, *"Percy, we're starting to suspect the guard you boast about is merely an imaginary friend. Have him add his thoughts from time to time, would you?"* Strangely, once Senna began adding his own annotations, Captain Calloway seemed to write *more*.

Senna had read the latest letter what seemed like a thousand times. With the sun warming him through his thin traveling clothes, his lip quirked at a tiny note squeezed underneath Princess Thea's instructions: *"Not all of the guards have been informed of your visit, so try not to stop and smell the royal roses for too long. — E.C."* What did such a man look like?

"Come now!" Percy announced. "We are unharmed from thieves, underneath an open sky, and there's a princess who awaits our arrival. If we lie here forever, we won't ever get to meet our friends." Then, with a meaningful sigh, *"Or* visit Elora."

Senna sat up, folding the letter and sliding it into his pocket.

"There's no need to rush. I wasn't going to let us get this far without coming prepared," he replied.

Holding his palm face up to the sunny sky, Senna drew one of the highest level sigils he knew into his hand with his pointer finger. He tossed a silent prayer to whoever would listen, hoping that all of the invisible lines were correct. After the final sweep of his fingertip, the entire sigil glowed bright red, the color of hot iron, but without the pain. Percy poked his head over the marking and frowned.

"Is there—is there a *horse* in that sigil?"

"We'll be attacked if we appear right by the castle," Senna explained. "Captain Calloway suggested we start at the stables and ride in on horseback."

More questions threaten to burst out, but Senna grabbed on to his arm and pressed the sigil onto the grass. The air and light around them folded in. Senna squeezed his eyes shut against the shrinking sensation.

When he opened them, his heart soared.

"Sun slay me," Percy murmured in awe. "Welcome to Redwind."

EMRYS

I T WAS IMPOSSIBLE TO burn a hole in the floor from pacing, but Emrys Calloway Rosecroft was gifted in stretching the limits of possibility.

"They're truly and officially *late*," Emrys said from the hallway. He had been pacing near the window, letting his eyes sweep over the royal garden where the Talsurans were set to arrive. But Thea had banished him from the study after telling him, *"Your incessant footsteps remind me too much of our exile march and it's making my head ache."*

As Thea's completely-real-and-not-at-all-fake guard, he was obligated to remain within earshot. Thus, the hallway.

"They have to navigate a maze of trade channels, travel to the outer stables to hire a horse, and then ride thirty minutes here," replied Thea. "Of course they're late."

Emrys could not decipher if Thea was self-assured of their friends' fate, or if she really didn't care for their safety. He paused in the doorway long enough to confirm that his sister had, indeed, not looked up from her book, then rolled his eyes.

"They could be drawing their last breaths as we speak, and you can't even be bothered to stop reading your—" He poked his head in over the threshold. "What on *earth* is that? It's huge."

Thea lifted the tome for Emrys' appraisal, but all he could make out was that the book was made of green cloth and had gold dragons embossed on the front. He wasn't able to say if it had come from this study's ceiling-high shelves—he wasn't much for reading. Cracking open a book at a time like this seemed impossible.

"You're not impatient because you're troubled over their safety. You're well aware that Goldheart Kane would rather die than let anything happen to Percy," Thea observed. "You're impatient because you developed an infatuation for a man you've never met and it has given you hives."

Emrys' feet came to a halt. There was no point in denying it, but he so hated when his sister was right.

"You might want to be careful about airing the future king's embarrassing secrets."

Thea dropped her book face up in her lap and fixed Emrys with a stern glare. *Oh, now you drop your book,* he thought impatiently.

"*Me?* You're the imbecile who just announced this kingdom's best-kept secret to the entire castle. What if someone heard you?" she hissed.

Emrys' lip curled down. As a teenager, Emrys wouldn't have thought twice about letting his anger bubble up and spill over in a loud declaration.

Guess what, Redwind Castle! Your princess is just an orphan my mother plucked off the streets to act as bait for all those who would assassinate the true heir to the Redwindan throne: me.

He could remember a few instances where he almost *had* confessed it all. But he was older now and anger was no longer a weapon he kept strapped to his belt. As for their situation, Emrys would carry the truth of it to his grave if it meant he and his sister could one day get the futures they wanted. Besides, it was a believable enough ruse. The richness of Thea's brown skin was nearly identical to his and his mother's, and her eyes were the same mahogany as the queen's.

Thea was still looking at him expectantly, so Emrys shrugged and continued his marching.

Then immediately stopped again.

"Do you think he knows?"

Thea huffed a frustrated sigh, dog-eared the corner of her page, and slammed the book shut. This was her *bratty sister* manner of giving Emrys her full attention. Emrys took that as an indication his banishment had ended and sulked back into the study.

"Do I think that a man, whom you've never met, knows that you harbor Islevaria's most pathetic torch for him?" she deadpanned.

Emrys frowned. "You're terribly cruel to me, did you know?"

"I'm only saying that was a lot of pacing for a man you've never seen. What if he's spoken for? What if he's *married*?"

"Do *not* speak like that," Emrys begged.

He plopped down into the armchair across from Thea. At the corner of his ear, he felt a bloom sprout without his consent. Plucking the nuisance away, he found it was a daffodil and scoffed. The flower of unrequited love.

The trouble was that Emrys didn't know Senna Kane, but he'd analyzed every word Senna had written in Percy's letters in a desperate attempt to try to know him. From Percy's explanations and the goldheart's rare sidenotes, Emrys knew that Senna was the prince's only guard and the highest-ranked knightheart because of it. Percy had mentioned that Senna held on to his words like they were rare coins, meant to be traded at the last possible moment. He also knew that Senna prized Prince Percy as a little brother, that he favored spiced treats instead of sweet, and that he was a man of fierce honor.

Yet, the things Emrys could list off about Senna were vastly outnumbered by the things he did not know. Emrys thought that ought to make him less susceptible to pining, but it only seemed to worsen it.

He *wanted* to fill in the empty spaces. To meet Senna. To sit with him and crack open his mind, letting all of the man's hidden truths fall right into his lap. Emrys had a feeling that if that ever did happen, this pathetic infatuation would worsen into something he could not venture back from.

"My feelings are perfectly legitimate," Emrys said crankily.

Thea leaned her chin on her knuckles. "What if his looks aren't to your fancy? Will you abandon this foolishness then?"

Emrys waved his hand in dismissal. "Looks are fleeting when measured up against a man's handwriting. What does it hurt to pine helplessly over a man I can't have?

"You, probably."

Though he had just sat down, Emrys bolted out of his chair and stomped over to the window. Anything to get out of Thea's knowing stare.

All the way across the pristine garden, the guards had detained two men. The first was much taller than the second, practically looming over him and the guards in his travel armor. The second was a scrawny fellow, though Emrys couldn't make out either of their faces. Strangely, the smaller of the men was gesticulating while the taller stood completely still.

Emrys drew closer to the window, pushing aside the flowering vines that obscured the pane's clear view. An unexpected jolt shot through his nerves as one of the garden sentries suddenly drew his saber, aiming its poison-laced tip right at the smaller man's chest. The taller man was between them in a second, a threatening hand on his own blade. To unsheathe it would be a declaration of battle.

A curse erupted from Emrys' tight lips. Pushing back from the window, he snatched his sword from where it collected dust against one of the looming bookshelves and broke toward the door.

Thea's book dropped into her lap as he passed.

"Are they here?" she demanded.

"Yes, but the damned guards won't let them in!"

If there'd been more time, he would've brought Thea with him to scare the guards with a stern word. Thea was always inscrutable, and the guards assumed her displeasure with so much as a downwards curve of her mouth. For threatening their guests, Emrys would evoke that same daunting awe himself.

Dashing through the castle was an easy feat. He knew the long hallways and flower-edged corridors like the back of his hand. He knew which railings he could ride all the way down if he hopped on them, and which were covered in decorative swirls of living greenery and blossoms. He knew which hallways would be bustling with servants preparing the royal lunch like bees in a hive and he knew how to pass them undetected.

His arrival to the garden was not a moment too soon. As he yanked open the tall, stained glass doors leading outside, Emrys could see yet another guard poise himself ready for battle.

"Stand down!" Emrys bellowed. The words boomed across the lawn like a command from a holy canon. For a split second, the sentries seemed to mistake them as such, because they looked around the cloudy sky for a looming deity.

Emrys bounded forward and placed himself clear in view, planting his feet firmly in the dusty path.

"I thought I commanded you to *stand down*," he repeated. "Or are you in the habit of ignoring orders from your captain?"

A pallor rivaling death washed over the sentries. In a picture of Redwindan tradition and training, they each fell into a low bow and crossed an arm over their chests to clap a shoulder.

"Our apologies, Captain. We're under direct orders from Queen Casta to forbid any Talsurans from gaining entry by whatever means necessary."

Emrys ambled forward, hands fixed on his hips. As he passed each of his men, they turned their faces away, likely hoping to hide in shadows that weren't there.

Then, finally, Emrys allowed himself to look up at Goldheart Kane.

Oh, cursed canons. Hope was lost for good.

Later, he'd think of how he must've looked like a fool, admiring the bow's curve down Senna's long nose and the warm golden skin that surely was meant to drink up all of the Redwindan sun. Long hair fell onto his dark rose lips as he looked down at Emrys. Senna had to have been around Emrys' and Thea's age, in his late twenties. He donned leather traveling armor that did not mask the muscle and long, hard planes Emrys would daydream about putting his hands to.

Cursed canons, what were they putting in that Talsuran water to make their guards look like that?

"*Mud,*" came his sister's voice in his mind. "*Mud and dying fish.*"

Senna seemed to be appraising Emrys in return with his amber eyes, expression controlled and mild. Emrys tightened his jaw against the urge to fidget and instead turned his assessing gaze to Senna's clothes, on the lookout for any tears. If Senna had touched a drop of the toxins laced onto the sentry's swords, he'd be temporarily paralyzed within the minutes—and the guards would be fending for their lives in the dungeons. Emrys' shoulders relaxed—the fabric was clean.

"You must be Goldheart Kane. I'm glad to see you aren't a human skewer," he said lightly. "My apologies for the scare and the miscommunication." He reached across his chest, clasped his shoulder, then bowed. "I am Captain Emrys Calloway. We're thrilled to finally welcome you to Redwind."

He waited for Senna to reply, but his jaw remained steady, lips pressed closed. Yet, Emrys thought he could see the barest hint of a smile at the corner of Senna's mouth.

"Hullo, Captain," Senna's companion cut in. "Um, this is the second time my feet have been bound in the last hour. I'd be polite and say I don't mind it, but I'm afraid it'd be a lie."

Emrys blinked. He'd forgotten Prince Percy was meant to be here at all.

Confused, he peered down and found both Talsurans were fixed to the ground by thick roots. Those wrapped around Senna's shoes were muddy and barbed with thorns, but it seemed the hearty leather had protected him.

The blood in Emrys' veins turned to fire. He spun to the sentries so quickly, they flinched as though they'd been struck.

"You used your inflorescence on our guests?" he demanded. Silence fell over the sentries, each waiting for the others to speak up first. Emrys cleared his throat. "Well?"

"It seems there's been a—a miscommunication, Captain," one of them finally answered with an expression of dread. "The queen said no Talsurans. Period. We didn't hear anything about guests."

"If you need formal introductions, then I shall clear the air," Emrys said sarcastically. "Gentlefolk, allow me to present to you Prince Percy of Talsura and Goldheart Senna Kane—*personal* friends of Princess Acathea. Her Majesty the

Queen has given these two express permission to pass through into the castle for a visit. You would *know* if you read the reports before changing posts, as is required of you."

"Yes, Captain."

"Now, must I ask you a third time *to stand the fuck down?*"

The root anklets disappeared instantly.

Emrys heaved an annoyed sigh, gesturing for the Talsurans to follow him inside.

"Somehow you look just like your handwriting, Percy. Pleased to have you here, friend," Emrys said, clapping the prince on the back. "Now, what's this about having your feet tied up?"

"**I**'VE NEVER SEEN ANYTHING so *beautiful,*" Percy said as they ambled down the castle's main corridor. He hadn't blinked since they'd stepped foot inside. He certainly hadn't stopped rambling. "The way the flowers blanket all the walls, it's as if they're the artistic focus, rather than the artistry of the columns. Absolutely stunning."

"Seeing as I'm the one who grew most of them, I appreciate the admiration," Emrys said, mildly amused. "If I didn't know any better, I'd say you'd never seen a flower before in your life."

"You'd be surprised," Percy answered. "Artificial sunlight is so draining to our mages, they reserve their power for growing food. Any decorative plants in our castle are merely lackluster illusions." He glanced at Emrys and laughed. "No, go ahead, you can scowl. It's ghastly."

Emrys smiled sheepishly. "I didn't want to offend you."

"You couldn't. Why do you think we were so eager for a visit?"

"Indeed." Emrys folded his hands behind his back and turned his gaze to Senna. "And you, Goldheart Kane? Are you finding Redwind to your liking?"

The goldheart nodded, but did not elaborate. His eyes were locked at the top of the grand staircase where Thea was waiting for them. She leaned against a marble pillar, anxiously plucking browning leaves off of a tress of inflorescent vines that wound all the way up to the ceiling. When she noticed them, she straightened and brushed her hands over her skirts.

Before she could make a formal introduction, Percy cocked his head and said warmly, "Hullo Thea. I imagined you were beautiful, but you look as though you were plucked right out of one of Hickorae's portraits."

Emrys flinched in anticipation of his sister's response. But, in very un-Thea-like fashion, she grinned and rushed down the stairs. Percy caught her with a small stumble. She was much taller—taller still in her heeled shoes—but Percy merely reached up higher and held on tighter. To Emrys' amazement, Percy had gotten away with cupping the back of her head, eyes closed in contentment.

The ease of their intimacy would have confused anyone who didn't know that they were meeting for the first time. He would've been confused himself, if he wasn't already aware that Percy was seeing one of the royal artisans and that Thea preferred women.

"I watched the whole thing. You must accept my apologies for our guards," Thea said, pulling back to hold Percy by the shoulders. "We've just appointed a new regime of knights and I'm afraid they are awfully by-the-book. I think if the sun rose at a time that contradicted their schedule, they'd threaten it right out of the sky. I'm sure your own guard went through a similar acclimation phase."

Three pairs of eyes drifted to Senna, who said nothing.

Percy gave Thea a gentle pat on the arm.

"It's my fault we're late. I was kidnapped—or rather, *snatched* by thieves." Thea gasped, but Percy waved a hand. "Not to worry, not to worry. Senna is incapable of letting me fall into any harm."

"You didn't need to stay and handle the breach?" Emrys asked Senna.

Percy waved dismissively. "That's what the silverhearts are for. Everyone probably assumes that Senna is with me in protective hiding. Really, the timing couldn't have been better."

"As long as all is well," Thea said slowly. "It's a pleasure to meet you, Goldheart."

Senna dipped his head.

Silence settled over them, no one quite certain how to break the ice and bring their on-paper friendship to the tangible world. Emrys caught Thea's gaze from behind the Talsurans and made a *drinking tea* gesture.

"Would you . . . care to see the study and have a cup of tea?" Thea asked.

"That sounds magnificent," Percy said, weaving his arm through Thea's. "We have so much to catch up on. Lead the way, darling."

"*I'd* like to know why on earth you played cards with the thieves," Emrys commented. "You left that part out earlier."

"It was 'deal in or die.' I'm quite decent at cards when I put my education to the task," Percy replied.

"Did you win?"

"Of course I won," replied Percy, sounding almost offended. "Some people are formally educated and some people are thieves—it shows in their card skills."

Emrys pressed his lips together. He doubted it had even occurred to Percy that someone could be low class *and* quick-witted. Emrys' own mother began as a milliner and ascended to queenship a year later. But then, Emrys supposed Percy didn't owe the people who had kidnapped him the benefit of the doubt.

Despite being a guest, Percy held the door for Thea when they arrived at the study. The only one who didn't filter into the room was Senna. He stationed himself in the hall, fingers at the ready on his sword's hilt.

"You *are* invited to join us, you know," Emrys murmured to him.

Senna gave a nod, though it seemed like more of an acknowledgement and less of an agreement. Crestfallen disappointment sat like lead in Emrys' stomach. All of the anticipation of seeing the goldheart, only to spend the entire time completely separate.

Emrys set his jaw. If Senna thought they'd simply allow him to stand outside the meeting room as nothing more than an armed statue, he had another thing coming.

"You leave me no choice," grumbled Emrys. "I'll wait out here with you."

This caught Senna's attention. His back stiffened. He opened his mouth, snapped it shut, then took a deep breath.

"You shouldn't"—another pause as Senna's throat worked—"miss out."

"Neither should you. But if you're intent on being a proper guard, then it makes me look bad if I don't join you."

"That's—" Clearing his throat, Senna turned his face forward. "Suit yourself."

"You're both being ridiculous," commented Percy, sticking his head out the door. "On royal orders, get your armored behinds in here this instant."

At Senna's reluctance, Percy placed a hand on his shoulder.

"For canon's sake, Senna, I didn't invite you on this trip so that you could be my guard. I brought you along because you're my *friend*."

Without preamble, Percy turned back into the door, leaving it open behind him. Emrys guided Senna into the study. As he turned to release him, he caught the goldheart taking in the—well, *everything*. It almost made Emrys feel like he was seeing it all for the first time too. The ivory pillars along the room that were encased with vining white roses. The humble amount of books lining the shelf. The high ceilings that Thea had spent her royal allowance having muraled with portraits of those who'd died in the exile. In the paintings, they were dancing in the same moorlands that had taken their lives—their bodies whole, the lands sunnier.

"Very good," Percy said, smiling as Senna took a seat near the shelves. He looked uncomfortable, but made no comment. A maid slipped in and served hot tea to each of them. When he'd received his, Percy took a polite sip and said, "Now, I suggest we continue the conversation we were having in our letters. Where did we leave off?"

Thea looked down at her notes.

"Ideas on how to repair relations between the Talsurans and the Redwindans. Our best idea was to begin a council with representatives from each kingdom. Perhaps a dozen from each to ensure that each kingdom's residents are fully represented." Thea looked up through her lashes. "Emrys said that it was a terrible idea."

"You want to talk about politics? Wouldn't you rather—I don't know—gossip, or something?" He poured a tiny spoonful of sugar into his cup. "And that's *not* what I said."

"Talking politics *is* gossip. But I'll set the record straight. You said, and I quote"—Uh oh, Percy was reading directly from the page—"*'If I decided I was going to drive a carriage of plow horses off a cliff to see if they would sprout wings, it would still be a better idea than starting a joint council with the Talsurans.* A bit harsh, in my opinion."

"Well!" Emrys sputtered. "First off, it would be an utter bloodbath. The Talsurans would say something insensitive about how *unnatural* they think it is that the Redwindans use inflorescence. They might even insist that we don't use our inflorescence while the meeting is in session, which is like asking us not to breathe. I'm naked without the flowers in my hair." To prove his point, he gestured at the side of his forehead where a patch of purple flowers bloomed. "Then it would be Redwind making all the compromises, and we have tolerated enough Talsuran abuse."

Percy opened his mouth, but Emrys cut him off. He couldn't stand to listen to the prince pretending the Talsurans wouldn't at least *start* the inevitable argument.

"*Second*, what would such a council even discuss? What could two dozen people do that would begin to rectify what Queen Phaedra has done to us?"

"The Talsurans suffered too, Emrys," Percy said quietly. His pale eyes were clear through his glasses. "They're *still* suffering."

"But they *survived*, Percy," Emrys pleaded. "Did you know, when thousands of people with sun sickness travel together, the bloodied pollen from the flowers on their skin turns the air red. That's why we call this land *Redwind*. Because we cannot forget what was lost."

"I know!" Percy exclaimed earnestly. "I was only a baby and I can't begin to imagine what it was like. But I have to *try* because it's my responsibility to make it right." He drew in a deep breath, nudging his glasses up to rub his eyes. "What would *you* suggest, then?"

Emrys plopped into one of the empty chairs across from Senna and folded his hands across his lap.

"I don't know," he grumbled.

The truth was, he probably could come up with something if he set his mind to it. But he refused to do *anything* resembling diplomacy. If it ever got back to his mother that he was suggesting strategic inter-kingdom compromises, she'd *never* stop insisting he should ascend to the throne. That was for Thea.

No, he needed to play the part of *incompetent fool* long enough to earn his freedom. Long enough to convince his mother that no amount of lessons or tutoring would prepare him to be a prince.

"Make it a necessity," Thea said suddenly.

"The council?" Percy wondered.

"No, not the council. Our resources. Our skill. *Collaboration.* We need to find a way that forces our kingdoms to join forces. If you dangle something they *really* want in front of their faces, they may be willing to suck up their pride and their animosity so they can have it. What would the Talsurans want?"

Percy slumped against the side of the desk. "Brighter sources of light that don't turn our mages fallow. Then there's fresh produce that doesn't have an enchantment aftertaste. A *cure*."

"Your food is enchanted?" Emrys blurted.

"We have no sunlight," Percy said flatly. "How do you think we *live*?"

Without hesitation, "Badly."

Senna snorted. Emrys' eyes shot to him, latching on to a smirk lifting the corners of his lips. It made Emrys feel like he was so light, he might float up into the high ceiling and hit his head. He scrambled to think of something else that would make Senna laugh, but Thea tapped her pencil loudly on the table's surface, and Senna's face dropped.

"Focus," Thea said, throwing Emrys a knowing glance. She sat down, drawing her note paper closer to her. "Percy, what do you mean 'a cure?'"

Percy shifted uncomfortably.

"Of course, mastery over inflorescence is one way to avoid sun sickness," he said cautiously. "But there are Talsurans who are so *terrified* by the sun sickness, I don't think they'll ever agree to being inflorescent. If Redwind could develop and provide a cure that would make the Dam arbitrary, it would prove to Talsurans that Redwindans are concerned with their well-being and not . . ." Another flinch. "I don't know, an agenda that pushes inflorescence onto them."

Emrys scoffed, but Thea shot him another dirty look.

"It's about restoring goodwill. Not about being right," she warned him.

"There's nothing to restore. There was never any goodwill in the first place," Emrys countered. Then, to Percy, "Say Redwind goes out of its way to give your people its miracle cure. What would the Talsurans give us in return?"

"Diversified skill in magic," answered Percy immediately. "We'll re-teach you how to be masters of sigil magic."

"Sigil magic?" Thea wondered.

"Magic in the traditional sense," Percy explained. "Performed by writing sigils and runes onto a surface. Some take hours to write but are powerful enough to raise the Dam. Some spells are fit for household use. Behold, the easiest spell." He held up his hand and snapped. A flame as small as a match lit on the top of his thumb. "The rune is just a swooping line. I'm not very skilled at sigil magic, but Senna studied it at length when training to be the goldheart. He managed to cut half a day from our trip today with a travel sigil." Percy blew the flame out. "There is a whole magical history that Redwind isn't utilizing. We could—*remind* you how."

Emrys frowned. It was true that Talsura had always been the epicenter of sigil magic. They might not have been able to develop a cure for the sun sickness in time to save the exiled Redwindans, but they had raised a wall that *literally* ate and nullified sunlight. Redwindans were masters of inflorescent magic, but the masters of sigil magic had been lost to the sun sickness. Any tradition that remained had been neglected, then forgotten, after the exile. There hadn't been any time for magical study in the midst of building a kingdom from the ground up. As tempting as it was to think about now, he wasn't sure if his people would share the desire.

"Goldheart Kane," Thea noticed. "Do you have any thoughts?"

Impossibly, Senna sat up even straighter than he already was. He looked as though he wanted to blend into the wallpaper, into the shadows, or maybe out of existence entirely.

Senna shook his head.

"I have a hard time believing that. Your opinions are worthwhile here," Emrys said, not unkindly. "Would it be easier if you . . . wrote them down?"

Clearing his throat, Senna fixed his eyes to the floor and nodded. Thea rose from her desk and produced a clean sheet of paper, handing the quill to Senna when he sat down. Emrys watched his fidgeting hands in an effort to keep his eyes off of Senna while he wrote. Senna handed the finished page to Percy, who read aloud.

"If a cure was possible, Phaedra probably would've discovered it already. But it doesn't rule it out entirely," he read. "As for sigil magic, Redwindans probably won't see the value in it right away, but it would be the greatest show of goodwill Talsura could give. Historically, Talsura's magical expertise is what made it the most powerful kingdom on the island, over Mount Livia. Sharing that knowledge with Redwind would be our way of proving we mean to right our wrongs. It'd be like giving Redwind the key to our treasury and saying 'help yourselves.'" Percy paused, shoulders slumping. "Which is why I think it would never work. The mages answer to Phaedra, and only Phaedra. She would never agree."

Percy placed the paper back on the desk.

"Fortunately, she won't be queen forever. If we decide to find a cure, then it'll take time," Percy said. "If Redwind can provide Talsura the option of choice over whether or not to become inflorescent, then, when I'm king, Talsura will give Redwind the option of magic. The choice to *grow* as powerful mages."

"It's worth a try," said Thea, scribbling notes in her notebook. "If it doesn't work, we'll revisit the council idea."

"We might be able to establish a council after the exchange begins," Percy added.

Emrys nearly snorted, but thought better of it. Percy and Thea already were wading through nearly two decades of their kingdoms' animosity toward each other. They didn't need anyone else to spoil their optimism.

"I've been searching for a 'cure' of my own by looking at restorative potions," Thea said. "Perhaps we could start in the apothecary?"

Percy's eyes lit up so brightly, they could've rivaled the moon. Emrys knit his brows. His sister researching magic? That was news to him.

"Can we start today?" Percy said.

Thea shrugged. "I don't see why not."

Emrys couldn't help but smile. Percy might have been young, and he might've had bigger dreams than he could bring to fruition, but no one's friendship had made his sister come to life like this before. If the truth about Thea's fabricated rule broke, she might not have anyone except Emrys and this optimistic Talsuran prince who didn't care who she was.

"We're going to have to find you a cotton apron. All the potion tenders wear them," Thea continued.

"Are we going to get terribly dirty?" asked Percy, hopeful.

"I'm afraid not. One must work up to dirt underneath their fingernails. But you'll feel much smarter with it on." She patted Percy's hand. "Come with me. The apothecary is by the kitchens. I've heard mutterings that there are extra custard tarts."

Grinning brightly, he followed closely at Thea's heels with questions of what he'd be learning first and whether or not he'd have to speak spells in a foreign language.

If Percy and Thea were distracted, then that meant . . .

"I think I'll sit this one out," Emrys called after.

Thea nodded. "As you please."

Senna turned without hesitation to follow Percy wherever Thea would lead him. Before he could cross the threshold, though, Emrys called the prince's name. Percy paused so quickly, Senna almost crashed into him.

"Would you like us to save you a custard tart, Em?" Percy asked.

"No, it's not that," Emrys stammered. "It's only—Well, I don't suppose I can convince you to spare your guard for an afternoon?"

Senna's whole body tensed, enough that even Percy paused to look up at him. To an outsider, it might've seemed that Percy was reluctant to let his goldheart out of his sight. But Emrys knew that Senna Kane was on no leash. Both Talsurans could take care of themselves—in their own way.

"I've no arguments, but shouldn't you be asking him?"

"Ask where he's taking you, Goldheart Kane," Thea called.

Emrys rolled his eyes, shifting his weight.

"If I didn't know any better, I'd say you expected me to tie him up by his ankles and drag him through the streets for a laugh," he said. Senna shot his brows up, so Emrys sighed dramatically. "I only mean to take you for a walk so you can get some of the fresh air you haven't received in—well, maybe ever. It's better than being in that stuffy apothecary and playing wallflower—no pun intended."

The warm color seeped out of Senna's face. Was the notion of walking with Emrys so horrifying? he wondered. Maybe not. Maybe it had been the inquiry and the focus of attention that had accompanied it that petrified Senna. Emrys had asked the question, but now there were three people awaiting an answer. He'd gone and done the most insensitive thing he could've.

"I'm—" Emrys tried.

Percy gently touched Senna's elbow. "It's up to you," he whispered. "If you're worried about me, I think I've met the number of kidnappings a person can encounter in a single day."

"That's not encouraging," Senna grumbled back. He turned to Emrys, chest rising in a subtle deep breath. "A walk sounds nice. Thank you."

It didn't matter that the words seemed to stutter and catch on their way out—they were *beautiful*. They settled light and hot as embers in Emrys' chest, overcoming his ability to breathe. He hadn't expected Senna to agree, and now that he had, the inevitability of their proximity had Emrys—hopeful? Eager for more before they'd even started? His mind suddenly filled with images of them walking alone, hands brushing like they were meant to naturally be close together. He imagined all the fascinating things Senna could reveal about himself without uttering a word. Emrys would observe him and catch a hint of Senna's musky scent on a wispy breeze and—

Steady, Captain, Emrys told himself. For one, his long silence had left Senna shifting uncomfortably, as if he regretted having said anything at all. Even worse, the more he daydreamed about it, the less likely it was to actually happen.

"Not to worry," Emrys said finally. "We'll stay so close, Percy will practically be able to hear you think. If it means you'll be able to enjoy yourself, I'll station my best men outside the apothecary to ensure no harm comes to our wards in our absence."

Thea mumbled something like "Not your ward," but she was already headed away, pulling Percy along.

Emrys eyed Senna head to foot. "You'll be uncomfortable walking if you don't take off some of your armor. The sun gets quite warm in the afternoon."

Obediently, but perhaps uncomfortably, Senna undid his leather tunic, revealing the plain white shirt underneath.

Senna lingered in the doorway. Emrys felt the base of his neck turn the same shade as his family's crested roses, and he was suddenly thankful for all the layers his mother mandated that the knights wear.

"Do you have something else in mind?" Senna was standing close enough that Emrys could hear the mumble. "Besides walking?"

"I do, actually," Emrys said, lips curving up. "You're clever, Goldheart. I want you to try something that may challenge that cleverness yet.

SENNA

"I'M GETTING THE IMPRESSION that I've ruined your day," Emrys Calloway told Senna on the way into the town.

No. Seeing Percy tied up and threatened by bandits had ruined Senna's day. His first experience with controlled inflorescence being a thorny attack had ruined his day. Hearing Percy talk so passionately of an impossible future ruined his day.

Emrys asking him to go on a walk to clear his head had actually been one of the highlights—especially with late spring views like these. They were ambling along one of the hilly paths that overlooked the residential quarters of Redwind. From their high perch, Senna could see the Sellair River winding through the houses, crowned with arching bridges to connect the stone paved streets. Sloped roofs peeked through the treetops fringing the streets, and flowers and leaves lined the individual shingles.

"You haven't," Senna said, but even to his own ears, it wasn't very convincing. He took a deep breath, mustering more command over his own voice, and tried again. "I like to walk."

Warm sunlight lit Emrys' grin. "Then I am glad to have asked."

Senna usually preferred to be better acquainted with those who would monopolize his time and attention. It was easier if a person already knew they'd carry the burden of the conversation when they began one. Otherwise, they expected Senna to contribute more than he was able, and that, he found, led to disappointment.

But Captain Calloway had given Senna no expectations. He didn't raise his eyebrows expectantly, urging Senna to speak faster than he could. He didn't draw attention to the stutters or the mumbles. It was strangely . . . comfortable. *He won't punish you for speaking to him*, his mind told him. It didn't remove the tightness from his throat completely, but it lessened.

They'd walked in amicable silence, venturing into the shopping district where dozens of shops enticed guests to wander inside with bright signs and ornate pots of blooming flowers. Senna guessed Emrys was about to steer him into one of the clothing shops—Emrys so often wore fashionable, embellished clothes instead of armor. Instead, Emrys guided Senna through an alley which led to a street lined with small houses.

It was strange to be able to see the details of the buildings in perfect light. Senna was accustomed to needing to get up close to ensure he was in the right place. The Talsuran mages could only make the lanterns that lined the streets so bright without it draining their abilities.

Here, he could see how every building was engulfed with a shower of blossoms and verdancy. They spilled over the sides, drinking in all the light they could get, and pouring into the streets. The sheer variety of them was overwhelming. Senna didn't think he could learn all their names if he tried.

"Those are all the houses that were abandoned when we arrived on this land. There are only a few. It took ages to fix them up, but now you'd never know they sat vacant for so long. We built the rest on the block based on similar floor plans to prevent issues of fairness," Emrys explained. "You can decipher which family belongs to each house because of the plant life they've chosen to cover the outer walls and roof in. We believe every person has an innate inclination toward a certain plant and members of the same family bear the same inclination. Is it not fascinating?" he concluded with pride.

Senna's brows furrowed. Fascinating? The same power that had torn his friend's mouth from his skull?

"Look there," Emrys continued. "Orchids for the Standridge family, members of the royal court. Difficult to grow on their own, but when the Standridges were overcome with their sun sickness, it was the orchid's blossoms that bloomed on their skin. Now they can grow them whenever they please."

Senna's stomach roiled. He'd been apt to defend and agree with Redwind on the principle of disagreeing with Phaedra, but he couldn't help but feel sick at the thought of celebrating something that caused such harm and trauma. Poison hemlock had been the downfall of his parents—administered by a vengeful man who had blamed them for a wrong they had never committed. If he lived here in Redwind, would he be expected to hang sprigs of hemlock out of his window like a prize?

"Ah, I can see this upsets you. I apologize. I regret to say I'm quite accustomed to the way we do things here and I forget others are not," Emrys noted. "Try not to think of the inflorescence as a weapon, but instead as a tool or a symbol of strength."

Senna shook his head. He couldn't. Yet Emrys persisted.

"Imagine you'd never seen a kitchen knife before. Imagine you walked into a room overflowing with them. Everywhere you stepped, they'd cut you. Force you to bleed out. But then, imagine you learned that you could *use* the kitchen knives for good. That you could clear them out of your way, change the way they existed in your life, and utilize them in ways that served you. Food preparation, protection—hell, even decoration, if you thought they were pretty enough. Inflorescence is no different."

"It's unpredictable," Senna countered.

"Not if you can control it. It's not a weapon, or a curse. It's merely a source of specialized magic. Mastering inflorescence takes time, especially when you don't know what it is or why it's happening in the first place. It was difficult to learn when we were busy choking on thorns and trying not to starve. But now, we *understand* it. We've become strong enough to not only will the inflorescence to grow from our bodies, but from the ground, sometimes from *nothing*. Can you possibly imagine?"

"I—" Senna's throat closed.

Emrys stopped in the path, placing just his fingertips on Senna's chest.

"I understand your apprehension. But look around you, Goldheart."

Senna turned his gaze to the courtyard. Children leaned over the edge of a trickling fountain, laughing as they grew tiny lily pads for a small frog to leap about on. One woman used her inflorescence to turn the side of her home into a mural, growing a thousand tiny flowers to create one cohesive image of a hummingbird. A group of old men lounged on benches, sipping fragrant coffee from a pot. Beside them was a tiny peach tree, which grew more fruit every time one of the men plucked one off to eat.

"These people have endured the worst days of their lives and clawed their way to the other side. Isn't it a miracle that we seized control of the roots at our throats?" Emrys plucked a handful of tiny blue flowers from the ground and let the wind carry the petals off. "We do not air the flowers that killed us simply because they are pretty. We utilize our inflorescence to prove that we went against every deadly hand dealt to us and we *lived*. If I had to guess, I'd suspect you know something about that."

"I never had the sun sickness."

"No. But you could be inflorescent."

Senna shook his head. What a ridiculous suggestion. "There's nothing in me to grow."

"*That*, Goldheart Senna Kane, is why I've brought you out here—to prove you're wrong. There is more in you than there is in anyone I've ever met."

It was only then that Senna realized Emrys' hand on his chest was still lingering over his heart. Up until he processed the touch, the feeling had been warm. Almost pleasant, like it could have lingered in place indefinitely and Senna would have been content to sit still. See how long it could linger. But the second Senna's attention was drawn to it, his skin burned painfully.

He stepped back, pressing on up the footpath, though he knew not where they were headed. Emrys fell into easy silence beside him. As their steps began to match rhythm, they ambled up Redwind's streets—Emrys smiling and offering pleasantries to those who passed, Senna avoiding every curious eye that landed on him. He had to admit, uncomfortable conversations aside, it was nice to be in the open air.

"You speak so easily," Senna said, at last.

"And you do not," replied Emrys without judgment.

"No, I don't."

"Why is that?"

"It's not my job to speak."

"Working an occupation in which you quiet yourself and remain at the ready does not require that you suffer difficulties of the tongue."

Senna almost stumbled over his own feet. No one had ever said it so plainly before. He didn't realize how raw it would feel for someone to go prodding around his open wounds.

"Then again," Emrys continued, "for all your words won't come, mine pour from a faucet that can never be turned off. Forgive me."

"I'm jealous of your skill," Senna stammered.

"Don't be," laughed Emrys. "It's not a skill if it's just blabbering out whatever comes to mind. You should try it sometime."

"I think it's going to rain."

Emrys blinked. "What?"

"That was me trying it. I think it's going to rain."

A peculiar glint lit up Emrys' eyes, amused enough that Senna felt uneasy.

"Well done, Goldheart. You are a fast study. And I think you might be right about the rain."

Senna pressed his lips against a scoff. What a silly compliment to pay a person who only observed the weather. But for someone who was not acquainted with praise, giving or receiving alike, Senna could not help the sudden urge to speak more. To comment on how even clouds rolling over the sun were a thing of beauty. How he'd thought they ought not to be, considering it was what the orphan mother had named her orphanage for—*It was gray skies when I got the deed and gray skies when I opened my doors.* How they'd later found out that his true surname was Kane, so he'd gone from being Senna Gray, who belonged to no one, to Senna Kane, who had at least belonged to someone, once. He wanted to know which of his childhood notions of the sky were real, if clouds truly were soft to the touch.

But now Emrys was looking at him, as if he too wanted to hear Senna's voice utter foolish observations. All at once, the words were gone.

Damn it all.

Emrys only offered him an understanding smile and began up a short ramp. He occupied the open air easily, as if claiming it. Making it his. The adorned layers of his Redwind-style clothing caught on the breeze, pushing the fabric of his tunic away from where strong calves worked in their leather. He stopped at the top of the ramp, taking a moment to realize that Senna was still at the bottom. Even through the rain clouds, there was enough dependable sunlight to illuminate the captain's face.

It was easier to look at Emrys from a distance. Up close, one might miss how Emrys' angled face was really quite soft when he was at ease. The eyes that were usually rich mulberry reflected something closer to the Standridge's orchids when paired with gray clouds. He was more beautiful than Senna had imagined he'd be, with his thick brows, full pink lips, and high cheekbones. From the top of the ramp, he looked like a canon who commanded the entire earth and sky.

"Come, there's something I want you to see," he called down. When Senna hesitated, he continued, "What's the point of journeying all the way here if you won't enjoy Redwind with an open mind?"

Senna wasn't sure if Emrys had a point or if he was just very convincing, because a compromise rose in the back of his mind. He didn't have to drop his guard entirely. He could follow Emrys into the unknown without opening himself fully. The noise of calm, murmuring villagers and the cascading water grew stronger the higher he rose. When at last he reached the top, Senna's gaze widened.

He had never seen so many people outside in the open air before. They filled the grassy space at the foot of a statue-fountain depicting one of the canons. He was not familiar enough with the large assembly of canons to recognize which one this was. He rarely gave any thought to the minor deities. He understood enough that they were *real*, but he couldn't fathom how some were tangible and visible, and others were as present as imaginary folktales. As an adult, he was silently of the opinion that the canons were merely glorified humans, often bearers of responsibilities they themselves were not adept enough to use. It was more productive to accomplish things on his own than resort to prayer.

Here, in Redwind, things were different. Some of the villagers were already placing offerings at the foot of the fountain, baskets of fresh vegetables and herbs wrapped in twine. It struck Senna what a waste it all was, but he kept his face neutral—this seemed sacred to these people.

When the villagers noticed Emrys, they immediately parted, allowing him to walk easily through the crowd. Senna followed behind, gazing up at the statue to avoid meeting anyone's eye.

Up close, Senna could glean why some mortals took comfort in the worship of this particular canon. Even in stone, she had an aura that might draw a person close to seek refuge under her outstretched arms. From those open palms, a gentle cascade of water poured out, gliding between the canon's stony fingers into the mosaic basin below. There was no nameplate at the foot of the statue.

Emrys seemed to be reading his mind, because he leaned over and whispered, "This is Varyan, canon of inflorescence."

Senna nodded slowly in understanding. That explained why he didn't recognize the canon's statue. Varyan was of little use to the Talsurans, who hadn't had verdancy of their own in almost two decades.

Emrys took his place at the base of the fountain. He freed himself of some of the restrictive layers required of Redwindan knights, first stripping off the one-shouldered cape with ornate embroidered details along the edge. As if it were second nature, he folded the cape and draped it onto the fountain's edge. Then, he untied his cotton shirt, exposing the deep brown skin underneath. Senna remembered a second too late to tear his eyes away.

With easy grace, Emrys turned to face the crowd head-on. His warm eyes commanded their attention, silencing the talking until all bowed in respect.

"May Varyan favor us this day," Emrys announced. He paused, allowing the crowd to murmur their own *Varyan, favor us.* "Thank you all for venturing out, especially under the impending threat of rain. I am Captain Emrys Calloway, right-hand knight to her Royal Highness, Princess Acathea. It is with pride that I declare this exchange officially commenced."

Murmurs of excitement rumbled over the crowd as all the villagers fell to form a single line. Those at the front bounced on their toes and gnawed on their lips, eager to receive whatever Emrys had to offer.

Rolling up his sleeves, Emrys grinned at Senna. "You're about to see firsthand that inflorescence is more than a disease. It can cure ailments, protect against evils, soothe the mind and heart, increase your luck. We share it gladly."

He reached out to the first person in line, a short, fat girl who rolled up her own sleeve and stepped up to meet them.

"What we grow from our bodies is more than just symbolic," Emrys explained to Senna, smiling down at the girl. "There's magic within us that gives our inflorescence power. An ordinary wildflower can act as a miracle cure when grown from inflorescence. But most people's bodies only know how to grow one thing. However, a person can be taught to grow something new if someone grows it for them."

At this, Emrys smiled down at the girl. She blushed under his warm gaze, her face, full of freckles, becoming beat red.

"What's your inflorescence, dear?" Emrys asked her kindly.

"Lavender," she answered timidly. To prove her point, a sprig of fragrant lavender appeared from behind her ear.

"Ah, I'm sure you sleep beautifully."

"That's just it, sir. I sleep throughout the night, but I'm plagued with awful nightmares. I wake up well-rested but completely terrified."

"I understand," Emrys said softly. He smoothed his hand over her forearm, gently rubbing the same spot over and over until it had to be warm to the touch. "Watch closely."

To Senna's horror, a small yellow bud poked from the girl's skin. It unfurled, revealing a few silky petals and a flurry of thin stamens. A tiny bead of blood dripped from where the root embedded into her frail skin, but she did not seem to be in any pain.

"This hypericum is known as 'Evil's Scourge.' It will purify your mind and ward off unpleasant influences," Emrys explained.

The girl squeaked out her thanks. Senna opened his mouth to ask if she was alright, but her father stepped forward, holding her shoulders.

"If you don't already know it, I can give you comfrey, sir."

Emrys' face lit up in delight.

"I can't say I've heard of that one. What does it do?"

"It's a travel aid, sir. We spread it around during the exile and all who grew it had safe passage."

Emrys extended his arm eagerly.

"Then by all means," he invited. The villager turned Emrys' arm so that his palm was facing down, then rubbed their own firmly over the skin. When they pulled away, purple bell-shaped flowers dangled from Emrys' fingertips. He smiled at them. "It makes me want to embark on an adventure. Thank you!"

As they departed, Senna's heart raced as all the pieces fell into place.

"I understand," he breathed. "It's an *exchange*."

"Yes," Emrys agreed, already working on the next people in line. "Giving someone else a new plant to grow can be taxing and difficult, but I became skilled as a child. It costs me barely anything to come here once a week and encourage others to gain more power for themselves. It's beneficial for me too, as you've just seen."

Senna cocked his head. Why would Emrys want to bring him here and show him this unless—

He stumbled back a step.

"Is that what you want to do to *me*?"

"If you've a mind for it. I suspect that in your case, you're not really immune. I think your body simply doesn't *know* anything to grow. I can teach you, both how to grow and how to avoid it escalating into sun sickness."

A rush of adrenaline began to course through Senna's veins. It was indecipherable from a nearly two decade-old terror that he sometimes forgot he had. The hurtling of his pulse was paired with memories of Conall's unhinged jaw—how the blood had dried brown against his cold skin.

"... Senna?"

Senna gasped, looking up and finding Emrys right there, cradling his wrist in gentle fingers.

"I will not force you to do that which distresses you."

A familiar tenseness held Senna's words tight in his mouth. It took a few subtle, deep breaths to loosen the tightness in his throat.

"I'm immune," he managed to say.

Emrys' fingers wrapped more securely around Senna's wrist, soft skin pressing up right against his racing pulse.

"That's what I'm trying to disprove," Emrys said softly. "I think all people can be inflorescent. It's just a matter of time and skill. I want to teach you how to call upon it. Then, I want to teach you how to make it go away."

Senna's jaw clenched. "It'll overtake me."

"It won't. While you're in my care, no harm will come to you," swore Emrys. "Can you find it within yourself to trust me?"

The question was lost in the roar of Senna's reeling mind. His own blood crashed and wailed in his ears to the same deafening pace it raced through his veins. He squeezed his eyes shut against pain blossoming behind them, but all he saw was Conall's bloody bed and broken skin.

"No." Senna shook his head. "No. No. I can't. I—" His throat closed, and he dug his nails into his palms to force it back open. "I need to find Percy."

He slipped out of Emrys' grip, steeling himself for whatever insult he'd earned for his reaction. But Emrys folded his hands in front of himself where Senna could see them and gave a sad, but comforting, smile.

Then, Senna was pushing past shoulders and elbows toward the ramp. The air was easier to breathe at the back end of the crowd. He paused to catch his breath and clear his mind, but something at the front of the fountain made him pause.

Two women had stepped up to Emrys. The taller of the two, with pale skin and a long red braid, presented a baby completely swaddled in a bright blanket. It was only when the second mother politely uttered the name of the plant that Senna realized the inflorescence wasn't for them. It was for the *baby*.

They pulled the blanket away from the child's face. Senna's heart sank into his stomach. How could they willingly do this to a baby? Emrys rubbed a single fingertip over the tiny forehead.

Senna held his breath as a patch of miniscule white flowers bloomed on the baby's skin. There was no blood this time, nor flinching or crying. To Senna's amazement, the baby *laughed*. The mothers matched Senna's deep sigh of relief, immediately cooing praise and compliments to their child.

Emrys looked up, meeting Senna's gaze. He smiled, a genuine, happy thing, as if to say, *Take your time. I know you'll come around.*

PERCY

I F YOU ASKED PERCY his earliest memory, he would tell you that it was being bathed in light, held by a person who had come into his life and never left.

When Percy confessed this to others, they often assumed he spoke of his mother. In truth, it was Senna who had first held Percy.

To explain their friendship would've been easier if Percy didn't have to sidestep all the nosy questions the gentry asked. They saw love as a weakness to be exploited, even the love of their prince. If Percy had the opportunity to speak freely, then he might've explained how Senna Kane was as a brother to him—beyond the bond of blood or the commitments of royal vows. No one had loved Percy better. Not even his mother.

It was because their friendship left no unfilled desire that Percy found he didn't have other friends. Those in the ever-dark Talsura found his sunny disposition a nuisance. They wanted a prince who could complain with them, *for* them. A prince who would luxuriate in the darkness and gripe about misery, a mirror of their own bellyaching. But Senna had never asked Percy to be anything but himself.

In a way, that was why Percy had immediately warmed up to Thea. She had taken one look at Percy's letter and assessed him for exactly who he was. In return, she was exactly who she said she was. Today's meeting had proved it so.

The rub? Thea didn't offer much by way of self-information, knowing both her brother and Senna read her letters. By now, she had confessed that she was not the true heir to the Redwindan throne. Percy had sworn on his father's grave to carry that secret with him under staunch lock and key. He hadn't even told Senna.

"But . . . didn't the Redwindan people know they had . . . well, a prince? Not a princess?" Percy had written. Thea's response had come quickly.

"You know the tradition of allowing children to choose their place on the spectrum of masculinity to femininity. That practice didn't change when we left Talsura. Mother allowed Emrys to choose his gender when he was ready. When we were in exile, Emrys chose not to subscribe to any label. The people didn't even know his name because the family wasn't important yet. Of course, he later chose to be the prince, but that was never formally announced."

Really, that was more a truth about Emrys than it was Thea.

She was much of a mystery in every other regard. Where she came from, what power she possessed, what her hopes and dreams were . . . It was all blank. She was far more content to read Percy's letters. This was a practice that translated into a preference toward listening to him ramble. As for him, he was accustomed to those who preferred to listen.

It did not quell his curiosity. Throughout the years after they had met, Thea had written things in her letters that did not add up. Not in a deceitful way—more in the way a person speaks when they feel their lives are at stake with the very words they utter. Percy loved Thea enough not to demand the truth.

But no one was perfect. Sitting on the apothecary worktable, peeling through an old tome on basic herbal cures, Percy's reins slipped.

"Why *have* you been dabbling in restorative magic? It doesn't seem like you have anything that needs"—he gestured vaguely—"restoring."

Thea looked up from where she was measuring dried lavender flowers in a quarter teaspoon. The only evidence he'd caught her by surprise was the way the spoon shook, spilling little purple pebbles onto the table.

"I—"

She closed her lips shut, like Senna did when he had nearly said too much.

"Are you ill?" Percy pressed, gently. "Because, if something ails you, then we ought to search for *that* cure first."

After dumping the lavender into the mortar, Thea placed her spoon down very, very carefully.

"I'm not ill. At least, not in the common sense."

Percy waited, knowing the rest was on its way out. Thea gnawed on her lip in a very un-princess-like manner and it endeared him so much, he rounded the table and took her hand.

"My dear, there is no judgment among friends. Especially none so devoted as us."

Thea found Percy's gaze, but only for a split second. Carefully, she peeled her hand away and began to wring her fingers into the skirts of her dress.

"Do you know why the Redwindans chose Queen Casta to lead them when we settled here?" she asked quietly.

Percy admitted he didn't.

"It was because she and Emrys had traveled their exile with a woman named Ceday Lespryn." She gave Percy a pitying smile. "Your aunt, I think."

"She was, though I never met her." A distant ache squeezed inside Percy's chest, but he ignored it and nodded for Thea to continue.

"Ceday was on the verge of understanding that inflorescence could be used as a gift instead of a death sentence. She died before she could make the discovery for herself, but not before telling Emrys about it. When she passed, he and Casta were the first to master inflorescence. It saved their lives. It saved the lives of everyone in Redwind. *That* is why they chose her as their queen."

"That's beautiful," commented Percy. "But, forgive me, I don't understand what it has to do with you."

Thea picked up one of the lavender buds and began to roll it around between her fingers.

"When Casta first became queen, I'm told that the land was quite desirable—*especially* for kingdoms overseas."

"The lands overseas are so dreadfully far away. They'd have to sail for two years just to send a legion," Percy noted.

"It seemed like a price they were willing to pay. They thought that a land of people with untrained powers could make an easy conquest of soldiers for their armies. Or, if we could not be useful, we could simply be removed from our lands. Casta did whatever she could to prevent this from happening."

"I admire her for that."

"As do I. One of the things she did was hide the true heir to the throne. At the time, supporting a legitimate line to the throne was integral to establishing our credibility as a nation. You know that much."

"But why did she choose you? I mean, I'm glad she did. But was it because you were—" *An orphan*, is what he almost said. Senna hated that word, so Percy tried something else. "Without parents?"

"Yes. Very few people had seen Emrys enough to know what he looked like. Or if they had, the exile had caused them to forget. The queen found me and realized if she *said* I was her child, our people would believe her. She trained me in the ways of being a royal, which was strange, because it was still new to her too. Eventually, she announced my existence and hid Emrys in plain sight. It was only days later when she discovered she'd made a mistake."

"A mistake?"

"I have no inflorescence. I am completely powerless."

Percy's brows cinched together.

"But . . ." He cleared his throat. "You wear the Rosecroft roses on your head. Why, they're in your tiara and all over your dress!"

"Emrys grows them for me in the morning. He tried to teach my body inflorescence once, but it failed. Miserably. Along with any hope Casta might decide I can be a real princess and a member of this family."

With that, Percy understood perfectly.

Well—not exactly. He understood the way Thea was feeling, that gnawing desire to impress. To be accepted by someone whose attention always turned toward the well-being of their kingdom. It was no wonder Thea craved Queen

Casta's approval. Even someone with an empty heart would feel the connection with a person they'd acted as daughter to for over a decade.

What Percy did not understand was the apparent notion that Thea was not already considered a *real* princess. She certainly looked the part, known for her unique creative style that had a habit of stealing the attention of anyone who passed. It was aided by the very air with which she carried herself, the manner with which she wore her clothes.

The dress she had on today was one of her own designs, given to a seamstress who had replicated it magnificently. Percy remembered seeing the sketch in a letter, but the real thing was the stuff of magic. The free-flowing dress was a sunbeam yellow that complemented the richness of her dark skin. Most notable were the ribbons and pins that configured her braided curls into sculpted beauty. It was all crowned with a tiara of gemmed twigs—and of course, the royal roses.

"I doubt that a lack of inflorescence would keep the queen from accepting you," he said slowly. "*You've* been the one in the manners classes, and the history lessons, and really all the other education a proper heir receives. Your studies have been as thorough as mine, if not more."

"She knows that," Thea huffed. "But it's all for the sake of appearances. She keeps me at arm's length. Barely acknowledges that I exist. The worst part is, I think she does it to protect herself, so that it doesn't hurt as much when I leave. Because she *knows* she'll make me leave. And what will I do then?"

A dark, hazy cloud came over Thea's eyes. What could Percy say that would compare to all that Thea had and would endure? All he could do was stand beside her and hold her hand. He did just that.

"I'll help you find a way to be inflorescent, Thea," he promised. "For what it's worth, I really do believe that your mother will see things your way eventually."

Thea pressed her lips firmly together. Gingerly, she removed her hand from Percy's and he smiled at her. There were moments he didn't like being touched either.

What he could not abide was the sour taste in the air.

After giving his hands a few short claps, Percy skirted to the bookcase's counter and poured two more cups of tea. It had to be tepid, but it would serve for their purpose. He placed both cup and saucer in Thea's waiting hand, already noticing that her shoulders had relaxed, then took the stool beside her at the workbench.

"Oh dear, am I sensing more gossip about your chambermaids?" Thea said, reading Percy's mischievous glance.

He took a luxurious sip before clacking his cup onto the table.

"Sabrina and Astrid are involved again—*finally*."

Thea practically dropped her teacup in relief, releasing a momentous sigh.

"The two of them, I swear! I had half a mind to sneak into your castle and force them to sit down for an adult conversation. Did Sabrina finally explain why she was alone with Cosimine?"

"I haven't the foggiest!" Percy lamented. "All I know is that Sabrina avoids Cosimine in the hallways like the plague. *And* . . . I might've caught Sabrina and Astrid greeting each other with their lips in my chamber bathroom."

"You beast!" Thea scolded, smacking Percy's chest with the back of her hands. "You should have opened with that! I'm so relieved. How lovely it is for them to have each other again."

"You know . . ." Percy began.

Thea caught the impish glimmer in Percy's eye and groaned. "Don't finish that thought, Percy Laurent."

"Cosimine is *very* beautiful."

"I would not impose myself in that sordid affair for all the world. Besides, I have far too much to be worrying about and no time to woo Talsuran women." She glanced at him, the dreadful cloud nowhere in sight now. "Speaking of your maids, don't *you* have a sordid affair you're late to? Your goldheart will be back any minute and you've not yet seen your Elora."

Percy could not hide the grin that swept over his face. Just the name . . . Was there any word so lovely as *Elora*?

Then a tiny memory of the last time he'd seen Elora rose to the forefront of his mind, and the smile slipped away.

"First off, it is not sordid, nor is it an affair," he stated primly. He set his teacup back on the tray, only to wrap a few biscuits with his handkerchief and stuff them in his pocket. "Secondly, I am not the sort of fellow to leave behind a loyal friend in her time of need. Therefore, I cannot go until I know without a doubt that your mind is at ease."

"It is," deadpanned Thea.

Percy lowered his brows pointedly. "*That* lacked conviction."

"I shall rehearse diligently," the princess replied shortly. "I thought you'd be intent on seeing her, but you haven't mentioned her once."

"Writing about seeing her is one thing. Actually seeing her is another thing entirely."

"I've asked about her a few times, but you've never opened up. You don't have to, but maybe talking about it will put your mind at rest before you visit her."

Percy stirred his tea, watching the powdery bits at the bottom swirl.

"There's not much to tell," Percy said softly. "A year ago, Elora worked as a palace maid, tasked with cleaning my branch of the castle. I'd always see her and—well, it's embarrassing to admit now—but I'd taken to hiding behind illusionary plants to catch a glimpse of her while she worked. One day, she caught me and said that if I wanted to be friends, I could act my age and ask. So we talked. And then eventually, we kissed." He chuckled, embarrassed. "A lot."

"How did she end up here?"

Percy pressed his lips together sadly. "Elora was always an extraordinary sculptor. She kept a private studio in Talsura's capital and crafted whatever she pleased, including controversial artwork. Eventually, my mother found out that someone on her own staff was raising statues that criticized both her and the Dam. I'll never forget how terrifying it was helping Elora flee, but Emrys helped. He met her at the Agora of Alpedis and promised he'd find her employment. He made good on his promise. She was able to flee before my mother even learned what she looked like.

"After she settled, Elora wrote to me and said that if I didn't mind that our relationship existed solely on paper, then neither did she. Lately, I rarely hear from her."

Thea hummed. "My mother has commissioned several new pieces for the local parks. Perhaps Elora's merely busy."

"Maybe. I'm worried that if I see her tonight, she'll say she's changed her mind. Not that I could blame her, but . . ." He scrubbed his face. "I'm quite certain I'll die alone if Elora breaks off our courtship."

"You won't die alone," Thea scoffed. "But it's like she said. If you aren't sure, act your age and *ask*."

Percy crossed his arms onto the workbench and heaved a breath. "Do you think Senna will be back soon?"

With a weary skyward look, Thea shot off her stool and grabbed Percy by his arms, dragging him along.

"Wait! Hold on—Thea! Let go of me this instant!"

"You'll thank me later!"

Thea opened the door.

"Goodbye, Your Highness. Visit again soon!" she exclaimed.

—and promptly slammed it shut.

As soon as he was alone, blazing hot anticipation began coursing through to his furthest corners. He stood before the closed door, willing himself to take a slow breath.

Then, he was a blur, racing through the empty castle halls, into the open air, straight for the palace gardens.

WORD MUST HAVE SPREAD about the garden confrontation, because the guards let Percy navigate the grounds without any trouble. He wove through the hedged maze and past all the glowing, nighttime blossoms, trying to decipher which of the many buildings was Elora's artisan studio. Above him, the glittering sky stretched for miles. It couldn't have been more different than the Dam—open, bright, and starry. Percy tilted his head up and drank in the expanse of it. How would he ever be satisfied with home now?

At the far end of the grounds, a stony building was lit by burning lampposts. A tall woman came out with a handful of paintbrushes, which she washed with soap under the well pump. When she was done, Percy smoothed back his tousled hair, pushed his glasses up his nose, marched up to the door, and knocked.

It swung open, but Percy's smile dimmed. The person who had answered was Elora's opposite with jagged blonde hair, a pointed chin, and no eyebrows. They leaned their hip against the doorframe, arms crossed.

"Who are you?" they demanded.

"Hullo," Percy said with all his royal charm. "My name is Percy. I'm here to see Elora—if she's available, that is."

The artist narrowed their eyes, before recognition dawned.

"Elooora," they called back into the studio, drawing out all the pretty vowels in the worst way. "Your *prince* is here to grace us with an unannounced visit. He's short in person!"

Another artisan appeared beside them—still not Elora, but someone with a friendlier expression.

"He's not short! I think he's taller than you are," she rambled.

"By *at least* an inch," agreed a third artisan, standing on her tiptoes to see Percy's face over the first person's shoulder. "Luca, You're just huffy because everyone would rather consort with a Talsuran than spend a minute listening to you brag about your watercolor landscapes."

"Get out of the way and let him in," another person shouted from inside the room.

Throwing up their hands in defeat, Luca shuffled out of the way, muttering something about *uncultured Talsuran swine* and *can't even send a bloody messenger bird.*

Before Percy could utter so much as a greeting, half a dozen hands reached out and snatched him wherever they could grab hold of him—his wrists, his belt, the collar of his silk doublet. The artisans pulled him into the studio, asking him a million questions at once.

"Where's your guard?"

"Why did you wait so long before visiting?"

"He's a king—he's very busy!"

"He's not a king, you blockhead. He's just a prince."

"And you're just a painter who still muddies her yellows, but—"

"Didn't you write about your guard? Is he here? I was so looking forward to seeing if he was handsome! Do you think he'd ever sit for a portrait?"

"Better yet, you should sit together! I bet a guard would be marvelous at sitting still! The last man I painted wiggled about like a cocker spaniel in desperate need of the loo—"

At the back of the room, a familiar voice cut through the commotion. "Hello, Percy."

Elora.

The sight of her made him feel wide awake. She was wiping her hands dry with a towel, though Percy could see the flecks of dried gray clay that she'd missed with the soap and water. The sea of her black hair took on strands of gold in the studio's warm candlelight, cascades of silk waves tumbling down her back. Against her glowing face, Elora's eyes were bright and blue. It was a wonder Percy could breathe at all.

Elora tossed the towel over her shoulder and smiled sweetly.

"Don't tell me you're speechless," she teased. "You're the one surprising me, remember?"

Percy shook his head. "No. I—*wow*. You are . . ."

She tilted her head, an amused glint in her eye. She crossed the room in three graceful strides and folded herself soundly in his arms. Her warmth against his body quieted the parts of him that worried for the future. None of it mattered when her gentle fingers stroked his hair.

Percy buried his face in the crook of her neck, breathing in the honey scent of her skin. She hummed contently as he clung to her, letting their bodies sway from side to side. *When you hold me like that, it reminds me how much you treasure me,* she'd told him once. And he did. More than all the gold and jewels wasting away in his coffers, he loved her.

"It's okay if you've changed your mind," Percy murmured.

Elora released him and smoothed her hands over his face.

"Is this because I haven't written as much? Queen Casta commissioned half a dozen statues and barely gave me any time to get them done. I've been working all day and night on them."

Percy dropped his forehead onto her shoulder. Of course Thea had been right.

"Why do I get the sense that you've had a taxing day?" Elora asked fondly.

"Well, I survived capture by thieves, stepped outside the Dam for the first time in my life, traveled dozens of miles in a blink, survived a *second* capture by Redwindan guards, *and* plotted with my political enemies against my mother. So, it's been a rather typical day, really."

"My poor lad." She kissed his cheek and then his lips. "I'm so happy to see you're alright. And I really am sorry I've been too busy to write. I had a feeling that if I had told you how hard I was working and how stressed I've been, you'd do something silly like come here yourself."

"I wanted it to be a surprise, in case Senna changed his mind about letting me come," he admitted. "It was like trying to persuade a brick wall."

Elora chuckled. "Is he still being too strict with you?"

Percy sucked his lip under his teeth. Speaking poorly about Senna always made his mouth taste sour. But sometimes it seemed like his goldheart had forgotten Percy wasn't the newborn Senna had been given charge of. He was eighteen now, old enough to be king.

"He only wants to make sure I don't make a mistake I can't come back from," he said finally.

"For that, I'm thankful." She tucked herself into his side and began leading him through the hallway. "Now, come sit for me. I've been wanting to practice my busts."

"I wonder if you could put that talent to good use and make my nose three times smaller. You might give me a squarer jaw while you're at it."

"Percy Laurent, I've never known you to be so vain!" Elora scolded. "Keep speaking like that and I'll chip away all your hair to make your forehead the size of Talsura. They'll chart maps across it. Maybe even the stars." She punctuated this with a firm kiss, then planted a second at the corner of his mouth.

"I haven't much time to sit for you, I'm afraid," Percy stuttered, moreso a reminder for himself. "Sen is off doing canons-know-what with Emrys Calloway and he's due to return at any moment."

He pulled them to a stop. The corridor was a swatch of dark green paint with only a few oil lamps flickering quietly on the wall. If anyone had looked at them, they would've seen two silhouettes bleeding into each other, no distinct border where one stopped and the other began. The lamplight was just bright enough that Percy could count the tiny splash of freckles on Elora's long nose.

"You have no idea how happy I am to hear that you haven't changed your mind about being with me," he began. "I've been wishing for so many impossible things that I worried this was merely another hopeless dream."

"When it comes to me, if you want something, you only need to ask," she said softly.

Percy smiled, eyes sad. "I would trade all my kingdom to be able to stay here forever. It's hard to enjoy myself when I'm counting down the seconds."

Elora caressed up and down Percy's sides. "There is a lifetime for us, Percy, and in it, too many seconds to count."

Percy licked his lips, tasting the honey balm Elora wore.

"El," he began, voice trembling. "Would you ever leave here to be with me in Talsura? Is *that* impossible?"

Elora's eyes fluttered, like the question had been a sharp gust to the face. Before she could say anything, Percy rushed to continue.

"What I really mean to ask is . . . Do you think you could stand being queen consort of Talsura?"

Elora's face did something strange.

"That . . . is the natural conclusion of this relationship," she said in a strange voice. "But . . ."

Her hands fell away, dropping helplessly at her sides. Percy restrained himself from grabbing them again, instead allowing her space to breathe.

Footsteps echoed from down the hall. Percy ignored them, focusing all of his attention on Elora. Desperately, he tried to think of anything that would undo all the shadows and worry lines on her face. But the question had been asked. Now it was time to await her answer, whatever it would be.

The footsteps stopped—then came a familiar voice.

"Percy."

Percy's eyes slipped shut.

"Just a minute, Sen."

"No, now."

Percy spun around, a fiddle string pulled too tightly. "It will only take a moment."

"We don't have any moments. We're already late."

"Which means we'll be late no matter when we leave," he spat, frustrated. "You've been gallivanting all day through Redwind's streets, but I get a single minute with Elora and suddenly it's time to leave? We can head off when I'm finished here."

It would've been easiest if Senna turned angry with him. Percy knew he wouldn't. The expression on his face now was of sadness. Maybe even hurt. It made Percy want to tear his heart out of his chest, just to stop it from pounding against his ribs.

"I'm not your keeper," Senna said finally. "But if we don't leave now, I can't promise you'll be able to return."

Percy's hands balled into fists. He couldn't leave Redwind yet. Not when Elora hadn't given her answer. All that waited for him in Talsura was a barricade of black, smoky death and his mother's ever-shortening leash.

At Percy's trembling silence, Elora stepped out of his space. She held her arms, rubbing them up and down, eyes glued to the floor.

"You should go, Percy," she said quietly. Then, looking up from underneath a strand of her curled hair, she offered him a small smile. "I'll—I'll think about what you asked."

With the same gentle touch he'd use to hold a baby bird, Percy brushed the loose strand away from her face. She took his hand, just as softly, and pressed a kiss to the knuckles.

"We're alright," she promised.

"We're alright," Percy echoed.

He pressed one last kiss to the corner of her lips, then disappeared away to Senna's side.

"It's good to see you, Senna," Elora called out. "Come visit anytime."

He froze, then nodded.

The studio was silent when Senna and Percy departed. The silence persisted as they made their way to their horses. Then to the outer Redwindan stables to return them. Finally, Senna cast a sigil that dropped them at the front of the trade channels that had nearly been Percy's downfall hours ago. How could there be so many hours in the bloody day?

"Because it's tomorrow," Senna answered quietly, making Percy realize he'd asked the question out loud.

Percy pressed a knuckle to his sleepy eyes. "Do you think we'll ever be able to come back?"

Senna chuckled. "Part of the reason I waited so long to allow this trip was because I knew I'd never be able to keep you away again. I wanted to make sure you were ready for the responsibility."

Percy squinted up at the Dam, then into the dark trade channel. "I don't feel ready," he admitted.

Senna's hand fell on Percy's shoulder, the most steadying thing Percy knew. Together, they crossed through the veil of the Dam.

THEA

ACATHEA ROSECROFT'S STORY BEGAN with survival.

As a child, she didn't know it as such. No one had told her it wasn't meant to be that way—scrounging for food in the empty orphanage cupboards and always sitting on her hands to keep them warm. As an adult, she would long wonder what it was about *her* specifically that made the canons favor her above all the other children who scrounged and sat. What had she done to enter the exile an orphan and emerge a princess?

Life was a beautiful gift when no one else around her had it. Thea remembered feeling the terrible burden of her own beating heart and the fullness of air in her lungs. The morning the exile began, her own pulse became a treasure more valuable than anything in the world. The other children in the orphanage were not as lucky, each succumbing to the sun sickness. Even Mister MacBennal—Orphan Mother Mabel's assistant who led the orphans during the exile—was eaten alive by a million thorny pink flowers.

Thea's testimony was not that she was the only survivor among a mass grave of helpless orphans. The miracle was that, in the early days of Redwind's genesis, the new queen had knelt beside her and told her that she could be Redwind's princess. All Thea had to do was become a very, very good liar.

So she did. She lied to the Redwindan people for over a decade, telling them with untruthful lips that she was their heir. The person who would one day bear the burden of their concerns, their sorrows, the prosperity of their futures.

That was why Thea needed to find a way to restore her magic—even if it had never been there in the first place. Because if she didn't, then it was only a matter of time before she shrunk back down into the starving orphan girl who no one wanted. If that happened—if Queen Casta removed Thea as princess—the people of Redwind would learn she was merely a fraud who'd come from the same dirt they had and gotten to play pretend.

A round of applause for the actress, everyone. What fools you all were for believing her.

THE TROUBLE WITH TRYING to become inflorescent was that everyone else was attempting to cure it.

Conducting research on restorative magic by herself was as peaceful as it was lonely. She was sure Percy would have helped if she'd asked, but she couldn't. Not when she knew that all of his hard work would probably amount to nothing. This was her undertaking. If she was going to find answers, she needed to do it herself.

One thing was for certain, though: the apothecary lab had run dry on its support. Thea had read all of the apothecary's books and learned all there was to know about curing the common cold and a queasy stomach with a few well-grown herbs. Yet, in matters of inflorescence, the ancient tomes were of no assistance. She'd have to find her answers elsewhere.

"Why don't you start at the library?" Percy had suggested off-handedly during their conversation earlier. *"I'm always sneaking into my library about one thing or another. Though, I suppose it's not really sneaking when I'm the future king. It*

just feels so naughty, somehow. Being in there when no one else is, for my own trivial purposes. When I get interrupted, the invader always seems to think I am perform-ing some type of solemn research. Really, I'm satisfying some morbid curiosity and looking up the phallus size of the average draft horse."

Thea hadn't met the librarian assigned to Redwind's collection yet, despite having lived in the castle as long as they had. Rumors had grown that the librarian was protective and did not appreciate having their space invaded. If Thea wanted to search its shelves for something that could help her, she'd have to go when the librarian was out.

This was where Thea's maids came in. They knew, with perfect accuracy, the comings and goings of all who passed the castle perimeter—including that the librarian would be away for the next few days on collection-related business. The news thrilled Thea so much, she offered sweet tea biscuits and a tiny jar of her perfume as thanks.

After her conversation with Percy, Thea could barely keep still with the desire to get closer to her cure. To finally be accepted as a real Rosecroft.

Creeping toe-first into the Redwind Library, Thea now felt like the books were all observing her in the librarian's absence, daring her to pick them up. The last, and only, time she'd been here, Emrys had been showing her around the castle. Back then, the library had been a massive, empty room with a stack of ten books on a middle table. Now, it was transformed.

Like most of the rooms in the castle, the library was mostly windows. Where there weren't panes edged in green inflorescence, there were shelves, all filled with a wide variety of books. Trees stood tall at each of the cardinal points, stretching up and closing over the domed glass ceiling. A spiral staircase led to a balcony with a large worktable, the contents of which were a mystery from the floor.

It wasn't a library of many books, by any means. Thea suspected that this was the amount of books a person might possess in Talsura if they had even a small amount of wealth. But the librarian, whoever they were, had been curating this particular collection themselves, ensuring each book had earned its shelf space, for twelve years.

Thea perused the stacks. Up close, she could see that each book had a ribbon lying over its spines like a bookmark. Attached to the end of each ribbon was a small tag, upon which was inscribed a combination of letters and numbers. In the back of her mind, she remembered Percy complaining in one of his letters about the complexity of the Talsuran library. This had to be the same system. If she was right, there should be a large cataloged index containing all the titles listed alphabetically.

Skimming a few stray books, Thea searched for the index. If she could locate it, she'd be saved the trouble of opening every individual book. Yet, the catalog was nowhere to be found on the first floor.

Next, Thea tried the balcony. On her way up the stairs, the floorboards creaked at a grievous volume, sending an unpleasant shiver down her back. She was always aware of the way her body existed in a space—even now, when she was completely alone in the quiet. The world, it seemed, was always trying to get her attention and Thea was frightfully attuned to it. Every chirping bird or dripping faucet captured her full focus. The bright light of the castle's windows were worse because they were even needier and often came with a headache. It made her feel like she could tear someone's throat out with her teeth. But that was unbecoming of princesses, so she refrained.

There was complete silence at the top of the balcony.

Better still, the index was there too.

It was almost as she imagined it, big enough that it'd be able to spill over the edges of her bedside table, and crafted from fine light-brown leather. The leathersmith had embossed floral designs along the pressed edges. It must have been maintained with a conditioner, because the book smelled of lanolin.

Thea opened the catalog, delighting in the pleasant way the ivory pages crinkled. Temptation nearly drove her away from remaining on task—there were so many topics to be discovered, titles she'd never heard of before. With an impressive amount of restraint, Thea flipped to the section labeled *Inflorescence*.

It was a humble assortment. Where other sections could boast dozens of pages of records, the section about inflorescence contained all of seven books. Thea ran her finger down the page as she read through the titles—*Wanderer: A Firsthand Account of Talsura's Oldest Exile*. Another titled *What is Inflorescence, Really? Origin Theories by Redwindan Experts*. Even *Blooms and Balance: A Redwindan Guide to Inflorescent Interior Design*. Nothing helpful. Nothing of use.

Then her finger paused, eyes catching on a title in a completely different sub-heading:

Basic Sigil Spells for the Beginner
Edited by Morrison Kagner

Thea's heart leapt. She only needed a clue, a hint of where to begin with her magic. If any book in this library could provide that, it was going to be this one. With a spare scrap piece of paper and ink pen lying on the table, Thea jotted down the book's whereabouts, knowing she'd never remember the random location code on her own. She scurried back down the stairs to where the *T-I's* were located, eager to get her hands on that book before the librarian returned.

It took her longer than she cared to admit to locate it, but once it was in her hands, it felt like all the library windows had spread wide open. Possibility lay perfectly flat in her palms, waiting to be explored. Thea returned to the worktable so that she could record any notes worth remembering. Hands trembling, she opened to the first page.

The beginning of the book required some patience. It had vocabulary to learn. Basics to cover. If Casta had cared enough to give Thea any sort of magical lessons, she might've been able to skip to the first spell. But Casta had seen Thea fail one too many simple enchantments to invest any of her valuable resources.

Thea refused to cut corners. If learning magic meant sitting through monotonous mountains of text, then she would endure it. She would read about how the source of all magic was internal, how it required a very practiced concentration.

The sun had shifted to the opposite wall by the time Thea felt prepared to step into the first spell. It was a simple igniting spell, suitable for lighting candles and rolls of smokable hemp, but more advanced than the snapping spell Percy had demonstrated.

First, lay your hand flat open before you. Then trace the following symbol into the heart lines of your hand. Use a feather-like touch. The caress should tickle, then start to warm. Think strongly of the intention of the spell.

Thea followed the instructions like a reverent acolyte tending to a canon. The touch *did* tickle, but no warmth followed it. Perhaps she was drawing the symbol wrong. It seemed like a tailed numeral six, sweeping off like a treble clef. Maybe it was best to read on.

Once the symbol is complete, sweep your finger off your hand in the direction of your candle, up the middle finger. Utter "Ignite."

If you've performed the spell properly, the candle will light. If the candle remains unlit, focus your concentration. Smoldering is a good sign, but be careful not to burn your hand.

Thea drew the symbol once more, this time following the instructions and trailing the tail all the way off her middle finger.

"Ignite!"

No flame appeared. No warmth on her skin either—just a terrible urge to itch her palm from all the strange sensations.

She tried again. And again. And again. Until her voice was trembling from the strain and frustration.

How *blasted* hard was it to utter a single word and draw a canon's damned sigil?

Letting her anger bubble to the surface, Thea pressed the symbol hard into her skin and hissed out, "Ignite, damn it!"

Without a breath of warning, an arrow whizzed from thin air and caught Thea by the sleeve. Its momentum was powerful enough to force her arm above her head, affixing the fabric to a wooden beam beside her.

Thea stood completely still. She didn't dare move. Who knew what sort of hemlock poison was dripping from the arrow tip. One accidental nick, and life as she knew it would fade away.

As carefully as she could, Thea scanned the room for the assailant.

There, on the bottom floor, standing in the doorway, was a woman. Her bow was still poised at the ready, another arrow already notched. She was dressed in fine scarlet Redwindan clothes and her strong jaw was pointed upward in defiance. Kohl-lined eyes glared beneath two full brows down her long, curved nose. Her black hair was loose on one half of her head. The other side was cut close to her scalp, with swooping designs shaved out of the hair that remained. If she hadn't been aiming a potentially poisoned arrow at her face, Thea might've thought her beautiful.

She raced to utter the first word, but the woman beat her to it.

"I'd thank you kindly if you didn't attempt to burn down my library, Your Highness."

So *this* was the librarian. Thea didn't care if this woman was the queen of the entire world, she did not appreciate being threatened. Especially when she was so close to getting the spell to work.

"*Your* library? You ought to reconsider who this library really belongs to. You just tried to kill me!" Thea spat, drenching her voice in her own venom. "My mother keeps dungeon cells that are especially dank and abominable for occasions such as this. I suggest that you lower your weapon and explain yourself. Or should I call for my guard?"

This was a bluff—Emrys wasn't anywhere within earshot—but the librarian didn't know that. With a huff, the librarian dumped her bow on the notch to the right of the door and slung her quiver off her shoulders onto the floor.

"If I was trying to kill you, you'd know," the librarian explained crankily. "I was merely trying to keep you from burning down the castle."

"Is this arrow poisoned?" Thea demanded.

"No," said the woman, gritting her teeth. Thea smirked. At least the frustration was mutual. "Only ranger knights carry poison arrows. I'm just the librarian."

"I can see that," Thea replied, plucking the arrow from the beam. She snapped it in half, then sent the broken pieces sailing over the edge of the railing. They landed with a hollow clatter at the librarian's feet.

"Well?" Thea demanded. "State your name."

"Nare Demira, Your Highness."

"I should report you directly to Captain Calloway, Nare Demira. Do you have any idea what the usual punishment is for threatening the crown princess?"

A shadow crossed over Nare's face, curling into a deep frown. Thea's skin already crawled whenever someone didn't say what they were feeling. Trying to interpret a grimace on its own was gambling between whether its cause was humiliation, anger, or fear.

"Answer me," Thea pressed.

The librarian narrowed her eyes. "You're worse than they say you are. How's that for an answer?"

Red flared behind Thea's eyes. She tore down the stairs, picked up the tip of the broken arrow, and held it up under Nare's face. Nare peered through her lashes at the sharp tip, a challenge in her gold eyes.

"I don't think you understand the gravity of what you've done," Thea snarled.

"I don't think you understand how dangerous it is to practice flame runes in the presence of some of the most important, *flammable* materials in the entire kingdom," Nare shot back. "You could've blown the castle into the blasted sky."

"Yet here we are."

"Unscathed," Nare pointed out, nodding at the arrow.

"Unscorched," Thea dared back.

They appraised each other for a long moment. Up close, Thea could smell Nare's perfume, a mix of autumn apples and spiced honey. A closer inspection revealed tiny saffron blossoms in Nare's loose hair. The tiny, crimson threads were sewn into the individual strands, lending their fragrance to their wearer. Her smile lines placed her a few years older than Thea, maybe at around thirty years old. When Thea looked back at Nare's eyes, she found the librarian sizing her up from her skirts to the crown on her head.

"What *are* you doing here?" Nare said. The sharp edges were gone from her voice, leaving only sheer curiosity and the ever-present notes of a challenge.

"What does anyone do in a library? I was conducting research."

"I have a feeling if I ask you to share, you'll suddenly become speechless."

Thea pressed her lips together, annoyed. She kicked the arrow aside, pushing past Nare to head toward the door. This was getting nowhere quickly and Thea had better things to do than argue with someone who wouldn't help her.

"Ah, the princess is a secretive thing," Nare teased, halting Thea in her tracks. "Who would've guessed?"

The sharp points of Thea's nails dug into her palms. If only this impudent librarian had any clue. She spun around, gaze sharp.

"Is there some law that says I have to report every little thing I want to study?" Thea snapped.

"Actually, there is," Nare drawled, sauntering away to sit on one of the round tables. Legs kicking easily in their loose trousers, she gestured at all the unorganized books. "I'm the only one who knows where everything is in here. Name any book, and I can tell you what canons-cursed pile it's collecting dust in. If you need a book, you have to go through me to find it."

"I didn't need you for the first book I found. What if I want to take my chances?"

"Then the queen will be very curious about what you're doing by yourself in here that you want no one to know about."

Thea narrowed her eyes. The longer this conversation dragged on, the more concerned Thea became that this was somebody she might not be able to outwit. No one had ever spoken to her this way, much less threatened her.

"I've nothing to hide from my mother," Thea pointed out. *Only my pathetic desire to be recognized as a member of this family. And sometimes the truth of what Emrys is getting up to when he disappears. Oh, and that really unfortunate affair I had with my ex-lady's maid a year ago.* "But if it's all the same to you, I'd like to wait until I have solid findings before I present them to her."

This was apparently reasonable enough to Nare, who opened her arms wide.

"Alright, then. Let's have it. What's this mysterious project that's got the Princess of Redwind all up in arms?"

"You want . . . to help?"

Nare shrugged. "Isn't that what you pay me to do? Provide research help?"

Thea's gut reaction was to tell the librarian to stuff her questions and mind her bloody business. But Thea needed someone who would understand the way the Redwindan people would turn their backs on her the second they learned she was fallow. Percy would try to understand—for that Thea would always be grateful—but he had grown up in a kingdom that despised anything having to do with inflorescent magic. He supported Thea's quest for magic because he supported her, not because he gave it much value.

After a long moment, Thea closed both of the heavy library doors. Only when they clicked shut did she spin around, holding them in place.

"I really will burn down your library if you breathe a word of this to *anyone*," she said, low.

"Relax, princess," scoffed Nare. "I'll try not to tell my diary."

At Thea's pointed stare, Nare held up her hands.

"My lips are a steel cage," she swore.

Thea toyed at a white rose fixed to her dress, rubbing the silky petal between her finger and her thumb. It'd been so long since she'd admitted the truth out loud, she'd forgotten how hard it was to say.

Finally, Thea said, "I'm fallow. Possibly completely incapable of inflorescence—*and* sigil magic, apparently. I'm looking for a way to restore"—Thea gestured vaguely—"whatever it is I wasn't born with."

Nare blinked. "You're fallow," she repeated.

Thea rolled her eyes in exasperation.

"Yes."

Strangely, Nare craned her head to look at the bookshelves, as if they were able to tell her whether or not she'd heard Thea correctly. Her lips pursed together, the words on the tip of her tongue not quite making it out.

"But that's not possible," she said slowly. "*No one* is fallow. We only use that word to describe Talsurans who can't use inflorescence because their sun is literally blocked out."

"It *is* possible," Thea said, annoyed. "Because *I'm* fallow. Do you think I'd make that up?"

"You're—you're literally wearing the royal family's flower on your head and on your dress. I'd recognize the Rosecroft white rose anywhere."

"My mother grows them for me," Thea lied tightly. She was spilling secrets, but she could not explain it was really her brother who was the *true* heir to the throne.

"*Every day?*"

"Are you going to help me or not?" Thea snapped loudly.

Nare's wide eyes gave way to a wrinkled brow. Thea already knew what was coming. This was the part where Nare explained that she believed inflorescence was a gift from the canons and whoever wasn't inflorescent must've displeased them somehow. *Sorry, but I can't help you*, Nare would say. *If you're cursed by the canons, I don't want to get cursed myself.*

"I . . . don't know anything about restoring magical abilities," confessed Nare. "There aren't any texts here that even skirt near the subject. They all just assume—"

"—that a person is inflorescent. Yes, I know," Thea said bitterly, rubbing at her throat.

Nare's eyes skimmed the shelves, squinting at the books. She sighed, then turned back to Thea.

"Do you want a librarian's professional advice?"

"If I did, would I have snuck in when you were away?"

Nare shot her an annoyed look. "You have to yank yourself from whatever shallow pool of pity you're drowning yourself in and ask your mother for her help. She has access to the best mages in the kingdom. I'm sure any of them would fall over themselves to help the princess." She switched into what must've been her impersonation of a snotty male sorcerer, straightening a nonexistent collar.

"The acclaim! The plaudits! How nice it would be if someone else stroked my ego for once."

Nare's smirk betrayed that she was dying for Thea to snatch up the opportunity to make the dirty joke, but Thea was wholly uninterested in imagining men stroking anything.

"I can't involve my mother," Thea said.

"Why the hell not?"

Because she's technically not really my mother. Also because telling her about my long-standing plan to convince her to make me her real daughter would make her laugh in my face, and I simply don't have the will to withstand that.

"She's already tried," Thea said. "She's insisted it's futile and that we never speak of it again, but I'm not inclined to give up."

Nare crossed her arms over her chest, tapping her finger against her round biceps. Thea could practically hear rusty gears churning in Nare's mind as her thoughtful gaze darted from the shelves to the glass ceiling. If there was any hope to be found, it was hiding under a fog of distant thought. Thea thought it best not to interrupt.

Then, all the twisted muscles of Nare's face dropped their tension and her expression lit like a candle. Without explanation, she vaulted off the table and hurried around the stacks of books on the floor to where a thick ledger waited in the middle of a table. The pages fanned in a blur as she searched for something with hawk-like intent. When at last she found it, Nare held the book open and pointed at the page. From across the room, it didn't bear much significance, until Thea realized Nare was pointing at the only lines on a page that was otherwise completely blank.

"Laurentine Saville. If anyone in Islevaria can help you, it's him. Or, more specifically, his journals. He's been writing about magical equality for eons. I've been trying to get my hands on them for over a decade."

"For what purpose?" Thea wondered.

"For this library, of course. That's how *all* of these books came to be. I ask folks what books are in their possession. Sometimes they make generous donations." At Thea's incredulous look, Nare shrugged. "What? It's not like the queen emerged from her exile with a full library."

Thea's frown lost heat. This she knew all too well. Queen Casta had made quick work of transforming Redwind into a kingdom that was as reputable as Talsura. Of course, Talsura had the benefit of taking its time, growing as slowly as a flower that only bloomed once a year. The people of Redwind recognized that every day without their own fortified society was another day left completely vulnerable. The birth of the city was nothing short of miraculous—rising from the ground up in a matter of months.

Thea would never forget how the Redwindan people raced against the approaching winter, scrounging for supplies, warm shelter, and control over their inflorescence. They'd come to this land with all they could carry. Books had occupied valuable space in their packs where a person could have brought more clothes or food. That made every book in this collection *intentional*. A treasure in its own right, given up to a greater cause.

When Thea had been trapped among her memories for too long, Nare plucked a small throwing knife from her bodice and whipped it at the wall beside Thea's head. Thea jolted away with a yelp.

"How many blasted weapons does one librarian need?" Thea cried.

Nare didn't dignify that with an answer. Not now that she had regained Thea's attention.

"I want you to come with me and convince Laurentine to donate his books," she said resolutely. "I've stuffed his mailbox with letters, but he hasn't answered a single one. He'll listen to a princess."

"*A* princess? Not his?"

"He's not from Redwind. His village, Claewick, used to be one of the outer Talsuran villages that didn't make it inside the Dam. I heard it suffered a fair amount of devastation during the height of the sun sickness, but if anyone survived it, it'd be Laurie. I bet he expects that Redwind is interested in the Claewick lands."

Thea plucked the throwing knife from the wall and tossed it onto the table. "Do I understand correctly that you want me to intimidate this man into making him believe that I'll seize his home if he doesn't comply with our demands? That's practically Talsuran."

"I never said you had to intimidate him yourself. I'm only saying that if you show up and ask for something and he jumps to terrible conclusions, that's not your fault."

Thea fought the urge to rub her hand over her racing heart. Though she couldn't decipher if its cause was surprise from the throwing knife or the intense gaze with which Nare regarded her.

"They're *his* journals. Why should he donate them if he doesn't want to?" Thea pressed. "Just because he's of low birth doesn't mean that the throne can simply demand his belongings."

"Says Miss High-and-Mighty who threatened me with her station not ten minutes ago," Nare challenged. "Look, you have his name. You could leave right now, waltz up to his door, and take care of matters yourself. I bet he'd let you copy the books down just to get rid of you. But his work is far more advanced than simple runes. You won't know where to begin and Laurentine won't help you. He's far too cautious."

Crossing the room on soundless steps, Nare once more hovered in Thea's space. She plucked the knife from the table and tucked it back into her shirt.

"But if you help me secure the journals, then I will allow you to read them as much as you'd like. *And* I will instruct you in their ways."

The idea tossed around in Thea's mind. She knew her own strengths. As unpleasant as it was to put herself in a social situation with a stranger, she knew how to be cordial. Convincing. But what good would it be to obtain information she couldn't really touch? Nare was right that she'd need help.

Then, Thea remembered who she was. Nare might've believed she had the upper hand, but at the end of the day, Thea was the princess. She had all the time in the world.

"I'll think about it," Thea said.

Nare's displeasure was immediate.

"You'll think about it," she deadpanned. "When will I have an answer?"

"Not *when*. If," Thea answered smoothly. "If I have an answer, then you'll hear of it when I deem fit."

Thea turned and marched off—but not before hearing Nare wheeze out a laugh, murmuring sarcastically, "Yes, Your Highness."

PERCY

IF SOMEONE KICKED PERCY in the head and left him in the dirt to count the stars behind his eyes, it would not have felt different than standing in the Talsuran streets.

Percy had been living in this dimness for eighteen years now, and still, the dense *black* had a maddening way of throwing daggers into his equilibrium. He'd insisted on no lanterns for this outing for fear he and Senna would be recognized. That left them relying on the pitiful glow shed by the dim street lamps and watching their own feet. They slipped into alleyways and murky passages to make it to the meeting point. Above them, the Dam flickered and churned, like ink stirred with a quill.

The dark was overwhelming, despite the artificial lamps that lined the streets. Percy had met the mages who powered the city's lamps and maintained the Dam—witnessed how drained they were from paying the price of maintaining a base level of glowing light. It required a mage's constant, unbreakable concentration, along with the acceptance that one day their magical abilities would run dry.

Once, Percy made the mistake of suggesting that they increase the number of mages to allow them all to share the burden together and preserve their power. Phaedra renounced the idea immediately. To her, advanced magic like that was privileged knowledge, not to be shared. She didn't mind that Talsura was darker for it.

The darkness did have its benefits, though. It meant that it was easier to sneak out of the castle undetected. It meant Senna could keep a furtive hand on his blade, ready to dampen the soil with the blood of anyone who looked at them wrong.

Percy's fingers tapped against the side of his leg. It was one thing to *talk* about finding a cure with Thea—but actually pursuing it? Percy couldn't help but feel like he was playing pretend. He'd wanted to start easy—discover what other kingdoms did to survive the sun. It'd made him realize he didn't know what their neighbor, Mount Livia, did to avoid sun sickness. Uncovering that answer required hiring someone to visit Mount Livia for him to see what they could find. A week later, he was asking Senna to dismiss Snake-Eyes' trespassing charges in exchange for the information he needed, and the whole thing had unraveled from there.

"Is no one in this kingdom punctual?" murmured Percy underneath his breath.

A shift in the darkness. An annoyed click of the tongue. A swish of fabric. Two steps in the dirt. Then a round face materialized from under a coal-colored cloak. Senna raised his blade out of instinct, but Percy was just as quick. He caught Senna's wrist, attuned to exactly where it would be, and squeezed.

"Mr. Meskill?" The words sounded unnatural. Either Percy's voice wasn't meant for these underground dealings or Mr. Meskill wasn't meant to be called by his legal name.

Snake-Eyes took a long moment to appraise Percy. The rag he used to cover his face was still missing, revealing his crooked grin and his tattoos, sharp and vivid in the darkness.

"The prince has called on his gritty toy thief to play—to play—to play a game!" Snake-Eyes crooned.

Senna shifted closer to Percy, allowing a rare swath of light to hit his face.

"The prince brings his shadow. My, it's taller and bigger than he is. Perhaps the prince is a magician with tricks and shadows up his sleeve," Meskill continued, head tilting.

Percy had suffered through years of rigorous royal negotiation training, but it couldn't serve him here. He nearly missed Meskill's hand shifting under his cloak, unhooking something from a holster. Senna did not. This was his training—to paralyze and disarm with only a sharp-edged glare. Or in this case, draw his own knife.

Snake-Eyes unleashed an uneasy snarl on Senna.

"Think you're real sly, do you? Pulling a knife on me when I wasn't looking."

"Then open your eyes," Senna snarled back.

"Easy, old fellow. He doesn't bite." Percy hummed, though he wasn't positive which one of them he was referring to. "Now, shall we conduct our business? The sooner you deliver the information you promised me, the sooner you won't have to worry about ending up on the wrong side of Talsura's blade."

A loud *bang* rang out in the lamplit street across the alley. Percy tightened his hold on Senna's cloak in alarm, only to find two drunken fishermen being heaved from a tavern onto the cold stone road. They tumbled over each other, tangled their soupy legs, and landed in a heap in front of two copperheart guards on patrol.

A royal knight, a prince, and an underground spy did not often see eye to eye. Yet, it seemed to occur to them all at once that when in proximity to overzealous copperhearts, a dark alleyway was a terrible place to be. Snake-Eyes turned to Percy with such an urgency, Percy believed for a heart-stopping moment that they'd already been seen, only to realize they hadn't.

"I picked the clues you wanted from the mountain folk and put them into the basket of my mind." He uncurled his hand so the dirty palm lay flat in the open air. "But I shan't shake out the contents until the price is paid."

Percy's mind reeled, trying to make sense of the man's words. Coin wasn't the agreed-upon payment—Meskill's freedom was. But there wasn't time to argue.

Eyes trained on the guards corralling the fishermen out of the street, Percy produced a fine linen sack and placed it in Snake-Eyes' open hand.

If Meskill was going to betray them, he would have to do it now. To his immense annoyance, Percy would have to let him—else he would risk turning the guard's attention to them.

But Meskill merely poked a finger inside the satchel, pushing the coins around.

"The riddle given me, the answer found for thee. He wants to know how mountain people outrun, out-scream, outlive the sun sickness." He spun on his heels and spread his arms wide open. "They don't."

"What do you mean, they *don't*?" pressed Percy eagerly.

"Sun sickness deaths in Mount Livia," Meskill said, then held his hand in a zero motion. "When a sprout pops up, a person pops up—the mountain. Then the sprout pops down, down, down when they see the mountain town."

Percy scrunched his eyes together.

"So, the people recover, but only when they stay on the mountain." Percy exchanged a disbelieving glance with Senna. "How is that possible?"

Meskill bristled.

"Specifics you should want, specifics you should pay for." He jingled the bag like an instrument. "Sweeten the money pot, and my mind might patch itself right up."

Meskill threw an expectant look at Percy, like he assumed the prince to reach into some secret pocket and offer him more. But Percy pushed his glasses further up his face. He barely paid any mind to the spreading tussle on the street when he fixed himself with a polite smile and said, "Right. Well, Senna and I have dinner plans."

Then he turned up the alley to leave. Senna left Snake-Eyes with one last unimpressed glare before following along.

"Hold on now!" Meskill stammered. "That's—that's it?"

Percy paused. *Now* Meskill was cognizant? Percy held up a finger as if to say, *I just remembered something.*

"You're very right, sir. You'll want to wipe the grit off your fingers before spending the royal coin. I'm afraid us royal sorts are dreadfully fond of soap, and you'll be found out in a blink."

The familiar blustering of a man realizing he'd been bested echoed off the walls. As they disappeared up the alley, Percy caught a glimpse of Senna in the stale Talsuran darkness—he was smirking.

"You really gave him coins with the royal emblem?" Senna whispered. The poor bastard wouldn't be able to use the coins anywhere without being questioned about how he'd gotten them.

"I'm tempted to feel poorly for it, but I believe it's a fair trade since the man *did* tie me up a week ago," Percy said, lowering into a long-forgotten grate into the trade channels.

Senna snorted, following behind. "You're the textbook definition of forgiveness."

"WHATEVER YOU DO, DO not panic," Thea said, panicking. She strung her arm through Percy's the second he crossed the threshold into the palace. "My mother is joining us for dinner."

"How wonderful! I'm great with all mothers except my own."

"You don't understand. She caught wind we were having *you* as a guest, and she insisted on hosting." She grabbed Percy by the shoulders. "My mother doesn't *host*."

"It's no trouble at all," Percy said, patting her hand. "She only wants to make sure I'm not a spy, and there's nothing to worry about there. I hire out all my spies."

Thea threw an agonized look at Senna.

"He's joking," Senna stated professionally. "Mostly."

"Truly, Thea, I'll be delighted to meet her. I know how you so like to impress her. As your friend, I will make it my mission to be the perfect guest," Percy insisted. "But I'd hate for lateness to be my first impression. Would you mind leading the way?"

Thea clung to Percy's hand as she guided them into the dining room. It was as big as the banquet hall he was used to at home, but its ceiling touched the sky, framed by equally lofty windows. The table itself was beautiful under the window's light, the stained marquetry depicting a swath of white roses and sharp thorns.

Queen Casta stood from her place at the head of the table. Her eyes and mouth, which she'd passed to her son, made her familiar. She was dressed in typical Redwindan fashion—layers and layers of elegant fabric billowing out, the purple rich against her brown skin. When Percy was close enough, she squinted at him, a frown tugging at her lips.

"It's these glasses, isn't it? They're dreadfully big on my face," Percy said. "My court says my nose should be a national monument."

Casta pressed her mouth against a laugh.

"Forgive me. You look, and *sound*, terribly like my late best friend, your Aunt Ceday." Her smile grew sad. "She'd be thrilled to hear we were all dining together today. No doubt she's terribly jealous, wherever she is."

Percy's heart squeezed so hard, it stole all of his rational thought. He crossed the room in eager strides and wrapped his arms tightly around the queen.

Emrys choked on his wine. Thea and Senna gaped. But Percy paid them no mind.

"I'm so sorry for your loss," he said quietly. "My mother says I hug like her. You can just pretend that it's Ceday giving you a long-overdue squeeze."

Casta stood completely frozen, hands hovering over his back. Then, finally, she patted Percy's shoulder.

Remembering himself, Percy stiffened and then inched back.

"I always forget to ask permission to hug before I launch myself onto some-one," Percy said, embarrassed. "Forgive my impudence. It's only that no one has mentioned Aunt Ceday in some time."

She smiled fondly and tapped his cheek. "I'm used to it. She was the same way. I am very pleased to see your mother hasn't killed Ceday's spirit after all."

Percy's heart settled softly. "It's nice to meet you too."

Clearing her throat, Casta gestured to the table.

"Please, take your seats. Dinner will be served shortly."

Behind him, Senna dipped into a low bow, then stood against the window.

"That includes you, Goldheart," Casta called out, unfurling her napkin across her lap.

A flash of hesitation flickered on Senna's face. He did not move.

"If the goldheart is going to skip his dinner," Emrys began dramatically, "then, as the princess' guard, I have *no choice* but to—"

Senna pushed away from the wall and took the empty place beside Emrys. He murmured something in Emrys' ear that Percy couldn't make out. Emrys barked a laugh, patted Senna's knee, and said, "Who knew Talsuran knights had such good senses of humor?"

With the ring of a bell, dinner was served. Percy eyed his plate eagerly as it was placed before him—peppercorn steak surrounded by vegetables of every shape and vibrant color. The staff laid even more choices at the center of the table—golden potatoes, lemoned asparagus, and broccoli in a smooth orange sauce.

"You mentioned how unsatisfying your vegetables were the last time you were here, so I requested that the chef go heavy on the produce," Thea confessed politely. "Make sure you leave room for dessert. I snuck a glance at the fruit custard tart and it looks divine."

"Acathea, what have I told you about snooping around the kitchens?" Casta scolded lightly.

"Apologies, Mother," Thea murmured, her smile dim.

"Thank you," Percy said quickly. "No one has ever decided a menu with me in mind before."

"No one? Ever?" Emrys deadpanned. "I'd expect your staff to make meals to your taste daily."

Percy hovered his fork over his plate, unsure of where to begin. "All menus are to my mother's taste. I only request special additions when I'm having a stubborn craving. I try not to trouble the staff. My sweetheart—Elora, you know her as your royal sculptor—made me learn years ago to be kind to my staff. You never know when the young lady dusting the royal portraits is going to be your true love."

He took the first bite, a heavenly taste filling his mouth.

"Sun slay me," Percy gasped. "Is this how you eat *every day*?"

Casta chuckled. "I hadn't realized this would be your first experience with fresh vegetables. This is indeed how food tastes when you grow it with natural sunlight." She nodded at Senna. "How about you, Goldheart? Is it how you remember?"

Senna straightened in his seat. It took him a few moments to pull the words out. For a second, it looked like Casta might repeat herself, but Emrys cleared his throat.

"My—" Senna's voice cut off, so he politely took a sip of his wine. "My cook wasn't nearly as imaginative."

Percy grimaced. Senna's childhood meals consisted of bitter vegetables boiled in plain water. He hadn't even tried butter until he'd moved into the castle.

"We are known for imagination," Casta agreed. She tossed her hands up. "I simply can't get over how strange it is to have Talsurans at our table. Though, I have to admit, I feel more at rest meeting you in person. You'll forgive me for being nervous about my daughter exchanging letters with someone she'd never met for so long. I see you are harmless."

"Your Majesty!" Emrys laughed into his cup.

"She's right," Percy lamented. "I couldn't hurt a fly. And Senna wouldn't, unless that fly hurt me first."

"It's not surprising," Queen Casta said comfortably. Everything about her was that way—smooth and easy. Her full lips were almost always upturned into a charming, wise smile that reached moon-bright eyes. "I feel like I know so much about you after all I've heard from Acathea. She tells me you've begun your formal sword training? By my standards, you're practically ready to be king."

"If my ascension to the throne rests on the level of my swordsmanship, then Talsura is surely doomed. I can't seem to get used to the weight. They insisted that I learn to wield my father's blade, which has diamonds embedded into the hilt. You can't imagine how pitiful I look lugging it around the training grounds."

Casta tsked placatingly. "You've only just begun your training. You must be more patient with yourself."

Percy gave a half-hearted shrug. He'd never expected to become overly skilled at the battle arts, but then, that was what his goldheart was for.

"I'm not concerned either way. My mother, on the other hand . . ."

"How *is* your mother?"

Percy was able to do the necessary reading between the lines: *I absolutely despise your mother and I'm only asking about her because I want to make sure she isn't starving you or planning Redwind's demise.*

Percy placed his fork down. "She's positively dreadful, I'm afraid."

"Oh dear, is she sick?" replied Casta, in a poor attempt to sound concerned.

"Not at all. She's merely a nightmare to be around. I've got the benefit of never having to see her, but she's a terror at parliament meetings and seems to find keen pleasure in tormenting Senna." Then, turning fully to Senna. "I think it's the fish."

"The . . . fish?" Thea faltered. "Does your mother eat a lot of fish?"

Percy waved a hand. "No no, not that. She earned her disposition all on her own merit," was all he said, before stuffing his mouth with a bite of steak. "The fish thing is about the—" He glanced up at Casta. Had Thea told her about their research? "Nevermind."

Queen Casta had a strange, corkscrewed expression set on Percy. The delicate hand holding her wine chalice hovered midair, halfway to her face. She set it back down without taking a sip.

"Alright, darlings. I can discern when I'm the reason the table is silent," she sighed dramatically, tossing her napkin onto her plate. "No one wants to gossip around their queen. I understand."

"Your Majesty! But you so rarely come to dinner. At least finish your wine," Thea pressed, but Casta was already pushing back from the table. As casually as a person putting on their boots, she plucked her bronze circlet from the table and laid it atop her mountain of coils.

"No no," she said. "I was young once. I remember what it was like having secrets."

"Your Majesty, you know the only reason I can't gossip with you is because I've already got *one* mother who disapproves of everything I do," Percy said.

Casta tossed down an amused smile.

"Then perhaps you should consider adjusting to mother-approved behavior."

"And stop sneaking away from home to visit your beautiful kingdom? I couldn't."

Casta squinted at him affectionately.

"It's a pleasure to have you visit, Percy. When you've got all your hush-hush chatter out of your system, I'd love to have a substantial conversation with you. Come see us anytime."

Percy smiled in agreement. His eyes followed Casta as she disappeared. He craned his neck back to stare down the closing door until it finally latched shut.

Then he spun to the rest of the table, opened his hands, and declared, "I think it's the fish!"

"You said that already," deadpanned Senna.

Emrys leaned into the goldheart's space.

"Has he lost it?" Emrys commented. In the same voice he might've used to placate someone who'd accidentally eaten a hallucinogenic mushroom, he enunciated, "There are no fish on your plate, Percy. There are no fish in this kingdom."

Percy scowled. "Oh, shove off."

"I'm afraid you've been having a conversation in your head that none of us have been privy to," Thea said, snatching a handful of candied oranges from the dessert centerpiece. "Care to fill us in?"

"I'm getting to that! A fellow can't get a word in edgewise."

He moved to take Casta's seat and folded his hands.

"Before arriving here, Senna and I made the acquaintance of a snake-eyed Grit Finger—"

"Of a *what*?" Emrys whispered to Senna.

"A guild thief," the goldheart replied.

"—who happened to be the same thief that tied me up a week ago. He charged a *ridiculous* amount of coin for the pittance of information he actually offered. Not to worry, though, I hoodwinked him and showed him what happens when you attempt to swindle a prince. You know, he smelled distinctly of rotten cheese, and it quite ousted any appetite I had, which made me wonder—"

"*Percy*," Senna said pointedly.

"Oh, yes. Off I go again." Percy shook his head and adjusted his glasses up his nose. "I asked him to tell me about how Mount Livia handles suffering from sun sickness. He provided. In short, they don't. Suffer, that is. No one in Mount Livia has ever had sun sickness."

Thea leaned forward. She always struck Percy as a sprig of belladonna when she was like this—beautiful to look at in her cascade of light purple skirts and flowery bodice, but dangerous to get too close to. Best to leave her simmering with her ideas from a safe distance.

"I . . . hadn't considered looking into Mount Livia. They keep so much to themselves and we trade with them so rarely. Do they really not suffer sun sickness?" she asked.

Percy explained all Meskill had told him, wringing his hands.

Thea pursed her lips thoughtfully. "If it took royal coin to squeeze that much out of your informer, then Mount Livia must be keeping their secrets under lock and key. I've heard nothing of this."

"That's why I've been trying to discover for myself what they're hiding. There has to be something that sets Mount Livia apart from both Talsura *and* Redwind. Something that would make it possible for their citizens to walk among sunlight without fear of becoming sick."

"Maybe their sovereign made a deal with some bored canon," Emrys suggested with a cynical smirk.

Percy didn't think so. If the canons were bored, it was because they didn't have enough power to do anything of substance. The canons probably couldn't stop the sun sickness, even if they pooled all their power together and wished on a shooting star. But Percy prized Emrys' friendship too much to spurn the idea completely.

"I like to think that if the canons were so bored, they would've come to our aid decades ago," Percy replied carefully. "Really, I think . . ."

He paused, the path of his thought swept away in a storm of distraction. He tried to correct it, but his mind was completely empty. His hands clenched on the table. No matter how tightly he tried to hold the reins of his own thoughts, they always vanished. Trying to find them again was like crawling in the dark, not knowing what he was searching for.

"You think it's the fish?" Senna prompted.

"*Yes!* I think it's the fish," Percy exclaimed, relieved. He could've leapt across the table and smacked a kiss to Senna's handsome face. Instead, he spun to Thea, who responded to his enthusiasm with a quirked brow. "Do you remember when we first met, and I wrote that I was excited to visit and have fish that wasn't from a dying, diseased river?"

Thea frowned. "I told you that, during the exile, we saw all of the Redwindan fish swim up the river to the mountain."

"They were avoiding the sunlight," Percy explained. "Or, at least I *think* they were. Haven't we always suspected that the sun's elevated power affected more living creatures than just us?"

Emrys threw a glance at Senna, almost as if he wanted to see what Senna thought before voicing his doubts.

"There's no guarantee that the fish found the salvation they were looking for on the mountain. For all we know, they swam up the river and died anyway," Emrys pointed out.

Thea was still a pillar of thought and concentration. "Then wouldn't they have washed up on our riverbanks?"

"Maybe the Mount Livians netted them in," Emrys suggested with a shrug.

"I don't know *anyone* who would willingly bring a full net of dead fish on shore and eat them."

"Oh, apologies. Do you know a lot of fisherfolk?"

Percy cleared his throat. He didn't like asserting himself at a table where he was the guest—and the youngest person present, at that—but they wouldn't get anywhere if Emrys and Thea started up one of their pointless spats.

"Senna, you've been quiet," declared Emrys. "Do you think it's the fish?"

Senna's back straightened. He'd gotten better at speaking with their Redwindan friends, but catching him off guard like this was a sure way of shocking the man to silence. Yet, to Percy's surprise, Senna sat back and tilted his head to the side.

"No, probably not. If the fish had some kind of immunity, they wouldn't have journeyed up the river in the first place. We don't even know for sure that the sun is what sparked their migration in the first place."

Percy spluttered. "Senna! I can't believe you!"

"I think it's more likely that there's something on the mountain itself that draws wildlife there," Senna continued. "But it's impossible to know for sure unless someone actually journeyed up the mountain and saw for themself."

"Then I'll journey up the mountain and see for myself," answered Percy without a hint of hesitation.

"*Absolutely* not," Senna shot back. "It's hard enough to get you here without anyone noticing you're gone. Mount Livia is all the way at the edge of Islevaria. A half-day's journey from Redwind, at least."

Percy drew in a deep breath through his nose, loath to allow his friends to see his composure wane. It was a heavy burden to be filled to the brim with so much *appetite.* He didn't think anyone else craved a *good* world the way he did. But then, maybe no one else could see it. Maybe no one else dared imagine the simplicity of a world without its sorrows, for fear that it would never come to pass.

But Percy could see it. Every time he closed his eyes, it was all Talsura without the Dam. Redwind without its decade-old trauma. People who trusted him. The favor of the canons. It wasn't fair that Percy had to dream away his days imagining what he *could* be doing to help all the people of Islevaria. At this rate, he wouldn't be able to do anything to help anyone until after his coronation. And who knew when that would be?

Senna was right. As much as he ached to stretch his adventures even further to the mountains, a day's long journey would put his entire enterprise at risk. If his mother noticed he was missing, it all would be over. He'd never be able to leave Talsura's dark Dam again—not as long as she was queen.

Around the table, his friends watched him warily.

He knew what he needed to do. After all, the first rule of being royal was knowing which tasks only he could accomplish and which tasks to cast off.

"You're right, Senna," Percy said. "You will go."

The goldheart held Percy's gaze. Percy was asking a lot of him. He knew better than to think Senna feared the unknown that would await him outside Redwind. But Senna did tread carefully around Percy's mother, as if he thought the queen could scent the fear in his blood.

And yet Senna would jump into a dragon's open maw if Percy asked. That was what being the goldheart meant to him.

So it came as no surprise when Senna's worries disappeared somewhere un-traceable and he uttered, "It is done."

"Emrys will go with you," said Thea. "He is accustomed to traveling the moorlands at the base of the mountain."

Emrys dropped his chin in disbelief.

"I'm not some loyal pet waiting for your command," he argued.

From the corner of his eye, Percy saw Senna frown. From his perspective, that's *exactly* what Emrys was, even if Senna might not have phrased it that way himself.

"I'm sorry," said Thea, sipping her tea and generally sounding very not sorry. "I can find someone else to take on the mantle of traveling at Goldheart Kane's side, if you prefer?"

Emrys pressed his lips together. He seemed to be fighting for his life to look anywhere except at Senna. Bringing his own chalice to his mouth, Percy glanced between the two guards.

Now *that* was interesting.

"I only meant," seethed Emrys through his teeth, "that you should ask the goldheart if he minds company on his travels."

Thea played along, cocking a head toward Senna.

"Are you an anthrophobe, Goldheart?"

"No," Senna replied, unbothered.

"Then it's settled," declared Thea decisively. "Emrys and Senna will depart tomorrow."

7

EMRYS

THERE WAS NOTHING MORE unsettling than walking around the Alpedis Agora before the waking of the sun. As Emrys made his way through what used to be the bustling streets of vendors and socialites, he scanned the immediate perimeter. He'd heard rumors that guild thieves prowled about the now abandoned market square—eager to take advantage of desperate civilians trying to sneak between the kingdoms. If there were rogues about, it'd be easy for them to slip out of detection behind a pile of broken bricks or a wall of pervasive ivy.

Emrys turned a keen ear to the wind, listening for anything unnatural. A sharp rustle of leaves. The scraping of light footsteps on the gravel. But there was nothing.

What a bleak loss, Emrys thought. Everything was right where he'd left it nearly twenty years ago. But, somehow, it was entirely different. He'd never seen a place so contaminated by the wear of nature, the kind that came after so many years of neglect. As a boy, he never would've been able to imagine that the never-sleeping agora would become void of laughter and dancing. No stalls selling hand-crafted treasures. No knights sparring for entertainment and coin. No getting lost in the crowds, finding something new to discover at every corner. All that was left were the dusty roads and the eerie ghosts of memories of days before the exile.

Emrys only hoped that Senna had arrived safely. The agora had made the most sense as a meeting ground when they'd been plotting out their trip to Mount Livia. The temple of Alpedis, located in the center of the agora, was the halfway point between Talsura and Redwind. When Talsura had exiled all of its inflorescent citizens, Queen Phaedra had ordered her engineers to build a tunnel connecting the trade channels to the temple's underground crypt. The intention had been to allow traders to continue to meet in the agora, without forcing Talsurans to face the bright sun. They could simply meet within the agora—no threat of sun sickness.

Emrys didn't pretend to know what had changed the queen's mind. As soon as the tunnels had been carved, Phaedra had forbidden most of the traders from venturing into them. Now it was only used for the bare essentials to come in from off the coast. It was a wonder they were still safe for travel at all. But who knew—maybe they weren't.

At least Senna didn't have to walk all those tunnels to meet Emrys. In his latest letter, he'd written that if he walked part of the distance, a well-cast sigil spell would carry him the rest of the way without tiring him out.

"I'll have to wait several hours before casting the spell again. Unfortunately, this means we'll have to walk to Mount Livia," Senna had written.

Oh no, not that, Emrys had thought, a cat's grin wide on his mouth. *Anything but more alone time with you.*

No thieves beset Emrys as he made his way up the temple's marble steps. They'd seemed so tall in his boyhood, like climbing a mountain. There were different mountains to be climbed today, ones he'd never reached the tops of.

Without constant exposure to the natural elements, the temple's interior was mostly untouched. In its prime, it served as a shrine of justice—a place where the Talsuran magistrates could mete out justice on behalf of the canons and the law. Ghosts of judgment haunted the lofty ceilings, a proclamation that had never stopped echoing. Though Emrys had only seen a trial once in person, hundreds of souls were doomed to the Talsuran jail right there on the platform in the center of the room.

The platform that Senna Kane was currently sitting on.

He hadn't noticed Emrys yet, holding his wrist up in front of his face with a scrunched frown. His thumb rubbed aimlessly back and forth over his pulse point—the same spot Emrys had chosen for the exchange attendants. Was he—thinking about inflorescence?

Emrys approached him and cleared his throat.

Senna's face snapped up. His hand dropped to his lap, sliding beneath the cover of his cloak as he stood up.

"Are you ready?" he asked.

Not really. What Emrys truly wanted was to sit beside Senna and teach him a dozen inflorescent tricks until the sun had wafted from one end of the temple to the other. But time was limited. Senna would need to make it back to Talsura as quickly as possible to avoid anyone noticing his absence.

Emrys adjusted the strap of his pack on his shoulder.

"Good morning to you too, Goldheart. I hope you weren't waiting long?"

Senna hoisted his own bag, situating it diagonally over his chest. "I intentionally came a little early—before the change of the guards. The copperhearts assigned to night patrol are easier to slip past, always half asleep by sunrise."

"Can you blame them?" Emrys said, stretching his arms sleepily. "I feel like I could curl up on a smooth rock and drift back to sleep"

"Out late dancing at the local taverns?" Senna asked with a small smirk.

Emrys blinked. "I was, actually. How'd you know?"

"A well-informed guess. You often write to Percy about what you get up to when you venture out of the castle. It seems like it brings you joy."

"It does," Emrys said slowly. He gave Senna a long look, then said, "Forgive me for pointing it out, but you seem to be speaking more freely than usual."

Senna frowned.

"I'm delighted!" Emrys rushed. "It's new and unexpected, and it makes me curious to know what changed. That's all."

Senna smiled, only for it to dim as he retreated deep into his thoughts.

"I don't know what exactly it's tied to," Senna said, the words stuttering quietly on their way out. "Sometimes it seems like—like unfamiliarity. Other times, a lack of safety. But I'm familiar with you. Now."

Emrys fought the urge to take Senna's arm. "Do you feel safe with me too?"

"I do, I think," Senna replied. "But the reminder that—that the impediment exists has a way of . . . triggering it. It'd help if you—If you didn't—"

"I understand. I'll not ask about it again unless you want me to. Why don't you and I start over?" He cleared his throat, offering a dramatic bow. "Good morning, Goldheart. I hope you weren't too lonely waiting for me."

Senna smiled. He swallowed once, but when he spoke, the words flowed easily. "Not at all. I'm used to mornings alone. Percy doesn't wake up until half past ten."

"Oh, the luxury! My mother would *never* allow that in a million years."

A second too late, Emrys remembered that Senna didn't know his true identity. Though, it wasn't like he'd said *"my dearest mother, queen of Redwind, canons save her."* To derail even the possibility of heading in that direction, Emrys started toward the entrance and asked, "What's *your* mother like?"

Senna followed dutifully behind, though he didn't answer right away.

"I don't know what she was like," he admitted honestly.

Emrys turned to him, only to turn straight back when he saw the tight look Senna wore. The goldheart seemed to be working up to something else, so Emrys focused on his leisurely pace and held his tongue.

"My orphan mother, on the other hand, is a terror," Senna stated finally.

He didn't elaborate, but Emrys had heard all he'd needed to. He wasn't sure what to say to him—if there was anything he *could* say that would soothe the discomfort of the confession. Emrys thought back to his own unpleasant memories. When the occasional outsider offered their pity for all he'd suffered in the exile, he'd always prayed they would just change the bloody subject. So, as they stepped foot back into the open air, that's what he did.

"The agora is different than it was when we were kids," observed Emrys. "Do you remember that one artisan who used to throw pots right over there? Canons, she used to flick clay at me whenever I got too close. I think she was worried I would stick my thumb into her masterpiece. She was right to be suspicious, because I definitely thought of it."

Another moment of quiet from his traveling companion. Had Senna forgotten they had grown up in the same city, citizens of the same sun-hungry kingdom?

"Unless . . ." Emrys started uneasily. "Unless your orphan mother never took you to the agora."

"Why would she?" Senna's steps seemed to fall even harder. "We were children. We didn't have money to spend on trinkets and entertainment. Most of us were too young to consider knighthood, so the demonstrations only *filled our minds with violence.*" He spoke the last words like they'd come verbatim from the orphan mother's scowling lips.

The terrible thing was, Senna sounded like he found logic in what he was saying. But parents were *supposed* to gift children with money for trinkets and take them to see frivolous performers among cheering crowds. Even if the orphan mother didn't have the extra funds to give all the children, attending the agora was free. All a person needed was an afternoon of time. Surely the orphan mother could have afforded that. Emrys thought perhaps it was kinder to keep all of this to himself, though.

"I'm really muffing this conversation, aren't I?" he sighed.

Senna made a thoughtful noise. "I'm only—acclimating. No one speaks so openly to me, except Percy." Emrys shrank down a little. Senna glanced over at him, eyes glinting. "It's nice."

The corners of Emrys' lips tipped up, widening even further when Senna echoed the smile. The goldheart averted his eyes, scanning the open fields.

"What *was* the Agora Market like? Vigilant artisans aside," he asked.

Emrys clicked his tongue. He hadn't really thought about the agora in detail before. He tried not to think of the time before the exile at all if he could help it. But today, the memories weren't as painful as they usually were. Maybe it was because they knew that they'd be gifted to someone who deserved them.

"You couldn't walk without bumping elbows with *someone*. But that was sort of the charm. Trying to force a way through the crowd and ignoring how awful everyone reeked in the heat. My mother liked to purchase soaps from the agora. She liked the way they smelled. My father—" Emrys' throat closed. When was the last time he'd spoken about his father? "My father had dreams of becoming a knightheart, so he liked the demonstrations. The goldheart at the time—Ilias—even told him he'd be able to become a copperheart, if he applied himself enough."

"He must be very capable. That's not a compliment casually given. Did he ever achieve his aspirations?"

Emrys folded his hands behind his back and smiled sadly at the sky.

"I'm afraid not. He was an early victim of sun sickness."

"I see," Senna said softly.

He did not apologize, for which Emrys was exceedingly thankful. That was the way it was between people who had both been forced to be creatures of loss. It was its own language, one that could only be learned with the spilling of blood or tears.

Emrys squeezed his eyes shut. They were leaving the agora now. It would be wise to leave the strongest dregs of his bitterness here for the ghosts to play with.

"I suppose it all worked out," he said, forcefully. "My mother is seeing this horribly splendid fellow now. Hezra. He's a delight to be around. It's awful. Positively worships the ground she walks on."

"Isn't that a good thing?"

"Oh, it's a wonderful thing." Emrys grinned. "A little less so when you're stuck in the same room as them, though. When he's not growing her a bouquet of roses from his own hands, he's actually quite noble."

"I don't suppose *he'd* like to become a copperheart."

Emrys' mouth scrunched. "No, I don't think he wants anything to do with Talsura, I'm afraid. No offense."

"None taken," Senna answered with a small snort.

"But if he *did* want to become a copperheart, how would he? I mean, how did you become the goldheart?"

Senna's head tilted back in thought. By then, the morning sun had begun to stretch over the tired trees, shedding its soft-hued light over Senna's face. Emrys felt his heart give a lurch, like it wanted to be closer to the sight. To drink it all in. He averted his gaze to the path and swallowed.

"I . . . don't know," Senna admitted. He looked down at his own traveling armor, at how gold all of its components were—a symbol of his status. "I have often asked myself the same question."

"Start from the beginning, then. What made you decide to attend training?"

The goldheart stopped dead in the middle of the path. When he looked at Emrys, he wasn't angry. Only . . . lost? Defensive? Whatever it was, it poured from his gaze, spilling between them so tangibly, Emrys felt it on his skin. Senna struggled for his words, rubbing frustratedly at his throat when they wouldn't come out.

"I was sleeping. And I woke up to—" He paused, a haunted look crossing his features. "Well, once I was awake, the orphan mother came out of nowhere, dragging me by my hair to the parlor where the queen sat. She informed me I would become the goldheart that would protect the queen's newborn baby. So I did."

"That—" Emrys shook his head. "That doesn't make any sense."

"I know," agreed Senna.

"Doesn't it . . . worry you? You know her better than I do, but I never would have believed Phaedra capable of doing something so . . . haphazardly. My—queen says Phaedra is always conniving about something. To include a child who can't choose for himself . . ."

"I *know*."

Emrys had to believe Senna did know. The goldheart shared the castle with the royal family, after all. Percy had once written in a letter that Senna's room was right next door to his, practically equal in luxury and comfort. If anyone knew the inner machinations of the queen, it would be the one person who was always present. Always listening.

But even if Senna could read Phaedra's mind and learn her true intentions, would it make a difference? Senna wasn't exactly in a position to deny the queen's command. To contradict her was the same as asking to be hung for treason.

It reminded Emrys of his Aunt Ceday. Princess Ceday had been Emrys' mother's best friend but Phaedra's sister by birth. When Phaedra had first begun talking of exiling the Talsurans suffering from sun sickness, Ceday had been the only one who'd been brave enough to stand up for those who couldn't stand up for themselves.

Ceday had been the first to be exiled because of it. She'd risen to the occasion, the first leader of Redwind. The one to lead the bleeding and the dying from Talsura. To think of ways to feed her hungry and cross the wide moor. The first to garner some control over inflorescence and teach it to Emrys. He would never forgive Phaedra for the way Ceday had *nearly* made it, but choked on thorns and leaves before she could save herself. Not as long as he was alive.

He sped up the path again so that Senna would not see the dark clouds fall over his expression.

"I hate to think that she's taking advantage of you," said Emrys finally. "You're too good for that blasted kingdom."

"I don't care if she *is* taking advantage of me. I accepted long ago that Phaedra would always be scheming and lying about something. All I care about now is taking care of Percy. I keep him safe. Besides, Percy and I have our own secrets. I take him to Redwind to make sure he doesn't die of loneliness. Then, I return him safely to his room without anyone noticing."

"I'm sure that's not what Ilias would've done."

"No, but Ilias was wrong."

Emrys kicked a loose stone, counting the number of times it skipped across the overgrown road. Whatever Phaedra knew about Senna that he didn't, she'd gone and chosen the best possible guard for her son. He had to give her credit there.

"Well," said Emrys, eager to lighten the mood, "if you ever have any interest in leaving your hopeless kingdom behind for somewhere with a little more sun, our gates are always open."

Emrys meant every word of the offer. If Senna fled Talsura, Emrys could make him a knight and see him every day—no more wasting away a fortnight with only glimpses of Senna's modest smile every time he closed his eyes. Maybe Emrys could ask Senna if he'd like to be courted.

But that could never happen. As long as Percy remained heir to the throne, Senna would always have his priorities set within Talsuran boundaries. He was incapable of doing anything else.

Senna tilted his face up toward the sun.

"Who knows? Maybe we'll take one look at Mount Livia and leave both our kingdoms behind."

"Don't tempt me, Goldheart," replied Emrys. "I can never say no to a good time."

T HEY'D BEEN WALKING FOR half a day when Emrys finally suggested they rest to eat lunch. They'd chatted a little more, but spent most of their journey in silence.

For Emrys, being back out on the moorlands reminded him of the exile. The victims of the exiles had traveled this exact path when trying to decide which patch of land to settle on. The patch of trees and heather nearby were right where they'd been decades ago, still catching swirls of wind and remaining strong against them. Emrys remembered hiding among the tall sunset-colored flowers to avoid the cries of the dying. He squeezed his eyes shut and drew in a shaky breath.

They'd survived, he reminded himself. As long as he continued to master inflorescence, he'd never have to watch someone suffer like that again.

"Calloway! I think I found somewhere to have our lunch."

Senna's voice came from a dip in the hill. Emrys followed the sound, wading through the tall grass until he came upon the goldheart sitting on a large boulder. It was situated at the bottom of a valley where the land swallowed them up on all sides.

"We'll be out of sight here," Senna said.

Emrys plopped onto the stone beside him. "Good find, Goldheart."

Senna reached into his pack and pulled out a tin canister, a loaf of bread, and a corked bottle. To Emrys' surprise, Senna snapped his finger and produced a very small, but warm, flame above his thumb. He stirred the flame on the bottom of the canister, heating it. Emrys had known that sigil spell once, but any memory of it was long gone.

Smelling the savory aroma coming from the canister, he laughed. "Did you bring *stew* on our adventure?"

"It's what the kitchen servant packed me," admitted Senna sheepishly.

"My kitchen staff packed me a loaf of stale bread and two pieces of dried jerky. Any cook who leaves you with stew, fresh bread, and—what's in the bottle?"

"Orange juice."

"*Orange juice?* Canons damn it all, man. Whoever is in your kitchen is terribly in love with you."

The flame on Senna's thumb flickered out at a strong breeze, so he snapped it back to life.

"She might be," Senna granted reluctantly. "I hate to take advantage of her affections, but there was no one else to ask. She's the only one who would keep my leaving a secret. I asked her for travel food and this is what she gave me."

"I'd hand-squeeze fruit juice and bake fresh bread for a man I loved too," Emrys laughed.

"I feel awful," Senna lamented.

"Why should you? It sounds like the start of a fun romance. The goldheart and a sweet kitchen maid who pours her heart into cooking for him. I bet you're the object of the entire staff's gossip." Emrys took a bite of his jerky, feeling a swell of bitterness in his gut. Why couldn't he keep his mouth shut? "Tell me you at least properly compensated the poor girl for all her trouble."

"I thanked her and told her I'd pass along compliments to the prince."

"Ah, what a bore," Emrys sighed. Though, if Senna had said he'd given the young lady a kiss on her cheek and made her blush, Emrys would've started gnawing more than just his jerky.

"Women are not my preference, so her efforts were in vain—appreciated as they are," Senna added.

Emrys went very still. All at once, his mind began to race at leagues a minute, trying to ascertain whether or not Senna had mentioned his preference with a *purpose*, or if he was merely making conversation. Did Senna Kane *make* conversation?

Senna was entirely unconcerned with the pure torment he was putting Emrys through. He unscrewed the lid to the canister and began scooping spoonfuls of lukewarm stew into his mouth. Emrys reminded himself he needed to keep eating too.

Emrys tore his stale bread apart and grudgingly took a bite. He felt Senna watching him from the corner of his eye, then tore into another mouthful.

"I would've forced you to come with me on an adventure months ago if I'd known I was going to learn so much about you," Emrys said.

"There's not much to know," Senna replied. He dug back into his stew, only this time, held the heaping spoon out to Emrys and nodded down at it. "For your dry bread."

Emrys blinked, allowing Senna to pour the beefy soup onto the open part of his sourdough. The bread absorbed the stew instantly, reviving it into a realm which resembled "appetizing." The first bite alone was enough to make Emrys fall back onto the boulder and groan in satisfaction. Senna smiled and rewarded

Emrys with another spoonful, and another, until they had polished off the entire canteen. When they were done, Emrys leaned his back flat onto the rock.

"I've been . . . I've been thinking about your offer," Senna began.

Emrys' brows knit together. Then, realization struck him and he sat bolt upright. "To give you inflorescence?"

"Yes." Senna wrung his fingers together. "I think it'd be okay if you did it. I won't be at risk in Talsura and when I *am* outside the Dam—I'll mostly be with you, won't I?"

"I certainly hope so." Emrys beamed. "What made you change your mind?"

"There's something my mentors taught me in knightheart training that I haven't been able to stop thinking about. As the goldheart, I always have to have the upper hand." Senna tapped his canister against his knee. "In this endeavor of ours, I need to have the upper hand above Phaedra. She's—she's slippery. The magic Percy is offering you—access to our knowledge and our mages—it's not his to give. He needs to seize it in a way where Phaedra can't stop him. But those mages answer to her only, and she has more money than she knows what to do with. Inflorescence is the one thing she'll never have. *That's* my upper hand—even if I have to wait for the Dam to fall to use it."

"You're a marvel," Emrys said quietly. Warmly. "I'd be honored to help you. May I have your hand?"

Reluctantly, Senna let Emrys take his hand, his pulse racing against Emrys' fingers.

"Inflorescence is a lifelong commitment, one that bears responsibility. Once awakened, it will take root in your blood and urge you to use it. It will use itself if you don't wield it properly. But"—Emrys smiled warmly—"it is the most wonderful gift, one that I hope will inspirit you. However, there is still time to change your mind if you're uncertain."

"What will it be?" Senna asked roughly.

"The first thing you grow should be something meaningful. Something that when anyone sees it, they'll know it is yours."

Emrys squinted his eyes thoughtfully.

"Amber lilies, I think," he decided. "It's a flower of protection. If you intend to spend your life protecting Percy, then you'll need some help protecting yourself. Amber lilies provide strength and courage, among other things. It'll amplify the good things in your life when you need them. If you need vigor in your heart or strength in your muscles, it will be right at your fingertips. Would you like it?"

Senna relaxed and nodded his consent.

"Verbally, if you please," Emrys muttered.

Senna swallowed. "Do it."

"Yes, Goldheart."

Emrys rubbed his free hand up Senna's forearm, releasing tension and spreading warmth. His arm needed to be *ready* to be a foundation—waiting and willing.

"May Varyan favor you," he murmured and began to work.

Initiating an exchange of inflorescence was second nature to Emrys. Where Aunt Ceday had been the one to suggest that inflorescence could be wielded and controlled, Emrys had been the one who'd accidentally discovered it could be gifted. He'd been playing a game of tag with other noble children in the palace courtyard. In his desperation to claim victory, he'd grazed his friend's shoulder and grown a white Rosecroft rose. It'd taken years for him to understand how it had happened, but once he had, he'd taught everyone he'd known.

Now, he would do it a hundred times to experience the rush of the first step—establishing a connection. It involved briefly communing with his own magic, recalling the unique quality of each type of inflorescence within him. He drew the amber lilies to the surface, recalling the dewy scent of the flower that came to his nose whenever he grew it. Senna would experience it differently in his own body—his own intimacy with the flower would be entirely his own.

Emrys centered his focus to the point in Senna's skin where the flower would grow. He sensed the intrinsic magic of Senna's blood, pulsing with his racing heart. Emrys imagined that the magical foundation in Senna's blood was a bed of soil. Then, he imagined himself planting a seed.

"The first time can be strange and uncomfortable, so I'm going very, very slowly," he explained softly. "There should be no pain. Only a sense of fullness right underneath the surface of the skin. The second it starts to sting or itch, I want you to imagine a very tiny root being dragged in a river current. I want you to imagine that the root begins to exist in harmony with the river around it, not against it. Not rooted into it. Just—there, present and real."

Through his own magic, Emrys felt the inflorescence take root. Senna drew in a deep breath.

"Now, the slightest prick. You'll barely feel it," Emrys whispered.

Senna stared down in astonishment as a tiny bud emerged from his skin. He turned his hand, as if looking for a bleeding hole, but there wasn't any. To someone who didn't know better, it might've seemed as though the flower was sitting on top of the skin.

Emrys's hand began to pull back, allowing the bloom to come to life on its own. It opened, a bright orange lily with streaks of yellow and brown.

"I've never seen anything like it. It doesn't hurt nearly as much as I thought it would. It almost tickles," Senna laughed, and it was the easiest, clearest thing Emrys had ever heard him say.

Senna blinked rapidly, eyes a little wet.

Emrys smoothed his hand over Senna's. "What is it?"

Senna sniffled. "The difficulty isn't entirely gone, but it's *easier* to speak. I don't know if it's ever been this easy."

Emrys grinned, nudging the petals, urging them to unfurl. As if prodded, the flower multiplied, doubling and tripling, until there was practically a full bouquet growing out of Senna's arms. The magical effects seemed to rush through him, and he stumbled back. Emrys let out a surprised laugh.

"You're a powerful thing, Goldheart. The amber lilies want to spread, but remember, *you* control it. You can compel the inflorescence to amplify or die away entirely by just focusing on what you want it to do. The body knows how to listen."

"It was surprisingly effortless," Senna chuckled.

Emrys laughed. "It's easy because it had a master's hand guiding it. But if you had to discover it yourself, as we did, you'd find it much more difficult. It is, of course, a living and breathing thing."

Senna plucked one of the petals off and rubbed it between his fingers. "It needs cared for?"

"In a way. An inflorescent person exposed to sunlight cannot staunch their abilities for too long, or they will inevitably lose control of it. It's like stepping on a stubborn sapling—stomp too much and it will defiantly sprout up. The cure we're trying to find will hopefully give choice to those who want nothing to do with it, even if I think they are foolish for denying the benefits."

Wordlessly, Emrys pressed down on Senna's skin by the sprouts and pulled the flowers free. "Removing it is much easier when it's been grown properly." He offered the flower to Senna. "You'll not suffer in Talsura, but it might be wise to practice while you're with me so I can help you. It takes some getting used to and plenty of practice in self-control."

At once, Senna closed his eyes and concentrated. His hand remained empty.

"I'm . . ." His chest rose. "I'm not sure what I'm doing wrong. I imagine it growing. I imagine it—flowing in my arm. Nothing happens."

"Did you remember to prepare the skin?" Emrys asked gently.

Senna's face scrunched into a deep frown, and he shook his head.

"Not to worry. I think your hesitance is causing your body to fight it," Emrys said. He took Senna's hand and began to smooth over the skin, just as he had during the exchange. "But you're with me and I'm not going to let you hurt yourself."

Senna's breath fanned over Emrys' hand as he exhaled.

"I trust you," Senna whispered.

Emrys smiled.

"Good. Now try again."

There it was, a tiny bud. Not even a full leaf. It emerged from Senna's wrist as simply and easily as if it'd been waiting. Emrys kept his voice soft as he continued, careful not to break Senna's concentration.

"Lean into it. Imagine your blood has been blocked by a dam, and you are removing the stones one at a time. More energy and power is flowing through."

The bud took size, blooming smoothly. When it was fully grown, Emrys gently pulled Senna's hand closer to his face to examine it. It was not as big or bright as the one Emrys had grown, but it was an excellent start. There was no blood around the root, a sign that the inflorescence had been performed successfully. The flower's effect must have been setting in, because Senna sat up straighter and stared down at his masterpiece with less and less apprehension.

"How does it feel?"

"Natural," Senna said, a little surprised.

"Would you like to learn another one?"

"Yes." The reply was immediate. "Yes, I would."

Now it was second nature—focusing on the natural energy pooling in his core and willing it to prepare for a new body. Without speaking, he reached out and rubbed Senna's temple with his thumb. The movement made Senna drop his shoulders as he stared into Emrys' focusing eyes.

Emrys nodded, a question.

Senna nodded back, an answer.

The energy surged from Emrys' fingertips, like water from a well spout. It poured into Senna's body, coming out again in tiny white flowers.

"Needle yarrow," Emrys explained, pulling his hand back, though Senna's eyes never left his. "In Redwind, this is one of the first herbs we teach children to grow because it's one of the easiest to produce and bears the lowest risk. It's also one of the most useful. If you're ever wounded, it will staunch the bleeding and seal your skin like a needle and thread."

"What if I'm not wounded?"

Emrys grazed his fingertip under one of the bright blossoms.

"Then it makes for excellent decoration."

Senna touched the patch of flowers on his face. "I can't see it myself."

Emrys chose to remain quiet that all Redwindans carried a compact mirror to fuss over their inflorescence at all times. Instead, he shrugged and said, "You'll have to grow it yourself somewhere you can view it."

"I see how it is," Senna chuckled, but his smile was bashful. "Thank you, Calloway."

"You should know by now, Goldheart, that I am at your service." Emrys plucked one of the wilting flowers from his forehead and urged a new patch of purple verbena along his temple. "I do have to ask, why do you call me Calloway?"

Senna blinked. "Out of respect for your station."

"My *station*," Emrys scoffed, waving a hand dismissively. "You're not one of my knights. Call me Emrys."

"If you say so," was all Senna said. He might not call Emrys by his first name now, but maybe he would the next time he needed it. Emrys craved it, the sound of his name on Senna's lips.

Then, at the top of the hill, the grass rustled.

Emrys craned his neck, only to find a deer standing at the top of the hill. It stood at the highest point, muscles poised to bolt at the slightest indication of danger. But the sight that astounded Emrys the most was its antlers—a bony rack made of molten sunlight. Liquified light dripped from the bones, like someone had poured smelted white gold over the antlers.

"Senna," Emrys whispered, giving him a gentle nudge. "*Look.*"

To his credit, Senna remained completely still, moving only his eyes to where Emrys had pointed. But instead of commenting on how lovely the creature was, or about the magical nature of its antlers, Senna dropped his hand to the inside of his cloak.

"Don't move," he instructed very slowly.

There was a heart-dropping moment where Emrys believed Senna might launch himself up the hill and charge at the poor creature. But then, something clicked. The mystical doe had not looked at them once. Its alarmed gaze was fixed on something behind them. Something that terrified it so much, it could not move.

As slow as a final breath, Senna turned around and looked up the valley behind them.

"Don't panic," said Senna. "It may yet pass us by."

Emrys wished he had taken hold of his own blade when he'd had the chance. His voice dropped. "What is it?"

"I don't know. I have a guess. I hope it's wrong."

Emrys heard the beast now. Facing the wrong way, he could only listen to the grinding sound of broken bones and unnatural breathing—a wheeze that was part human, part dying animal.

"A dre'malor," Emrys whispered in horror.

It was an ancient word meaning *dreadful misfortune*. They were the only beasts that roamed the moorlands who struck enough terror to make a man go still. They were the violent retaliation of nature, the natural result of the death of an animal when brought about by a human's violent hand.

Emrys had first seen a dre'malor during the exile, when a group of men had tortured an innocent fox to release their grief and anger. The fox had been unrecognizable when they had been through with it, but in the night, it had transformed. With meatless limbs and disjointed bones, it had prowled into camp and eaten the men alive. Like all dre'malors, the tortured beast had melded forms with its tormentors, creating a monster that rivaled Emrys' worst nightmares. It was the physical manifestation of an animal's suffering and a human's evil nature—a bloodthirsty abomination.

"What kind is it?" Emrys asked, quiet as the grave.

"Another deer, maybe," Senna replied. "But it's hard to tell."

"Has it noticed us?"

"Yes. It is deciding."

A shiver ran down Emrys' spine. Not being able to see it for himself was agony. He could feel the dre'malor's gaze on them, though he wasn't sure what he dreaded more—the monster choosing to prey on them or that the helpless creature of light and magic still hadn't moved.

"What do we do?" Emrys asked. It was an unfair question. He was willing to bet Senna had less experience with dre'malors than he did.

"It may yet pass us by," Senna repeated.

Emrys realized the statement didn't come from a place of insight, but desperate hope. It was possible the goldheart didn't know what to do if the dre'malor did select its prey. The doe, at least, might stand a chance of outrunning the dre'malor. It was of the same stock as the monster, but with all of its working limbs and muscles. As for Emrys and Senna, they couldn't dream of outrunning it. The only option would be to fight. Senna was allowing the beast to decide for them.

The dre'malor leapt. Despite its rotting muscles, it propelled itself mightily through the air and landed in the empty space between the humans and the white deer. It was even worse than Emrys had imagined, with its sickly, deformed flesh and antlers on its half-decayed human face. The longer Emrys looked, the worse it was—a body of flesh *and* fur, hands of hooves and fingers, and eyes as scarlet as the red blood around its gnashing maw.

Emrys' instincts unleashed a wave of adrenaline through his body. He spared enough effort to sprout an amber lily on his throat for strength and endurance. Senna followed suit. The flower's effect was immediate, but before Emrys could draw his sword to defend himself, the decision had been made.

The dre'malor chose the doe.

Emrys let his shoulders drop, but the relief was too quick. Because before he could chance another breath, Senna was on his feet, racing up the hillside. Emrys called after him, but could not penetrate whatever force drove the goldheart to protection. Emrys chased after him, leaving behind their packs and cloaks in a messy heap.

At the top of the hill, the doe of molten sunlight bolted full-force toward the tree line. The dre'malor began to sprint after it, but Senna picked up a large stone and chucked it at the beast with all his might. It smashed against the creature's face, sending shards of bone cracking apart like fractured glass.

Then, with hell-like fury, it turned to Senna.

The dre'malor charged before Emrys could make it to Senna's side. He watched in abject horror as Senna braced his feet and allowed the beast to surge toward him.

"What are you doing? *Move*, damn you!" Emrys cried.

Senna and the dre'malor met. Emrys nearly closed his eyes, unwilling to see the monster tear its antlers through the person he desperately wanted to survive. Miraculously, Senna grabbed the beast by its antlers before it could gore him, and threw himself onto its back as if he were taming a wild horse.

The dre'malor bucked and screeched, but Senna's hold was unbreakable. Whatever Senna had planned seemed to be working, because with each of the dre'malor's wild thrashes, more bone and skin and fur broke off.

Emrys tried to get close enough, but its hooves warded him back. He knew of only one way to kill a dre'malor—he needed to cut off its head. If Senna could somehow get the beast with its back to Emrys, then he might be able to sneak up behind it and seal its fate.

The dre'malor gave a shriek and bucked its hind legs with centuries' worth of violent rage. Its skin under Senna's hand slid off its body, but before Emrys' gut could churn at the nauseating sight, Senna flew off the beast. His back thudded into the grass, his sword flying somewhere out of reach.

It was strange. The goldheart didn't yell for help. He only set a fierce glare on the monster as it spun to him.

There—an opening. Emrys seized it without a second thought. The dre'malor was quick, but it was angry and messy. Emrys was quicker. He positioned himself behind the monster, drew his sword back, and sliced at the dre'malor's throat with all his strength.

The blade cut clean through, sending the dre'malor's head ripping through the air and shattering against the ground in an inglorious *SPLAT* at Senna's feet.

All was still. Senna's chest heaved as he stared wide-eyed at the mess on the ground before him. Emrys fell to his side, scanning his arms and legs for injuries.

"Are you alright? Are you hurt?" he gasped.

Senna produced his arms for Emrys to appraise, stretching them out and turning them over.

"I'm not hurt. I thought I'd have more cuts and scrapes, but . . ." Senna gestured at the needle yarrow on his temple. A few of the tiny blossoms had been ravaged in the fight, but they remained rooted nonetheless. "I guess there's something to this inflorescence thing, after all."

"What on earth were you thinking?" Emrys scolded.

He sat back on his haunches and laughed. Now that the fear of death and injury had passed, he could look at Senna—*really* look at him.

"You're positively disgusting," he finally said.

Senna had the grace to appear offended for all of two seconds, before he glanced down at his own body. Every inch of his clothing was covered in pungent mud that Emrys didn't want to try to identify. Some of it was even on Senna's face, clumping in his hair.

Senna groaned. "Where do you think the nearest body of water is?"

Emrys offered him a pitying smile. "Up the mountain."

In other words, at least two more hours of walking.

Senna stood up, wiping his hands on his pants. His lips were parted, as if he were about to say something, but a flicker across the field caught his attention. For a second, Emrys remembered dre'malors sometimes traveled in packs and feared there was another. But it wasn't another monster.

It was the doe with the weeping-sun antlers. Its bright eyes reflected sparkling light in their direction. It lowered its head in a slow bow—a gesture of thanks.

Emrys returned the gesture, letting his arm extend to the side the way his mother had taught him. Senna's bow was much more stilted. Emrys frowned. Was Senna not accustomed to being the recipient of such holy respect, or indeed, any thanks at all?

When they both straightened upright, the doe was gone. Senna stared at the spot where it'd been standing with wide eyes.

"You alright there, Sen? You look like you've seen a ghost."

"Did you hear anything, just then?" Senna whispered.

Emrys frowned. "No. Do you think you heard another dre'malor?"

Senna hesitated, gaze still fixed to the spot where the doe had been, the molten gold pooled on the ground where it had dripped off the antlers. Then, he smiled tightly at Emrys. "It was probably nothing." Emrys felt like he should press on, but Senna was already changing the subject. "I didn't know deer could look like that."

"Humans weren't the only ones affected by the sun. I've heard of other animals suffering side effects of the sun's growing power," Emrys replied, jogging down to retrieve their belongings. "Come, daylight is wasting."

He clapped Senna on the shoulder, but immediately regretted it when his hand came away brown and sticky. "Let's find you some soap."

THEA

"I F YOU WANT MY help getting those journals from Laurentine Saville, then it has to be today," declared Thea from the library doorway.

On the balcony, Nare was standing hunched over her work table at a strange angle. She looked at Thea through the long strands of hair curtaining her face, but didn't turn fully around.

"Does it now?" Nare crooned, setting down her fountain pen. "What? Did you wake up this morning and decide it was a beautiful day for an excursion?"

Thea rolled her eyes. As if it were that easy. In reality, today was the day that Emrys and Goldheart Kane would travel to Mount Livia to do research on the cure for inflorescence. Usually when Emrys disappeared, Thea had to hide away in the castle and pretend that she was wherever her guard was. At first, she'd had the idea to suggest she travel with Emrys and Senna herself, where they'd drop her off to visit Laurentine. Anyone would be more likely to offer help when staring down two heavily armed guards. But she had a feeling that if she encroached on Emrys' alone time with the goldheart, her brother would never forgive her.

"It's hardly a road trip if Claewick is only two hours on foot."

Nare hummed in approval. "Someone has been doing her research."

Thea huffed, crossing her arms over her chest.

"I said I would think about it." And she had. Ever since her conversation with Nare, Thea had known she'd wanted to implore Laurentine Saville for his help.

She'd been scheming, trying to uncover a way to make it to Claewick without her mother discovering where she'd been or what she was up to. The only way to not draw Casta's attention was to disappear at the same time Emrys did. That's why it had to be today. "I'm going whether you join me or not."

Nare leaned on her elbows, squinting suspiciously.

"Where's your guard?"

"The captain is predisposed today," Thea replied evenly, trying to give off the illusion that it was completely normal for her guard to abandon his station. "But I have it on good authority that my traveling companion is proficient in arms of her own?"

Nare hesitated, tapping her finger against her book and glancing out the large windows to her right at the weather beyond the library. Thea wasn't sure what Nare was looking for, but she had a feeling she knew the answer.

"Oh *alright*," Nare said, pulling a pencil from behind her ear and throwing it onto the table. "Let's ready the damn horses."

Thea met Nare down in the stables some time later. She'd snuck away to her chambers and changed out of her ornate emerald gown, leaving behind its breezy, embroidered skirts for comfortable trousers and one of Emrys' shirts. It was true that she loved the lavish gowns in her wardrobe—they were her way of creating beauty where her lack of inflorescence failed to. But she had to admit that these traveling clothes were surprisingly comfortable, complementing the little curves she had without constraining her movements.

Nare took one look at Thea, then immediately focused on saddling the horse. Thea could almost swear that the back of Nare's throat was turning an incriminating red. Strange.

"Hello to you too," Thea grumbled. She reached up and gave a friendly pat on the side of Nare's horse's haunches. "I so rarely ride anymore, I'm afraid I'm unfamiliar with the horses we have here. Which do you recommend I saddle for our trip?"

"None of them," Nare stated. "You'll ride with me."

This gave Thea pause.

"If you think the princess of Talsura is unable to ride a horse on her own, then—"

"Don't get your knickers all twisted up, Your Highness," said Nare, fastening the saddle. "Anyone taking a royal horse from the stable has to record its purpose in the ledger." She gestured to a leather book near the door. Then, lowering her voice, "We have to log a single horse under my name to avoid suspicion."

Nare draped her bag in front of the saddle and hoisted herself up. She situated herself with a graceful ease, though Thea supposed Nare had ridden this horse dozens of times in search of books to add to her library.

"Up with you. Charlie doesn't bite." A mischievous glimmer sparkled in Nare's eye. "But she's got a *mean* kick."

Thea bristled, but moved away from the horse's legs. She had to admit that Charlie was one of the lovelier horses Thea had encountered. Her chestnut coat and midnight hair boasted an impressive sheen, and she stood with a confident steadiness that suggested she'd prove reliable for their journey. Nare, it seemed, didn't just lend her vigilant attentions to her books.

Gripping onto the pommel, Nare offered Thea an arm. Thea accepted it, despite how little she liked to be touched. With barely a grunt of effort, Nare hoisted Thea up off the ground and over Charlie's back. Now the contact really was too much—Nare's backside caged safely in between Thea's thighs, Thea's chest pressed flush against Nare's back.

Thea was blushing in earnest now, thankful her companion couldn't see her. She couldn't scoot back any farther, not if she wanted to avoid sliding off the horse's ass. Unsure of what to do with her hands, she laid her fingers loosely on Nare's sides.

"You'll have to hold on tighter than that if you don't want to vault off the back," Nare scolded. With a huff, she guided Thea's hand until it was wrapped tighter around her waist, pressed against her flat stomach securely. Thea expected her skin to crawl, but somehow, she didn't mind the closeness.

Charlie cantered on, eventually falling into an easy gallop. The castle faded out of view, followed by the Redwindan streets. Thea should've enjoyed the sights of her land and people, which she so rarely got to observe, but her mind was too full of possibility. She'd left her fallow self behind, now carrying the possibility that she'd become magical at long last.

THEY DIDN'T TALK ON their journey. Thea wasn't sure what she'd say. She didn't think they were friends—not yet. Maybe two people whose meeting had been marred by fired arrows and royal threats could never be friends. Maybe Nare believed they were merely collaborators, and temporary ones at that. People who would cross paths for the sake of their overlapping goals, never to interact ever again. Thea wasn't sure how she should feel about the distance between them. All she was certain of, strangely, was that she wasn't eager for this trip to end.

Maybe they could make the most out of it. She'd invite Nare to lunch. Food and wine always made friendships develop more naturally—right? The last time she'd made a friend, it had been Percy, and she'd taken a gamble that he even existed in the first place. He'd done most of the hard work taking their acquaintanceship and heaving it into a place of genuine friendship. Thea couldn't remember the last time she'd made a friend all on her own.

For the short miles they rode, Thea prepared to make her peace offering. It all drained away, completely forgotten, when they arrived at Claewick.

"Sun slay me," Nare breathed as she steered the horse over the village border. "I knew it was bad, but this . . ."

Claewick was utterly, completely destroyed. It wasn't the overgrown destruction that other abandoned Talsuran villages had suffered. Claewick looked like it'd been the very fragile object of a canon's righteous fury. There were structures along the sides of the untended streets that were so demolished, there could be no telling what purpose they had served or even how big they'd once been. Evidence of the desolation littered the ground in broken bricks, shattered glass, and other debris that was stained with something that looked suspiciously like old blood.

Nare threw herself off Charlie, taking one wary step, then another, before crumpling to the ground. Thea came behind her, giving her space, but drawing close enough to hear whatever Nare would say next.

"It's—it's—"

Nare pressed her face into her palms and squeezed.

"I'm so sorry," Thea whispered. What else was there to say? "I know you thought he might still be here, but do you think this is why Laurentine hasn't answered your letters?"

The hands that clawed against Nare's eyes dug into the littered soil.

"He would never have left his home, even if—" She heaved a crackling breath. "Even if it was destroyed. He must be alive. He has to be."

"Nare, maybe he didn't have a choice," Thea said delicately. She was frowning up at a home to their left, where the walls on the upper walls had been torn away like a curtain, exposing a slanting floor. Its rug was dangling in the open air where the rest of the floorboards should've been, but instead they were a heap on the ground.

"*No,*" Nare hissed. In a flurry of desperation, she was on her feet, jogging up the street, crunching over debris and rubble. Thea called out for her to wait, but Nare was like a storm unleashed, unable to be wrangled or subdued. Thea had no choice but to tie Charlie's reins to the nearest sturdy post she could find and follow after.

Through side paths and across overrun gardens, Thea followed the blur of Nare all the way to a small house at the top of the hill. Of all the homes that Thea had seen so far, this one was in the best condition—almost as if whatever had ravaged Claewick had skipped this acre of land all together.

Thea could feel Nare's hope spilling out of her in waves as she rushed up the hill and peered in through the window. She only looked a second before tearing in through the front door. Thea entered with more respect, hesitating at the threshold before inching inside.

The good news was, everything was intact. The bad news was, nothing had been touched in a very, *very* long time. Every surface was coated in a thick layer of dust, with dirty dishes in the sink that were long past smelling bad. Nare patted one of the armchairs by a reading gas lamp, causing a cloud of gray to plume over the cushion.

"Maybe he fled when the village was destroyed," Thea suggested, voice low so as to not disturb the ghosts that lingered.

"He never would have left his books," Nare murmured back. "They're far too precious to be left behind, rotting."

"It would have taken a lot of work to move this many books. Maybe it wasn't possible. It seems like a storm passed through. Maybe he just—" Thea shrugged. "Needed to get to safety."

"But he didn't," she gasped out.

"You don't know that for sure."

Nare eyed one of the armchairs like she wanted to sag into it, but was too uncomfortable to—*settle*. She hovered in the space, wringing her hands. Thea watched quietly as Nare oscillated between sneaking glances at the unfinished writings on Laurentine's desk and turning away.

"When was the last time you saw him?" Thea wondered.

"Hells," Nare cursed, shoulders dropping. "Eighteen years ago. I was just a kid."

"Maybe we should explore the rest of the village and look for any indication of what happened to him."

Nare shook her head, but she didn't elaborate further.

Thea had no choice but to stand and wait for Nare to say what came next. She could try to guess, but figuring out what people were thinking based solely on their body language came as easily to Thea as performing magic. One thing was for certain, though: Nare wasn't going to let this go. Maybe all Thea needed to do was be there for her, just like Emrys and Percy were always there for her. Would that be enough?

Shattering the quiet of the cottage, Nare spun around to Thea with a gasp and balled her fists at her sides.

"There might be a way for me to find out what happened to Laurentine. If I share it with you, you can't tell anyone else what you've seen. It's—it's an illegal spell."

Thea should've at least thought it through. She should've asked what type of secret she was being asked to protect and why it needed to be kept to begin with.

But she didn't. Because for some reason, she *trusted* Nare. She trusted this abrasive woman who had once thrown a knife at her just to get her attention. It settled in her as a gut feeling: *Nare trusts you and you are the safest you have ever been.*

It was for this reason Thea met Nare's determined gaze with her own and asked, "What do you need?"

Nare reached out both of her hands, inviting Thea to take them. She did, but nearly jolted away as soon as their skin made contact.

It was *magic*. Tangible, hot, and crackling—hovering above the surface of Nare's palms like a halo or a rain cloud, barely visible. Sensing Thea's reluctance, Nare strengthened her hold.

"Relax. I know it's a capital offense to hurt the crown princess," Nare murmured with an anxious chuckle.

Thea relaxed into the magic's sensation, realizing that even though it felt like sparks jumping against her fingers, there was no pain.

"There's a way for me to access the memories this house holds. I need you to act as a mediator between the past and the present. When the magic takes hold, I'll be locked away from the present, but you'll be able to see what I see *and* have an awareness of what's around us. If something goes wrong, you'll need to shake me out of it."

"But I'm fallow," Thea argued helplessly.

Nare squeezed Thea's hand. "That's why I'm the one casting it. You only need to do what I've asked."

Thea had a hundred questions. How would she know if something was going wrong? What happened if the vision was too strong and Nare *wouldn't* snap out of it?

There was no time for doubts. The magic in Nare's palm was only growing, and with it came a dizzying sensation. Nare began to murmur an incantation in a language that was all soft consonants and long vowels. Thea focused on the firmness of the ground beneath her feet, even as it felt as though it was slipping away. She kept her eyes wide open until the very last second a vision closed in around her.

*L*AURENTINE SAVILLE'S POOR BACK *had a crick from leaning over his desk all afternoon, and no amount of twisting or stretching would ease it. He stuck his quill back into the inkwell and scrubbed his eyes.*

What a mess.

This was all the king's fault. Laurentine had never met a man more infuriatingly selfish than His Royal Majesty Mathis Laurent. The worst part was, Laurentine had once believed his king was the very best of men. He'd been thrilled when Mathis had sent a wax-sealed invitation, wondering if maybe Mathis had finally read his work on magical equity. Maybe after all this time, the king finally wanted to acknowledge Laurentine's royal blood—after all, his mother, Haether Laurent-Saville was Mathis' cousin. She'd given Laurentine his name based on the royal surname to honor their monarchical blood.

What he hadn't expected was Mathis to send another summons to Talsura and demand Laurentine act as royal mage.

It went against everything Laurentine stood for. Laurentine had told Mathis so when he'd refused. He hadn't spent his whole life mastering magic for it to be monopolized by the king. "It's to ensure the royal court survives this famine," Mathis had said. "The civilians are not my priority."

Laurentine had returned home to his husband in tears, more determined than ever to ensure that the common person knew how magic could serve them—provide and protect for them when their king did not.

He'd been hoping that with this treatise, he could present Mathis with the figures and research to prove that magical equity was in everyone's best interest. It wouldn't be a detriment to the privileged royals if the commoners knew enough magic to keep them protected from starvation.

He just needed to get the bloody paper written to prove it.

Tapping the excess ink from his quill, Laurentine got back to work. For hours, it was only his roaring mind and the scratch of the quill tip against the paper. When he finally felt like he was making progress, his focus was broken by horses clomping up the drive. At first, he suspected it must be his husband, back from his daily ride through the mountain forests. Judging from the noise, though, it had to be three horses at least. Maybe four.

Laurentine bent by the window and peered out. It wasn't four horses, but seven, each carrying a royal knightheart. On the largest steed was Goldheart Ilias Griere, donning the same gold-trimmed armor he always did. Laurentine scurried to the mirror, pulling his waist-long straight white hair out of its ribbon and straightened his mage robes. The tips of his fingers were still smudged with ink, so he folded them behind his back.

Three thunderous knocks pounded the door.

"Laurentine Saville, by order of the king, you will open the door."

Something sank in Laurentine's stomach, but he carefully unlatched the door and looked through the crack of open space.

"Hello there, Goldheart Griere. To what do I owe the—"

Ilias kicked the door, sending it slamming into Laurentine. He fell hard to the ground, pain radiating from the impact, then again as Ilias' boot crushed into his ribs. A gasp of hollow air heaved from Laurentine's lips, phlegmy blood spitting out with it.

"Ilias," Laurentine begged as the goldheart unsheathed his blade. "Ilias, why are you doing this?"

But the goldheart didn't answer. He took the back of his blade and slammed it down on Laurentine's head, making the mage's consciousness flicker—a flame not fully snuffed out.

Through the onslaught of heavy blows, Laurentine came to the realization that he was about to die.

"My husband—" he gasped, tears and sweat and blood pouring down his cheeks. "My husband will end you. Do not underestimate a canon's grief."

Ilias paused then—just long enough for creaking to come from the back stairs. Only, Laurentine didn't hear it.

Thea did.

Someone else was in the house with them.

The present crashed over Thea's consciousness like a storm-rallied tidal wave. She gasped, breathing in the stale, dusty air of Laurentine's home. Beside her, Nare's eyes were still glossed over, hands glowing with magic so bright, it hurt to behold.

Another creak on the stairs sent Thea spinning toward it, pulling an arrow from Nare's quiver and holding it out like a blade.

It was a woman. The first thing Thea noticed was that she was dressed in the same robes Laurentine had been wearing in the vision, only they were older, sullied by a thin layer of dust and dirt. The second thing she noticed was that the woman's hair was on fire. No—not on fire, but fiercely red. Red enough to look aflame in the midst of the stairwell's shadows, long and messy along the entire length of her back. Her hand was cupping an orb of crackling magic the color of an opal—white, but flickering bright green, then yellow, then blue and orange. She was older than Thea, maybe by a decade, but her ferocity was just as dangerous as Thea's own was.

"Drop the arrow, you fool. I could snap it in half by breathing on it," the woman said. Thea gritted her teeth, but complied, leaving her hands up in the air in surrender. "Good girl. Now state your name and business."

Thea considered lying for a few furious beats of her heart, only to settle on the truth just as quickly.

"Princess Acathea Rosecroft of Redwind."

The magic orb shrank, like the woman's focus had taken a hit.

"What are you doing with Nare Demira?"

All at once, Thea became deathly curious how this woman knew Nare, but asking would be fruitless.

"She's my librarian," Thea said, instead.

"No," the woman growled. "I mean, what spell is she doing and why are you acting as mediator?"

Thea slowly lowered a hand to Nare's shoulder, but the magical orb flared bright red.

"I'll be dealing with just you to start, thanks," the woman said.

"Who are *you*?" Thea pressed. "Why do I owe you anything?"

"Because I'm the one with the orb of death floating in my hand."

"You've got a lot of gall to threaten someone who could choke you in thorns with the snap of her finger," Thea threatened, hoping beyond all belief that the bluff was convincing.

The woman hurled the orb with a mighty snarl. Thea pushed Nare out of the way just in time to avoid being grazed. The magical sphere crashed into a wooden side table, exploding it to woody chunks. Thea held up an arm to protect them both, frowning against the sting of the impact.

Then, Nare's spell was broken. She rolled over, pulling her bow from her back and notching the arrow Thea had dropped on the floor. The arrow's point was encased in magic of its own, smoky and scarlet as death.

"I'd prefer if you didn't throw explosives at my friends, Lane," Nare hissed. Another orb started forming in the center of Lane's palms. Nare sighed. "Put that away, would you? I can't—" Nare's voice grew rough. "I can't be happy you're bloody alive if you're threatening to kill me."

Lane dropped her hand, face going pale beneath her slurry of freckles.

"No thanks to you," she spat, voice just as rough. "I should have known you would've given yourself over to the royals eventually. Laurentine would've been utterly ashamed."

"The Redwindan royals aren't the Talsuran royals. You think I would travel around with one otherwise? You know me better than that."

"I don't know you at all, Nare," Lane said. Nare didn't react, save for the wrinkle in her brow. "I never wanted to see you again. Much less in Laurentine's house performing taboo magic. What were you looking at anyway?"

Thea narrowed her eyes. Lane might've judged Nare for performing taboo magic, but she'd been able to recognize it just by its effect and color. Whatever illegal enchantments Nare had stored up her sleeves, Thea was willing to bet Lane knew every one of them.

"I wanted to know what happened to Laurentine," Nare admitted. "I came here to get his help on something and found . . ." She gestured all around her. "Were you here? When it happened, that is."

Lane hesitated.

"Not when it happened. But I came to warn Laurentine that he'd angered the king a few days after. I found him tied to a post in the village square. He'd been beaten to death. It was all the villagers could talk about."

Thea shuddered, remembering Ilias' sword pounding into Laurentine's head over and over. She'd seen horrible things happen to other people, but it was always the sun sickness that brought about tears of blood. Never another person. Judging by Lane's sick expression, maybe she felt the same.

"I went back home to tell the others what had happened, but when we returned, Laurentine's body was gone and the village was destroyed. We didn't tell you because you were so young. The elders and I planned to avenge Laurentine's murder, but—"

"The sun sickness," Nare realized.

"And didn't you come just in time to save the day. Only to fail. We never did make it back, and every day I live on this earth without my family is a day I wake up and curse your name."

Nare set her jaw, frown even more disturbed than it had been moments ago.

"What, did you think you were the only one who survived?" Lane seethed. "Little Miss *Abandon-Her-Friends*. You were never smart enough to save us. Everyone believed you could, but I never did. They made the mistake of trusting you."

"What is she talking about?" Thea cut in impatiently. She could only tolerate being ignored for so long, but Lane was a woman on fire.

"Only one of us had to watch our friends die off thorn by bloodied thorn and it wasn't you, Nare. You made sure you were long gone by the time the first drop was spilled. But *I survived*."

"Lane—" Nare begged. Now she really did slump into one of the chairs. Lane came down the rest of the stairs, fists balled tight.

"I was ready to die along with them. I waited in that house, waited for the sickness to take me. It turns out, staying out of the sun was all I needed to live another miserable day. *But no matter*, I thought. *I'll run out of food eventually. I'll let myself starve.* I nearly did, too. Until a little Redwindan child found me in the Academe Grove and taught me how to survive without becoming inflorescent."

"But why are you here? Now?" Thea asked quietly. She still didn't quite understand what was going on, but she knew that Lane hadn't explained why she had been hiding in a dead man's attic.

"Because if I stay in hiding and refuse to use my magic, I'll lose it. I needed somewhere safe to practice my craft. I ensure that the Talsuran royals will never have what they spilled blood trying to control."

"What a pretty little sob story," Nare sneered bitterly. Her head was hung low against her chest, a mess of tangled hair obscuring half her face. "But I've heard enough. Let's go, Your Highness."

Without even a glance at Lane, Nare stomped in slow, heavy steps toward the door. Thea had no choice but to follow her. It was only when she stood in the threshold that she remembered they hadn't gotten what they had come for.

"Why don't you go get Charlie?" Thea suggested carefully. "She's tied to one of the posts near the village gate."

"If you don't want to walk, I'll bloody carry you like the prim prig you are. Now, let's *go*."

Thea set her jaw and then her tone. "I said, *get the horse*."

It was a battle of sternness—a joust between two women who were highly trained in the art of making words cut like steel. But Nare had already been fighting and her resolve was weaker because of it.

"Oh, *fine!*" Nare growled and stomped off down the hill.

Then Thea turned to Lane and smiled like a princess should.

I T TOOK LONGER THAN it should've for Nare to ride the horse back up the hill. Thea wondered if perhaps Nare had sought out the post the Talsurans had tied Laurentine's body to. There hadn't been time to grieve before Lane had accosted them.

Nare didn't come inside the hilltop house when she finally did bring the horses round. Thea slipped out the front door, her teeming bag heavy at her hips. Nare went to great lengths to avoid Thea's gaze, keeping her red-rimmed eyes fixed on the noon sun shining over the hill. She didn't ask what Thea had stayed behind to do. Maybe Nare had assumed Thea had wanted to hear all about her sins from the person who seemed to suffer most from them. But that wasn't it at all.

"I fit as many as I could into my satchel, but you'll probably have to come back with a wagon and some crates to collect the rest," Thea said.

This caught Nare's attention.

"What?" she said thickly.

"Lane has agreed to donate Laurentine's books to our library."

Nare's expression warmed at the word *our*. But it was such a simple admission. A truthful one, at that. The Redwind Library was just as much Nare's as it was any of the Rosecrofts'.

The librarian spared a glance into the dusty window of the house, then nodded for Thea to mount Charlie. This time when Nare hoisted her up, she groaned at the extra weight, situating Thea in front of her.

"How many books did you manage to fit in that blasted bag?"

"Enough to make me worry about the seams. Ride fast."

It was only when Claewick disappeared in the distance that Thea realized just how much quieter this silence was compared to that of the journey in. There was so much to talk about now, so much Thea still didn't understand. Nare's muscles were drawn tight under Thea's hold, like she was a pulled bow string that hadn't fired, but she still was quiet.

"Are you alright?" Thea wondered. She wasn't sure what she'd say if Nare gave her the truthful answer—*of course she wasn't alright*—but it felt wrong not to ask.

"How did you convince Lane to donate Laurentine's books?" Nare asked quietly, sidestepping the question. Thea drew closer over Nare's shoulder to hear her voice. "I thought she'd rather let them mold over than give them to me."

Thea tightened her hold on her satchel.

"I pled a very compelling case. I explained, in depth, what I needed them for. Then I told her what a waste it would be to let the books rot on the shelves, especially if she didn't plan to use them herself."

Nare threw a suspicious glance over her shoulder.

"*And* I might have told her that you would never appear in Claewick again once all the books were in our possession," Thea admitted.

Nare's ribs pressed into Thea's back as she drew in a deep sigh.

"I guess all those princess lessons paid off," Nare conceded. A pause, then, "You probably have a lot of questions."

"Of course I have questions. You involved me in taboo magic and nearly got me exploded by some hermit who hates you."

At first, Nare was quiet. Charlie slowed her canter, as if sensing her riders needed to stretch out their journey. Tall wildflowers grazed Thea's feet as the horse followed the untrodden path. They were the same flowers Thea remembered seeing strewn about the moorlands during the exile. These fields weren't on the path the exiles had traveled, but they looked so similar, Thea had to swallow back acidic dread to keep it at bay.

Finally, Nare sighed and said, "Have you ever heard of the Academes?"

Thea replied that she had not.

"They were an ancient, elite order of mage scholars. The group was formed before the first king of Talsura was born."

Thea's eyes widened. That had been nearly a millennium ago.

"I'm not surprised you don't know about it. We went to a hell of a lot of trouble to make sure that no one discovered us."

"*We?*" Thea cut in. "*You* were part of this order?"

"And Laurentine. And Lane. There weren't many more than that—less than one hundred total on Islevaria. We had to be selective about who we allowed into the order. Lane mentioned the Academes were her family. I felt the same."

"But Laurentine was gone for nearly two decades. You would've only been a child."

Nare tugged the reins tighter in her grasp, somehow drawing Thea closer to her chest. "I was. I was seven when I joined. My parents weren't sure when the recruiter encouraged them to let me enlist. But then they told us all about how I could grow up to be one of the best mages on the island, unearthing my full potential in a safe environment. My parents agreed and I moved in. It was . . ."

Her eyes lit, like she could see it.

"It was *incredible*. I went from feeling misplaced among my schoolmates, and uncomfortable in my own skin, to belonging to a family of people who were just as bright as I was. They respected me, even though I was young and learning. They *listened* to me when I spoke of my frustration and discomfort. They were the ones who suggested I try living as a girl with a new name. They even held a celebration where I announced the name that *I* had chosen: Nare. That was the first time I ever knew true joy."

"That's wonderful," Thea said sincerely, secretly a little envious. "What about your parents, though? Didn't they miss you?"

"I visited them from time to time. They were surprised to see how much happiness had helped me blossom. I still visit when I have a chance. Not often, though. They keep—" She cleared her throat. "They keep asking why it all fell apart."

Thea continued delicately. "Why did it? Fall apart, that is. The sun sickness and the exile?"

"Sort of," Nare answered dubiously. "For centuries, the Academes believed it was vital for us to stay hidden. We were more powerful than Talsura's royal mages, which made us a threat, even though we took great responsibility for the magic we wielded. Except, one day, Laurentine got the idea to start sharing our secrets with the public. He wanted them to be able to defend and sustain themselves from all threats. At the time, I was a naive fourteen-year-old who saw Laurentine's suggestion as a threat. If we revealed ourselves and shared what we knew, then nothing would stop the king from controlling us. For me, it wasn't about the magic. It wasn't even anything against the commoners, who I do believe have a right to protect themselves. It was about keeping *our* people safe."

"It seems you were right," Thea said gently. "Mathis did kill Laurentine when he revealed himself."

Nare shook her head. "I should've been there to stop it."

Thea was glad Nare couldn't see her face when she said, "I'm sure you had a good reason not to be."

Nare scoffed. "We had a fight—all of us—about Laurentine's idea. I refused to entertain the notion of sharing our best-kept secrets with the king. Our argument was so catastrophic, I left our home. I think it was during that time Mathis ordered Laurentine to be killed." By now, Nare's voice sounded like it had been rubbed raw with sandpaper. "I returned when I heard word of the sun sickness. The order had put out a message to all members, asking for immediate help to discover a cure. Academes all over Talsura were already dying.

"I got arrogant. I thought that if I could create the cure, show just how valuable my power was, I could convince Laurentine to change his mind. No one told me he was already dead. I worked and worked and *worked*, but I had the sun sickness all wrong. I was so mistaken about what caused it, I never would've been able to cure it. And while I wasted time, the Academes died off, one by one. Some of us lived long enough to be exiled. I had believed I was the only one who survived long enough to see Queen Casta establish Redwind."

"I still don't understand why Lane despises you so much."

"Because I *insisted* I could find a cure. I convinced everyone else to focus on surviving, and they trusted me—despite how I'd left them—because they loved me. I failed them when they needed me most."

"The sun sickness was so new. No one could have uncovered what was really going on so quickly," Thea said over her shoulder.

"My family could have."

"You can't know that. Maybe all of you would've searched for the solution and still never found it."

"If you really believed that, we wouldn't have come all the way here for Laurentine's journals."

Thea didn't know what to say to that. Could she not reject Nare's perception of her failures *and* believe that Laurentine's journals could help?

"For what it's worth, my friends and I are looking for a real cure to inflorescence now. We want to give all the kingdoms on Islevaria a choice without having to make the sacrifices that are demanded by inflorescence or the Dam."

Nare paused. "That's quite the taboo undertaking. Who did you manage to convince to help you with that?"

"My guard. The Talsuran prince and his goldheart. It's a long story. We only want to do what's right for our people, even though it goes against both of our kingdoms' rulings. I only thought—" Thea thumbed the saddle horn. "If you're still feeling guilty about not being able to find the cure the first time, you'd be welcome to help us. We've only just begun, so we don't have any leads but—"

"I'm in," Nare rushed. Then, with less eagerness, "Truly, I'd be honored to help. The opportunity to make up for what happened is more than I could have hoped for. Thank you."

Thea smiled privately to herself. "I'm sure we'll be the ones thanking you."

Nare let out a frustrated huff. "I'm only sorry we couldn't get Laurentine's journals this time. I'm certain he knew something that would've helped us. When I return, I'll try to convince Lane to part with them. I can't promise she will, but maybe."

"How little faith you have," Thea chided. She opened the flap of her satchel and retrieved the top text—Laurentine's single, *massive* journal. "He only had one. I *might've* swiped it when Lane was collecting the rest."

Thea craned her head to see the full effect of Nare's dismay.

"Acathea Rosecroft, you *thief*!" Nare laughed. "For the record, she definitely saw you. But she probably thought it was too much effort to stop you."

"Maybe she's hoping we'll find what we're looking for."

"Or maybe she's certain I'll fail again and believes that it doesn't matter." Nare kept her voice light, trying to pass it off as a joke, but Thea wasn't convinced.

It never got easier—comforting people. She could offer encouraging words just fine. She could change the subject and sit quietly without any trouble at all. But *knowing* what someone needed was another issue entirely, and she so very often got it wrong.

But then, maybe her and Nare weren't terribly different at all. They both had complicated relationships with the family they loved. They were both focused, but low on companionship. They both had responsibilities and would lose everything if they failed. Maybe Thea needed to comfort Nare like she would have wanted to be comforted.

With a flick of her wrist, Thea tugged Charlie's reins from Nare's hands. Before Nare could stop her, Thea flicked the reins and gave Charlie's haunches a kick. Charlie brayed, then threw herself into full speed like she'd been waiting for it.

Nare laughed in surprise, throwing her arms around Thea's middle as Thea leaned forward and urged the horse faster and faster. Heavy gusts of wind crashed against the pins in Thea's hair, unfastening her braids and sending them sailing through the air. Charlie found her rhythm, soaring over tall grass and patches of heather.

Tentatively, Nare let one arm loose from Thea's waist, then the other, and finally threw them out to her sides. She tightened her thighs' hold around Thea to keep steady, making the princess' mouth run dry.

Nare let out one ferocious crow—not a cry of victory, but the roar of someone who'd had it building in them for a long time. It echoed across the trees, awed the birds into flight, and settled in the pit of Thea's chest. The cry fizzled into something weak and wet. At first, Thea was afraid Nare might be weeping. But when she turned around, she found the librarian laughing.

"My friend is dead and everything is awful," Nare said honestly, without bitterness. "But it's a little easier knowing Redwind's princess isn't the killjoy everyone thinks she is."

Thea handed the reins to Nare.

"You might as well start getting used to it."

THEA WAS QUIET BY the time they returned to Redwind. It was like that sometimes after a day of excitement and social intercourse—Thea found herself drained of the desire to talk. Nare didn't seem to mind the sudden quiet. She fell into it easily, wordlessly helping Thea unload their spoils onto one of the library tables. When the books were all spread out, Thea sat on a nearby stool and waited for Nare's initial observations. The view of Nare working, her strong arms stretching across the table, was a pleasant one, indeed.

The first problem arose when Nare finally picked up the journal.

"Oh Laurentine, you son of a bitch," Nare cursed.

Thea crept forward.

"What's the matter?"

"He *locked* his journals. That's probably why Lane didn't stop you from taking it. She knew we wouldn't be able to get into it." Nare threw the journal across the table. "*Fuck.*"

"Let's not panic yet. We just need to find the key," Thea said.

"There is no key. It's a magical seal. Laurentine had these enchanted glasses that would reveal magical seals when he wore them. It was like the glasses showed him the safe's code and let him in. I bet that's how you open the journal." Nare's hands pressed flat on the table. "Did you see them when you were going through his things? Similar to alchemy goggles, with thick rims that look like constellations. I think the lenses were amber glass."

Thea's heart sank.

"There was nothing in Laurentine's desk except for the books and the journal," she said. "Do you think Lane took them?"

"It's possible. When I go back for the rest of the books, I'll see if she knows where the goggles are."

"And if she doesn't have them?"

Nare's shoulders slumped.

"I don't know. But between the both of us, I'm sure we'll figure something out."

"It won't be just the two of us," Thea said. "When my best friend gets word of this, he'll lose his mind if he can't help. He's a package deal with his goldheart and I'm a package deal with my guard. That makes five of us."

Nare barked out a laugh. "The more the merrier."

With that, the quiet returned. Thea excused herself to bathe and change back into nicer clothes. The dress she chose today was an ivory gown of a dozen layers of fabric. The top tier was paper-thin lace embroidered with a sea of flowers.

When she returned to the library, she found Nare right where she'd left her, on the balcony, bent over her leather inventory, cataloging Laurentine's books.

"Are you in the middle of something?" Thea asked.

Nare didn't look up from her work. "I haven't found anything about restoring magic to a fallow person, if that's what you're going to ask."

"No, um—" Thea shifted her weight and found Nare watching her from under her long lashes. "I brought something else back from Laurentine's house. I thought I ought to show you."

Nare moved to the railing and lifted a brow.

From behind her back, Thea revealed a pot of pink begonias with scarlet-hued leaves.

"Lane said they were Laurentine's favorite because they symbolize a love for knowledge. She's been having trouble keeping them alive, so I said I'd take care of them for her. I'm going to have them planted in the garden to ensure that they're always cared for." She set the pot on the table, like a peace offering. "So you can remember him."

"That—" Nare cleared her throat. "That's very thoughtful, Thea."

Thea's heart swelled almost painfully.

"Well, until tomorrow," she rushed, snatching up her pot and fleeing the room. Nare murmured something after her, but the words were lost in the distance.

When she was certain she'd escaped anyone's gaze, Thea leaned her back against the hallway wall. She peered down at the begonias and wondered if one day she would grow flowers this beautiful

CIARAN

N o one in the world recited the holy invocations better than Ciaran Lynwood, but no one was hungrier either.

He wasn't trained in medicine, but he had a sinking feeling that if he stood here and prayed a second longer, his profound hunger would gnaw a hole through his stomach and he would start bleeding all over the marble floor.

"Oesyth, canon of favor, you see into the depth of our desires."

He doubted anyone would notice until it was too late—his black robes would hide the bloodstains. Don't ask him how he knew.

"Observe the vespers of your worshippers. See how they crave your divine favor."

He stumbled over the last word, too busy trying to remember the last time he'd had a good meal. Three weeks ago, before prayers, his mother had made porridge. The only thing he'd had since was watery broth and tea that tasted distinctly of dirt. He'd been gulping it down by the potfuls, eager to fill his empty stomach with *something*—until he'd vomited it into his chamber pot right before evening benedictions. Now he was even emptier than before.

"Only you can mold clay into bread. Only you can sprout roots from stone."

The altar wasn't empty. In the ravenous flames of the thurible, their dinner was burning to ashy bits. Ciaran was so hungry, he felt like a small slip of his sanity would send him lapping up the ashes like a dog. He hadn't seen what the votary put into the thurible, but it smelled like fresh turkey and sprigs of rosemary.

That should have been his meal. Why did they have to burn their limited rations? Weren't their prayers enough for the canons?

"Ciaran!"

Ciaran almost repeated the word out of habit, until he recognized the aggravated tone of his father. He knew better than to tear his gaze away from the thurible, which spilled out alternating wisps of bone and coal smoke. Breaking focus from the thurible was a sign that his devotion was imperfect, and the canons accepted nothing but perfection. Confusion swirled in his mind like the opposing smoke. What had he done to make his father risk imperfection just to scold him?

Then he realized he wasn't praying anymore—only thinking the prayers hazily as if the words were whispers of thick mud. His father had noticed his silence.

"Unto you, we lay our adoration and thanks for your good deeds," he recited. Somehow speaking was making the ache in his stomach feel dire.

"Oesyth, favor us!" the votary bellowed over the gathering. Ciaran was always curious what the votary's name was, but his family said the man's identity wasn't important now that he'd given his entire being to the canons.

"Oesyth, favor us," chorused the rest of the adorers.

Ciaran held his breath as he waited for the prayer to continue. It wasn't uncommon for the votary to go through the entire index of canons. There were at least a dozen more after Oesyth, including Varyan, whose prayer was especially lengthy. Ciaran didn't think he would last that long. The ground was already starting to churn like ocean waters under his feet, and it was all he could do to blink away the hazy blackness encroaching on his vision.

But if he passed out, he'd be punished for his impudence with an even longer fast.

The votary began to sing words in the ancient tongue, and Ciaran nearly sagged in relief. He was skipping the lesser canons. It was over.

He'd never been so happy to hear unintelligible gibberish in his life.

It was a good thing the canons couldn't read his thoughts, Ciaran mused as he quietly left the rite chamber. He loved the Canonized Cloth. When he wasn't fighting for his life, he was truly and indubitably happy to be at the basilica.

Spending his days in devout adoration of the canons wasn't an honor many could boast. He couldn't imagine more meaningful work than empowering the canons—The Canonized, as they were formally called. The Cloth's work was the most reverent thing a person could do—worshiping the canons to bolster their power. Their holy prayers served to empower the canons. In time, the canons would repay their followers for their veneration in blessings.

Ciaran had long ago stopped asking what those blessings would be. When he was a boy, he used to daydream a lot about what the canon's grace would be like. Having been born within the walls of the basilica, he'd had a lot of time to wonder. He hoped it would be a cure for the sun sickness so that real, genuine sunlight could shine on the basilica as it had in his memories. He had only been four then, but he remembered it being so *warm*. So all encompassing. The basilica wasn't built to retain its own heat, so when Ciaran wasn't distracted by his hunger, he was held hostage by the cold.

Ciaran rubbed his numb fingers together as he made his way back to his family's dwelling chambers. The lodgings were small, barely big enough to fit Ciaran and his parents. The three were crammed together, always sharing the same stale air and listening to each other's growling bellies.

It was homey—in a way. His parents had grown to know him extraordinarily well. When the nights got cold, his family's warmth was never far away.

Ciaran was sure there were other things to be thankful for, but he couldn't quite think of them at the moment. Not when he was this hungry.

It dawned on him all at once that he was walking completely alone. His parents had gotten lost in the crowd of worshippers leaving the rite chamber, hundreds of bodies wriggling through the narrow corridors but not quite getting anywhere.

Seizing an opening between two children, Ciaran had slipped into a nearby hallway toward the back route to his family's room. He could feel the glares of a few other Cloths as he disappeared, but he was too poorly to care. The Cloths liked order, but Ciaran preferred breathing fresh air.

It was only when he had ventured to the end of the corridor that he realized his mistake. Because at the end of the hallway were the open doors to the kitchen.

Ciaran's mouth began to water as he beheld the food that hadn't been selected for the rite. A wheel of cheese and a link of cured sausage.

It was more than temptation that came over Ciaran. It was mania. *Delirium.*

Like a feral dog on the scent, Ciaran stormed into the kitchen, grabbed the cheese in shaking fingers, and buried his teeth into its soft flesh.

It was so delicious, he could have died.

He'd filled his mouth with it, barely remembering to swallow, until there was no room for any more. But that was no matter. He clutched the sausage, ravaging it right down to its center. The food landed unpleasantly in his stomach, but Ciaran could not stop. Who knew the next time he'd get a chance to eat his fill?

He lost himself in the frenzy of the feast, entranced by the worship of savory flavors and the way his stomach felt like it was sinking to the floor. He'd never felt so *satisfied*. Maybe he never would again.

The door creaked. Ciaran looked up, eyes wild. If anyone—*anyone*—tried to take his pillage from him, he would eat them. He would bury his teeth into their throat where their pulse was strongest and tear the veins from the muscle. He would—

The craze faded.

Marit was watching him.

She was still in her ritual robes, the oversized sleeves that gave way to billowing skirts. It was cinched at her waist with a corset, from which dangled strings of beads that represented each of the canons. Though she covered her face with a white shell mask, Ciaran could still make out her horrified gaze. She held the thurible close to her, which released a string of smoke into the kitchen.

The sight of her slammed him back into reality and reminded him who he was. He was no ravenous beast, but a man. It drew his attention to the nausea of too much food on a profoundly empty stomach. There were crumbs of cheese on the corners of his mouth and even a drop of blood where he'd accidentally bitten his lip.

It was a blessing from Oesyth herself that of the hundreds of people who lived in this basilica, the one who'd found him had been Marit. No one else loved Ciaran the way Marit did. They'd been fast friends since the day they had confessed to each other as children that Marit wasn't a boy and Ciaran wasn't a girl. They'd changed their identities together, stood shoulder-to-shoulder when they'd announced their decision to the rest of the basilica. The other Cloths had supported them—it wasn't uncommon for children to discover their identities at such a young age—but Ciaran never forgot that Marit had supported him first.

They'd looked out for each other ever since. Marit, protecting Ciaran from the judgmental eye of her father, the votary. Ciaran, giving Marit a place to be herself without the strict eye of her parents telling her what robes to wear, what songs to sing, what thoughts to have.

"Come. You must be hungry too," Ciaran whispered. "Close the door behind you."

He expected Marit to come along without a second thought, but she remained firmly planted at a safe distance.

"Marit," Ciaran pressed. "What's the matter?"

"That food is for the sacrifice," Marit said shakily.

"No, it was an option for the sacrifice, but it wasn't selected. It will just go to waste if no one eats it. Not even the canons will enjoy it."

"Have you *been* stealing food?"

"What? No. I'm—"

"Just because you're training to be the votary after my father doesn't give you the right to take what isn't yours."

"I—I know," Ciaran stammered. "But you must understand—"

"I understand that we all eat equally," Marit pressed, becoming more frantic. "You eating the remains is wrong. You're stealing from your family, Ciaran."

Frustration boiled in Ciaran's gut. The Cloths certainly did not get equal to eat. He was sure *Marit* got plenty to eat, as daughter to the votary. But when the rations were few and there were hundreds of members of the Cloth to feed, he was one of the people who was asked to skip meals. *It's a holy sacrifice*, the votary told him. *It will demonstrate how deep your faith runs. Every votary must learn sacrifice.*

But if it was such a holy act, then why didn't the votary—the holiest of them all—shoulder the loss himself? He ate better than the entire basilica combined.

"I haven't eaten in nearly a month," Ciaran grit out between his teeth. "I feel like I'm dying. I *am* dying, Marit."

"Don't lie to me."

"I'm not," Ciaran swore.

He surrendered his hands before him, showing Marit the way his pale skin was drying against his bones, flickering off in scales. It was his way of yelling, *Look at the way hunger has ravaged my body.* The dark circles like disease under his eyes. The way he'd lost all of his strength from his bones. He'd even lost his monthly cycle. Something about its absence made him sick, despite how much he hated the bloody rags and the muscle cramps.

Marit indeed looked at Ciaran long enough to observe the shell of her friend—and turn against him.

"You're not starving," she said finally. Disgusted. "If you were, you would've told my father. He would've fed you. It's what the canons call us to do. You stole because you're *greedy*. Everything there is here, you want *more*."

Ciaran's stomach dropped.

"What?" he gasped. "Marit, no. No, I just want to live. I'm *trying* to live. Don't you see? How can I serve the canons if I can't even stand on my own feet? I'm no good to the canons if I'm dead."

Even through the ache in his own body, Ciaran could see the words were falling on closed ears. Marit shook her head.

"Look," he entreated. "I know I made a mistake. Why don't I put everything back and we'll pretend nothing happened. I—I'll skip meals for the next two weeks to make it up to the canons. To *you*. You're my best friend, Marit. You know I'm not perfect. Just—don't tell your parents. Please."

Ciaran reached for her, but Marit lurched back as if she'd been stung. She jolted, tripping on her long skirt and landing on the ground. The shell mask dropped from her face, cracking into three whole pieces. Underneath, Marit's face was splotchy red.

"I don't know you at all, Ciaran."

Ciaran foresaw what would happen next, but not quick enough to stop it. Maybe that was the first sign he had forfeited divine grace forever.

"*Thief!* Ciaran Lynwood is a thief!" Marit shrieked. The roar soared down the long corridor of the basilica, filling any empty space it could find. It seeped into the bricks of the walls, the marble of the floor, the stained glass of the windows, reaching every member of the Cloth as if they were just *waiting* for Ciaran to be caught.

The damage had already been done, but it didn't stop Ciaran from dropping the half-eaten link of cured sausage and launching after Marit.

"*No!*" he cried.

"*Thief! Ciaran Lynwood is stealing sacrificial food!*"

"Stop! Please!"

But Marit did not stop. She scrambled to her feet through the many layers of her dark robes and took off down the hall. Ciaran snatched out a hand, but the fabric of her robes slipped through his fingers before he could seize her and pull her back down.

Ciaran's legs screamed as he tore after Marit, his thin muscles and unprotected bones no longer possessing the strength they'd once had. It was only when he bumped into one of the display pedestals lining the hall that he realized where Marit was headed. He'd been so determined on quieting her that he hadn't realized until it was too late that he was in the heart of the basilica. The Ritual Chamber.

Someone's hand snatched out of the crowd and grabbed the dusty train of Ciaran's robes. Momentum propelled him forward, but he couldn't stop in time before he was sent rolling to the ground, knees scraping against the floor.

The taste of iron on his tongue churned his stomach. Ciaran managed to push himself up to look at the crowd before him. From the ground, it was difficult to tell just how many people there were, even harder with his swimming vision. But he could see well enough to know that he was surrounded on all sides with no hope of escape. They must've all come running when they heard Marit's screams, who now stood beside her father, weeping.

"*Please*," Ciaran whispered. He wasn't sure what he was begging for.

It didn't feel real. Just minutes ago, he had been standing next to his parents in prayer. Now, he was a lame animal lying on the floor, waiting to be put out of his misery.

"Ciaran tried to hurt me because I caught him stealing food," Marit sobbed.

His arms shook with the effort, but Ciaran still held himself up.

"I would *never* hurt her. I love Marit like my own family!" Ciaran cried, tears welling in his own eyes. "I did eat the sacrificial food. I admit that. But I didn't hurt Marit. She tripped and fell on her own. You have to believe me."

Marit's claim seemed so ridiculous to Ciaran that he didn't consider that anyone would believe it.

Fingers buried into Ciaran's hair, yanking him up. Pain exploded on his scalp, stripping his legs of the strength to stand on their own. From the corner of his vision, he saw tufts of his own dull blonde hair sinking to his feet.

Through the burn, Ciaran mustered the nerve to look up into the eyes of the person who had grabbed him.

A chill ran down Ciaran's spine. He'd never seen the votary so furious. Rage had transformed him into a monster, a creature with its lips curling up around his teeth, ready to strike. Along the walls, candles in crimson holders shed blood-colored light onto the votary's face, making his eyes glimmer red.

"You partook of the sacrificial offerings?" the votary seethed.

It was futile to plead his case. Ciaran's bones could have spiked through his paper-thin skin and the votary wouldn't have cared. If he had any hope of making it out of this mess alive, he had to appeal to what the votary cared most about: the canons.

"Remember who I am, Your Excellency. I am your most reverent acolyte. I am your successor," Ciaran said carefully. "You have trusted me to lead your most sacred rituals. You have enlisted my aid as scribe, as servant, as messenger of the canons, and I have served you dutifully every time. I have given my entire life to the canons and this basilica." Each word felt like nails down his throat, but if he didn't speak now, it wasn't guaranteed he'd have another chance. "*Everything* I do is to serve the canons. If my actions today are the first moral failing I've committed in my twenty-two years of life, then isn't that a blessing from the canons? A sign of their approval? I am their favored."

The edges around the votary's eyes softened. Ciaran drew in a sharp, silent breath.

Then, the teeth returned.

"My, how pious he is," the votary sneered.

Ciaran's hope crumbled away like a clay statue beneath a hammer.

The votary continued, "This must be a new method of worship I haven't heard of—glorifying the canons by gluttonizing the food that is rightly theirs, in the sanctity of their own home. How blessed I am to be in the presence of the canon's most favored zealot! Maybe *he* should be the votary."

Laughter exploded from the onlookers. Ciaran felt like he was going to be sick right all over the holy floor. Horror clutched his throat, but still he rasped, "Let me pay for my crimes. Please. And I'll show you I'm still worthy."

"Why would I punish you? I know your worth. Why, let's make you the votary of the canon of thieves. How *beautifully* you have served Jasrath this day."

Hot tears trickled down the sides of Ciaran's face. The Canonized Cloth revered all the canons, even the ones who hadn't been heard from in centuries. The only one they ignored was Jasrath, the canon of thieves. He was their wretched outcast.

Ciaran had asked about Jasrath as a boy. His child's curiosity wondered what a canon could have done to earn the Cloth's displeasure. But his parents scolded him, saying that Jasrath was an evil canon that hadn't been heard from in decades. Praying to him would urge his evil nature out of hiding—the exact opposite of what the Cloths had set out to do.

"But first, a test. A test to see if your canon will honor you."

The votary's hold tightened. He produced a thin, small blade from inside his robes, and sliced it down the front of Ciaran's. The belt holding the clothing in place exploded, sending glass beads raining down. The votary tossed aside the tattered robes, exposing Ciaran's thin body to the basilica's cold air and dropping him to the floor. His nails closed around Ciaran's ankles a second later. He began to drag Ciaran through the halls like a slaughtered lamb.

Ciaran clawed at whatever his fingers could reach—someone's boots, the train to a long robe—but he was not strong enough to break free. A howl bellowed from his lungs, dissolving into coughs the farther he was dragged.

It was then the canons had the grace to take his consciousness. It was the best blessing he could have hoped for in this tragedy. This recognition that he'd behaved beyond the pale, but they still loved him enough to spare him the heartbreak of being awake while he was dragged past the garden monuments. Past the statues of all the canons he so loved and worshiped.

When he came to, he was kneeling before Jasrath's altar on the abandoned corner of the garden. Moss and lichen devoured the headstone, filling in the letters and making it impossible to read the original text. Like the other altars, Jasrath's monument featured a full-sized statue, only the long hair and one of its arms were broken off. The remaining arm was outstretched, dangling a set of lock picking tools from a hooked finger. Dead vines partly covered Jasrath's stone, shrewd eyes, but they looked down at Ciaran with judgment all the same.

In the next minutes, Ciaran was tied to the statue, attached to Jasrath's extended wrists. His arms were bound above his head and his feet barely scraped the ground. Sweat dripped down his bare skin, chilled by the mild summer air. Before him, the Cloth members cheered and laughed, a cacophonous sound that shattered the peace of the grotto.

Ciaran tried to lean his head back and close his eyes, but hanging mid-air meant there was nothing behind him.

He was so *tired*—too tired to wonder what had come over him in the kitchens. To mourn that Marit's friendship had been far less loyal than he'd realized. To hate himself for running *toward* Marit when she'd revealed his crime, not away. If he'd accepted his fate sooner, he could've disappeared into the black Talsuran streets and been lost forever. Losing his parents would've chiseled out a permanent cavern in his chest, but at least he wouldn't have been chained by this altar, cast out by the people he loved most.

It felt like there was a hole in his gut where his strength poured out of him like blood. The last thing he saw before letting the world go black was his parents. They did not cheer, nor did they shout. They merely stood expressionless and watched.

And watched.

And watched.

Ciaran closed his eyes and let the darkness swallow him whole.

O N THE FIRST DAY: Ciaran woke to birds singing from Jasrath's ivory head. His entire body burned, inside and out, so he did all he could think to do. He prayed the holy incantations, just as the votary had taught him. Just as he had yesterday when his hunger had gotten the better of him. He began at the start of the index, *"Blessings be to aerial Alpedis, canon of the skies and sun . . ."*

No one came to watch, but if they had, they would've noticed that he skipped Jasrath entirely.

On the second day: He prayed the holy incantations again. They took longer this time, muddled by the distraction of his pain and starvation. Without water, the words chafed against his throat, but still, he spoke them. The canons were simply testing him, he told himself. They wanted to bring him to the very brink of death, then demonstrate their holy splendor by saving him. It was all to show him what his sacrifices were for. To teach him a lesson about stealing from the canons.

That day, he prayed to every canon he could think of, murmuring feverish apologies for what he had done. He even spared a prayer to Cevyn, the greedy canon of lost things—often ignored by the Cloth, and yet the only canon to *live* physically in Talsura. *"I will serve you in your den,"* Ciaran had raved desperately. *"I will let you take me as one of your lost things."* There was no answer.

On the third day: It occurred to Ciaran, through a dry mouth that tasted of blood, that perhaps the canons would not save a man chained to their traitor canon's altar. They weren't coming to help, he realized pitifully. He was going to die.

He hung in silence, his broken faith festering inside him, until the air began to smell of nighttime dew.

Then, he lowered his chin and prayed the unholy invocation.

"Cunning Jasrath, lord of larceny and woe, hear my plea. I have stolen what was not mine..."

That night, when Ciaran slept, a man who had white clothes and long, raven's-wing hair appeared to him in a dream and told him that if he could be obedient, then he would live.

In the morning, when he woke, he was leaned up against the monument, sore, bruised wrists crossed in his lap. His bindings were shorn into slivers at his side, frayed from a dull blade. He picked up one of the bloodied ropes, his cracked lips parting as he assessed the severed ends of the knot.

The dream was real. Ciaran would *live.*

Something rustled in the copse of trees in the grotto. A man cloaked in shadows and bloodied wools emerged from the darkness, eyes tattooed like a hungry snake. He appeared like a ghost, with only the basilica's distant light to reveal him, but Ciaran did not tremble. He was past the point of fear.

The man assessed Ciaran, tsking at what he found. From the pockets of his cloak, he pulled out a sweet roll and threw it to Ciaran.

This time, Ciaran did not pounce on the food.

"Eat it. It's a welcome gift," the man said.

"For what?" rasped Ciaran.

"To the guild. You're a Grit Finger now, thief."

PART
TWO

Emrys' mother could not stop telling them how strong they were for a nine-year-old child. They were *so strong* for carrying all the rations on their back. *So strong* for saying goodbye to their house in Talsura without crying. *So strong* for wiping the bloody mucus from the corner of their father's mouth every time he vomited poison plants up on the side of the path. *So strong* for building their tent each night when the exiles stopped to rest at the end of the day.

Emrys wished she'd stop saying it already. It wasn't like they had any choice but to be strong. With their mother worried about Aunt Ceday and their father teetering on the edge of death more each day, Emrys had needed to rise to the occasion and protect their family. Without Emrys, who would raise the tent and cook their family's supper? Emrys had seen what happened to families who slept under the stars and skipped their meals. It had given Emrys nightmares.

Tonight, Emrys had to reduce the size of their tent so they could double up the roof protections. The extra fabric would go toward catching rainwater and keeping them dry. The last thing his ailing family needed was to catch a cold. The tent was wide enough to squeeze his unrolled map of the island next to Father's bedroll.

"What do you think, little butterfly? Where are we?" Father asked from his bed where he lay. His brow was flushed and damp with sweat. Emrys patted the beads away with the edge of his sleeve.

Father had started calling Emrys "little butterfly" because they were small creatures that survived long periods of migration. Emrys hadn't even known what the word *migration* meant before the exile.

Emrys trailed their finger along their exile path on the map—past the mountains, into the wide green area where no one had settled yet.

"The air smells salty," Emrys noted. "And my feet hurt. We're probably by the sea."

Father closed his eyes and let his head sink into his pillow. "I've never been to the northern sea before."

Emrys sat beside him, gently rubbing his father's brow. His mother would hate them if they said so, but they weren't sure his father would survive long enough to see the northern shores. They hadn't thought about what that meant yet—there just wasn't time to.

Right then, the tent flap flew open and through it burst Aunt Ceday. Emrys always thought Aunt Ceday was prettier than the portraits they'd seen of Queen Phaedra, her sister. Unlike the queen, Ceday had a head of chopped brown hair and a strong nose. Her eyes sat deep in her head and her lips smiled bright and long. Looking at her pale face, it was hard to tell if the redness was a result of the unrelenting sun or the sun sickness setting in.

Collapsing on her knees before her pack, Ceday began to rummage through her things until she found her sewn journal.

"I *knew* I was right. We missed our chance," she said, exasperated. "We should've settled at the base of the mountain by the forests when we had the chance. Now we've gone too hard and there aren't enough trees on these moorlands for us to build the kingdom with."

Emrys' mother was close at hand. She kissed her husband on his clammy head and said, "It's worth it to settle near the shore. Trading off the island will be so much easier if we're right on the sea. The building logs can be transported."

"*How?* Our people can barely carry their own packs. No one will risk their lives to walk back the way we came—under the *sun*—to carry materials."

"Settling at the base of the mountains will leave us exposed to Mount Livia. Any imports we get from overseas will have to travel an extra week. Not to mention, it's practically within sight of Talsura. What if Phaedra decides she wants to eradicate us completely?"

"She won't," Ceday swore confidently. "That would involve her leaving the safety of her fucking Dam, and she's too much of a coward."

"Language," Father groaned.

Ceday rubbed Emrys' back. "Sorry, sweetheart. The sentiment remains." She grabbed Mother's hands and drew them close to her chest. "Listen to me, Casta. Our people are desperate for as good a solution as we can find. Encourage them to turn around while they can. Let us find shade, water, and lumber. We'll grow food. We'll humble ourselves to Mount Livia and see if there is any aid to be spared. Most importantly, we'll *survive*."

"We'd better, Cee."

Ceday opened her mouth to say something else, only to cut away in a bout of coughs. The hand covering her mouth came away bloody with tiny roots. She hid it behind her back before Mother could see, but Emrys had seen it plain as day. Their stomach sank. Was Aunt Ceday going to die too?

Heaviness swelling in his chest, Emrys tore out of the tent. They stomped ferociously to a tiny puddle where yesterday's rain water had accumulated in a dip in the ground. The long grass floated easily in the muddy water. They couldn't drink from this water without boiling it, but Emrys liked to dip their feet in. The coolness soothed the half-scabbed sores. They tilted their face up to the open, starry sky and hummed a song they'd been scribbling down the night before the exile.

"I am no good at short goodbyes. I linger 'til the daylight dies . . ."

"I like that," Aunt Ceday called behind them. "Did you come up with it?"

Emrys shrugged shyly. Around them, the other exiles began their nightly routines, setting up their own tents and washing with jugs of water. With a short sigh, Aunt Ceday knelt next to the puddle and dipped her bloody hand in.

"I know you saw," she said. "Sorry about that. I hope it didn't frighten you too badly. Sometimes it's easy to forget that anything scares you."

Emrys didn't think it would do either of them any good to admit that they were so scared they could hardly sleep. Instead, they said, "I miss home. Being scared won't bring it back. Nothing will. But I can't help but miss it anyway."

It was deeper than that. Emrys missed their bed, their favorite snacks, their cittern—though they didn't say so.

Ceday dried her hand on the loose shirt. The fabric was stained with sweat and old blood after so many days of wearing it to help the other sick refugees.

"That's natural, I think. I miss my nephew terribly and I haven't even met him. was born the week we left," she admitted quietly. "But I have hope that someday I'll be able to meet him—talk with him, even if he's an old man." She smiled down at them. "It may not be the way you imagine, Emrys, but you will go home again one day."

Emrys plucked at the clover underneath their hands.

"You know," Ceday began. "It's not lost on me that every night when your mum and I go talk with the other refugees, you build our tent so beautifully. And, to my own shame, no one has said thank you. So thank you, Emrys. Thank you for taking such good care of your parents and I."

"It's not hard," they mumbled. "I'm getting taller."

Ceday leaned her cheek on the top of Emrys' head. "That you are. Not to mention, older. That's why I want to show you something. Something I haven't shown your mother yet. Can you keep a secret for a little while?"

At this, Emrys perked up. They'd never been trusted with a secret before.

"I swear!" they said.

"If I'm right, this secret will save our lives," she whispered sincerely. "I don't want the others to know because I don't want to get their hopes up. But you're strong and you're smart."

"Show me," Emrys pressed eagerly.

Aunt Ceday held out her arm, palm up, and pointed to the spot where her purple veins were visible under her pale skin. Emrys squinted at the veiny juncture, not noticing anything at first. Then, to their horror, a teensy sprig of clover broke through her skin, unfurling with tiny, bloodstained leaves.

Emrys pulled the growth out without thinking. "Aunt Ceday! You're—"

"—controlling it, sweetheart. I urged it to bloom there, so it did." To prove her point, another four-leaf clover grew in its place.

"Why would you do that?" they said, voice shaking.

"Because if I can command it to grow, I can probably command it to leave."

Emrys glanced at where her wrist was bleeding like it'd been pricked with a needle. "It hurts you."

"Being separated from my family and watching everyone around us suffer hurts me. *This* gives me hope." She caressed Emrys' face the same way Mother did. Their skin prickled like fluttering pixie wings when they felt the soft clover petals skim their cheek.

"What do you think?" Ceday asked, curious.

"It's amazing," Emrys admitted. "I hope you know what you're talking about."

Ceday barked out a laugh. "Me too," she agreed.

They sat there by the puddle for some time. Emrys leaned against their aunt's steady shoulder while she grew a dozen clovers from her skin, over and over and over. She practiced controlling the size and the point where they sprouted—even dragging a helpless chuckle from Emrys when she grew them in the shape of a smiling face.

For the first time in days, Emrys felt the soothing allure of peace and relief wash over them. Their eyes grew heavier by the second, the weight of their exhaustion landing over them like a warm blanket.

"What do you call it?" Emrys asked sleepily. "It can't be called sun sickness if you control it."

Ceday hummed. "You're right. How about inflorescence? It means the process of flowering."

"I like it," Emrys said with a yawn. Their eyes fell closed. Before sleep could drag them under entirely, they felt Ceday shift their head into her lap.

"Go ahead and rest," she murmured softly. "I'll carry you to your bedroll once you're asleep."

Emrys welcomed the offer. In the morning, they'd be back to analyzing maps and raising their makeshift tent after a long day of walking. But they would enjoy this while they could.

SENNA

ONE OF THE ONLY stories Orphan Mother Mabel told Senna as a boy was the story of Flynn the Filthy—a young boy who played in the mud with his friends once and could never, ever get clean again. It didn't matter how much he scrubbed his ears or how long he pruned away in the bathtub, he was filthy forevermore. Senna imagined that the story began as a silly way to make children laugh before bedtime. But Mabel had weaponized the story, turning it into an agent of fear. It must've worked, because any mess, any layer of dirt on him, made Senna feel like he could crawl out of his skin.

"Are you alright?" said Emrys beside him. How he could stand to be within three feet of him without vomiting was beside Senna. He'd tried to tell Emrys hours ago that, "I wouldn't be offended if you wanted to stand further upwind." But Emrys had only laughed, as if the offer had been nothing more than an amusing joke.

"You seem uncomfortable," Emrys continued.

"I'm fine," lied Senna.

Emrys gave a lightless smile, but he didn't argue.

Senna was glad. It wouldn't do either of them any good to say he wanted to claw his contaminated skin off his body. He hadn't told Emrys what he'd heard the deer say to him, either.

"You are the one with the heart of gold who has my favor. You must be my blade."

The voice had thundered in Senna's ears and echoed down into the pit of his lungs, like thunder traversing miles of stormy skies. It'd been clear he'd been the only one to hear it. But why? Who was the deer, and what did it mean to have its favor? It sounded like a canon, but Senna had imagined them much less powerful than the way the voice had made him feel. He'd never heard of the canons taking on an animal's forms before. Perhaps it was a spirit of the moorlands? Or maybe the overpowered sun had given a normal doe the ability to communicate.

The possibilities were endless. Senna knew telling Emrys would only distract him from their quest. If the doe had wanted Emrys to hear it, then he would've. Still, Emrys had proven to be more loyal than Senna had earned. Maybe Senna wouldn't be so plagued by the *unknown* if he trusted someone enough to bear it with him.

Before he could consider the idea further, the murmuring, echoing sound of a city rang across the path. Senna blinked the haze away from his eyes to find a large stone gate and a big sign overhead reading, Mount Livia, Birthplace of the Canons.

They had arrived.

Emrys led the way through the gate, walking with an air of ease and familiarity when it was his first time here too. Senna couldn't help but envy him, even if he was glad Emrys would steal any focus with his starlight smile and bright, titian eyes.

The city was distributed across steep hills and valleys. The architecture was tall compared to Talsuran buildings, which were wider. The Mount Livian citizens filled the streets, bustling in and out of more shops and businesses than Senna could count. Above the main road, half a dozen bridges connected the steep points of the mountain, adorned with architecturally perfect flourishes and swirls. The sand-colored stairs, which connected the different ground levels, were sharp and clean.

A flurry of young children rushed by Senna, fast enough to make his cloak catch wind. The smallest of the group bumped into Senna's legs, stumbling over their own small feet to regain balance. They turned a horrified look on Senna, craning their face all the way up to see him.

"It's a mudman! Run for your lives!" they bellowed. Some of the children screamed, others laughed. They all disappeared in a herd of pattering feet and cacophony.

Senna felt his heart tug at the sight of children having harmless fun. Emrys must've mistaken Senna's frown, because he gave Senna a hearty pat on the shoulder.

"Don't mind the kids. Their imaginations are five times bigger than they are." He pointed up the road. "I think that's an inn over there. I've got enough money if you'd like to rent a room and clean off. We could order some food before we start asking around."

Senna nodded, unsure if Emrys would be able to hear him above the bustle of the crowd.

When they got closer, the inn's hanging sign came into view: Crag's Kegs and Saloon. Now that it was dinner hours, the place was a madhouse, serving all manner of folk trying to find a drink and a meal after a long day of work. None of them showed a sign of inflorescence—even the ones sipping their ale outside in the golden-hour sunshine. Emrys had to journey inside shoulder-first to make enough room for them to pass. Senna fought the urge to pinch Emrys' cape so as not to lose him. That proved unnecessary, because once the bystanders got one look—or whiff—of Senna, they cleared the path immediately.

Incidentally, this gave the bartender a clear view of the outsiders as they approached the bar. She was a woman of incredibly strong build, hair shaved close to her scalp. A long scar journeyed up her throat, ending in a tattoo of a wilting rose. Senna felt her gaze as soon as it landed on them.

"Oh, no. Absolutely not," she spat. "Not today, fellas. Get out of my inn."

"Now, just a moment, ma'am," stammered Emrys, sounding as perplexed as Senna felt.

"I don't like to be ignored. I said, get out of my bar, you *filthy* Talsuran waste."

The last insult was spewed directly at Senna.

The room went silent. Even the chatter outside the threshold rumbled away. All at once, dozens of eyes fell on them. Senna clenched his fists, willing himself to breathe. How did they know he was Talsuran? It must've been his clothes. Talsurans dressed so darkly, not willing to waste precious money on frivolous things like dye that couldn't be seen properly.

Senna grabbed Emrys' elbow, tugging him, but Emrys wouldn't budge.

"I don't like being ignored either. My friend was attacked by a dre'malor. He's desperate for a wash. Are you so unkind as to turn us onto the street?"

The bartender didn't get a chance to respond before someone among the drinkers threw their pewter tankard at Senna's head. He managed to catch it before the sharp embellishments on the handle could hit his eye.

Senna placed the tankard on a nearby table. He snatched Emrys by the collar and dragged him out of the tavern.

"You shouldn't let them talk to you like that," Emrys seethed once they were outside.

"*Your* people talk to me like that, and they have every right to. Talsura is not a good place," Senna hissed back. People were still glaring at them from the tavern's porch, but he paid them no mind. "We came here to find information and no one will talk if they're too busy throwing cutlery at us. There's no time for your Redwindan sense of justice."

Emrys blinked, his harsh expression fading.

"Miracle of miracles," he said dubiously. "You've got a little bite in you after all."

"They don't make defenseless lambs in knightheart training."

"No, they do not," Emrys teased, gaze raking over Senna's body.

Someone tapped on Senna's shoulder. He snapped a fierce glare at whoever had touched him, only to soften when he gazed upon a young woman with a gentle countenance and waist-long locs.

"Sorry to bother you, Goldheart" she said quietly. "I was Talsuran too. It's how I recognize you. I used to be a member of the queen's court, but I moved here with my Redwindan sister. I just wanted to apologize for the way they treated you in there. Lots of folks here moved after the exile, so you can understand their apprehension. But, still, I'm sorry. You weren't the one to exile them."

She waited for Senna to say something, but he didn't. Nervously, she brushed one of her locs back.

"Anyway, there's a bathhouse at the top of the hill. It's what Mount Livians are known for—the baths. I think you'll find the attendants there more accommodating."

The girl glanced up at the bar, and it was then that Senna realized she had a tray tucked underneath her arms and an apron around her waist. She'd snuck out of work to help him.

He held up his hand and imagined a lily growing from his wrist. There it appeared, easier than the last flowers he had grown, as bright as the warm sun overhead. Careful not to draw blood, Senna plucked the lily at its stem and handed it to the girl.

"Thank you," he said. He couldn't express what her kindness had meant to him. He only hoped the bloom would extend the sentiment, just the same.

The girl held the flower, eyes wide. But then she smiled, slipped the lily into her hair, and skittered back into the inn.

Emrys let out a low whistle.

"Cursed canons, I'm starting to see how you ended up torturing your poor kitchen maid. Excellent use of inflorescence, though. Grown and given like a true Redwindan heartthrob. I'm taking notes."

Senna doubted that Emrys needed any help in the wooing department, and at any rate—

"I wasn't flirting," he said. "I didn't know how else to say thank you."

"No, I think you did just fine, Sen," Emrys said genuinely. The nickname did something to Senna, landing on his chest like a warm stone that would not be moved.

Shaken, Senna started up the street.

"Let's go find the bathhouse. There's only so long I can take covered in sludge."

"*There* it is," Emrys cheered. He bounced along behind, his steps light. "I have to say, assertiveness looks good on you."

THE MOUNT LIVIANS APPARENTLY had never seen a Talsuran before. Senna could feel their eyes on him while he moved, like ants creeping over his skin. If someone was not looking at his dark travel clothes, then they were glaring at the back of his head, or squinting to try to get a look in his eyes. He tried to do his best not to pay them any heed, but their gazes were like sun through a looking glass, hot and piercing.

He didn't have to suffer long. Built directly into the mountainside, the bathhouse was indeed not far, nor was it difficult to miss. From the street, it was impossible to know just how deep the bath buildings went into the mountain's core. Senna could at least see different floors, stacked like flat mushrooms on a tree. For a moment, Senna thought that they'd been led astray—surely the building before them served a more royal or parliamentary purpose. But then, as they got closer, Senna could make out steam rising from the tiered levels and people moving around in nothing but bath towels.

"What *is* this place?" Emrys whispered as they entered.

Senna didn't know. There was certainly nothing quite like it in Talsura. He tried to make sense of it, but the longer he looked, the less he understood where he was.

Anywhere else, the bathhouse would have looked like a temple's courtyard. A marble path curved around a large basin of steaming, floral-smelling water in the center of the room. Pillars surrounded the pool, ornate figureheads at the tops spilling more fresh water into the bath. Senna guessed it was merely decorative, because it was empty of bathers. The bathers seemed to be milling about between the doors along the walls—sometimes wrapped in towels, and sometimes air-drying their steam-flushed skin in the open spaces.

All of this matched perfectly with what Senna assumed a bathhouse would be. What did not match were the signs above the doors that decidedly did *not* fit in a bathhouse: Parliament Chambers, Judiciary Tribunal, Their Majesty's Throne Room.

"They conduct all of their civic business in a bathhouse?" Senna whispered back.

Emrys scoffed in mock disbelief. "What, don't you?"

A smile crept up Senna's mouth at the joke, only to disappear the instant they were approached by one of the bathhouse attendants. He was dark-skinned and thin, wearing a floor-length chiton made of emerald chiffon. When the man stepped closer into the light, Senna tore his gaze to the pool—the fabric was see-through.

"Welcome, sirs, to Mount Livia's Bathhouse. It is rare we host first-time guests such as yourselves"

Unbothered that the man seemed to know them—and equally unbothered by his nudity—Emrys gave the attendant a smile.

"How pleased we are to be here. As you can see, my friend is well overdue for a good scrub. We ran into some trouble on our journey, and he's been quite uncomfortable for many hours."

Senna expected the man to fawn over them and offer his finest baths, but he merely ignored Emrys entirely and continued, "You've been requested in their majesty's chamber."

Senna exchanged a look with Emrys.

"But I'm filthy," said Senna.

"Lucky for you, this is a bathhouse," the attendant deadpanned. "Right this way."

They were led down a long corridor with tiled art embedded into the walls. It wouldn't have been accurate to describe the bathers in this hallway as finely attired, as many of them weren't attired at all. But Senna could sense an air of wealth around him—softer towels, expensive soap, and chocolate-covered fruits.

He barely noticed the attendant ushering them through a pair of massive doors and into the throne room. Emrys shrank closer to Senna's side as they took in the space.

It matched the rest of the bathhouse, only grander in size and decoration. The pool at the center of the room was surrounded by half a dozen plush daybeds. Instead of a spigot filling the tub, a small stream of water poured into the bath, starting from one side of the room and ending in a grate on the other side. The small river branched off, leading to private baths along the edge of the room. Bridges connected divided sections of the throne room, pouring water from their guardrails. In the corners of the space, soaps and oils and flower petals waited to be poured into the steaming water. The air was humid, making the slime on Senna's skin feel even stickier.

"It's not often I have Talsuran guests in my home."

The voice pealed across the domed ceilings, difficult to track.

Then a figure emerged from the bath, grand and nude. This time, Senna felt he could not look away from the bather—the sovereign of Mount Livia—as they sauntered over to their robe and tied it around their waist. Under the candlelight, Senna could better make out their features. They were fat, with skin the same olive color as Senna's, only golder under the low bath light. Their beard had been trimmed a few inches from their face, but perfectly sculpted to match its shape. They had low lids, but bright, wide eyes and a smile one could only display after they had spent most of the day in the bath.

"My companion is Talsuran. I am from Redwind," Emrys clarified. A rose appeared from behind his ear, solidifying his point. "I'm Captain Emrys Calloway. This is Goldheart Senna Kane. We thank you for your hospitality."

"Oh, I see. Not just any low-dwellers, but *knights*. It's rare to have such entertainment on short notice."

Senna had never heard the term *low-dwellers* in person before. He'd seen it a few times in his reading, used to refer to those who lived below the mountain's high peaks. Perhaps he'd never heard it because he'd never had a reason to. From the ruler's tongue, it sounded like it should've been an insult, but wasn't.

"I am Sovereign Sascha Oakcage, but I beg you to just call me Sascha."

Emrys nodded respectfully. "Well, Sascha, we didn't mean to intrude on your evening or cause alarm. We've only come so my friend could have a bath."

"I've never met anyone who would journey to such lengths for a bath." Sascha turned their eyes to Senna. "Though, one suffering from your plight might crawl a thousand miles for hot water."

Senna could not tell if they meant the dried dre'malor slime or his general Talsuran citizenship.

"You are very quiet," Sascha observed. They began to smooth lotion onto their arms and throat. Its jasmine scent wafted across the bath to Senna. "You should be the one to tell me why you are really here. But first . . ." They gestured vaguely to the baths about the room.

Senna's muscles tightened. Was he expected to bathe right here? *Now?*

Memories came crawling from the back of his mind—visions of bathing with the other orphan children under Mabel's care. The memory of being stripped bare and thrown into the tub like a sullied kitchen apron was imprinted in his mind.

Sascha noticed Senna's discomfort and set down their salve.

"Ah, I didn't mean to make you feel like a voyeuristic object, Goldheart Kane. Here, it is culturally understood that your preference for modesty comes first in the baths. I forgot that you were not accustomed to our ways." They gestured to a standing screen off to the side. "You should bathe however you are comfortable. If you are uncomfortable being in public view—" In other words, the central bath. "—then the private baths are clean and ready for use."

Senna bowed awkwardly in respect, then made his way to the nearest private bath. Once inside, he slid the silk curtain closed and hooked it in place. The private bath was probably small for Sascha's standards, but was the most luxurious washroom Senna had ever encountered. An impressive assortment of soaps stood ready for use on the edge of the in-ground tub, with towels nearby on heated stones. If there hadn't been a kingdom's ruler waiting for him on the other side of the curtain, he might've been able to relax all day here. Still, undressing felt like a miracle, his skin able to breathe for the first time in hours.

When he was fully bare, someone knocked on the wall outside the bath.

"Only me," Emrys murmured. He slid a basket under the curtain. "You can put your dirty clothes in there. Sascha is going to have them cleaned."

Senna murmured his thanks, then finally sank into the water, willing himself to grow accustomed to the way his body was relaxing without his consent. He couldn't remember the last time he'd been able to bathe for the luxury of it. Usually he showered before finding Percy for the day, too quickly to even let the water heat. Now, he was enveloped in steaming warmth that took all the tension of their journey and eased it away.

Another knock.

"Are you decent?" Emrys called through the curtain.

"I'm . . ." Senna sloshed his hand through the water while he searched for the right word. "Submerged."

"Would you mind a little company, then?"

Senna chose to blame the blush rising on his cheeks on the hot steam. He'd bathed with the other knighthearts a few times, and though it reminded him of the orphanage, it was tolerable. But it would be different with Emrys. Emrys was . . . well, he was beautiful. Senna hadn't ever stopped noticing it. With just two of them in the bath, it would surely feel rather intimate.

"You can say no, Sen," Emrys added earnestly. Patiently.

Senna drew his knees up under his chin.

"Come in," he called out as loud as his voice would allow.

Emrys emerged from the curtain slowly, as if he were giving Senna time to change his mind. When his eyes landed on the goldheart among the steam and soap, he smiled warmly.

"There's the man under the mud," Emrys observed, stripping out of his own clothes. "I was worried about getting into a bath filled with your dre'malor guts, but Sascha assured me the bath cleans itself."

Now that Emrys had told him, Senna did feel a pulse of . . . something in the water. Something alive enough to remind him of the very basic magic all Talsurans knew. The more he focused on it, the more the strange feeling engulfed him. It felt like a thousand feathers running along every inch of his skin. He swirled his finger in the water, but he could see no visible traces of the magic.

"I told Sascha all about our run-in with the dre'malor. They weren't surprised we'd encountered one. Apparently, the dre'malors have always gathered in herds at the base of the mountain, but lately they've been wandering up here and wreaking havoc on the poor civilians."

"What reason could they have to come all the way up here?"

Emrys shrugged. "Do they need a reason? They're dre'malors. Maybe the human part of their souls keens toward civilization. If I was half-monster, I'd want to be as close to my old life as possible."

Senna looked up from the bath to find Emrys completely bare. His back was to Senna, giving the goldheart the perfect view of his ass. Senna was strangely transfixed to the planes of smooth brown skin when Emrys turned around, but he looked back at the water before he could get caught staring.

The image remained in his mind, though he tried to turn his attention to anything else. There might have been other feelings simmering further out of reach, but Senna ignored them. To let himself acknowledge even a flicker of want was to entertain the impossible.

"Are you—" Emrys' voice broke Senna out of his thoughts. He bent over the bath and looked into the water. "We've come to the kingdom of magical, luxurious baths and you're sitting in plain water?"

Senna sank deeper, letting the surface lap against his shoulders.

"It didn't cross my mind to add anything else. But—you can? If you want?"

Emrys was already appraising the stocked racks. He pulled the cork from a glass jar, then poured a few splashes of eucalyptus oil into the water. Hints of the eucalyptus' honey and mint lilted on the steam, but Emrys wasn't finished. He held out his hand over the water, growing individual flowers and letting them drop into the bath like water from a leaf. They swirled around Senna, a mixture of red and white hues.

When at last he was pleased with his work, Emrys took a seat in the bath. Senna did not allow himself to watch Emrys' strong thighs or his cock from the corner of his vision. He didn't.

"Now I see why you wanted the bath all to yourself," Emrys sighed, stretching his arms out on the edge.

"I invited you in, didn't I?" The words came out forced.

Emrys paused, giving Senna a long, assessing look. Then he smirked, wide. Senna was beginning to understand why Thea found her guard so insufferable. Everything the man did made Senna's blood rush.

"I should like it if we could be friends, Senna," Emrys said at last.

This made Senna sit up straighter.

"Are we not?"

"You tell me. It seems you keep me at arm's length."

Senna caught one of the flower petals in his hand, then dropped it back into the water.

"I keep everyone at arm's length."

"Not Percy."

"That's different."

"How?"

Senna wished there was a way he could tell Emrys that he didn't easily share his past because of his own shortcomings—not because of the company he kept. He ached to tell Emrys that he'd try any magic that would let him speak the way he wanted to, without succumbing to memories or fits of pained breathlessness. But then, that magic *was* at his disposal.

Remembering all the steps to inflorescence, Senna called an amber lily to the center of his palm, letting its magic soothe him. The flower came with more resistance than the others he had grown—a result of his anxious heart? Emrys noticed the small bead of blood spilling down Senna's wet hand and moved closer. He took Senna's hand in his and pressed a thumb against the bleeding root.

"I'm listening, but only if you want me to," Emrys whispered.

"We *are* friends," Senna promised. He dug his nails into the meat of his palm. "Companionship wasn't something I was allowed as a child. The orphan mother said that speaking with other children fostered bad behavior. We were . . . We were punished for the impudence of speaking with our bedmates. I grew into the habit of muteness for fear that something terrible would happen."

"Sounds like a very quiet childhood," Emrys said softly.

"Have you not wondered why I don't speak?"

It took a second for the meaning to sink in. Emrys rested his cheek on his knees, still holding the root on Senna's palms. The bleeding had stopped moments ago, but Emrys didn't let go. He only softened his hold.

"I only wondered until I remembered it wasn't my place to," he said, at last. "Besides, you speak to me just fine now."

Senna paused. Hearing the observation felt like getting caught with a shameful secret, though he wasn't sure why. There was nothing shameful about a growing acquaintance with Emrys. Ease of speech was what he'd been chasing for decades. If there was something about Emrys that loosened Senna's tongue, then it was only wise to embrace it, no?

Senna folded his fingers around Emrys', barely holding them. He couldn't tell Emrys what it all meant to him—not yet.

"I figure, if you were going to kill me for being a traitorous Talsuran, you would've done it by now."

A delighted, lopsided smile bloomed on Emrys' face. His eyes searched Senna's.

"Your propensity to break Talsuran law is what I like about you, Senna," Emrys mused. "For what it's worth—and you didn't ask my opinion—but I think if you let yourself leave Percy's side from time to time, you might find company out there you really enjoy. I mean, have you ever gone for drinks with the other knighthearts? Taken a lover?"

Senna leaned back in the bath. "It's not safe for me to leave Percy's side. Even if it was, the other knighthearts despise me."

"What on earth for?"

"I am nearly a decade younger than they are, yet I outrank them all. I joined their training when I was nine years old, hand-selected to guard Percy days after he was born."

Emrys let out a whistling breath.

"It's their loss," he said. "I can't help but notice you didn't answer my last question about a lover."

Senna met Emrys' eyes, gaze narrow, though he felt a warmth climbing up his neck.

"I've never met a guard with your philosophy before."

"The outrageous philosophy that you should be allowed to have an ale and release pent-up stress in the warm embrace of a beautiful man? Senna, you've been brainwashed to think that your entire existence is to be spent serving the royal family. That every breath you breathe is given immediately to people who have more control and power than you ever will. You are a person down underneath all of that, but right now, everyone treats you like a tool with a single purpose and you *let* them," Emrys said passionately.

They looked at each other for a long moment, before Emrys let out a sigh.

"That's . . . that's not what I meant. I mean, it *is*. I think you are a terribly good person and the queen's leash snuffs out the brightest parts of you, but . . ." He scrubbed his eyes. "Really, I think I'm accidentally talking about me. I want so badly to be free of my station that it gives me hives to see you simply—endure it."

"I didn't realize you were so unhappy."

"It's not that," Emrys murmured. "How unhappy can a person be when they have their needs met and a career worth boasting about?"

Senna squeezed Emrys' hand. "As unhappy as they need to be."

"What I *need* is to help Thea find the cure. I need her to step into her role as princess so I can finally be unshackled from following her around everywhere she goes."

Senna wasn't sure he knew what Thea's cure search had to do with Emrys' appointment as her guard, but there were so many things about Redwind that were a mystery to him.

"Don't misunderstand me. I *adore* Thea as a sister," Emrys continued. "But there are so many other things I could be doing with my life. I want to travel. I want to be able to make trips to Mount Livia without having to sneak out or rush back." His words were gaining traction, growing brighter with every breath. "Don't you ever get curious about the culture that's out there? The world that we don't get to see because we're too busy stuck in the same castle, doing the same thing, day in and day out?"

Even though the bath water flowing into the tub was just as hot and fresh as it had been when he'd first gotten in, Senna couldn't help but start to feel a chill.

"That curiosity is a luxury. One I don't have," he replied.

"But it could be, if you chose to prioritize yourself."

Senna couldn't imagine it. To entertain the idea would mean leaving Percy helpless under the inadequate protection of some silverheart who only cared about jumping up the status ladder. If something happened to Percy because Senna made a selfish decision, he wasn't sure he would ever forgive himself.

Not to mention, what would he even *do* with free time? The realization that he had no hobbies or amusements outside his job should've come as a comfort, but it only made Senna feel like he'd failed at something. Which was ridiculous, because his lack of diversions was proof that he'd done exactly what he'd sworn to do.

"Close your eyes," Senna said. The request was polite around the edges, but it didn't leave room for Emrys to say no. Emrys didn't bristle, though. He complied without question. When he heard Senna rise out of the bath, he frowned.

"I didn't mean to offend you, Sen," Emrys swore.

"You didn't." It was the truth. No matter how uncomfortable it had made him feel, Emrys' honesty was just as refreshing as the exquisite bath he was leaving behind.

Senna dressed in the linens Sascha had left out for him. The clothes were simple—a translucent cream-colored shirt and trousers, completed by open-toed sandals. Without all of his armor on, or even his heavy traveling clothes, Senna couldn't help but feel exposed.

As he slipped back into the main throne room, Senna heard Emrys lift himself out of the bath. Senna didn't realize he was turning to Emrys until he was looking at the man, his expanse of soft brown skin on full display. Senna kept his eyes resolutely on Emrys' face. But Emrys was frowning at Senna's abdomen.

"What?" Senna asked, somewhat self-consciously.

Emrys blinked and schooled his face. Quickly he wrapped himself in a warm towel, fixed his gaze to the floor, and said, "Nothing at all."

Senna glanced down at himself, only to realize that through the thin fabric of his shirt, Emrys had probably seen his scar. He couldn't blame Emrys for staring. It was alarming to behold on a first glance—long and thin across his stomach.

"I don't remember getting it," Senna admitted. "I don't even remember when it appeared."

Although it was meant to settle Emrys, the man only curled his lips into a complicated frown and continued to dress.

"It looks like it must've been incredibly painful."

Senna shrugged. "Perhaps that's why I have no recollection." He stepped forward and righted Emrys' own shirt so it sat correctly on his shoulders. "Take your time. They want to speak with me first, after all."

Senna found Sascha lying in one of the daybeds reading a book barely thick enough to have a spine. They'd dressed in a blush-colored robe of soft, layered tulle—transparent around their shoulder and opaque at the abdomen. The fabric fell off the edge of their ample stomach and cascaded gracefully to the floor. They caught Senna hesitating at the corner of the room and gestured casually at the text.

"I prefer books that are shorter in length. They make the little free time I have far more productive." They gestured for Senna to follow them over one of the bridges into the side parlor.

Senna tossed a nervous look back at the private bath where Emrys was still dressing.

"Your friend can join us when he's ready," Sascha said. "But it's you I'd like to speak with first."

A sinking feeling settled in Senna's stomach, but he nodded and did as he was bade. It was only when he'd crossed the bridge that Senna realized his sword was nowhere in sight.

SENNA

"Imagine my surprise when I found out the Talsuran prince was asking after me," said Sascha. They lounged in an easygoing fashion in one of the ornate couches across from Senna, who still hadn't relaxed into his own seat.

He knew he was right to keep his instincts sharp. Everything about the room urged him to relax—the soft cushions on the round couch, the fur rug warming his damp feet, the torches lit with cozy flames along the edges of the room. But Senna refused to settle into the soft comforts around him. He'd gone this long without them and his apprehension had kept him safe.

Sascha raised their eyebrow as if to say, *Well?*

"I'm—" The word coughed out of him. He grew a small amber lily in his palm, rubbing the silky petal between his thumb and finger. The magic lifted the chokehold on his throat, but only infinitesimally. He'd have to manage the rest for himself. "Speech does not come easily to me."

"Ah." Sascha sat back. "My apologies, Goldheart. I've put you quite on the spot then, haven't I? But you agree we should talk, yes?"

Senna nodded.

"Then what do you suggest?"

A bead of sweat dripped down Senna's temple. If the sovereign cut their conversation short because of Senna's speech difficulty, or even his lack of conversational finesse, he wasn't sure how he would face Percy. He had to remind himself that this was not Phaedra. Not every royal behaved as if life were a bloodied battlefield—proceeding sword-first. But Sascha had no reason to trust anything they said and every reason to closely guard their secrets. Senna wouldn't be able to blame Sascha if they turned him away, even if he wasn't sure how he'd handle going home empty-handed.

"Patience," he said finally.

"That, I can do. Don't worry, Goldheart. I have judged your character. I won't think you a liar if your words arrive unsteadily."

Senna cupped his hand around the amber lily, letting it ground him. Sascha only wanted to hear his side of things. If this conversation became dangerous, he would leave. He wasn't alone. Emrys was here.

Drawing in a long breath through his nose, Senna tried again.

"Prince Percy wasn't enquiring about *you*, my liege." His free hand stretched for the hilt of his sword out of a nervous habit, but with nothing there, it was forced to settle on his knees.

"But he was enquiring about my land and its magic," Sascha agreed plainly. "He may not have been curious about what I wear in my sleep or what my favorite genre of book is, but all interest in Mount Livia is my concern." They leaned back on the center banquette and peered at Senna. "I imagine he sent you when his contact proved sparse. Believe me, I was appalled when I found out a member of my staff provided privileged information to a Grit Finger. I'd like to give you the opportunity to ask me directly. Tell me, what does your prince wish to know?"

A bitter, familiar inadequacy washed over Senna. He'd not been trained in the art of negotiations and scrutiny the way Percy and Princess Thea had. Could he trust the wisdom of his instincts to be truthful? What if this leader turned everything he said back on them, and Percy was the one to take the blame? Senna's mouth opened and closed as he searched for the right thing to say.

"Whatever notion you have of Talsura is probably true. But not when it comes to Prince Percy. The queen is entirely ignorant to Prince Percy's interest in Mount Livia, as well as the larger quest behind that interest."

"Sounds adventurous."

"Percy intends to cure the sun sickness."

This caused Sascha to lean forward, as if the news had been the very last thing they had expected.

"Adventurous indeed," they murmured dangerously. "From where we sit, it seems like you Talsurans are content with the arrangement of darkness that you went to such great lengths to conjure. You tell me this assumption is incorrect?"

"Percy isn't content. I'm not. You wouldn't be either if you were forced to live in complete, magical darkness. It's more than just the darkness itself. It's . . ." Senna wet his lips. "The exile separated families, you know. Friends and neighbors. I met one such woman today who fled Talsura to live here with her sister." Senna dug his fingers into his knees. "Phaedra might have commissioned the Dam under the ruse of protection, but many Talsurans aren't fooled. It was a strategic move to gain control over her people and take advantage of their fear."

"You hold no love for your queen."

"None," Senna replied immediately. "And, I'll admit, he might not have given you the strongest first impression by sneaking behind your back, but Percy isn't anything like his mother. That's why he sent me here—to uproot everything Phaedra has done."

Sascha nodded. Their gaze drifted to something behind Senna's shoulder.

"You've no reason to lie for the Talsurans, Captain Calloway. Is Prince Percy what the goldheart says he is?"

Senna peered behind him to find Emrys leaning up against the archway entrance, arms crossed.

"Afraid so. He's painfully endearing," Emrys answered casually. "I wouldn't have followed Senna all the way here otherwise."

"Then what is it you'd like to know?" The question came with a tilted nose and a curiosity that they failed to hide.

Senna expected Emrys to jump in as he had been, speaking on his behalf. But it seemed he was finally willing to hand the reins to Senna.

"Well." He straightened his back. "We heard that none of your people suffer sun sickness. You live freely without inflorescence and without magically blocking out the sun. We'd like to know how."

Sascha folded their fingers under their nose, regarding the both of the knights keenly. Then they whipped to their feet, stepped behind a dressing screen, and emerged wearing breezy linen pants and a cropped plum shirt.

"Follow me, gentleman," they said.

Senna and Emrys exchanged a wary look, but did as they were told.

As Sascha led Senna and Emrys deeper into the bathhouse, an unexpected draft wafted up into the cape, billowing it up under Senna's feet. He had to fall back to keep from tripping.

Eventually, the luxury of the bathhouse fell away into a simple cavern. Pointed rocks reached from the ceiling, close enough to Senna's head, he could feel their pointed tips grazing his hair.

"I wondered how deep the bathhouse went into the mountain," Emrys murmured, but his voice carried on the empty walls. "Now I've got my answer."

"It's quite the stronghold for our secrets, yes," Sascha answered. They tossed him an amused smile, one without rancor or suspicion. "A little farther now."

They'd been traveling so long that Senna didn't know what to expect to be waiting for them. A trap? A cliff edge looming over the end of the realms itself? Maybe this all was a lengthy trade channel and all of this had merely been an elaborate, *Get the fuck out of my kingdom.*

Yet Senna's instincts remained calm. Trusting, somehow.

At long last, the path gave way to a wide open room. Sascha gestured for them to come stand at the railing. Senna lingered in the shadows of the cave, gnawing on the inside of his cheek as Emrys easily took the space next to Sascha and gasped.

"*Sen,*" Emrys sighed. "You must come and see this."

When Emrys reached out a hand, Senna was powerless to leave it empty. He obediently twisted his fingers with Emrys' and allowed himself to be pulled to the looking point.

And, *oh*, what a sight.

This was the heart of the mountain.

Looking down over the ledge was like peering into the screaming mouth of the underworld. But looking up was all sunlight, as if the mountain were completely open and hollow at the top. Senna squinted, sparing a thought that maybe a canon had struck their staff right down the middle of the mountain. Effervescent light bounced around, fracturing back on itself from the thousands of crystals growing off of the walls.

Beneath and above them, a dozen more looking points surveyed the open basin, connected by narrow paths. Guards patrolled the areas, speaking to each other as they passed, though all sound was muted by the rush of roaring water deep at the bottom of the mountain's core.

"This is the secret you have come so far to discover," came Sascha's voice beside them. "This is the reason my people are not inflorescent, nor do they suffer sun sickness. It's this mountain "

"I can feel the magic," Emrys observed. "There's more of it here than air to breathe."

The same inadequacy from before settled in Senna's stomach like acidic nausea. He didn't sense the magic—not at all. He closed his eyes and drew in a breath, paying attention to every sensation on the surface of his skin, but there was—nothing. Just musty air and the essence of damp dirt.

Senna gnawed on the inside of his mouth. He'd spent endless days of his childhood with his magical masters, drilling some of the highest-level spells Talsura had to offer. What was the point of all those wasted hours if it could not serve him now?

Emrys took another step closer to the ledge and held his hand over the abyss. He caught something Senna couldn't see, holding it reverently.

"I think I understand," he murmured.

Sascha lifted a brow.

"You trust us. But even if you didn't, you probably would've still brought us here. Because if our intentions were bad, there'd be nothing we could do about it. Your cure to sun sickness *is* the mountain and it's the one thing we can't take from you."

"As steady as the ground you're standing on, it's not going anywhere," Sascha confirmed. "In truth, even my best mages don't entirely understand the origin of the power. Our best guess is that the mountain somehow acts as a magnet to the sun magic. It funnels into this center, grows the crystals you see on the wall, and siphons into our water supply. We call the crystals 'basks,' because—" They chuckled, leaning their arms on the railing. "Well, we like to bask in the sun and so do our crystals. We believe that because the mountain acts as a siphon for the sunlight's magic, it doesn't exist in the air to hurt us. That's why when my people stray too far from the mountain, they experience inflorescence. Luckily, they've been able to return before becoming gravely sick."

Senna lifted his hand to one of the crystals and ran his thumb over the smooth, glassy surface. It thrummed under his touch, the magic pulsing like a racing heartbeat. Was this what Emrys meant? Was *this* what he could feel in the air?

"Mount Livia is what it is today because we've worked to understand the power the sun graciously bestows upon us," Sascha continued. "There, you'll see my harvesters collecting the basks, which we then grind up and use to supply energy to anything we can. Our lights, our stoves. The magic in our water supply reaches the kingdom's limits, but doesn't require any preparation on our part. You might have felt its effects for yourself in the bath. It's restorative and healing. " A mischievous glint reached their eye. "I could tell you how to grind up the basks to light your own homes, but I'm afraid *that's* Mount Livia's secret."

"How *do* you keep it a secret? Your people's lack of inflorescence, I mean," Emrys asked. "Redwind and Mount Livia have been trading since we settled at the foot of your mountain and we didn't know. And surely some desperate Talsurans have already come wondering before we have."

Sascha crossed their arms over their chest, tilting their head back in thought. "Can you really call it a secret if you share it openly?"

"How open could it be if the Redwindan queen doesn't know about it?"

Sascha shrugged one shoulder offhandedly. "Of course she knows. We do still engage in *some* trade. Queen Casta merely does me the courtesy of handling matters discreetly."

Emrys looked taken back, but Sascha was already continuing.

"As for Talsura, when the sun sickness began, King Mathis of Talsura had been desperately trying to acquire Mount Livia to help build his empire. I was only freshly sovereign at the time, elected by my people, but I staunchly refused. The sun sickness stopped what was a nearly inevitable invasion. Mathis died and Phaedra demanded our secrets, threatening us with all of her knighthearts."

"But Ilias had just died," Senna realized.

"Precisely. I knew that with him gone, her army was weakened. I called her bluff. Truthfully, at the time, we didn't know why we were being spared from the sun sickness. We attributed our survival to the canons. It took some years before we noticed the connection between the mountain, the river, and the crystals." They shrugged. "The mountain isn't a secret, not really. If someone wants to share the knowledge, we tell them. But the Talsurans are too afraid to leave their Dam to see for themselves. The Redwindans have no interest in moving."

Emrys nodded. "When you build your home from the ground up, it's difficult to leave it."

"I'm also told the mountain makes inflorescence more difficult, since the sun's magic is not as readily available."

"As for your immunity," Senna started. "It can't leave the mountains, can it?"

Sascha's smile was apologetic. "I'm afraid not."

Senna felt his shoulders drop.

So that was it. The cure they'd traveled so far to discover wasn't a cure at all. It was the miracle that allowed the Mount Livians not only to survive, but to flourish in luxury and comfort and safety. It didn't matter how hard he tried, Senna would never be able to imagine what that felt like.

"What are you going to tell Percy?" Emrys muttered beside him.

"The truth. What else is there to say?" Senna replied.

From the corner of his eye, one of the crystal basks flickered an ivory-hued blue up the path. It caught Senna's attention, but when he turned his head, there was no light at all. Only a dark corner.

Senna's intuition set off like a war gong. Narrowing his eyes, he focused on the corner, keen to any movement. Any sound.

Then, light erupted into the shadows, like someone had poured moonlight from a bucket over the dirt in diamond-sized drops. The bright, glowing tears melded together along the ground, drawing up until they formed a human figure made of translucent moonbeams.

A man.

He was wispy around the edges, like wind-blown smoke, but the features of his face were clearer than life. At first, Senna mistook the spirit for a canon making an unwelcome appearance, but then he noticed the apparition wore the same robes of the Mount Livian guards.

The spirit looked around furiously, only to catch Senna's gaze from across the chasm. His expression hardened from desperation to determination. He pointed down at his feet, right where Senna had been scrutinizing.

There, illuminated by the spirit's light, a cloaked man with snake eyes tattooed onto his face aimed a readied bow at Sascha. The bandit noticed the light shining above him, then snapped his attention to Senna.

It was a warning. But now that Snake-Eyes knew he had been caught, he had no choice but to fire.

The whistling arrow had only just pierced the air when Senna jumped into action. He didn't spare a moment to think before shoving Sascha out of the line of fire, snatching the bolt straight from the air. The arrow's splintering wood bit into his hands like a wasp desperately trying to escape someone's hold.

Snapping the arrow in two with a single hand, Senna spun around to the attacker, only to find a dozen more Grit Fingers emerging across the different levels. Metal scraped behind him. Three more Grits with their blades turned on Emrys and Sascha.

Senna reached to his side, only to remember that the sword that had dutifully served him had been taken. He balled his fists as tightly as he could, looking around for anything else he could use.

Emrys acted first. With the force of an angry bull, he rammed his knee into the groin of the nearest bandit. The bandit doubled over, heaving out a gasp. Emrys swiped his dual rapiers with deft finesse. He slammed the hilt on the poor bastard's head and the entire mountain erupted into battle.

More Grit Fingers emerged from the caverns, surrounding Senna as he held his fists before him. The first Grit swung a curved blade downwards, but Senna sidestepped—directly into another bandit. He rolled around them, dodging the jab of their knife.

"Goldheart, incoming!" Sascha called.

Senna tore his gaze away from his opponents in time to see Sascha brandish four thin needles in the spaces between their knuckles. He dropped to the ground, allowing Sascha to unleash the needles like throwing darts.

He only touched the ground for a second, before leaping back up to his feet. His enemies crumpled to pathetic heaps beside him.

Emrys was at his back in a blink, handing him the second rapier.

"I don't know about you, but this is the most eventful day I think I've ever had," he said, parrying another incoming blow. "And I was exiled."

Senna was not accustomed to casual conversation during fights, but he found it . . . pleasant? Comforting, maybe? Like perhaps Emrys was not the least bit concerned about the outcome of this battle.

"I've met these bandits before," Senna called out in between clashes of his sword. "They're the Grit Fingers. The guild thieves. The one who fired at Sascha was Percy's informant."

Sascha allowed a brick-shaped man with a hammer to draw dangerously close to them, only to ram another small needle somewhere Senna couldn't see. The brick-man dropped to his knees and planted face-first into the damp soil.

"What on earth could they want?" they demanded, hurling another dart up the mountain. It lodged into the shoulder of a bandit who was about to tackle one of the workers harvesting crystals.

"You?" Emrys guessed. "The first shot was aimed at you."

"Only because they don't want to wind up on the other end of these poisoned needles."

Senna kicked one of the prone bodies, flipping it so he could open the satchel hiding under the bandit's cloak. The leader's pouch was stuffed entirely with crystal basks. This time, when he touched one, it shocked him with a bolt of pure energy that traveled up his arm and nearly made him drop his blade.

"They're smuggling basks out!" he shouted.

Another body dropped hard onto the ground beside him, this time with a needle centered between their brows. Discolored foam frothed from their lips, spilling onto the dirt, drawing the light from their eyes with it.

The sight sent Senna leaping back to his feet. He adjusted his grip on his sword, throwing a look at Emrys that meant something like, *Remind me not to get on the other end of an angry ruler's needles.*

Time seemed to hold still as more and more Grits poured in down the path, spilling around Senna and his allies. Before he knew it, they had slashed and pierced their way up the path, closer to where Snake-Eyes was poised on a stray rock, loosing arrows over the cavern like a hailstorm.

Senna withdrew into the shadows when no one was looking, eyes locked on Snake-Eyes. Pearls of red blood scattered from the tip of his blade onto the ground as he slowly approached the Grit Finger. The bandit looked exactly as he had the first time Senna had seen him—a filthy black cloth over the lower half of his face, the same dark tattoos piercing his eyes. He had to admit, the bandit was an excellent shot, notching his next arrows before the previous could meet its mark—and it did, each time with heart-racing accuracy.

But with his focus so fixed to his task, Snake-Eyes failed to see Senna round the corner on him. Though the rapier in his hand was meant for fluid, light-handed movements, Senna couldn't help but heave all of his strength into the single slash he aimed directly at Snake-Eyes' bow. The blade grazed the top of the bandit's thumb, then sliced through the upper limb of the bow and through the string.

Snake-Eyes hissed, tripping over himself to stumble back, but with the mountain's cold stone behind him, there was nowhere to go. In a last-ditch effort, he reached into the back of his boot and pulled out the smallest dagger Senna had ever seen. Scoffing, Senna swatted the blade away. It skittered across the floor and over the ledge, plummeting into the hungry abyss. Senna turned his ear, but he never heard it land.

Hands fumbling over his pockets, Snake-Eyes searched for a miracle, only to freeze when Senna brought the rapier under the man's chin.

Behind him, Emrys clung to a thief in a hood. The captain strained against the bandit's strength, gritting his teeth against the effort it took to stop himself from being flung over the side of the railing. The thief clawed down the side of Emrys' face, though Emrys seemed to be giving as good as he got, if the thorns strangling the bandit's wrists and throat were any indication.

There was a second Senna was prepared to leave Snake-Eyes with his broken bow and throw himself to Emrys' aid. But before he could, Sascha was there, stabbing something that looked like a knitting needle straight into the bandit's throat. Blood gurgled over the bandit's lips, spraying over Emrys' face. Emrys spun him around, flinging the lifeless body over the ledge.

Emrys grinned when he noticed Senna watching him, but the bloodthirsty pride drained away in an instant.

"Senna, behind you!"

Snake-Eyes was on him faster than Senna could turn around. He jumped onto Senna's back, arms wrapped tightly around his throat. Senna cursed as he failed to keep his balance, tumbling to the ground, bringing Snake-Eyes with him. They rolled in the dirt, the blade threatening to slip from Senna's hold. Eyes red with rage, Snake-Eyes climbed over Senna, aiming a readied fist at Senna's face, but Senna kicked him off.

It was Senna's turn to demonstrate speed. Snake-Eyes pushed up onto his elbows, spitting blood and dirt into the soil. Anger swelling to the surface, Senna stepped in the center of the bandit's chest, slamming him back into the ground.

A low snarl rumbled from Snake-Eyes' curled mouth.

Senna leaned all his weight into the foot holding the bastard down, wondering if he should question Snake-Eyes or put an end to it while he had the upper hand.

To his dread, Snake-Eyes began to laugh. Deep, hysterical, deranged laughter that echoed down into the abyss, until it sounded like a savage god preparing to upend the earth.

"I've found the goldheart!" he shrieked with delight. "I found the bloody goldheart!"

The bandits froze as if compelled by a holy command. An entire roomful of blades and hammers, which had once been fixed on the Mount Livians, now turned to aim right at Senna.

Emrys took the opportunity to close the distance between himself and Senna. He fixed the sharp end of his sword toward Snake-Eyes' stomach, stretching his free hand out to the side. Thorns twisted from his fingertips like hissing snakes, brandishing their sharp teeth at anyone who drew too near.

"What do you want with the goldheart?" Emrys hissed. Maybe it was the drying blood on the man's cheeks, but Senna hadn't known Emrys could be so—*intimidating*. It was almost a little . . .

Snake-Eyes started to chuckle again, the sinister sound a disturbing interruption to his thoughts.

"My loooord waaants him," warbled Snake-Eyes. "Ask him what he is hiiiid-ing."

Senna's mouth went dry. What—what *he* was hiding? He wasn't hiding any-thing, and certainly not anything a lord could desire.

"Don't look so confused, baneheart. Do you really think we came here just for the crystals? We came here because we knew *you'd* be here," Snake-Eyes snarled, eyes gleaming when Senna frowned. "He's a fool, he's a fool, the goldheart is a fool." In a jeering voice, he crooned, *"They're guild thieves, they* must *be here for the castle jewels. They're Grit Fingers, they're here for the crystals.*" He lifted his head up from the ground, a pool of blood forming beneath his hair. "We're guild thieves, Goldheart. We know a real prize when we see one. We may not have you today, but we *will* have you."

"I'm no prize," Senna hissed. "Certainly not for any thieving lord."

"You *will* hand yourself over to the ruler of sky and slick hands," Snake-Eyes threatened. "He will make you scream so loudly your ancestors will cry blood and you will never. Speak. Again."

A chill crossed over Senna's skin, one that closed his throat tighter than any amber lily could touch.

"Alright, I've heard enough," Emrys grunted. "I can't wait to see what Sascha does with you."

Emrys flipped his sword so the hilt was poised in his hand, ready to meet its mark. He dropped to a knee, hovering the blunt end in between the bandit's eyes.

"Sweet fucking dreams, you scum," he sneered.

Snake-Eyes didn't waste a second.

"*Fire!*" he bellowed.

It happened quicker than Senna could follow. There was a gasp from Emrys' lips. The clatter of his sword as he tossed it aside and spun around. Throwing his arms out in front of him, Emrys let out a bellow and—

Cursed canons.

A wall of dense thorns—higher than the oldest Redwindan trees—and briars the size of deadly icicles. It burst from the rocky mountain floor so quickly, Senna thought he was hallucinating it. But it was very, very real, catching all the incoming arrows and swords before they could shower over the Mount Livians. Through his stunned gaze, Senna almost thought the wall was thickest right where he was standing.

A curse fell from Sascha's mouth. They approached the wall from farther up the path, angling around the wall's edge to see the dozens of arrows sticking out from the vines. With a forceful yank, they tried to pluck one out, but the arrow was fixed firmly in the woody surface.

"Remind me not to get on Redwind's bad side," Sascha whistled.

Senna turned back to Emrys, expecting some cheeky reply, but—

He caught Emrys before he could collapse to the ground. The wall had captured every single arrow, every thrown knife—

But not the one lodged deep in Emrys' stomach.

"Emrys," Senna said tensely. The captain's eyes grew heavier and heavier with each slow blink. For a man with an arrow sticking under his ribs, he wore the gentlest smile. "Emrys, you need to stay awake."

The captain followed orders, but barely. His eyes were heavy slits, the amethyst color dull and wan. They would not waver away from Senna's face, though they did shake, as if Emrys was waging a losing war to maintain his focus.

Behind them, Sascha was unleashing a thread of commands over their men. Some of them had sprung into action without needing to be told, binding Snake-Eyes in heavy cuffs and patting him down. The wall of thorns must've scared the rest of the Grits away, because through the sharp protrusions in the wall, Senna could make out the unmistakable sight of cowards fleeing. He turned his attention back to Emrys, though the distraction had only been a second.

He found his own shaking hand pressed over the flesh around the damp puncture wound. Senna didn't remember calling upon his medical training, but his instincts must've done the thinking for him. He pressed down, ignoring the way the wound gushed blood over Emrys' stomach and made scarlet mud on the ground below. Vaguely, he wondered if the wound was too deep. If too much blood had been lost.

How would he return to Redwind and tell Thea that her guard had died on his watch?

"Courage, friend," came Sascha's urgent, but soothing, voice. "Can you carry him?"

Senna didn't answer. He wound his free arm under Emrys' knees and supported his shoulders. Arranging his hold so as not to jostle the wound, Senna carried his injured friend back through the caves as if the captain were as delicate as a newborn chick. It was with great courage that Senna avoided looking at the worsening wound, but he knew his boots and fresh clothes were staining crimson.

"This way," Sascha directed, nudging Senna toward a set of channels he hadn't yet traveled through. It wasn't the way to the throne room, but as Sascha hurled open the doors at the path's end, Senna understood why.

This had to be the infirmary. It was almost hard to miss, what with the dozen baths lining the walls. But within reach of the baths were just as many loaded carts and shelves filled with medical supplies. One part of Senna's mind nearly forgot that he was leagues deep into a mountain, because the walls were painted with a mural that was realistic enough to mimic the beautiful sight of Mount Livia out a real window. The images even glowed—that same daylight hue that the crystal basks let off.

The other part of Senna's mind, the louder of the two, could not shake the terror of holding Emrys—dying—in his arms.

"Get him into one of the healing baths," Sascha instructed. It was barked along with a flurry of other orders for the healers, but Senna recognized that this one was for him.

The water was warmer than Senna expected as he lowered Emrys into the bath, but not hot enough to further scorch his open wounds. Strings of blood branched into the water like bursting veins, sinking to the bottom of the shallow basin.

For a few seconds, the sovereign and the healers rushed around the tiny station, preparing tonics and bandages. Senna could only stand off to the side, his fingers itching to get closer. To *do* something.

Unable to help it any longer, the goldheart knelt into the water beside Emrys, snatching a cloth straight out of someone's grasp and pressing it to the wound.

Sascha was in the bath a moment later, laying their hands overtop Senna's and gently pushing them aside. Senna's instincts told him to remain steady, to do what he was trained to do, but when a shred of Emrys' skin appeared from underneath his hold, he gasped.

12
EMRYS

I T WASN'T THE FIRST time Emrys had brushed up against death. He liked to think he kept what he called *a companionable distance* between himself and the entity that would one day detangle him from his earthly body. They were ships in the night, always passing but never getting close enough to actually meet. There was one time he'd rolled out from underneath a horse's wild hooves after being thrown, seconds before he could be trampled. Another time, he'd accepted a muffin from a child made with what they'd *thought* had been edible sweet fairy drops, and instead was poison foxglove. Hell, Emrys was sure death had kept a good eye on him during the exile.

If all those instances had been *brushing up against death*, then this was *being grabbed by the bloody shoulders and shaken within an inch of his life.*

Literally.

He realized it must be bad if he could only think about one thing at a time. Trying to stay conscious was like wading through burning mud, and his mind so badly wanted to go to sleep. He vacillated between trying to remember what had happened, squinting up at Senna's worried face, and listening to the healers scrambling for supplies. Distantly, he was aware he was in another bath, though it felt the way it might've if he was only *dreaming* he was in a bath.

Then, the feeling sharpened. The hazy struggle to stay present in the moment faded into a sort of relief. With it, the searing pain below his ribs ebbed away, dragged from his body like it was bloodied water circling down the drain.

"The wound is almost healed," Senna gasped. "How?"

"The water possesses medicinal properties. When your friend is out of hot water, I'll tell you all about it," said Sascha.

A pause.

"Is that supposed to be a joke?"

"That depends. Was it funny?"

Another few heavy blinks and Emrys felt well enough to keep his eyes open for more than a flickering second. Above him, Senna glared at Sascha, who ignored the daggers being thrown their way and popped the cork to a bottle of pale pink fluid. They poured it into the bath. Instantly, numbness bloomed around where Emrys had once felt throbbing pain.

"Who is he?" Senna asked.

This time, Senna's question was directed at a young man sitting by the edge of the bath. Unlike the rest of the Mount Livians, he was wearing long black robes, held together by a belt made of a dozen beaded strands. The man held a bead chain in one hand, and dipped his free fingertips into the bath's water. His features were small, his figure worryingly thin, and his straight blonde hair was smoothed away from his face. He was as pale as Percy was, which made Emrys dizzily wonder if the man was from Talsura.

"This is Ciaran Lynwood. He is our new resident votary. We like to invoke Hedela at all our healings."

Hedela was picky about who she healed. If this votary thought she'd help Emrys, he was in rougher shape than he had realized.

Senna must've read Emrys' mind, because he asked, "Will she help?"

"Maybe. But there's a chance this won't be a successful healing without her aid, so the prayer is necessary," Ciaran answered.

"I thought your river was enchanted," Senna said.

"The water can only offer so much," Sascha explained. "It can stitch a wound of his magnitude loosely, enough to slow the bleeding, but not enough to heal the gash completely. I'd stitch the skin together, but I fear he'd only bleed out from the inside. We need something that can accelerate the healing where the wound is deepest."

"That's where Hedela comes in," Ciaran said.

Emrys would believe it when he saw it.

"You need needle yarrow," Emrys slurred. Whatever numbing agent was swirling around his bath had turned his tongue to lead.

Sascha's brows raised to their hairline at the strained sound of Emrys' voice, but the expression washed into contrition.

"Needle yarrow doesn't grow well around the mountains and our supply ran dry ages ago," they said. "We'll have to find something else to amplify the water."

"It's my own fault," Emrys groaned.

"Of course it's not your fault," Senna murmured.

Oh, how Emrys wished that were the case. But he remembered when his mother had asked him what he thought about increasing inflorescent exports. Emrys did not care to think about anything that could be considered a princely duty. He'd given a half-hearted answer about how, *"If Mount Livia wants inflorescent flowers so badly, they can come down the mountain and learn it for themselves."* To his current horror, his mother had agreed. The thought made him grimace.

"He's still in pain," Senna pressed, mistaking Emrys' frown.

"The prayers *will* work," the votary insisted. "Hedela has sent her sign. His pain will begin to alleviate any second now."

"No," Emrys hissed, voice strained. If his life was in the balance, he wasn't leaving it up to a canon who *sometimes* healed those who sought her out. He seized Senna's wrist under tight fingers. "Senna can grow the needle yarrow. He's—"

A pause as a sting of pain radiated up his side under his skin. It almost felt like the wound was trying to stitch itself closed, veins and guts pulling and straining together, but not drawing close enough.

Emrys sucked in through his teeth. "He's inflorescent."

Surprise filled Senna's expression and Emrys realized it was probably the first time anyone had called the goldheart inflorescent. Senna's shock washed away as quickly as the dirty bath water, replaced by heated tenacity.

Around the bath, the Mount Livian healers drew closer, eager to see a Talsuran willingly perform inflorescence. Senna paid them no mind, placing a steady hand under Emrys' back and letting the water buoy him so his wound broke the surface. A pain-twinged shiver ran through Emrys' body as Senna gently rubbed the skin around the wound. The touch's tender brush made Emrys' mind dizzy enough to dull the sting of being prodded. Then, Senna set his palm over the wound and closed his eyes. Realizing his efforts were better utilized elsewhere, Ciaran laid a hand on Senna's shoulder, prayers shifting away from Hedela into murmurations for Varyan.

Emrys felt the roots as soon as they sprouted under his skin. He prepared for the inevitable twinge that always came with unpracticed inflorescence, but pain never came. Instead, the deepest part of his wound shifted from a burning sting to a dull ache. It meant that Senna had done exactly as he was supposed to.

A sigh of relief spilled from Emrys' lips, his breath no longer a burden in his lungs. Senna's brows wrinkled together, and he lifted his hand away to reveal six patches of needle yarrow. The biggest was in the center of the now-scabbed gash. The remaining five were spread apart like star points, right where Senna's fingers had been. The tiny white flowers were still unfurling, expanding over Emrys' skin so far, Senna had to brush the blooms away in order to examine the healing taking place underneath.

"How do you feel?" Senna muttered.

Emrys hadn't quite gotten around to paying attention to how he felt. None of that was important. Not as the last minutes become clearer in his mind. Being carried in Senna's tame hold. Feeling his inflorescence take root in his body. Knowing that, for a few beautiful moments, the Goldheart of Talsura had cared *about him.*

That was all he could think of when his lips fell into an easy grin and said, "*Well done*, pupil."

For a terrifying—exhilarating—moment, he thought maybe Senna could see through him. Past the transparent fabric of his soaked clothes. Under his dark, smooth skin. Beneath the web of his nerves. Into the very depths of whatever made Emrys the person he was. The place where the desire to love Senna ran molten hot like lava, fueling him and making him ignite with only a single look.

What would the goldheart do, Emrys wondered, if he knew just how much someone burned to adore him?

"He'll be a bit woozy until his body can replenish the blood he lost," Sascha explained. Emrys wanted to shout that he was perfectly cognizant, but while the pain had drained away, so too had his strength.

Ciaran rolled a wheelchair up to the edge of the healing basin. There was a dark plum robe folded neatly over the chair's back.

"We're giving you the royal treatment, young sir," Sascha said. "Your robe has been warmed and everything."

"Oh canons, anything but the royal treatment," Emrys moaned.

"You don't want to feel like a prince for the day?" Sascha chuckled. "I'd say you've earned it. You didn't mention you were a genius at inflorescence."

"I'd rather get run through by another arrow than *ever* be prince of anything. Besides, a man has to maintain some humility."

"My apologies, friend. I'm afraid you'll have to be the prince of your sickbed until you've healed enough to travel home. Are you well enough to stand?"

Emrys was, so he did—delicately. Sascha looked as if they were about to hold out the robe for him, but Senna plucked it from their hands.

"I'll do it," he said. He was back to quiet, chopped tones now that the panic was over. Sascha didn't argue.

Heat crept up from the hollow of Emrys' throat as Senna offered his hand to guide Emrys out of the basin. Emrys had known the baths refreshed themselves, but he was still surprised when he looked down and found it was filled with crystalline water. Senna held the robe open, causing Emrys' blush to darken. How was he expected to make a speedy recovery with Senna's breath on the back of his neck making him absolutely feverish?

Emrys should have known it would've only gotten worse. He should have insisted that he tie the robe himself, but when Senna's arms wrapped around his waist to knot the soft cord, Emrys could only stand there and hold his breath.

WHEN HE WOKE, EMRYS found reality better than the murky nothingness of his dreams. Pleasant saltiness wafted into the air, carried by a gentle breeze that ebbed and receded like sea waves. It reminded Emrys of where he was—on Mount Livia by the eastern coast. Swaths of orange and fuchsia on the walls spelled the passage of time. Emrys traced the dusky light across the room to the wide balcony, where open accordion doors exposed the room to the entire mountainside and the ocean beneath.

There, taking it all in against the ancient summits and lapping waves, was Senna. He leaned his arms against the railing, open fingers catching flitting gusts of wind. It was the most relaxed Emrys had seen him. The muscles of his hard back were finally loose and at ease. He was dressed in his regular goldheart travel clothes again, all traces of the dre'malor's muck gone.

Emrys watched Senna for a long moment. His affection for the goldheart had been like an earthquake, unmistakable from the surface. But now that he'd seen Senna fighting—witnessed the way he'd unleashed the full breadth of his loyal protection—Emrys realized how deep that affection shook his core.

It would never work, of course. *They* would never work. If, by some miracle, Emrys managed to convince his mother to let him abdicate the throne to Thea, it would only solve half of the problem. Percy wasn't like Emrys. He didn't have a backup heir, and without a backup, that meant he *had* to be king and Senna would *have* to be his goldheart. Even if Emrys moved all his earthly belongings to Talsura to be with Senna—the thought of which made something in him rot—Senna's priorities would always lie with Percy.

Emrys tried not to fault Percy for it. None of them could help it, really—how hopeless it was to want Senna. But Emrys did. Canons help him, he *wanted*.

He had learned more about Senna in the last day than he could have dared to learn in the past year. It wasn't only that Senna had opened up about his past. It was also that Senna could go from fighting with the ferocity of an angry god to becoming the most tender creature in the realms without a second thought. Emrys didn't just yearn for the pleasure of Senna's companionship. He ached to know what Senna could be without being tied down to Talsura. Most of all, he wanted to know what they both could be together, without restraints.

"I don't think I've ever seen you enjoying a moment to yourself before," Emrys called out.

Senna spun around as if he'd been struck. The worry in his brow smoothed away when he found Emrys looking back with a tired smile.

"You're awake," he noted, perhaps a little stunned. Then, "I'm hardly enjoying waiting around and worrying about you."

"*You're* worried about *me*? Sen, I'm touched," teased Emrys. He tried to push himself up to lean on the headboard of the bed. He'd been lying down so long, all he wanted to do was sit up. But the movement yanked painfully on his wound and his arms didn't have the strength they usually did.

Senna was by his side in an instant.

"Here, allow me," he said. Gently, he guided Emrys into the sitting position, bearing the brunt of the burden so Emrys wouldn't have to. Senna's hands holding him up reminded Emrys just how strong he truly was—how disciplined Senna had to be to keep that strength dormant, ever at the ready.

"Are you still in pain? Should I call for a healer?" Senna continued.

"No pain. Just sore. A bit weak, but nothing a common cold hasn't done to me," Emrys rasped. He looked up sheepishly, then said, "We're late."

Senna didn't deny it. "I already sent word to Princess Thea. She's going to cover for us until we return."

"And Percy?"

"Not entirely thrilled about being stuck in his room for longer than we planned, but relieved we're both alright."

"Won't Phaedra question that her son hasn't left his room?"

Senna scoffed. "That would mean she'd have to care enough to notice."

He went on to explain how Sascha had been so grateful for their help, they'd given Emrys the nicest guest room in the mountainside palace. Emrys couldn't help but ask a thousand questions about what he'd missed. How could he not, when Senna's usual difficulty of speech was completely absent?

"How *did* you know Sascha was in danger?" Emrys asked.

Senna rubbed at his knuckles for a second, then confessed, "I saw a spirit visit."

"Really?" Emrys hummed, intrigued. Spirit visits were rare. It was presumed that they only happened when a deceased person could not move on to the next life without resolving whatever plagued them—unfinished business that was so substantial, it kept the soul from moving on to whatever life came next. The spirit would have one—and only one—chance at peace. They could manifest visually and their hands could touch and take hold of things, but rarely could they speak.

"After we ensured you were safe, Sascha's guards and I investigated the mountain to see if we could find the weak spot where the Grits got in. We found a body, freshly slain, near the coastal entrance to the mountain. It was the same man from the spirit visit. I think he returned to warn us about the attack. When he appeared, he pointed right to Snake-Eyes to draw my attention to the ambush. But Snake-Eyes fired when I saw him."

"So, we're just going to gloss over the fact that you caught that arrow midair?" Emrys said.

"It's not worth mentioning. I should have been able to stop the attack before it happened," Senna murmured with a frown. Emrys opened his mouth to argue, but Senna was spiraling ahead. "They were after *me*, and I have no idea why. They said some lord was after me. I can't think of who would want me. Can you?"

"No, but I'm not acquainted with Talsura's court like I am Redwind's. Maybe it's a political move. I imagine targeting the goldheart is a sure way of hitting Talsura where it hurts." Emrys frowned. "But they said *you* were the prize. Not Talsura. Not the riches. Not even Percy. *You*."

"What a joke." Senna leaned his elbows on the mattress, hands folding over his mouth. "Sascha tried to pay me, you know. Like I was a hired mercenary. Like I *did* something for them."

"Sen, you *saved* their life. You protected Mount Livia, even after its citizens treated you with contempt and its ruler interrogated you like you were a criminal."

Senna didn't argue, but he didn't agree either. It was possible he was having a moment where it was hard to speak, so Emrys waited and watched Senna pick at the scabs on the back of his hands.

When the silence stretched on too long, Emrys sighed.

"How much did they offer?" he asked nosily.

"It doesn't matter. I didn't accept it. It wouldn't have been right—not when I'm the reason the ambush happened in the first place." Senna scrubbed his fingers through his hair, and Emrys felt the urge to smooth the tangled strands away from Senna's face. "It makes me sick to think about what would've happened if Percy would have been there."

"You won't have to find out. We'll get to the bottom of what these Grit Fingers are after, and put an end to it."

Senna's smile revealed he wasn't convinced.

Emrys leaned forward and said, "We will."

"I don't know where they got the foolish notion that I have or—or *am* something of value. They'll be bitterly sore when they find they're mistaken."

Emrys' heart dropped.

This was the real Senna Kane. The highest-ranking guard in Talsura—the very best of all men—who still thought he was insignificant. Emrys would've laughed from the irony of it if it didn't make him feel sick to his stomach. He couldn't fathom what Senna had endured to look at himself that way. To see himself as someone whose existence was a means of provision, and nothing more.

Emrys caught Senna's hesitant gaze and held it, sincerely, like he would not let it go for all the money in the world. He took Senna's hand, warmth radiating from the place their palms pressed together.

"Before me, I see a man who does not use his blade to intimidate or harm. I've found he's rather thoughtful and gentle by nature. He chooses his words carefully and has sacrificed the glory of his youth so that he can be *good*. Does that not sound like treasure to you?" Emrys asked sincerely. "I don't pretend to know what those thieves are up to. But you *are* singular, Senna Kane, and you deserve so much more than what you've been given."

Senna was cut wide open. Every ounce of his humility and hesitance was embedded into the lines of his face, crowned by the prettiest blush Emrys had ever seen. Senna searched Emrys' gaze, as if looking for any sign that it had been a lie. Something to confirm his worst doubts. But he wouldn't find it. Emrys had meant every word.

"I can't," Senna confessed. Emrys knew what he meant. *I can't believe that yet. I can't believe that of myself.*

"You will," Emrys answered, certain. "I'll help you."

Then, he rose out of the bed—ignoring the soreness in his body—and pulled Senna to the balcony. Before them, the sunset overflowed into the ocean, making the gentle waves swirl with a thousand colors. Emrys kept Senna close to his side, their arms brushing.

"We have to leave in the morning," Senna said quietly.

Emrys swung himself up to sit on the wide stone railing, his feet dangling over the slope of the mountain.

"It's funny. We've almost died twice today and yet I still don't want to leave," he confessed.

Senna leaned onto his elbows. His eyes were molten gold as he watched the day ease below the horizon.

"No," he said. "Me neither."

THEA

T HEA WAS BEGINNING TO understand why Emrys paced around whenever Goldheart Kane was late. She sat on her sofa, trying to finish the book she'd started the day before, but her gaze kept drifting to the door. She'd almost missed the letter that had appeared and dropped into her lap. One look at Senna's familiar, blocky handwriting and she'd torn the letter open.

Your Highness,

I am writing to inform you that Captain Calloway and I will be late in returning to Redwind. We encountered some trouble. We're both safe, but the captain will require a day to recover before he is well enough to travel home. We'll provide a full report when we return tomorrow morning. Please rest assured that we have been privileged with the full extent of Mount Livia's renowned hospitality.

Your Servant,
Goldheart Senna Kane

Thea pressed the letter to her cheek. She knew that Senna wouldn't have lied about being safe, but she was intimately aware that safety was fleeting. She tried to pass the time by reading in her study, only to scan the same lines over and over. After an hour passed without progressing a single page, Thea made her way to the library, where she knew Nare would still be working late into the night. It'd only been a few hours since they'd returned from their own adventure, but Thea felt like it'd been months.

Nare took one look at Thea—the silk bonnet, the soft night clothes—and set her quill down. "You're about to ask for something. What is it?"

"If I wrote a letter, would you be able to send it off? Obviously, I can't send magic missives."

Nare fixed Thea with an unimpressed look.

"I was recognized as a child prodigy in a very elite group of underground geniuses," she deadpanned. "I think I can send your letter."

Thea was too anxious to give Nare as good as she'd gotten. Without asking, she swiped a piece of parchment from the table and commandeered the quill. Nare grumbled, but didn't dare stop her.

The reply to Senna was short: Thea had received the message and would cover for him until they managed to make it home. When she was finished, she folded the paper the way that was customary for magically-delivered letters and handed it to the librarian.

Nare, to Thea's immense irritation, unfolded the letter, read it completely, then folded it back up. Then, with a snap of the finger, the letter ignited into bright flames, then vanished.

"Your guard got himself into a spot of trouble, did he?" Nare chuckled.

Thea knew there was no point in lying. Not after Nare already possessed so many of her secrets already.

"The goldheart didn't give any details. But it seems that way. Not that I'm surprised. Trouble finds Emrys wherever he goes."

"He's your guard. If you'd been there, I'd have said the common issue would have been you, princess." When Thea only offered a tight smile, Nare tapped her shoulder with a book spine. "Captain Calloway has a reputation of being unbearably stubborn. I'm sure he won't let a spot of trouble be his demise."

"He better not," Thea said stiffly. Then, remembering her manners, "Thanks for sending the letter."

"What else would I have done? Missed an opportunity to serve my princess?"

Thea expected to find the words dripping in Nare's usual sarcasm, but there was truth in them too. Something about the way Nare said *my princess* made Thea remember the last time she'd lain with a woman very long ago. She gnawed on her lip, swallowing back the appetite to be touched. *Strange*, she thought. That was a memory she rarely had interest in reliving.

She supposed she should probably return to her quarters and do her best not to worry over Emrys. She'd never hear the end of it if he found out she'd doubted, for even a second, that he could take care of himself. What she needed was a distraction.

How convenient it was that one was looking right back at her with a quirked brow and a decade's worth of research.

"How late do you suppose you'll be working?" Thea said in her polished princess tone.

"It'll be a miracle if I finish before dawn," answered Nare warily. "Why?"

"I think I shall make myself comfortable and begin sketching what those magical glasses look like. It may help us find them."

"You have no idea what they look like."

"I know the description you gave me. I've quite the hand for drawing, if I put my mind to it." Thea took another stack of paper and traded her quill for a pencil. "You won't notice I'm here."

Whether or not that was true, Thea didn't know. From her perch high at the balcony's desk, she was able to sketch without disturbance. Fatigue strained her eyes from focusing on all the tiny details of the elusive goggles. Between sketches, she watched Nare work. And if she let herself idle on Nare's round ass or the sweat pooling at the small of her back, it was royal business and no one else's.

Thea woke on the library's window bench, a thin blanket draped over her. She didn't remember how she had gotten here or where the blanket had come from.

But she didn't care. Because Emrys was leaning over her, a bit pale, but grinning in that familiar way he always did.

"Not rid of you quite yet, I see. What trouble did you get yourself into this time?" she murmured, sitting up all the way.

"What trouble *didn't* we get into?" Emrys laughed, hoisting Thea into his arms and giving her a squeeze. She groaned and squirmed away, swatting him like a fly. "Would you believe me if I told you it was Senna's fault?"

"Never in a million years," Thea stated. "He could throw you into the ocean with leg irons and I'd still find a way to blame you."

"He's right, though," came Senna's voice behind Emrys. He was hovering awkwardly, trying to give Nare a wide berth. "It was my fault."

"Oh for canon's sake, I was kidding," Emrys admonished. "You weren't the one who used me like an arrow pincushion."

"*What?*" Thea said, rubbing her eyes.

"Kind of badass, if you ask me," Nare commented.

"Don't encourage him." Thea fixed Emrys with a look that demanded obedience. "Tell me now if I should be concerned for your well-being."

"Your concern is such a rare resource that is not to be wasted, my dear. Rest assured, Mount Livia's sovereign gave me the best care they could offer," Emrys said. He sat in the free space beside Thea on the window bench. "But Senna was the real hero. He healed me with needle yarrow when I wasn't well enough to grow it myself. I was good as new overnight."

Thea tossed Emrys a wary expression.

"I hope you didn't coerce him into becoming inflorescent." She glanced at Senna for confirmation. He shook his head. Thea narrowed her eyes at him. "Are you well?"

"Yes," he answered simply.

"Never thought I'd live to hear about an inflorescent Talsuran," said Nare. "Convenient he was right where you needed him, Captain."

Emrys gently scrubbed over where his wound must've been. "He only learned yesterday. I'd have gotten him started earlier if I'd known our lives were going to be repeatedly at risk."

"The thought makes me sick," Thea said. "Percy and I never would've sent you both off if we'd known you were going to get into so much trouble."

"You don't know the half of it," said Emrys with a cynical chuckle. He spiraled off to tell the whole tale: how Senna had faced a dre'malor (and, to Thea's astonishment, *lived*), how the sovereign of Mount Livia had shown them the truth of their magic, how the Grit Fingers had been waiting like vipers ready to strike—apparently for Senna.

"That sovereign owes you one hell of a favor," Nare commented, kicking a boot up to lean on the tree beams. "Also, hi. Hello. I'm Nare Demira—royal librarian and the princess' royal adventure escort."

"More like royal headache," Thea grumbled, but Senna still shook Nare's hand. "It does sound like you both made a valuable ally. It's disappointing that you weren't able to discover more. I hope Percy won't be too upset."

"We found jack shit ourselves," Nare said, annoyed.

Thea wasn't sure what the difference between jack shit and regular shit was, but she thought she caught the meaning just the same. At Emrys' piqued interest, Thea told her own story—how they'd managed to bring back some of the books, but Laurentine's journal had been magically sealed shut.

"We think the journal may have some answers we're looking for—including how to cure the sun sickness," Thea concluded.

"The only way to open it is with the magical glasses Laurentine made himself," Nare jumped in. "I rode back early this morning to see if I could find them, when uh"—she shot Thea a careful look—"when the house's current resident was asleep, but they weren't there."

"You don't think Lane could have them herself?" Thea wondered.

A sheepish smile lifted Nare's lips. "I might've woken her up accidentally looking for the glasses."

"*Nare!*" Thea groaned. "I'm shocked she didn't kill you!"

"Oh, she tried! But we talked in a way that could almost be classified as peaceably. Anyways, she doesn't have the glasses. She didn't even know what I was talking about, which only pissed her off more. I tried to calm her down and *that's* when she tried to kill me."

"So the glasses are lost for good," Thea sighed.

"No surprise there," Emrys said, crossing his arms. "The canon of lost things is one greedy bastard."

Thea's gaze snapped up to Senna, the same idea seemingly forming in his mind as he looked back at her.

"The canon of lost things lives in the Pocket District outside our castle," Senna mentioned carefully.

Emrys' smile faltered. "I was kidding." When Senna's gaze only intensified, Emrys bristled. "Oh, I don't like where this is going. There's no evidence Cevyn's Den even exists. And even if it did, doesn't the legend say that the den is designed to destroy all those who would steal back the lost items?"

Thea hugged her knees under her chin. In the days before she had been an exile or a princess—when she had simply been an orphan—Mother Mabel had told her the story about how the canon of lost things, Cevyn, would sneak into locked homes during the night and take treasures that children forgot about. Appraising the story as an adult, Thea believed it was just a scare tactic to keep her from losing her socks or her single bed shirt. But there was truth in every story, wasn't there?

"The den exists," Senna said, assured. "Only one person has gone in and made it out alive. They came out with their lost item as proof. I was there."

The news didn't make Emrys any less uneasy.

"I don't like it at all. If you really think there's something in the journal that'll help us cure the sun sickness, then we can find another way to open it. We don't need to go angering the canons, no matter how worthless I think they are."

"Don't forget the goal is twofold. We're not just looking for a cure for the sun sickness," Thea pointed out. "Talsura's part of the deal is to provide us with their superior magical knowledge. Laurentine was apparently keen on sharing his genius with the Talsuran people. There might be something in his journals that would make that easier." She folded her hands in her lap. "If we need to try to locate those glasses in Cevyn's Den, then that's what we'll do."

Emrys opened his mouth, but Thea threw him a withering glare.

"That's final," she stated. Then, "Pending Percy's agreement."

"Why include the prince at all?" Nare wondered. "Let's just do this thing ourselves."

"If we decide to go looking for the glasses, we'll need his help. Won't we, Goldheart?" Thea said. Senna frowned, but she charged ahead. "Percy is the one who made it into Cevyn's Den. That's one of the only ways you would have been there."

"*Shit*," Emrys swore.

Senna set his jaw, but nodded. "It happened by accident. He was very young. We both were. We almost didn't make it out."

Thea could tell there was more to the story, but she didn't press further. If she wanted to find out what the goldheart couldn't say, she'd have to wait until she could ask Percy herself.

"Are we seriously talking about going *back* to Talsura?" Emrys sputtered. "Because when I watched hundreds of my own people die, I sort of vowed to never return."

"You don't have to go," Thea replied. "But I'd advise you to make up your mind about whether or not you want to have a hand in this endeavor. I won't allow you to have one foot in and one foot out."

"You don't *allow* me to do anything," Emrys shot back without thinking.

Thea had to hold herself still to keep from flinching. Emrys hadn't taken such a sharp tone with her since they had been teenagers. Back in those days, Thea had cried herself to sleep wondering if her brother would ever learn to love her. Now that she was older, she knew Emrys loved her as well as he should. He just hadn't ever figured out how to feel about hating his lot as *true prince* and taking orders from someone who shouldn't have the authority to give them. And, of course, he hadn't permanently shaken his anger—he'd only kept a tight lid on it.

Thea fixed an unimpressed glare on her brother and waited. Emrys sighed.

"I just don't like talking about going back to Talsura like it's nothing," he said. "Like it won't cost us anything."

"No one said it would be easy," Thea murmured.

Emrys leaned over his knees and tilted his head back to meet Senna's eyes.

"I'd feel better if you came," was all Senna said.

And weren't those the magic words?

Emrys dropped his head again and groaned.

"Hells," Emrys huffed. "Let's go rob a canon."

14

PERCY

Percy Laurent could not sit still. This was part of his everyday reality, something he expected, but he couldn't remember the last time it had been this unceasing.

In boyhood, his tutoring lessons had been an ongoing battle just to remain seated and keep his knees from jumping endlessly. His attention had skipped around, fixed on this thing and that whenever something flashier or more exciting had crossed his line of sight. It was only a few months ago when he'd become a man—legally speaking—that he'd noticed at some point he'd found ways to redirect his overflowing spigot of energy.

Not today. Ever since Senna had been over twelve hours late returning home from Mount Livia, Percy had been agitated enough to give a wild horse a run for its coin. He'd known something was wrong—had feared the worst. He'd thought that once Senna reappeared in one piece, the itching dread would have subsided. It had—only to return a few moments later when Senna had explained to Percy what was needed of him.

Currently, he was surrounded by his personal collection of books, which looked as though they'd been regurgitated by his shelves all over the floor. He'd gotten the bright idea to reorganize his bookcases by color. As soon as he'd gotten the books off the shelves, though, he'd lost interest in the task altogether.

Now he was cross-legged on his rug, trying to decide if the book in his hand was indeed green, or perhaps a lying hue of aquamarine. Sometimes it was so hard to tell in the artificial candlelight of his room. He missed the sun.

Percy tossed the book aside, snatched it back, and huffed.

"You're certain you've redirected the knighthearts' schedules away from the trade channels without raising suspicion?" he said in exasperation.

Senna didn't flinch at the sudden break in the silence. He was sitting casually at Percy's desk, halfway through a letter addressed to Emrys and Thea. His head was still dipped toward his paper and he looked up through his lashes.

"I mandate training every year as part of my duties. It makes no difference to the other knighthearts *when* the training is," Senna answered. "The channels will be well and clear by the time our friends arrive. And I'm detailing an alternate route in case of emergency."

Percy flopped back onto the floor, smothered his face with the green-aquamarine book, then tossed it aside again when it smelled too strongly of dust.

Senna frowned.

"I . . . haven't sent the letter yet. It's not too late to change your—"

"No no," Percy interjected, halting hand raised high in the air. "I am quite capable of jumping into a river and retrieving something from the bottom. I'll not have our friends thinking otherwise."

How ridiculous it was to suggest a change in plans. No, he *had* to do this. He'd done it before—and he'd lived. That was more than anyone else could say about venturing into Cevyn's Den. Had it been the ordeal that had contributed to most of his recurring nightmares? Possibly. Had Cevyn warned him to never step foot within their cache again? Yes, but so much time had passed. Maybe the canon of lost things wouldn't recognize him.

But if they did, they would want him. A canon so greedy for all things lost and forgotten would not let him go so easily. Not when they'd met Percy's eyes, his brown ones to their black, and said, **"You're a lost thing, Percy Laurent."** It was their way of saying, "*I will have you.*"

The thought of it made Percy shiver. His body remembered just how *cold* the river was. How a thirteen-year-old Senna had held him up by the fire to warm him, whispering, *"I'm sorry. I'm sorry."*

Across the room, Senna murmured a few magical words and snapped his fingers. Percy turned his head just in time to watch the letter ignite in blue flames and disappear into nothingness.

"The letter is sent. All that's left to do is wait a few hours until they arrive."

Somehow, knowing that the letter couldn't be stopped now made Percy's lungs feel smaller. Back still against the cold floor, Percy tapped on his knee, trying to focus on that sensation over literally anything else in his body.

"What if they're caught?" Percy said suddenly.

"They won't be. The shift in the schedules, remember?"

Percy barely remembered, which was ridiculous, since Senna had just told him a few minutes ago.

"What if they get lost?"

"They won't. I'll be meeting them right at the entrance to transport them with my regular sigil spell."

"But what if you're not there in time and they accidentally go down a wrong path and Grit Fingers are waiting for them, except they didn't bring their cards this time, and Emrys isn't fast enough because he isn't done healing, so all of them get tied up all the way—not just their feet."

"Percy."

"Oh, canons, what if my *mother* finds them? She'll figure out how we know them and then she'll kill them, Senna. She won't hesitate. She's a murderous, *bloodthirsty*—She doesn't care about me. She doesn't care about this kingdom. I don't think she has any love in her heart for anything at all. What if something goes wrong today and she doesn't let me rule? I can't fail the kingdom. I can't—"

"Percy."

Senna was inches before him now, one knee to the floor, holding him by the shoulders. Percy's brows tensed together. He didn't remember Senna coming to him. He must not have remembered how to breathe either, because he was gasping, clinging to any air he could squeeze through his mouth.

"What color is this book?" Senna asked, placing a small tome in Percy's shaking hands.

"G-green," Percy stammered. "Mostly."

"What is it about?"

Percy's eyes squeezed shut. He couldn't remember. He couldn't focus.

"It's—" Percy drew in another shallow gasp. "It's a love story. About an orphan boy and a knight."

Senna paused. Percy had squeezed back just enough clarity of the mind to see a flicker of something cross Senna's expression.

"Are they happy at the end? This orphan and his knight?"

"I don't know. I never finished it."

"I see," Senna said. He flipped through the book until he found where an old slip of parchment was nestled into the pages like a bookmark. Then, he began to read. "*Jonesy thought about the first time he'd seen Dame Ruth with her sword drawn, the bright sun reflecting off her silver armor. He'd always known justice and grace were a woman. How amazing it was that the same woman loved him.*"

Percy tempered his breathing, fighting against his shaking frame to focus on the sound of Senna's voice.

As the end of the chapter drew nearer, Percy felt more like himself and less like a troubled spirit trapped in a tempest's body. When the final words rang out, Percy reached up and gently closed the book.

Senna watched him, giving Percy the space to speak.

At the end of the bout of worry, an idea had lit in the back of Percy's mind.

"Cevyn won't let me just waltz into their river and take something again," he said quietly. "But we *need* those glasses to open Laurentine's journal."

"We do," Senna agreed, urging Percy to continue.

"So, what about an exchange? The toy boat for the glasses."

Senna did not need clarification for what toy boat Percy meant.

"You think they'll agree?" Senna said.

"No," replied Percy honestly. "But what other choice is there?"

Senna seemed to toss ideas around in his mind, only to come up empty-handed. He squeezed Percy's shoulder and smiled—a small, rare thing.

"I'll be right there," he said. Percy knew what Senna was really saying. *I won't let anything happen to you.* "As will our friends."

Percy rubbed his ribs, over his heart, feeling his own steady pulse and the way his lungs expanded with the deep breath.

"I'm indebted to you, Sen," he said finally.

But Senna shook his head, as if to say there were no debts among family.

Some hours later, Senna had gone to retrieve their friends. Percy was alone.

He still hadn't managed to get any of his books on his shelf. Would it be rude to ask a servant to clean his mess for him so that when he returned from his ordeal, he could retire to a clean room? Probably. Not to mention, then he'd have to explain why he was leaving his suite without his guard.

By now, Senna would be arriving at the meeting point. Percy had argued he should remain in his room to cover for Senna if anyone discovered him missing. Really, he didn't want to witness his friends' faces when they stepped back in Talsura for the first time since the exile. His imagination did an excellent job filling in the blanks. Thea would keep her expression as hard as stone, but Emrys would air every bit of his disgust. Percy hadn't yet met Thea's friend, Nare, but from the way Senna described her, he suspected she'd complain loudly, and he—

He just didn't have the strength to shoulder their pain. Not today. He wondered if that made him a terrible friend—for not wanting to support them. For leaving Senna to bear it by himself.

Someone knocked at the door.

Percy froze. It couldn't be Senna. He would've never knocked unless it was after dark. Carefully, Percy stood and prepared himself to handle whatever stone in their plan was waiting for him.

"Enter," he called in a stately tone.

Elora Wright walked in with light feet and clay-stained clothes and Percy could have died. Her eyes brightened as soon as she saw him, not noticing the garden of books at his feet. She was the most beautiful, wonderful, *spectacular* thing Percy had ever seen.

"Sun slay me," he gasped.

"I'd rather it didn't," Elora said, shyly.

Percy didn't waste another second. He crossed the room in two long strides and took Elora into his arms. His body caged around hers, his face burrowing into her neck. Underneath the scent of clay, Elora smelled of floral perfume. He murmured as much into her shoulder.

"I think it's because the studios are so close to the royal gardens," she laughed, combing her fingers through his hair.

She tugged him back to kiss him.

"How are you here?" he wondered, voice wet.

"A little gold birdy mentioned in his letter that I may be of help to you, so the princess invited me on official business. I have to say, I'd never met the princess before so it was quite the surprise to have her on my doorstep. We had a friendly chat on the way here. I can see why she's your best friend." She ran the back of her hand over his face, smoothing away the bead of anxious sweat on his temple. "I had no idea you were taking all of this on."

"I should have told you. I didn't want to make a fuss until there was something fuss-worthy." He kissed the inside of her palm. "You're here now though. Thank the canons for it."

Elora scoffed. "Don't thank that worthless lot. Thank Senna. He's twice as helpful *and* doesn't ignore me when I talk to him." She slid her arm through his. "Now, what can I do to help you relax? We have a little time to dawdle."

Percy flushed. He could think of a few things.

Once Percy had gotten Elora in his bed, he was loath to remove her from it. It was so much nicer to be swept up in her arms than thinking about confronting Cevyn. But Elora insisted on getting dressed and seeing this thing through.

"*You'll regret it later if you worm out,*" she had told him wisely. He hated when she was so right.

Dutifully, Percy and Elora met the rest of the group in the trade channels leading into the city. The meeting point of choice was the basement of an abandoned mill, long abandoned since Talsura had stopped being able to produce grain. With one tug on a sliding wooden door, the group became visible before them.

They were all huddled around an old barrel. Thea was sitting in the middle of the group, scribbling a pencil furiously over a small sketchbook. At her feet, Emrys sat against the barrel, carving something into a scrap of wood. His expression was stormy. Senna was beside him, a hand secretly on his shoulder, almost out of view. He watched Thea work intently. At Thea's other side was someone Percy didn't recognize, so it must've been Nare. She towered over Thea, shooting commands and instructions into Thea's ear like a knightheart captain.

The sound of the door drew everyone's attention to Percy and Elora.

"Oh, good," Thea said. "I was starting to think you'd changed your mind."

Elora shrugged. "We got lost."

Senna lifted a brow. He knew damned well Percy hadn't gotten lost. But if he didn't want Percy to take advantage of the rare privacy with his lover, then he shouldn't have sent Elora up to Percy's room.

"*This* is the prince of Talsura?" Nare bleated.

"Yes," Thea hissed. "And you should speak to him as such."

"Oh, please don't. It makes my skin crawl to hear my friends call me *Your Highness*. It only makes me remember how blessed short I am and that it would be more accurate to say *Your Lowness*." He reached out a hand. "I'm Percy Laurent. I'm indebted to you for being here today."

For a librarian, Nare's handshake was bone-crushing.

"What can I say? The princess already owes me a few favors. Figured I'd collect the entire royal set." Then, with a gutty laugh, "Oh, and I'm Nare."

"Elora, dear, you're a qualified artist," Thea cut in. "Could you look at this and tell me what you think?"

A bewildered, but honored, expression overcame Elora, and she tossed Percy a look that said, *The princess wants my advice?*

"It's not something you're taking artistic liberties with. It's supposed to be as accurate as possible," Nare pointed out.

Still, Elora took the drawing, holding it out so Percy could see too. On the paper were half a dozen lightly sketched depictions of the glasses. Each had the same constellation motif on the temple hinges and circular rims.

"Nare says this one is the closest to the real one," Senna said, coming up behind them and pointing at a larger pair drawn in the center. "But the glass lenses are bigger."

"The drawing is even throughout. Excellent technique, Your Highness," Elora praised shyly.

"Can we just *go* already?" Emrys snapped. "Being here makes my head swim."

Silence fell over the group, a few cautious pairs of eyes landing on Percy. He wanted to tell Emrys that this wasn't easy for him either. The thought of doing this had made him feel like he was dying. If Emrys was uncomfortable being back in the kingdom that had exiled him, Percy was in just as much agony. But then, he'd been privileged enough to be the only person in the entire kingdom who had never had to fear exile, so he held his tongue.

"I want this over with too," Percy admitted.

Emrys scowled. "Then what are we waiting for?"

"Nothing." Percy crossed the room where stone steps led to a hatch in the ceiling. He heaved it open, peering out into the open air. Nearby, the Sellair River coursed parallel to the abandoned streets. "Let's go rob a canon."

IT WAS FITTING THAT Cevyn, the canon of lost things, lived in the sector of Talsura that was almost completely deserted. Unlike the thriving market center, which was lit aglow with a thousand lamps and magical strings of lanterns, the Pocket District was bitterly dark. It had earned its name for being the home of most of the Redwindans—the people in Talsura's pocket who had been let go like loose change. After the exile, it'd come to light that the only reason the Pocket District had been hit so hard with the sun sickness was because it was void of the tall buildings of the urban square. Its farmland was tended by people who worked in the verdant fields under the open sky, making them the very first people who'd been exposed to the sun's hyper-magical power. They'd been the first to go, leaving all their belongings behind when the queen had driven them from their lands.

Percy was sure those abandoned belongings were floating around right next to Laurentine's glasses—more lost things for Cevyn's greedy hands.

The group crept up the dark streets in unsettled silence. There were a handful of lampposts, but they were distant and dimly lit. Elora stuck close at his side, holding tightly to his arm as if she were afraid he'd disappear into the shadows.

"The entrance to the cave is a branch off the river. We'll need some type of boat or raft," Percy said quietly.

"Over there," Nare called out. "We can use one of those if they're not damaged."

It took Percy a few moments of searching to find the rack of rowboats stationed at the side of one of the piers. Senna and Emrys got to work setting one on the river's shore without uttering a word.

Percy pressed his lips together. When had they gotten so—synchronous?

"Are you alright?" Senna asked.

Percy turned, but found the question wasn't directed at him, but Emrys. He should have felt pleased to hear his friend watching and speaking with someone else for once. But Percy was the one who would be risking his life, tempting the patience of a canon that had already tried to kill him once. Didn't Senna want to know if *he* was alright too?

Senna lifted his small lantern, illuminating every ounce of pained horror on Emrys' face. His gaze was fixed to a cottage across the river. It was hard to make out the details in the dark, but the silhouette revealed that the roof had caved in.

"I—" Emrys swallowed. "I realized where we are. It was hard to tell in the dark."

Senna followed Emrys' gaze. "Do you know that house?"

Emrys was quiet. Then, "I lived there."

Percy's stomach sank.

It was hard to imagine that Queen Casta and Emrys had ever lived in a place so small and lifeless. Under the Dam's thick darkness, it was hard to imagine that anywhere in the Pocket District had ever been someone's home. Percy wanted to ask questions, but he got the sense that the admission had been for Senna's ears only. Percy went and searched for the oars. But he couldn't help himself from glancing over his shoulder to find Senna rubbing a hand up Emrys' back.

It was intimate. Percy didn't think he could recall seeing Senna intimate with anyone.

When the rowboat's nose dipped into the water, the group took their seats. By some miracle, they all fit, which meant that no one would be left behind. Percy handed oars to Nare and Senna, then took the empty space beside Elora. That left Emrys and Thea fighting for space on the middle bench. Senna tied his lantern to the front of the boat. At Nare's nod, they eased the boat into the water with one heave.

Without much wind getting through the Dam, the river's current could barely push them along. Percy still felt a bit dizzy and seasick. The only thing keeping him from pitching over the boat's side was Elora holding his hand.

"I've got to say, I'm all for group outings. But maybe next time we should plan a vacation somewhere relaxing," Nare said, breaking the silence. "Ay, Captain. Didn't you say that Mount Livia is a spa city? I could use a goddamn spa day. I feel like I'm crawling out of my skin here."

"It's the darkness," Senna said. "You'll get used to it."

"I better not! Take me where beautiful girls put little cucumber slices on my eyes and make me smell like a summer's breeze. That's what I'll get used to."

"Tell you what, you get us to and from Cevyn's Den in one piece and I'll pay you enough money to spend a week in Mount Livia," Thea chimed. "The sovereign owes Emrys and Senna a favor. Maybe you could cash it in."

"Excuse me, *I'm* the one who nearly died. If anyone is 'redeeming' a favor, it's me."

It was spoken like a joke, but if Percy didn't know any better, he'd say that Emrys was dead serious. That, or his usual joking nature couldn't hold up in Talsura, where black skies and shadows abounded. Percy couldn't blame him. If he tried to crack a joke right now, he suspected it would come out just as bitter. Not that he wanted to laugh, either. He wanted to get in, get the glasses, and get the hell out.

"Can I see that drawing again?" Percy said, cutting off another of Nare's tirades.

Thea scooched forward so that her knees nudged Percy's, then unrolled a piece of parchment across them.

Percy leaned close, trying to make out the details, but with Senna's lantern lighting the river before them, there wasn't enough light. With a dramatic sigh, Emrys held his palm open and grew one big, luminescent rose. Pearly light poured from its petals over the rest of the boat.

"I would've done that if I could've," Percy grumbled, miffed.

"Exiles only, sorry," Emrys spat back.

Senna twisted at the waist, set his brows, and *glowered* at both of them. Percy had been on the receiving side of hundreds of those glares, but Emrys hadn't. His cheeks reddened and he shrank back onto the boat's bench, holding his hand out petulantly over the drawing.

"Elora was right. I had no idea you had such a talent, Thea," Percy couldn't help but comment. "I'm glad you drew this. Whatever I was imagining was completely off the mark."

"Do you think you'll recognize them in the water?"

"Maybe," Percy said reluctantly. "It's hard to see anything anywhere in Talsura, much less in a swamp cave."

"*Swamp cave?*" Elora hissed.

"Don't worry about the darkness," said Emrys, waving his glowing hand around. The light smeared through the open air. "I can line the entire cavern with them."

Senna stopped rowing and threw a disapproving glance over his shoulder.

"You'll get yourself drowned that way," he said. "Cevyn is very particular to begin with, and they'll be even more irked when Percy and I show up in their territory. There's a reason no one tries to find what they've lost."

"Other than the fact that they, you know, *forgot* about it?" Emrys deadpanned.

Senna didn't dignify this with a response.

"We need to go about this as wisely as possible," he said instead. "No one touches the water except Percy. Don't touch anything that doesn't belong to you. Actually, don't even look Cevyn's statue in the eyes."

Percy ran his thumb over Elora's knuckles to keep his nerves at bay. Senna had acted so strong, but it seemed even he wasn't unaffected by going back to Cevyn's Den.

"If you aren't going to let us help, then what was the point in us coming in the first place?" Nare cut in.

Senna was quiet. Percy guessed Senna didn't have the heart to admit to everyone how much danger they were putting themselves in over some foolish glasses.

"Moral support," Percy said finally.

There was another reason, of course. If anything went wrong, Senna wouldn't be alone to stop it.

Emrys' lips parted, an argument surely about to roll off his tongue, but something gave him pause.

It was the air, which had gone from smelling of stale city air to smelling like sappy balsam. Emrys carefully stood and lifted his hand, shedding more light on the environment around them. The grassy hillsides had given way to a copse of trees. From the dark ground, it was hard to see just how far they stretched above them, but Percy imagined you could stand on the top branch and scrape your fingers across the Dam overhead.

"Where did you say Cevyn's Den was?" Emrys whispered.

Senna rowed as carefully as death.

"A cave."

"It's hard to believe you found this place all on your own when you were so young. How on earth did you manage it?" Thea murmured. Her hand was clutched to a small blade Percy assumed Emrys had loaned her.

"In the stories, all you have to do is follow the river," Percy said unevenly. "Maybe that's what I did."

"You don't remember?" Emrys asked.

"I was four!" Percy hissed, alarm rising in his chest.

Without warning, Senna blew the lantern closed and made a *shhh*-ing sound that was nearly lost in the rustling trees overhead.

Percy felt it the second the boat coasted into the swampy cave. What had been crisp air muddied into something thicker, more difficult to breathe. Beneath them, the water smelled of stale sewage and lapped with spoiled cream against the ship's short walls.

Senna snapped his finger and a small flame balanced above his thumb. It wasn't very bright, but the thick blackness was at least penetrable now. Emrys uncovered his own hand, meeting Senna's eyes over the white glow.

"Percy needs to *see*, Sen," Emrys whispered, barely audible.

If it had been Senna going into the water, he probably would have insisted on working in darkness. But the blackout posed just enough danger to Percy's safety that he relented.

"Leave the lights on the edge of the boat," Senna instructed him. "We'll prop it up on the shore."

Without further thought, Emrys placed his palm flat against the boat's edge. A vine of glowing white roses expelled from his palms, creeping around the perimeter of the ship as if it was what it had always been meant to do. Percy, who had been gripping the rim of the boat for dear life, snatched his hands away when he felt his fingers intertwining with thorny stems.

"Remind me to ask you why the captain can grow the royal roses like a professional," Nare told Thea, a little breathless.

"Don't look a gift horse in the mouth," Thea said back.

It wasn't until Senna and Nare had eased the boat onto the sliver of shore that Percy was brave enough to look around him.

It wasn't at all like he remembered it. (But then, he hadn't had two dozen inflorescent roses lighting his path the last time he had been here.) To start, it wasn't a cave at all. It was just an alcove of rocky walls that gave way to open air and vegetation. Swampy sludge churned in the center pool, strings of dirt weaving through and around forgotten human belongings. Percy couldn't tell if the pool was shallow or if it was just so filled with misplaced junk that the depths were long buried.

At the crest of the pool stood a statue, larger than life and leagues taller than the walls of the alcove. There was no question who it was. Whoever had carved the statue had even painted Cevyn's eyes black. Around them, mounds of half-broken, dirt-smeared objects covered the shore—a treasure trove fit for a monster.

"Careful not to touch the water when you step out," Senna advised.

"What's wrong with the water?" Thea hesitated.

"Don't know. Let's not find out."

Nare stepped out first, more fearless than the rest of the lot combined. Senna was next, offering a hand to Thea and Elora (who accepted it), then Emrys (who ignored it in favor of patting Senna's face). When it was Percy's turn, he found his legs felt like his bones had turned to swamp water. But Senna was there, grabbing his forearms and guiding him. Percy should've felt the shame of not being able to help Elora, but there wasn't any time for embarrassment.

Nare squatted down by the wall, one of Emrys' flowers between her fingers.

"There's a whole pile of wedding rings," she noted. "How do this many people lose and *forget* their wedding rings?" She reached out to grab one, but Thea swatted her hand.

"Are you trying to get us killed?"

"Let's just get this over with," Elora said, hand curled tight in the back of Percy's shirt.

Percy drew in a *long* breath. The chill was starting to set in.

Then, Senna stepped closer and the edge of the chill waned.

"I'm right here," Senna murmured.

Maybe it was because he'd never felt more sick, more like a shell of a person. Maybe it was because the words were such a balm to his pounding heart. Maybe it was because underneath all of his manners and big ideas, he was the worst thing of all—a coward.

But Percy took a step forward without even acknowledging his goldheart, reached into his pocket, and retrieved the toy boat.

This would be the last time he ever saw it.

"Fair winds, old friend," Percy whispered and set the ship floating into the sickly basin.

For a few seconds, the poor vessel's winds were fair. It bobbed and floated as if it were on regular seas and not some twisted canon's swamp pool.

Then, for seemingly no reason at all, the boat stopped amidst the lapping water and sank.

"*Shit*," Nare and Emrys cursed at the same time.

Elora squeezed Percy's arm. "Maybe it's a good sign. Maybe Cevyn is accepting your offering."

Heart racing, Percy took the spare rose from Nare and knelt beside the shore.

"Is swamp water *supposed* to move like the ocean?" wondered Thea.

"Nope," Nare answered with a pop.

"Can we all just—still our tongues for a second?" Percy snapped.

They did, but only after Nare had whistled and grumbled sarcastically, "*Sorry, Your Highness.*"

Percy turned his attention back to the water. The unnatural waves lapped up like dying heartbeats, rolling forgotten items closer and closer to the surface. They reeled and eddied, until finally, a constellation glistened off of the rose's light. Percy scrambled forward, watching greedily as the constellation twirled, revealing another. And another. Then finally, two round amber lenses.

"Sun slay me, I see the glasses. Cevyn accepted the offering," he gasped. He spun around to Senna. "W-what, what do I do? Do I just take them?"

"Nare, you're the genius. Does he take them?" Thea sputtered.

"I-I don't know! I'm a mage, not a blasted acolyte."

The glasses tumbled closer, and closer, then ebbed away from the surface.

"You're losing them, Percy," Emrys rushed.

"Oh, for the love of everything!" cried Percy.

He lunged forward and snatched the glasses. He didn't pay any heed to the freezing water or the way it smelled like a dre'malor's toilet. All that mattered was that the glasses were in his hands, and he wasn't about to let them slip away.

"I've got them! I've got—"

A hand of bones sprung from the pool, anchored a death grip on Percy, and dragged him into the water.

*P*ERCY SAW HIS FATHER.

Not the static version of Mathis, immortalized in oil paints on canvas in the royal study, but real. *Breathing and moving, standing amidst waist-high grass and a sky full of crystalline stars. The inside of Percy's mouth tasted of stale sand*

and cotton, but he still tried to call out, "Father! Father, it's your son! We've never met, but here I am!" No sound rumbled from his urgent lips—barely the huff of his breath. His limbs wouldn't move either, holding him in this place where reality was the past, but the past was out of reach. Percy knew who he was, but he couldn't quite get his mind to hang on to the truth of why he was, or when.

A strange thing happened then. Percy's father held his palms open to the sky, screaming words that were old—older than the roots of grass and the rings in the trees. A whirlwind of smoking, glittery air churned over Mathis' hands, picking up speed so quickly that sharp wind scraped across Percy's cheeks.

When Percy thought the magic couldn't grow without whisking his father with it, it settled. In its place, standing in the sky, was a canon of long black hair and frown lines.

"You have gall to summon the canon of thieves after what you stole from me," the canon—Jasrath—bellowed furiously. The words sat like thunder in the air, reverberating through Percy's bones. But Mathis didn't flinch.

"I summoned Alpedis," Mathis answered, commanding the same respect.

Percy grabbed hold of his elbows. Alpedis? What could his father need with the canon of the skies?

"I'm surprised that you do not kneel before me and beg me to spare you the agony I have contrived for your weak flesh," declared Jasrath. "But perhaps you don't know the extent of my power. Perhaps you aren't aware that Alpedis no longer controls the sun and skies."

Mathis held his chin high. "And you do?"

"Take a guess, wretched kin!"

Jasrath threw his arms and head back. Lightning exploded from his fingertips, stripping the sky of its nighttime glory and smothering the stars. When it faded, the stars hadn't returned. In its place was a dull expanse, a pathetic whisper of what had once been swaths of moonlight and a sea of cosmos.

"You're still the one I have come for." Percy heard the words, despite that they were spoken on a whisper. "I'm sorry. But it's for my kingdom."

Standing behind his father, Percy couldn't tell just how the king did it. Whether there were words, or potions, or scrolls of incantations. All Percy saw was Mathis reaching a hand forward to lay on Jasrath's chest.

And then Jasrath began to scream.

P ERCY CAME TO WITH a gasp—but instead of drawing in the stale Talsuran air, his throat choked on thick, noxious swamp water.

All at once, his instincts took over. He thrashed, trying desperately to make it to the surface, only to find that his ankles were caught in forgotten things. He blinked, scouring the pool's floor for some type of escape.

As his lungs began to burn, Percy's chest filled with despair. Where was Senna? Had Senna abandoned him like he had the first time?

Gathering all the strength he could muster, Percy heaved himself up, freeing one ankle. It allowed him just enough movement to spin behind him.

There was Cevyn—a slow, sinister grin crooking over their face. Their human teeth were silver and gold, like they'd come right out of the mouths of human people. Their skin possessed the pallor of someone three days gone, but their unblinking eyes belonged to death itself.

Percy was so struck with terror that he didn't fight when Cevyn reached out, a hundred forgotten bracelets jangling on the fleshless arm, and plucked the glasses. For a sickening second, Percy thought that the canon would snap them in half. But to his surprise, Cevyn put the glasses on, the constellation-rimmed temples tangling in Cevyn's endless muddied hair.

"You're a lost thing, Percy Laurent," they told him. **"No one's prince at all. No one's son. No one's brother. No one's king. Lost lost lost. That makes you MINE."**

By some miracle, Percy found enough control of himself to keep himself from flinching. He didn't squirm against his need for air, but he did let his face fall into careful neutrality. He shook his head. *You can't scare me again.*

Cevyn squinted in response, gaze piercing Percy down to his marrow.

"A lost thing, but claimed," they growled. **"Claimed by another canon. Strange. Unnatural."**

Percy wasn't sure what that meant, but it didn't matter. He reached out, hand open, as if to say, "*Give them back.*"

"A trade," he said. The cost of the words was great in his lungs, but he support-ed them with enough air that they bubbled in front of his face.

Cevyn's cockeyed smile flipped.

"You ARE the lost thing. You don't TAKE a lost thing," they growled.

Oh yeah? he thought. *We'll see.* Because the vibrations of Cevyn's voice had been strong enough to rattle Percy's bone marrow, but they'd also been enough to jostle the rubbish at the bottom of the pool—including the mess at Percy's ankles.

With the last of his strength, he yanked the glasses off Cevyn's face and pro-pelled himself toward the surface.

He was so close. The light from Emrys' roses lay close enough to touch. If he could just get there—

But he was running out of air. He'd used too much strength on freeing himself, too much determination to keep the glasses tucked in his hands, and Cevyn wasn't going to let him get away that easily.

They dug their nails into his calves, roaring waves from the watery depths, and Percy had a thought that, at least, he'd gotten his hands on the glasses. If he'd failed miserably in every other way, he'd managed that.

Then, strong hands hooked under his arms and dragged Percy above the sur-face. He gasped, greedy for as much air as he could gorge himself on, nearly choking in an effort to *breathe.*

"Pull him up!" ordered Senna, and it was only then Percy realized the familiar hands keeping him afloat were his goldheart's.

The number of hands on him multiplied, his friends working in tandem to haul Percy free. He should have thanked them, told them how glad he was that they were all there. He nearly asked what had taken so bloody long, but he wasn't in his own body, much less his own mind. All the sensations desperately trying to ground him to this moment were far away—the icy cold air that assailed his wet skin, and the chattering of his teeth.

His friends laid him in Elora's arms and she clung to him, petting his hair and squeezing him against her chest. She shielded him, tugging him so his feet were as far from the pool's shore as possible.

"You're alright, you're alright," Elora whispered, frightened. Chest heaving, Percy didn't have the strength to do anything more than shake in Elora's arms.

With a soft handkerchief, Elora wiped the muddy water out of Percy's eyes—just in time for him to see Cevyn emerge from the water like a tidal wave and close their fingers around Senna's throat.

15
SENNA

Senna wasn't sure what happened when a human killed a canon—didn't know if it was even possible—but he was seconds away from finding out. The rage in his blood craved it. Death to the canon who had burdened Percy with nightmares. Death to the canon who had tried to trick and drown him in their swampy waters. Death to the canon who had their fingers of ice and bone clutched around Senna's throat.

Behind him, he heard Emrys call his name and unsheathe his sword, but Senna raised a hand to stop him. He couldn't risk anyone else getting close to the water.

Cevyn, on the other hand, turned Senna this way and that, like a trader ascertaining the authenticity of a treasure. It gave Senna enough time to brainstorm a way to set himself free without involving anyone else.

The canon of lost things was half-bone, half-forgotten objects. Even though they wore some of their treasures, like the bracelets clanking the entire length of their arm, there were other things lodged where they shouldn't go. Rusty keys wedged into shoulders. Forks stuck in pelvic bones. Stringed toy puppets tangled in ribs. If Senna managed to dislodge one of the objects holding the body together, it might dislocate the body enough to give him a chance to make it on shore.

If Cevyn could follow them on land, though . . .

He'd worry about that if they got there. For now, Cevyn's grip was weak. He could still breathe—barely. He could still get out of this.

"I am glad you're here, Goldheart. You're a worthy trade for what was taken from me. I cannot take the Talsuran youngling. He has been claimed. But I can take you," said Cevyn.

"Me?" rasped Senna.

"You are the lion of all the lost things. The one no one will ever claim. The one no one will remember. Not your friends. Not your prince."

"You're wrong!" Percy yelled. He made no effort to hide his fear. "Senna isn't a lost thing for you to claim. He has a *family*. That means you have to let him go!"

"Yoooou," Cevyn crooned, pointing at Percy with a crooked finger, ***"are not the prince I meant."*** They slid their hand up Senna's face to cup his chin, tilting it up. ***"Not even the one who loves you will keep you. When that day comes, I will add you to my collection."***

Senna had heard enough. Cevyn could be as vainglorious and greedy as they liked. Because if they were lost in the sound of their own voice, they weren't paying attention to him. The claws piercing his jaw lessened infinitesimally. Senna seized his opportunity.

Before Cevyn could realize what he was doing, Senna grabbed their arm in both hands, set his jaw, and snapped the bone in half.

Cevyn howled in agony, jewels and splinters of bone spilling into the water like pieces of hail. The pain made them rear away, but Senna forced them farther with a strong kick to the breastbone. Senna had just enough time to crawl up the shore. His feet slid on the slick stones, but Thea was there. She grabbed him the same way he had Percy, putting all her strength into bringing Senna to his feet.

They were fast, but the canon was faster. If Cevyn's cries had been deafening before, they grew only sharper as they unhinged their jaw and released their wrath in a high-pitched wail. Too late, Senna felt the magic the canon had released—like pockets of fresh, clean air against the swamp.

Senna only had half a second to guess what the magic would do, before trinkets began to rise up from the pool's dark floor and encase his legs, pulling him down.

He jerked his leg, using the heels of his boots to force stray toy blocks and belt buckles away, but the effort was as fruitless as it was tiring. The magic tore apart the shore, trying to snare his friends as well as the boat.

"I'm *really* tired of this," Emrys hissed, kicking a sailor's net off his ankle. He aimed a hand poised with inflorescence at Cevyn.

At first, Senna thought Emrys' power had missed. But then strands of ropey pondweed shot through the water and tangled in all of Cevyn's spare bones that they could reach. Emrys yanked back, straining as though the pondweed was in his own hands. Sure enough, the pondweed, too, seized back, taking Cevyn flying with it. Whatever enchantment Cevyn had over their trove waned enough for Thea and Nare to pull Senna the rest of the way out of the water.

"Senna's out! Get the boat in the water!" Nare commanded.

"*What?*" Thea cried.

"Do as she says!" Emrys yelled, voice straining with the effort to keep Cevyn subdued.

Body shaking and throat burning, Senna wrapped his arms around both sides of the rowboat and flung it into the water. They made quick work of throwing themselves into the boat next, nearly capsizing it in the process. Emrys was the last to jump in. With barely a glance, he took two steps and leapt. Senna caught him. He clutched at Emrys as tightly as Cevyn had held his neck.

Something about seeing Emrys Calloway alone on that shore, standing his ground against a raging canon who wanted nothing more than to drown him and pluck his bones like spare coins . . . It had stolen Senna's breath in a way that had nothing to do with the bruises on his throat.

Senna stared in Emrys' eyes. He couldn't bring himself to let go. Not even as Cevyn turned the alcove's echoing walls into booming thunder.

The moment was shattered when Nare leaned over the edge of the boat to dip her fingers beneath the water and draw a sigil. She bellowed an ancient word Senna couldn't distinguish, before the rowboat propelled like lightning, skidding across the water back out the way they had come. Senna gripped the edge of the boat, watching as Cevyn's Den disappeared into smudgy blackness behind them.

Below, the waters calmed, far enough away from Cevyn's thrashing to return back to their stasis.

Senna scanned the boat, not quite believing that everyone had made it. It was only when his gaze lingered on Emrys that he realized the captain was still concentrating on his inflorescence. He should have told Emrys he didn't have to strain himself anymore. They were practically back to the edge of the forest.

Over the roaring gushing, he said, "You can control it this far away?"

"He's the most powerful inflorescence mage in Redwind," Thea answered, arms wrapped around herself. If Senna didn't know any better, he'd suppose that she sounded bitter.

"Kinda rude to say when the *other* powerful mage you know is saving your bloody life," Nare chimed in. Spurts of water gushed into her face as she held her hand over the boat's stern. "I could take the captain any day of the week."

A bead of sweat dripped down the side of Emry's grinning face.

"Yeah? Prove it!"

Releasing a brutish cry, Nare sent the boat reeling faster than before. Senna's stomach rose into his throat. Then he saw a bend in the river, and the dread amplified.

"Wait, Nare—" Elora shrieked, but it was too late.

The speed and power of Nare's magic forced the rowboat over the riverbank, up onto dry land, and crashing nose-first into what seemed to be a pine tree older than all of them combined.

Senna flew from his bench the same time Percy did, allowing him to catch the prince before he could go rolling too far into the thicket beyond the line of darkness.

They sat up on the forest floor. Emrys' glowing roses, now torn apart by the splintering boat, flickered like candles losing their wicks. When the last one went out, they all lay silent, blanketed in the Talsuran darkness Senna would never be able to escape from.

"I hate this bloody kingdom," Emrys declared crankily into the solemn air. With the same energy one puts behind a vulgar gesture, he slapped his hand onto the tree and lit more roses up the thick trunk. Senna lifted his head off the ground just enough to find everyone else lying in a tangled heap across from him and Percy. "Also, not to break the spirits of our Talsuran friends further, but you all *reek*."

This was followed by more silence until—

A sharp bite of laughter cut the air—from the *princess*, of all people. Nare joined in, howling, then Percy, until even Senna couldn't help but cover his face and laugh, and laugh, and laugh.

Then Percy's laughter shifted to a deeper, gasping sound. He was crying—bone-deep, like a tapped spring, releasing every feeling he'd been smothering back.

Everyone's laughter snuffed out. Elora was by Percy in a heartbeat, guiding him close and holding him to her, as sweet and gentle as she always was. Percy wouldn't let the others see his face, though it was impossible for them not to hear him. He wept, face nestled above Elora's heart.

Elora—for all Senna knew that she was kind and good—did not seem to know what to say to him. So Senna gently nudged Percy until he was leaning back. It'd been a long time since Senna had seen Percy's face so wet and splotchy.

Percy stared back at Senna through the tears lining his lashes. He sniffled, drawing in deep breaths to regain control of himself, but the effort was a wasted one. That was okay, though. Percy could cry as much as he wanted. Senna let him know as much with a small smile.

Senna placed his hands on Percy's temples. Then he rubbed his thumbs underneath Percy's brow bones and over his red and puffy eyelids in long, careful strokes. The tension between Percy's brows was the first to go. Then his breathing steadied. Senna kept at it until Percy's cheeks were dry and he could breathe without shuddering.

"Why did it take you so long to help me?" whispered Percy.

Senna's hands dropped to his lap. "What?"

"They called me a lost thing again, Senna," Percy whispered, haunted. "They almost had me. I—I couldn't get away."

"You're not a lost thing. We got you out," Senna insisted, grabbing Percy's knee. "The canons lie and cheat all the time to get what they want. Cevyn is among the greediest. They only called you a lost thing as a way of trying to keep you."

"The goldheart is right. What better treasure for their collection than a prince?" Thea added bitterly.

Percy shook his head, lips curling down.

"I thought you were going to let me die," he admitted.

"*Never*," came Senna's answer immediately.

"How could you leave me fighting for my life, *drowning* in a swamp, fighting off an angry god?"

Senna flinched back. Was that what he had done?

"I jumped in as soon as I saw you struggling. It—it was only a few seconds."

"It was *minutes*."

It definitely wasn't, but Senna didn't think it would do any good to argue. It was possible that time moved differently in the canon's domain.

"Percy," Senna began carefully, "I don't know why it seemed that long to you. I can't imagine how terrifying it must've been. Especially given—everything. But I promise on the oath I took when you were born that I didn't wait as long as it felt. I had eyes on you the entire time, and when you needed my help, I was there."

"Fat good it did me!" Percy snapped.

Emrys threw a broken piece of the rowboat to the side and barked out a cynical laugh. "What a way to speak to the person who has given up his life for you."

Senna sighed. "Emrys—"

"No! You've given up everything for Percy. And from where I was standing, it looked like you would've let Cevyn kill you trying to save Percy, so my apologies if I won't sit here and listen to him scold you!"

Percy spun around to Emrys. "What do you know about Senna?"

"What do *you* know about Senna that isn't the leash you keep him on?"

"*Quiet*, both of you!" Thea shrieked, rising to her feet. "If you don't stop arguing, I will waltz myself back into that cave and let Cevyn drown *me* so that

I don't have to listen to you whine. Percy, it really was just a few seconds. I'm sorry if it seemed like more, but it wasn't. And *you*!" This was directed at Emrys. "Percy has just been through something extremely traumatic. Could you at least wait a *minute* before making him the target of your misplaced frustration?" She paused, drawing in a deep breath, this time speaking more calmly. "I understand that today has been stressful and that none of us want to be here, but it's over. We get to go home now and never come back again."

Nare jumped to her feet and plucked out a dead leaf stuck in the long side of her hair.

"Actually, that depends. Did anyone manage to grab the glasses?" she said.

Percy furiously felt around the ground beside him, found where the glasses had landed when the rowboat was pitched aground, and threw them at Nare's feet.

"Take them. I hope they were worth it."

Emrys scoffed, another gripe seemingly on the tip of his tongue, but Senna shot him a stern glare. Emrys' lips snapped shut, gaze dropping immediately to the ground.

Something complicated churned in Senna's stomach. He loved Percy like the brother he'd never have. He was so proud of everything that Percy was. The type of prince who could swindle the thieves he'd played cards with. The type of friend who wasn't afraid to show his affection in embraces and loving words. The type of person who acted when he heard that his friends needed something, even if it meant going to the one place that scared him the most.

But he *was* behaving in bad form, even if he was still reeling from the ordeal. Maybe with some rest in his own bed, Percy would go back to being the version of himself that Senna would go into dangerous waters for.

In quiet, careful tones, the group decided what they would do next. Nare and Thea would head back to Redwind to bring the glasses to safety as soon as possible. Percy, still shaken to his core, needed a little time before he could be of any use to the quest of opening the journal. Elora declared she would remain in Talsura until Percy was feeling better.

That left Emrys, whose uncertain gaze lingered on Senna.

"Elora will need someone to escort her back home. I know I've been—cranky, but if it's alright with you, I'll stay in Talsura until she's ready to leave," he said.

Senna's brows knit together. "Are you certain? I thought you didn't want to be here."

"Who knows? Maybe Talsura's like cheap wine and tastes better the more you drink?"

The honorable thing to do would have been to inform Emrys that Talsura actually got *worse* with age—something about the unending darkness that drove its residents to feeling like their brains had been stirred with a spoon. But the thought of Emrys lingering around, with his bright smiles and warm sugar scent, was convincing. So Senna agreed.

Later, Thea gave Percy a squeezing embrace before disappearing up the mill's trade channels. Nare, to Senna's surprise, clapped Percy on the back and told him he "*hadn't done half-bad.*" But something told Senna that she didn't think Percy had done half-good, either.

At his side, Emrys took Senna's wrist.

"I'd like to visit my old home. Would you go with me?"

"Of course," answered Senna without hesitation. Then to Percy, "Do you think you make it back to the castle without running into trouble?"

Percy set his jaw, expression still stony.

"Oh, *now* you permit me to travel by myself," he said. "I suppose I'll have to make it back safely, won't I?"

The sharpness of the words hit Senna immediately. It squeezed on Senna's throat.

"You're right. I'm sorry," he said slowly. "If Emrys doesn't mind waiting, I can escort you and Elora back to the castle and write a sigil to travel back out here." To Emrys, he added, "It won't take long."

Percy scoffed. "Emrys' wish is our command." Then he disappeared back up the trade channels.

Elora looked at the passageway helplessly. She tossed Senna an apologetic glance and dropped her hands at her sides. "He doesn't mean it, Senna," she said, before following behind.

Senna knew better than anyone that Percy didn't take to anger quickly, but when he did, he shared it as generously as he did anything else. That didn't mean he'd ever figured out how to weather the storm of Percy's ire.

Senna spun to Emrys, torn between taking off right after Percy and ensuring that Emrys would be safe here.

Emrys waved his hand and pulled a flask out of his pocket.

"Go. I'll wait for you on the path above. I'll be in better spirits when you return." He took a swig of his flask. "It's only up from here."

EMRYS

Emrys heard Senna's footfalls on the path behind him before he saw him materialize out of the dark. He peered up at Senna from where he leaned against a low-lit street lamp, finding the goldheart's jaw tight.

"All is well?"

Senna gave a half-shrug. He said nothing.

Emrys had been under the mistaken impression that he'd been making progress with Senna. Now, he saw that it was only the influence of the easy, relaxed city on Mount Livia that had lessened the tension between them. The strain had returned, rearing its angry head, making the air in the tiny mill so thick, Emrys thought he might choke on it.

Senna didn't seem to be faring any better. He fidgeted with the hilt of his sword, thumbing over the jewel embedded into the gilded metal. He refused to meet Emrys' gaze.

Why would Senna behave kindly to him after the way he'd kicked Percy when he was down? Emrys had no business inserting himself where he did not belong. He could see that now that the initial frustration had worn off. To imply that Senna did not understand the depth of his unfair situation was to insult his intelligence and the choices he had made of sound mind. Would Senna forgive him if he knew that the wick of Emrys' anger was short and burned quickly—sometimes more than he could help it?

Emrys needed to apologize. He couldn't step foot in his childhood home until he had. Someone just had to break the silence first.

Like an arrow string pulled back too far, they both snapped, nervously speaking at the same time. Their words met like clashing swords.

"I am unbelievably sorry, Sen."

"You're not hurt, are you?"

Senna and Emrys froze, regarding each other cautiously. Then the tension gave way, and Senna smiled. Emrys was helpless to do anything but return it.

"I'm just fine," he said warmly. "And you?"

Senna blinked, as though he hadn't quite thought to consider his own well-being, but then shrugged. "I'm wet."

The statement came out so casually, it shouldn't have made Emrys envision other scenarios where Senna might utter the same words. But it did, bringing with it a flurry of imaginations of Emrys' hand cupping Senna through his pants. His fingers would caress right where wetness gathered at the tip of his cock, seeping through his dark cotton clothes, sweet enough for Emrys to put his lips to.

Emrys cleared his throat, leading the way up the path.

Walking through the open, abandoned fields of the Pocket District did not bring the same cool-wind ease that the moorlands outside Redwind did—but then, that was a freedom only a lack of borders could bring. Emrys opened his hand to another one of his family's famous roses, urging it to fill the palm until every inch of skin was covered by glowing petals. He ought to grow another for Senna to carry, but using so much inflorescence from such a distance had drained his strength.

Grabbing Senna's elbow, he said, "Hold on a moment, Sen."

"What—do I have a trinket in my hair?"

Damn him, that smile was lovely. Lovelier than the glowing rose in his hand. Lovelier than all the flowers in Redwind—hell, even the sun in the late evening sky.

"No, you goose wing, your hair is frustratingly perfect, as usual. I just thought . . ." By way of explanation, Emrys opened Senna's own hand and rubbed his thumb on the palm. By now, Senna knew what it meant when Emrys touched him like that, so he did not stop him. Perhaps Emrys caressed the calluses there a moment or two longer than he should've, but by the time he pulled his hand to hold Senna's wrists, there was another glowing rose that matched his own.

"Don't tell the princess I shared the royal flower with you," Emrys said quietly. "It's a secret that it glows. Makes for a fun party trick with the right guests."

Senna beamed at the creation, the product of his own flesh and blood.

"If I'd known that's what I was accepting, I would have stopped you," Senna admitted.

"Consider it atonement for the ghastly way I behaved to Percy. Being here has been a trial for my good mood and I fear it was made worse by . . . well, you know. I don't care for you to endanger yourself on Percy's behalf." Emrys slid the fingers still resting on top of Senna's palm to cup the underside. "Sometimes I rather think I get angry *for* you, because you're never angry for yourself."

Senna had no words, lips parted as he stared at the point where their skin touched. Emrys became acutely aware that if he stood this close to Senna a moment longer, he would kiss him.

Hells, he *wanted* to. More than anything, he wanted to taste Senna's lips, even if they were still stained with swamp water and forest mud. Emrys forced himself to step back. He pulled some tangling weeds off the wooden spindles of a nearby bench and took a seat.

Senna hesitated. "I thought we were visiting your old home."

"We are," Emrys assured. "But I think I'd like to work up to it. I expended a lot of courage just now riding in a boat captained by Nare Demira—the realm's quickest shipwrecker."

Senna let out a barking laugh and it was sweeping music to Emrys' trained ear. The goldheart took the seat next to Emrys, stripping away his sword and kicking his feet far into the empty path.

"You were right, you know," he said. His head was tilted back to the churning dam, as if he were imagining stars.

"Of course I was," Emrys said. Then, "Right how?"

Senna chewed on the inside of his cheek, taking a long moment before answering.

"I'm not angry at Percy for the way he spoke to me today. It's because, for a long time, angry was *all* I was."

Emrys leaned forward, brows furrowing. "I can relate to that."

Senna shook his head. "It was different. It was—" He scrubbed his day-old stubble. "You remember that I was young when I was stationed as the goldheart. Barely nine years old."

"Yes, you told me of . . ." Emrys hesitated, choosing his words carefully. "Of the queen finding you in your home. Did you even *want* to become the goldheart?"

"At first, I was excited. What little boy wouldn't be? I had all these notions of traveling in big groups of silverhearts, saving lives, and fighting off the disease that had killed my best friend. There was one silly notion of another knight watching me spar and—" He cut off, sheepish. "And fancying me."

"I think I've had a fantasy or two like that," Emrys said, not clarifying that all of them had included Senna. "I take it that reality wasn't like you thought."

Senna shook his head. "The sun went first. Then I was introduced to the other knights in training, boys almost ten years older than I was. Men, really. Their instinct was to torment me, but they couldn't because I outranked all of them. So they did something worse."

"They ignored you," Emrys realized.

"It was like being at the orphanage all over again." A stormy expression crossed Senna's face. "When I had completed enough training to give Phaedra confidence that I wouldn't get Percy, or myself, killed, she gave me the order that I was to never leave Percy's side. But he was quiet company too."

"Hardly sounds like him."

"Well, he *was* a newborn."

Emrys' shoulders dropped. He supposed he'd known factually that Senna had been caring for Percy since his birth, but he'd never given thought to what that meant. Emrys couldn't imagine if his mother decided to switch his station from *Captain* to *Glorified Babysitter*.

"You had no company at all?"

"There was no one my age." Senna shrugged. "I was aware of it every second of every day. In the quiet moments sitting over his cradle, all I could think about was how I hadn't spoken a word in weeks. Not a single person had addressed me in the corridor, inquired how my day was, or even asked about the prince. To the members of the castle, I was nothing more than an empty suit of gold armor."

Emrys had a sinking feeling that, whether he knew it or not, Senna felt that way about himself now.

"Then, one day, I was rocking Percy's cradle and it occurred to me that my life would never change. I'd be the prince's silent shadow forever." A swath of gloom shaded over Senna's face, the Dam flickering even darker above them for the briefest moment, like moving clouds. "I was violently furious. I couldn't do anything about it, so I made Percy the object of my silent contempt. I pictured a thousand ways of fleeing the kingdom, but in the end, I was only a child. One with too much responsibility and altogether too long to wait before adulthood."

Emrys could picture it: Senna, the embodiment of a spark, ever threatening to combust and tear everything down with him. It was how he'd felt when he had been exiled, how he'd felt when his mother had asked him to temporarily give up his birthright to a pretend sister. Except Emrys *had* burned—he'd terrorized everyone around him for years until he'd managed to transform the anger into something he could live with.

"How long was it like that?" Emrys wondered.

"Until Percy was four."

"When he found Cevyn."

"Yes," Senna agreed. "It was a few months after his birthday. You see, there's a tradition in the castle that its staff must provide offerings to the royal family every year in celebration of their birth. Some of the staff don't want to spend their carefully earned wages on pointless gifts, so they don't give one. After all, who notices a few items missing in a pile of toys that large?"

A sad smile rose on Senna's face.

"I didn't want to give a gift either, but everyone would have noticed if the goldheart didn't offer anything. Percy didn't care about the toys. But he cared about the one *I* gave him, because he idolized me, even though I never graced him with any attention or care. Because I was the goldheart, I had to give him something. So I picked the first toy I saw in the market."

"That toy boat from earlier?" Emrys guessed.

"The price was reduced because of a chip in the sail's paint. But Percy adored it. He carried it everywhere he went. It made me sick to see him enjoy it so much. For me, it was just an obligation. An undear toy for village peasants. Yet, it was his treasure. I guess I had wanted him to see it as the trash it was, so he would see how little I cared. He didn't, so I threw it into the river."

"Oh, Senna," Emrys said in understanding.

"Percy wailed for a fortnight, searching for the toy everywhere he went. I knew he would never find it, so I didn't help him look. I got into the habit of leaving him alone just so I wouldn't have to listen to him crying."

Senna clutched his hands. His nails bit tiny moons into his skin.

"This is the part I'm the most ashamed of," he warned.

Emrys covered Senna's fingers so he couldn't hurt himself further.

"You could murder a man and I'd still sit beside you," Emrys assured him. "Always."

Senna drew a breath and continued.

"Phaedra couldn't stand Percy either. It's the only thing we've ever had in common." He spoke the words like it horrified him to admit that he'd ever shared the same depths of selfish evil as his queen. "Finally, when she couldn't stand it any longer, she told him that his boat had been stolen by Cevyn, the canon of lost things, who would never give it back. Her mistake was telling Percy the legend, which included directions for how to find Cevyn. All he had to do was follow the river to the forest until he found a treasure trove. So he did."

"I have to say, I'm impressed."

"I wasn't," Senna laughed bitterly. "I hadn't even noticed he was gone. When his maids realized he wasn't in his room at meal time, it became my business to locate him. In my gut, I knew where he'd gone and knew I had to follow him. I can't stomach thinking about what would've happened if I'd continued searching the castle like I had been advised."

"It seems you've always been a skilled guard, despite everything. You found him, after all."

"Only after the danger had passed. When I arrived, he was stumbling out of the cave, the wretched boat clutched in his hands, crying the way people do when they're afraid they'll die. He said Cevyn had called him a lost thing, something no one wanted. I heard that and it all sort of . . ." Senna swept his hands away from his lap. "All the bitterness and the hate and the loneliness was gone. Because here was this child with no more strength or bravery to spare. A child who had faced a canon and somehow tricked them, all to find the thing that I had purposefully thrown away."

Senna tilted his head up to the black sky.

"But I was the thing he really loved. It scared me because he *was* me. A lonely, pitiful thing with no parents to love him. No friends to talk to. All he had was a guard who despised him, even though he'd been nothing but nice to him. He had no hand in my fate. We were . . . tangled together, though neither of us had asked for it, and I was unfair for blaming him for it.

"From then on, I decided I would take my position seriously. I would become Percy's friend—his brother—and we would stand against the world—together—because it was obviously standing against us."

Emrys drew their hands into his lap, the glow of the white roses falling over their faces.

"It seems to have worked out for the best. Percy worships you, Sen. No matter what he said tonight. If you think anyone could protect Percy as well, or love him as much as you do, you're wrong. I feel the same way about my—" Emrys paused. "About Thea."

He wanted to thank Senna for trusting him enough to speak so much. To praise him for being brave enough to relive what must have been one of his greatest moments of shame. But every time he attempted to shape the words, they felt lacking. He stood up, stretching his hands up, then out.

"Emrys," Senna said softly.

At the sound of his name, Emrys dropped his arms and turned, only to find Senna standing right behind him. Canons, the man was tall.

"Yes?"

If Emrys didn't know any better, he would have guessed that Senna knew he was making him squirm—and *enjoyed* it. The big, infuriatingly beautiful man.

"Thank you for being angry on my behalf," he said.

He might as well have kicked Emrys in the chest for all he lost the ability to breathe. It practically knocked Emrys back onto the bench in a heap.

"W-what are friends for?" Emrys stammered.

Senna's lips spread into a smile.

"What for, indeed?"

This time Emrys did sit. Anyone else might've rushed him along, told him to stop wasting time. But Senna said nothing when he took his place next to Emrys once more.

It seemed they were always stealing time together. As soon as they left this empty, peaceful pocket of the world, he would have to confront the memories of his childhood. And afterwards, he'd have to brave the Talsuran castle and the rest of their hopeless quest. It was easier to sit here with Senna and pretend the moon was just covered by clouds. To share secrets of the past without fear of judgment, all in hopes of a better future.

"You do remember I said I'd go with you, right?" asked Senna when the silence had stretched on too long. Emrys didn't have to ask what he meant.

"Can't a man live in the luxury of his own dallying in peace?"

"Is that what we're doing? Dallying?"

"Definitely dallying. I don't suppose it's quite a dalliance yet."

Senna stiffened imperceptibly.

"... Yet?"

Emrys' face ignited in bright heat as he realized what he'd said. Like a cat doused in water, he jumped up and started marching up the path, urging his cheeks to cool.

"The darkness is making you hear things, Goldheart," Emrys spluttered. "Come along now. Dallying time is over."

The sound of Senna's laughter followed Emrys all the way to the decrepit patch of land where his father had built their house. These were the nailed boards and planks where he'd been born. Any warmth that had bloomed in his stomach from his talk with Senna drained away, spilling over the tall grass and onto the untouched path like blood from a wound.

Emrys had forgotten how humble his beginnings had been. Sometimes, when he drew upon the memories of his childhood, they seemed like someone else's—planted into his mind to trick him. But standing mere strides away from his old front door, Emrys was nine years old again, humming a song and spooling his spinning reel on the bottom step.

"I used to like to fish," he stated. "I completely forgot."

"Be kind to yourself. Things like that are easy to forget when they were so long ago." Senna bent over and picked up a wood shingle that had blown off the path. "Were you a skilled fisher?"

"*Canons*, no. I don't think I ever caught anything. I liked—" He laughed wetly. "I liked watching the reel spin. Or rather, I liked the sound it made. What a simple thing to adore."

Senna stood at his side, the heat of his body grounding Emrys.

"Do you want to go inside?" Senna asked.

"No," Emrys answered immediately. Then, "Maybe. I think so. Yes?"

Fingers like molten glass intertwined with Emrys', equal parts strong and gentle, ready to be molded into whatever Emrys needed.

"Lead the way."

Emrys was aware of every step, the very way his weight fell on the porch, the creaking of the neglected floorboards. He tried to shift that focus to the man at his side, but found he couldn't linger on Senna long enough before the overwhelming flood of memories swept over him once more.

The Rosecroft house was a skeleton frozen in time. Everything was exactly where his family had left it the day they had been forced to leave Talsura—only now, there was a digit's worth of dust over everything.

"My father built this house," Emrys heard himself say.

"Then it's no wonder it's withstood twenty years on its own."

Emrys hadn't quite worked up to moving past the threshold, but Senna stepped in, taking in everything with a reverent gaze.

"It was nicer back then. Humble and simple, but cleaner," Emrys said, picking up a sketched portrait from the windowsill. He hadn't only forgotten about his own hobbies, but his mother's too. She hadn't painted a sketch like this since becoming queen. He didn't even think Thea knew she shared that in common with their mother. "I'm surprised to find some of our things still here. I would have thought Cevyn would've come and taken everything for themself."

"I don't think that's how it works. Cevyn is only the canon of lost things. If someone in your family *remembers* where they left something, then it isn't truly lost, is it?"

Emrys looked around the room again and realized that Senna had to be right. His mother would remember where she'd left her paintings. A first glance at the bookshelf made it look as if it had been scoured by canons or thieves, but there were some texts still on the shelf—the family favorites. The books that the Rosecrofts couldn't have forgotten about if they'd tried. He hadn't realized how much he'd missed the things he'd left behind, or how silly he felt for missing them in the first place.

He was a prince, dammit. He wanted for nothing. Yet, he desired to fit all these abandoned artifacts of his childhood into his satchel and bring them to Redwind.

Across the room, Senna was rubbing his hand against a doorframe, eyebrows knit together.

"What is it?"

"Everything is in exceptional condition except for these scratches," Senna explained. "They look too purposeful to be accidental."

Emrys held his hand up to shine light on the scratch and barked out a laugh. His amusement was immediately followed by guilt. How could Senna be expected to know about common family traditions when he'd grown up in an orphanage?

"The marks *were* on purpose, Senna. My parents carved these markings to keep track of how tall I was growing," Emrys explained. He waved Senna closer. "See, the number shows how old I was when my parents measured me. My father chiseled the last marking on my ninth birthday, even though he had measured me a few weeks before. I insisted I *must've* grown overnight. That's why the lines are so close together."

Senna ran over the mark with the pad of his thumb. "Is it common to stop measuring at nine years old? You've obviously grown since then."

"It's common to stop when the child stops growing." Emrys tossed Senna a pointed, but kind look. "We were exiled the same year, Sen."

"Oh." Senna turned his gaze down, expression humbled. "Of course. Forgive me."

"It's just as well," Emrys said, kicking a foot up on the opposite side of the doorframe. "I had high hopes as a child that I'd grow tall enough to mark the top of the door. I'm sure nine-year-old Emrys would have been quite disappointed to realize he didn't have much further to go."

Something like an idea shone in Senna's expression. He guided Emrys so that his back was pressed up against the knife scores. His breath fell on Emrys' mouth, through his skin, and down to his knees.

Senna slid a hand behind Emrys' back and pushed, urging his spine to straighten. Now they were touching—the barest hint of tunic on tunic.

"At attention, Captain," Senna scolded playfully.

"Yes, sir," Emrys breathed on instinct.

Then Senna produced a small knife from somewhere along his belt. With the same gentle precision he might use to shave his face, Senna aligned the blade with the top of Emrys' head and made a long incision.

"I'm trusting you not to cut any of my hair," Emrys said with a lopsided grin. He couldn't look away from Senna's face, searching the goldheart's gaze over and over, uncertain when he'd be this close to Senna again.

"Not even a little off the top?" Senna grinned. Emrys nudged him in the stomach. Senna glared at him warningly, but his lips were still curved up. "Hey, now. Jostle me and you really will end up with a haircut."

When he was done, Emrys stepped away and appraised the workmanship.

The mark was impeccably straight, the number twenty-seven inscribed beneath it in careful writing. Emrys looked at it and looked at it, until his vision blurred.

"Did I—did I do it wrong?" Senna asked nervously.

"No, Sen. It's . . ." Emrys scrubbed his eyes. "It's wonderful. You did exactly right. I think my father would have been so happy to see how much his son grew. I didn't realize how strongly being in this house would make me remember him. But perhaps I was naive. I can feel him in everything he built: these walls, the furniture, and my cittern . . ." Emrys looked up. *"My cittern."*

Without a second thought, Emrys was breezing down the hallway into his old bedroom. He stumbled back as soon as he crossed the threshold, as if he'd been shocked.

Protruding through a massive gash in the ceiling was a large oak branch. It had pulverized Emrys' childhood bed, piercing through the mattress. Rotting strands of straw spilled over onto the floor like entrails.

Emrys let out a pained noise. The room was ruined. He'd known without doubt that his family would never move back to this house, but realizing they *couldn't* because of the damage the house had sustained . . . It finally wrenched the grief from its hiding place deep in his stomach.

"Emrys," Senna said behind him. He sounded distant, but his hand was on Emrys' shoulder. *"Look."*

Dropping his head into his hands, Emrys shook his head. He couldn't look at it a second longer—this place where he'd grown up. The birthplace of all of his dreams, songs, and rest.

Senna brushed past Emrys, careful not to hit his head on the large branch or slip on any debris. Then he grabbed something from behind the mess of bark and wreckage: Emrys' cittern.

"I thought I saw the glimmer of the strings," Senna explained, offering Emrys the instrument like a king bestowing a sword to an honored knight.

Emrys blinked down at it, like he couldn't believe it was in his hands again. By some miracle, it was perfectly untouched. Emrys would have to clean a substantial amount of dirt from the frets, and likely even more inside the body. But none of the strings had snapped and the wood showed no signs of water damage.

"Let's go sit outside. It's probably not safe for us to be in here if the roof's structure is compromised," Emrys said flatly.

Before leaving the house behind him for good, though, he mustered the courage to retrieve a folio of sheet music from his father's desk. It took several minutes of searching—he was unable to avoid reading every stray note and document he came across. So foreign had his father's handwriting become.

Senna was waiting for him on the front stoop. Emrys' chest expanded when he realized Senna was doing his best to clean between the cittern's frets. He couldn't imagine where Senna had found a clean rag amongst all the mess, only to discover Senna was using the damp ducktail of his shirt.

Emrys sat beside Senna, who handed the cittern to him.

"The worst of it is gone, but I have a feeling a proper cleaning will make it shine like it used to."

Emrys let his hands slide up the neck, making the strings whine. "You're very thoughtful, Sen. Did you know?"

Senna shrugged.

"You can't play it if it's so filthy."

"Not just this." Emrys held up the instrument. "You marked my height. You followed me into my family home, even though it's falling apart. You've treated everything here with more respect than anyone else would have and I want you to know I'm thankful for it. Thankful for *you*."

Senna seemed like he didn't know quite what to say. He rubbed his throat, then gestured restlessly at the cittern.

"Play something," he stammered.

"You don't know what you're asking for. I haven't picked up a cittern in almost six months." Still, he plucked the first string and twisted the tuner.

If Senna was this rapt while Emrys merely tuned the cittern, he wondered what the goldheart's reaction would be when he actually played it.

"How do you know what pitch to tune it to?" wondered Senna.

"I listen." Emrys strummed all the strings, resulting in a harmonious chord. "I know how it's supposed to sound."

It took some time for Emrys to find a song he knew in his father's folio of music. He feared he'd have to sight-read the music after not having practiced in so long, and he so badly wanted to impress Senna. Finally, he opened to a page that had once been blank and was now filled with handwritten notation: a song of Emrys' own making.

Emrys gently pulled a glowing rose from his hand with the same ease as weeds from loose soil. He set the rose next to the sheet music, letting its light wash over the paper. It would retain its shine for another half hour at least and was bright enough that Emrys didn't have to squint down at every tiny note on the page.

Then, he began to play.

The strings bit his un-calloused fingers, but his hands danced up and down the fretboard, muscle memory recalling each measure of music before his mind did. The cittern's tuning hadn't been perfect, but the sound it produced was unlike anything Emrys had heard, because the instrument was *his*. Each chained chord of notes yielded bright harmonies that reverberated over the empty fields.

He was approaching the portion of the music where the lyrics joined the fray. Although he'd practiced with his cittern in Redwind, Emrys couldn't remember the last time he'd sung. For a moment, he was terrified that he'd lost the smooth-ness of his voice in adulthood and considered ending the song early, but Senna was looking at Emrys like he was the canon of music, the very inventor of sound itself.

So Emrys sang. When he did, it was as natural as breathing. The lyrics told the story about a young boy who'd had to let his pet bird go free. The song was formed from a naive grief—the sadness that comes the first time a child faces a loss—but Emrys found that perhaps he had not changed so much, after all.

"I am no good at short goodbyes.
I linger 'til the daylight dies,
to try to get my friend to stay
each time he wants to fly away.

I love him so I'll let him go.
Farewells are hard, I know he knows.
But I'd give anything to say
Please fly home to me one day."

As he sang the final phrase, Emrys dropped the support of his lungs, letting the final note reverberate quietly until it was a whisper he could sigh away. He hadn't sung like that in years. The muscles in his chest felt good—satisfied, even—to have been used to bring the song back to life.

He looked up at Senna, eager to see if he felt it too—the rightness, the beauty of music in the dark, the promise of all the songs to come. Senna *must* have, because his eyes were cloudy with amazement and desire, and it wasn't the first time he'd looked so *starved*, but it was the first time he'd let Emrys bathe in that hunger.

So really, Emrys had no choice but to lean over the body of the cittern, give the man what he wanted, and kiss him.

Senna tasted the way sunlight might if you ladled it into a glass and drank of it. That warm honey only tasted stronger as the goldheart returned the kiss, closing his lips over Emrys' like he had a sweet taste of his own.

All at once, Emrys understood why his people grew flowers that would intoxicate them, because feeling Senna run his tongue along the swell of Emrys' lips was like being drowned under a thrall. Emrys would've stayed in Talsura forever if it meant that they could unendingly grow drunk off each other's taste.

He wanted Senna to put his fingers in his hair. To tug until Emrys felt those pinpricks of pleasure hot on his head. He needed Senna to *stake his claim* so that Emrys would know, without a doubt, that he could keep this thing forever. Whatever it was.

Senna tore away, pushing Emrys back by the shoulders. His eyes were wide and glassy, but the second Emrys tried to search them, Senna looked down.

And froze.

Emrys waited. The wise thing was to give Senna the space he needed to speak, so Emrys held back every urge to open his blasted mouth. It didn't help that Senna looked so confounded.

"You—" The words were a gasp from Senna's mouth.

Emrys braced for the other shoe to drop.

"Is your name Emrys *Rosecroft*?"

Now that can't be right, Emrys thought at the same moment as, *Oh no.*

He tilted his head, blinking, hoping that clearing his eyes would rid his mind of the sudden ringing in his ears. His heart throbbed like a warning in his chest, and if he hadn't been so acutely aware of all of his senses, he would have thought he'd been kicked by a horse.

"What—what makes you think that?" Emrys stammered.

Senna pointed down at the sheet music where a young Emrys had written, *"An original song by Emrys Rosecroft."*

"Oh."

"*Oh*," Senna scoffed. He was—he was *mad*. Emrys didn't think he'd ever seen Senna Kane properly angry. Frustrated, to be sure. Stern, definitely. But the ire brewing on his face was uncharted territory for Emrys. It was clear that Senna had more to say, more questions to throw in Emrys' face, but the anger had brought back his old self. The one that couldn't speak.

Senna scrubbed at his throat, a frustrated sound working its way out of his lips.

Emrys grabbed the wrist and moved it away from where it was scratching red lines into Senna's throat.

"Don't force yourself to speak when you can't. I'll—I'll explain. I'll tell you everything."

Senna looked at him expectantly. Emrys had no choice but to follow through and tell him the truth. He didn't think he could have lied to Senna if he'd tried.

"My full name and title is Prince Emrys Calloway Rosecroft of Redwind. Queen Casta is my mother by birth and Thea is . . ." He chewed his lip, searching around for the right word. "My stand-in. For now. And for all intents and purposes, my sister, as well."

Senna released a long breath of air, eyes falling shut.

"When Redwind was still just tents in the moorlands, everyone was searching for a leader," Emrys continued. "Someone to tell the crowds where to go, someone to keep them alive. Someone to make the hard decisions. But half of us were already dead and most had lost hope that the rest of the refugees would survive. Whoever stepped up as our leader would take the blame for whatever misfortune befell us, even if it wasn't their fault."

Senna's brows knit together. "Queen Casta—your mother—volunteered?"

"Not exactly."

This was the hard part. Quelling a cresting wave of grief, Emrys told Senna about Ceday, Phaedra's sister. How Ceday had discovered the secret of mastering inflorescence too late, how she'd passed that miraculous discovery to Emrys and Casta. How Casta had shared that knowledge around the entire encampment after Ceday's passing and become the natural leader.

"Before she died, Ceday knew the wise thing to do was to keep us on Islevaria and develop Redwind near the base of Mount Livia. She knew how badly the majority of the people in our care wanted to sail away from the continent. But we were sick and dying. Too many wouldn't have survived the journey. So, after Ceday passed, my mother established Redwind in the middle of the continent. Close enough to Talsura and Mount Livia to facilitate trade. Far enough away so that we wouldn't have to see your Dam over our own horizon."

"But why keep your identity a secret?"

"We were an injured lamb surrounded by wolves. Do you realize how many kingdoms on other continents wanted our land, who saw Redwind as a conquest easily won? We had no army. No defense. My mother has never been so terrified as she was the first few years as queen. She instilled a passion for survival among our people that made it possible to build our homes and our castle. To fend off the initial attacks. All the while, threats on our land and *my* life arrived. They weren't only threats to the queen's child, but the future of the kingdom. The *bloodline*. That's when she found Thea, the only survivor of the Gray House Orphanage, and made her the counterfeit princess."

If Emrys hadn't been so tangled in the choking tresses of his bad memories, he might've realized Senna had gone as still as death.

"The other children had all died by the time Thea arrived here," Emrys continued. "The orphanage mistress apparently sent her assistant to care for the children. Thea, the last remaining child, outlived him. My mother says she found Thea alone, sleeping in the unfinished orphanage because she had nowhere else to go."

"The Gray House was *my* orphanage," Senna snapped.

Emrys had the good sense to look ashamed. "I know."

"The princess and I would've been there at the same time. I understand why you kept your birthright secret, but I deserved to know that someone I grew up with survived. For years, I thought they had all died. Do you have any idea how hard it was to carry around the guilt of surviving?"

"You're right. You did deserve to know. I'm so sorry, Senna."

Emrys told Senna the rest—that no one had known the chosen gender of the queen's child, so no one had known any different when their heir turned out to be a princess instead of a prince or princet.

Senna tore away from the porch, putting several hearty steps between them. He rubbed his chest, though it didn't seem to bring him any relief.

"So, you're a prince."

"To my utter displeasure, yes," Emrys breathed out a sardonic laugh. "To be honest, I'm surprised Percy didn't squeal about it years ago."

"Percy—?" The words blustered out of Senna. He lifted his sword from the scabbard and slammed it back in. "You *should* have told me. I never would have taken you with me to Mount Livia if I'd known what I was putting at risk."

This Emrys could not abide. A surge of anger roiled in his gut so profound, it swept him onto his feet.

"What would that be, exactly? Because I can promise you it's not the fate of Redwind. I may be the true crown prince, but I will not reveal my birthright and I will not ascend to the throne. I don't want to. I've *never* wanted to." Emrys fixed Senna with a stern look. "For your information, I'm a grown man, Goldheart. I've kept myself intact this long and I am perfectly capable of executing my will without jeopardizing my safety."

Senna crossed the distance in two easy steps, then touched the pads of his fingers over the place Emrys had been stuck with an arrow. With a look of pure knowing, he pressed down on the tender flesh and scoffed when Emrys flinched at the dull throb.

"You may think you are indestructible, but I am well acquainted with how easy it is to ruin you."

The anger churning in Emrys' gut turned into something else. Something hot and tinged with desire.

"I wish you would," Emrys breathed.

Senna huffed out an annoyed breath, eyes lifting to the Dam.

"This is serious. Do you know how it felt to turn around and see your blood soaking your clothes. You have so much *life* in your face, but as you bled out . . ." He shook his head. "In case you have forgotten, *I* held you in that healing tub. *I* bound your wounds. If you hadn't taught me needle yarrow earlier that day, you would have died."

"But I didn't!" Emrys moved Senna's hand so that it hovered above where his heart raced, and dropped his tone. "I kissed you because—"

"It doesn't matter," Senna cut in, stiffly. "That can't happen again."

Another kick to the chest. It was a wonder Emrys was still standing.

"You're right," he agreed solemnly. "I should have asked. I violated your trust. I—I thought I was sensing something that clearly wasn't there and for that, I beg your forgiveness."

Senna's shoulders dropped. "It was there. And you didn't violate my trust. I wanted it too."

"In that case, I can't imagine why it *shouldn't* happen again. What's changed?"

"You're the prince of Redwind!" Senna cried emphatically.

"My darling man, I was the prince of Redwind when I kissed you. That hasn't changed."

Emrys grabbed Senna's face, forcing him to look directly into his eyes.

"The choice isn't made yet, Senna. This is what I've been trying to get past those good looks into your painfully thick head. You belong to *yourself*. You don't have to turn something down because you *want* it. Because you think there isn't enough of you to have it. The decision is yours, Sen. *Make it*."

A rush of cold swept over Emrys' skin when Senna stepped back.

"The choice is made."

Emrys scoffed. *The* choice. Not Senna's choice. Emrys had rather hoped that in showing Senna how highly he cared for him, Senna would see that he didn't have to waste his life serving

"No," he rushed. "I'll be damned if I let you walk away from a good thing just because you're the most infuriatingly selfless man this side of the canon's forsaken mountain."

Senna's smile was edged with *I cannot help who I am or the responsibilities I have pledged myself to. And I'll not have you damned for my sake.*

There was something in the way that Senna said it—something that tasted of finality. Moments ago, Emrys had kept his emotions steady by deciding that Senna would come around eventually, he just needed to be patient. That was only because the kiss had given him a *drop* of hope, a slivered look into what Senna wanted beneath his responsibilities.

But there was something in Senna's *face*—like he was already grieving.

"It is an utter waste, Senna," Emrys said definitively. "And it breaks my heart."

"I didn't mean to hurt you—" Senna swore, but Emrys silenced him with a raised hand.

"That isn't what I mean, though I can't say I'm delighted by the way that this has played out." He sighed. "I mean that I look at you, and I see enough brightness and talent and potential to fill the bloody sea. It's all wasted."

Senna didn't have a response for that. Despairing, Emrys suspected that Senna *agreed* with him.

"No one has ever cared for me to get this angry on my account," said Senna. Emrys scoffed.

"You haven't a clue of how much I care about you."

Of all the things he'd said, that was the one phrase that seemed to crack Senna's stubborn exterior. Devastation flashed across Senna's face long enough for Emrys to catch it.

Emrys reached for Senna, who instinctively took a step back.

"We should return to the castle," Senna stated grimly.

Emrys thought he could practically hear his heart sinking into the pit of his stomach, crashing into a million bloody pieces. Setting his jaw, Emrys rallied.

"Maybe I should stay here. It'd be dangerous for you to be seen with me in the castle, given the, uh—" He gestured to where his usual fuchsia flowers were wilting on his temple, loose petals stuck in his heavy hair. He'd have to regrow them as soon as he crossed the Dam, or all his knights would think he had some strange potency problem.

"If you think I'm letting you sleep in a house that is losing its war against ballista of nature, you're mistaken," Senna barked. Emrys opened his mouth to argue, but Senna cut him off. "*And*, it isn't because you're a prince."

Emrys dropped his hands at his sides. "Then tell me, oh revered Goldheart of Talsura, where I am to spend the night."

Senna set his jaw.

"My room," he said. "It's as I said: I am often left alone. You won't be seen. You'll sleep in my bed."

Emrys' jaw dropped. "Oh, will I?"

"I'll find other sleeping arrangements. In the morning, you'll escort Miss Wright back to Redwind."

Emrys let out a defeated huff.

"I suppose while in Talsura, I have no choice but to yield to the goldheart's command," Emrys said sarcastically. "Lead the way to your *room*."

Senna squared his shoulders and started for the castle. Emrys was too busy glaring at his back to realize he was walking away from his childhood home, maybe forever. But in the darkness, he glanced over his shoulder one last time, holding to the song still lingering on its front steps.

SENNA

I F ANYONE WONDERED WHY Senna was stationed outside Percy's chamber door for the first time in almost a decade, they didn't ask. Maybe they didn't notice him. He kept his countenance stony, unable to help but feel that every member of the staff that passed him knew that he was hiding a Redwindan prince in his bedroom.

His mouth was still warm with the sensation of Emrys' kiss. It had been laid upon him so carefully—so *intently*—that Senna couldn't help but think that perhaps Emrys had been carrying it around in his pocket, waiting for the right moment to entrust it to Senna's care. Now that it was soundly in Senna's possession, he couldn't shake the charged eagerness to plead for more.

He *could* go to Emrys, gracefully hidden in his own private quarters . . .

No.

He needed to remain at his post—away from temptation, away from beautiful men who always seemed to know *exactly* what to say, away from the first thing he had wanted in a very long time, but couldn't allow himself to have.

He wondered if Emrys was comfortable. His room was spacious, though he had very few personal belongings. Having an unexpected guest made him glad that he'd kept it clean, a lingering side effect from living under Mother Mabel's roof. He imagined Emrys rummaging through his drawers, searching for any hint of Senna in the space. But there was nothing to find. The only thing that was truly *his* was the bed—and even that would smell like Emrys come morning.

Held captive by an image of Emrys' bare skin tangled up in his sheets, Senna didn't notice the door swing open behind him.

Percy made it two steps into the hallway before jolting back. Senna, steadfast and numb to surprises, remained perfectly still. The prince's eyes fluttered behind his favorite glasses—the ones that rested the most comfortably on his face but, in his royal opinion, didn't do his nose any favors. His shirt was open to the fourth button, half tucked into his fine trousers, leaving a ducktail drooping down his leg.

Senna waited expectantly for the question that would surely come, but Percy said nothing as he swept past and disappeared down the hallway.

With a sigh, Senna sank to the floor. Reeling from the kiss, he hadn't had time to ponder how he'd make up his failure to Percy. He supposed he could have asked Emrys what he thought, but Senna could guess what he'd say: *You've given him your entire life! What more can you possibly do?*

In truth, Senna didn't know if there was more to give. Not if Percy couldn't accept his apology.

As sudden and shrill as a stroke of lightning, a tray dropped over Senna's lap.

Percy fell to the space beside Senna with a *plop*, arms crossing over his knees. He nodded down at the tray.

"All of your favorites. Cream custard tarts, sticky pudding, and a slice of honey cake," he said scientifically, pointing out each sweet as if he were a teacher labeling bones in the body. "The tea is to my liking, but I suspect you only take yours black because you think it is too much luxury to add the cream and sugar. Believe me, it is worth the effort."

To prove his point, Percy sipped from one of the teacups and sighed.

"Yes, that is quite the thing," he stated.

Senna couldn't help but feel like he was looking at a different version of Percy than the one he'd spent the day gallivanting around the Talsuran forests with. His friend noticed him looking, because he nodded down at the tray and said, "If I've misjudged your tastes, I'm happy to make a second trip."

"What is this?" asked Senna, uneasy.

"It's an apology," answered Percy, as if it was obvious. He met Senna's gaze from above the rims of his glasses. "Eat, Goldheart." To anyone else, it would have sounded like an order. But there were enough hints in the command of the *brother* and *friend* version of Percy—the *real* Percy—that Senna knew it wasn't an official command.

Senna took a bite of the honey cake first, shoulders drooping in relief at the first break through the gooey, almond-encrusted upper-layer. He let the flavors sit on his tongue for a long second, washing the bite down with a sip of tea.

". . . Well?" Percy pressed.

Senna swirled the tea, lips tilted up into a smile. "Far too rich."

"More for me, then," Percy scoffed, collecting the cup from Senna's grasp and gulping it all down in a few hearty mouthfuls. It was only when the cup was drained that Percy seemed to realize he had taken what was *supposed* to be Senna's apology tea.

He smiled sheepishly. "Let me go down to the kitchens and pour you a new cup the way you like it."

But before he could, Senna reached over to Percy's cup and repeated the crime—only, instead of a sigh of satisfaction at tea well consumed, Senna grimaced.

"Now we're even," he said, coughing through the last swallow.

The foolish ordeal reminded Senna of distant days, when the only things Percy had worried about had been good-humored jokes and sneaking around the castle without getting caught. But that was all it was—a reminder. Because Percy's smile, amused as it was at bantering like old times, was stained with the troubles of the day. It only lingered on Percy's face for a few seconds, before sinking into a frown. He slumped against the wall.

"Actually, we're not even." He gestured vaguely at the tray of royal desserts. "This is my way of procrastinating the actual apology that I planned in my room with Elora. I finally worked up the nerve to give it to you when I found you sitting here." He paused, brows furrowing. "Why *are* you sitting here? Where's Emrys?"

"You mean *Prince* Emrys?" Senna deadpanned.

"Ah," Percy said sheepishly. "I owe you two apologies, then."

Senna shook his head. "It wasn't my business and you did well to respect his wish for privacy. But I . . ."

"You were surprised."

"That's one way of putting it."

Percy twisted so that he could face Senna directly, something he did when he was trying desperately to wrangle his focus.

"I understand that I've acted dastardly to you today and I would not blame you if you remained cross at me for a full eternity, but I'd like to ask you something. I hope that you answer honestly." Then, added as an afterthought, "But I don't require that you do. It is my *hope* that you'd still trust me to regard you with respect and care, enough that you'll feel comfortable—"

"You can ask the question," Senna cut in patiently so Percy didn't ramble himself into a panic.

Percy's expression scrunched in on itself.

"I really ought to give you a proper apology first. Do you think this is another form of procrastinating? You *can* hold me accountable for my behav—"

"*Percy.*"

"Oh, blessed be—Are you in love with Emrys?" Percy said exasperatedly. "Because I watched you both today and it seems to me like there's *something* there. Up until recently, I had rather thought you were the sort of fellow who wasn't disposed to romance, but . . ." Percy shrugged. "You look at Emrys the same way you looked at the sunny side of the Dam all those years ago. Like he—he's taken a weight off your chest. So, I only thought . . ."

Senna dug his nails into his thumb, rather at a loss for words.

Did he love Emrys?

He'd never been able to tear his attention away from Emrys—even when Emrys had been only a few witty words on a page. Something in the way he walked around as if he trusted the world had put Senna on edge. Now, it occurred to Senna that perhaps the unease had been envy that he could not do the same. How close he'd come to letting that jealousy fester. The only reason it hadn't was because—well, because of Emrys.

Emrys, who had taken Senna out into the world time and time again, each new experience like a gift gracefully given. Stranger yet, Senna had *let* him. He'd gone against everything he'd believed and allowed Emrys to make him inflorescent. Not out of curiosity, but because when Emrys had said it would be a good thing, Senna had believed him. He trusted Emrys enough to *speak* to him—easily, with words that had long since been stored away, not to be unearthed or witnessed. And Emrys hadn't touched any of Senna's confessions; instead, he'd listened.

But Emrys *had* touched Senna. Emrys had taken his hand and held it over his heart, letting Senna count the pulse underneath. He'd kissed Senna as the Prince of Redwind—fearless, because he was brave enough to seize what he wanted. More than that, Emrys had kissed him because he'd known it was what they both wanted.

But did Senna *love* him?

He licked his lips. "Why do you ask?"

"Because I'm your best friend and I want you to be happy," Percy answered easily. His expression was earnestly curious, like he was prepared to sit against this wall all night until his friend finally gave his answer.

"I don't know," Senna answered, finally.

Percy hummed thoughtfully. He inched forward, taking Senna's hand between both of his. "That isn't a no."

Senna looked into his lap. He supposed it wasn't.

"What's holding you back? It isn't—It isn't *me* is it? Tell me you're not holding back on my account," Percy pressed. "You are allowed to have your own life, Sen. I rather prefer that you do."

"I do have my own life." The response burst out of Senna before he could process that the words were on his tongue. "There's nothing wrong with the life I've chosen."

"That's the rub, Sen. You didn't choose it." Percy smiled sadly. "Maybe you'd choose it now, after knowing how you and I would be, but you didn't choose it at first. Not at the beginning." Senna heard the unspoken words: *Not when we were both children.*

"None of us can change the past," said Senna. It was what he told himself when he let himself imagine too closely how his life could have looked if he hadn't been chosen as the goldheart.

"I know. The only thing we have any sort of control over is the here and now. It makes my behavior today all the more unacceptable."

"Percy—"

"No, please let me speak. I've put it off long enough," he insisted. "You have to understand, it's been so long since I felt *this* terrible. I'm afraid I laid all of that on you. I'm terribly sorry, Senna."

There was no reality in which Senna could stay sour at Percy forever. Really, he'd forgotten about his own frustration when Emrys had kissed him. For this, he said, "It happens so rarely, I think you're allowed a pass."

Percy tenderly pulled their joined hands until they were resting on his thigh. They sat that way for a long moment, as if letting their friendship and the feeling of being together again equilibrate. Senna felt like he did the rare times he went swimming in the sea—a few careful steps, wading into waist-high water. A quick bite of cold. Then, the rightness of being submerged in a good thing.

Without Senna realizing, Percy had laid his head on Senna's shoulder, still holding their hands together.

"You really like him, don't you? Emrys?" Percy clarified quietly, though he didn't have to.

The urge to lie was at the tip of Senna's tongue, equipped and ready to strike. But if he could not be truthful to Percy, then who?

"I do like him," Senna agreed, somewhat miserably. He liked that careless Redwindan prince and his crooked smiles and his eagerness to feel and live.

"What will you do about it?"

There was no precedent for something like this. Senna couldn't remember the last time he'd ever felt so drawn to someone. There had been, of course, flitting attractions, granted only to the starry-eyed, handsome knights that Senna could bring into his dreams without guilt—and rarely, his bed. But he'd never let someone sneak past his defenses and earn the affection he so rarely entrusted with anyone. The only person who had successfully made a home in his heart was Percy, but the love there was different, and there was no chance of him leaving.

But Emrys . . . Not even the kingdom's most canny scholars could sum or cipher a way to let two guards from cutthroat lands be together.

Senna let his head fall on Percy's with a small sigh.

"I will allow one night to feel sorry for myself, and then I will readjust my focus onto our task," he said.

The answer did little to please Percy, though they'd done enough arguing today to make him press the issue. "After that?"

"Nothing."

Senna paused. He nearly asked Percy if he'd be alright after reliving his worst childhood fear. But he could imagine the way the prince's shoulders would sag, the fear falling over his eyes like a storm-blown thundercloud.

No—it was best to seize the modicum of peace while they still had it, eating sweets and pretending the entire world around them did not exist.

E ACH OF THE TWENTY-SIX candles that lit Senna's quarters were blown out when he returned some hours later.

He'd put off returning long enough. He had only allowed himself the comfort of Percy's company for the half-hour chime of the hallway's clock before sending him back into the arms of the woman who was waiting for him. He'd originally planned to bring the extra sweets to Emrys, who was sure to be hungry after a long day of traveling, but the thought of returning to the room had made it difficult to speak, even to Percy. So he'd finished off the sweets and walked around the castle's perimeter with a sugar-induced stomachache.

It was only when his own limbs were heavy, each step a thousand tons, that Senna ventured back to his quarters.

As quietly as he could, Senna snapped a flame into his fingers. Brushing the thumb against the tips of the other fingers on the same hand, he spread the flame so the light it shed was brighter. In its orange glow, he could make out Emrys lying on his stomach, his shirtless back rising and falling with the torpid speed of sleep. Situated on the left edge of the bed, he'd left an expanse of empty space on the right.

But Senna couldn't trust himself. The temptation to rouse Emrys awake with his lips and curl around his warm body would only fester in these conditions—sleep-deprived, touch-starved, and drowning in darkness.

So he moved onto the small balcony and brushed dirt and dust off of his iron frame bench. It could not boast that it was beautiful or comfortable, but Senna sat down anyway, leaning his head on the brick of the outer castle walls. Blearily, he peered out over the little he could see of Talsura, lamps going out one by one throughout the city streets. Then, he let his gaze slip to the Dam.

In the safety of his mind, the exterior of the Dam—the side he couldn't see— was washed with white lunar brightness. In its silver glow, he imagined Redwind in the distance and the open moorland teeming with cricket song. Then, he remembered Emrys' song, imagined it lulling all the land's creatures to sleep.

When sleep at last overcame him, that was where he was—in a field of moon-white roses, with nothing but open sky above him and Emrys' song on the air.

The only indication that morning ever came was the growing glow of lantern lights and magical lamps—arriving in slow, blooming flickers as quietly as they'd gone. It was nothing like waking up in Mount Livia to a face full of sunshine.

Stirring awake, Senna realized that the usual outside chill of Talsura's nights had never settled on him because someone had covered him with a blanket.

Emrys.

Wrapping the blanket around his shoulders, he padded silently into the room, heart pounding.

Emrys was gone. In his place, a folded note waited for Senna on his own cold pillow.

Until next time, Goldheart.

Part
Three

A CATHEA GRAY LEARNED WHAT she knew about nesting by watching the birds. During the long days of the exile, Thea had chosen to keep her eyes fixed to the young skylarks to keep herself from staring at those who were dying. The skylarks fascinated Thea as they picked up spare straw and strings to meticulously build their nests in the treetops above.

In the abandoned foundations of the Redwind Orphanage, Thea was a bird who had a nest of her own. It was as humble as it was precarious, but she was proud of what she'd been able to accomplish with the spare planks of wood and tools that the builders had left behind. Sometimes, when passersby walked too close to the half-built orphanage where Acathea lived, she thought the architects had returned. But they'd arrived one day and realized that everyone at the orphanage had died, even Mister MacBennal. Thea had watched them pack their tools and leave. They hadn't noticed Thea hiding in the wood piles, nor the hammer and nails they'd left behind.

Thea's burrow was situated in the back corner of the open room, underneath the unfinished stairs. She managed to hammer the wooden planks together to look somewhat like a rowboat. Then, over the poky, unfinished edges, she laid forgotten clothes and blankets she'd found in the street. She'd even managed to swipe a pillow off the back of someone's carriage. It wasn't much, but it kept her dry and nearly warm.

She was tucked neatly in her burrow under a bloodstained quilt when she heard voices from the skeleton doorframe.

"I can't fathom why the project isn't complete already," said a woman's voice. "I was assured that the building wouldn't take more than a few days to assemble. Where's the orphan father and the children?"

"I've heard rumors that they died," replied a masculine voice.

"What about the children orphaned every day by the sun sickness? Did the builders truly think that they didn't need to complete the work I hired them to do because there was no one here?"

"I'm not sure. Seems that way."

"There's no telling how long this structure has been exposed in the rain like this. It's possible new builders will have to eradicate any faults to the structural integrity before the new foundation can be raised."

"I'll contact the builders this afternoon, Your Majesty."

Thea made a tiny chirping sound in surprise. The *queen* was here? And she wanted to *tear the building down*?

"Did you hear that, Hezra?"

Hezra paused. "Afraid not, Your Majesty."

Thea shifted lower to keep the top of her head out of sight. The nest's wood creaked under her weight. She flinched.

"Over there. In the corner."

"It's probably just a stray cat taking shelter from the rain."

"Maybe," Queen Casta assented. "But I have a feeling..."

The queen's steps approached. There was nowhere to hide. In a last-ditch effort, she dove underneath her blankets and curled up in one corner of her hollow. A shiver erupted up Thea's spine as she felt the queen's gaze heavy on her through the thin fabric.

"It's a child," Hezra blurted. Casta shushed him.

"Hello there," she said. Her tone lifted, airy and light, but Thea didn't know why. "We see your little feet. Do you want to come out from underneath there? Maybe we could find you some shoes."

Thea didn't dare move. With painstaking delicacy, the queen drew back the cold blankets from Thea's shoulder. Thea gathered enough courage to peek through her squeezed eyes and found the queen kneeling close by. Even in the dark, she was very pretty. The man, Hezra, was a foot or two away, nervously rubbing his downy beard.

"This is quite the hiding place you have. Who made it for you?"

Thea covered her mouth with the quilt. "I did. I'm a bird."

The queen and Hezra shared a surprised look. Queen Casta's face was difficult for Thea to make sense of.

"Even little birdies have parents," the queen said. "Have yours already flown the nest?"

A twinge of pain bloomed in Thea's chest like a thorn. "They died."

In the silence between them, Thea was sure the queen would scold her. Mother Mable always had, even when Thea hadn't been sure why. But the queen didn't raise her voice.

She offered a hand to Thea, helping her stand up. The clouds had parted, shedding a patch of yellow sunlight on the unfinished floor. Thea's head swam, but the queen held her upright and steady.

"What's your name, child?"

"Acathea."

"When was the last time you ate something, Acathea?"

Thea shrugged. She couldn't remember.

The queen muttered something Thea couldn't hear to her companion. He fumbled in his bag, pulling out a canister. With a gentle smile, the queen poured water into her hands and smoothed it over Thea's face. Drops of brown and red slipped onto the ground.

"I'm very impressed that you've been so brave on your own. Are you here to avoid the sunlight?"

Thea cupped her hands out for water, drinking when they were full. The water was heaven on her parched throat.

"No," Thea answered, speaking more smoothly. "The sun doesn't make me sick."

The adults exchanged another look.

"At all? Not even a tiny clover or a little snowdrop?" the queen pressed.

Thea nodded obediently.

"It's not unheard of," Hezra said. "Phaedra chose her son's goldheart from the Talsuran orphanage. They say he's immune too."

Thea hadn't thought about herself being immune from the sun sickness. She rather thought she was just a girl nothing wanted anything to do with—good or bad. She especially didn't think she'd be the type of person a queen would want to talk to.

"Acathea," the queen said slowly. "Do you know what a princess is?"

Thea flicked her fingers over and over. "The daughter of a royal? In a castle? With a tiara?"

"Well done." The queen tried to meet Thea's gaze, but she darted her eyes around. "Would you like to be a princess?"

Thea flicked even harder. That was a strange question. If a princess was the daughter of a royal and Thea's parents were dead, how could she *be* a princess?

"You're not my mother," she said, confused.

"Sometimes mothers and daughters choose each other."

Thea pursed her lips. "So I get to . . . choose?"

The queen nodded.

Thea had never been able to choose anything in her life. Usually Mother Mabel or Mister Macbennal chose things for her—her clothes, how much food she got to eat, when they took out the warm quilts in the wintertime. Thea didn't know her queen. But she supposed the other queens she'd read about in storybooks were nice more often than not. Being a princess would be nice and all, but having a *mother* . . .

"Okay," Thea said softly. "You can be my mum."

Queen Casta reached out then—not to hit her or grab her hair, but to *hold* her.

In the warmth of the queen's arms, face nestled into the softness of her shoulder, Thea imagined that all of her bird's feathers were molting. One after another, revealing the little girl underneath. On her fresh skin, she'd wear pretty dresses and take bubble baths. She'd lie in her mother's bed and listen to her read stories.

"You know," Queen Casta said, "you have a brother. And this man here is my close friend."

Thea snuggled even closer. A *brother*. A brother, a mother, a Hezra, a home.

THEA

THEA WAS GOING TO have to send for a tonic for the ache in her back. If Nare was here, she'd likely tell Thea to take a break from hunching over the table and let someone else have a turn with the journal's magical ward. But Nare was snoring away in her room, loud enough to be heard from the side door.

Thea didn't think sleep would find her until she figured out how to open Laurentine's journal. She squinted down at it in the peachy morning light filtering through the window and the library's trees. The glasses they'd retrieved from Cevyn—now washed and polished—sat a little too tight on Thea's face to be comfortable. Yet she refused to take them off until she found something.

Through the glasses, the world was awash in orange and pink light. It was obvious what they'd been enchanted to do—show the wearer things that were there, but could not be seen through the unmagical eye. From her arched position at the library table, Thea had already seen magical sprites flittering around the treetops and spirits like smoke billowing from particularly old books. Besides other people's inflorescence, it was the closest thing to magic that Thea had gotten to experience firsthand. She was drunk on it, eager for more.

At first, she had imagined that *she'd* be the one to unlock the journal, all alone in this library without anyone's assistance. She'd torn off in a chase, desperately trying to turn her daydream into reality. That desire had quickly died when she'd looked at Laurentine's journal and seen nothing.

Drawing in a thin breath, Thea gingerly took the glasses off her face. What was she doing wrong? She huffed a hot breath across the orange lens, then rubbed the fog away with the skirt of her dress. The glasses were no more comfortable, nor any clearer, when she deposited them back onto her head.

She'd done everything she could think of—attempting to open the journal outright, uttering the words *"open please,"* and looking for some type of magical lock to unhook. Her pitiful knowledge of magical anything had finally caught up to her.

Mumbling out a curse, Thea straightened up and rolled her shoulders. Losing faith, she lifted the journal in a grumpy hand and flipped it upside down.

Her chair jerked forward, the legs scraping on the floor equally as loud as her startled shriek. She stopped short of her stomach ramming into the edge of the desk, though now her back was aligned with the chair's wooden spokes.

"You can fuck up your back all you want, just not in my library," Nare said, appearing over her shoulder. "Never met a princess with such shitty posture, and I have to say, I'm delighted."

"Laugh all you want," Thea snapped, though it lost its bite as she stretched her arms out, and subsequently her words. "I had half a notion to tear my spine right out of my back, but I thought bloodstained floors would be garish alongside the walnut molding."

A surprised chuckle bubbled out of Nare.

"I do try to keep violence out of my library, though I'm afraid library *injuries* are not as easy to dodge."

Thea's brows knit together. "What trouble could you possibly encounter in a library? Do the books fly off the shelves and strike you when you nod off?"

"Have you forgotten that our first meeting included a near miss with a bow and arrow?"

Actually, Thea *had* forgotten. These past two months of spending days in Nare's company had cast an easy cloud over the memory of their first meeting. Nare had spoken her joke in the spirit of their usual banter, but it drew Thea's attention to something peculiar happening under her ribs—a painful urgency that almost throbbed. It worsened with a single glance at Nare's toothy grin.

"Canons, you look sour," Nare grumbled. "If your back was hurting you so badly, you should've spoken up."

Thea was about to brush off the pain, when Nare's sturdy hands pressed firmly into her shoulder blades. A rush of relief edged in tingling gooseflesh sparked under Nare's touch, causing Thea to melt into it.

"Not just anyone can simply walk up and touch the princess," she sighed, desperately trying to sound annoyed, and failing.

"Oh, I know." Nare dug her thumbs into the tight knotted muscle and pressed with the brunt of her whole weight.

Thea pushed back against the force, eyes slipping closed in pain-edged relief. The castle's healers had pressed knots out in her back before, but they'd never elicited the tingling sparks at the base of her spine. Nare had to be using some type of magic.

"You didn't rest very long. Are you sure you don't want to go back to sleep?" Thea breathed forcefully.

"I could feel you fuming through the walls. Are the glasses giving you that much trouble?"

Nare's hands were lighter now. Touch for touch's sake. Strangely, Thea let her continue.

"I can feel myself on the verge of a breakthrough, but I can't quite get over the precipice."

Nare snorted.

"Damn, you really haven't been touched in some time, have you?"

Thea knit her brows together. Why did Nare say that all of the sudden? She replayed the last thing she'd said in her mind, realizing several seconds too late how suggestive the statement sounded. Clinging to the last shreds of her pride, Thea set her jaw and fixed her gaze to the journal.

"That's *not* what I—" Nare's hand trailed down the length of her spin, causing her to shiver. "No, evidently not."

Nare's touch lifted away and she sat backward in the chair at Thea's right.

"Give 'em here," she said, fingers grabbing in the direction of the glasses. Thea fixed her with a dirty look. "Don't take it personally, princess. If you're fallow, then it's possible nothing you try will work."

Thea was bloody tired of being fallow, but she rather expected Nare had guessed as much, so she handed the glasses over and shrank back in her chair.

If the glasses were tight on Thea's face, they looked even more ridiculous on Nare.

"It's not my fault Laurentine had the realm's smallest head" she grumbled, then lifted the journal squarely in front of her eyes. The features of Nare's face were not delicate to begin with, but the withering stare she fixed at the book would frighten a dre'malor into submission. Finally, A low hum rumbled from her throat. "Laurie, you absolute pain in the ass."

"You don't see anything, right?" Thea pressed eagerly.

"No, there's something. I bet you could see it if you looked really hard. Give it another gander."

In a second, both journal and glasses passed hands once more. Thea, predispositioned to distrust her own abilities, at first did not note any difference through the amber lenses. The high walls of the glasses prevented Thea from seeing Nare lean closer, but she still sensed her hot breath on her ear—a warm invitation to be curious and to discover.

"I don't see anything," Thea griped. Nare clicked her teeth in disapproval.

"Turn the book on its side," Nare instructed. Thea gingerly followed orders. "You're not going to hurt the thing, I swear. All I want you to do is look very, *very* closely at the fore edge. Yes, the edge where the book opens. There are hundreds of thin little magical strands all tangled together."

Thea frowned, an objection halfway out of her mouth, but Nare placed an encouraging hand on her shoulder.

"They're hard to see because the pages pressed together make thin lines of their own. You have to look past them for tangled threads, like the hair of a ghost. Look for curves and intersections, something that doesn't look quite right."

Thea wanted to tell Nare that she'd seen a ghost's hair during spirit visits amid the exile and *this* was hardly a worthy comparison, but—

Just there—a single wavy strand, its end caught somewhere against another thin strand, which was tangled up with another, unceasingly. Thea traced the mess and watched the magical threads move, though her finger felt only air and the edges of the uneven pages.

"The lock is the tangle of threads?" Thea said in awe. She stripped off the glasses to find Nare's smile both impressed and exhausted in equal measure.

"Sure is. If we want to crack this journal's secrets, we have to detangle each of them. And if I know Laurentine, we'll need to make sure they're *all* untangled. Leaving a handful to rip open by force won't do it."

Brute force was something Thea hadn't even considered, but then, she and Nare were rarely on the same page.

"That's why we needed the glasses. We won't be able to see and untangle the threads without them," Nare continued. "I had expected some type of ward, something would just need a quick counterspell, but this is another beast entirely."

"You make counterspells sound so easy," said Thea, leaning on her elbows.

"For me, or any other Academe, it's a walk in the bloody park." Nare slumped in her chair, like a puppet whose master had dropped her strings. "I know you wanted the book opened quickly, but this is going to take forever. Like, literally forever. We will be bones in the ground still untangling these strands."

Thea's stomach dropped.

"Is it really as bad as all that?"

Nare pouted and gave a single shoulder shrug.

"No," she grumbled. "I merely hate things that take a long time."

Thea's eyes glinted. "Things like building a library from scratch?"

"Oh, shut it, you," Nare said, bumping Thea's shoulder. Her joking demeanor slipped off her face like a mask. She laid a hand on Thea's knee, strong and firm.

Nare cleared her throat. "Listen, Thee. I wondered what you thought of the idea of me and—"

"Acathea," called a voice from the doorway.

Recognition hit Thea and Nare like the sky was falling down. Thea shot to her feet, quickly looking down at her dress to see if any of the endless twill tiers were out of sorts. Nare looked around frantically at the utter mess that was the Redwind Library, only to straighten her back to accept her fate.

Standing completely still in the threshold, Queen Casta could have been mistaken for her own royal portrait. Someone who didn't know better would not have guessed how young Casta's reign was by looking at her—pin-straight back and a demeanor of regality that would part the seas if she so much as uttered a command.

Thea lowered herself in a curtsy that would have made her tutors weep in pride.

"Hello, Your Majesty," she said evenly.

Behind her, Nare made a throaty noise so unladylike that it would have made Thea's tutors weep for an entirely different reason. As discreetly as she could, Thea tossed Nare a wordless message—something to the tune of, *What's wrong with you? Greet the damn queen!*

"Welcome to the library, Your Majesty," Nare murmured, blushing.

"Thea, I'd like to speak with you." A glance at the librarian. "Privately, if you please."

Thea gnawed her lip, praying to whatever worthless canon could hear her that Nare wouldn't put up a fight about being thrown out of her own library. And she supposed miracles had to happen eventually, because Nare snatched some loose parchment from the table without even so much as a dirty glare.

"I, uh, better write to our friends. Percy will be wanting to know—" She glanced at the journal, then nervously at the queen. "That you're indisposed."

With one fortifying nod at Thea, she disappeared back into her quarters.

The door had barely clicked shut when Casta said, "Acathea, I don't need to remind you what your expectations are in terms of your marriage."

She really, really didn't, but had somehow managed to work a reminder in nonetheless. As if Thea could ever forget the day her mother had taken her aside when her menses started and made Thea promise she would marry someone of high status. She'd held Thea's bloody rags in one hand, Thea's shoulder in the other, and told her that it was alright if she started to fall in love with people, so long as they were "suitable."

At the time, Thea was practically still an orphan, dreaming of marrying some far-off princess somewhere. It wasn't until she'd grown some that she had come to understand her mother had manipulated a child into signing away her own freedom.

But why would her mother remind Thea of that agreement *now*? Unless . . .

"It isn't like that with Nare," Thea said, swallowing in a pitiful attempt to keep her voice steady. Vaguely, she wondered if this was what Goldheart Kane felt like all the time.

Casta stepped into the room, her own guard closing the library door behind her. Sometimes Thea forgot there even *were* real guards. So often they blended into the scenery of the castle, soundless statues.

"Emrys should be here with you," said the queen.

"I was not aware I needed a chaperone to speak with a librarian in a library."

"I was not aware you had suddenly taken to the academic arts. I suppose it is *academic support* when she places her hand on your knee and looks longingly in your eyes."

Stomach roiling, Thea suddenly wished Emrys *was* here after all. He had a way of softening the weapons of Casta's words—something about being her first, and only, born. But there were just two doors in this library and her mother was blocking the exit.

Casta sensed her panic—frustratingly, as she always did. She was, after all, a mother. In three long strides, she took a seat at the main table. Only, instead of choosing Nare's seat, still pulled out at Thea's side, she situated herself at the other end of the table.

Thea refused to sit.

"I'm only trying to save you the heartache of having to give up an unsuitable choice when the time comes."

A response was fast to the tip of Thea's tongue about how she was starting to sound like Percy's mom—manipulative and calculating—but then her mother's words caught up with her racing mind.

"When the time comes for what?"

Confusion flashed across Casta's face—the pull of her brows, a few shallow blinks, a twisted frown—but it disappeared instantly.

"For the transition of power," she said plainly.

Thea blinked. "The what?"

Casta shook her head gently, folding her hands before her.

"I'm sorry darling, I thought you knew. It's rather my fault for not being as forthright as I should have been, but I thought surely one of your instructors had informed you of our—our intention for your future. Forgive me."

"Tell me now," Thea said, voice fragile. Then, remembering herself, she added, "Please."

Hope burned Thea's knuckles white as she clutched the edge of her chair, but she could not read her mother's expression.

"In three years, your time as princess will conclude and Emrys will ascend to his rightful position. By then you'll both be thirty years old, so the transition is only natural."

It was as though one of the library's tall, ancient trees split the ground with a mighty root and sent Thea plummeting—down, down, everlastingly down.

"We will, of course, mitigate the damage of the surprise to our people as best we can. We will first announce Emrys' rightful claim, then you will 'abdicate' the throne to him, wanting to pursue personal passions." The queen said *abdicate* like it was some fictional thing and not the violent slaughter of everything Thea had ever dreamt for. "Your occupation will transition from *royal* to *nobility*, and if you wish it, *wife*."

"Occupation?" Thea choked out.

Casta blinked. "Sweetheart, that's what this is. Your occupation."

The back of Thea's throat began to burn—worse than the time she'd been sick and tasted bile and acid for hours. Worse than the night she'd gotten her finger stuck in hot wax trying to write a letter to Percy. But she refused to cry. Princesses didn't cry. It wasn't in the *occupational description*, she thought bitterly.

"There is no room for negotiation in this plan?" Thea wondered, eyes stuck to the center of the table.

"Negotiation for what? Among the noblewomen, you will be regarded with the utmost respect. Your residence will be royally guarded and you'll possess a large enough dowry to secure a marriage with any dignified lady of your choosing. What else could you want for?"

A real purpose. A *mother*.

How had Thea gone nearly eighteen years disillusioned that Casta was her mother? Was the queen playing a part? Thea couldn't recall all the times she'd gone to Casta for comfort, for council. It was *real* to Thea.

"After all the tutoring I received, would I not be an aid to Emrys as princess? Second to his command, of course. No one knows the trials of being in that station as acutely as I do."

"That sort of aid would be best provided by a family member."

Thea put a hand on her chest. It was distinctly possible that her heart had stopped working. That she would never draw a breath again.

"I thought you'd gladly receive this news," Casta said gently.

Thea slipped into the tumultuous storms of her mind to take stock of how she was feeling. But even with a mind of chaos and tossing waves, Thea could not feel anything. She was perfectly, utterly numb.

"I do gladly receive it," Thea managed to say. It was a miracle she hadn't vomited all over the hardwood table. She cleared her throat. "Forgive my impudence. Is—Is that what you came to tell me?"

"No. There are other prevailing matters at hand." Casta folded her fingers across the table. "I'd like you to tell me where Emrys is."

Like navigating a mountain of fog, it took Thea several long seconds to orient herself. To hear and comprehend the question.

There was no use in lying—Casta had eyes everywhere and surely knew the truth already—but Thea couldn't disclose the full truth either.

"He's visiting Percy and Goldheart Kane in Talsura. I expect him back any moment," she explained stiffly.

"Is that where he ran off before? When he was gone for two days?"

She was, of course, referring to the days Emrys and Senna had gone to Mount Livia. The days when Emrys had nearly died. But the first lie made this one easier, so she said, "Yes."

"Alright," Casta said evenly.

"That's it? You're not going to ask what he's doing there?"

"It isn't your fault that Emrys is struggling with notions of independence. It wouldn't be fair to ask you to disclose your guard's secrets. Besides, I've seen the way that he looks at Goldheart Kane. One doesn't need a royal education to guess what he's doing in Talsura."

Thea nearly squeezed her eyes shut in relief. The very last thing she could do right now was admit they were risking their well-beings on some quest that—apparently—was pointless.

"I merely wanted to ensure he was safe and you were the only one who would know," Casta concluded.

The bitter taste of acidic rust grew on Thea's tongue. It was only when she recoiled against it that she realized she'd gnawed through the inside of her cheek. Queen Casta had only come to ensure that her *son* was safe. She didn't care about seeing Thea, talking to her, hearing about her new friendship with Nare.

"He is safe," Thea said, swallowing back the blood. "When he's with Senna, he is always safe."

That same expression of disapproval soured Casta's face.

"I know that this life is not what either of you had expected. But we've been here for two decades now. It is our reality. You'd both do well to remember what your future may and may not possess." Casta lifted herself from the table with very little effort at all. "I hope to see you *and* Emrys at dinner this evening."

When Thea's vision cleared, Queen Casta was gone.

Distantly, she hoped she remembered to say goodbye, because she could not remember anything from the last several minutes. In truth, she could have been standing there for another three years, three decades, minutes away from the end of her life, and she would not have known.

But once reality set in, it fell over Thea in a deluge. She felt like she was underwater, unable to draw breath that wouldn't drown her. Her legs gave out, and she crumpled to the floor. Tearing with all her strength, she clawed at her bodice until the fabric relinquished under the attack. Sharp nails met her skin, shredding over and over until she bled. Tears spilled down her cheeks, coming out her nose and gathering at the base of her chin. One of them dripped into the open wound over her collarbone, burning with the salt.

Distantly, Thea realized that the last time she had cried this hard, all the children in her orphanage had died of sun sickness. This must've been how you wept when you lost a family, she thought—raw, wide open.

Behind her, the door swung inward. Thea squeezed her eyes shut, clinging to the rungs of her chair to stay upright.

"I know portal scrolls cost a barrel of canon's piss to buy, but can we not invest in *some* if we're going to be making this journey every fucking week?" cried Emrys, barreling into the room with a wild wave of his hands. "Please tell me you figured out how to open that—"

Thea looked up, barely able to see Emrys noticing her on the ground in a heap of fabric and tears. He fell to her side so hard he had to have skinned his knees.

"*Canons*, Thea, what on earth is the matter? Come now, come here."

For a brief second, Thea forgot it all and let Emrys bundle her into his arms, pushing her head where it fit on his shoulder. He rocked her like *she* was the younger one, shushing into her hair. Thea was sure she was staining his shirt with her blood, but couldn't get the words out to warn him.

The words she did manage were all spittle and devastation.

"*Momma*," she cried. "She doesn't love me, Emrys."

Emrys pulled her back, hands fully cupping her face.

"*What?* What gave you such a silly notion?"

Thea's face crumpled.

"She said . . . She . . ."

Thea dropped her chin.

"Whatever it is, we'll figure it out together," Emrys swore. "You're my sister. I'm not going to let anything hurt you. Alright? Just—tell me what's wrong."

Thea shook her head, the motion making her dizzy.

"I'm not your sister," she murmured.

"What are you talking about?"

"All I am to you is a hired actor. My whole life is a bloody stage, Emrys, and you're the leading man. Congratulations. A dozen thrown white *royal* roses to the star of the show."

"Thea—"

"Get away from me," she hissed. "This is all just pretend. It's a *fucking game.*"

Emrys was stunned enough that Thea was able to push herself up and away without him keeping hold. She fell onto the table, catching herself with sweaty, flat hands.

"All of this," she shrieked, waving wildly at the table of research and the glasses. "It's all wasted time. It was never going to work in the first place and we should have never deluded ourselves that we'd actually *accomplish* anything. I won't ever be princess, not even if I stop death itself. And when you're king, you won't care a fucking bit about this kingdom or its people or restoring any sort of goodwill with Talsura. All you care about is yourself and your pathetic romance with a man you can't have. Then we'll *both* be failures. How about that?"

The caring, comforting brother was gone, vanished as if he had never been there in the first place. His body turned to icy stone.

"What a fucking thing to say," he spat. "You don't know anything about me or Senna or about what I think. About what I *want*. You're so busy trying to be mother's perfect little princess that you never can spare any mind for anyone else. You think anyone believes you were helping us out of the kindness of your heart? You've *never* had a selfless motive."

"Oh please," Thea laughed bitterly. "You wouldn't know what selflessness looked like if it wrapped around your throat and grew thorns."

Like a thunder gall, he rushed into her space, peering right into her eyes. The Emrys of ten years ago—the one with anger in his veins and ire in his voice—had fully taken over. But Thea was well acquainted with him. She refused to back down.

"You listen, Acathea. I *won't* be king. But if I was, Redwind would rejoice that they'd finally gotten rid of their cold, heartless princess."

The only thing that stopped her from slapping him was his tight grip on her wrist. Instead, she inched forward, filling her breath with all of her pain, all the wrong that had ever been done to her.

"Then Redwind doesn't need me to save it, does it?" she said as low as death.

She reached down, grabbed Laurentine's constellation glasses, and hurled them across the room. Amber glass shattered, raining in fiery fragments along the floor. She crossed the room in wild strides, coming up to the mess and stomping it with her boot. The metal bent like a deformed root beneath her feet, but Thea relished in the sensation of ruination caused by her own brute strength.

"Have you lost your mind?" Emrys cried. "Percy and Senna almost died to get those glasses!"

She twisted her gaze to the ruins, and smiled to see the metal bent and out of place. But that smile slipped as quickly as it had risen onto her face. The wreckage was as repulsive as it was spellbinding.

"*Oh*," she whimpered. "Oh canons, what have I *done*? *What have I done?*" It might've come out in a scream, but there was no breath in her lungs. The words were forged of heartbroken sincerity as they tumbled out over and over.

Thea tripped over to the pile of broken glass, clawing into it to scoop up the pieces.

Emrys hadn't moved. He merely looked at her with a complicated mix of pity and fury.

"What do I do now?" Thea begged. *"Emrys."*

He shook his head. Of course he didn't know. Because Thea had broken everything beyond repair.

Her legs were carrying her away before she could catch up with her thoughts and the blood roaring in her ears—out the library, down the hallway, knocking into someone without apology. Tearing open a linen closet door, Thea fell inside, beneath the shelves and soaps and towels. On instinct, she inched as far as she could into the corner, drenching herself in shadow and dust.

It was where she belonged. Mother Mabel had told her so when she had been just a girl.

All you're good for is what you can give others. What else would anyone want a dirty thing like you for?

She'd lost count of how many days and nights she'd spent sleeping in the orphanage's linen closet then—starving and hollow.

The wound on her chest burned. It stitched her to the present, forbidding her from slipping into the past. A past, at least, that was over. She rested her head against the dusty wall and counted the seconds between throbs of pain in her scratches.

The door reluctantly cracked open, as if caught on a stray breeze. But towering against the bright hallway was Nare.

On instinct, Thea covered her face with her hands, not wanting Nare to see as it crumpled again. But Nare gently guided the hands into hers and squeezed.

"Not here," she said fiercely. "You're not a thing to be used. You don't belong in the closet."

Thea shook her head.

"You didn't hear," she moaned. "You don't know what I've done."

"I heard. I saw."

"You must hate me."

Nare held out her hand. "Come on, Thea."

Thea let herself be led through the castle. Later, when she remembered this moment, she'd notice how Nare had chosen all the quiet hallways, the ones least traveled. She'd remember how the flowers in the garden smelled so familiar, like home, as Nare guided her through the open gate.

The outside air did not heal all of her open wounds, but it was easier to breathe. It did help her feel things that weren't pain—soft grass beneath her bare feet, cool wind on her marred skin, Nare's steady hand in hers.

They came to a pond, the one beneath the wisteria grove along the back edge of the royal gardens. Thea tried not to think about how, just a few paces away, Oesyth's Grove waited—a place where those desperate for a favor could beg for one.

"I don't want a favor," Thea rambled. "Even if I did, I can't, I'm fallow, I—"

"I'm not here to take you to the grove," Nare promised gently. "I brought you for a swim."

She let go of Thea's hand, but only to slip her shoes off. She stripped her shirt off too, revealing the graceful planes of her flat chest, then stepped into the pond. The water eased up around Nare's waist, inviting and mild.

"When I first started here, I was so angry all the time," Nare explained. "I was still angry at myself for my failures, angry at Talsura for exiling us, angry at the Redwindans for not giving up their books for the library. Then I was angry at myself again for asking them to give up their prized possessions in the first place. My rage felt so *hot* in my chest, that during one of my fits I jumped right into this pond for a modicum of relief."

Nare smiled, holding out her hand.

For the first time since speaking with Casta, Thea felt a hint of herself breaking through. She took Nare's hand.

Together, they fell back into the still water, letting it hold them up. Nare hadn't yet let Thea's hand go. Thea's dress bobbed in the calm waters. Above them, long purple branches caught on the breeze, whispering against each other.

"Aren't you mad?" Thea whispered. "I broke the glasses."

"No, I think you've been holding all that in for a long time. I would've done worse if I was you." Nare turned her head, her hair swirling around her. "I *have* done worse."

To her own surprise, the pond's pleasant chill did cool Thea's anger. It drew away her mind's attention, focusing it on the unexpected sensation. The betrayal and despair were still there, only now they weren't sitting on her lungs and heart.

A tear slid down the side of Thea's cheek. "What are we going to do?"

Nare let her feet touch the bottom of the pond. She reached over and spilled a handful of water over Thea's bloody chest. Then, she grazed her fingertips over the tender skin, uttering the soft words of a healing spell.

"You tell me," she said simply. "The world is all yours."

Thea didn't know if she believed it. But as the wound sealed, skin sewing together in a strange, painless sort of way, she knew that even if the world would not relinquish itself, she would not rest until she had seized what it owed her.

19

PERCY

The roaring in the Alpedis Agora reached an ear-piercing peak. Percy wrinkled his nose against the sound, but a sunburn caused a twinge of pain with each move of his muscles. He held his arm up to his face, trying to ascertain how bad the burn would be, but every time his blurry eyes focused, a shoulder or an elbow jostled him.

An exploding roar of cheers surged through the crowd. Percy couldn't remember what they were here to see—jousting? Fencing?

"I'm getting a little dizzy, Sen. Can we find some shade and something to drink?" The question sounded like it had come from beside Percy, which was strange, since he thought he had been the one who'd spoken. A bead of sweat dripped down into Percy's eye, but he squinted it away and spun around. "Senna?"

Senna was not easy to lose in a crowd, but somehow Percy couldn't find him among these yelling faces.

Tripping over large stones and shifting feet, Percy stumbled over to the first shelter he could find—the Agora of Alpedis. His weight came down hard on the stone stairs, but the surface was cool in the shade. He pressed his palm to the marble, then to his flaming cheeks. Certain he wasn't going to collapse in heat exhaustion, Percy started scanning the crowd for Senna. The goldheart wouldn't let Percy stay alone for long. If he stayed put, Senna would come to him.

Beside him, he heard the unmistakable sound of ice clanking against itself. Percy twisted his face up to find a vendor pouring shimmery red liquid into a group of tankards. A thirst suddenly burned at the back of Percy's throat so profound, he almost thought he tasted blood.

"Would you mind letting me—I'll send coin later. I promise. I promise," he murmured, not quite aware enough to know whether or not the vendor heard the slurred vow. Then he reached up, fingers wrapping dazedly around the tankard. Without sparing a glance for what was inside, Percy clamped his mouth over the goblet and chugged the liquid down.

The first sip came burning like scalded tea, and thick enough to choke on. The chalice slipped out of Percy's fingers, hands grasping at his throat with each lung-burning cough. Splatters of red spackled the white stone, sending Percy into another fit when he realized the taste in his mouth was copper. Blood. He'd been drinking boiling blood.

A hand snatched out, clamping around his throat like a vice, and pulled him to his feet. His ankles scraped the ground, but he found he did not have enough strength to kick himself up or away.

"Sen—Senna!" Percy choked, wringing all the air from his lungs he could manage.

Senna never came.

At first, the arm that held him was bitterly familiar, torn apart like a corpse's, with half-broken items squeezed in between algae-stained bones and rotting muscles. A scream clawed up Percy's throat, caught on the way out when the limb had shifted. Now it was as pale as ivory, nearly luminescent.

Attached to it, a pale face framed by pin-straight black hair stared back at him with eyes as dark as death.

"Don't you know the sentence for stealing is DEATH, boy?"

Percy recoiled as rancid spit and breath hit his senses.

A stream of apologies overflowed out of his mouth with such speed, they lost their consonants, turning into a garble of vowel sounds and agonized wheezing.

"Your father tried to steal what was mine, but you can't TAKE from the CANON OF THIEVES."

A shiver like frozen lake water sluiced down Percy's spine. Jasrath, the detested canon of thieves, grinned in hateful delight. Percy tried to speak, to ask how he could right what had been wronged—he didn't know, no one would tell him; how could he fix things if no one told him what had been done—but his lungs had long since used its last dregs of breath.

"Your goldheart won't be able to save you when I come to settle my debts. He will weep and you will water the soil with your blood." Jasrath pressed a kiss to Percy's forehead, a twisted paternal gesture that made Percy nauseous. "I'll see you in Redwind, Prince—"

"P ERCY."

Pain rippled down Percy's spine as he hurtled backward, his head hitting his bed's hard backboard with a solid *thunk*. Before he could register his own response, his hands felt frantically around his throat and the base of his neck for sharp fingers, for thorns, for blood.

Another hand landed on his hair, combing through the small tangles. The unfamiliarity of it had Percy wrenching back even further, but he barely managed any extra space, legs tangled up in sweat-damp sheets. Tears blurred his vision, and his mind was thick with enough disorientation, that he almost believed the dream hadn't ended—that the hand in his hair belonged to the canon of thieves. But it was too gentle for it to have come from his dreams.

"Senna," he whimpered. Pressing the heels of his hands into his eye sockets, he bit out a curse word. He couldn't remember the last time he'd cursed.

The hand in his hair tightened.

"He's doing his rounds, sweetheart."

Percy didn't realize how quickly he swatted his mother's hand away until he registered a short sting on the back of his palm. He cupped it against his chest, waiting until his vision cleared to finally meet his mother's gaze. He noticed the dark circles under her eyes at once, and felt a guilty surge of justice that he wasn't the only one missing sleep.

"What rounds?" he managed.

"At the orphanage."

It took everything in Percy not to allow his face to crumple again. Senna had never told Percy just how much performing the orphanage inspections troubled him, but Percy knew regardless.

"That's strange," he commented with a fake sort of lightness. "It hasn't been half a year yet since his last inspection."

"His last inspection was incomplete. I've asked him to redo it."

Percy set his jaw. It was a dangerous thing to stand up to his mother, but with the adrenaline from his nightmare still coursing through his veins, the prospect was perilously appealing. But he couldn't. Not when his mother could punish him by taking her cruelty out on Senna.

Calling upon his manners, Percy put on his glasses and said, "Could you please call him to return? I'd like to take a walk to clear my head."

"No," Phaedra stated flatly. "If I retrieve your goldheart, you'll only try to leave the kingdom again."

Bile rose to the back of Percy's throat.

"What?" he said, small.

"I know you've been wandering through the trade channels, eager to leave the safety of your home. I must be honest with you, I do not understand why you would want to do such a reckless, traitorous thing." The petting in his hair landed harder with each pass until she was pulling it, pricking unpleasant needles into his scalp. Percy was beyond trying to keep his face neutral. He didn't have to hide his horror—like any good predator, his mother knew when she'd caught something in her claws.

"Senna didn't put you up to it, did he?" she continued, keeping the same, sickly-sweet voice.

"Of course not!" This was quickly turning into a concrete confession, deftly manipulated out of him via his desperation to keep Senna safe. "He begged me not to, but I ordered him to escort me."

"I should have known it wasn't his idea. The goldheart is loyal, but he is not brave."

It took every muscle of control for Percy to keep from jumping again to Senna's aid. Trying to compel a positive opinion out of his mother was like trying to stop a dre'malor with a commanding word.

"I try not to be offended at your ventures out of Talsura," his mother continued. "I don't dare mention your absconding to anyone else for fear they'll expect the worst—as I do."

"The worst?" Percy murmured, fingers clutching his sheet.

"Don't play ignorant. Anyone catching you slipping out from under the Dam would suspect you were transporting our secrets to our enemies in Redwind. Your disappearances have become frequent enough that I can no longer ignore the possibility."

"That's not it at all!" he cried.

"Then have you rejected the Dam?"

Percy clenched his teeth, trying desperately to disguise the lie.

"I'm thankful for the Dam."

She narrowed her eyes. Percy's mind blanked. He wasn't transporting secrets or plotting Talsura's downfall like his mother suspected. But he *was* planning on reforming Talsuran policy and reconciling with Redwind. To her, that was the same thing.

"I met a girl," he blurted. "A Redwindan girl. I'm in love."

That was true enough. Anyone with eyes could tell as much.

"In love," Phaedra deadpanned.

"Terribly so. I ventured out the first time due to curiosity and got lost. She helped me," he rushed to explain. "I know I've breached the kingdom's trust, but—well, you've been in love, haven't you? With father?"

An undecipherable cloud covered Phaedra's expression. Percy dug his nails into his palms, pulse hammering at a frantic pace.

"I knew you were naive, but you've proven you're still a stupid child. I have no choice but to treat you as such."

"Mother . . ." Percy quavered.

"I forbid you from leaving Talsura. If you give me any reason to suspect that you've betrayed my trust again, I will remove Goldheart Kane from his station and repossess the last five years of his wages. Do you understand me?"

Tears pooled in Percy's eyes. The thought of living without Senna at his side was painful enough, but without a goldheart, Percy would likely be confined to his room—imprisoned until the next goldheart could be sworn in.

He couldn't cry now. Not when she'd already accused him of being a child.

"I understand," he murmured.

His mother stood from the bed, crossing to his bookshelf and eyeing his collection with a frown. "I came here to inform you that I've decided to move the Canon Masquerade from this fall to next week. Doesn't an early summer party sound far preferable?"

Percy curled his lips down. The Canon Masquerade was Talsura's pathetic effort to remain in the canons' good graces. It involved all the guests donning overly embellished masks to yield deference to the objects of true beauty—the faces of the canons. There was dancing and food—half of which was sacrificed over the gaping maw of an open flame. Percy doubted that any of Talsura's food tempted the canons, and while he was sure that the tradition had begun in good faith, it'd just grown into a fashion sport.

"But why?" he asked.

"Is there ever a poor time to offer thanks to our gods? Your attendance is not optional."

Mood already spoiled, Percy wanted to snap that one day he would be king and she might be careful of what unpleasantries she forced upon him.

But then the door opened, squeaking with a desperate need for oiling.

Senna was dressed in his casual clothes, long hair tied back in a ribbon. Percy suspected he'd done it in an attempt to blend in with the citizens north of the Pocket District where the orphanage was located—but the splendor of the goldheart's sword would have given him away in a heartbeat.

"We would be happy to attend," Senna said quietly.

"We would?" Percy chirped, surprised.

Senna met Percy's gaze. Though his expression didn't change, Percy had grown accustomed to reading the silence around it. It said, *"Keep your mouth shut for once and trust me."*

The goldheart produced a folded piece of parchment sealed shut by the royal knighthearts' wax seal. He submitted it before the queen, offering a low bow as he did.

"The report, Your Majesty," said Senna.

Phaedra's brow cocked. "You successfully completed the report?"

Senna did not waver. "Yes, Your Majesty."

Phaedra clicked her tongue. She accepted the sealed report and made to leave, pausing in the doorframe.

"Remember what I said, Percy," she warned.

When she was gone, Percy wiped his eyes and fell at Senna's side, glancing to make sure the door was closed all the way.

"Did you really conduct the inspection of the orphanage?" he whispered.

Senna dropped flat on his back onto Percy's bed with a long laboring sigh.

"Of course not," he admitted. "I'm taking a gamble and calling her bluff."

Percy frowned. "My mother doesn't bluff."

"The last time I didn't complete the report, your mother threatened to dispose me from my position."

Percy's stomach sank. Did she *want* to discharge Senna?

Senna propped himself up on his elbows. "However, recently I was telling Emrys the story of how I became your goldheart and it made me think of something: there's a reason she made *me* the goldheart."

"Do you . . . know what it is?" Percy hesitated.

Senna shook his head. "But she deliberately chose a child from an orphanage, when she could have picked any of her capable, fully-trained knights. Whatever her reason is, I suspect it's enough that her threats were only that: threats. She needs me as your goldheart. Even if she discovers I passed the inspection on to the actual inspector, she won't remove me. She can't."

"Good," replied Percy, heaving a deep breath. "Because she knows we've been visiting Redwind. She said if we ever go back, she'll dismiss you and repossess your wages."

Senna flopped onto the bed, his boots hanging over the edge. Percy drooped beside him, the mattress still warm from where he'd been sleeping.

"What do we do?" he whispered.

"What we've been doing," Senna said resolutely. "But this time, we won't get caught."

"**A**M I LOSING MY sanity or is the Dam . . . *thinning*?" asked Percy the afternoon of the masquerade.

He was standing atop a stool while one of the royal tailors adjusted the cuffs of Percy's trousers. Their assistant, a wiry girl with an endless braid, repeated the process on his dark vest, adjusting the fabric so that it lay evenly. Percy had grown weary of avoiding her eyes and staring at the top of the tailor's head, so had instead fixed his gaze out of his window.

It wasn't anything like looking out of Thea's window in Redwind, where the Mount Livia peaks crested the horizon and the rest of Islevaria seemed to stretch out as far as the sea. His own view was like looking at the night sky—endless black with flickers of small golden lights in the capital. No amount of concentration or squinting would reveal the blue sky that waited on the other side of the Dam.

Or, at least, until today.

Today, there was something to the black sky. Something that suggested an expansive presence *behind* it.

"I swear it's thinner," Percy said again, this time more confidently.

Senna kicked away from where he'd stationed himself along the wall and moved to the balcony doors. His expression twisted in barely-concealed hope before he turned around and shook his head.

"I don't mean the whole thing," said Percy. "I mean—Well, look at that north-eastern corner of the sky. It's almost indigo, is it not?"

"Please don't move, Your Highness," the girl at his vest whispered.

"Forgive me. I'll hold still," he replied in his best princely tone. Then, meeting her mousy gaze, "Could you please look outside and tell me if you think the Dam is thinning?"

Senna rolled his eyes, but the seamstress did as she was told. To her credit, she looked long and hard.

"Maybe it's wishful thinking, Your Highness. It would be nice if it *was* getting thinner." Under her breath, she mumbled, "Don't know what I'd give to see a hint of the sky again, though."

Percy pressed his lips together. He was inclined to agree.

Eventually, the tailors finished their work, leaving Percy standing in one of the most uncomfortable masquerade suits he'd ever been put upon to wear. The piece fit all of his unimpressive contours like a glove, but the *feeling* of the clothes was nearly agony. The vest was an awful velvet texture, his trousers rubbed too much on the insides of his thighs, and his sleeves had embroidery that itched on the interior of the fabric.

Senna wasn't in better shape. For formal occasions, it was customary for him to wear his decorated armor—the plate mail he'd be expected to don in battle. Like the silverhearts, Senna's breastplate and pauldrons were forged of gleaming iron. But where the silverhearts' iron was smooth and clean, Senna's was magically embellished with gold. The intricate gilded linework was etched into every minute inch of the armor, and when Senna stepped under the light of the castle's hundreds of candles, it was as though each one began to glow.

A tiny whizzing noise struck the air above Senna. On instinct, he stuck his hands out in time for something to fall from the empty air. It was lit with flames when it appeared, but was a perfect, crisp letter by the time it floated into Senna's hands. He began to hand it to Percy, before his eyes caught on the name written across the front.

"It's for me. It's . . ." He set his jaw. "It's in Emrys' handwriting."

Percy tugged at his collar, begging it to loosen. "Well, what does it say?"

Senna's eyes skimmed the message, then hopped back to the top and skimmed it over again.

"Percy," Senna began slowly. "Did you write to Thea or Elora about your mother changing the date of the masquerade to tonight?"

"I mentioned it to Thea because I wanted her artistic opinion on what mask I should wear? Why?"

"Because Emrys says they're coming to the masquerade. They're practically here already."

"They're *here*? All of them?"

Senna brought the paper closer to his face. "No. Just Emrys and Elora. They're waiting for us at the agora so we can help guide them through the rest of the trade channels."

"Well, write back right now and tell them to turn around!"

"*We already boarded our horses at a stable nearby, so don't think of telling us to turn around,*" Senna read, despairing. "Why is he like this?"

"Elora was chased out of Talsura because my mother wanted to publicly execute her. Now she wants to be in the same room as her?" Percy cried. "Why would she want to come in the first place? Is she unwell?"

With a huff, Senna dropped the letter in Percy's lit fireplace. He waited until it was consumed to ash, then poked it again with the stoker for extra measure.

"I'd bet anything it was Emrys' idea," he grumbled.

"Because he kissed you and you let him sleep in your bed alone?"

Senna spun around, jaw dropped. "That's—!" He flung the stoker back into place with a *THUNK*. "If that truly is the reason, then he and I will exchange words. I can't believe he'd endanger Elora's safety to get a reaction out of me."

"No, Elora doesn't do anything because of someone else's ulterior motives," Percy moaned. "I fear they're both equally to blame. As are we, for being so predictable."

Senna fastened his scabbard to his belt with a sour frown.

"Where are you going?" Percy demanded.

"If we don't escort them in, they'll try to sneak into the party themselves and get caught by one of the guards. I'm going to meet them, if only to try to convince them to wait for us in our quarters, away from your mother's gaze." He paused, glancing up at Percy's wild look. "Well, put on your shoes!"

E MRYS WAS APPARENTLY EMPLOYING the *act now, beg forgiveness later* tactic, which Percy respected. Except, Emrys didn't seem to realize he'd reached the *beg forgiveness* stage. His head snapped up when he heard them approaching the agora seats where he and Elora were waiting. His bright violet eyes were lit with a grin. He kept the rest of his face neutral and poised on Senna, who marched up to him with pounding footsteps.

"Have you utterly lost your mind?" Senna demanded.

"Oh dear, Senna's unhappy," Emrys commented dramatically at Elora. "You know, Sen, it's customary to say hello when seeing someone after a period of absence."

"I cannot believe you put your kingdom, yourself, and Elora at severe risk merely to prove a point—a point that is still lost on me."

"Actually, it's my fault," Elora admitted. "I was worried about Percy after everything that happened in Cevyn's Den. He mentioned a masquerade in his letters and I figured, what better time to visit again than a party I can wear a mask to? I asked Emrys to accompany me in case something happened."

"I'm sure you were all too willing to go along," Senna huffed at Emrys.

The mask of Emrys' haughty air cracked. "Is it a sin to want to see you? *You* were the ones who invited us to Talsura the last time. Can we only visit when you need help?"

"You can visit as much as you'd like," Percy cut in, "but you *cannot* be in the same room as my mother. You don't know what she's capable of."

"Our entire lives are evidence of what she's capable of," Emrys said, gesturing between him and Elora. "Besides, I've been wanting to see firsthand what we're dealing with."

"No," Senna deadpanned.

"I wouldn't mind seeing it too," Elora added cautiously. "Given what you asked me, Percy."

Percy's shoulders slumped. It was a low blow to bring up the uncertainty of their engagement. It wouldn't be fair to keep Elora away from Talsura if it helped her make an informed decision on whether or not she wanted to eventually be his queen. As for Emrys, if they somehow managed to keep him away this time, Percy had a feeling he would only attempt to come back again and again until he was successful. If Emrys saw the ugly truth *now*, maybe it would stop him from trying something rash in the future.

"Alright. You can attend."

Senna's head snapped over to him. "You're serious."

"Very," Percy said. He fixed a stern look on Emrys. "But it must be on our terms. No inflorescence. It'll be a dead giveaway. If anyone asks, you're my invited guests—actors from the Talsuran theatre."

Emrys rolled his eyes, but he nodded. He glanced at Senna, waiting for him to argue, but Percy knew he wouldn't—not now that the royal decision had been finalized.

"We better leave," Senna grumbled. "If Percy and I are late, it will only raise suspicion."

"Do you have enough energy to—" Percy drew a pretend sigil aimlessly in the air. "Save us some time?"

Senna tossed Percy an annoyed side-eye, then plucked off one of his leather gloves. He drew the sigil with his finger and pressed it to the ground, whisking them away before the mark even lit. The sigil placed them at the beginning of the trade channels underneath the castle.

"Come on, all the knighthearts will be surveilling the ballroom, but they'll make rounds at their usual posts soon," Senna said, taking off.

Percy's legs strained in an effort to keep up. The ferocity of Senna's pace succeeded only in placing distance between him and Emrys. Percy thought that resolving things with Emrys—an unspoken look that said, *We're both sorry, we both were fools, we aren't going to dwell on it*—would break the silence. But whatever was going on between Senna and Emrys was awkward and tense enough to lie tangibly heavy in the air.

"I'm surprised Thea did not come with you both," Percy commented lightly. "She so loves an excuse to commission her modiste."

Emrys' jaw tightened.

"She's—under the weather," he replied, stiffly.

"I see. I'm sorry to hear that."

Well done, Percy Laurent, he grumbled in his mind. *Somehow, you've made it even* more *awkward.* He tried again.

"How is the weather in Redwind, Captain?"

"Rainy."

"Ah."

Sensing his agony, Elora offered Percy a red-lipped smile. She was carrying the long scarlet skirts of her dress that made her skin look like expensive ivory. Her black curls were, for once, loose down her back, a single strand falling demurely against her temple.

"What should we expect from this masquerade?" she asked.

"Masks?" Emrys guessed dryly.

Elora snorted. "How astute, Captain. I daresay you're onto something."

"It's like any other ball," Percy assured. "Though, don't be unsettled when you see members of the Canonized Cloth. At my first masquerade, I took one look at the votary and wet myself."

"You were six," Senna pointed out.

"You had to change me like a baby and carry me around for the rest of the night," moaned Percy. "I'd be lying if I said I didn't shiver a little every time I saw them."

"I can't imagine what could possibly be frightening enough to unsettle you still," Elora commented.

"It's the—the *air* around them. They do either altogether too little or too much. It's like they want to remove their personhood and be mindless beings of worship."

Elora frowned. "Mindless?"

"Senna and I once toured the basilica and it was like watching statues come to life—barely moving, barely talking. Repeating the same prayers over and over, crowded together without room to breathe. They hold in contempt any clothes that aren't their plain robes, and practically starve themselves. But it's their eerie masks that are the worst part—plain and white. It's why the ball is a masquerade in the first place."

"Seems like they're the center of the party. Why's that?" asked Emrys, though the question was directed to Senna. Senna looked at Emrys long enough to acknowledge that he'd been addressed, but then faced forward without answering.

"They're the experts in canonical worship," Percy replied instead, throwing Senna an unsure look. "They'll facilitate the presentation of the offerings to the canons and then perform a sacramental dance."

Emrys let out a snort. "I can't wait to see that."

Percy turned his gaze ahead, music and the rumble of a crowd lilting through the closed hatch ahead.

"Be careful what you wish for."

SENNA

IT WAS A CENTURIES'-OLD tradition that all attending members of the masquerade ball wore masks—all except the goldheart. This placed the annual ball among Senna's least favorite responsibilities, as there seemed to be nothing so interesting as a face among a crowd where there were none. It wasn't that wearing a mask would disguise Senna. It was that if he was going to draw attention in his gold-embellished armor, he preferred something to hide behind.

Tonight, Senna had only allowed himself a passing glance at the ballroom before dizzyingly splitting his attention between Percy, Phaedra, and Emrys. He didn't need to peer around in gaping awe to know that the servants had practically broken their backs waxing the emblem in the middle of the dance floor. He didn't need to crane his neck to count the thousands of candles that had been hand lit and hung along the domed ceiling. Nor did he need to prod his nose into the bright flowers stationed around the room to know that his touch would slip right through the lifelike illusions.

Phaedra's throne was sheathed in the same spectral blooms. Senna was sure she felt the illusory designs demonstrated a superior wit to all *real* inflorescent people, but the colors were too dull and the petals weren't nearly silky enough. The illusions rippled as she leaned over the arm of the throne, whispering something to the votary, who craned his ear to listen. Her gaze slipped to the side and—

A shiver sluiced down Senna's spine. Phaedra had caught him staring.

He returned the stare in kind—blankly, as if to say, *Yes, I was staring. I am watching you.* She smirked, an intangible, unreadable thing that made Senna turn back to Percy for fear that her pleasure alone was enough to put the prince in danger.

Heart racing, Senna assessed everyone Percy spoke with for signs of ill intent. His job was easier than usual. Percy didn't seem to have a stomach for talking to strangers tonight with Elora's hand in his elbow. Several partygoers had already approached the prince, the hungry glints revealing a curiosity about his female guest. But Percy brushed them aside, every one, and led Elora back to the dance floor. He was altogether too happy and in love to trouble himself over trivial things like manners and gossip. He wore that love like it made him untouchable.

And Senna—

Senna was jealous.

On instinct, he looked at Emrys. The seal keeping his hopeless desire at bay cracked at the sight. Now that he had started looking, it would be impossible to stop.

The Redwindan prince was waving around a flute of something star-colored and bubbling. For the first time since Senna had met him, Emrys looked well and truly like a prince. The mask he'd chosen for the party covered half of his face in intricately woven silver designs. He wore a billowing silk shirt the color of fresh snow, cut deeply enough to reveal the smooth planes of his brown skin and the gemmed body chain underneath. His shirt was cinched in at the waist by a corset embroidered with golden thread to look like the night sky and tucked into loose trousers. Matching chains dangled in sweeping loops from his narrow waist down his hips. In his heeled boots, he commanded attention and demanded devotion.

What else could Senna do but adore him?

Currently, Emrys was offering his brightest smile to a blonde-haired woman wearing standard Talsuran dress clothes—equal parts doleful and dark. Her mask covered the top half of her face, leaving her flirtatious smile exposed and ready to be wielded.

Without regard for who was watching, Emrys leaned close to his companion and whispered something in her ear. It offered Senna the perfect view of the side of Emrys' head and—

Cursed canons.

Senna should have expected it. Emrys was, after all, a man who refused all ordinances of behavior. *Of course* he had grown a patch of tiny purple flowers. They were arranged to look like they were affixed to his mask, but the blooms had a vibrance and life to them that all the pretend flowers did not.

This risky behavior was exactly why Senna didn't want Emrys here—especially around Phaedra, who knew that Percy had friends in sunnier places. Emrys had likely done it as an act of defiance—almost as if he *wanted* Phaedra to catch him in her midst. Almost as if he wanted to remind Talsura what their queen had taken from him.

But that was Emrys. He couldn't seem to help but toy with his safety like life was a gambled game of dice. Even so, his confidence was mesmeric.

Heat burned in Senna's gut, bright, then brighter still when Emrys laughed at something the woman said and placed a coy hand on his shoulder.

To Senna's horror, Emrys offered his hand for a *dance.* They disappeared behind a crowd of giggling ladies and waving fans.

Clenching his jaw so hard a throb resonated up his temple, Senna moseyed along the wall, his gaze never leaving Emrys. Guests parted ways, whispering about *the patrolling goldheart* and something about falling on a knife just to look him in the eye and hear him say hello. But Senna didn't hear them—Emrys was getting away, dipping behind a potted plant and fleeing Senna's sight.

"*Oh*, you blundering, slovenly halfwit!" cried a woman's voice beside him.

Senna broke from his thoughts, readying himself to neutralize the collision, only to discover he *was* the collision. Though he didn't remember doing it, he must have knocked the woman hard to spill her dark wine all along her deep brown gown. She had not yet looked up at him and instead was pawing at the damp spot, which only succeeded in spreading it around.

"This gown was made with imported batiste that took three months to hand stitch, and you've ruined it!" she screeched. "My servants will have to scrub it for a century just to get the stain to lift. I can't believe they let such imbeciles amble around the—"

A slap across his face. Fingers wrenched in his hair, uprooting strands in stinging bursts. An exclamation: "Senna Kane, you clumsy imbecile!" A whispered apology made of words stuck in grief and mud and terror. Another slap. "Do you have any idea how long it will take to scrub out all this ink from your trousers?" More pain in his hair, on his face, resonating like a throbbing pulse. And he is only five years old. His hands barely work and he hadn't meant to knock the ink well over. Please, Mother Mabel. I'm sorry!

A hand landed on his shoulder. The feel of it was familiar enough to tear Senna from the waking nightmare, but disorientation swirled his vision. All he knew was the touch was *safe*. Senna focused on the tangible weight, drawing in a long breath. The vision of the orphanage dissolved around the edges, until all that remained was Emrys, stern-faced and *beautiful*.

"You'd be wise to notice who you speak to with such disrespect," said Emrys to the woman.

Mother Mabel's snarling teeth. "How dare you speak to me with such disrespect!"

Breathe, Senna told himself. *You are the master of your lungs. Of your mind.*

The woman gasped, stumbling back. Her heel caught something, and she tumbled to the floor in a heap of brown-stained skirts, face veiled by all of her hair. Now that she was sprawled on the ground, Percy came into view. He clutched Elora's hand, but was poised to jump to Senna's rescue. Around him, the crowd had ceased dancing to watch the spectacle unfurl. The musical ensemble flanking either side of the throne had ceased playing.

There was no need for a rescue—not with Emrys' hand pouring support and strength into him. Adrenaline was still thick in his blood, threatening to dredge more unpleasant memories to the surface, but he urged it to disarm itself. To temper its rage.

Shaking, the woman removed her mask. Tears spilled over her lashes, dripping more wet blotches onto her skirts.

"Goldheart Kane, I-I didn't realize it was you. I'm so sorry. *I* ran into *you*. I'm the clumsy one. It's my fault."

He stared at the woman, then glanced up at Emrys.

"You left your dance partner," Senna said.

Emrys crossed his arms over his chest and gave a lopsided grin. "Why dance when I can leap to your aid?"

Senna looked back at the woman—her tense shoulders and her quivering lip. Strands of her straight red hair were stuck messily to tear streaks drying on her cheeks. Senna took to one knee and offered her a hand. The entire room watched raptly, their attention making his throat feel thick.

He took a deep breath and murmured, "I was watching the prince, not the path. The transgression is mine. Forgive me."

"You won't—punish me for yelling?"

Senna was met headfirst with the memory that Goldheart Ilias had been a knight of justice. His pleasure had been making the culpable bleed after even the smallest of transgressions. And when he'd died, Senna remembered hearing rumors around the castle about how Ilias hadn't suffered nearly enough when he'd been whipped to death after King Mathis' passing.

"I'll not punish you for yelling," Senna swore firmly. Then, directly to the partygoers, to the knighthearts, to Queen Phaedra herself, "No one will."

The words were still ringing out as Senna excused himself, sliding easily past Emrys and Percy, who called after him. He stumbled on the hidden balcony overlooking the Dam, hands clutching the railing.

He should have expected the footsteps that trailed behind him.

Senna kept his gaze forward, knowing that if turned around, his compounding emotions would display plainly on his face. The desperation to be close to Emrys. The certainty that he would say something wrong, no matter the words he chose.

"Are you alright, Senna?" asked Emrys.

Senna's shoulders dropped. "I thought you weren't talking to me."

"I was *trying* not to talk to you and you can see how bloody well that worked out," Emrys said, appearing at Senna's side. He removed his mask, revealing all of his expression's kindness in full. "Tell me to go and I will go."

"Don't," Senna said immediately.

Emrys' fingers bravely crossed the space between them and skimmed down the back of Senna's arm. They hooked around his wrist, lying on his pulse. "Then tell me what I can do. Anyone can see that you are troubled."

Senna shook his head.

"I'm only catching my breath. I don't care for being the center of attention."

"I know," Emrys said sincerely. "But it was more, wasn't it? I turned around and your face . . . You were somewhere else entirely. Where were you?"

Upon a first meeting, it was easy to mistake Emrys for a man who simply didn't care. To the rest of the world, he ignored his duties protecting Thea, snuck away to parties, and disappeared for days at a time. But here, his fingers wrapped around Senna's pulse, Senna could see who he really was: the sort of person who approached obstacles like they were pieces in the royal gallery—something to momentarily appreciate, then navigate away from. He wasn't lazy at all. He merely wanted to help.

This was why Senna pointed to the sea of lanterns still lit in the city. The lights revealed hints of the buildings—a barred window, a half-open door. His own focus was fixed where the light was dimmest, a corner over by the Pocket District.

"I was there," he said.

Emrys approached the railing, lilac gaze narrowing, before widening in understanding.

"The orphanage," he realized.

"That woman called me slovenly and mentioned—well, scrubbing." Senna shook his head. "I know it makes little sense."

"It makes perfect sense. She insulted you the way you were insulted as a child." Senna sagged forward.

"Yes," he breathed, voice thick with relief. "I don't know what draws me so readily back to that place. I-I *hate* that I can be summoned with a few careless words. It isn't just the memory. I was there, ink stains on my clothes, face stinging from being slapped. It was twenty years ago, and yet, it happened just now."

Emrys hummed, then hopped up to sit on the balcony's ledge. Senna couldn't help himself—he reached forward and held Emrys steady by his corset so he wouldn't fall. Ever an opportunist, Emrys placed a hand over Senna's, caressing up and down. The hairs on Senna's skin stood up.

"When we went to Mount Livia, you might recall I wasn't eager to go," Emrys began.

Senna smiled, small. "I tried not to take it personally."

"Please, the possibility of having your sole attention for a day was a temptation beyond my own human strength and comprehension." At this, Senna blushed, but Emrys was unperturbed. "But I didn't want to cross the moorlands."

Senna understood immediately. Sometimes when he was in Redwind, it felt like the exile was sewn into every home, every interaction, every relationship. He'd known that the trip would be difficult for Emrys, but perhaps he'd underestimated how much.

"Don't look like that," Emrys complained good-heartedly. "If I had wanted to take a shovel and dig out my childhood injuries, then I would have sought out your company and we would have cried into our kerchiefs together. But I didn't want to spend my time with you dwelling on things that ruin my mood—just as you have come out here to shake off your own pain. It wouldn't have been fair to myself to waste time I was meant to be relishing. In the end, I rather enjoyed myself."

"You almost died," Senna deadpanned.

"Yes, but it was *fun*." Emrys tilted his head, the beaded chains on his face catching a new strand of light. "I want you to have fun, Senna. We can enjoy the fresh air and poke holes in whatever brought you back to a place that hurts you. Or, I can distract you. So I'll ask again, what can I do?"

The answer tumbled out of his lips like a child's first word, unconscious and anxious to be spoken.

"Distract me."

Emrys' brow shot up. "The last time I distracted you, you fled my company and left me to sleep in your room alone," he murmured quietly.

"Was that what that was? A distraction?" Senna breathed.

He was teetering on the precipice of danger. On one side of the line was Emrys' touch—the taste of his lips, warmed by the comforting heat of his skin. On the other side was more fighting, more time apart, more longingly wringing his heart dry of blood and feeling.

"It might have been a distraction to you, maybe. Not to me," Emrys replied. He'd gotten close—close enough that the chains hanging from his corset were now brushing Senna's leg.

Swallowing, Senna breathed, "A different distraction." Then, hearing how pathetic he sounded, added, "Please."

The answer came to Emrys easily. "Dance with me."

Senna had expected that Emrys—the prince of burning daylight—would've had more creative means by which to distract Senna.

"Have I affronted your sensibilities with the mere suggestion, Goldheart?" Emrys asked with an amused smile. "You don't want to talk. We're at a masquerade. The next logical solution is to dance."

It occurred to Senna then, that possibly there wasn't any way to spend time with Emrys Rosecroft and not feel like he was betraying his oath. When Emrys had kissed him on the stairs of his childhood home, Senna had felt like he was giving too much of himself away. Perhaps naively, he'd assumed that if they drew a platonic boundary in the invisible space between them, that he'd be able to be around Emrys without giving those parts of himself away. But he'd been wrong.

With Emrys' hand extended, eyes bright and captivating, Senna knew that he'd never be able to share Emrys' air without offering everything that he was.

"I can't dance," Senna whispered.

Emrys' hand drooped, but did not drop entirely.

"Haven't you been to dozens of these stuffy balls?"

"Only on patrol." He shrugged. "I wouldn't want to step on your feet.

At this, Emrys tilted his head back and *laughed*.

"I'm insulted that you think I'd come to a ball without the right footwear. You could step on them a hundred times and I wouldn't feel a thing."

Emrys grazed the underside of Senna's wrist, letting the other hand fall on his shoulder blade.

Emrys' voice dropped as he continued, "If I didn't know better, I'd say you sounded a little intimidated—which would seem entirely out of character for a man I once saw leap onto the back of a dre'malor. Rest assured, dancing is the easiest thing in the world when you have a partner who lives and breathes the steps."

"And you can?" Senna wondered softly.

Emrys' eyes gleamed.

"Would you care to find out?"

Senna unshackled a lifetime's worth of restraints. With confidence he didn't know he possessed, he pressed his strong hold to Emrys' back and urged him closer.

A surprised glint lit in Emrys' eyes.

"Listen to the music," he instructed. "Feel the natural pulse in its rhythm. *One*, two, three. *One*, two, three." He tapped the beat over Senna's heart. "You'll feel me guide you. Don't worry about what your body is doing. For once, darling, let yourself be led."

Senna did. He took to his task with complete focus and reverence, amazed when Emrys successfully guided him around the veranda. Somehow, they danced close enough to brush ribs without losing their ability to move in tandem. Emrys buried his face in the warm nook of Senna's throat, breath damp and close. For months, he'd wondered what it would be like to be warm and safe in Emrys' arms. Now he knew.

Maybe Percy would be okay without me.

This last thought fired through Senna like a stroke of lightning at the last second. He nearly tripped over his feet forcing himself back.

"I didn't hurt you, did I?" Emrys said, concerned.

"No," Senna rushed, hands running up and down his arms. "The dancing has ended."

Emrys tilted an ear toward the door. The rolling music had dispersed like fog on a warming morning, leaving behind the murmurs of the crowd.

"So it has," he agreed flatly.

Senna felt like cold water had been poured over his head. The *want* had not disappeared, but it had fallen into the background—like the murmurs of a person speaking from two doors over. He was at once the child of his past, shivering in a bloody bed among thorns, and a stranger he'd never met—a selfish creature that craved things beyond shelter and the goldheart station.

"I am feeling quite myself again," he lied, clearing his throat. "Thank you for the distraction. I need to return to my post."

Emrys' face fell, like he knew that it was pointless to argue. He distanced himself away a few paces and nodded. Wordlessly, he returned his mask to his face. The moment was well and truly ruined.

They slipped back into the ballroom. If some of the silverhearts had seen the goldheart return to his lookout with a beautiful man, they knew well enough to keep their lips shut. Senna skimmed the crowd, but Percy was either perfectly camouflaged in the sea of black and brown formal wear or hiding from his mother, for all Senna could find him.

"I'm not over there, if that's what's got you looking so hard."

Senna spun to Percy, then heaved out a heavy sigh.

"I'm going to petition your mother to create a new law in which the prince must wear bright yellow to the masquerade ball," Senna whispered, eyes still on the crowd.

"If you hadn't disappeared with your paramour, perhaps you would not have so easily lost me," Percy replied.

"I'm still standing here, you know," Emrys said, leaning out with a smirk.

"Oh, hullo, old fellow!" Percy chimed in fake surprise, loudly enough that a pair of ladies turned around to glare. "I didn't see you there hiding behind Senna's *dreamy shoulders* and *strong chest*."

Percy caught Senna's elbow before it could nudge into his side.

Emrys didn't seem fazed by Percy's teasing. The plain hurt from moments ago was now masked away behind his usual facade of confidence and aplomb.

"Speaking of paramours, where on earth is Elora? I'm meant to be her escort," Emrys continued.

"And a perfect escort you have been—leaving her completely alone and un-bothered for the evening." Percy's words came out easily, without a drop of sarcasm, much to Emrys' apparent amusement. "I sent Elora up to my room so that she didn't have to suffer the rest of the party. The ballroom gets rather smoky and she has trouble breathing when the air is thick."

Emrys tossed a confused glance at Senna. "Don't tell me. This is when the badly dressed cultists come out and show everyone how bad they are at dancing."

"Careful, Em. You're beginning to sound like you're from around here." Percy's expression dropped. "Oh, hells. My mother is giving me wraith eyes. That means I'm late." He darted forward, then halted a few steps away and whirled back around. "Emrys, I know things between you and Senna are more uncomfortable than the time I accidentally caught my maids bare-breasted and trysting in my own bathroom, but could you *please* be a terrible escort for a while longer and wait to bring El back home until tomorrow? I'd bribe you but—" He lowered his voice. "I don't think I could offer you anything you don't already have, except—Well ..." He glanced meaningfully at Senna, cringed again, and disappeared into the crowd.

"I'm surprised you're not going to follow him," Emrys commented.

"Percy doesn't usually remain for the complete duration of the offerings. With Elora waiting in his quarters, I have a feeling he won't make it five minutes."

"That doesn't explain why you're still here."

"If I'm still present, then it gives the queen and the rest of the guests the impression that Percy remains in attendance." Senna gripped his belt. "Besides, I prefer not to be standing just outside the door when he and Elora are alone. It's a rather unpleasant reminder that the boy I knew is long gone."

Emrys smiled understandably.

"But you don't consider him a man yet, do you?"

There were precious few people who could understand Senna without his needing to utter a word. It reminded Senna of when he'd been in Mount Livia and he'd felt the chilling gaze of a spirit visit watching him. But instead of an icy bite down his spine, there was only a warm tingle at the base of his neck—like nails raking through his hair or lips tasting the dimple there.

"I think this year is changing us all," Senna answered finally.

A flicker of hope crossed Emrys' gaze. Senna might have greedily drank in the sight forever, but three loud rattles of a staff at the front of the room shattered the spell. The crowd's murmurs silenced.

Senna leaned over to Emrys' ear, ignoring the citrusy rose smell of the purple flowers there. "I shall return momentarily."

Emrys cocked an amused brow. "Shall you? In that case, I'll be your wallflower waiting to be plucked."

With any luck, Senna had disappeared into the crowd before Emrys could witness how his flirtations had turned his face into an overripe tomato.

Senna joined the other congregating knighthearts in time for the votary to rise from his seat beside the queen. He looked simple next to the queen's opulence and Cloth acolytes flanking his side. The worshippers lifted the censors above their heads, sending smoke billowing into the Votary's grasp.

He swirled his hands through the gray exhaust, and projected over the crowd, "We call upon a reverent silence over this convocation of devoted citizens."

The crowd rumbled. To them, this was nothing more than a performance—a group of actors in boring clothes putting on theatrical airs for their entertainment.

"We call—" the votary tried again. Still, the crowd chattered. "We—"

Three loud bangs echoed from the dais, shuddering all the way to the soles of Senna's feet like a pulse. At once, the crowd silenced. This seemed peculiar—most votaries had to wrangle the Talsuran nobility's attention like a wild horse. But when Senna braved a glance up, he saw that Phaedra had stolen the votary's pure black staff. Her lips were parted in a snarl, as if another breath from the crowd would send her gnashing.

When every gaze was rapt, every heart held still, Phaedra twisted her gaze to the votary.

"I don't have time for your failure. It is the votary's duty to command respect. Kneel and I will show you how it is done."

"Your Majesty—"

"Kneel."

The votary stumbled away from the dais. He stepped on the long hem of his robes and tumbled to his knees. But before he could right himself, Phaedra laid the obsidian staff on his shoulders, forcing him lower. Huffing wet breaths, the votary bent down, down, down until his nose grazed the floor.

Senna held his expression perfectly neutral as he waited for whatever would come next. He caught eyes with Percy, who imperceptibly shook his head as if to say, *I have no idea*. There were supposed to be opening prayers, dirge-like hymns that the votaries were required to memorize.

Indeed, Phaedra didn't bother with speaking the verses properly.

Drawing thunder into her lungs, Phaedra bellowed, *"Alpedis, canon of the sky and sun!"* The words roared into the empty dome of the ballroom and Senna swore he saw the candles overhead flicker. *"Talsura has no use for you. We have neither sky nor sun. Spare us your favor."*

Beside him, the knighthearts shifted uncomfortably. They all knew the proper refrain. They'd droned it a thousand times over dozens of masquerades. Senna remembered how hard he'd struggled to get the words out when he'd first become goldheart: *"Confer on us your favor."*

"Your Majesty—" moaned the votary, as if the blatant disrespect hurt as badly as a gut wound.

"That isn't a *reverent silence*," she hissed. The votary's forehead immediately smacked against the ground. "Refrain!"

"Spare us your favor," echoed the crowd meekly. Obediently.

Lifting the staff high, she said, "*Cevyn, canon of lost things. We offer you our land. In times when the mighty of Talsura seized power, you took the filth of our population and turned every inflorescent scab into another lost weed. You expelled their corrupted possessions and took them into your righteous care. Cevyn, seize the lost people. The traitors. The foul inflorescent offscourings of our greatness. Confer your wrath.*"

"*Confer your wrath.*"

Senna's heart dropped into his stomach. Percy stared at him, face pale.

Phaedra knew Redwindans were here. Of course she did. She wasn't ignorant. She'd seen Percy toting around a pretty girl all evening. Emrys was unplanned, but he'd come right with her. Maybe she didn't know who exactly he was, but it wouldn't matter. Because Percy had only admitted to knowing Elora—and now there was another traitor in their midst. One Percy hadn't accounted for.

This was Senna's fault. Despite his gut telling him to force their friends to return home, he hadn't been able to help himself. How could he deny Percy Elora, who took Percy's buzzing energy in both of her artful hands and made him still? How could he deny himself Emrys?

"*Varyan, canon of the sun sickness,*" Phaedra scoffed. This time there were no waxing speeches. "*Spare us your favor.*"

Emrys was somewhere behind him, taking in every hateful word. All because Senna was a selfish creature who failed to deny his own desires.

"*Rira, canon of extermination and destruction.*" Her eyes slid to a point behind Senna, past the crowd, to where Emrys leaned up against the wall. "*Eradicate the Redwindan scum in our midst. Lay your righteous hand upon him and raze the air in his lungs. Pry his skin from his muscle and bone. Spill the marrow of his being onto the ground, mix it with his blood, spit in the sludge. Rira, confer your wrath.*"

Dread cut through Senna like a knife.

Then Phaedra smiled at Senna. "Goldheart, highest knight in the land, most respected champion, confer your wrath."

One by one, the knighthearts looked down the line at Senna, hands on their blades. Waiting for an order. Waiting to see how the goldheart—the only knight without blood on his hands—would obey the queen.

Pain roared up Senna's throat, the impossibility of what Phaedra was asking him to do settling like fire in every nerve in his body.

Senna needed to act. He needed to act *now*.

"Knighthearts!" he declared, voice rasping. He couldn't remember the last time he'd managed this volume to his knights. "Scour the crowd for traitors. Leave—" *Come on, Senna Kane. Don't lose your words now. No matter how awful they are.* "Leave no survivors."

Chaos unleashed like a flock of carrion birds.

A drop of relief hit Senna to the core. This would have to be enough. The terror of the guests, the determination of the knights, the outrage of the queen—all of it would be loud enough for Emrys to slip out the back doors, away from danger, away from those who would notice the flowers on his face were *real*.

Percy rushed up to Senna, but Senna caught him by the shoulders and spun him around.

"Go to your quarters. Don't leave until I come and say it's safe," he whispered in Percy's ear, then pushed him off into the commotion. With any luck, Phaedra would lose sight of her own son.

Senna spun on his heels, hand poised on his blade. Around him, knighthearts grabbed partygoers by their sleeves, demanding to know if they were inflorescent. He hunted through the crowd, making his way to the point where Emrys had been standing. He drew his sword for good measure, hoping to find Emrys long gone.

Emrys wasn't gone, though. He was twisting a copperheart in a bind of thorn-sharp vines.

Senna forced his way through the rushing bodies, praying he reached Emrys before anyone else noticed.

"He's here! Goldheart, help—" the copperheart moaned. The words could barely make it through the gag of leaves and spurs, losing volume the tighter the vines twisted. Face damp with desperation and sweat, the copperheart lunged for his dropped blade, but Emrys tightened his ivy, briars growing ever sharper.

Senna drew close to Emrys' ear. He did not care who saw—only spit out the words "Release him" with the same authority that he might wrangle his knighthearts into submission. "We must go."

The revelation that the goldheart was fraternizing—*longing for, craving*—the Redwindan intruder was lost on the copperheart, whose eyes had rolled into the back of his head. Emrys could not have missed Senna's plea, always so carefully paying attention to everything the goldheart had to say. Yet, the vines stretched out onto the floor, threatening to ensnare the next unfortunate victim.

"Emrys," Senna pressed. "You're angry with the queen and you're taking it out on a probationary soldier who has wet himself with fear. *Release him.* I have to get you out of here."

Finally—*finally*—Emrys broke away from the copperheart. He looked at Senna with a tortured expression, eyes red around the edges. Senna understood. Phaedra had insulted his kingdom. His *family*. Above all, Emrys was a thing of loyalty—every mortared brick and stone in his soul that made up his very essence had been cast in the need to protect what he loved. Emrys likely wanted to kill Phaedra with his own power. To watch thorns drain her blood and marrow just as she had wished upon him.

Senna would not allow this to happen—not today, at least.

"If she finds you, I will never see you again," he whispered.

"Do not act as though that makes a difference," Emrys gritted through his teeth, his days'-old anger melting into his current rage.

"It does," Senna stated definitively. "I *want* to see you. Do not make me live without you."

Immediately, the vines draining the life from the copperheart withered away into nothing but a wisp of dust. He dropped to the ground, clutching his throat, blood spilling from over his closed hand.

Emrys' chin dropped. The fingers that had once strained against the demands of the inflorescent magic now found their way to Senna's.

"Get me out of here."

Senna did not waste a second. He clutched Emrys' hand and guided him through the side servant door. It was a dangerous gamble to choose this route. They would pass most of the staff on their escape—sun-deprived servants who would have to choose between the goldheart, who was kind enough to them during the little he spoke, and the queen, who could decide whether they lived or died.

Yet, they all cleared the path for Senna and Emrys—not out of fear, but perhaps in solidarity for the defiant act itself. Abetment to the transgression of bringing a Redwindan into the castle right under the queen's nose.

When they'd reached the kitchen, Senna hoisted the rusted hatch to the trade channels. Before he could jump in, a small touch landed on his shoulder.

It was the kitchen girl. The one whose name Senna still did not know. The one who had packed a lunch worthy of royalty when he'd asked for the barest sliver of something to eat.

"We won't breathe a word," she whispered.

Promises rose on Senna's tongue, the kind he couldn't keep. He wanted to tell her that one day he would repay her kindness by bringing her through the trade channels, show her that she could taste a bit of sun without fearing for her life. He wanted to turn to all the scullery staff and swear that he would tear down the Dam with his own hands. Confess that his dealings with Redwind were for their benefit, to undo all the insidious acts Phaedra had forced upon their land.

Instead, Senna cupped her hand on his shoulder and said, "Thank you."

THEY RAN TO THE border where the tunnel dirt met grass, forgoing any sigil spells in case the castle mages were alert for magical surges. Past the tunnel and the Dam, the grassy patch beyond the trade channels was awash in the golden hour, turning the tall strands of wildflowers into rolling strands of gold. Sometimes Senna forgot that the sun set so late in the summertime.

Emrys dropped Senna's grasp and marched ungracefully forward. For him, such sights were available every day.

"Well, as they say, fare thee well," Emrys said bitterly, turning in the direction of the outer Redwindan stables.

"Emrys, let me escort you home," Senna called out reasonably.

The prince paused. Against the golden light, he was the thief of all of Senna's rational thought, all of his breath. It rendered his thin white shirt translucent, catching the chains along his slender chest and making them glint as radiant as starlight. He was not impressed with Senna right then, but he *was* lovely—unspeakably so.

"If you want to walk all that way just so you can turn down my affection in the comfort of my own castle, I'd kindly ask you to save yourself the trouble."

"Is that what you think I intend to do?"

"I haven't a bloody clue what you *intend*, Goldheart." The words were sharp, but his gaze was soft, a bit desperate. "Do you?"

No—though he felt himself on the cusp of a decision. He just . . . wasn't there yet.

Emrys' frown settled. "That's what I thought."

This time when Emrys turned to go, he only made it two steps before he spun back around, a finger held in the air as if to say, *"Actually, I'm not finished."*

"Do you know the part that is the most maddening? Because it isn't your viper queen trying to have me killed. It isn't having to run for my life through the dark tunnels." He drew close to Senna. If he hadn't been a whole head shorter than the goldheart, they might have stood nose to nose. "It is this expression on your face. The one that says you know *exactly* what you want. The one that contradicts all that you've told me. It gives me hope—something I have desperately tried to leave behind the day I kissed you."

Senna shook his head. "I have despised my own confusion as much as you have. It is not for my own pleasure or amusement that I've displeased you. You must know it kills me to disappoint you."

Emrys sighed.

"*You* were the one that told me the decision had been made. Yet, I don't think it was."

Sometimes Senna thought possibly Emrys knew him better than he knew himself.

"Why?"

"Because for once, you didn't go to Percy."

Senna blinked. Emrys was right. Senna supposed he could counter with any logical requital—the queen's threat had been only directed at Emrys, no one would think to search Percy's rooms for an intruder, Emrys was closer and easier to protect—but he hadn't been thinking of any of those things when he'd shoved Percy off and dashed to Emrys' side. He'd only been thinking that Emrys *needed* to be safe.

Senna wasn't sure what to make of that.

"I am a stranger to myself," said Senna finally. "That is why I seem of two minds. I am of many. I cannot offer to you that which I myself can't comprehend."

The jagged line between Emrys' brows softened. For the first time, he not only seemed to understand the boundary Senna had drawn, but also agreed with him.

"Well, you aren't a stranger to me. I know exactly who you are," replied Emrys gently. "When you figure it out for yourself, you know where I'll be."

It was as clear a dismissal as any Senna had heard. But if he had not gotten the message then, it was even clearer when Emrys began to walk on.

Senna undid the straps of his armor and refastened them so they hung looser on his body, more comfortable for travel.

"I will escort you."

Emrys sucked his lip under his teeth but he did not argue. He led the way, wading through the waist-high grass.

Beyond the crest of the hill, nearly farther than Senna could see, the land sloped into blue mountains against the watercolor sky. If he thought too long about all the memories he could have had of this land, memories that had been stolen from him, his throat would burn.

They didn't speak on the journey back to Redwind—not as Senna finally drew a sigil to shorten the distance, not as Emrys passed over an extra coin to the stablemaster for Senna's horse, not as Redwind's overlook broke the horizon. The silence was not unpleasant, though it could not boast the same easiness they'd once shared between them.

"Thea would tell you of how brightly my anger burns," Emrys said finally. "I shouldn't have been so harsh with you."

Senna shook his head. "I deserved it."

Emrys urged the horse ahead, seemingly still brooding in his own thoughts.

"There's something I'd like to show you," he called over his shoulder. Emrys didn't wait for an answer before leading him on.

This untrodden path reminded Senna of the park where he'd first become inflorescent. Crossing its boundaries was like entering a haven of reverent magic, passing into an aura that made everything—the dirt road, the overgrown wildlife—something *more*.

Emrys tugged on his reins, easing back so as to ride beside Senna. The rest of his anger had drained away from his face. It was no wonder. Senna wouldn't have been able to be angry in a place like this.

"You look contemplative," Emrys commented.

"You look calmer."

"Being here reminds me how wrong your queen is. She wants a *reverent silence*? Here it is, among the whispering leaves and sun-blessed wildlife. I nearly pity her for her delusions." Emrys glanced at him out of the corner of his eye. "What are *you* thinking about?"

"I'm thinking that I'm glad you are feeling more yourself. I thought I'd lost the privilege of your company for good."

"You think I'm fickle?"

"No. I think you are wise beyond what I will ever know."

Attempting to hold back a frown, and failing, Emrys gently kicked the horse along. "It's up over the hill."

Over the crest of the valley lay a sight that made the entire evening feel a little like it had been leading up to this moment. What had been a dirt and stone path was now laid with smartly chiseled crystal bricks. It was what lay along it, though, that demanded the most attention.

Wisteria trees. Or, rather, wisteria vines wrapped around dead trunks and branches, giving them the appearance of new, full-grown trees. There were dozens of them, older than the canons, spilling out their sweet-smelling blooms. They were as beautiful and hazy as rain clouds from leagues away, shedding flowers without any rhyme or reason. Some of them had been wound up high on the tall trellises crowning the walkway until the sky above them was blocked by leaves and silken petals. Through the rifts in the branches, wild dusky light poured over the sparkling bricks, fractured like stained glass or intricate lace.

Emrys dismounted his horse. "This is Oesyth's Grove."

Senna threw his leg over the side of his horse and took a few tentative steps.

"Aren't you a little curious?" Emrys pressed.

"About what?"

"Why each branch bears a different type of flower?"

"Are they not supposed to?"

Emrys gave an endearing smile and shook his head.

"I've only ever seen drawings of wisteria in books," Senna continued. "Pen and ink on paper. Never anything with color."

Emrys nodded in understanding. "They're usually purple. Sometimes pink. But look closer."

Senna reached out, letting the breeze carry one of the branches into his open palm. The white rose-like blossom in his hand didn't match the purple ones that overwhelmed the arboretum. Nudging them aside, Senna found yellow blooms hanging from their own strand underneath.

"When Talsurans speak of Oesyth, the canon of favor, they're referring to favor in the sense of a feeling of approval. Redwindans subscribe to a different definition. We see Oesyth as the canon of favors, *acts* for a person in need."

"I didn't know distinctions like that could exist."

Emrys scoffed. "If the canons are not powerful enough to enforce a unified image, then discrepancies are inevitable. Redwind has the right of it, though."

"Oh, does it now?"

"It's said that when the kingdom was first being built, a widow came to this grove to weep—she had no food for her children, no materials or money for her home. Oesyth appeared to her and said that if she grew her heart's flowers from the branches of the wisteria tree, she would be granted a favor. At first, the woman didn't know what Oesyth meant by *heart's flowers*. But then she thought of the man she'd lost, how his sun sickness had manifested as snowdrops. So she grew those from the wisteria's branches. At first, she thought nothing had happened."

As if demonstrating proof, Emrys reached into one of the trees and pulled out a length of tiny white flowers.

Emrys plucked one off and tucked it behind Senna's ear.

"When the woman returned home, she found a patch of fruits and vegetables growing in the yard where her children played. Her neighbors heard her cries of joy and came to see what had passed. They discovered she'd been so happy at the provisions, that she hadn't noticed the bricks and mortar that had also been left to build her home. Overcome, the widow returned to the grove to thank Oesyth, but when she arrived, Oesyth and the flowers she'd grown were gone."

One of the tree branches caught wind and grazed the back of Senna's neck. He shivered.

"It is unknown exactly who that woman was," Emrys concluded. "Or if she even existed. But still, Redwindans visit here in times of trouble to grow flowers related to the things we most wish for. It is said when the flowers disappear, your wish is granted."

"Do flowers often disappear?" Senna asked.

"I hear that they do. I don't visit often enough to see which branches have remained the same and which have faded away. I don't really have any use for favors."

Emrys ambled forward, hands falling open to prepare for inflorescence. The gesture was such a simple thing, as though Emrys was collecting magic in his palms like dandelion seeds sailing through the air. His movements were all grace, light-footed steps, lazy swaying hips, intention, and confidence. He glanced back at Senna over his shoulder and—

Senna was up to his throat in aching want. He didn't realize how much until he couldn't breathe. His mind was at once standing along the path, clinging to the elegance of Emrys' smile, and simultaneously in another reality entirely. One where there weren't miles and a magical barrier between them. One which consisted of *their home,* and *their bed,* and *their life.*

The want was damming in his lungs. It was the hammer smashing against the one weak spot of his resolve. It was forgetting about anything else in the world except this man, this place, his eyes, the triangle of his chest through his translucent shirt, the possibility of touches and mouths, the promise of them both knowing Senna Kane truly, the vow that this love would bring him to life, would make him *exist.*

Emrys' eyes narrowed knowingly, his smile growing.

"Maybe I do need a favor, after all," he remarked lightly.

Without the effort or concentration it took for Senna to call upon his inflorescence, Emrys reached a hand up into the trees. Through the kaleidoscope branches bloomed a new, long sprig. Emrys caught it and eased it forward.

Senna's breath hitched.

The branch was *covered* in bright amber lilies.

Emrys smiled. "Can you guess what I'm hoping for?"

Senna was on Emrys like a surge of heat-swept wind. This kiss was beyond the scope of what their first had been, beyond the scope of the island, beyond the scope of the damned sun itself. Emrys let out a desperate noise—something sweet that was both a moan and a sigh—and Senna slanted his mouth over it so he could feel its vibrations. His hand fit against the small of Emrys' back, the other cradling his head, holding him in place. They fit together better like this than they had when they'd danced—like every odd curve and line of their bodies had been created to fit against the other.

The terrible—*wonderful*—thing about it was that this kiss was all Senna. The dissonant parts of him—the goldheart's vow, the love-starved orphan—had all fallen somewhere Senna couldn't, *wouldn't*, touch them.

This was the first time Senna had ever done anything for himself.

"*Senna*," Emrys whispered, hot against Senna's mouth. It was the only word he seemed to be able to utter, but it was no trouble. Senna heard the plea for more as though it'd come out of his own mouth.

Protecting Emrys' head, Senna marched him backward, pressing him hard against the trunk of the wisteria tree. Emrys curved into its twisted bark, falling back as far as he could go with the full breadth of Senna's weight on top of him. He hoisted his leg up around Senna's hips, hands slipping from his shoulders down to press against Senna's ass, pushing him further into place.

It was the one spot in Senna's armor that Emrys' heat could bleed through. The first brush of Emrys' hard length against him drained all of Senna's restraint. He dropped his face into the hollow of Emrys' shoulder, kissing and nipping and breathing and cursing. He was repaid in full with purposeful rolls of Emrys' hips, which only spurred Senna on more.

Voices echoed up the path. They pulled back, huffing hot breath into each other's faces.

Emrys' eyes were half-lidded, blown black, but he still had the wherewithal to ask, "Knighthearts?"

Senna brushed the branches that hid them aside, peeking out.

"No, just visitors looking for favors."

"I don't want to disturb them." Emrys pulled Senna forward by one of his leather straps. "Tell me you mean this. Tell me you won't take it back."

"I mean it. I *mean* this, Emrys," Senna promised, nuzzling his nose against Emrys' cheek.

Emrys kissed him, barely a graze of his lips before he was sliding away. His flushed cheeks curved up in unfettered exuberance.

"In that case, I know a place."

EMRYS

WHEN EMRYS HAD BEEN a teenager undergoing his knight training, his instructors had told him, *"When you move from place to place, take the shortest route. Stay on your guard. Do not give in to distractions."*

Senna sucking on his lower lip was *definitely* distracting.

Somehow, Emrys had been managing to cling to the last vestiges of his self-control, guiding them through Oesyth's Grove and into the furthest borders of the castle boundaries. Senna was ravenous, though—not that Emrys minded, actually. But it did mean he had to occasionally break away from Senna's intoxicating ardor to glance around and ensure they hadn't gotten lost.

By some miracle, they'd arrived in one piece.

"Senna," Emrys whispered, using the fingers tangled in his lover's hair to gently guide him back. "We're here."

Senna blinked slowly, lips parted and eyes bright. This was the Senna who was unguarded and seized what he wanted. Emrys had never seen him before, and to behold it now was surely a reward for all the kisses and touches Emrys had showered him in.

The goldheart took in their surroundings. Emrys' back pressed snugly against the glass wall of one of the Redwindan greenhouses. The manicured, florid garden drinking up the last of the daylight. A presence of familiarity and calm after an evening of commotion.

When the haze cleared his gaze, Senna asked, "Are we back at the castle?"

Emrys caressed the side of Senna's face with the backs of his fingers.

"Not quite. This is still just the royal gardens. The caretakers have ended their work for the day and Elora's art studio is all the way across the grounds, so no one will be around to bother us or ask questions." He produced a key from a satchel tucked into his corset. "*And* it just so happens that I have the master key."

Amusement danced on Senna's face. "Who gave you *that*?"

"Probably the same fool who made me captain."

Senna drew his lip into his teeth.

"So we're alone," he said.

Emrys' hand curved around the side of Senna's face and guided his chin forward. He went willingly.

Like honey straight from a comb, Emrys said, "We are *very* alone, Senna."

He punctuated the words with a weightless kiss, letting the light graze of skin ease all tension from Senna's muscles. Perhaps it was because he was a man of plenty that he did not mind taking his time, luxuriating in the sweetness of Senna's touch. In a way, it felt like it'd been what Emrys had been put on the earth to do. His duty wasn't to disappoint his kingdom with decades of failures, but to give this man—this *singular* man—more than he could hold.

This man, who was currently vibrating in an attempt to let Emrys take the lead.

"You look as though you're afraid I'll disappear. But I'm not going anywhere," Emrys swore. Then, considering the alternative, let out a breathy laugh. "Why would I want to?"

"I'm—" Senna paused, swallowing. "My mind won't shut off. I keep thinking—"

Emrys kissed him, smiling fondly, hands rubbing up and down Senna's sides to ease the worries about them, about the future. "We don't have to do anything if you're not sure."

A sigh blew out from Senna's lips, a lifetime's old dread departing like a last dying breath, shuddering and heavy. He buried his face into the hollow of Emrys' throat, above the gold-cast collar, like the real treasure was the pulse of his blood. Then, Senna hoisted Emrys into his arms. A flash of a memory crossed Emrys' mind—these same arms clinging to him as they raced through the Mount Livian tunnels, his life in the balance—but this was nothing like that. The hold was too reverent. Too wanting.

"I'm sure," Senna vowed. It was truer than the goldheart's oath.

It was a mess to get inside—lips on lips, hands on keys, keys scraping around keyholes—but when they did, Senna deposited Emrys on a chaise. Around them, a thousand different flowers unleashed a harmonious mix of fragrances, establishing a unique sweetness to the air.

Senna descended upon him. The pillowy chaise remained steadfast beneath the weight, giving Emrys the confidence to throw his hand back and grip the carved rose motif at the top. The pads of his fingers itched, the telltale sign of magic urging to break free. He wasn't certain what brand of inflorescence would wreak havoc if he let loose his control, but he wasn't willing to find out. He squeezed his fingers, urging the feeling to pass.

The direction of Senna's kisses shifted, trailing lower and lower, to the open V of Emrys' shirt where his body chains lay cool against his skin. Senna took them between his teeth, grazing against Emrys' nipple. Then, grinning at the first taste, Senna closed his mouth over it. Emrys might've sighed, but his blood roared too loudly in his ears for him to hear.

Fingers trailed along the edge of Emrys' corset, skimming the sensitive skin of his abdomen.

"May I?" Senna inquired ardently.

"You *must*," Emrys nearly growled. He reached behind his back and deftly undid the laces. Senna pulled the corset from the front, interest seeming to ripen as he watched the chains drag against the planes of Emrys' chest. With the bodice fully removed, Senna was able to undo the airy trousers, which whisked off of Emrys' body like a loose scarf on the wind.

Senna swore—an ancient word so foul, so dirty, Emrys was surprised it was even in his vocabulary. Senna didn't seem sure of where to put his hands—Emrys' smooth thighs, the bulge straining against his undergarments, or the lace knickers themselves—white as snow.

"If you wanted me dead, I would have handed you the knife myself," Senna said. He mouthed at the length, his damp spit bleeding through the fabric.

Emrys let out a breathless laugh and glanced at the knickers. "Aren't they pretty?"

"They're my ruination." He said it in a way that made Emrys believe Senna was seconds away from tearing them off with his teeth. The idea thrilled him.

He wasn't sure he'd ever been *known* like this—his scent, his taste, the untamed manner with which he gasped for breath, keened for more. His past lovers hadn't cared enough to catalog such things. Yet every sordid detail spurred Senna on, until it was undeniable he was the hungrier beast, poised to strike.

Biting the inside of Emrys' thigh, Senna's quiet lips unleashed a flurry of marveling words. Lust had smudged the words beyond articulation, but Emrys still caught *lovelier than the mountains* and *warmer than the sun*.

"I'm sweet to the tongue too." Emrys yanked Senna forward by his pauldrons. "Do you want me to beg?"

Senna bit a particularly deep bruise into Emrys' skin.

"I want you to madness. I won't make you beg." Senna unclasped his pauldrons and tossed them aside. He guided Emrys' legs so that they rested on his shoulders. "I need to taste you too badly to make you ask for it. I need you to know that Phaedra was wrong. You're *precious*, Emrys. You're incomparable. *Exquisite*."

Senna's hair was pure silk when Emrys combed his fingers through the wavy strands.

"How funny. I always thought the same about you."

Senna looked up.

"Really?" Without a word of warning, he pulled Emry's snowy lingerie down. He made no move to take it off all the way, instead leaving it tugged tight against Emrys' spread legs.

"From the first time I saw your handwriting in one of those letters," Emrys confessed. He opened his mouth to elaborate, only to choke on a gasp the second Senna swallowed him whole. *Bleeding hells.* You're straight to the point."

Senna came off of Emrys' cock slowly, letting his tongue drag like the skin was coated in expensive honey.

"When have you ever known me to maunder?"

He kept Emrys' cock so close to his mouth that it scraped against his chin as he spoke.

"I almost wish you would," Emrys groaned. Attuned directly to his desperation, Emrys' length twitched, tapping on Senna's mouth to beg attention.

This pleased Senna. "I am yours to command."

Emrys did not have to command Senna to take him by his hand and stroke in time with each pass of his mouth. Nor did he have to instruct him to unhinge his square jaw and hollow his cheeks so that his mouth was nothing but soft, wet skin and sucked air.

It was the first time he rode a horse at full speed, wind whipping his face and howling in his ears. It was the strength and wakefulness that came when his fatal wound sealed shut in the Mount Livia baths. It was sitting in the sky among the stars, feeling their burn.

Every inch of Emrys' body was alight with pleasure and humming magic. It was strongest in his core, where it built ever closer to the crest. But he still felt it along the miles of his nerves leading to his sensitive fingertips. Emrys squeezed his fist shut, fighting to keep the pleasure at bay with every sweep of Senna's tongue, but the damage was already done.

"Oh, fuck," Emrys cursed. It must've sounded too much like frustration and not enough like a groan of pleasure, but Senna broke away, holding Emrys' thighs in place on either side of his head.

"What's the matter? Have I done something wrong?"

Emrys dropped his head against the chaise. "No no. You are possibly the most devastating creature I've ever encountered. It's just . . . Well, look." Resigned, he positioned his hand before him and squeezed his eyes shut against the humiliation.

There was silence—Senna likely deciphering what on earth he was looking at.

"I've—never seen something like that before."

Humiliation settled in full force. He'd said it like he was looking at some magical deformity or an art piece he couldn't quite find the beauty in.

"It's whimfruit," Emrys said. "It's perfectly natural for this sort of thing to happen. It grows in the height of passion sometimes. It's meant to—assist it."

"Assist what? *Passion*?" Senna looked as though he wasn't sure whether to be embarrassed at his own performance or amused. "Were you in need of assistance?"

Senna drew Emrys' palm closer, observing the fruit's dark crimson color that shimmered with every stray sunray. It was not altogether different from a raspberry, with full drupelets. The leaves were smooth like velvet, the same softness Emrys had found between Senna's thighs.

Emrys yanked his hand back.

"Definitely not. It would only be . . . more."

That was plenty convincing to Senna, who reached out for Emrys' hand.

The filthy image of Senna putting his hand to his mouth and letting the whimfruit juice drip down his chin with every satisfying bite was nearly enough to conquer Emrys' resolve. But he bolstered his self-control and pulled his hand back.

"I know it seems like we should use it whenever possible. After all, it's available to us at no cost." Emrys cupped his hand over the fruit. "But I'm the sentimental sort. I'll like it best if it's *you*. Just you. At least, for this first time." He paused. "Does that disappoint you?"

"Of course not," Senna insisted immediately. "I have enjoyed every second of learning your body and I don't find you at all lacking. I certainly don't need—" He nodded down at the whimfruit. *"Assistance."*

Relief surged through Emrys' heart. It reared and roared inside him, building power like a summer storm until it wasn't just relief, but lust and adoration and want. Mindlessly, he plucked the fruit away and dropped it in the pot of a nearby pot. Then he pulled Senna down for another kiss, stretching his tongue deep into Senna's mouth. He tasted like the Talsuran cider he'd sipped during the masquerade. Emrys was already drunk with Senna's taste, but not so overwhelmingly that he could not pull off the goldheart's shirt.

Emrys steeled himself for the scar he knew he would find. Seeing it outside the Mount Livian baths, he had noted that it ran vertically from where Senna's ribs ended, all the way down into the trail of hair leading to his cock. Emrys kissed the top, letting the scar guide him lower and lower, until eventually, he unfastened the strings of Senna's pants.

Hard and demanding, Senna's cock sprang into Emrys' waiting hand. He'd held all of his lovers in his hands—their cunts, their cocks, their breasts—but Senna's cock was the prettiest of any that Emrys had the pleasure of worshipping. He was not as long in length as Emrys, but he made up for it in girth—wide enough that Emrys could only graze his finger against his thumb when he wrapped his entire hand around it. He gave a few tight strokes, delighting in the way Senna had to catch himself on the headrest to hold himself up.

"Has it really been so long since someone has lavished such a pretty cock?" Emrys mused, voice silken. He twisted his wrist, wetting his lips. "I've been imagining you with the sweetest taste. Am I right, Senna? Do you taste as sweet as whimfruits?"

Senna gasped out a choked breath, the answer losing all shape against what Emrys hoped was building pleasure.

"Step out of your trousers and sit down."

Senna did as he was bade, cheeks flushing when his cock stood at proud attention between his sizeable thighs. Emrys knelt in front of the chaise, facing the object of his want. He grasped Senna's cock, then closed his mouth over the damp head. Senna's back bowed, desperate hands finding their way to Emrys' neck. It seemed to take every ounce of strength he had to not fuck into Emrys' wet mouth.

Emrys couldn't allow *that*.

He cupped the thick, plush muscles of Senna's ass in his hand and urged him faster, harder, deeper into his mouth. Senna moaned so low in this throat, the sound barely resonated loud enough to be heard.

Emrys craved more of those noises, to watch Senna greedily soak in every building drop of pleasure. He wanted to feel Senna's muscles tighten and grow hot with the sensation, to know his orgasm's taste. How long he'd dreamt about this, and now he had it all.

To his delight, Senna watched him, loosening the reins of his own restraints. He fucked Emrys' willing mouth unlike any other person Emrys had ever been with—taking care as much as he took up space.

Yet it only took one gag for Senna to pull back.

"I like choking on it," Emrys promised the second his mouth was free of Senna's flushed, wet cock. "You haven't hurt me. Come here now. I want you to bruise the back of my throat. I want to hear it on my voice tomorrow."

As soon as the words were out, he realized it had been the wrong thing to say. The lust on Senna's expression cleared enough that Emrys could see he was remembering his own choked and raspy voice. Those tainted and cruel memories had no place here.

"Or," Emrys suggested, "I could lie with you and you could take us both in your hand."

He draped himself over Senna, using an elbow to prop himself up. The chaise was barely big enough to fit them both, but the size only meant Emrys had to lie closer. He clasped into Senna's heat, warm enough to daunt the wintertime.

"Touch me," Emrys commanded.

He obeyed. Emrys felt the desperate pulse throbbing in Senna's fingers as he took them both in hand. The contact set Emrys alight. Losing all sense of self-control, he jerked his hips up. The first brush of friction made the magic at his fingertips tingle and burn.

Emrys closed his open mouth over the cut edge of Senna's jaw, kissing and nibbling. He squeezed his hand overtop Senna's, urging the pace on. Senna gasped brokenly at the speed, hitching into Emrys' kisses.

"You like that?" Emrys asked.

"I want—" Senna gasped hopelessly.

"You can tell me," Emrys swore breathily. "Whatever it is, it's yours."

"I want to *tell you* how—But I . . ." He cut himself off again, his groan of pleasure tinged in frustration. He settled with capturing Emrys' mouth, centering the force of his frustrations into the kiss. The power seeped down to his fist and Emrys felt the intensity of his hold like flames to his nerves.

Finally, his words spilled out, precious molten ore boiling over.

"You're so beautiful it makes the canons sick with envy. I can't look away from you when you speak, when you fight, when you think."

"*More*," Emry began to plead, but Senna kissed the begging away with damp lips and stroked them harder, faster. Emrys moaned and pressed his forehead to Senna's. "Tell me what you want, Senna."

"I want others to look at you and know they can't have you—because you're *mine*. Mine to protect, to hold, to honor and cherish. To *fuck*. I want to reside in you. I want your taste on my tongue day and night. I want you to come so I can see how pretty you are with your seed on your stomach."

Emrys, powerless to give Senna anything less than what he asked for, came hard, spilling thick pearly beads over both their hands. Senna stroked him through it, grinning through heavy breaths, then sucked his fingers into his mouth.

"Nectar from the royal roses."

The sight jolted Emrys from the haze of his orgasm—Senna wasn't the only one who wanted to taste.

Emrys slid down the length of Senna's body, kneeling at the end of the chaise. Suddenly, they were back where they had started—Senna's cock wrapped in the fierce warmth of Emrys' mouth. Senna tangled his fingers on the honeysuckle climbing up the windowed walls beside them, unleashing the vanilla scent like a spray of perfume. Emrys moaned and lapped him up until *finally* Senna came with a moan. Emrys swallowed each wave of Senna's pleasure, drawing out the climax in an effort to keep him teetering at the height of it. But it ebbed back, leaving Senna hissing away in oversensitivity.

When he looked down at Emrys, he was no longer the beast who had been unleashed after years on a tight chain. Nor was he the loose-tongued lover who could lavish praise as easily as he catalyzed blinding pleasure.

He was the goldheart, who seemed to be remembering each of his responsibilities like a tallied list, gaze clouding over with each silent moment that passed.

Quietly, he extracted himself from Emrys to collect his clothes.

Insecurity dulled the pleasant feeling in the base of Emrys' stomach.

"Don't tell me I'm so easy to regret," he said.

Senna looked up from where he was buckling his boots and frowned.

"I would never tell you such a thing. Have I given you the impression I have regrets?"

"You're in a rush to get dressed, and meanwhile your seed hasn't yet dried on my chin."

"Oh." He blinked, then leaned over and kissed Emrys sweetly on his chin. His tongue flickered over the offending spot, then was swept dry with his thumb. He punctuated it with a kiss, only to go back to fastening all of his straps. "There."

"I only mean that your signals are a little mixed, my heart," Emrys said earnestly. "If you want whatever this is between us to end when you walk out those doors, I will respect your decision. But you must know I would have you forever if you allowed it. And it sounded like you wanted that too."

"What I want and what I can promise are two different things." Senna slipped his hand into Emrys'. "But forever sounds nice, if it's with you."

"It does, doesn't it?" Emrys said, poorly attempting to keep his voice more coy than hopeful.

Senna chuckled. To Emrys' surprise, he produced a bright orange amber lily and held it out. At first, Emrys thought Senna was trying to distract him with some poor excuse for a romantic gesture. But then Senna said, "What? Isn't it customary to make vows with flowers here?"

Warmth bloomed throughout Emrys' chest.

"It is," he agreed cheerily, unable to fight back the smile overcoming his face. He accepted the blossom and tucked it behind his ear. "Maybe there's something to Oesyth's Grove after all. This is just what I wished for."

SENNA

L ATER, THEY WALKED HAND in hand back to the castle. Senna's chest felt so light and easy that he'd almost forgotten the events of the masquerade. A part of him wondered if he should be getting back soon. But no one would suspect him if he took his time *tracking down the interloper*. As long as Percy stayed in his room and kept Elora hidden, Senna could rest a night and let his sigil power reenergize.

When they made it to the castle, Emrys disappeared into his room.

"I just need ten minutes to hide my other lover," he'd said, rushing up the stairs. "Wait for me in the library?"

Senna didn't mind. He stepped into the empty room, able to appreciate more than he had the last time he had been here. It smelled remarkably like the one in Talsura. Senna supposed that this was because most of the books Nare kept in the collection had come from Talsura during the exile. If it weren't for the large trees stretching high into the domed ceiling, this library might've even matched Talsura's in appearance as well. Its plentiful lamps shed warm light over the tall shelves, making the books' foil embossing glimmer.

He began to amble around, scanning the shelves to see if he'd recognize any of the books. Before he could get a look, a chair behind him creaked.

"Goldheart Kane. I didn't hear you come in."

It was Thea. Her thin frame was swallowed by a silken robe that matched the bonnet holding the mountain of her long twists. She was hunched over Nare's desk, an assortment of craft materials spread out around her—vials of cloudy glue, spools of thin wire, pliers and hammers of strange sizes. In front of them all, there was a pile of cracked glass and twisted metal. With the pieces in a pathetic heap, it was impossible to tell what it had once been.

Senna sat in the chair across from her and folded his hands on the table somewhat awkwardly. "I hope I haven't disturbed you."

"It's always a delight to see you," Thea replied firmly, but sincerely. "Even if it is a surprise at this hour. Is Percy with you?"

Shame boiled up Senna's throat, but he swallowed it down and shook his head.

Thea's brows knit together. "How was the masquerade?"

"A disaster," he answered, honestly. He told the tale about the queen's sacrilegious prayer in muted words, as if its corruption could follow him here. Thea didn't seem surprised when he reached the part about Emrys nearly running a Talsuran knight through with his thorny inflorescence, but she did squeeze her hands together.

"Ah, so you must be here avoiding Emrys, as well. If he was short with you, try not to take it personally. He was already riled up after rowing with me. Anger tends to sit long in his chest." Senna opened his mouth, but she threw him a silencing glare. "And I'd prefer *not* to talk about it, if it's all the same. But if you want to vent your frustrations with someone who has been on the receiving end of Emrys' righteous fury, by all means."

Senna cocked his head. It dawned on him then that he'd left the part out about him and Emrys kissing and making up. "I don't think it could classify as anything so serious. It was more of an . . . aftershock. I'm only here because he requested I make myself scarce while he hid his other lover in his wardrobe."

Thea blinked, then her face softened with a small laugh.

"For a moment, I thought you meant that seriously."

It was the sincerity in her voice that made Senna recall that sometimes, Thea struggled with simple social mannerisms. Things like eye contact, small talk, and—in some cases—taking words literally when they were meant to be metaphors or sarcasm. Thea was likely imagining some poor bloke stuffed amidst all of Emrys' clothes, waiting to be released and ravished.

"I think he wanted a few moments of privacy to clean the mess inside his room. He knows how much they vex me. Messes."

Thea considered this for a moment, pulling a pencil from her ear and twirling it between her fingers. "You said, *other* lover. Does that suggest you are his lover now?"

Senna hadn't realized the confession had slipped out. But now that it had, he felt no shame in admitting it. Quite the opposite. It felt—natural.

"There's no name for it yet."

Thea hummed. "Affection that big often doesn't." She nudged the pieces apart, aimlessly picking up one of the bent scraps of metal, a faraway look in her eye.

Senna squinted down at the metal, getting a better look this time. His stomach dropped.

"Your Highness," he began gently. Kindly. "Is that . . . ?"

Thea's face snapped up. The change in her features was immediate. Senna recognized that raw terror. It was the unique abject dread that came when someone expected the backside of Mother Mabel's hand. The reflex now meant she expected to draw his wrath. The tiny pile of broken metal and glass made it clear, a fractured constellation glimmering in the heap.

She hadn't just broken the glasses. She'd destroyed them.

"Mistakes are human," he said.

Thea ran her tongue over her lips. "It was on purpose. But I regretted it as soon as I did it."

"Okay." Senna's neutral expression did not change. "I'm not angry, if that's what you're afraid of."

"You should be."

Senna sighed softly. "There's something you should probably know. Emrys hasn't told you because he thought it should come from me. He waited too long to tell me, and I fear I've waited too long to tell you."

Thea steeled her face, but Senna smiled and shook his head, "It's good. I think it'll help you trust me when I tell you I'm not mad."

Her shoulders relaxed only a little. She nodded for him to continue.

"Emrys told me the truth about who he is and . . . where you come from."

Thea's eyes fell shut. She picked up one of the serrated shards of glass and squeezed it. Senna reached across the table and nudged the glass away, replacing it with his own hand.

"Thea, I'm from the same orphanage. I shared your chores and ate the same pitiful meals. And I'm not Mother Mabel. I didn't survive her to become like her. I'm not angry at you."

Thea's expression was empty at first, then understanding beamed triumphantly through. History seemed to rewrite itself, playing over her eyes. Suddenly the fingers beneath Senna's were squeezing like a vice. Tears gathered at her lashes.

"You—you lived at the Gray House Orphanage?"

"In the upstairs bedroom."

Recognition bloomed in her eyes. "You were the boy in the storeroom. The one who hid from Mother Mabel. The one who didn't talk. The queen came early one morning. We all whispered about it in secret after you left, but—no, you didn't leave. Did you? She *took* you. She came to make you goldheart."

Senna nodded. A memory itched at the edge of his mind—thorn scratches on his arms scabbing over, the scent of iron imbued with floral undertones, the floorboards under his bare feet and their permanent lack of warmth.

"Oh, Senna." Thea leaned forward. "Do you remember me at all?"

He smiled, a sad, heavy thing. "I wish I did. But I only remember the terrible things. You're not among them."

A tear charted course down the side of Thea's face. It was a perfect match to Senna's own.

"I thought I'd left everyone behind to die. I thought there weren't any survivors," he admitted quietly.

Thea sucked in a shuddering breath. "There weren't. You saw, the orphans were among the first to get sick, the first to get exiled. By the time Queen Casta founded Redwind, all the other children were dead. All except me."

"I'm unspeakably glad, but—*how*? All that time in the sun and you didn't get as sick as the other children."

A sad smile rose on Thea's lips. "I'm fallow. I can't produce any magic at all, so the sun sickness couldn't affect me. The queen found me and mistook my fallowness for resilience. It was a mistake."

Senna frowned. "A mistake?"

"She thought that I possessed the strength to give the perfect image of a rightful heir. But my fallowness wasn't bravery or skill. She was so disappointed when she found out I could never be inflorescent. The other children were the brave ones. Any one of them would've been better suited for this position, succeeded more than I have done. I am—" She cut off, eyes lifting to the dark windows above. "I am so unworthy of this station."

"You're wrong," Senna swore. "I know we were taught to reject all notions of fate entirely. But don't you think it's a little strange that the only two survivors of that orphanage are—*here*? The most eminent figures among our people?"

"*Eminent*," Thea scoffed bitterly. "I'm a counterfeit!"

"You're a *princess*. When I first met you, I saw your poise, your strength, your wisdom, and knew you could be nothing else."

He crossed over to her. A hand on her elbow, he guided her to stand beside him. She was not as tall as him, though she stood taller than most women. He took hold of her shoulders, drawing focus to their perfect posture. She tilted her head up, somewhat defiantly.

"See?" he said. "The very air around you changes when you refuse to cower. You are power manifest, Acathea."

Then, Thea did something that surprised him. She slid her arms around his waist and tucked herself into his chest, her silk bonnet nestling under his chin. It was only as Senna gently wrapped his arms around her thin frame that he felt the tension drain from her shoulders. It was the shaking arms and tight squeeze of a child who'd had an unlucky start—a hurt spirit who only wanted to be held. Senna held her and held her and held her.

The library door creaked open. Emrys was waiting, a silhouette in the doorframe. He'd changed into his nighttime clothes, arms crossed casually over his chest.

He glanced nervously at them. "Aren't you both a sight? Is all well?"

Thea drew back with a sniffle. "Quite." She patted her eyes with the sleeve of her robes. "Senna, you've had a long day, I'm sure. I should leave you to rest."

As if he'd done it a million times, Emrys tucked himself into Senna's side. "The room is ready for you if you'd still like to stay." To Thea, he said, "You'll get some rest tonight, as well, I hope."

The words took a second to seep in, passing through her stony, royal exterior. They were the words of a brother who genuinely cared, no matter how bitter their squabble had been.

There was still more for them to discuss, more painful memories to make sense of. But for the first time ever, Senna looked forward to talking about his childhood. It would be the only time in his life he'd dredged up his pain with someone who understood.

"Goodnight, Thea," he said.

The line on Thea's forward softened. "Goodnight."

S ENNA JERKED AWAKE VICIOUSLY, nearly thrown off his straw bed and onto the orphanage floor. Cold air burned in his nose as he heaved for oxygen, but none of his breaths were big enough. His own calloused hand clamped over his lips, pressing hard enough to seal away any spare oxygen he might catch. It was his fault Mother Mabel wouldn't let him make any noise. She hated the sound of his voice, and yet he'd disobeyed her—he'd *spoken*—and now he might never breathe again. He might never—

A knife tearing into his stomach, from his navel to his ribs. Blood overflowing out over the open rift. A dizzying nausea with every minute of drained blood. Magical words whispered over him by a dozen different people in bloodied robes. The feeling of something filling him up—past the agony, past the cold. A word repeated over and over and over: siphon, siphon, siphon, s—

"Senna? Sweetheart, are you alright?"

The world around him adjusted, a telescope coming into focus. He wasn't lying in a straw bed but one of soft silks. He wasn't cold, either, besides the freezing sweat drying on his skin.

Emrys leaned into Senna's vision, face illuminated by the moonlight filtering through the gauzy drapes. Gently, he took hold of the hand clamped to Senna's mouth. Senna wasn't back at the orphanage—he was with Emrys.

"Did you have a nightmare?" Emrys asked. Senna nodded.

Emrys sighed. He caressed the backs of his fingers over Senna's temple. "What good is being a knighted captain and prince of this kingdom if I can't scare away the things that plague you?"

Every sinew of taut tension in Senna's shoulders dissipated. Emrys seemed to take this as a good sign, because he carefully eased Senna's own hand away from his mouth. Senna heaved a deep breath, filling his lungs to the brim with the floral air.

Senna clung to that which affixed him to reality. The softness of Emrys' fingertips. The breeze coasting through the tall, open windows. The aubergine sheets draped easily over his bare skin. Though the terror of the dream was still diluting in his racing blood, he knew exactly where he was.

Dampening his lips, Senna rubbed his throat. He'd gone so long without struggling to speak, he'd almost forgotten how tightly his throat latched to any word he might try to utter.

"Can you speak?"

When Senna's face dropped, Emrys took it and pressed a kiss to each cheek, saying, "That's okay. We don't have to talk."

Senna could feel his words in the pit of his stomach like resilient smoke in a rainstorm, fighting beyond all possibility to surface beyond the tempest. They grated past his tongue.

"It'll pass," Senna rasped roughly.

"I'll be here to keep you company in the meantime."

Emrys guided Senna's head until it was nested under the shelter of his chin. Senna burrowed deeper into the soft skin, relaxing at the familiar scent.

Senna was untouchable here. Emrys held him like he was more precious than all the canons' glory. He held him like if Senna gave the command with a word or a glance, even a beating heart would be compelled to stand still. That made it less somehow—the physical strain and bad memories, all of it seemed smaller with his ear on Emrys' heart.

When Senna could speak again, he uttered against Emrys' breastbone, "Tell me something good."

Emrys hummed.

"When I was a boy, I used to steal my father's lap harp from where he hid it underneath his bed and take it by the river to serenade the frogs . . ."

THEA

R AIN CLOUDS VEILED THE sun the next morning. Thea ambled on tired feet to the castle's parlor, rubbing a knotted muscle in the back of her neck. She'd spent yet another night in the library, head pillowed on a dusty book. She could already hear the royal physician scolding her for neglecting the bed that had been tailored for her body and sleep habits. But she couldn't help but crave the peace the library brought—hearing Nare's snoring from her quarters, seeing Nare's notes scribbled on the strewn papers around the tables, the warmth of Nare's sweater when it was draped around Thea's shoulders. Indeed, the library was becoming one of her favorite places.

At the first hint of Nare stirring, Thea had snuck out of the library and crept to the parlor. For reasons she couldn't place, she needed to be out of the library before anyone saw her sleeping at the table. She had every intention of curling into the cushions of one of the parlor settees, forgetting about Laurentine's broken glasses in the pages of a romance book.

But when she plopped into the soft chair, she found Senna hunched over a desk across the room. There were dark circles shadowing his eyes, and his pen moved slowly as he wrote words on a piece of plain parchment.

Thea couldn't always read the unspoken language of the body, but she knew the look of a man who was tired to his bones.

"It's hard to sleep away from home, isn't it?" she said.

Senna's head snapped up.

"Yes," he confessed tiredly. "I've done it once before in Mount Livia, but I slept a bit better here."

"Because of Emrys?" Thea wondered.

A soft smile for himself only. "Because of all of you. Though, he goes to exceptional lengths to care for me."

As if summoned, Emrys appeared, carrying a tray of breakfast treats and hot coffee.

"I couldn't remember how you like your eggs, darling, so I had the cook make them three separate ways. There's blood sausage, too, which is all yours if it's to your fancy—I can't stomach the stuff. Just seemed like something you'd like. The coffee should be extra strong so you won't be too tired on your journey home."

"I'm spoiled," Senna said warmly.

Emrys kissed the side of Senna's head, deposited the tray on an accent table, and looked up, seemingly realizing seconds too late that his sister was also in the room.

"Morning," he said stiffly. Thea pretended she did not hear him. Emrys returned the scorn in kind and returned to his lover. "Are you finished with your letter yet, Sen?"

Senna put his pen down a little sheepishly. "Not quite."

Emrys rounded behind him and plucked up the letter, his free hand holding Senna's chest between his heart and his shoulder.

"*Your Royal Majesty* . . .' That's it? That's all you've written?"

Senna shrank down a little, embarrassed. "I have to be thoughtful with what I say."

"Why? It's only Percy," Thea wondered.

"It's a letter to Queen Phaedra," clarified Senna.

"What?" cried Emrys. "Why on earth would you write to *her*?"

Nare bounded into the room like a storm unleashed, dressed in her traveling clothes—a sure sign that adventure was not far behind. A smile erupted on her face when she beheld everyone, turning joyous when it landed on Thea.

"Oh, fantastic, you're all assembled already!" she beamed. "I had a *dream*."

Emrys tightened his hold on Senna. "You too? Who poisoned the water?"

Thea glanced alarmedly at the teapot, before realizing her brother—*surprise surprise*—was being dramatic again.

"What kind of dream?" Thea said, tired.

"A memory sort of dream. Or, mostly memory. I think my brain was trying to fill in the missing pieces, which meant I was wearing one of Thea's outlandish dresses. Percy was there, too, but he was half horse. Except, his *head* was the horse part and I could only recognize him by his tinny voice and his royal pantaloons."

"*Nare,*" Thea chimed in, fighting back a smile.

"What? Who knows if the horse imagery will become relevant later!"

Senna was holding back his own smile. "Like a premonition?"

"I certainly hope not! Any event involving horses that is worthy of a premonition is not one I'd like to endure."

She sat on the edge of Thea's seat, knocking their ankles together. Emrys poured out a few cups of coffee, handing one to Senna and the other to Thea. Nare held out her hand for one, but Emrys scoffed. "I think you're plenty awake already, thank you."

"*Anyway,*" Nare grumbled. "In the dream, Percy was having tea with Alpedis. When I woke up, I remembered that Laurentine used to invite Alpedis into his dreams whenever he had a research problem he couldn't quite crack. They'd spend hours in his head discussing it, talking through possible solutions. We used to think that he would try to become a canon to be with her, but then we found out he was already married."

"Can you *become* a canon?" wondered Emrys.

Thea snorted into her cup. "Why? Are you hoping to become the canon of aggravating brothers?"

"Honestly, right now it'd be fairly convenient to be the canon of *senselessly broken rare magical objects*, wouldn't it?" Emrys griped.

Nare turned pleading eyes to Senna. "Stop them, I beg of you."

Emrys opened his mouth, almost certainly to allow his morning irritability to lash out once more, but Senna took Emrys' hand and pressed the knuckles to his lips. The tempest quieted immediately, loosening the tension in Emrys' shoulders and softening his hard gaze.

"Well *that's* a new development," Nare said with pleased amazement.

Senna ignored this. "You were saying? Laurentine and Alpedis?"

Smacking her hands together, Nare settled in one of the open chairs. Her knees took up all the space they could, spread a league apart. She gestured wildly in the open gap, like the memory lived there, right before her. "For the canon of the sky, we knew that Alpedis was *smart*. I suppose that's par for the course when you're an immortal deity who's been dealing with powerful magic for millennia. Everything Laurentine knew about complex, taboo magic, he must have learned from her."

"We may not be able to have Laurentine open his journal, but maybe we could ask Alpedis," Thea realized.

Emrys frowned. "She's the canon of the sky. Do you think she'll just drop down for a chat?"

"If it's to keep Laurentine's research alive, maybe," Nare said.

"She's one of the few canons we regard positively in Talsura," Senna added. "Maybe she's reasonable? But if she is, how do we even summon her?"

Thea cocked her head. "Would one of us have to summon her in our dreams?"

"Controlling your dreams well enough to summon a canon takes years of practice. Even if you do, there's no promise that she would answer a summons," Nare countered. She opened her hands before her, officially in *librarian mode*. "All canons have some earthly form, even if they aren't human. I think we imagine Alpedis as some invisible creature of the sky, but that's wrong. She *can* be on the ground. Sure, my dream was a little—*eccentric*, but don't you think it's strange that it came like that?"

"You think she's helping us?" Thea wondered.

Nare sucked on her teeth and dropped her hands. "It's an intuitive feeling."

"Then we should listen to it," Senna chimed in. "Where do we start looking for her?"

Thea folded her hands in her lap. "Isn't summoning a canon difficult?"

"It can be, but if Alpedis is purposefully trying to contact us, then we won't have to go to such lengths. It may be a matter of—" She made a vague motion with her hands. "*Encountering* her."

With the swiftness of someone pursuing a good idea, Nare pulled Laurentine's journal out from her satchel. The inscription of the ivory deer wasn't nearly as bright in the daytime.

"You've all held the journal," she rambled. "You know its tangible feeling of magic, even Thea. Surely one of us has noticed something with that same magical affect. It would be strong, impossible to ignore. Almost like it found *you*, instead of the other way around."

Senna and Emrys exchanged a meaningful glance.

Nare groaned.

"Oh, come on. *Really?* You two are always having all the fun." She waved them on. "Alright, let's have it. What'd you see?"

To Thea's surprise, it was Senna who told the story about the deer they had protected during their encounter with a dre'malor. For someone who'd been plagued with unbidden silence, he possessed a natural storytelling ability.

"At first, we thought the deer was simply impacted by the sun's magic. But I heard the deer . . . say something to me," Senna confessed.

"What?" Emrys sat up. "You never told me that."

"I wasn't sure if there was anything to tell."

"A magical deer *spoke* to you? Darling, that is definitely noteworthy."

Thea leaned forward. "What did it say?"

"You are the one with the heart of gold who has my favor. You must be my blade."

Even secondhand from Senna's lips, the words had an ethereal quality to them—like there was *more* hidden underneath each consonant. Thea rubbed at her chest, suddenly feeling as though there was an emptiness inside her lungs that the words drew to the surface.

"Nare was right," came Emrys' voice into the extended silence. "She's watching us. She favors you, Sen."

The thought seemed to make Senna uncomfortable. "I can't imagine why."

"Oh, please, you are easy to adore." This time Emrys was the one to kiss Senna's hand.

"But what do you think she means by *'You must be my blade'*?" Thea asked.

Nare's eyes glinted like she was already plagued by daydreams of Senna rubbing elbows with a canon. "Does it matter? The only canon who can *do* anything likes Senna. This means she'll talk to us."

"It doesn't guarantee anything," Thea pointed out.

Nare was already off to the races. "Where did you see her again? In the moorlands?"

Emrys moaned dramatically and draped himself like a rag doll over Senna's shoulders.

"Why do I feel like this is leading up to another venture into the vast wide world?"

"Oh no, another adventure. How dreadful," Senna teased in his smooth, quiet voice.

"I am definitely keeping you away from my sister. You're beginning to sound like her."

It stirred something that was still ached in Thea's chest to hear Emrys call her his sister after their fight. They'd have to talk about it soon—discover what in their fight had been truth and what had been insults motivated by hurt.

"Senna's not wrong," Thea commented. "Knowing you, you're actually itching to leave right this second.

"We *will* depart now," Nare said flatly. "While Senna is still here. Thea told me last night about what happened at the masquerade. It may be some time before the Talsurans can make another trip here."

"Shouldn't we wait for Percy and Elora?" Thea wondered.

Resting his chin on his hands, Senna leaned forward. "It's unlikely Percy will be able to sneak out of the castle with all the heightened protection around it."

Nare's face scrunched together. "How are you here, then?"

"I'm '*hunting the interloper*,'" he answered. "That's what the letter to Phaedra will explain, at least. It will make my delay more believable."

"More like you're *bedding* the interloper," Emrys mumbled.

Thea coughed uncomfortably. Nare pretended as if she hadn't heard a thing.

"Then it's settled. We'll gear up right away and scout through the moorlands. Who knows? Maybe Alpedis will be waiting for us when we get there."

"Or we'll be wandering like fools through a wasteland littered with dre'malors?" quipped Emrys.

"Worry not, princeling," Nare said, patting Emrys on the shoulder. "I'm a great shot."

"T ELL ME AGAIN WHY all of this is necessary?" Thea asked. She was stationed with her back to Nare as the librarian—Thea had to continually remind herself Nare was a *librarian*—fastened the leather bands of her armor along her shoulders. "It's not like the armor is going to do a damned thing against a herd of dre'malors."

Nare tugged one of the bands a little snugger than she probably needed to.

"Just put it on, Princess. It'll help me sleep at night."

The extra weight of the armor was eerily similar to the heft of some of her dresses. Every step she took would have to be intentional because of the energy it cost. In a way, it made her feel comfortable, despite that she was moments away from venturing out into the wilderness—the same wilderness where half of her people had died.

Yet, at the same time, she worried she should have felt braver. It was possible that when the queen had taken away her sense of family and belonging, she'd taken away *more*.

"Maybe I should stay back," Thea said quietly. "I don't know the first thing about fighting."

"We don't know for sure that we'll have to fight." Nare fastened another belt, this one securing the leather around Thea's waist. "You're more resourceful than you give yourself credit for."

"With thoughts and words! Not with weapons."

"In a crisis, resourceful thoughts can be life-saving." Her touch disappeared from Thea's skin, something she didn't realize she'd miss until it was gone. "There. All finished."

Thea looked at her own reflection in the window. Beyond the glass panes, gray clouds roiled against one another. "Aren't I missing the scabbard to holster my weapon?"

"I thought you said your weapon was here?" Nare tapped the side of Thea's temple. Thea scowled. "I'm only joking. Emrys and I decided it would be best to give you a staff. Once we get out in the fields, I'll give you a crash course on how to use it. It'll help herd things away from you and give you an opportunity to escape."

"Oh, delightful," Thea deadpanned grimly. "Help me unfasten the straps. I'm staying."

"No, you're not!" Nare sat on the window ledge before Thea and looked her straight on. "Look, when I joined the Academes, the very first thing I was taught was *balance*. Our council leaders were insistent that we weren't just vessels for great knowledge. We also had to defend it and ourselves. So for every rare spell and dead language I learned, I also was trained in the art of combat."

"I wondered what business a librarian had with a bow and arrow," Thea said under her breath.

"It's why the queen chose me. There were plenty of scholars who survived the exile who would've been perfectly adequate in my position. But none of them had the ability to protect it—which, in a brand-new kingdom, means the world."

Thea looked down, smoothing out the freshly oiled leathers.

"You're very open about your time with the Academes," she commented.

"I've got nothing to hide."

Thea looked down. "Not even from your princess?"

The air turned heavy. Where eye contact was a constant point of contention, now Thea found she could not turn her gaze away. There was treasure in Nare's gaze, things she didn't want from other people—the fractals of color, the widening of the pupil.

The door swung open. "Senna is in the kitchen begging travel food off the cook because he has better luck with the—Oh!"

Just like that, the moment shattered. Thea floundered among the broken pieces of it, desperately in search of her composure. She spun around to Emrys, who was slinging a pack over his shoulder.

"You look—formidable," he commented. "Glad the armor fits."

Nare kicked her foot up onto the window ledge, tucking her knee under her chin. She watched the unfolding scene with rapt interest, like she was waiting for Emrys to step out of line, an opportunity to strike. "Had to tighten it to the last hole, but it'll do."

Emrys' face scrunched up when he found Nare hiding behind Thea on the window.

"I came to talk with you alone," he said to Thea.

Nare preened sarcastically. "An audience with the guy who's secretly our prince. How bloody honored you must be."

Thea swatted Nare's knee. "It's alright. I'll be fine."

Nare dropped her foot back to the ground with a *THUD*. "Alright, but just know, Your Royal Secretness—" A jabbed finger at Emrys. "That I overheard the last conversation you had with the princess, and I was not impressed. I won't be quiet this time if you put your foot in it. By that I mean, I'll *really* put your foot in it."

She was gone before Emrys could utter a reply.

"I deserved that," he said sheepishly. "She's more of your guard than I am."

Thea couldn't argue with that. She only stared at him—waiting. Emrys shifted uncomfortably

"I came to apologize," he said.

Thea waited. She wasn't delusional enough to believe she was blameless in the matter of their falling out, but she hadn't quite forgiven Emrys for how quickly he'd abandoned her.

Something caught Emrys' eye.

"Oh, here, let me."

Thea knew what to expect before he even approached. She allowed him to grow his family's white roses wherever he felt they would be seen, while keeping them out of her way.

"This is pointless, you know," she murmured, watching one of the roses appear under her shoulder strap. Somehow he managed to get the roots tucked in between the strap, so that they never pierced her skin.

Emrys stepped back, his expression hard. "It's not pointless."

"I didn't think our subjects would want to see their cold, heartless princess wearing the royal roses so proudly."

The words struck their target with frightful accuracy. Emrys sighed, hands falling to his sides.

"I shouldn't have said those things."

"You only said them because they're true."

"No, I said them because I knew they would cut you where you were most vulnerable. But Mother had already done that, hadn't she?"

Thea swallowed. "She said this was my *occupation*. That in three years, I would go off and leave you as the true leader. She—insinuated that I wasn't really a member of this family. That I didn't belong."

Devastation tore across Emrys' features.

"She said that?"

Thea couldn't meet his eyes. This was enough of an answer for Emrys, who pulled her into his arms and held her as tightly as his strength allowed.

"She's wrong. She's *wrong*, Thea. You are family. You're my sister. I won't let her take you away from me." He buried his eyes into her shoulder and Thea felt a hint of dampness. "I can't believe she would say that. I'm sorry, Thea. I'm sorry."

It took everything in Thea to hold herself together. Pieces of her resolve chipped away, but Emrys clutched her tight enough to keep her from breaking.

"I'm sorry I broke the glasses," she murmured. "I'm sorry I said you weren't my brother. I'm sorry I said that you'll be a failure. You could never be a failure."

Emrys' tight hold squashed his own white roses, but neither of them cared.

"I'm sorry you went even a second thinking you weren't the pride and joy of this family—to me especially," he said.

Thea's courage returned like the first warm day of spring—welcome and overdue. She could roam the moorlands of her exile. She could find Alpedis and seek her help. She may not have been princess of Redwind, but that didn't mean she wasn't a violent storm, the uncatchable refraction of stars. Senna was right. She was formidable. She would prove today that she was power made manifest.

"**T**HEA, I'M ABOUT TO send this off," said Senna while their group rode up the path leading away from Redwind. "Could you read it over and tell me if it's believable?"

From the front of their line, Thea craned to look over her shoulder. She'd been keeping pace with Nare and Charlie, who liked to ride with a little more whipping wind. Emrys and Senna had been falling behind on their own royal draft horses.

Senna was seated atop a chestnut stallion. Apparently, Emrys had tried to convince him to wear Redwindan armor for the excursion, but Senna was content in his formal goldheart plate.

"Have you been riding and writing all this time?" Nare asked him.

Senna only shrugged. "In a sense. I brushed off one of my old sigil spells so the words scribe themselves on the page. It's too bumpy of a ride to write the old fashioned way."

"Is that the kind of ride *I* am, lover?" Emrys crooned from his own horse.

"I'm going to stuff beeswax in my ears," Thea groaned. "I'm happy to read your letter for you, Senna, but wouldn't you rather have Emrys read it instead?"

"Why? Emrys doesn't write royal missives."

Emrys sputtered. "Excuse me? The missives I write are royal by default!"

Thea ignored this. "Unlike you, I can't read and ride. Why don't we take a break so I can read it over? You said we're nearing Mount Livia."

"Yes, we passed the valley where we first encountered Alpedis. That means the mountain is close," Senna confirmed, pointing to the peak of the hill.

"Then we'll need all eyes on the moorlands. No distractions because we're too busy reading or writing any letters."

Like a puppet cut from his strings, Emrys dismounted his horse and plopped into the soft grass, extending his limbs wide away from himself. "Don't have to tell me twice."

They all followed suit, Senna sitting close enough that Emrys could lay his head in his lap. Nare pulled off her jacket and laid the light fabric across the grass so that Thea could sit on it. Thea shot her a surprised look, but took advantage of the gesture anyway.

Senna handed Thea the letter shyly. It read:

Your Royal Majesty,

I'm on my second day in search of the interloper. I've tracked his movements to the western Redwindan shores. I hope to intercept him

*at the harbor before he can board a departing ship. His identity is
still not known, as the locals have never seen him before.*

*In the meantime, I'd like to humbly request that the silverheart cap-
tain assign two copperhearts to the task of Prince Percy's protection.*

I await your orders.

*Your Servant,
Goldheart Senna Kane*

"I'm a little disappointed," Thea admitted, handing the letter back to Senna. "It's perfect and doesn't contain any of the sarcastic, underhanded remarks I'd hoped it would."

Senna scratched a hand up and down Emry's arm, leaving the prince practically purring. "I can't afford any underhandedness. Not when I'm not there to stop her from taking it out on Percy. Besides, she's already threatened to remove me from my post twice this year."

"What?" Emrys' eyes snapped open. "She can't dismiss you from your post."

Thea wrapped her arms around her legs. "She absolutely can. You'd know if you paid attention—or, you know, *attended* your diplomacy lessons."

"Why would I do that when I have you to fill me in?" Emrys grinned. The curl of his lips possessed a sardonic bite.

"Play nice," said Senna. To Thea's amazement, Emrys sighed in dramatic frustration and closed his eyes again.

Holding the letter away from Emrys' face, Senna snapped and sent it off. It whisked away to the queen in a quick flicker of flame and smoke.

"This letter should buy me a few days at least, but then I have to return to Percy. He's probably worried sick, especially if he doesn't know what came of Emrys."

Nare unrolled a map and held it in one hand off to the side. "In that case, we better keep searching. I think we should continue in the direction we're in. If

Alpedis wants an audience with us, I don't think she'll make us wander. But I also don't think she'll stoop to our level just for a conversation."

Thea brought her horse up to Nare's side. "What are you thinking?"

Nare shrugged. "She's the canon of the sky and sun. Where's the best view?"

Ahead of them, Emrys and Senna exchanged a glance. Then a bright grin exploded over Emrys' face.

"Well, Madam Librarian, it looks like you're getting that spa day after all."

B Y THE TIME THEY'D neared the foot of the mountain, Thea was ready for a trip to the spa. Normally, the thought of a masseuse made her shiver uncomfortably, but after hours of stiff riding muscles, she would've endured anything for hot water and the sweet feeling of relief.

But with one look at the base of the mountain path, Thea's stomach dropped.

"Oh fuck—not again," Nare whispered.

Littered among the tall grass at the moorland's border were hundreds of makeshift tents and tall, waving flags. They filled the base of the mountain, with armored soldiers milling in and around them—some training, others lying on sickbeds, their wounds being bandaged. The largest tent was at the head of them all, closest to the foot of the mountain trail. Waving from its highest beam was the emblem of Mount Livia—a black bear roaring on its hind legs, claws poised to strike.

"Not every camp is a bloody exile," came Emrys' voice from behind her, but even he sounded disturbed. "Ride on. Let's find out what's happening."

A few paces into the encampment made it abundantly clear that visitors were not welcome. Thea itched to keep a hand on her staff, but she gritted her jaw and reminded herself that Emrys and Senna were friends of the Mount Livians. There were no threats here.

"Something feels off," Thea murmured. "They're letting us ride in too easily."

"Maybe they recognize us," answered Senna. "If Sascha is going to be any-where, it's the main battle tent. That's the first place we should check."

Emrys looked like he'd barely heard Senna, but still he said, "Why have a battle tent and an army camp with no battle?"

"There's no battle *here*." Senna pointed up the path. "Something made them evacuate."

As they rode, Thea regarded the faces of those she passed. Many of them scowled, ducking into their tents at the first sign of contact, but not before Thea could see the blood and muck stains on their clothes.

The battle tent at the head of the encampment was guarded by two sentries who looked as though they'd barely survived the first week of their training. Instead of guarding the entrance to the main tent, it seemed as though they were merely acting as an inconvenient obstacle. A fat olive-toned person shoved through them, not minding how the short train of their dress dragged through the dirt.

"You're meant to keep dre'malors *out*, not trap *me* in!" they said, pushing through. "Now what's this I hear about—" They stopped, gaze landing on the party of riders before them. "When I prayed for a miracle to arrive, this isn't exactly what I had in mind."

"Surely you're not talking about *me*, Sascha!" Nare chimed, jumping off her horse.

"As I live and breathe, *Nare Demira*? You've grown so much! Where's that little girl who used to run circles around the enclave? Oh, don't stand there like a dead tree, come here!"

Nare dissolved into Sascha's hug with such relief, Thea felt it roiling off of her several paces away.

"I heard you all died," Sascha said, voice hoarse.

"They did. Except for Lane and I. And you too, apparently. Thank the canons!" She hugged him again like a child going in for seconds.

Emrys scoffed petulantly. "How is Nare the miracle? I'm the one that survived the near-death experience the last time I was here."

"Oh, my friends, you are all a beautiful sight for these sore eyes. But I actually meant the *goldheart* is our miracle. I find things tend to improve when he's around." Sascha laughed, pulling back from Nare. "How on earth do you all know each other?"

"After the exile, some ill-advised person put me in charge of the library in Redwind. Can you believe it?" Nare explained. "This mangey lot needed my help doing research."

Sascha turned to Senna and Emrys.

"More work in your quest to cure inflorescence, no doubt? I'm eager to hear all about it, but I'm afraid I just don't have the heart, nor the time. I wish I could be welcoming you all under better circumstances, but obviously, we're a bit frayed at the moment."

"What's happened?" Thea asked.

Sascha turned, mouth open to answer, but they paused when they looked at her. "Ah, forgive me. I don't think we've met." The manners were well practiced, despite the fact that they probably didn't have the heart for pleasantries.

She'd said it a million times—*I am Princess Acathea of Redwind*. But the more her conversation with the queen stewed in her mind, the less those words felt like they belonged to her. Instead, she offered Sascha a small smile and said, "I'm Thea. Emrys' sister."

"Hello, Thea," Sascha repeated, equal parts warm and sad. They took Thea's hand in both of theirs and held it. She got the impression it was more for their benefit than hers. "We've been forced to evacuate after a herd of dre'malors came up the mountain and set siege to the city."

Emrys dismounted his horse. "That must explain why we didn't encounter any in the moorlands all day."

Sascha's expression clouded into a mournful anger. They dropped Thea's hand, face turned to the trampled ground. "We had it under control at first. It would take several soldiers to fell a single dre'malor, but we had the resources. We assumed, perhaps naively, that they were merely a stray few that had followed each other up the mountain. But then the scales tipped and they just kept coming and coming. We were quickly overpowered."

They pulled a map out of their satchel and spread it across one of the open tables. It was a drawing of the entirety of Mount Livia. The craftsmanship captured Thea's attention immediately. The cartographer must have spent at least a year on it, capturing hundreds of the mountain's details. In the drawing, Mount Livia was divided into three sections. Sascha pointed at the gates that separated the middle section from the top and bottom.

"There are gates that close the middle tier off from the top and the bottoms. We managed to confine the dre'malor hoard to the middle tiers, while evacuating most of our citizens either up or down the mountain. The dre'malors won't be able to penetrate the gates to get to them." Sascha scratched their stubble. "It's only a temporary fix. Eventually my people on the upper tiers will need supplies. Not to mention, we estimate that at least forty-five percent of the middle tier residents weren't able to evacuate in time. They're cornered—the dre'malors prowling their streets."

"*Canons*," Nare cursed.

"We haven't found a way to get up to the middle tier without sending my legionnaires to their deaths." Sascha pressed their soft collar into their wet eyes. "There's been no reprieve to collect our dead or take our wounded to the healing baths."

"Why didn't you send word to us? You know I would have summoned my men to your aid in a heartbeat," Emrys said.

"With all due respect, aid like that only comes after negotiations and signed agreements. I couldn't beg your help without knowing what your queen would require of us in return."

Emrys' eyes flashed. "We know better than anyone what it's like to be forced to flee your home. Redwind wouldn't have exploited your suffering."

"Maybe you're right. But what can I do now?" Sascha gestured an exhausted hand at the field of tents. "The damage is already done. I tried to beg the aid of my votary, Ciaran. But he won't leave the chapel."

"You can let us help you now," Nare chimed.

Sascha's shoulders dropped. "I couldn't place myself in your debt again."

"Then don't. When all is said and done, there's a matter we need help with. But your people and their welfare come first."

"Well, hold on!" Thea stammered, panic rising up her throat. This wasn't what they had come to do. When she'd strapped on her armor, she hadn't expected they'd actually come head to head with any danger. She definitely hadn't expected to go courting it. "What if Alpedis is waiting for us?"

Senna drew closer. "What if this is *where* Alpedis is waiting for us?"

Thea exchanged a wary glance with Emrys. Maybe they were both cautious because they'd both been raised under direct orders to protect their well-being. But then she remembered her brother feasted on adventure—spent his spare time collecting runaways and giving them hope—and she knew the battle was already lost.

"Look, Thee," Nare said, grabbing Thea's elbow. "I failed Laurentine in a way that I can never make up for. I failed the rest of the Academes because I was prideful and selfish. What good am I if I let the people around me down all the time?"

"I know you're skilled with your weapon, but we're only four people."

"Four extremely skilled people," Nare reminded her. "You included."

"But—" Thea was floundering. She could feel her argument's validity dissolving. "Going up the mountain guarantees that you'll be putting your life at severe risk. What will I do if you get hurt?" Something intense lit in Nare's eyes, so Thea heard herself say, "Any of you?"

"We'll play it smart," Nare said, squeezing her shoulder. "When you told me why you were planning to find the cure for inflorescence, what did you say?"

Thea scoffed, trying to break free of Nare's hold, but it remained affixed.

"You *told me* that you needed to do what was right for your people. Helping the Mount Livians is what's right."

Thea skimmed the expanse of the camp. Under a tent's ineffectual shade, a legionnaire nibbled at a wild apple with tiny bites. She was trying to make it last as long as possible. Thea knew because she'd done the same thing during the exile.

"Fine," she breathed finally.

"If you help us, we'll help you. No negotiations or signed contracts. Just—just my word," Sascha swore.

"Your word is plenty," Emrys declared with a firm nod. "If you could spare another day, I could rally my own recruits."

"With my people trapped among the dre'malors, we don't have a day."

Nare marched forward, extending her hand.

"Then it's decided. It would be an honor to help an old friend."

Sascha shook her hand once, resolute. Thea took her staff and squeezed the smooth wood until her hand shook too.

She felt Emrys' gaze from the corner of her eyes. He leaned in close, meeting her eye in a manner that demanded she not look away.

"You can stay here and no one will judge you for it. No one will think you cowardly or weak."

"They'd be foolish not to," replied Thea, ever-reasonable.

He scoffed. "Let them try. The choice is yours, sister."

It was then that Thea felt the worst thing she'd ever housed in her body and mind—temptation. Temptation to remain at the foot of the mountain, bandaging wounds and helping strategize. Temptation to let Emrys risk his life, to hand it over willingly over this futile cause. Temptation to give Queen Casta no choice but to coronate Thea for real.

The thought struggled like a person drowning—breaking through the surface, trying to grab air, to live. Then it sank back down where Thea would not help it thrive. She felt despicable—utterly sick at the mere consideration of such a betrayal.

She set her jaw. "Where you go, I go."

"We'll not let any harm befall us," Senna swore. "If it seems we're overwhelmed, we'll retreat."

"I'll leave you to your preparations," Sascha interjected. "When you're ready, you'll find my legionnaires patrolling the lower tier by the gates. Tell them I sent you for assistance, and they'll let you into the secondary tier. If you're successful, I'll owe you everything. But if you're not, I need to be prepared so . . . excuse me."

The panic of what Thea had agreed to began to settle into her stomach like hot stones, but before she could spiral off into a terror, a whistle sounded from across the field.

A rider—no, two—came galloping up the path.

It was such an impossibility that Thea didn't recognize the rider until Senna darted forward and cried out, "*Percy?*"

Terribly, it was. Percy was taller, bigger, more imposing than he'd ever been before, mounted atop a chestnut horse. Behind him, Elora expertly rode as passenger, matching each galloping stride with trained ease. The horse's reins were coated in a brilliant gold, the same polished cast as the horse plaque resting between its eyes. But it wasn't until Percy drew close enough that Thea realized that the crest had been embossed with the image of a hand wielding the sun itself—the symbol of the goldheart.

Percy was riding Senna's horse.

"He sure knows how to make an entrance," Nare mumbled.

Percy looked—for the first time since Thea had met him—like a real Talsuran. A hard-edged frown. A propensity to squint like everything was too bright. The general affectation of someone who had lost a little of what made life bright, possibly for good. He looked nothing like the young man who favored embraces with his friends, compliments, and long stories with winding sidetracks.

The prince yanked the horse's reins upon reaching his friends. His eyes were rimmed red—the kind of claret red that only occurred after a lengthy bout of tears. Percy looked expectantly at Senna, who awaited his own cue. The silence between them ran thick as blood.

"Are you alright?" Senna asked, finally.

"Am *I* alright?" Percy scoffed in disbelief. "You ask me if *I'm* alright?"

"I—" Senna swallowed, glancing at the rest of them with a lost expression. "I feel I've missed something."

Rage swelled on Percy's face, but he turned to Emrys, mouth twisting strangely. "You're unharmed?"

Emrys tossed an unsettled look at Senna. "Uh, yeah, mate. I'm tip-top."

"I'm glad to hear it," Percy replied. It sounded sincere, if not a little prickly. "Senna didn't tell me one way or the other, so."

Senna's face dropped like he'd been slapped.

Emrys gently touched Senna's elbow, a gesture of comfort. "How did you find us?" he asked Percy.

Percy turned back to Senna.

"Everyone in the castle is convinced you're dead, you know."

Senna winced. *"What?"*

"Apparently a few of the silverhearts found pieces of your armor covered in blood near one of the trade channels."

"T-there was a copperheart. Emrys, he—" Senna shook his head. "The blood wasn't mine."

"I didn't know that. I asked all the staff if they had seen you or Emrys. No one had seen either of you. Maybe I wouldn't have worried, but all I could remember was that the Grit Fingers have been hunting you!" Percy's shoulders dropped. "Then my *mother* made a comment about how if Senna had aided the 'interloper' in any way, she'd be forced to give him the same punishment as she would any traitor. I was *sure* she'd already caught you both and killed you—fabricated some story to keep me calm," Percy cried.

Elora squeezed Percy's shoulder. "Even in the morning when she showed Percy Senna's letter, we still thought it was magically forged."

Percy pulled the missive out of his jacket and threw it to the ground at Senna's feet.

"I spent all night *sick* with grief, trying to convince myself I was mistaken. And because *someone* made such a scene at the masquerade, I had to wait for the changing of the knighthearts to sneak away through the trade channels. Imagine my surprise when we arrived in Redwind, only for the knights to tell us that you're *alive*."

"They said you might not return for a few days," Elora explained. "We put together that you might've been returning to Mount Livia, but we weren't sure."

"Whatever you're doing here must be pretty canon's-damned important," Percy shot out.

Thea knelt down and grabbed the letter. Percy had to have left immediately after it had been delivered. It was crumpled, some of the magical ink smudged with dried tears. She looked to Senna, an unspoken invitation to allow him to explain. But he dropped his gaze to the ground and rubbed the base of his throat. Offering a hand for Elora to dismount, Emrys began to explain what they knew so far—about the dre'malors, about the people trapped in the mountain.

"Of course you're here to play the hero," Percy grumbled. He dismounted and immediately began rummaging through his horse's saddlebags for his shortsword. "Fine. You'll need every extra pair of hands you can get."

Senna snatched hold of the blade before Percy could pull it out of the bag all the way. "But not yours."

Percy's jaw twitched. "Let go of the blade, Senna. I'm helping."

Senna did not relent.

"Be wise. I know you were worried and I am so sorry to have frightened you. It was too dangerous to write to you directly." Percy shoved Senna back, only for Senna to tighten his grip. "But I have a reason to be away from Talsura. You don't. If your mother discovers you've escaped again, she'll eventually come to the conclusion that you're *helping* Emrys."

"Which I am. Earnestly so."

"As am I. But surely you must see that there is too much at risk to allow even the slightest suspicion that you're colluding with any Redwindans. Remember her threat."

Whatever frustration had been reaching a boiling point inside Percy finally bubbled over. He hoisted his shield with a furious yank, brandishing the ornate barrier like a war hero.

"What *really* happens if I allow her that suspicion?" Percy exclaimed. "Is it truly the end of the world?"

Senna looked the way people do when they've caused a child to cry unexpectedly and they haven't any idea how to make it stop.

"It's the end of *ours*," replied Senna earnestly. "It's an easy excuse to dismiss me from my station like she's been threatening to. It's an invitation to watch your every movement with hawkish precision until you can't even blink without her knowing."

"It's a risk I'm willing to—"

"It's more than a risk. It is the active decision to sacrifice your throne and the future of your people. If you remain here long enough for her to realize what you're up to, our entire undertaking is a failure."

This time Percy grabbed his sword, as resolute as ever.

"I'll petition the council. Find a loophole that allows me to become king sooner."

"Which will take *time*, and your mother will not go down easily. What if she's ahead of you, already conniving to keep you hidden away? Convincing the council to forfeit your right to the crown? All that risk, and for what?"

"To help people in need!"

Senna drew in a long breath.

"I understand your passion to protect those who need it, but you'll protect them best by getting back on your horse and going home."

"I'm not going home! Not after it took so long for me to get here. To ensure that *you* were safe!"

"You've seen I'm safe. Return home," Senna repeated, his patience held on a thinner thread with every passing second.

"I know what this is," Percy laughed sardonically. "You don't want anything to get in between you and Emrys. Don't you know the lives of these people are more important than your *thrilling* romance?"

Thea's heart sank. This wasn't about any of that. This was about Percy—who wanted nothing more than to be *worthwhile*. Percy, who wanted so badly to stretch the limits of what he was capable of and fix everyone's problems with a snap of his fingers. Percy, who underneath it all had a fragile pride and a fear of being alone. Thea knew Percy's heart like her own. Him leaving now would be his way of admitting he was the most controllable and powerless among them.

Senna laid his hand on Percy's sword so gently, it was easy to lose the sheer strength of the grip. Percy held no chance when Senna yanked it away.

"This isn't up for discussion. You will go home. *Now.*"

Percy scoffed, rolling his eyes. "I don't have to listen to you."

He took one step forward, but upon attempting to pick up the other foot, he found it clamped to the ground by smooth vines.

Percy choked, stunned.

The goldheart seemed equally stunned. He turned to Emrys, who merely shook his head and said, "That was you, Senna."

This only empowered Senna more. He reached out his hand, as if to hone his inflorescence, and locked Percy's other foot to the ground. Bitterly, Percy fought against the bindings.

"Release me at once! I want to fight! That is a direct order, Goldheart."

"You aren't skilled enough with a sword to take on the dre'malors and you know it. You'll die up there. I don't know where all this has come from, but it isn't you. You're acting like a spoiled child!"

"*Fuck you!*" Percy exploded, frustrated tears spilling over his eyes. "*Fuck you,* Senna Kane. I wish my mother had picked some other stupid orphan who could obey his ruler's directives!"

Senna stilled, stone-cold.

It was this—this specific combination of cruel words—that made him unbind Percy at last. Thea looked at Senna long enough to see his eyes fill with tears.

She couldn't bear to watch any longer. Her own eyes were already brimming, the aftershocks of Percy's words catching her in the crossfire.

But Emrys was already there. He threw his strength into giving Percy a righteous push. "How *dare* you speak to him like that!"

Percy only shoved him back, poking his head up over Emrys' shoulder to scoff at Senna.

"What? Nothing more to say? What a shock."

Elora gasped. Thea couldn't stand another blasted minute of it.

"That's *enough*!" she yelled.

Silence spread throughout the camp, save the echoes of her voice sitting in the air.

"You." She pointed her staff accusingly at Percy. Her voice's edge was even sharper. "That *orphan* has dedicated his life to your care. And it's an *orphan* who has given you even an ounce of your freedom in Redwind. Do not forget that for a single second."

Percy had the decency to look positively devastated. But Thea was already forging on.

"If you want to join us on the mountain, fine. You're a grown man. No one, not even your goldheart"—this she directed sharply at Senna—"can tell you what to do. But if you want my opinion, which you should, Senna is right. You're acting foolish. You're acting cruel. Follow us if you must, but leave this heartlessness here or you will quickly find yourself without friends."

Percy's chest heaved, more hot tears spilling over his eyes. With a huff, he snatched his sword and shield from the ground.

"I'm going. That's final."

A curse spat out of Senna like a mouthful of blood. He shook his head and stomped up the path to the city, leaving them all watching him go. Emrys was next to follow, then Nare. To Thea's surprise, Elora bounded past them, sprinting to catch up. Percy tried to grab her arm, but she shook him off and fell into pace with Emrys, wiping her eyes with the back of her hand.

"What's happening to me?" Percy said bitterly, almost to himself.

Thea didn't answer. She didn't know.

23
CIARAN

I F CIARAN LYNWOOD HAD let himself die the day he'd been tied to Jasrath's altar, at least he would have been useful, spread around the vast world that would never know the weight of his footfalls. He imagined himself not as a lost, hungry man, but a wealth of carrion. Bones used to compose birds' nests. Flesh served as an ample feast. The most organic parts of himself consumed, carried across the sea, used to fertilize new life somewhere the ground didn't already know the taste of his blood.

But Ciaran had been weak. He'd made a deal with the canon of thieves, one that stitched his existence with impenetrable thread to the Grit Fingers. If he'd known what would happen, what he'd be asked to do, maybe he could've mustered up enough courage to let himself die. But desperation had its way of giving the righteous hope they didn't deserve.

Ciaran's hands shook as they cupped around the warmth of a single stick of incense. The muscles in his legs had begun to go numb with the ache of kneeling on the cold ground, the only indication that this prayer—this pitiful, humiliating exhortation—had been going on for hours.

This wasn't the way things were done—Votaries kneeling on the floor, begging, shivering. He'd wanted to do this the right way and light the hearth behind the altar. He'd wanted to stand and pray the way he was meant to. Any plan for normalcy had been shattered when the dre'malors had roamed the Mount Livian streets. To keep them from seeing him through the windows, he'd had to drop to his knees in huddled wretchedness just to continue his prayer.

Dragging his stinging eyes away from the incense's burning end, Ciaran found the neglected temple darkening with the waning sun. It'd been a few hours after noon the last time he'd let his eyes focus, yet in all this time, Jasrath hadn't answered.

"Jasrath, end this siege," Ciaran whispered. He'd prayed so much that the words had run his throat raw, like a well-trodden path. Now, he was just speaking to the canon like a person in the room. His parents would have bled his knuckles with a switch if they'd heard him addressing his patron canon without any devotion. But the time for reverence was over, his patience even more drained with every breath.

"Call off the dre'malors. The people of Mount Livia have done nothing wrong."

The incense continued wafting upwards, undisturbed. Ciaran laid his forehead on the temple ground. More negligence from his patron.

"Canons *damn it all*!" Ciaran pounded his fists onto the ground. He almost hoped the beasts prowling outside would hear him. "I have done *everything* you asked. I delivered the Grits to Mount Livia the day of the goldheart's arrival. I risked my life shepherding these—these *beasts* to terrorize these innocent people. But the goldheart isn't coming. He isn't coming this time."

The incense went out. Ciaran snatched it all in his hand—the leftover stick, the ceramic burner, and the silver ash—and hurled it across the room. It crashed into the desolate hearth, the burner splitting clean in two.

It was pointless. Trying to reason with a vengeful canon of thieves was *pointless*. There had been days when Ciaran had thought he could work beside Jasrath, find out the purpose behind the canon's madness, and uncover a solution that suited them all. But something had devolved Jasrath into chaos beyond what Ciaran could touch. Any effort to seek reason underneath the capricious plans and unnecessary bloodshed would fail.

Ciaran struggled to stand, legs weak. He didn't want to give up, but what more could he do? If Jasrath wouldn't listen, then he was worthless. He couldn't seek the help of the other canons—not when his patron was their pariah. All he could offer was his own two hands and his willingness to lay down his life to give Mount Livia a chance. He would keep praying until his body gave out.

Behind him, something gasped.

Ciaran paused, squinting into the dark temple.

He could feel the rasp on his voice before the words came out. He couldn't remember the last time he'd had anything to drink. "Come out into the light."

Then, into the meager glow cast across the floor, a boy emerged. He looked younger than Ciaran by at least a few years. His fear-twisted features were too big for his face, and the glasses balanced on his nose were cracked. Ciaran had lived in Mount Livia for months now, hosting regular prayers for the citizens, but he didn't recognize the trembling boy before him.

"Who are you?" Ciaran asked.

A pause, long enough for someone to choose between retaining their secrets or revealing all of them.

The boy took off his broken glasses and stuffed them in his pocket. "I'm Percy. I'm helping survivors evacuate." When Ciaran didn't answer, Percy looked at him closer. "Are you alright? You look a little worse for wear. I'd escort you out now, but erm—" He ducked from the window. "There are three dre'malors passing through. We'll have to wait them out, I'm afraid. But we'll be safe here until the path down the mountain is cleared."

"I don't intend to evacuate. I have to pray."

Percy knit his brows. "Pray?"

"I'm Head Votary Ciaran Lynwood. Though I don't feel much like it at the moment. Actually, it rather feels like all of this is all my fault. My patron *refuses* to listen."

A beast's shadow crossed the window. From just the silhouette, it was impossible to decipher what animal had consumed the person's body to make the monster. From the corner of his eye it seemed like a beak and feathers, but upon a second glance, the shadow shifted into something horned. Percy scuttled across the room, dragging Ciaran out of sight from the window. They sat together against the wall. Percy put his ear to the weathered planks, listening for movement on the other side.

Silence.

"Take heart, friend. Failed prayers aren't the fault of those who speak them. Your patron is the one to blame." Recognition dawned as Percy studied Ciaran's face. "You must be the votary who helped Emrys."

Ciaran had tried to help a great number of people. The name held no meaning to him, until he remembered the Redwindan captain from the healing baths. The one who had helped save Sascha when Ciaran had snuck the Grits in through the mountain channels in preparation for Senna Kane's arrival. Jasrath hadn't been planning for the goldheart to arrive with company—magically formidable and protective company at that. The Grits had thrown everything they'd had at Emrys to eliminate that protection, but if Ciaran had sent a silent prayer to Oesyth in the captain's defense, no one needed to know.

"I remember him," Ciaran answered. "I hope he is well." He found he meant it.

Percy's lip twisted. "Me too. He's here, fighting the dre'malors."

"Then he should leave," Ciaran said immediately.

"I'd tell him myself, but we got separated. My goldheart slipped down an alleyway. I think Emrys and my partner followed."

Something pieced together inside his mind then. The realization came easily because Ciaran was, at heart, a Talsuran.

"You're the *prince*."

"I'm afraid so." Then, with a forced, teasing smile, he added, "Don't feel like it much at the moment."

"To be blunt, Your Highness, I can't imagine what on earth you're doing here. Even *I* don't want to be here."

"Then let's go. If we're quiet on our feet, I think I can get you to the mountain path without drawing the dre'malors' attention. There's a safe house above the midway gates."

It wasn't as strong a temptation as the food in the basilica's kitchen, but it was a near thing. Only this time, there were lives at stake. If he gave up trying to contact Jasrath, then the Mount Livians were doomed. He'd been selfish once, and it'd cost him everything. He wasn't going to make that mistake again.

"I can't," Ciaran replied, his torment bleeding into his voice. "I have to pray. I have to pray or we're all dead."

Percy's hand found his wrist.

"The canons aren't listening, Ciaran."

Ciaran knew this. Once he'd sworn his allegiance to the canon of thieves, he'd sealed the disdain of the other canons. Now none of them responded to his pleas.

"What else can I do? Prayer is all I know. I'm *good* at it."

"You can't be good at it if you're dead. You can *leave*. We can go now and give you a chance to return to your prayer somewhere safe." Percy shot a sneer at Ciaran's prayer materials, still littered across the floor. "But if begging was what the canons wanted, don't you think you'd be saved already?"

Ciaran banged his head against the wall, savoring the sting so much he did it again.

"Look, I–I understand that Talsurans despise most of the canons. But haven't you ever thought that maybe you're forced to live in darkness *because* you've not sought out the canon's blessings? I can't give up now. I can't."

A sorrowful expression crossed the prince's face.

"To tell you the truth, friend, you don't look very blessed."

"I'm not. I know I'm not. But I still have to pray because I *know* the dre'malors were brought here as a result of a canon's wrath."

"All the more reason to leave them alone."

"No, you're not getting it! I *can* convince this canon to change his mind. I just have to establish a strong enough connection."

"Alright. What can I do?" Percy asked.

"W-what?"

"You're trying to establish a connection with a canon. What can I do to help? You won't let me take you into the mountain."

"Only because the prayer has to be given in a holy place. The connection will be even harder to sustain the further into the mountain we go. But this isn't my preferred temple, believe me." Ciaran banged the thumbed end of his fist to his forehead, desperately trying to concentrate. What would he do if he was still home at The Cloth?

"I need the magic of another person." At Percy's uncertain expression, he rushed, "It's not much magic! You wouldn't even need to be an ordained votary through the Cloth. I could just teach you, the prayers and spells and the connection would have to grow stronger. The prayer will be so loud my patron won't be able to—"

"I don't know if it'll work," Percy cut in nervously. "I'm dreadfully bad at magic. I can barely manage the most basic sigil spells and I've never been inflorescent. Not once."

Ciaran's stomach sank with a grimace. "We'll make do. Now kneel."

Unwilling to risk dre'malors spotting them from outside, Ciaran assumed the proper kneeling position. Percy remained frozen against the wall. Patting the spot on the cold ground beside him, Ciaran did his best to exude confidence—like the votary he never would be.

"There are people starving in the moorlands and you won't attempt a prayer?" Ciaran prodded.

At this, Percy crawled in front of him.

"Lay your palms open like—yes, exactly." Ciaran heaved out a sighing laugh. "I forget how many Cloth rituals you must've attended in your lifetime."

"Later, you'll tell me what a Talsuran Cloth cultist is doing working for a foreign sovereign," Percy grumbled.

"I'll tell you anything you want to know, but first, clear your mind."

The rumors of Percy's intellect were true. He was a lightning-quick learner, innately following each step of the spell before Ciaran could instruct him. Although his face betrayed his uncertainty, the prince moved his hands to draw the connective sigil as though he'd done it a hundred times before.

But that was the strange part. Percy was performing the spell with complete accuracy, better than many of Ciaran's own pupils had after months of training. Yet, the power didn't *feel* amplified. The connection was just as distant and intangible as it had been when they'd begun.

"Focus inward," Ciaran murmured, urging his connection with Jasrath to solidify. He strained, murmuring the incantations stronger and quicker, until Percy couldn't keep up.

And then—Jasrath was right before him. Hand in hand. Breath on breath.

Percy's expression had gone utterly slack. His lips moved around the shape of the incantation, but the voice that came out said, *"Hello little pet."*

Ciaran saw it all then, as if the magical sinews of his mind that formulated thought in Jasrath's mind now fired in his own—one mind, one memory, one basin of thought. He saw Jasrath's past, bloodstained and clawed open. He saw the present, nothing more than a fragile illusion, already cracked, waiting for the final blow. He saw the future, which was awful beyond anything Ciaran could comprehend, but equally inevitable. It *would* come to pass.

Jasrath would not call off the dre'malors, Ciaran realized. Not until he had Senna Kane.

Ciaran stumbled back, the connection snapping in half. At some point, Ciaran had bitten his lip, and the blood filled his mouth with the taste of iron.

"*You!* You!"

Whatever hold Jasrath had on Percy disappeared. The prince fell back into himself

"Me? What's the matter? What did you see?"

A bead of sweat trailed down Ciaran's brow. "You—you don't remember what you said?"

"I didn't say anything. Just the incantation!"

Percy didn't know. He had *no* idea.

Ciaran clutched Percy's shoulders, drawing him so close, their foreheads almost slammed together. His hands shook, fingers pressing hard enough to bruise Percy's pale skin.

"Seek Jasrath's favor. Seek his favor, Percy. Your life depends on it. Seek it *right now.*"

"*What?*" Percy fell away like he'd been slapped. "What are you *talking* about?"

It was possible that Ciaran would later mourn all the energy he'd poured into changing an inexorable future, but he'd never forgive himself if he didn't try.

"Percy," Ciaran began fiercely. "Jasrath is—"

Outside, an ear-splitting scream. It was the sort of scream that ravaged the throat, coming out in blood and spittle. It was the kind of scream that was sometimes the last sound a person ever made.

Percy's face went pale.

"Elora," he whispered. He tore himself away from Ciaran, stumbling over his own feet, banging pews and statues in the dark in a desperate effort to get through the door.

"Percy, wait—"

"That was—I have to—"

"You'll *die*—"

"I'll come back later. Stay safe!"

Ciaran had enough sense to clamber after the door, heaving it shut once Percy disappeared into the unsafe streets. He deflated, hands still shaking as he clutched the doorknob. Exhausted, he turned his face to the incense in the hearth and whispered through the taste of dirt and dust in his mouth, "I won't do it, Jasrath. I won't."

The thing about lying to himself, Ciaran found, was that for all he knew his deceptions weren't true, he couldn't help but cling to the illusion like a lifeline.

"I won't do it," he whispered. This was his new prayer. "I won't do it. I won't do it. I won't do it."

PERCY

T HE STENCH OF FESTERING sickness and rot suffused the Mount Livian streets like pus pouring from a putrescent wound. This was the reek of a pack of dre'malors.

It was so strong, so nauseating, that Percy nearly doubled over, vision blurry. But he couldn't afford even a second of weakness.

Because for every dre'malor snarling in the streets, a civilian was nearby, fighting them off with a plank or a kitchen knife, slicing amateurishly through the air, clinging at whatever chance of survival they had left. It was fleet-footed chaos, unraveling so quickly Percy struggled to identify faces between slashes, dodges, and snarls. He snatched a door that had been torn off its hinges and held it by its knocker, wielding it like a shield as he desperately searched for Elora among the madness.

A roar echoed down over the mayhem. Across the street, a dre'malor crouched on a roof's ridge, perfectly poised for an ambush. The clouds parted, spilling just enough moonlight to reveal a dozen mangled birds sticking out of the rotted body by their beaks.

Relief flooded through Percy when he noticed the dre'malor hadn't seen him, only to run cold when he traced its bloodshot gaze to Elora.

It lunged before Percy could utter a sound. Its talons sliced through the air, aimed to pierce Elora from behind. A desperate sound choked out of Percy.

He threw himself between them, intercepting the beast and heaving it away with the door. Elora spun around, face pale and blood-soaked. She acted before Percy had fully realized what she was doing. Throwing all her strength into the sharp, pointed end of a mailbox stake, she crushed the dre'malor's head into the pavement.

"Get back, you blasted fuck!" Elora shrieked.

It erupted into an explosion of bone and feather and gore. All that was left of the creature—an arm, a half-exposed spine—twitched, before going still.

Elora spun to Percy, tossing aside her weapon in favor of taking his face in her blood-coated hands.

"Are you alright?" she demanded. "I was so worried when we got split up. But then the dre'malors found Thea and Nare with all the survivors trying to escape into the lower tier and I couldn't just leave them."

"You did everything right, you beautiful, astonishing creature." He pulled her into his arms, squeezing his eyes shut into her hair to get his terrified tears at bay. "My love. I hate that your last memory of me was almost my vile behavior. I don't know what's becoming of me."

"Don't trouble yourself with that now," she said, brushing his hair out of his face. "We have to finish off the rest of these beasts and evacuate somewhere safe."

"Evacuate? Why?"

Elora flicked her head so that her black curls slid out of her eyes. "I think the human side of the dre'malors are on to us. I don't know how, but they *know* we're trying to sneak the civilians through the gates. They're targeting the checkpoint. The Mount Livians are safer hiding indoors until Sascha can supply reinforcements."

Percy thought back to the votary in the temple. If this really was the wrath of a canon, then who knew how long they'd set their torment on the Mount Livians? He pulled Elora back, looking her over for wounds.

"What happened to the sword and shield I gave you?"

"I handed it to a mother trying to lead her children to safety."

Percy rubbed her arms. "Of course you did."

Further up the street, a dre'malor smacked a survivor, sending her skidding across the cobblestones to Percy's feet. Elora caught her, pulling her out of the way before the dre'malor could land on her. Percy set his door-shield in front of them like a barricade. Now that his hands were empty, he'd need to find another weapon—and fast. He skimmed around some of the ruin nearby, choosing a metal picket that'd been torn off a nearby fence. The embellishment at the top was sharp, so Percy held it like a spear and pointed it at the prowling dre'malor.

"Get her to safety, El," he said.

"What? No, come with me!" she demanded fiercely.

"Not until everyone has safely retreated."

 "Now is not the time for your heroics."

From the east side street, a stampede of footsteps approached. Percy tensed, aware of every inch of his flesh under his thin, unarmored clothes.

Then the cobblestone cracked, splitting apart under the force of a large, spiky root. It was too thick for any dre'malor claws to try to tear through, though the beasts tried. Percy traced the spikes back, all the way to Emrys. He was the picture of divine retribution—anger and righteousness laced in the ferocity of his sharp eyes. Senna was close behind him, sword drawn, along with a group of survivors and soldiers, each with weapons of their own.

Emrys lifted his hand, and the roots shot up from the cobblestones. More tendrils sprouted from the thick trunk, encasing two of the dre'malors before shrinking back down toward the ground. The beasts keened and roared, fighting against the inflorescence, their flesh tearing with the struggle. But the roots did not wane.

"Glad to see you both," Emrys said when he noticed Percy and Elora standing there. "Sorry to be cutting it rather close. But we've brought reinforcements."

True enough, his roots caged the dre'malor to the ground tightly enough for Senna to drive his sword clean through the monster's throat. The head smashed against the dirt, leaving a trail of gore behind as it rolled away.

Percy had only a second to catch his breath, because Elora had been right. With this one killed, three more broke through a nearby metal fence, roaring a sickly sound. Pieces of the fence stuck to their decaying bodies, spikes and metal rods poised in all directions.

The one nearest to the group eyed them, growling like the bear it used to be. But before it could strike, an arrow pierced the air, prodding the dre'malor in the middle of its open mouth. The scent of acrid smoke was the only warning. The arrow exploded on impact, blasting the dre'malor's head to bloody bits.

From farther up the hill, Nare sprinted down with Thea on her heels. Behind them, the survivors they must've freed from the mountain trailed cautiously after them.

"Did I get it?" Nare called out. "Oh, *hell yes*. Look at that, Thea! Is that not fucking badass?"

"That was your last explosive arrow, smart-ass!" Thea snapped. Then, "Emrys, are you all okay?"

"Never been better," he said, trying—and failing—to catch a dre'malor around the throat with a thorny vine. Noticing his struggles, Thea swung her staff with all her strength at the dre'malor's legs, knocking it off balance.

It dropped to its knees, allowing Emrys to finally get the vines around its neck. He pulled them tauter and tauter until the thorns cut through the gnarly flesh and sliced the head clean off.

As soon as there was an opening, Percy waved for more survivors to come behind their small barricade. Thea shepherded along some of the more frightened people, too focused to hear the wolf-like dre'malor leaning back on its haunches, preparing a leaping strike.

"Thea, watch out!"

She spun around just in time to slam her staff into the wolf's unhinged jaw. It went skittering across the ground, leaving the dre'malor trying to gnash and growl with only its top teeth. From across the courtyard, Nare drew a sigil in the air and aimed it at the staff. The staff began to glow red like molten metal.

"Hit it again!" Nare yelled,

Thea did, jabbing the staff clean through the back of the wolf dre'malor's throat. The flesh sizzled and burned like a brand. The dre'malor howled in agony, rearing back its head right in Senna's proximity. Without hesitation, Senna pulled a dagger from his belt and sank it into the back of the monster's brain. He stabbed it over and over, black blood spewing out and spilling across his face.

The dre'malor's legs gave out. It collapsed in a heap between Thea and Senna.

All of them looked at the dead monsters on the ground, then glanced nervously around the quiet streets.

It was over—for now.

The woman Elora had saved broke free of the barricade. She yanked away the picket in Percy's hand and, with a cry of rage, pierced through the eye of the first slain dre'malor. The woman spat at it, and stabbed it again for good measure.

"Bleeding fucking demon made us work for it," she murmured, face wet with tears.

The sadness lingered for only a moment, because as soon as she looked at the group Emrys and Senna had led, she gasped.

"Hana!"

The woman fell into her Hana's arms, weeping and uttering words of devotion. Percy looked away—directly into Senna's searching gaze.

"Hullo, Sen," Percy said weakly. "I think you and I have a lot to—"

The only warning was the stench of rotted flesh.

Percy didn't process the impact until he was already on the ground. When he lifted his head, his hazy mind took inventory of what he saw: half a dozen dre'malors exploding out of a shop door, seizing the street in an instant. Emrys desperately trying to tangle them up in weeds, but failing. Senna, on his back, holding the dre'malor that had attacked Percy at arm's length—but not far enough. Claws and teeth tore and scratched Senna's skin.

Percy stared in horror.

Ciaran was right. He would die. He'd die a bloody coward, and worse, Senna would die too.

"*No*, Senna!" Percy tried to scramble to his feet, but pain roared up his ankle and through his leg. He tried speaking again, but the words were barely a croak. "Emrys! Emrys, help Senna." He pushed up once more. The pain was in his arm this time, sourced by a long slice where the dre'malor must've gotten him. Any strength he had to hold himself up drained away. "Someone, help him!"

No one heard him. Not Emrys, with his concentration set on keeping a wall of thorns between the survivors and the monsters. Not Elora, who was trapped behind that wall. Not even Senna, whose chest was being torn into ribboned strips, face pale.

"I hear you, Percy Laurent of Talsura," said a tender, wise voice.

Percy's head snapped up. There was no one there. No one except—

On the hill something *glowed*. Its radiance was amplified by the dawning night, silvery and effulgent. Percy willed his swimming vision to focus. It was a deer. No—

It was a canon.

Thea followed Percy's gaze, lips parting.

"It's Alpedis," she said in awe. "Just like Emrys and Senna said."

"You're a canon?" Percy whispered.

The deer bowed its head.

"We need help. Please."

"You want to save your goldheart? Command the monster."

"W-what?" Percy panted.

"Command it!"

Percy pushed himself up onto his good elbow, a sob bubbling up his throat. He looked directly at the dre'malor fighting and winning over the last of Senna's strength.

"Let him go," he cried weakly.

"Mean it, princeling."

Percy pulled his legs under him, groaning. "Let him go!"

The dre'malor stopped thrashing. Courage surged in Percy's chest.

"Let him go! *Let him go! Stop attacking him!*" Percy was hysterical now, hobbling toward the monster, which by some miracle, had gone completely still. "Get the fuck away from him!"

Slowly, the dre'malor backed away, head bowed. Its attention was wholly on Percy. With a strange thrill, Percy realized that all of the dre'malors were looking at him—awaiting his command. Emrys seized the moment and rushed to Senna's side, face pale.

Every bloodthirsty dre'malor waited.

"How far does the command go?" Percy whispered.

"How far do you want it to go?"

Percy kept his eyes on the dre'malors as he said, "Emrys, bring everyone to this side."

Emrys did as he was told without an ounce of hesitation. At his beckoning, the survivors slowly fell behind Percy.

"You dre'malors who torment Mount Livia, assemble." Percy imagined the command echoing across the hills, over the peaks, through every forgotten dark corner that evil might burrow into. Then, to his friends, he said, "Trust me."

The dre'malors came—disgusting and deafeningly loud. They formed a perfect line, like knights falling in row one by one. Now that the command had been changed from *kill* to *come*, they were pathetically tame.

Everyone behind Percy prepared their weapons—all except Senna, who was held tightly in Emrys' arms.

The dre'malors filled every inch of the streets when they were all assembled—dozens and dozens of them drooling rancid breath, heeled like well-behaved dogs.

"*You want them dead?*" the deer's voice whispered. "*Command it.*"

Percy's body shook. Was this what it was like to be king?

"You, dre'malors who torment Mount Livia," he said. "*Die.*"

The first one dropped like Percy had cut its puppet strings. Then another. Then another. Until they were nothing but piles of flesh littering the street, shells of the torment they'd been wreaking all damned day, now rendered powerless. Percy held the feeling of the command until every blasted dre'malor was dead on the ground.

He beheld the carnage before him with a numb sort of awe.

He had done this.

Something in him had allowed him to rip the life from the dre'malors and compel them into whatever hell awaited monsters. That something was . . . was *furious*. The rage reverberated through him like thunder crashing against every tendon, every vein and nerve. He mistook it for his own anger, so embedded was it into his deepest essence. But his mind wasn't angry, nor was his heart.

Percy wasn't strong or skilled in battle, but he was wise. He knew the power he'd just used had merely been borrowed. He knew that whomever he'd borrowed it from had not wanted to share.

But it didn't matter. Not when Senna lay ripped apart on the blood-muddied ground.

Percy cried Senna's name, wincing as he climbed to his feet, and falling at his side. The goldheart was colorless under the gore on his skin. His eyes were thin slits, though Percy didn't think Senna was really awake. Percy moved to hoist Senna from Emrys' arms into his own, but Emrys put a hand on his shoulder. Thea, Nare, and Elora were close behind.

"Don't move him yet," Emrys said gently.

Tears burned Percy's throat. "This isn't what I wanted. Emrys, I didn't *think*—" A shudder tore through him. Then weakly, he asked, "Will he make it?"

Emrys' eyes were red and wide as he quickly looked over the damage to Senna's body. "I—I don't know. It looks bad."

"How did you do that?" Nare gaped.

Percy shook his head. "That's not what's important."

"You killed all those dre'malors with a single word. I think it *is* important."

What was Percy supposed to say? That he'd seen a deer higher up the mountain and it had communicated telepathically?

"Enough. Senna's not breathing," Thea cut in, gravely.

Percy scrambled to look, choking on a sob when he realized Senna's chest was bitterly still. Without thinking, he began unfastening the straps of Senna's splintered armor. Emrys joined, but he was too slow, stumbling over the leathers.

No one knew Senna's armor better than Percy did. He'd been helping don Senna in his armor since he was tall enough to reach the fastenings.

The breastplate scraped the ground when Percy finally managed to tear it free, revealing a wound underneath that nearly made him vomit.

Emrys keened.

"What do we do?" Percy whimpered.

"He needs a healer immediately," Thea said, her voice the steadiest thing among them. "These wounds won't keep for long."

"We can't transport him like this," Elora rushed.

Nare squatted to look at the wound herself. "Any healing spells I know won't touch this. It was never my area of expertise. But Sascha's a healer. If we bring Senna down, Sascha might—"

Percy shook his head, halfway to madness. "The healers are all the way down the hill. He'll never make it. The wound needs to be stitched."

Emrys was still gaping wide-eyed at the wound, hands pressing futilely to stop the blood. Thea fell on the ground next to him and grabbed his chin with her hand.

"You *know* what to do," she said fiercely. Emrys shook his head, but Thea kept her gaze calm and grounded. "He's not gone yet. Start with the needle yarrow."

Emrys swallowed, breaths coming out heavy and shaky. He hovered his hand over the strips of open flesh where Senna's blood stained the ground. Instantly, tiny, thin stems stitched the wound closed. Blood managed to spring between the tendrils, but not nearly as profoundly.

Nare shoved into the free space above Senna's head, drew a sigil onto her palm with her middle finger, and pressed it firmly onto Senna's sternum. Electrified, he arched up, gasping out thin breath. Senna's eyes fluttered slowly, wispy breaths coming out of his dry lips.

Emrys cursed out a shaking laugh. With a featherlight touch, he leaned over Senna and wiped the blood and sweat out of his eyes.

Thea reached up and grabbed the tails of Nare's shirt. "What did you do?"

"All I did was boost the healing properties of the needle yarrow with an amplification spell. Like oil on a fire." Incredulous stares turned to her.

"I think you just saved his life," Emrys said brokenly. Senna shifted in his arms, groaning pathetically. "Don't move, my heart. You're safe. Can you hear me?"

Senna's tongue dabbed at his lips, trying to damp them. Emrys wet his own lips and pressed them softly to Senna's.

"Are you hurt?" Senna croaked.

Emrys smiled warmly, pressing their foreheads together.

"I'm alright."

Senna's hand reached limply in the air. "Percy?"

Percy swallowed. "Tip-top, old friend."

"Everyone?"

"We're all with you, my love," Emrys swore. "We're going to get help."

"Good," he said. Then, his eyes rolled back into his head, leaving him unconscious in Emrys' arms.

"He's asleep. That's—that's a good thing, right?" Elora asked.

"I don't know," Emrys answered honestly. Now that he'd heard Senna's voice, seen him breathe, he seemed more like his usual level-headed self. "But I do know where the healing baths are. Nare, can you transport us there? I don't—I don't know the sigil."

"Yes, but you have to picture where you want to go exactly, or you could end up far off course. Stand up and hold him tightly."

He heaved Senna onto his back, supporting him by his legs. Emrys' face was as dirty as Senna's hair, but he pressed a kiss to the damp strands, then looked at Percy. "The dre'malors are really dead?"

"I—I think so."

Emrys nodded at Nare. "Then do it."

Nare drew a sigil on the bloody dirt, then gestured for Emrys to step in it. His toes had barely touched the ground before they disappeared like smoke on the air. Percy knelt in the spot where Senna had lain, staring at the stagnant blood staining the ground.

"They'll be alright," Thea said, grabbing Percy's shoulder. "Come on. I have a feeling Sascha won't believe the news unless it comes from all of us."

"We'll vouch for you," called out one of the survivors. It was Hana. She had her family tucked under her arms, a drying smear of blood like a scar across her face. She eyed Percy suspiciously, almost like he was too good to be true. "It's the least we can do."

Elora took Percy's hand. "There's no time to waste."

25
CIARAN

W HEN CIARAN WAS A young child in oversized zealot robes that hung loosely off his ribs, the votary had told him this: *"If a canon appears to you in your sleep, accept the blessing. They are as powerful in the dreamland as they are in the world of the waking."*

That was why his hungry subconscious had dreamt Jasrath the day of his expulsion—and worse, trusted him. Chained to the canon of thieves' altar like purchased cattle, it'd been easy to imagine that the canon in his dreams would give him *more*. But now, all Ciaran had that he hadn't before was anger.

Jasrath's anger, an old thing born from a lost love and a life he'd been cursed with. The anger of the Mount Livians, forced from their homes, fearing for their lives. The anger of the Canonized Cloth, his own people, who'd hated him for trying to cling to the last dregs of his life. It was all his anger now.

It came out of him in blood and spit and tears, warring with Jasrath's anger. Because among the many things the canon despised, Ciaran was now among them—a failure of a votary, a patron canon's worst nightmare.

He'd told Percy a hint of the truth because it was the right thing to do. At the time, he'd decided that if his actions went against Jasrath's depraved plans, he'd pay for it later.

Later had come.

Ciaran leaned, bloodied and beaten, against the altar in the Mount Livian temple. The votary had been right when he'd said that canons were more powerful in dreams.

In dreams after the fall of the dre'malors, Jasrath had claws and teeth and mire. Ciaran weathered it all.

That night, the canon of thieves confessed everything. Why conceal it anymore? Ciaran had already seen it, connected to Percy. Jasrath admitted that Mount Livia was only meant to be a conquest—a stronghold of protection for the things yet to come. He'd sent Ciaran, a vehicle of prayer and safety, and placed him as the marker for the dre'malors to draw toward. Then, when the people of Mount Livia were nothing more than gored victims in empty houses, Jasrath would move in—himself as king, Ciaran his votary, and a thousand dre'malors as willing toy soldiers. When the goldheart came to help, because he would come, Jasrath would finally take his power and lay siege to Talsura.

It hadn't gone quite to plan, but Jasrath wasn't deterred. What were thieves if not adaptable?

There were no illusions of Ciaran's love or devotion. Jasrath realized all of that desperate loyalty had gone the second he willingly made Ciaran the killing weapon against the Mount Livians.

Now, they merely tolerated each other. Until tonight. Until Ciaran had defied Jasrath. Now, Ciaran tolerated each punch and slash and insult that came to him in the dream—retribution for what he'd ruined.

When Ciaran woke, he was bloodied and hungry against the altar. All that was left was anger.

It fueled him, fueled his hatred, until the only person he despised more than Jasrath was himself.

All because the final words Jasrath had spoken were still ringing out in his mind—and Ciaran couldn't say no.

Tonight—the goldheart's drink. If you don't, I will burn the mountain to the ground with pure sunlight.

EMRYS

"I RECEIVED A LETTER from your mother," Thea murmured to Emrys the next day when she entered the healing chamber. "She wants us home by sunset."

Emrys had barely processed the sound of her voice. He dipped his hand into the water of Senna's healing bath, assessing the potency of the magic slowly stitching his lover's body back together. In truth, he wasn't versed enough in this type of magic to know if there'd been any type of change. Sascha had stitched Senna back together with painstaking precision, ever the master at needlework. They insisted that the potency of the mountain's power was consistent enough to provide a steady flow of healing magic to whoever lay in the bath. But when Emrys grazed his fingers along the surface, they only felt numb. He hoped, at least, it meant Senna wasn't in any pain.

"Emrys, did you hear me?" Thea pressed.

He lifted his chin away from his folded arms resting on the bath's rim.

"I'll return home when Senna is well enough to travel," he said tiredly. "Don't wait for me."

Thea crossed the room with a sigh and took the open seat at Emrys' side.

"Of course I'm going to wait for Senna to recover too. I only meant to ask how I should break the news that we plan to directly disobey her orders."

"Could you ignore it?" wondered Elora, bustling into the room with a tray of hot tea. "That's what I did with my mother. She told me *give those silly clay statues a rest and do something important with your life—like become a Redwindan farmer.* I ignored her for two months after that one. Everyone knows if I touch anything green, it dies."

"Is that why you don't use inflorescence?" Emrys asked.

"Not all of us can be prodigies, Captain." She placed her own teacup on a nearby table. "Anyway, you should ignore the letter, Princess."

"She's right. Pretend you didn't get it," Emrys agreed bitterly. "She's been ignoring you all this time, after all."

Thea folded her hands into her lap, wringing her knuckles. "What will she do if we disobey? She wouldn't send your knights to collect us, would she?"

Emrys snorted. "Oh please, I know my riders. They'd take one look at all the dre'malors littered throughout the streets and race home, horse tails between their legs."

"Alright. I'll ignore her." Thea let out a surprised laugh. She touched the letter's corner to the small flame that warmed the bath on the underside of the basin. When the flames had engulfed the paper, she dropped it in the rocks and watched it burn to nothing but ashes.

Elora came to Senna's side table. She gently nudged all the medical supplies over to make room for her tray. Her lips formed a thin line as she brushed a wet strand of hair off of Senna's forehead. "Any change?"

"Still resting peacefully," Thea answered. "He woke a few times, but we told him to go back to sleep. Sascha thinks that the longer he sleeps, the better chance he has of being well enough to travel back to Redwind. Really, I've never seen anyone recover so quickly."

Emrys shifted uncomfortably. He had a feeling that the moment Senna could stand on his own, he would insist on bringing Percy home once and for all.

"That's wonderful news." Elora handed Thea a cup of the tea. "I brewed Redwindan tea for a little bit of energy and a taste of home. Sascha made me promise to tell you that more substantial food is on the way. Apparently Mount

Livians celebrate with banquets in the streets? I'm not sure what all that entails, but I do love a good party."

"In the *streets*? The same streets we just killed a hundred dre'malors in?"

"It's quite the group undertaking. Some folks are currently cleaning the streets. Others are cooking. Others are tending to the wounded and burying the dead."

"Isn't it rather late for a party? It's nearly nightfall."

"I thought so too. I asked a man in the kitchen about it and all he told me was, *There's nothing like survival to make you feel awake.* I expect we have a long night ahead of us." Elora paused, nudging Emrys with his foot. "You're beginning to look as pale as Senna. Drink."

She poured another cup for Emrys, glancing at Percy from across the room. He'd been so silent, leaning against the wall on a bench across the room, that Emrys had to remind himself Percy was there. He hadn't spoken a word since Sascha had sworn that Senna would survive his injuries. Everyone had taken that as a message to leave him alone, but Elora ignored it.

She set Percy's tea at his table. "You drink too, my love."

Percy glanced up for a second, gave her a tight smile, then dropped his gaze again.

Elora sighed. She pressed her lips to his forehead.

Emrys swirled his own cup in his lap. The scent was familiar and calming, but he had a feeling a single sip would make him sick to his stomach. It was possible he wouldn't be able to down anything until Senna woke up for real.

The door opened once again. This time, Sascha and Nare walked in. They'd been inseparable since reuniting, but were considerate enough to take their reminiscing away from Senna's sick bed. Thea had filled the others in on some of the missing details—about Nare's past with the Academes and her atonement for the harm she felt she'd caused. Emrys couldn't help but relate to Nare—they both had taken on so much responsibility as a child.

With peaceful ease, Sascha traded the fine robes that denoted their royal status for a healer's apron. The clothes underneath—ankle-high pants and a cotton shirt—were more common than anything Emrys had ever seen a ruler wear.

"My, it's so grave in here. Did I not already assure you Goldheart Kane would live?" they said, rolling up their sleeves.

"You did, but forgive us if we're apprehensive. Redwindans aren't used to receiving so many miracles," Thea said.

"Our troubles come with a bit more walking," Nare agreed sardonically.

Sascha chuckled, uncorking a bottle of glimmering bath salts and adding a pinch to Senna's bathwater. "Believe me, you're the miracle. I still don't know how to thank you for saving my people." This, Sascha addressed to Percy, who kept his eyes in his lap. "How do you fare, princeling?"

"How does *Senna* fare?" Percy pressed.

Sascha placed a hand under Senna's back, using the water to lift his chest past the surface to assess the wounds.

"His wounds are healing quite nicely, if I do say so myself. I had wanted my votary here to invoke Hedela, as we did at Captain Calloway's healing, but he's been missing since the dre'malors' attack."

Percy shifted uncomfortably, turning his face toward the window.

Practiced concentration took over Sascha's face. They hovered their hand above Senna's body, summoning the familiar twinge of magic in the air—cold and tingly.

Sascha sat back and nodded thoughtfully.

"My original assessment remains correct. Goldheart Kane will be just fine. You may have noticed that he's healing much faster than he should've, given everything. I wish I could take the credit, but I believe he is being kept alive by something inside of him."

On instinct, Emrys reached out and held Senna's hand. "Inside him? Like, his heart?"

"Not quite. It's something magically extrinsic."

Thea sat forward. "Meaning what?"

"Meaning there's magic in him that isn't naturally produced by his body. He is the host of powerful magic that somehow has assisted his body in surviving a trauma he shouldn't have. Beyond that, I can't really ascertain the exact brand of magic, where it came from, or what its purpose is."

"That's extremely helpful," Emrys grumbled.

Thea snatched Emrys' knee, her nails digging into his skin.

"We're just happy he's alive. Thank you," she said.

"I know it's a little alarming to hear, but I'm sure the goldheart will be able to answer your questions when he wakes."

"Which will be when?" Emrys asked.

Intrigue glinted in Sascha's eyes.

"I sewed a thread of sleep amidst Senna's wounds to help his body recover from his injuries. It's why, if he's woken, he's been so drowsy. But now that it's been a day, I think the sleep thread has done its job. Now, all I have to do is . . ." They produced a pair of ornate silver scissors from their apron and brandished it. "Give it a snip."

A sailor's curse fell out of Nare's mouth. "I always knew you were the more impressive one of the two of us, Sasch. But this takes the bloody cake."

Everyone held their breath as Sascha found an invisible string among Senna's sutures and cut.

"Hey, Princess, you thinking what I am?" Nare murmured.

Thea sat back in her seat, leaning her head back against Nare's stomach. They looked chin up and chin down at each other.

"If we're right, this trip really has been a miracle," Thea said with a smile.

Emrys wasn't paying attention though, because there, in the warmth of the healing bath, Senna drew in a waking breath. Sascha got out of the way in time for Emrys to wrap an arm around Senna's middle, helping him come to a sitting position in the water. The back of Emrys' throat burned with each new part of Senna that moved—his legs, his arms, his face. All of him was *blissfully* alive.

In a flurry, they all surrounded Senna's bath with words of "Oh thank the canons" and "Hey now, don't push yourself!"

All Emrys could think was, *I love you.*

Senna returned to the world of the living very, very slowly—but when he did, his amber eyes were clear and bright. Emrys wanted to weep long enough that he tasted the tears in the back of his throat.

"Emrys," Senna said, carefully.

Emrys drew closer, not minding that the fringe of his clothes was growing damp. "Yes, my heart?"

"I'm in a bath."

"Yes, darling, you are."

"Why?"

"I know how much you hate being covered in dre'malor muck and thought you might like to wake up to clean hair," Emrys teased with a comforting smile. He gently caressed the side of Senna's face with his knuckles. "We were attacked in the street. Do you remember?"

"I . . ." Senna's eyes darted around Emrys' face, as if he were watching the memory play across his mind. Then he shot forward, chest wound be damned. *"Percy."*

It was then that Emrys realized Percy wasn't standing with everyone else at Senna's side. He was still watching from the chair across the room—only sitting up, chin to his knees, weeping as silently as a scolded child.

"He's here," Emrys said carefully, moving out of the way so Senna could see for himself. "Sprained his ankle, but he's in one piece."

"I'd like to speak with him," Senna said, rising from the bath.

Emrys wrapped a warm towel around Senna's shoulders, catching the water dripping down his back and arms. Once the towel was secure around his waist, Emrys helped Senna step out of his soaking underthings. "You've only just woken up. Don't you think that conversation will keep until—"

"Please."

In the end, Emrys couldn't deny Senna anything.

"Alright. Take all the time you need."

He pressed a kiss to his forehead, but Senna caught him with wet hands and pulled him down for a real kiss. It lingered long enough that Senna's hair and nose dripped down Emrys' face, but he didn't mind. Emrys treasured every moment he could feel Senna's pulse.

"How about I show everyone else the party preparations to give you both some privacy?" Sascha said. "I'm a vain creature and want to hear all the praises for how spectacular it looks so far."

Reluctantly, Emrys pulled away from Senna and followed behind Sascha. "How on earth did you prepare a party on such short notice? Don't tell me your mountain crystals are secretly party-planning pixies?"

Sascha let out a sharp laugh. "Believe me, Captain, a full day is plenty of time to plan a party. And why shouldn't we? We're all drunk on the wine of being alive, and we intend to celebrate to the fullest—Mount Livian style."

"When Redwind was established and the exile ended, we celebrated for forty nights straight."

"I know. I donated the wine." Sascha grinned.

"I remember that celebration," Nare groaned. "I couldn't move for weeks after all the dancing I did."

Sascha grinned, gesturing for the group to follow them out of the healing chambers. "Then you know half the merriment of a Mount Livian party. I hope you can all hold your drink. We're partial to mountain wine."

"What makes mountain wine different from regular wine?" Elora asked curiously.

"You'll see." Sascha paused, poking their head back through the door. "Goldheart, no strenuous activities. No matter how joyous the reunion." This last comment was directed to Emrys, who blushed.

He fled the room before he could convince himself to sit outside the door and wait for Senna to walk out of it. All would be well, he told himself. Senna would keep.

Besides, Emrys really, *really* needed a drink.

27
SENNA

ONE GLANCE AT PERCY tucked into the room's corner with wet eyes made Senna's stomach drop. The last time Percy had been like this, it'd been because he'd used Senna's personal journal as a sketchbook. He couldn't have been more than three years old at the time, but he'd already been conditioned to his mother's sharp, caustic reprimands. It was one of the rare times of their early relationship that Senna had thought, *He's just a boy. It isn't his fault.*

"It looks like they left a robe for me over there. Could you help me put it on?"

Percy sniffed hard, digging his chin more firmly into his knees.

"Come here, Percy. It's alright," Senna said soothingly.

"I can't." Percy shook his head. More tears fell down his face.

"Is it because you're still angry with me?"

"Of course not! Of course I'm not—" Percy dug the heels of his hands into his eyes.

"Then come here."

Furiously, Percy wiped his face and sniffed. He followed Senna's request in a businesslike fashion, face stern with the effort to contain his tears. More carefully than Senna had ever seen him do anything before, Percy supported Senna under his arm and helped him off of the bath's ledge and onto his feet. Senna watched Percy as he removed his towel and replaced it with the robe. The prince's hair was a mess, and he wore his fogged glasses hooked over an unbuttoned shirt.

Senna opened his mouth to say that all was well. That they'd survived another terrible thing. That they were one step closer to the future they'd dreamt about.

But then Percy said, "I was the worst thing to ever happen to you."

On instinct, Senna pulled Percy into his arms. Percy squeezed tight into the fabric of Senna's wet shirt, tears mixing into the leftover damp of the bath. "I'm so sorry, Senna. *Canons*, I am so sorry. Forgive me."

"There is nothing to forgive," he said, still taken aback.

"How can you *say* that? Don't you know what being with me has done to you?"

Senna sat on the flat ledge of the tab, wearied by the standing and confusion. "What are you talking about?"

"What are your hobbies, Senna? What do you enjoy? Singing? Writing? Drawing? Hunting?"

"I—" Senna paused. He—he didn't know. "What brought this on?"

Percy ignored him. "You don't have any, because you don't have any *time* for hobbies, because you're too busy following me around with *my* interests."

"Or maybe I've just never found a pastime that suits me."

"What's your most prized possession? The thing you couldn't live without."

The answer came easily. "My coat of arms."

"A tiny golden plaque that you received not out of your own merit, or because you overcame great knightly challenges, but because it was bestowed on you—randomly—all so that you could protect me." Percy kicked Senna's shield, which was resting at his bedside, sending it clattering to the ground like a gong. "What do you have that is *Senna Kane's*? What do you have that isn't of me?"

Silence draped between them. Senna wanted more than anything to remember some odd trinket he adored, some secret hobby for collecting rocks, but he could think of nothing. Percy would see through a lie in an instant.

"I have inflorescence," Senna said finally.

Percy drew back. "You—you what?"

"Emrys is teaching me to be inflorescent," Senna repeated steadily. To prove his point, he willed an amber lily up into the palm of his hand. It was a small, powerless thing because of all the energy he'd spent healing. But it blossomed nonetheless, evidence that he spoke true. "I have that."

Percy shook his head mournfully. "Even *that* is not your own, Senna."

He opened his trembling hands and held them out

"You are the reason I'm alive," Percy said. "And I need to set you free."

"*What?* Percy, no—"

"You've sacrificed enough for me. You've given me enough. More than enough now."

"Where is this coming from? This—" The wound at Senna's chest felt like it was on fire, the pain deep to the very marrow of his bones. "Is this because I crossed a line before? Because I only did it to protect you."

"It's because *I* crossed a line. The things I said to you, Sen. I don't have the stomach to remember them."

Senna took Percy's hand. "You thought I was dead. You hadn't slept, hadn't eaten. It wasn't you."

"That's just it. It wasn't. I mean, it was. It was and I own up to my behavior completely, but—" He shook his head. "I don't feel like myself."

Senna's brow pinched. "What do you mean?"

"I *mean*," Percy huffed, frustrated, "that lately I'm angry all the time. It's like there's this aggravation in the back of my mind that won't cease yelling. I've no clue where it's come from, but it *wearies* me. It makes me a beast to be around and I've taken it out on you twice now. I refuse to do it again. I've made the conscious choice to do better, to do the right thing. *This* is the right thing."

Senna's pulse hammered underneath his skin like a warning.

"Maybe this whole endeavor—the sneaking around, the fighting—maybe it's all been too much," he suggested desperately.

"It shouldn't be. I'm going to be king. If I can't handle one small adventure, then how can I rule my kingdom? How can I undo the damage my mother's done?" Percy's gaze dropped into his lap. "I'm no longer ignorant of your circumstances, of how much has been taken from you. I am immensely guilty of taking advantage of you. These past months, I've been trying to find a way to atone for your wasted life while also keeping you by my side. But even that is selfish of me."

"No. Absolutely not. *No.*"

Tears burned his eyes. How could he explain that this wasn't the solution?

"When we return to Talsura, we'll begin the process of assessing silverhearts. You'll leave me in the care of someone trustworthy," Percy trudged on.

Senna curled his robe into his grip. "If you find another goldheart, you may not be able to leave Talsura. You'll be kept in the castle, without light. Without Elora, or our friends."

"That's for me to figure out. You've sacrificed so much for me. It's time for me to return that favor." He squeezed Senna's hand, looking him straight in the eye. "Be with Emrys. Overwhelm yourself with friends and freedom. Find things that fuel your passion, that bring you *joy.*"

A tear trickled down Senna's cheek. "You're my *family*. You're all I have."

"I want you to have *more.*"

"You are enough!" cried Senna.

Percy swiped away Senna's tear with his thumb.

"I want you to have everything," he said softly. "The swoony love affairs with Redwindan princes. A treasure trove of fond memories to recall when you're old. I want you to have a single day that doesn't revolve around my schedule."

"Throwing me jobless into the streets is the way to do it?"

"Oh please. You and I both know you haven't touched your wage account. There's enough money there to support you for years. Besides, Emrys and Thea will make sure you're well taken care of. You'll want for nothing." Percy smiled tearfully. "I'll always be your family, Senna. That won't change."

It was all spiraling out of control so quickly. Senna had lived his entire life under the assumption that he would always belong to the royal family. That was his future. He didn't consider anything else for himself like other people did. Now, presented with the possibility that his future would change, he felt he was suffocating, choking on his own heart.

"Percy, you have to know that I don't blame you for the way things are. You were only a baby when I swore my life to your service. I confess, there were times I regretted it—times I cursed your mother for picking *me* out of every child in Talsura. But that was years ago. I love being your guard. If you asked me to pick another fate, I would still choose being the goldheart. It's what I want."

Percy smiled, small. "Is it what you want, or is it what you *know*? You and I are the same, old friend. Neither of us care for change."

"I don't see why those things have to be different."

Percy deflated, shoulders falling forward.

"I'm trying to do the noble thing."

"The noble thing is to trust me," Senna shot back emphatically. "You say I don't have a life of my own. Perhaps I don't. It's true that if you're asking me what I want, I'll tell you I do want a life with Emrys and with our friends. But I also want you there. There has to be a way where you and I can still work as we have, and have more too."

"You make it sound so easy," Percy said exasperatedly, shaking his head.

"Trust that I know my own mind. Trust that we can find the difficult solution. It isn't just the two of us anymore."

Percy wore the expression that people do when they witness someone lost in delusion. He wanted to trust Senna, that much was visible, yet he couldn't. He was protecting himself from the reality that one day, it would all fall apart.

"This is really what you want?" Percy asked warily.

"I swear."

At last, Percy sighed. "As you wish."

They would have a future together—all of them. Senna would make sure of that. He opened his arms and they embraced as brothers do—heart to heart.

"I didn't mean any of those cruel things I said to you," Percy apologized, cheek squished on Senna's shoulder.

"I know."

"You're not a stupid orphan. You're so smart it puts me to shame, and you are far from an orphan. If my mother has only given me one good thing, I'm so glad it was you."

Senna chuckled, laying his own cheek on the top of Percy's head. "She had you. That's two things right."

"Can we go back to the way things were? Before we fought?"

Senna nodded. Things *wouldn't* be the same, not exactly. But they would be close enough. If Percy wanted his goldheart to start doing things for himself, Senna would—he would pretend nothing at all had changed. At least then he could enjoy himself at the celebration.

After, it took some time for Senna to hobble into the streets where the celebration was taking place. Percy remained dutifully at his side, providing a strong shoulder to lean on. True to Sascha's promise, the Mount Livians indeed knew how to throw a party on short notice.

The Mount Livians had lined a miscellany of dining tables in the middle of the street to create one massive banquet table. Each was different, from the type of wood and shape, to the cloth coverings and dishes. Centerpieces of flowers spilled out of mixing bowls and vases at each table's center, each punctuated with a white, glowing rose. The banquet table snaked all the way down the sloping avenue, and above it, garlands of flowers and lanterns hung between the houses. Their warm orange light fell over the streets, the perfect pairing to the fiddler bowing a jaunty tune nearby.

Senna found Emrys perched on Nare's shoulders, arms outstretched to grow more garlands between the houses. His face erupted into pure light when he caught sight of Senna out of the corner of his eye.

Instead of demanding to be put down, however, Emrys pointed at Senna and cheered, "Bring me to him! I must see that he is hearty and hale for myself."

With a bark of raucous laughter, Nare clamped Emrys' thighs to her shoulders and hiked up the hill. They both bobbled and wobbled, but somehow made it to Senna without crashing. Emrys carefully leaned down and positioned himself for a kiss. Senna flushed, but obliged his lover, leaning up on his toes to press a chaste kiss to Emrys' waiting lips.

Senna drew back, ignoring the lovesick thing his face was doing. "Do I meet your expectations?"

"Hmm, I'm not sure. Let me try again."

Nare let out a moan of disgust. "*Alright.* Not that this doesn't remind me of a disgustingly romantic painting I saw in the royal galleries, but I will not be your bloody horse, Emrys. Off you get." She bent over, leaving Emrys with no choice but to leap off. He tumbled directly into Senna's arms, who caught him around the waist and pulled him close.

Emrys shoved back. "No thank you, I will not be the cause of your wounds reopening." He grazed the front of Senna's chest. "How are you feeling? Shall I call for Sascha?"

"I am well recovered. A bit tender, but not enough to trouble the healer," replied Senna, brushing his thumb over Emrys' cheek.

Emrys sagged, dropping his forehead to Senna's chest.

"Thank the canons. We were worried about you, you know. "

It occurred to Senna that it was the first time anyone other than Percy had been concerned for his well-being. More accurately, it was the first time anyone had spoken it out loud. Logically, Senna knew that Emrys had probably been concerned about him endlessly since they'd met. But hearing it—that was a different thrill entirely.

It was because of this that he couldn't bring himself to sound too regretful when he said, "Forgive me for worrying you. I'll not do it again."

"You'd better not. I was a bloody mess, weeping over you in your healing bath. I looked regrettably pathetic in front of my sister," Emrys said grumpily.

"Don't worry, you always look pathetic to me," Thea chimed in, setting the table with regal ease. "Percy, come make yourself useful and put the forks in the correct order. No one else knows the right of it."

Percy hesitated, an ashamed expression twisting his mouth.

"Percy," Thea said pointedly. "The bygones? They're bygones. Come now."

A sheepish smile, bright and honest, grew across Percy's face. "I've been summoned," he said with a happy shrug, before wandering off.

"I can't help but notice you've stopped working too, brother," called Thea.

Emrys waved a hand. "Ignore her, let me see what's under those robes." The robe in question was deep red and woven with expensive cotton. One of the assistant healers had helped Senna exchange it for his bathrobe, explaining that the light, clean fabric was safest for his wound.

Emrys slipped his hands underneath and Senna reeled back.

"Emrys!"

"Oh, stand down, soldier. I'm not ravaging you quite yet. I only want to see your wound."

At first, something sick and foreboding clutched around Senna's heart at the thought of airing his wound where everyone could see it. But a quick glance around revealed that all the Mount Livians were too busy with party preparations to notice him. Even if every eye was on him, he was safe here, vulnerable as he was after his scrape with death.

Emrys stood still, waiting for Senna's word of consent. Carefully, Senna brought Emrys' hands just below his collar and let him tug. Emrys' lips drew into what could only be called a lovesick smile. He pulled the top section of the robe until the tender red scars underneath touched open air.

"Sascha spoke true. You really are a miracle," said Emrys softly. With enough reverence to make a votary jealous, he grazed his fingers at the edge of the redness. No pain followed the touch, only a sweet tingling sensation. "How was your conversation with Percy?"

"It was productive," said Senna. He said nothing about Percy's wishes to discharge him. Although Emrys and Percy often disagreed, Senna had a feeling this would be the matter that united them. "We've righted our wrongs."

"Can't say I'm surprised. I've never known two people more bonded at the hip than you and your prince. I confess I was almost jealous when I first met you both."

"Jealous?" Senna coughed. "Whatever for? You've never had any competition."

"Percy was the only one you would speak to! Meanwhile, I pined for you for weeks on end and only squeezed two words out of you when I finally did see you. Thea used to tease me endlessly for how gratified I was just to have that much of you."

"I had no idea it was as profound as all that."

"I was pathetically smitten. You've no choice but to make up for it now that we're . . ." Emrys trailed off, palm pressing into Senna's waist. "Why don't you tell me what we are, Senna."

Senna clasped his fingers together at Emrys' back, pulling him closer. "We're courting," he said definitively. Then he turned to the lantern-lit streets and unleashed a bold declaration that crashed down the hill. "Emrys and I are courting!"

All the Mount Livians looked up, surprised, and laughed. For all Emrys pretended to be embarrassed, Senna knew he was pleased as a peach to hear him declare his affection so loudly. He was pleased with himself, so much so he began to laugh along. It quickly cut off into a groan, though, his muscles twinging in protest.

Emrys' face fell in an instant, but Senna held up a hand.

"I'm okay. Just—don't make me laugh." Then, because Emrys' frown lines deepened, he added, "Impossible, I know. But please endeavor to be as dull as you can."

Emrys' frown didn't waver. "Maybe you should be resting. Sascha has reserved one of their villas for us to stay in. Why don't I show you where it is so you can go back to sleep?"

"I've been asleep all day," Senna pointed out. "I want to join the celebration."

Emrys eyed him warily. "Really?"

"You don't believe me?"

"To be honest, I didn't think you were the celebrating type," Emrys admitted.

Senna shrugged. "I don't know if I am."

"You want to experiment with your social side the day after you survived a deadly attack?"

"Mount Livian celebrations wait for no man—even its heroes."

Emrys had the look of a person who would rather impale themselves on a poison lance than agree. But after all the weeks he'd spent *begging* Senna to declare his desires, he had no choice but to give his blessing.

"Very well," he said warily. "But if even a drop spills from that wound, I am dragging you by your beautiful hair to the nearest bed. Am I understood?"

"Aye, sir," Senna said lowly.

Emrys blinked, face reddening.

"Stop that."

"Stop what?"

Drawing close enough to fan his breath across Senna's face, he breathed, "Flirting with me when I can't get my hands on you."

Without further preamble, he spun around, a hand pressing against his blushing cheek, and stomped back down the mountain. Over his shoulder, he called out, "Your public awaits you, Goldheart!"

Senna fell into step with him, a satisfied smile on full display. Emrys slipped an arm around Senna's waist to support him, pressing a short kiss to his cheek.

"I wanted to ask you about something Sascha mentioned earlier," he said, bearing the brunt of Senna's weight with ease. "I wasn't sure how to bring it up."

Senna paused, peering curiously down at his lover. "I keep no secrets from you."

"I know, I know." Emrys smiled, a bit strained. "We haven't really had an opportunity to sit down and discuss what happened. So maybe you don't realize how close you were to dying in my arms on the street. You *were* dead. You stopped breathing and I lost your pulse. For a terrible moment, I thought you were gone."

Senna paused. "I can't imagine how that must've felt. I guess I didn't realize . . . I'm so sorry I frightened you. I really owe you and Sascha everything for such extraordinary care."

"That's the thing. They said there was something in you. Something that kept you alive. Something that wasn't me or Sascha."

Something deep in Senna's core twitched, like a sleeping dog that had heard its name. He tried to pinpoint the feeling, but it fleeted away, lost.

"Do they know what it is?" Senna asked nervously.

"I'm afraid not. All they knew was that some sort of magic is inside of you and it saved your life. They thought you might know what it is."

"I haven't a clue. But whatever it is, it must be something good."

"You sound surprisingly optimistic," Emrys said skeptically.

"Something I usually expect from you. And yet."

Emrys tossed his head to the side. "It's only that I've got a sinking feeling about it." Then, in a rush, "It's probably merely the lingering exhilaration from your injury."

Senna smoothed the worry lines out from between Emrys' brows with his thumb.

"I'd hate it if I was the thing that kept you from enjoying yourself. Would it put you at ease if we talked with Nare about it in the morning?"

Emrys' forehead drooped onto Senna's shoulders.

"It would," he admitted with a relieved sigh. "Now, come. It's not every day you insist on attending a celebration as raucous as I'm sure this one will be."

They skirted the length of the winding banquet table all the way down the mountainside, where one final table was angled perpendicular to the rest. A stately wooden armchair was situated at its head. It loomed over the spread of party foods, sculpted chimeras for arms and a mountain scene carved into the back piece. Sascha leaned against the side, chatting brightly with a woman who offered them a dish of fresh-cut apples powdered in cinnamon and sugar. Sascha plopped one of the apples into their mouth, humming in delight.

"Ruthien, how you outdid yourself on such short notice, I'll never—" Their gaze snagged on Senna and Emrys. "Ah! Goldheart Kane. You look spectacular for a man who recently walked out of his own grave."

"Thank you?" Senna said, chuckling a little.

He shuffled forward to shake Sascha's hand. The sovereign seized the opportunity to affix themself to Senna's other side.

"Now that I think of it, I don't recall giving you permission to amble about. Not to worry, not to worry, everything is nearly set. Everyone is bringing out their food as we speak. You can have the hero's seat beside me. The other is already reserved for Prince Percy. My aestheticians will serve your drink."

Emrys shot a flummoxed look at Senna. "I didn't realize cosmetic care involved waiting tables."

"Well, Captain, if you hadn't noticed, the spas are closed. I have to pay them to do something after so many lost hours with their clients. Ruthien!" The woman looked up from where she was spooning apples onto Sascha's plate. "Could I trouble you to fetch our heroes some ale? I'm going to round up our hungry feasters."

"I wish they would stop calling us that," Emrys murmured, helping Senna into his designated chair. *"Heroes."*

Senna eased down, pulling the chair open beside him, an invitation for Emrys to claim it. "If you don't want to be called a hero, stop doing heroic things."

"I think Percy is the real hero," declared Thea loyally. Then, realizing what she'd said, tossed an apologetic grimace at Senna. "You too, of course, Sen. Glad to see you up and on your feet. I'd never seen you fight like that. You've done us all exceedingly proud."

Percy rounded the corner, carrying a massive platter of crab legs. "The day you get Senna to accept any praise is the day that the Dam turns into a cloud of bubbles and my mother laughs at sweet little babies." He set the platter down, heaving a breath of relief. "I hope none of you have a crustacean allergy."

"Only one way to find out. I'm fucking *starving*," Nare said. She spun one of the chairs around before plopping down and scooping one of the legs onto her plate.

"*Nare!*" Thea chided, leaning over to look across the table. "No one else has sat down yet!"

"Rules of etiquette only apply to you, your royal princessness," Nare quipped, jabbing a lobster claw at Thea. "*I* spent the day comforting weeping citizens and cleaning up dre'malor bits. I think I deserve a crab leg. Elora, do you think I deserve a crab leg?"

"I'm not about to get in between a woman and her meal," Elora laughed, taking her own seat. She crossed a leg over her knee and leaned forward to give Percy a quick peck. "Hello, my love. Are you feeling like yourself again?"

Percy set a look of wonder and soul-deep affection on Elora. That was how Senna knew everything was back to the way it should be. He looked to either side of him, a swelling growing behind his heart and his lungs. There'd been meals before, traveling and laughter. But nothing had ever felt as unbreakable and abiding as the group of people at his side.

He would not be leaving Percy's side. Nor would he leave Emrys'. He would do everything in his power to unleash all of his love and protection over his circle. They were in his care, and nothing would harm them. Of that he was certain.

Eventually, the Mount Livian people began to filter into the streets. They deposited their contributions to the meal, each dish more appetizing than the last, then found their places at the tables. Those who could not fit at the table settled themselves among porch rocking chairs, front steps, and the ledged edges of the mountain streets.

It was hard to believe that these were the same people who'd been harboring for safety in the mountain a day ago. They'd managed to return to their homes and scrounge through what remained to provide for the banquet. All in one day and without complaint. None of them left behind.

Senna voiced this admiration to Emrys, who explained that those who were not able to walk were brought home in horse driven carts.

"Nothing's left of the military encampment at the base of the mountain," Emrys finished a bit wistfully. "It's like it was never there."

"It's alright to wish that you'd had a miracle during your own exile," Senna whispered. "It doesn't tarnish your character."

Emrys shoved Senna playfully, looking quite caught.

"You could at least pretend to not know me so well," he chided grumpily. His face softened around the edges. "I do appreciate you, Sen. Whatever did I do to earn such care?"

Senna recalled the way Emrys had remained steadfast at his side. The feeling was quite mutual.

At last, Sascha took their place in their wooden throne. Respectful silence descended like a wave rolling across a shore, traveling up the mountain where the hungry citizens filled the tables. Sascha drew a sigil into their palm, touched it to their lips, then flourished it in a mighty gesture of welcome.

"Mount Livians!" With help from the rune, Sascha's voice resounded over the side of the mountains, heard to the farthest reaches of the city. "You are the face of resilience, the image of endurance, and the proudest nation on our island. Today, we proved that beasts of evil bear no agency over the strength of a united land that is blessed with powerful friends."

Sascha took hold of Senna's and Percy's shoulders.

"How long it's been, indeed, since we've all dined together. It's hard at a time like this to contain the magnitude of my appreciation—my *relief*—that we find ourselves at this table once more. Our situation was one with no deliverance. We planned for the worst, oppressed by a plague that we never could have anticipated. We owe our lives first to Mount Livia's legionnaires—brave citizens who risked their lives to ensure everyone evacuated to safety. We honor the six lives lost in the initial battle."

One by one, Sascha declared their names proudly over their people. They professed the names of their families, their hobbies, and their passions. It restored spirit to their memories, drowning out the loud circumstances of their deaths. When they were finished, Sascha waved above their head. The lights hanging above Senna's group brightened like stars coming into orbit.

"But we owe the greatest thanks, once again, to our friends from Redwind and Talsura. I'll admit, Mount Livia has long neglected our Redwindan and Talsuran neighbors to keep ourselves safe. Let this be the first proof that harmony between our people should be valued before all. We thank Nare Demira, Elora Wright, Thea Calloway, Captain Emrys Calloway, and Goldheart Senna Kane for defending the lives of our survivors.

"Highest gratitude we bestow to Prince Percy Laurent of Talsura for slaying the dre'malors with just a command. If he is the future of Talsura, then there is hope yet. Hope that we may one day eat like this with our neighbors again. Hope that the Dam holding Talsura captive will fall. Hope that the future of all of Islevaria is incandescently bright."

They swept their chalice of ale high in the air.

"To today's triumph and tomorrow's inexhaustible joy."

All of Mount Livia echoed the refrain. Senna picked up his cup, only to realize that it was empty.

"Allow me, Goldheart Kane," said a timid voice from behind him.

Senna followed the voice to a plain-robed fellow that was immediately familiar somehow, though he couldn't place where he knew him from. The boy had to have been around Percy's age, too young to be sporting the exhausted, pained expression plastered on his face. He was holding a merlot bottle, putting all his strength into popping the cork.

"Here," Senna said, taking the bottle and twisting the cork free.

"Thank you," the boy stammered.

Percy glanced up from over his own tankard, then began to choke.

"Ciaran?" he sputtered, pushing his glasses up his nose. "Why, I looked for you everywhere. Where on this beautiful earth did you run off to?"

"My home in the middle city," answered Ciaran, warily. "I wanted to assess any damage."

"It would have been appreciated if you could have let someone know you were alive, lad," Sascha said, clapping Ciaran on the back. "But we're glad to see you nevertheless."

Ciaran ducked into his shoulders.

"I'm honored, Your Excellency. And thankful, of course, to our guests for their rescue."

Now Senna remembered. This was the votary who had helped pray over Emrys during their first visit. The boy had been so quiet and unhelpful then (and Senna so concerned for Emrys' life) that Senna had forgotten he existed almost as soon as he met him. How Percy knew him, Senna couldn't guess.

Ciaran looked to Senna expectantly, gesturing timidly at his offering.

"Oh! Uh, thank you," Senna said, tipping his cup to be filled.

For the briefest of moments, Senna thought Ciaran had changed his mind. He held the bottle close to his chest, peering down at Senna's empty cup with an expression of pure dread. But the gloom vanished as quickly as it had arrived. Ciaran smiled awkwardly and filled Senna's cup.

The first sip settled heavy in Senna's stomach, slaking the profound thirst he hadn't noticed in his throat. The taste was sweeter than Talsuran cordial—not a surprise when Senna remembered the mountain had magical properties. Perhaps that, too, explained the magical aftertaste, the faintest bit of grit and sourness. The sweetness of the second sip promptly drew it away, forgotten.

Senna glanced up to give more thanks to the votary, but found he'd disappeared into the crowd.

"I always wonder why everyone finds you so intimidating," Emrys commented, draping himself over Senna's shoulder. "Then I remember how I trembled at your stern words when first we met. Now I see you're so softhearted—you make a stuffed bear look like stone."

"It feels like millennia ago," he confessed. "Recently, it feels as though I am a different person."

"Truthfully, Sen, I think you are simply yourself—maybe for the first time. But I quite like this version of you."

"Better than the man who made you tremble with a stern word."

Smiling softly, Emrys plucked up Senna's plate and began to load it with crab legs and the rest of the succulent dishes. It was filled with more food than Senna could have ever eaten on his own. Emrys presented the dish and kissed Senna's cheek. "There's not a version of you I've met and haven't adored."

Before Senna could process that every nerve in his body had ignited, Emrys was already shoving a fork into his hands. "Eat. Your body needs nourishment to finish your healing."

Senna looked up helplessly. "Em . . ."

Emrys pressed a kiss into Senna's hair, enveloping the gesture in so much affection, Senna felt the warmth of it down to his toes. Then he was gone, taking his own plate further up the table and mumbling something about, "Now where did I see the blasted onion jam and toast?"

Senna watched his lover amble easily through the crowd. With more finesse than Senna could dream of boasting, Emrys chatted easily with strangers and let them fill his plate.

"For the record, I think you both are positively disgusting."

Snapping out of his daydream, Senna twirled to Thea and found her scowling as she cut into a turkey leg with a fork and knife.

"Not enough to have taken your appetite," Senna pointed out obviously. "I suppose I should only be thankful that Nare is at the other end of the table."

"I haven't the slightest idea what you mean," said Thea.

Senna scoffed into his cup, but Thea turned to him fully.

"No, truly. I don't."

Quietly, Senna realized she was telling the honest truth. Senna gently placed his cup on the table and lowered his voice. "Do you not fancy her?"

"Oh, this again." Thea made a sharp sound with her tongue and teeth. She glanced down the table to ensure that Nare was distracted. "Percy has subjected me to relentless accusations of that sort. But I hardly know Nare. How could I care for her that way if I barely know her?"

Although he and Emrys had barely known each other when their attraction had first taken root, Senna didn't think it was unreasonable to require a little more time.

"I was under the impression that you knew her rather well," he said.

"I am beginning to," admitted Thea.

"But she *is* the type of woman who suits your fancy—that is, when the fancy strikes?"

Thea's frown cracked into a hint of a smile.

"I'm exercising my right to forgo answering. You and I should have never discovered we're siblings. You're apt to be just as insufferable as Emrys and Percy are."

"You liked it better when I didn't speak as freely?"

Setting her cutlery down with all the care of a princess, Thea looked Senna plainly in the eye—a rare thing for her.

"Let's set the record straight. I'd rather suffer a thousand of your good-natured quips than make you endure one second of not being in control of your own speech." The eye contact broke with a snap, Thea staring furiously at her own plate. "That is all."

Senna drew close across Emrys' empty chair.

"I rather like you too, Thea."

"Oh, hush," she replied, bumping his shoulder.

The party dissolved into a revelry that swept away every Talsuran gathering Senna had ever attended. He could barely hear himself think over the sonorous conversation and laughter, eating, and singing.

It quickly became apparent that if he tried to join the conversation, his voice would be overpowered by the loud merrymaking, so he trained his ears and listened. He listened to Emrys rave about the seafood, having forgotten the delight that was scallops and butter in his seafood-less kingdom. He listened to a lady legionnaire share about how her close encounter with a dre'malor had led to a split ear, asking for piercing ideas once the wound healed.

"Captain Calloway!" cried a jovial voice. Emrys straightened from where he was draping his legs over Senna's lap. Across the table, a performer held out a stringed cittern. "Rumor has it you're skilled with one of these."

Emrys fixed an accusing glare on Senna, who held up his hands.

"Stand down. It wasn't me."

"Thea!" Emrys cried.

"Sun slay me if I want to hear my very talented brother play his instrument every now and again!" Thea defended, laughing. "You're always sneaking away to play at the taverns and leaving me behind. It's only fair!"

Emrys pushed the cittern away like it was diseased. "I am outrageously out of practice! I promise it'll ruin the party if I play."

"I'm dying to see you try. Oh, tell him he has to play, Senna!" Nare jeered, sounding a little tipsy.

The table turned to the goldheart. Even Senna knew that one simple request from his own lips would put Emrys completely at his mercy.

But Emrys had his own weapon: his sweet, sparkling purple eyes. They blew wide, catching light in such bewitching ways that Senna had to rally himself to keep from turning into a lovesick fool.

"Senna, my heart. Have pity on me?" Emrys pleaded.

Indeed, Senna would not.

"He won't play for free," he declared finally. For a second, Emrys seemed to think he won. But then Senna added, "However, if he does play, *I'll* reward him for his performance"

And that—that was perhaps the only thing Senna could have said to get what he wanted fairly. Lust transfixed Emrys immediately. His face fell forward, hovering only a breath away from Senna's lips.

"How will you reward me?" he said eagerly.

Senna plucked a grape from his plate and bit it, letting the sweet juice spill over his lip.

"Play something pretty and find out."

Laughter and jeers exploded from the table of eavesdroppers. Among them was Percy's groan. He squeezed his palms over his ears, nose scrunched up in nauseous disgust.

"If I hadn't killed the dre'malors, I would've let them eat me just now. In case anyone was wondering," he declared.

Emrys heard none of the complaints. He snatched away the cittern. Short, wavering notes spilled from the instrument as its player tuned the strings.

Tall and proud, Emrys took his place among the band. Senna couldn't hear the quiet words they exchanged to presumably select a song they all knew. The band seemed to be waiting for Emrys' cue. Finally, he nodded at a burly lady sitting on a box drum. Her hands bounced in a skipping rhythm over the face.

Then, Emrys began to play.

Senna didn't know much about music. He couldn't say whether this particular tune was a jig or reel or air. But he observed what everyone else did: Emrys was remarkable.

The melody reminded Senna of their journey here, cresting easily up and down over hills and through valleys. Each note made his affection for Emrys build up, until he was up to his neck in it. There was no choice but to lower into its warmth and let it overtake him. The final notes of the song came reluctantly, listener and minstrel alike wanting the song to extend forever.

Face flushed red and glistening with sweat, Emrys handed the cittern back to its owner. He leapt off the stage and bounded through the cheering crowd over to Senna, the adrenaline of the song visible on his face.

"Senna, am I floating? I was dead on my feet before, but now I feel like I could run a mile. And the song! I couldn't remember how it started, but my hands knew the first sequence before I—"

Senna took Emrys' face in his hands and kissed him. This proved to stoke the cheers around them.

"Oh," Emrys said when he pulled back, dazed. "Was that my reward?"

"That was because I am very glad to be here with you," answered Senna honestly. He dragged Emrys into his lap, the weight warm against him. He kissed the column of Emrys' throat. "Expect your reward when we are alone."

"Goldheart," Emrys chided weakly. "You've been warned against all strenuous activities."

"There's no strain when you and I are together," Senna soothed, drawing Emrys in for another kiss.

After, the party did not wane. It merely changed. The ravenous hunger of the survivors shifted into the tangible need to forget the troublesome memories. Plates and tables were cleared away back into the houses from which they had come, leaving room in the street for a crowd of dancers, racing music, sweat, and joy. Senna watched them from the stairs, impressed at how they moved around each other, not letting obstacles like sloping hills or bumping elbows deter them.

Among them were his friends. Percy was the first to slide into the mix, spinning Elora under his arm, then pulling her close.

Nare followed, dragging an unwilling Thea by her elbow into the swarm of moving bodies. Thea was wary at first, dodging this way and that to avoid being touched by anyone else. But then she began to nod her head, nervous fingers tapping to the beat on her thighs. Nare leaned down, saying something for Thea's ears only that Senna couldn't make out. He watched, expression softening, as Thea nodded and allowed Nare to pull her close and guide her to the music.

"You're sure you don't want to join them?" Senna said, raising his voice to be heard over the music.

"And let you out of my sight? Not likely," scoffed Emrys, tucking himself into Senna's side. "Every time I glance away from you, I get this awful image in my mind of you lying in the street with your chest open."

Senna rose to his feet, ready to mask any lingering pain or strain, but there was none there. Cautiously, he pressed his hand over his wound. Though the flesh was rough with the scarring, it wasn't nearly as tender as it had been even an hour ago. It shouldn't have been possible. Maybe Sascha was right. Maybe there *was* something inside Senna healing him.

Whatever it was, he wasn't going to let it go to waste.

He spun to Emrys, eyes bright.

"In that case, where did you say our villa was?"

28
SENNA

I T DIDN'T SEEM THAT Emrys would ever truly believe that Senna had survived his injuries. On their way to the villa, he'd asked Senna over and over if he still felt well enough to make the short walk. He dutifully remained at Senna's side, though Senna was far from needing it. Sascha was right that there was something healing him from the inside out, because by the time they made it back to the guesthouse, Senna felt better than he had in months.

The sensation was foreign—having someone care for him so meticulously. Percy hadn't ever given him this level of attention, respecting Senna enough to trust that he could handle himself. Emrys knew Senna was strong enough to fight his own battles, but cared for him anyway. It was time Senna returned the favor.

Their room's door clicked behind them. The bedchamber was the same size as Senna's quarters in Talsura, though it was outfitted with tall, light-hungry windows. Through them, the sky was endlessly black, speckled with stars. Overhead, half a dozen glass-paned lanterns flickered, mimicking the stars outside. A large bed was positioned in the center of the room, dressed in a mountain of scarlet coverlets and pillows. Senna imagined a day where he might throw himself directly into the middle, allowing all the soft delights to swallow him up. But there were different soft delights he wanted this evening.

All of Senna's wildest imaginations of promptly ravishing Emrys flew out the window when his lover began undressing himself.

Senna crept up behind him, reaching around Emrys' back to catch his hands before he could untie his shirt completely. He brought his lips close to Emrys' ear. "Wouldn't you rather I did that?"

Emrys paused, but he did not free the laces for Senna's access. His back muscles were tense under Senna's chest.

Senna lifted his chin from Emrys' shoulder. "Is something the matter?"

Without breaking contact, Emrys spun around in Senna's arms and shrank into his chest. He tucked his head under Senna's chin, hunching over so his ear could rest right above his heart. Senna was sure he noticed how it kicked up speed.

"You were dead," Emrys murmured. "You keep acting like you suffered a scraped knee, but you didn't see what I did. You don't know how still you look when your breathing stops or the color of the stones when they're stained with your blood. You don't know what your ribs look like when they're visible through the slashes in your chest. My mind had already started convincing me I'd never hear your voice again, so forgive me if I'm a little clingy."

"Oh," Senna said, somewhat awkwardly. He returned the embrace, kissing Emrys' hair. "I didn't think—"

"I wouldn't want you to," Emrys said wetly. "It was a gruesome sight, even for the imagination. I never want you to have any idea how it felt."

"But I do." Senna drew Emrys back. "Don't forget what happened on our first trip here."

"You didn't care for me then."

"I did," Senna swore. "You hardly left me any choice in fixing my devotion on you. I don't know how anyone could know your warmth, your ferocity, and your passion, and *not* care for you."

Emrys scoffed shyly. "I'm a villain compared to you."

The phrase was spoken in jest, but Senna could hear the admission of truth in every word. He could not abide a single second that Emrys doubted his own precious value.

Senna burrowed his face into Emrys' throat and deposited an open-mouthed kiss where his blood ran hot. In a silky tone that exhibited the measure of his affection, he murmured, "You were kind to *me*. Everyone else is kind to the goldheart, the man they think I am because of what they see. But you were kind without reservation, without judgment to a man no one ever noticed. No one has addressed me the way you have. No one else has transfixed me either."

Emrys retreated slightly, running his hands down Senna's arms. "I haven't any idea why. I've so little to offer you."

"I disagree," Senna said gently. "This is unlike you. Normally, you're the picture of confidence."

With a frustrated huff, Emrys broke away, wrapping his arms around himself.

"You were lying in the street, bleeding to death, and all I could think was *What have I given him? What is he leaving with? A romp in a greenhouse? A few half-decent memories?*" he said exasperatedly. "Senna, you deserve the entire world. And what am I? A man who has two decades' worth of lies and deceit. What else can I give you? What else am I?"

"Aside from brave and unspeakably good? You're *mine*. Nothing in the world has ever been mine before." Senna advanced urgently. "You want to know what you've given me? You gifted me *your* inflorescence, the most beautiful white roses I've ever seen. You've encouraged me and protected me. Sascha told me that if you hadn't used the needle yarrow when you did, it would've been too late. You think you've given me nothing. You've given me my life. I expect you'll do it again, before all this is done."

Emrys' blush ran down his face to his parted lips, eyes bright and wide. He tried to speak around his speechlessness, but Senna couldn't wait a second longer. He seized Emrys' face and kissed him hard. It was steeped in everything he'd been bottling inside for the year, everything he wished he'd said before bleeding out onto the cobblestone streets. This was his decision, and he was committing to it.

Senna guided the intensity of the kiss, allowing Emrys to take and take all he gave. He swept Emrys into him, until his lover was completely at his mercy, rapt to every movement. Feather-soft, Senna trailed his fingertips down Emrys' arms to his hands. He pressed the heartlines of their palms together—pulse against pulse. Senna knew there was no hiding the undressed desire in his gaze.

He traipsed to the bed, pulling Emrys along beside him. Sitting easily on the soft mattress, Senna began to pull at the laces of his trousers, his knuckles brushing up against his own hardening cock. Emrys watched the gentle movement hungrily. He leaned forward, as if compelled, but his movements were stilted, betraying his lingering reluctance. Senna hummed in understanding. He didn't think there was anything he could say to assuage Emrys' guilt, no matter how unwarranted he thought it was. But perhaps he could show him how alive he was.

Reaching for the back of his collar, Senna pulled his shirt over his head and tossed it aside. A tear trailed down Emrys' cheek as he beheld the satin, red scars on Senna's chest. The new ones surely looked ghastly among the old one on his stomach.

"Come here," Senna said sweetly.

Emrys stayed entirely still, transfixed by the swollen discoloration.

"Emrys." Senna pulled him in. "You won't hurt me."

Sighing warily, Emrys perched on Senna's knee.

"Trust me," Senna urged. He guided Emrys' fingers to his scars and laid them flat against his abdomen. Emrys tried to flinch away, but Senna was already holding it down. He pressed deeper and deeper, but no pain came—only pressure against his ribs. "There's no pain. Not even a twinge."

The dread on Emrys' expression subsided, replaced by relief.

"Senna," he said helplessly.

"Let me submit to you."

Emrys fell forward until his lips were pressed loosely to Senna's temple.

"Alright," he assented. "But I'm taking the lead. And you have to tell me immediately if you're in any pain at all. Is that clear?"

Senna smiled, delightedly coy. "Yes, Your Highness."

Emrys tossed an expression of despairing lust up at the ceiling, but was matching Senna's wide grin when he looked back down. He lifted himself up, taking a moment to appreciate Senna's bleeding patience. Then, he glided into Senna's space, urging him further and further onto the bed, until Senna's back was flush with the mattress. Emrys shucked away the last of their clothes, tossing them in a heap on the floor. Then, he took his throne on Senna's swelling erection, grinding down as it filled out beneath him. Senna dug his head into the mattress, trying to arch up into the friction. Emrys paused, letting his burning heat linger where Senna needed it most.

"Give me your hand," Emrys instructed.

Senna complied swiftly.

Emrys kissed the center of the palm, nuzzling the callouses. His own touch was warm as it smoothed Senna's skin along the flow of his pulse. He worked the skin longer than usual for inflorescence, but Senna suspected that was to draw out the touch.

"What are you growing?" Senna whispered.

Emrys' eyes glinted. "Can I surprise you?"

Senna drew his bottom lip into his mouth and nodded.

With one final nudge, Emrys urged the inflorescence free. Senna couldn't see what it was with his hand facing away from him, but he felt it grow to the full size of his palm—round and velvet. Whatever it was, it gave off an aroma so sweet, Senna could practically taste it.

Emrys angled Senna's hand down so he could see. "Would you like to try whimfruit?"

Senna propped himself up on his elbow to get a better look. The whimfruit was more fascinating than it was the first time he'd seen it. Although it felt like a peach's velvet skin to his hand, the fruit's skin was practically crystalline. It was the same color as the jarred sunlight in Talsura, incandescently yellow and orange. Through the translucent skin, Senna could see a cluster of tiny seeds floating in the pulp.

Eager, Senna pulled his hand to his mouth. Emrys caught it before he could take the first bite.

"So desperate," Emrys said, amused. "There are traditions at play here."

Senna wet his lips, nodding eagerly.

"I'll eat the one you grew and you'll eat the one I grow. Just one bite. Eat too much and you'll come too quickly," Emrys explained blithely. "It won't hurt you.

As I said before, it won't impact your state of mind or your ability to consent. It will only heighten the sensation, while giving you a little . . . endurance. It's almost ritualistic."

"Have you tried it before?" Senna wondered.

"Once," Emrys confessed with a fond smile. "At one of the first exchanges I hosted, someone gave me the whimfruit. They had to whisper in my ear what it did, too embarrassed to speak too loudly. I was impatient to try it, so I went right to my paramour's house. We enjoyed ourselves, but she wanted to use it all the time. I discovered it was too . . . special to me to do with someone I was only casual with." He shrugged. "I haven't used it since."

"It grew the last time we were together. Does it often appear uncontrollably?"

Emrys dipped his head to hide his blush.

"Never. Only with you," he admitted. "Do you want to try it with me? I thought it might be a good way for you to enjoy yourself without straining your body."

It would be the most intimate and heady thing Senna had ever done. It would make even the most open-minded Talsuran wrinkle their nose in disgust.

He absolutely had to do it.

Senna sat up and extended his hand, the whimfruit still heavy and tender in his palm.

"For you," he said.

A smile lit Emrys' face, bright enough to outshine the lanterns overhead. He accepted Senna's offering, using both hands to bring the fruit to his lips. Keeping his gaze locked on Senna, Emrys bit into the whimfruit. His eyes closed and he tilted his head back. To see how immediate the effect was, Senna grazed his finger down the center of Emrys' chest.

Emrys shivered.

Senna couldn't have been more pleased. "Good?"

"Nectar of the canons," Emrys answered blissfully. He opened his own hand, allowing Senna to watch the fruit swell to life, then held it close to Senna's lips.

The scent was strong up under Senna's nose, like candied flowers and honeyed berries. He sank his teeth into the flesh. Sweetness exploded on his tongue, taking over his mouth and filling him completely. He felt like the taste had somehow branched out throughout him, reaching high into his mind and sinking into all of his nerves. He suspected that Emrys could've bit his thigh, his nipple, his arse and found his blood had gone sweet. The whimfruit's bright juice dripped down his chin, onto his chest, trailing to the line of hair that pointed to his full cock.

It was bliss and Emrys hadn't even touched him yet.

Emrys guided the fruit he'd grown above Senna's lap and squeezed. It crushed, spilling juice and crystalline pulp all over his cock. Each drop brought a pulse of brilliant pleasure, sending shivers down Senna's spine in time with the drops trailing down the shaft.

Emrys wet his lips, eyeing the sight with rapt interest.

"You may want to hold on to something," was all the warning he gave, before swallowing Senna whole.

Senna keened, unable to keep from bucking his hips up. Emrys anticipated this, because he pushed all his weight into keeping Senna fixed to the bed, sucking hard. Senna's vision was a million lit fireworks.

"Sun slay me." He gritted his teeth, the pleasure so intense his eyes watered. Yet, his climax felt a million years away. He felt so good he would die. "Is it always like this?"

Emrys pulled away with an audible *POP*, his lips wet and swollen. Senna wanted badly to kiss them.

"I like to think that some talent is involved." Emrys grinned. He kissed the inside of Senna's thigh, chuckling when the juice-smeared cock bobbed back against his nose. "I've gotten ahead of myself. Tell me what you want, Senna. My mouth? My hands?"

Senna's heart felt like if it raced any faster, it would explode out of his chest. "Your cock," he choked out.

Emrys lit up with delighted surprise. He hovered over Senna, stroking his hand up Senna's scarred chest and grazing his nipples. Despite all of his efforts to clench a moan back, it still hit the open air like a stroke of lightning.

"Don't quiet yourself, darling" Emrys crooned. "You were so talkative the last time we fucked. Tell me what you want."

"I don't want to."

Emrys paused, pulling back, confused but not upset. "Oh, alright."

"No, I—" Senna fought through the sensation to remember how to speak. "I don't want to fuck. I mean, I *want* this. But I want—I want—"

With a kind smile, Emrys caressed Senna's face. "Whatever you want, I want it too, alright? There's nothing to be ashamed of."

Senna held Emrys by the waist to keep his hands from shaking. He wouldn't get what he wanted if he lost his words, so he formed them very, very carefully.

"I want to be with you ardently. Intentionally."

"Oh, I see," Emrys said warmly. "You want to make love."

Senna covered his face with his free hand. "I do."

He couldn't hide behind his hand forever, because Emrys pulled it away and tucked himself neatly into Senna's throat. The first kiss landed with a dozen butterflies under his skin.

"You want to know how much I cherish you. How beautiful I think you are. I understand," Emrys said. He dipped his finger into his own whimfruit, the slickness practically sparkling under the lamplight. "Don't worry. The nectar won't harm you as a lubricant. This is one of its primary purposes."

He smeared the coating over Senna's hole. The first touch came with a cold sensation that made Senna squirm against the bed, too pleasurable to be unpleasant.

"Now, will you let me make love to you, my heart?"

"Yes," Senna breathed.

Emrys worked Senna open up with meticulous and reverent precision. It was unlike anything Senna had experienced, the intoxicating indulgence hitting him with even the most mechanical of Emrys' movements. The stretch that usually came with discomfort felt rapturous all the way down to his toes. If this was what it was like with Emrys' fingers, Senna wasn't sure he'd survive his cock.

At last, Senna felt the first building pulses of his climax within reach. It wouldn't overcome him yet—for this he was glad—but it did give all of his pleasure a sharp edge that left him panting.

When Emrys pulled his hand away, Senna hoped it was to lean up and kiss him. To his extreme displeasure, Emrys rolled to the other side of the bed and started rummaging through the bedside table.

Need seized Senna. He closed the distance between them, nibbling on Emrys' shoulder blade.

"Hells," Emrys groaned. He shifted back to brush his ass against Senna's aching cock, only to force himself away. Swatting Senna back, he tossed a disapproving glance over his shoulder. "You'll drive me to frenzied distraction if you're not careful."

"What if that's what I want?" Senna slipped his hand over Emrys' waist, brushing his cock.

"I'd not stop you," murmured Emrys brokenly. "I'd only ask you to use this while you do."

He produced a condom and relinquished it to Senna's care. Senna, on his part, was not going to turn down an opportunity to get his hands on Emrys. He rolled the condom over Emrys' considerable length with a tight grip. Emrys whined loud enough to draw a swell of pride to Senna's stomach.

"Lie back," Emrys gasped, chest heaving. Senna complied, knowing the sooner he opened the cradle of his thighs, the sooner Emrys would fill them.

Emrys guided the hand that held Senna's fruit so that it rested above his stomach and thrust his cock over the fruit. The sweet lubricant coated his member, shimmering and clear. Senna nearly lost the weak hold on his self-control and brought the enticing sight to his mouth. But he wanted Emrys closer still, to feel his body everywhere he could.

Caging Senna underneath him, Emrys slowly slipped inside until he was buried to the hilt. He stayed still, allowing Senna to settle into the feeling of their bodies joined together—not only to acclimate to the size, but the warmth too, the sensation, the rush of need to be even closer to Emrys.

Overcome, Senna opened his mouth, trying to lean up for a kiss but not able to move without molten pleasure tearing through him. Emrys recognized the need, though, because he covered Senna's lips in a deep kiss and began to move.

Senna cried out against Emrys' lips, eyes growing wet again. He'd never known this feeling—as if all of Emrys' adoration was a physical sensation he could burrow into his skin like inflorescence, a living part of him. It subdued him, dissolved him, pieced him back together. It stripped away his words, but for once Senna welcomed their departure, because it meant that every wire in his brain was transfixed on each of Emrys' thrusts.

It felt like Emrys moved in him forever—until the sun rose and fell a hundred times over—the pleasure drawing on and on. His climax was almost upon him now, within grasp. Senna's mouth began to form around sounds he couldn't find the breath to utter—pleas and praise, love and promises. Emrys heard the silent words over the sound of his own broken moans. Knowing exactly what Senna needed, he grasped Senna's weeping cock and stroked it in time with his movements. Each thrust into Senna's shaking body was harder than the last, drawing pulses of bright pleasure from deep within him.

"Open your mouth," Emrys rasped.

Senna parted his wet lips, tilting his chin up. Emrys squeezed the last vestiges of his own fruit into Senna's mouth. The magic struck him like lightning, amplifying everything he felt until it was all he was. He clung to Emrys' body with a vice grip and came with a yell. Emrys was right there with him, clutching him close and trembling in the cradle of Senna's thighs.

The whimfruit's magic drew out the sensation for eternity until finally—*finally*—Emrys rolled away from Senna to throw out the condom. He was back in an instant, curling into Senna's side, heedless of the sweat and leftover whimfruit juice.

Senna kissed the top of Emrys' head and pulled him close.

"I'm glad I chose to be with you," Senna said, voice raw.

"You're only happy you found a lover who could grow whimfruit," Emrys teased, his chest damp against Senna's.

"No, I mean it. I'd make this choice over and over if I had to."

Emrys snuggled in closer.

"Me too."

Part
Four

PERCY

YOU PROBABLY COULDN'T SUMMON a canon through sheer willpower alone, but that didn't stop Percy from trying. The night before they planned to venture back home, he perched on the bench underneath the wide window of his Mount Livian chambers, squinting into the dim mountainside. His eyes skimmed the shadowy canopy of trees, desperately trying to spy the glowing deer.

The Mount Livians had tried to do Percy the service of ignoring their curiosity, forgoing any questions about how he'd managed to kill the dre'malors. Possibly, they were too afraid to ask, but it did little to protect him from his own racing thoughts.

"Percy? I think my corset laces are knotted," Elora called out from the vanity, arms twisted around her back. "Could I trouble you?"

The hypnotic draw of his restlessness snapped at the sound of Elora's voice, fading away like the moon drawing back the lapping ocean. He smiled warmly.

"Of course, darling. I insist that you trouble me for the rest of our lives." He swept behind her and smoothed his hands down her bare throat until they grazed the soft fabric of her chemise. He pressed a soft kiss to the dip of her throat, lingering on the warmth. She tilted her head back, leaning sleepily into his chest. "I'm sure I don't have to tell you how amazing I think you are for volunteering with repairs all day in a corset."

"You don't. Your eyes are very loud on their own," she replied, wearing an affectionate smirk. "I was glad to help, as I'm sure you were, as well."

Though his eyes were blurry with exhaustion, Percy dutifully began to untangle the back laces. Elora watched from the mirror, a complicated expression veiled in candlelight.

"I know everyone has been stepping very carefully around it," started Elora cautiously, "but do you *want* to talk about what happened?"

Percy froze.

"With the dre'malors," Elora clarified.

"Yes, darling, I knew what you meant. I—I think I do." His throat tightened.

Elora met his eyes in the mirror with a soft smile, patiently waiting for him to continue.

"Everyone wants to know how I did it. To tell you the truth, I'm not sure. I saw a canon up on the hill who instructed me to do what I did. I merely followed orders. In the heat of the moment, I felt like a prophet. Like I was only wielding the canon's power on their behalf."

"Do you have any idea which canon it was?"

Percy fiddled with one of the strings, thinking. "Earlier tonight, Nare explained that they had come here in search of Alpedis because Senna had encountered her in the moorlands earlier this year. She told him that she favored him. Maybe she favors me too."

Elora's eyes widened. "Letting you possess her magic is one way to announce her favor."

"That's just it. The more I recall the moment and my experience of it, the more it felt like the power came from somewhere inside of me. Whatever I borrowed it from, it felt—offended and enraged. That means it couldn't be Alpedis' favor. But if it wasn't her, where did that power come from? What does it want?"

Reaching around, Elora took one of Percy's hands and held it to her chest.

"That must have been terrifying," she said.

"Yes, but I find that it gives me *hope*, something I sorely need just now."

"I never thought you'd be the one lacking hope."

Percy sighed and leaned his cheek into her hair.

"I am riddled with these grand ideas for the world and optimism that everything will work out. But I think I have felt rather inadequate at trying to make those ideas a reality. Who am I compared to skilled knights and geniuses? Knowing I have this power inside of me gives me hope that I'll be able to keep pace with my own dreams. I feel for the first time that I'll be a king worth his people's pride."

Elora took the hand on her shoulder and kissed it. "You always have been. You didn't need a canon's help or latent magical abilities to be a worthy ruler. I'll be proud to stand by your side."

Percy went completely still.

"Do you mean . . . ?"

Elora grinned, the candlelight illuminating the apple red of her cheeks.

"I put some thought into what you asked me all those months ago," she said. "I'll admit, the thought of being the queen consort is so overwhelming it turns my stomach. But it'll be *your* Talsura we care for, not the one I left. So, if a time comes when you want to ask my hand, take heart that you'll get the answer you're hoping for."

Percy shot around to the front of the chair, dropping to both his knees.

"Marry me, Elora," he begged earnestly.

Elora let out a loud bark of laughter. "I didn't mean right this second."

"Why wait? I have a ring that Thea's been keeping safe for me. It's Redwindan style because I didn't think you'd want to wear my mother's heirloom."

"Oh, definitely not."

"The jeweler let me choose any stone I wanted, so I picked a pear-shaped ruby. Do you like it?"

"I haven't *seen* it. But I'm sure I'll adore it."

Percy chuckled nervously. "I suppose you ought to. I've learned a thing or two from you about aesthetics these past years and my taste has greatly improved so—"

"Percy."

"—really there's nothing to worry about! Although, if you don't like it, I'm sure the kind fellow will switch it out for me. You can choose any stone you want, except for opals, which have a dreadful tendency to break and chip."

Elora seized Percy's face in her hands. "*Percy*," she said gently.

Percy blinked, his cheeks squished forward a little. "Yes, my love?"

"Ask me again."

The urgency remained, but his movements were slower, more purposeful. He needed to do this right.

Adjusting so that he was on one knee, Percy took Elora's hands and pressed a long kiss to her warm knuckles.

"From the moment we met, you've been setting me on the right path, guiding me and caring for me. Let me commit to the task of doing the same for you. I'll be a man you can be proud of. Will you marry me?"

Not even the Dam could have dimmed Elora's smile. She nodded, her affirmation muddying in a mess of happy tears.

Percy surged forward and kissed her. He'd never tire of her warmth, the familiar softness of her under his hands. Not for all the gold and power in the world.

They shifted so that Percy sat on the vanity stool and Elora was perched in his lap. He chased her taste along the column of her throat, the place where her sweat had gathered in the heat of their crusade. She'd since washed it all away, leaving behind the floral scent of the Mount Livian soap.

Percy returned his efforts to her corset. Distraction and lust lengthened the task, but with a gentle pull of his hands, the laces finally came free. The corset opened, two shells parting to reveal the chemise. She pushed it off and onto the floor, exposing the pearly-soft skin beneath. At Elora's nod, Percy ran his warm palm along the length of her sternum, caressing the sides of each breast. He let his fingers rest above the calm thud of her heart. Releasing a tired sigh, Percy kissed her hair, trailing down her chest. There, he laid his cheek against her breast and sighed.

"It's okay if you'd rather rest," breathed Elora gently.

"I do," he murmured. Voicing the desires made him feel like an over-needy hound, but he did it anyway. "I want this first."

But Elora tilted her head knowingly.

"What do you need, Percy?"

It was her way of saying the control was his. She pushed up onto her haunches just long enough for Percy to shuck away his trousers. He allowed her to encase him in her tight warmth and draw out a tired, love-laced climax. Afterward, they lay together, skin against skin. The rest of the world did not exist.

For the first time in weeks, Percy slept without nightmares.

THEA

"I HOPE YOU LIKE chamomile," said Sascha, sliding a cup of steaming tea to Thea.

The party had long since died down, with only a few people still lingering to talk and enjoy the quiet peace that came with being alive.

Thea had been dozing, leaning her face onto her knees tucked snuggly underneath her, falling asleep to the sound of Nare's voice as she debated a wiry man about the ethics of olfactory magic. At the sound of Sascha's voice, she jostled awake. Her feet dropped to the ground and she pinned her back to the chair.

Sascha waved their hand. "At ease, Princess. You needn't be straitlaced around me. Not after the day we had yesterday."

The title fell in and out of Thea's ears, until she remembered no one here was supposed to know it. Sascha chuckled guiltily.

"My apologies, Acathea. I should've told you I was aware of your title. There was a time when you were a young girl that your mother still invited me to dinners. I remember your extravagant way of dressing. I was always jealous of your elaborate gowns, but they're so impractical around my hot springs that I never had any made for myself. May I sit?"

The last time a stranger had spoken to Thea so casually, so familiarly, it was when she'd met Percy. She warily brought her knees back up under her chin and gestured for Sascha to take Emrys' empty seat. They did. In their hand, they swirled a ceramic cup of green tea. Thea was thankful for her chamomile. Drinking green tea as Sascha was would've guaranteed she would've been up all night.

"You don't plan on sleeping?" Thea commented.

"How can I? I can tell my body is tired. But my mind . . ." Sascha sighed. "Every time I close my eyes, my brain convinces me another beast will leap from around a dark corner. I fear it will take me a while longer to truly believe that things have gone back to normal."

"You still have no idea what drew all the dre'malors up the mountain?"

"None," replied Sascha easily with a shrug. "I always knew they prowled the moorlands at the base of the mountain. Naturally, a few would wander up and find us nestled into the mountainside. We can weather one or two, but there were so many—" Their voice caught, so they took a sip of their tea. "I can only assume they were summoned. But that is a problem for tomorrow."

Thea laid her face back onto her knees. Nearby, Nare was slamming her hand on the table and saying, "That's *exactly* what I'm trying to tell you!" Thea's lips lifted in a fond smile.

"She's always been like that, you know," Sascha said, gesturing to the librarian with their tea. "One of the most passionate, persuasive debaters I know, even as a teenager. I think she could convince a cow it was a cat if she tried hard enough."

Thea agreed, but her smile dropped. It was that same convincing manner of speaking that had persuaded the other Academes to trust Nare with the cure for sun sickness.

"She said all of you died," Thea commented lightly. "We were both surprised to see you."

She hadn't intended for the words to stumble out like an accusation. But in all the time Thea had spent with her, she'd seen how Nare had carried her guilt with her like another necessary supply in her pack. It was the weight on her shoulders, the shadow in her eyes, the briefest moment's hesitation before she rushed into things. If Nare had known Sascha was alive all this time, would her pain have been so profound? Could she have found closure sooner?

"I see we're equal on the scale of secrets." Sascha smiled fondly at Nare. "In truth, I broke from our branch of the Academes the first year Nare was sworn in. I'd had my own disagreement with the other mages and ran away from home before I could get to know her very well. But I think I made the right choice. Coming here, begging the Mountain Council to allow me to run for election—it saved my life." Then, without room for further questions, Sascha asked, "Nare mentioned before that you needed something from me."

Thea blinked, surprised. Folding her hands around her knees, Thea explained their quest, filling in the details Senna had left out. How they were researching the cure for the sun sickness—not to impose it on anyone, but to give them a choice. To give their kingdoms a chance to repair what had been broken and thought damaged for good.

"I hardly see where I come in. The last thing anyone needs is a third party telling them what to do," said Sascha.

Thea pulled the leather journal from her bag. She slid it across the table, the embossed deer on the front glimmering in the light.

Sascha fixed the journal with a confused look. Then, recognition dawned. "Is this—?"

"Laurentine's research journal? Yes. We think Laurentine knew something about empowering people magically. Something that got him killed. But the journal has this magic seal that we haven't been able to get past—a bunch of tangled threads. At first, we were going to use his glasses to untangle them ourselves. But they . . ." Thea pressed her lips together. "That's no longer an option. We saw you cut Senna's magical stitches with those scissors and thought maybe . . ."

Sascha held the journal by its spine, lifting it up to the light so they could squint at the fore edge.

"I suppose it's redundant to suggest that maybe the journal is sealed for a reason."

Thea could only guess as to what those reasons might be. The obvious one seemed to be to protect the most dangerous magical secrets from falling into the wrong hands. But it also might've been to keep others from taking the credit for his work. To take time to think about his findings without being pressured to act.

"Do you not trust us with Laurentine's secrets?" she asked quietly.

"I admit, when you first mentioned the journal, my instinct was to steal it away and hide it in a vault where no one would be able to find it. Then I imagined what it would be like if Laurentine was still here—he would be the one to make the decision." Sascha reached into their satchel and produced a pair of polished scissors. "But this cause of yours, this pursuit of the liberty to choose. It has Laurentine written all over it. I know the choice he would have made."

With an easy flourish, they opened the sharp blades.

"Without seeing the threads, it's impossible to tell how magically fortified the lock is. I can't promise the scissors will be strong enough, but I can certainly try."

Carefully, they sliced through the seemingly empty air where the pages were magically bound together. The book split open easily, fanning apart and revealing just a hint of Laurentine's notes, his sketches and cross-outs. Reverently, Sascha closed the yawning journal and placed it in Thea's gentle hands.

"Thank you," she said, hugging the journal to her chest.

"Laurentine's mind was a gift," they said in a low voice. "Please honor it."

There was none of the practiced manners when she spoke. Only raw authenticity. "I swear." Then, with a shy look at Sascha. "You made it look so easy. I labored over that seal for weeks."

"Who do you think taught him the thread spell?" they said, spinning the scissors around one finger. "Are you going to read it now?"

Thea drew her lip into her teeth.

"I don't suppose I can trouble you for some green tea?"

"No bloody *fucking* way!" rang Nare's voice. With absolutely no grace and even less finesse, she kicked away from her chair and bounded over to Thea, leaving her conversation partner with his mouth hanging open. "You opened it without me?"

Sascha barked out a laugh. "Blame me for that. I didn't know you were planning an unveiling ceremony. I'd have worn my nice clothes."

"I'll have you know it's been *my* blood, sweat, and tears that have gone into trying to open this delightful thing."

Thea rolled her eyes. "Are we reading it or not?"

Sascha settled into their seat, crossing their hands elegantly in their lap. Nare shouldered in next to Thea, eager to see the journal for herself. She gave Thea a short nudge.

"Well? Get on with it."

Thea opened the journal.

"I didn't miss his handwriting, I'll say that much," was Nare's immediate comment. "Why magically seal the book if your handwriting is comparable to an ancient scrawl?"

It was true that the handwriting was difficult to go through quickly, but Thea always took her time reading.

"It seems the first several pages are personal entries. It feels a little invasive to read them aloud. I'll skip forward," she said.

She flipped through the pages, skimming the words carefully until Nare stopped her. "Wait. Go back." Thea did. Nare's finger jabbed to the middle of the page. "There. Read that."

Drawing in a deep breath, Thea began to read.

"*Recently, I've been doing more research into the canons. It's always seemed strange that we have gods that we disrespect, yet we know not where they come from or what their purpose is. I never knew where to begin with my questions. Lane always advised against speaking to the canons directly, saying that they didn't have my best interests at heart. But I suppose no one could have accounted for my love, Jasrath.*" Thea paused. "He doesn't mean the canon of thieves, does he?"

"There were rumors among the Academes that Laurentine was sleeping with a canon. But he adored his husband too much for anyone to truly believe them. I don't think I ever learned his husband's name, though."

All at once Thea remembered the vision she and Nare had shared.

"Nare, do you remember what we saw in Laurentine's cottage?"

Nare shivered. "How could I forget?"

"Laurentine said his husband was a canon."

Sascha pressed their chin onto their fist thoughtfully.

"That explains why nothing came of the gossip. The canon Laurentine was sleeping with *was* his husband." They nodded at Thea. "Keep going."

Jasrath says there's a middle place between life and what comes after. Somewhere called Caenia. The Assembly of Canons is apparently the product of profound grief, the desperate kind that manifests as determination. Those who die but do not want to pass on linger in Caenia. Their raw desire to return to the life of the living keeps them from moving forward, wringing every last bit of time with their loved ones they can get, usually as spirits.

"Caenia is an arsenal of great magic. It's this magic that fuels the spirits and gives them the ability to appear to their loved ones—usually just once. But existing in this middle plane costs power. Some spirits both refuse to pass one and are compatible vessels of Caenia's magic. These are the canons.

"Holy shit," Nare breathed.

It turns out the magic the canons gorge on is a living thing—with desires and intentions, just as we have. Each canon's power craves a different purpose. Hedela kept her spirit alive on healing magic. Now she is forced to stitch wounds and cure disease. Oesyth spends her magic fulfilling wishes.

Jasrath says the canons simply use the resources Caenia provides them. If you ask me, it sounds a little like theft. I adore him, but the irony is not lost on me. But maybe he's right. Maybe the magic likes having the means to accomplish what it was meant to. After all, what good is healing magic without the hands to do the curing?

In the end, being a canon is just a challenge of endurance. How much power can one person's soul seize for themselves? How long can they bend to the whims of the magic that they host? Do some of them coexist peacefully with this magic? Is the cost of the magic—being the magic's hand to operate in the world of humans—too much for the canons? Or do they delight in it? It seems that the answer varies between the individual canon. Jasrath, for example, has forsaken his magic, gratifying it insofar that he may live happily with me—nothing more. I still have so much to learn, but now that Jas has given me a start, I feel I may actually get somewhere.

That was all Laurentine had written in that entry, using the remaining empty space on his page to sketch what he thought Caenia might look like—possibly based on his husband's descriptions. Eager, Thea forged on, reading passage after passage of what came next. If Laurentine's knowledge of the canons was this staggering, then whatever he knew of the sun sickness and restorative magic would have to be just as significant.

Laurentine wrote about the canons he managed to commune with in his dreams. He wrote about how offerings to canons were ineffective if they had already given up on trying to placate the magic they hosted. In some cases, it seemed the canons allowed themselves to give up their power and pass on—too burned out from being governed by their magic's whims to remember how badly they wanted to live.

All of it should've been terribly interesting, but none of it was of any use to Thea. She'd gotten her hopes up at a brief mention of Alpedis, who had apparently become the first canon by drawing her power from the sun that somehow still shone on Caenia. But in entry after entry, that was all Laurentine had to say about the sun. It seemed he hadn't lived long enough to experience any inflorescence.

They were more than halfway through the journal when Thea's patience finally wore out.

"Damn it all." She slammed the journal, deposited it unceremoniously in Nare's lap, and stomped a few paces away. Rubbing over her heart, she forced in several deep breaths.

Sascha's voice sounded so far away when they spoke. "I know it isn't quite what you were looking for. But it's a start. Knowledge is power, Thea, and knowing the history of the canons is a mighty thing."

"We haven't read the book all the way through yet," Nare reasoned. "He had this journal guarded with one of the strongest magical seals in existence. There has to be something he was protecting. Something that can be of use to us."

"We don't know exactly when he died," Thea pointed out bitterly. "We thought his village might've been destroyed during the sun sickness, but he might've already been killed by the time the sun sickness developed."

"That's for you to find out," Sascha said. "If I listen to you read a moment longer, I fear I'll be slumped over, snoring on the ground—not very dignified."

They smacked their hands to their knees and pushed themself up. The movement was demanding, requiring more energy and strength than they seemed to have left. Even upright on their feet, they slouched sleepily, pressing their lips together against a yawn. Holding the journal out in the empty space between them, they smiled at Thea.

They continued, "I suspect I'm not wrong in thinking that you won't sleep tonight until you've read the journal cover to cover. Linger here as long as you want or meet your friends in the guesthouse. I'll send a carriage in the morning to escort you home to Redwind. You can rest on the ride back."

"Thank you," Nare said, clasping Sascha's wrist.

"All I ask is that you come find me sometime soon. I'm terribly curious about your what you might discover."

Nare bumped Sascha's shoulder. "Oh please. You're going to see me so much, people will start to mistake me for a bad rash."

"I'll hold you to it," Sascha said with a sleepy smile. This time, they yawned in earnest. "If I don't want to end up sleeping in a bed-shaped shrub, I better start heading home. Goodnight, friends." They paused. "Oh! If you intend on enjoying the night air, the hammocks strung about are for public use. There are lanterns above them for your convenience. You only need to light them."

The women said their own goodnights, a cool breeze brushing over Thea's face. Around them, the crickets and frogs had begun their nightly chorus.

"Not that the cold, stone stairs aren't cushiony under my bottom, but that hammock is making my mouth water," Nare said, pointing across the road.

Thea wasn't sure if she would call the hammock in question mouthwatering, but she had to admit, it was better than the stairs. The hammock was tied between two sturdy trees, wide enough to fit three Nare-sized people across the woven berth.

"Alright then," Thea agreed thoughtlessly.

The thought only occurred to her as she sat in the hammock's hallow, wrapping her hair up with her satin scarf. By lying in the hammock with Nare, she was doing everything she hated—brushing arms, sharing air, letting someone be so close to her that she could feel every shift, every thud of their pulse. Astonishingly, she didn't mind a bit.

Giving a ginormous sigh, Nare stretched her long arms and legs out.

"I'm not going to read this entire thing to you," Thea warned.

Nare snuggled closer to Thea and said lightly, "I'll just read over your shoulder."

They started from the beginning this time, commenting under their breaths when something particularly interesting stuck out to them. For Nare, it was nostalgia. Every spell Laurentine found, every sparking discovery, Nare had been there. She told Thea about how she remembered him bustling into their assembly halls, remembered hovering around him to congratulate him on knowledge beautifully won.

But for Thea, Laurentine's journal was the key to the entire world. It had mentions of places that Thea hadn't known existed—far-off lands on continents it took nearly a year to sail to. Laurentine had been to them all, greedily drinking in everything he could learn about magic. In his travels, though, he never wrote about encountering any fallow people.

It didn't matter. Thea wasn't giving up hope until she reached the very last entry.

The sun spilled hues of soft yellow and pink over the mountainside when Thea reached the final pages. Nare had fallen asleep hours ago, letting her head nestle comfortably onto Thea's shoulder. Thea's eyes burned with the effort to keep reading, but she knew no rest would come until she reached the very end. The words blurred together, dancing on the page, but still she read.

This entry I write to Jasrath—my protector and my love. You have been a most patient listener, always dutifully lending your ear to endless ramblings about my research without complaint. There is no one in this world I trust more with my findings than you. Everything I have learned and discovered, I have placed tenderly in your hands. Everything except one hypothesis—but that ends today.

I have kept this from all of our conversations and I haven't written a word of it in my journals. This has been out of an abundance of caution, not because I don't trust you in every facet of my life, but because if I'm right, then I have the formula to seize more power than any man in Talsura should have. Frankly, it scares me.

Let me be clear. This is not power I want to possess. The very thought of having anything to do with it makes me sick. But I have to tell you now because I fear I have unintentionally shared the secret with my cousin, Mathis.

The mistake is mine. I have always given Mathis the benefit of the doubt, despite knowing wholeheartedly that he is a malleable man, susceptible to the manipulations of his ill-intentioned advisors. It's gotten worse since he married Phaedra, who has intimidated him into removing all goodness out of royal decrees. Naively, I've been keeping him up to date on my research, asking him for his input, hoping he would remember that underneath his weak spine, he is fiercely intelligent and a half-decent mage. In the end, he did, long enough to figure out my findings for himself. A truth that, if shared with his wife and his royal advisors, could be the end of Talsura.

It's this: canons can be killed. Because they can be killed, they can be controlled.

The formula of it is actually quite simple. A departed soul borrows magic from Caenia and becomes a canon. Take that magic away entirely and the soul is forced to move on just as regular souls do. That canon will cease to exist and the people who worship them will be none the wiser.

The process of seizing that magic is a little more complicated. I'll spare you the scholastic minutiae. But I believe that because a canon's power source comes from living *magic with its own will and purpose, to remove it requires one of two things: force or persuasion. Convince the power to seek a new host and you can do what the canons did in the first place—steal power that isn't yours and use it for yourself.*

I needed you to know. Not only so you may protect yourself—canons forbid anyone threaten you—but also so that you may also understand any prayers of those looking to "steal" power that doesn't belong to them. Canon of thieves, love of my heart, do not let the cycle of pillaging continue.

When I'm finished, I'll seal this journal so that only you may read what lies inside. (And my friend Sascha Oakcage too, I suppose, who taught me the seal. They can open any magical lock.)

The timing of things at least has worked out. I've just received a summons from Mathis. I haven't a clue what his intentions are, but I plan to seize the opportunity and appeal to his noble nature. He'll be responsible with the secret if I ask him to be. He is a reasonable man at heart—I am hopeful he'll listen to what I have to say.

Fear not, though. I am hurrying back home to you.

Signed Yours,
Laurie

The page after that was blank. As were all the pages that followed.

Thea didn't need to be told why that was. She'd already seen it in her vision—Laurentine beaten down by a forceful kick, scrambling for consciousness, and weeping because he knew how his husband would grieve.

After closing the book, Thea pressed it against her chest.

It hadn't been what she was looking for, but it felt *close* somehow—like a lost treasure that'd been right in front of her the whole time. She wanted nothing more than to figure out what it all meant, but staying up all night reading had taken a toll on her judgment. Maybe if she closed her eyes for just a second . . .

The swoony lure of sleep had nearly claimed her when clomping horse hooves approached from up the road. Thea's eyes snapped open, ready to jump into action, only to sigh and relax back into the hammock. It was only a sign of the waking morning.

But then two horses appeared, hauling a royal carriage. The driver tugged the reins when the horses fell in line with the hammock. They said nothing, only staring at Thea expectantly.

The carriage door flew open and out popped her brother's face.

"Canons, you look like you've just crawled out of your own grave!" Emrys cried in a voice that was far too loud for the quiet morning. "Why are you in a hammock?"

Nare rocketed awake with a mighty lurch. In an effort to grab her knife out of her pocket, her foot tangled in the ropes and she twisted out of the hammock, dropping onto the land below with a loud *SMACK*. Thea miraculously had held on, arms tight as twigs.

Senna's face appeared above Emrys.

"*Oh*," Emrys crooned meaningfully. "They're *both* in the hammock."

"Actually, I'm on the ground," Nare groaned, then spit into her hand and wiped dirt off her face.

"We waited for you at breakfast but you never showed. We've wrapped up a few patisseries and filled a tea canister so you can eat on the road," said Senna.

"The road? Where are we going?" Thea asked.

"Home, of course," replied Emrys as if it were obvious.

Thea blinked. Had she actually forgotten about the life outside of this one?

Brushing her wrinkled clothes, Thea slipped out of the hammock and helped Nare to her feet.

They stepped into the carriage. Thea had to admit, she had a serious, but momentary doubt that they would all fit inside. Most of the stagecoaches in Redwind could fit four people total. Yet the Mount Livian accommodations proved to be more spacious, fitting all six of them—with leg room to boot.

Currently, Senna was sandwiched between Thea and Emrys. As soon as she sat, her brother stretched his legs over Senna's lap, which left his feet resting primly on her knees. Thea sank tiredly into the spongy cushions, exhaustion stripping any desire to protest the imposition. Across from her were Percy and Elora. Nare situated herself at Elora's side, wasting no time in taking the journal out of Thea's bag and holding it on her lap. Percy squeezed his hands in his lap, eyes locked on the view through the window.

Then, as casually as if she were reposing with the morning tribune, Nare opened the journal and began to read.

Every gaze fell onto Thea and Nare, all traces of sleepiness gone in an instant.

"You *opened* it?" he sputtered in disbelief. "How?"

Thea picked at a hangnail. "Turns out, all you need to get past magical strings are magical scissors. Sascha had a few tricks up their sleeves."

"How fascinating. I've never heard of something like that before," Elora said.

"Eh, Sasch has always been one to take mundane, ordinary things and make them powerful. It's kind of their thing," Nare explained. "Makes sense if you think about it. Needles, scissors, baths, and soaps, they're all things anyone might have, no matter their status. When I was a kid, they enchanted these doormats that would judge the hearts of anyone who walked on them. The Dean of the Academes was so impressed, we put one on our own doorstep. Kept us from making some bad deals."

"If their passion is getting powerful magic to the everyday person, it's no wonder that they got along with Laurentine," Thea mused.

Senna knit his brows together. "How do you mean?"

"When we visited his house, we discovered Laurentine was killed by King Mathis for having progressive views on allowing strong magic in common households." Thea shrugged. "Laurentine wanted to use his knowledge for the people, Mathis wanted to monopolize it for the royal court."

Percy shifted uncomfortably in his seat, facing the window in a poor attempt to hide how pale he'd fallen. Thea narrowed her eyes at him in suspicion. Something was bothering him—beyond the mention of his father. Before Thea could wonder what it was, though, Emrys was already cutting in.

"Let me get this straight. We ventured out into the moorlands to beg a canon to open a magical journal for us. Then when we got here, we arrived in time to save Mount Livia from imminent destruction, completely forgetting about the journal in the first place. But it didn't matter, because miraculously, we managed to open the journal anyway."

Senna hummed. "You know what they say about the canons' design."

Emrys frowned. "I really don't."

"*Triumph is in remaining steadfast to the canons' design*," Thea quoted. When Emrys looked at her as if she'd grown another head, she shrugged. "What? One of us had to attend royal lessons."

"Well it makes me shiver. Sounds like something those Cloth cultists would say," Emrys griped.

Thea pressed her lips together. Now that she knew what the canons really were, she couldn't help but agree with Emrys.

"Nare, have you had a chance to read through the journal yet?" Senna asked.

"We read a little last night. I couldn't keep my eyes open, so I didn't get very far. Thea read on, though," Nare answered.

"Not all the way through," Thea lied.

The right thing to do would be to tell everyone what she'd found—to shake the carriage with the news that the canons could be killed. Confess that she suspected *that* was the real reason Laurentine had been murdered. The timing was right—they were all gathered, stuck with nothing to do but talk for several hours. But Thea had a feeling that as soon as she announced what she'd found, everything would change. They'd gone this long without knowing canons could die. They could last another day—or at least until Thea had been able to talk it through with Nare.

And yet—all her friends looked at her expectantly to say more. All except Percy, who still was glowering out the window.

"Percy," Thea started carefully. "Is everything alright, friend?"

The prince jolted.

"Oh, fine, fine," Percy mumbled dismissively. "Vacations never last quite so long as you hope they will and all that."

"If fighting dre'malors and nearly dying is your idea of a vacation, I hate to see what you actually do to relax," Nare said.

Senna and Thea exchanged a glance over Emrys' legs.

"Thea, would you be so kind as to share your insights on Redwindan real estate?" Percy continued, not looking up from where he was picking at a thread sticking out of his pants.

Emrys' lips fell flat. "Real estate?"

"I think I'd like to buy a house."

"In Redwind?" cried Thea.

"Yes."

"With what money?" Senna stated, somewhat incredulously.

"I'm a prince, Sen. I have—" Percy threw his hands up. "Well, I don't know how much I have, but I'm sure it's a lot. I'd like to get one with a studio space so Elora could have somewhere to work." He turned to Thea, eyes fringed with something akin to unrest. "Your answer, my dear?"

"I . . ." Thea looked helplessly around the carriage. "I would imagine there are residences to peruse, if you're serious."

"Do I not look serious?"

"No, love, you look ill," Elora cut in delicately.

"Oh, well, now that you mention it, is it not altogether too stuffy in here? Senna, you generate entirely too much body heat. It feels like eternal damnation in this tiny coach." Percy leaned his head against the headrest. "Canons, it's—hard to breathe. I heard mountain air is supposed to be thinner, but—*this*—"

Senna knocked the top of the carriage and commanded, "Pull over."

The driver complied. When the horses had come to a stop, Senna threw open the carriage door. Outside, the moorlands extended forever, green with gray, cloudy edges.

"Can you move?" Senna asked, a firm hand on Percy's knee.

Percy's eyes squeezed shut. "Afraid not, old friend."

Senna nodded. "Breathe then. You know how." He closed Percy's hands in on themselves, squeezed, then gently unrolled the fingers. He repeated the motion five times, ten, until the breaths falling out of Percy's mouth were steadier. Smoother. With them, color rose back onto Percy's cheeks.

Senna sat back again, giving Percy space.

"What is this?" Senna asked.

"We really made a mess, Senna." Percy blinked, wetness gathering at his lashes.

"It is a bit of a mess," Senna agreed.

"I wasn't thinking when I rode out here. I was just so, so terrified for you. And *angry*. And then there was everything with the dre'malors, and you being hurt, and the party. What if it's all ruined? What are we going back to? There's no possible world where my mother believes you're really out here *hunting* Emrys. Not after I followed you."

"I know," confessed Senna.

Thea couldn't help but notice the absence of an *I told you so*.

"We can't go back."

"We must."

"Why?"

Senna leaned forward so he could look Percy in the eye. "Because if we don't, your mother will come looking for us. And she will use it as an excuse to hurt our friends."

Percy dropped his face into his hands.

"You were right. I should have let you sigil me back home the second I arrived," he moaned. "We're as good as prisoners."

Now *that* Thea could not abide. She slammed the carriage door closed and knocked on the roof. She hoped the roll of the wheels on the gravel would be enough to drown out their voices from the driver's ears.

"You'll not be prisoners," she swore fiercely, taking Percy's hands and pulling them away from his face. "Not in your own kingdom by your own mother. Not if we have anything to say about it."

"That's right. We'll help you," Emrys agreed, though he turned his eyes to Thea, awaiting instructions. Awaiting her plan.

She thought he'd have more to say—his own plan for how to save his own lover. To place Senna's safety in her care meant that he trusted her more than she'd imagined he did. This was his way of recognizing that Thea's time in her royal classes hadn't been a waste—they had made her an authority.

"I will draft a letter," she said slowly, making it up as she went. "To Phaedra. In it, I'll say that you safely arrived in Redwind to solve matters diplomatically."

"Will Phaedra believe it?" Elora wondered.

"She will if I add in some familiar truths. I'll confess that we've knowingly allowed Senna and Percy to enter the kingdom since earlier this year. That you insisted on coming yourselves so that no one else would have to risk the sun sickness."

"When she found out we were running off to Redwind, we were forbidden from returning," said Senna. "Whatever you write in your letter should match that."

"Then I'll write that this is the first time we've seen you since your final visit. I'll explain that Captain Calloway was curious about Talsura after your visits and that the masquerade gave him the perfect opportunity to trespass into Talsura. I'll tell her that we've got Emrys in custody and that he's being investigated and punished for threatening our kingdom's security and well-being. It will buy Percy and Senna a little more time, while explaining where they've been."

"Will Mother agree to this?" Emrys said quietly. "Going along with a lie?"

"She will. She'll be the one to sign the letter," Thea stated. "Because if she doesn't, I'll tell everyone in the kingdom what she's been hiding from them this whole time. She's not the only one who can play games."

The laugh that rumbled out of Emrys was low with satisfaction.

"What has she been hiding?" Elora wondered warily.

With all the grace and poise that had been etched into her blood and bones, Thea said, "I'm not a real princess. I'm a decoy, poised to die in the real heir's place should anyone try to end Redwind's royal lineage."

She had to admit, the proud expression on Nare's face was worth the few drops of poison to her heart that came with saying it.

"*Real heir*," Elora said, like the words tasted bad. "Who?"

Emrys slouched back, flourishing his hand. "I'll give you one guess."

"Well, hells." To Percy, she said, "You knew about this?"

"I have a tendency of collecting secrets," Percy said nervously, brow still damp with sweat.

"Shouldn't we think this through more?" Senna interjected. "You're talking about blackmailing the Queen of Redwind. That's a decision that can come with serious consequences. She loves Percy. Won't she help if you ask?"

Thea and Emrys exchanged a dubious look.

"It isn't that she doesn't love Percy. She does," Emrys began. "But Redwind comes first to her. Above Thea. Above me. To her, it'd be more than a favor to a friend. Sending a letter to Phaedra—one filled with lies—endangers what we've not had two decades to create. She'll never choose anyone over her kingdom." He looked to Thea. "No matter who they are."

Thea knew her brother well enough to read between the lines: *No matter if you're her daughter. No matter that you're being cheated out of what is rightfully yours.*

"It's her own fault that we have to treat this like a negotiation," Emrys concluded. "She set that boundary herself when she refused to give Thea a chance to be the princess for real."

"Maybe. But extorting her like this sets a precedent," said Senna. "If what you say is true, then she has more leverage than we do. It isn't wise to have both queens as enemies."

Thea squeezed her hands together. Senna was right, of course. If she threatened to reveal the truth, her mother wouldn't take it lying down. Their relationship as she knew it would be ruined forever—what little was left. If there was no chance of Thea getting what she wanted, she might as well use the little power she still possessed to protect Percy and Senna.

She just wouldn't make them shoulder the guilt.

Reaching across Emrys' lap, she gently held Senna's wrist.

"You're right. I'll ask her first," she promised. "If she disagrees, I'll sign the letter myself."

Whether or not Senna actually believed her, Thea couldn't tell from his smile. But it seemed to give them all enough reassurance to make it through the rest of the carriage ride without descending into a panicked frenzy, and for that, she was glad.

"Does that reassure you, Percy?" Elora asked.

"Sure," he said, lying plainly. But at least he could breathe.

Tomorrow, Thea promised herself. Tomorrow they would worry about the journal, and the Talsuran queen, and filling the rift between their kingdoms. For now, she laid her head on her brother's shoulder and let the gentle rocking of the carriage lull her to sleep.

Before she drifted off completely, she felt Emrys' lips on her forehead.

"I might not agree with all of her choices," he whispered, "but I'll always be thankful she chose you."

Thea strung her arm through his and sighed, eyes still closed.

"Me too."

SENNA

The carriage dropped them off at the edge of Oesyth's Grove where Redwind bordered the northern moorlands. The driver had offered to deliver them closer to the castle, but Emrys had answered that it was safest—and would draw less attention—if they walked the rest of the distance themselves. Senna didn't mind. He was thankful for an opportunity to stretch his legs.

Emrys did, however, touch his fingers to the ground and urge a wild patch of needle yarrow to rise beneath them. The wispy stems pulled easily from the ground with a single tug. He took the sash from around his waist, wrapped up the bouquet of needle yarrow, and gave them to the driver.

"These will help those who are still healing. Sovereign Oakcage will know how to use them."

Now the group journeyed back to the castle in complete silence. There was too much to talk about, yet not enough energy among them to discuss any of it. Instead, Senna walked, greeted by waving wisteria vines. He couldn't help but remember the last time he had been here in Oesyth's Grove.

Beside him, brushing their arms together, Emrys wore a private smile, as if he were remembering the same. How strange that it was just days ago that Senna had kissed Emrys, felt the length of his body veiled underneath these long branches of a thousand desperate wishes. Senna didn't know exactly what Emrys had wished for, but the tendril of orange tiger lilies was gone, so he had a guess.

It wasn't long before the tree line gave way to the prismatic expanse of the castle's garden. This meant Elora was the first one to say goodbye. They each gave her a pleasant wave, except Percy, who walked her to her door and kissed her.

Percy returned to the group looking so lovesick and sad, Thea chuckled and slipped her arm through his.

"Oh, lighten up. You'll see her soon."

"Ah, but never soon enough," Percy lamented, only partly kidding. "I do have something to ask you. Come close."

He whispered something into her ear. Thea gasped. "*Percy Laurent.* You're only mentioning this *now*?"

A shy smile lifted on Percy's blushing face. "I want to bring it to her before I leave. Don't let me forget!"

"Sen, they're conspiring," Nare griped.

"It would seem so," Senna laughed, though he had a sneaking suspicion Percy's whispers were ring-shaped.

They passed through the garden gates, barely acknowledging the knights stationed there—the same ones who had trapped Senna and Percy to the ground all those months ago.

"You know what, keep your secrets," announced Nare. "Not that it hasn't been fun spending every waking moment of the last forty-eight hours with you weirdos, but I've got to get back to my library now before I break into hives. Give me an hour to commune with my books, then you can come and look at the journal all you like." She strode a few steps, then turned around. "Actually, uh—Thea. When you've got time, there's something I wanted to ask you too."

On paper, the words themselves would have suggested an academic inquiry, but the *tone* . . .

Emrys chittered beside him. "Scandalous."

"A question about the journal?" Thea said, entirely serious.

Nare blinked, mouth twisting downwards.

"Uh-huh," she said befuddled. "Yes. About the journal and not about anything else." She jabbed a thumb behind her. "Actually, I'm just going to—pip-pip cheerio, friends." She fled, bumping into a grand hydrangea bush, nearly falling face-first into its pastel blooms.

If Thea noticed Nare was more flustered than usual, she didn't let on. Instead, she slinked up the back palace stairs without preamble and called out behind her, "Might as well get the worst part over with. Emrys, make yourself useful and help me speak to Mother about the letter and getting our friends' lodgings sorted. Then I'm going to have a long, *long* lavender bath. I swear I still smell like canons-damned dre'malor intestines."

"I think I'll wait outside and enjoy the sun for a while longer. I can never seem to get enough," Percy said calmly. "Besides, probably best if we make ourselves scarce if the conversation doesn't go how you planned."

"Our home is your home. However you're comfortable," Emrys answered. He held the side of Senna's head and kissed him. "I'll send lunch out. You must be starving."

"I am," Senna realized, surprised. "Thank you for noticing when I didn't."

"The pleasure is mine, my sweet." With one last kiss, he was gone.

When the royals were inside, Percy turned to Senna and said, "I think I should like to take a turn through the garden. I could use some fresh air."

Senna heartily agreed, legs still stiff from several hours in the carriage. Together they embarked out to amble among the manicured garden rows. Mixed in among the fragrant blossoms, the royal horticulturist had added topiary sculptures. Instead of the magically maintained illusionary hedges Percy was accustomed to, these sculptures were the product of inflorescence, featuring depictions of Redwindan lore, stories told in hyper realistic twisted vines, flowers, and roots. In one, a woman wore an apron made of white magnolias, her rooty arm reaching up to the wisteria blooms.

"I think that one is the story of Oseyth, the canon of favors" Senna commented-ed.

Percy hummed politely, scratching his wrist.

That was strange. Usually he leapt at the opportunity to discuss history and folklore.

"Are you alright?" Senna said. "If you're still nervous about your mother—"

"*Ah!*" Percy hissed. He slapped the side of his arm. "Sorry. That was one hell of a bug bite. I'm alright. I just feel a bit strange. Maybe I've got a headache coming on. There's been a lot on my mind."

"There's no rush, you know," Senna said patiently. "I know the problems we're tackling seem urgent, but we've all survived this long under these circumstances. You can take your time to care for yourself. You won't be any help to anyone if you're unwell."

"Thank you," Percy said dismissively but sincerely. "That's why we're taking a walk. I'm gathering my thoughts. There's been so much, good and bad, I barely know where to begin."

"I see," replied Senna with a nod. "I'll be here if you want to talk."

"At lunch," Percy resolved. "I've something to tell you and Emrys. Don't worry, it's good news."

He was quiet for the remainder of the walk, only saying a polite *hello* to the groundskeepers. They came full circle, rounding back to the palace's back entrance. On the veranda, an iron table with three settings was lined with boards filled with hearty sandwiches and chilled wine. Emrys was setting out what seemed to be the last one, before swiping a piece of cheese and plopping it in his mouth.

"How did it go?" Senna called out. Beside him, Percy smacked another bug, this time on his neck.

Emrys glanced up and smiled.

"It couldn't have gone better. You were right. All Thea had to do was—"

A violent cough exploded out of Percy. He lunged forward, catching himself on his knees.

Senna fell to his side, placing a hand on his shoulder. "Percy?"

Percy spit. A sickly mix of blood and leaves sprayed the dirt path.

Senna's blood ran cold.

"Something's—" was all Percy managed to say, before he was taken by another fit of coughing. This bout stole the strength from his knees, but Senna caught him before he could crash the rest of the way onto the ground. He lowered them off the path into the soft grass, then brushed Percy's hair back in order to get a better look at his face.

Thorns, Senna realized with searing panic. There were bloody thorns spiraling out of Percy's ears and nose. He only looked for a second. Just a second. But in that second, the growth piercing through Percy's skin doubled, tripled—thick, thorny roots drilling through his arms, his throat, his legs. The bloody tendrils stretched up into the air like the desperate reach of a drowning sailor. They spilled over, threatening to bury into the ground.

Percy lurched again, retching more thorns out of his bloody lips. This time, a vine of briars stretched out of his mouth, as if it was rooted to his lungs.

"Emrys," Senna pleaded. "Emrys! Help me! *Help me!*"

Emrys was already there.

"Quickly. Move him to the shade and lay him in your lap," he instructed firmly.

Senna obeyed, hands shaking. In his arms, Percy looked up with terror in his eyes. He knew better than to try to speak, but it didn't stop the choked whimpers escaping from his lips. Tears spilled from the corner of his eyes, running red down the sides of his cheeks.

"Why is this happening?" Senna begged Emrys.

"Steady, Goldheart," was all Emrys answered. "Percy, keep your eyes on Senna. Look up at him and concentrate on breathing."

Emrys fixed his focus to Percy, placing one hand flat on his chest and wrapping the other around the thorny vine protruding from Percy's throat. He closed his eyes in concentration, let out a deep breath, and pulled the root free.

A scream tore out of Percy, growing louder the more Emrys uprooted the obstruction. It came all the way free with a spray of blood across Senna's face. Percy gasped, a terrible, choked sound.

A curse ripped out of Emrys' mouth. His hands flew to Percy's throat and chest again.

"I don't get it," he said. "We moved him to the shade. It should've slowed the sun sickness enough for us to get him inside. I've never seen it so violent with no influence from raw sunlight. It's like there's a secondary source of power."

"Senna," Percy rasped, terrified. "I'm scared."

"I'm right here. You don't have to be scared because I'm right here with you," Senna promised fiercely. "Emrys, what do we do?"

"I already called for help. I'm hoping that more inflorescent mages will be able to help me subdue the growth." The words cut off with a gasp. His muscles tensed, his own magic struggling to overpower the growth inside Percy's body. Through gritted teeth, Emrys called out, "When I yelled for help, I bloody meant it!"

Percy coughed again, mouth filling with bile-covered leaves and petals. Senna reached inside, pulling them out to clear his airways. The sun sickness raged on, pouring from every inch of Percy's skin and spilling onto the ground.

"What can I do?" Senna begged.

"What you're already doing. You're here with him."

"But I'm inflorescent. You taught me how to be inflorescent. Let me help."

"You can't, my love. I'm so sorry, but you can't. This is beyond what I taught you."

"Why did you teach me inflorescence if I can't *fucking* help?"

"You *are* helping," Emrys promised sincerely. He cupped Senna's cheek, opening his mouth to say something else, but he pulled back his hand with a hiss.

Slowly, Emrys looked down at his hand, then back up at Senna.

His palm was covered in thorns.

"Oh," he whispered brokenly.

"What is it?"

It was at that moment that help erupted from the castle—knights, healers, and mages. Among them was Thea and Nare. They led the crowd, only to rush forward when they caught sight of Percy's pale body in Senna's lap.

"Come no closer!" Emrys commanded.

"*What?*" Senna demanded. "What are you—? Let them forward!" He looked up at them. *"Help us!"*

"He's right, Emrys. Let us help," Thea called, voice shaking.

Emrys shook his head. "No. Just Nare." He reached out to the librarian. "Nare, you come, but very slowly."

Face twisted into horror, Nare broke away from the knights and stepped gingerly forward.

"Watch," Emrys whispered. Reverently, he ran his fingers down the side of Senna's face. This time, he didn't make any noise of pain when the thorns broke through his skin.

"It's *me*?" Senna wept. "*I* caused this?"

Nare's brows furrowed together. She raced forward and knelt before Senna.

"Look at me, Goldheart."

Broken, red eyes met hers. She hovered her palm over his chest, then over his head. When it neared his heart, she murmured a few ancient words. White light glowed like an aura around her hands. Tears gathered at her lashes. Her lips pressed together, like she couldn't bear to tell them, but she did.

"He's a siphon."

"What does that mean?" Emrys pressed.

"It means that the sun's magic has been siphoning into him for a long time, collecting in him like he's a—*jar* of magic. Somehow, the lid came off and the magic has been spilling over. Percy has probably never been exposed to the sun's magic before in his life with it siphoning directly into Senna. But with the siphon uncapped, there was nothing protecting Percy. With him being exposed and *touching* not only the direct sun, but all the unfiltered power from inside Senna . . ."

Emrys pulled the thorns from his hand, grimacing. "Is there a solution?"

"I found the source of the magic and was able to cap it off, but it's a temporary fix. He'll need a full incantation soon to reseal the rift."

"If it's fixed, let the healers come forward," Senna said frantically.

Emrys' gaze dropped to Percy, face falling. Senna wasn't strong enough to look down to see what he saw.

"Senna . . ."

"We'll take a carriage to Mount Livia. We'll put him in one of the healing baths. Sascha will have to help us."

Emrys shook his head. "I'm so, *so* sorry."

"*Stop that*," Senna spat. "You and I both nearly died. The healing bath saved us. We just need to—"

Emrys took Senna's hand and laid it over Percy's heart. There, a patch of red roses pierced through Percy's clothes, dripping blood onto the white shirt. The heart underneath the roses was still beating, but slowly, draining with each weakened pulse.

"You don't have much time," Emrys warned steadily.

Senna shook his head. *"No."*

Emrys took Senna's face in both of his hands.

"You're his goldheart. Remember what that means. Remember what you chose."

Emrys was right. Maybe he hadn't known what it meant, maybe it wasn't what he would've chosen for himself, but it was what he chose now. To be at Percy's side until the very end. To be his brother, his friend, his comfort—even if Senna was about to lose all of that himself. This was what he'd been chosen to do. This was what he'd chosen to be.

Trembling, Senna looked down at Percy. Instead of the thousands of freckles he'd collected on his adventures, his face was covered with tiny green sprouts. Instead of the chapped lips he chewed when he was thinking, Percy's lips were coated in crimson blood that stained down his throat and onto his shirt.

"S-Sen," Percy choked. Senna wasn't sure if it was the sun sickness or the weakness that had taken his ability to speak.

"I'm here," Senna swore. "I'm not leaving your side."

"I really"—a bloody cough—"don't want to go."

Senna swallowed. "I don't want you to go either."

"Sorry."

Senna knew it wasn't just an apology for going. It was an apology for all the things Percy still hadn't forgiven himself for. For all the things he'd taken from Senna. But how could Senna tell him that he'd sacrifice it all over and over again if it meant he could rewind time. If he could make this all go away.

"Don't try to speak, alright?" Senna said, trying to keep his voice steady through his tears. "Save your energy."

"I'm scared," Percy whispered. "Hate the dark."

"That's easily remedied," Emrys said gently. He reached up, waving a hand at the treetops above. The branches bent and parted, until their crowns of leaves gave way to blue skies and bright afternoon sun. He held Percy's hand. "I'll control the sun sickness from getting worse. There's nothing to be afraid of anymore."

Percy hummed softly.

"Are you in pain?" Senna whispered.

"No," Percy breathed. "I feel—light."

A sob clawed its way up Senna's throat, desperately trying to spit itself out, but he clenched his teeth against it. He looked up to Thea and nodded for her to come closer. Thea covered her face and wiped her tears away. She took a deep breath and knelt at Percy's side.

"All of your friends are here," she said gently. "You're not alone."

"El-Elora," he croaked.

Thea's face crumpled, before righting itself again. "She's with you here." She laid her hand on the rose over his heart.

Percy's hand reached up, floating in the sunlight, before weakly brushing tears off of Senna's cheeks.

"I'm a lost thing, after all," he whispered, eyelids fluttering.

"*Never*," Senna swore. "We belong to each other."

Percy breathed out a sigh of relief.

"That's right. Brother."

"Yes." Senna kissed Percy's sweat-damp forehead. "We're brothers."

With all the gentleness he possessed, Senna rubbed his thumbs over Percy's eyelids—the same soothing way he'd done it when Percy was a baby. The same way he'd done it when Percy had feared nightmares and canons and the terrible fate of being lost.

When Percy let out one last breath, everything sort of . . .

Stopped.

The world closed in around Senna and Percy, hiding them behind a wall of numbness. Outside of it, Thea let out a wail of grief. Outside of it, the healers approached and spoke something Senna didn't hear. Outside of it, Emrys' shaking voice said, "Give him a minute. He's in shock."

But inside that wall were Senna and Percy. Only them. Senna did not want to leave it. He did not want to leave Percy. He didn't want to exit into the place where there was finality and weeping and permanence. He would hold Percy to his chest and rock what was left of him, until Senna was allowed to follow behind.

Brother.

Outside of him, someone asked, "What's happening?"

"I—I don't know. Senna. Lean back." This was Emrys. But Senna didn't lean back. He didn't let in the outside world. "Sweetheart, you need to let go. Something's—"

The inflorescence that had killed Percy—bloody vines, roots, flowers, and thorns—exploded up out of his body, a roar of verdancy. At an alarming speed, the tendrils punctured the ground, enveloping Percy in a cocoon of greenery and flowers—almost as if they were mocking the death. Mocking what they'd taken.

Senna watched it all happen, but he could not move. Not even as the inflorescence tried to bury him too. They wrapped around his wrists, curling up his arm. Still, he did not move.

Distantly, Senna heard someone screaming his name.

"Grab him!"

Hands wrapped under his arms and heaved him back. Senna opened his mouth to scream *"No! Let go of me!"* but no sound came out. He tumbled back into Emrys, who held him tightly as more of the earth consumed Percy's body, shelling him away in a husk of roots.

Senna shook his head frantically, reaching forward for Percy. He needed to stop whatever it was from hurting him. He couldn't just sit here and watch it. He wanted it to stop. He wanted it to stop. He wanted it to STOP.

He slammed his hand on the ground and the inflorescence did stop.

Hands bloodied and dirt-smeared, Senna stared at the vined sheath.

One tiny root wriggled out of place, then the others, until the wild growth that had swallowed Percy was slinking into a new shape—a man. Made only of braided roots and ivy, the details of the figure were lost to the branches' curves and leaves. But it had a face and long willow branches for hair that swept along the ground.

When the figure moved, Emrys drew his sword.

Senna stayed completely still.

Impossibly, the monster began to speak.

"Goldheart Senna Kane," it crooned. "You are a difficult man to subdue." It waited, but Senna said nothing. "How ironic. The man of flesh and blood can't speak, but the man of twigs can." It howled out a laugh that echoed throughout the open sky.

"Who are you?" Emrys demanded, coming to stand at Senna's side, shielding him with his sword.

The man of thorns craned his head to Emrys.

"I am the gritty hand that empties the unknowing pocket. I am the hard-won bread swiped from the rich man's table. I am the bandit with gold-laden pockets."

"Jasrath," Thea whispered. Then, with all the command of a princess, "What do you want with Senna?"

"What does any thief want? To *take*. Now that I'm freed from my nettling host, I can. Relinquish the goldheart to me quietly and I won't call upon the dre'malors to ravage Redwind as I ravaged Mount Livia."

Several pieces fell into place in Senna's mind all at once. Jasrath's spirit had been residing inside Percy all this time. Jasrath commanded the dre'malors, so *Percy* had commanded the dre'malors. Senna didn't understand how any of that was possible. But it didn't matter, because now Percy was gone and Jasrath was unleashed.

"You killed Percy to free yourself and you think we're going to hand Senna over to you?" Thea snapped. "Laurentine would despise this."

A rush of wind and heat surged forward as Jasrath lunged to Thea. But Emrys was faster. He seized control of the vines making up Jasrath's body and affixed them to the ground, holding him in place. Behind them, all the Redwindan knights readied their blades.

"Do not *speak* to me about my husband," Jasrath hissed, struggling to break free. "You don't know anything about him."

"I know plenty," Thea hissed. "You're not the only one who can steal."

In a flurry, she reached into Nare's satchel and produced Laurentine's journal.

Jasrath gasped, arm shooting out to grab the book, only to fall short.

"Give me that," he demanded, desperate.

Ah, Senna thought darkly. For the first time since he'd laid Percy in the shade, he stood to his feet.

Calmly he held his hand out to the journal. A request. Thea hesitated, then nodded, placing the journal in his open hands.

Senna turned to Jasrath and snapped—hard. Flames erupted not only on his thumb, but along all his fingers, spreading into one substantial flame in the center of his palm. Everyone knew anger was sigil magic's best fuel.

"*No*," Jasrath gasped, straining against his own roots. Emrys and the inflorescent mages held him firmly in place. "Don't you dare! I'll kill you! I'll kill you all!"

Senna didn't say anything. He didn't have to. He just moved the fire the tiniest bit closer to the journal. He could feel how hard his expression was.

"*Stop!*" Jasrath screamed. The sun dimmed.

But what did Senna care? Percy was gone and this canon had been the one to kill him. Senna didn't know how, but he knew Jasrath bore the blame. It'd been Jasrath all along.

Senna waited. The corner of the book began to singe.

"Fine!" Jasrath bellowed. "Give me the journal and I'll give you time to mourn your prince. But I *will* come for you, Goldheart. When you are at your weakest, I will come for you and I will strip you of your pelt."

Senna blinked lifelessly. They would certainly see.

First extinguishing the flame in his palms, Senna placed the journal in Jasrath's desperate, thorny hands.

Then his spirit dissolved, and the figure of vines and branches collapsed onto the ground—broken. The canon of thieves and the journal were both gone.

Underneath the heap of misused inflorescence was Percy.

A wounded sound moaned out of Senna's mouth and he dropped to the ground, brushing aside all signs of inflorescence until he was holding Percy once again—cradling him against his chest. He buried his nose in Percy's messy hair and rocked him.

Behind him, he heard rustling. But he dared not move. Not while Percy's skin was still warm.

Emrys' footsteps were more familiar. "Leave them be. There is time."

Senna Kane closed his eyes. He didn't want time. He wanted to wake up from whatever terrible dream this was. He wanted to lie down next to Percy and never, ever wake up.

SENNA

Senna blinked.

He didn't know how long he'd been sitting there on numb legs, holding Percy's body to his chest, trying to keep him warm. The world around them was saturated with noise. The knights whispering among them, *I've never seen a canon in person before* and *What happens to a goldheart when their royal dies?* Nare drawing a long sigil on Senna's back to reseal his siphon. Thea petting Percy's hair, whimpering and sniffling. Emrys close at hand, breathing shakily, one hand on Senna's shoulder, the other on Thea's.

And Elora Wright, who approached them and keened like a wounded horse. Words babbled from her tear-soaked lips—a flurry of *no no nos,* moans of Percy's name, questions that couldn't be answered. Her knees hit the ground hard enough to make them bleed. She hovered her hands over his body far enough that Senna could see them trembling.

She looked at Senna then, eyes wide and pleading, begging him to tell her it was all a cruel joke, and pulled at her own hair. Distantly, Senna knew it was brutish to look at her like this, blank face and dry eyes, and not say anything. But he couldn't.

"Please let me hold him," she said finally, opening her arms.

Senna didn't move. Elora reached, attempting to scoop Percy away, but Senna recoiled.

"Sen," Emrys said beside him. "It's Elora. Let her hold him."

Against all he knew, Senna handed Percy into Elora's arms and listened to her weep.

Senna blinked.

He didn't remember standing up, but somehow here he was, legs holding up all of his body weight. Queen Casta was across him, holding him by the shoulders. He drowned out the condolences and sympathy, tuning in only when she said, "But we have to talk about what comes next."

"The paring comes next," Emrys said firmly. "We can worry about everything else after."

"I'm afraid we don't have the luxury of delaying our planning. I haven't written the letter to Queen Phaedra yet. I need your guidance on what I should write, Goldheart Kane."

Senna opened his mouth, but he already knew it was pointless. He wouldn't be using his voice anytime soon. Maybe ever again. Emrys read his face without difficulty.

"Speaking will be hard for him," Emrys explained. "What about yes or no questions, love?"

Senna's gaze drifted to the spot of the yard where the grass was stained scarlet. The royal gardeners gently poured buckets of water over the blood, regrowing fresh grass. In a moment, it was like it'd never happened.

He didn't want to answer any questions. He wanted to go back to where Percy was. Wherever that was—the healers had taken him away moments ago, wrapped in a white sheet that covered the worst of the injuries. The blood.

But this was about more than just him. It was about Redwind and Emrys and his friends. How they communicated with Phaedra would determine the very safety and sanctity of Redwind as a kingdom.

Senna met Casta's eyes and nodded.

She asked him questions then that he'd never fathomed wondering about. Did he want a funeral in the Redwindan tradition? *Yes.* Did he want to inform Phaedra about Percy's passing in written format? *No.* But Senna, don't you realize that means you'll have to explain to her yourself how Percy died? *Yes.* That means you'll have to speak. *Yes.*

Emrys rubbed between Senna's shoulder blades. "Once everything is sorted, Senna will still have a home here, right? If he doesn't want to stay in Talsura."

Oh.

So Emrys didn't know.

Of course he didn't.

With Emrys' gaze still fixed completely on his mother, Senna looked at Casta and very slowly, very deliberately shook his head. Her sure expression flickered.

"Of course Senna can stay here, sweetheart," Casta lied.

Senna blinked.

His hand dug into the harsh bark of a tree, holding him up against the strain of his revolting gut.

"It's alright," came Emrys' voice beside him. "Let it out."

As if commanded, Senna retched again into the grass. It drew barely any bile up, despite the violent twist of his stomach. He spat, but still felt the taste and burn of acid in his mouth and nose.

"It's just us now," Emrys said, wrapping his arms around Senna's waist. He laid his cheek on Senna's back, kissing his spine. "You don't have to be strong anymore. You're barely holding yourself together. But if you're tired, I'll take care of you."

Senna couldn't think about how much he'd miss Emrys when he went back to Talsura. There was only so much grief he could vomit up.

Senna blinked.

He was in a room in the Redwindan castle he'd never been in before. He squinted his bleary eyes at the sign above the door which read *Paring Room*. It was a small room with an arching, stained glass ceiling. In the center of the room, on a long marble pedestal, lay Percy. Senna stood close at Percy's head, with the rest of their friends circled around.

"This is a customary part of Redwindan burials for those lost to the sun sickness," Emrys explained carefully. "We call it paring. In gardening, paring means cutting off excess growth. That's what we do with our fallen. We'll remove all the leftover inflorescence so that Percy can be buried as he was."

"If at any point you feel like you need a break, all you need to do is give us a signal," Nare continued, squeezing Senna's shoulder. "We'll save all the inflorescence. You can either preserve it or burn it. It's usually up to the preference of the surviving family."

Senna looked up at Elora. He hoped she understood that the last thing he wanted to do was decide what should happen with the plants that had killed Percy.

"Burn them," Elora said lifelessly. Nare nodded solemnly and lit the fireplace.

Emrys handed Senna a golden comb with emerald jewels fixed to the top. The teeth were thin and close together. "This is a paring comb. I'll talk you through how to use it."

Slowly, Emrys pulled the white sheet back from Percy's body, folding it over his waist. Another small sob burst out of Thea's mouth.

"The intention is to remove the growth without causing further damage," Emrys said quietly. "Slide the comb into the base of the growth where it sprouted from the skin." Senna did as Emrys instructed, clenching his teeth. "Press the button on the side of the comb." A spring function pressed the comb's teeth close together, hooking to the tiny sprouts. "Gently, pull straight upwards."

Senna's stomach rolled again as he watched the thorny stem pull free of Percy's skin. He swallowed, feeling like he might be sick.

A gentle hand landed on his wrist.

"There's no shame in letting someone else do it," Nare murmured so only he could hear. "There are plenty of families who elect to leave the paring to the healers. We would do it for you, if you wanted."

Senna shook his head firmly and lowered the comb back to Percy's body. He needed to be the one to do this. He needed to see every last strand of *fucking* inflorescence eradicated from what it had ruined—from what it had taken from him. It was meticulous work, but it was possibly the most important thing he'd ever done.

He wasn't near finishing until dim blue light was peering through the stained glass ceiling. His friends—his steadfast, loyal friends—sat around the table upon which Percy lay. It was reverently quiet for hours, until finally, Thea said, "I lied. I read Laurentine's entire journal. That's why I was so quick to hand it over."

Emrys, who had both knees tucked underneath his chin, frowned. On any other day, he likely would've demanded to know what good her falsehoods had done. But Senna knew he wouldn't argue with Thea. Not in front of Percy like this.

"Senna, you're taking too long," Elora said flatly.

Senna paused. He wasn't daft. He knew she wanted a turn with the paring comb.

Too bad.

Nare was wiping dried blood off Percy's skin with a damp cloth. "I hope everything we went through was worth whatever Laurentine wrote in that journal. Hard to believe all we've accomplished when all I originally wanted was to add it to the library." She glanced up. "Was it—worth it?"

"Senna, did you hear me?" Elora pressed, voice harsh.

Thea sniffled. "I didn't think so at the time. But I found something that might prove useful to us, given the—well, frankly, I'm not sure what we're up against. I'm not sure what's going on. That's what scares me now. Not what I read in the journal."

Elora slammed her hands on the marble pedestal. "Hand over the *bloody comb!*"

Finally, Senna stopped. Whatever Elora saw in his eyes—evidence that he'd been broken beyond repair—made her sit back down. She crossed her arms over her chest, her trembling lip a warning to another onslaught of tears. And for once, Emrys and Thea were at a loss for words.

Ignoring the tense blanket covering the group, Senna leaned close and worked on the inflorescence around Percy's eyes. It was mixed with his eyelashes, strands of thin green against brown. He gently pressed an eyelid up for better access and—

Senna deflated. Percy's eyes were lifeless but they still saw right through him. Still commanded him.

With a tired sigh, Senna laid the comb on the marble in front of Elora and sat back into his chair. Emrys hugged Senna's arm and laid his cheek on his shoulder, almost as if to say, *I know what that took from you. Thank you. That was good of you.*

Nare cleared her throat. "What did you find, Thea?"

Thea sat up straighter, caressing a thumb over Percy's forehead.

"A way to avenge Percy," she said gently. "Laurentine learned how to kill a canon."

Senna blinked.

It took him a second to reorient himself, but he knew this room. He knew the endlessly wide bed stationed across from an equally vast window. He recognized the mess on the floor and the cittern propped up against the wall.

"You should get some rest," Emrys commented. Senna found his lover on the edge of the bed, stripping off his boots and clothes. "You must be exhausted."

Senna supposed he was tired. His mind was a machine with no fuel, sluggishly toiling just to keep him upright. He knew that if he closed his eyes, he would hover in vexatious wakefulness, unable to fall asleep. He did so anyway to see if his head could be tempted to give him a few hours of reprieve. But all he saw behind his lids were the tears of blood that had dripped down Percy's lifeless eyes. He shuddered.

A soft touch grazed his back, drifting forward to the laces of his shirt. He and Emrys were getting good at this, even in these circumstances—the unspoken language of the body. It was a question: *May I take off your sullied clothes for you?* Emrys waited for Senna's nod of assent, then gently untied the laces of Senna's shirt. He pulled the tails free from the leather trousers and lifted it above Senna's head.

Emrys kissed Senna's breast where his heart ran dangerously slowly. "Sit on the bed." These delicate commands were welcomed things. Senna didn't have to think if he was following instructions.

But then, this wasn't really where he wanted to be. Not when Percy was alone in a cold, lightless paring room.

He was not aware that Emrys had disappeared until he emerged again from his washroom with a steaming cloth. He settled on a stool before Senna, holding the towel before him close enough that he could smell the fine oils.

"Learned a trick or two in Mount Livia," whispered Emrys. "You'll feel better after a wash. Your hands . . ."

Senna looked down at them, but Emrys covered them in the towel before he could. A valiant effort, Senna granted, but a wasted one. He'd all but memorized the blood on his hands. No amount of washing would erase it.

"Are you still with me, Senna?" Emrys asked, carefully wiping away the dirt and blood with careful strokes. He waited, but Senna couldn't find it in him to reply. "I have to admit, I'm worried about you. Some things are so horrible you don't know what to do after they happen and that's okay. But I've been through this before and I survived. That's what I'm here for. To support you. To keep you alive. Beyond that, I—I really don't know what else to say. I doubt it would help anyway."

Senna let himself sink forward, dropping his forehead on Emrys' shoulder. Without hesitation, Emrys' set down the basin and wrapped his arms around him, molding into all of Senna's broken parts to keep them together. A fraction of the tension in Senna's shoulders released, barely enough for him to notice the difference.

"My strong man," Emrys whispered in his ear. He drew Senna back, careful hands holding his face. The corners of his mouth twitched down when he found the muscles in Senna's jaw tense and trembling. "Oh, my love. You can cry."

It was the heavy step on the frozen ice keeping Senna's composure intact, the words hitting him like a resonant crack. Through the fissure came all that he was forcing down. An avalanche of grief resurfaced from the dark place he refused to touch, shattering the rest of his willpower. It clawed up from his heart, through his throat, and threatened to come out of his mouth in a nasty roar.

Senna clamped his teeth down. He'd not been given permission to yell. He'd only been given permission to cry. So with his quivering lips pressed together, he did. He wept silent, wracking sobs that surrendered hot tears down the sides of his face. Yet he did not utter a sound.

Senna blinked.

He was too warm underneath too many blankets. Before him, the open window. Through it, a wall of black. All clouds and dark sky. There were no stars.

Behind him, Emrys was breathing—awake.

Inside him, there were memories.

Senna, I'm scared.

The blankets squeezed closer to Senna's chest. Pressed into his eyes. They grew damp, but at least the skin below his eyes would stop burning.

Senna, I'm scared. I'm a lost thing.

The words were a hot iron on the base of his spine, but he barely flinched.

Weight lifted from the other side of the mattress. Footsteps padded across the room. Emrys knelt on the ground beside the bed, face difficult to make out through the veil of the night and blur of his eyes.

"Let me help you sleep," he said, barely above a whisper. A hand, void of its usual opulent rings, reached for him across the empty space. Senna caught it.

No inflorescence. Not after—

"Please, my heart," Emrys pleaded.

Strangely, another memory found him. It was from the first day they'd spent together, the day that Emrys had shown Senna inflorescence. He hadn't realized he'd pressed Emrys' words to his heart for safekeeping, but they found him now, when he needed them most: *"While you're in my care, no harm will come to you."*

Senna released the hand.

It resumed its path, landing on his temple with familiar, delicate strokes. No pain bloomed where the inflorescence surfaced. Senna only knew it was there from the bare tickle of a silk petal he couldn't see.

"Thank you," Emrys breathed. "Rest now. You won't dream."

Senna closed his eyes. He believed Emrys when he promised miracles.

Senna blinked.

He and Emrys were standing in front of Thea's room, hovering in the doorframe. He didn't remember following Emrys here, but he was growing accustomed to all of the lost time. He didn't mind losing it—not when he didn't want to be living it in the first place.

"I'll respect your decision," Emrys was saying to her, "but remember that this is something you can't take back. Is this truly what you want?"

Thea was motionless on the ground in the middle of her chambers. Around her, a mess of handwritten papers were strewn about the floor. Despite being paces away, Senna recognized Percy's handwriting on them. Whether they were letters, research notes, or simple ramblings, he couldn't tell.

"I can't," she said, voice wavering. "I don't want to see him like that again. The paring was hard enough. The funeral will have too many people. Too many sounds. I don't want to get dressed. I don't want to pretend that I'm—" Tears overcame her voice.

"Alright," Emrys said gently. He crossed to kneel in front of her, then kissed her forehead. "Send for me if you need me. I am still your guard, after all."

Thea met Senna's gaze over Emrys' shoulder.

"You don't have to go either, you know," she said gently.

Senna shook his head. He'd never blame Thea for not wanting to attend Percy's funeral service, but it wasn't the same for him. He needed to be at Percy's side as long as he could, even if looking at him was hard.

Emrys squeezed Senna's shoulder. "In that case, we have to go or we'll be late."

Later, Senna would remember that he had not said goodbye to Thea before leaving her—and he would wish that he had.

Senna blinked.

Of all the time he'd lost, this was the moment he wanted to keep. The moment he wanted to be clearheaded. In the welcome clarity, he inventoried all the tiny details, committing them to the storming pool of his memory.

This was the funeral procession. Emrys had explained to Senna that Queen Casta elected to have it here, in the agora, to represent what Percy had been to them—the bridge between the kingdoms. Senna had been here several times before, had heard his voice echo along all the empty seats. Now those benches were filled mostly by those who'd never met Percy. Yet there were familiar faces among the crowd. Sascha Oakcage, Ciaran the votary, and all the Mount Livian people Percy had saved with a well-spoken command.

Elora led the procession, carrying a now completed bust of Percy's face. Her eyes were rimmed with dark, red circles, as if she'd spent the entire night completing what she'd started months ago. *"I had to get the nose right or he'd haunt me forever,"* she'd told Senna wetly. The marble bust had to be heavy, but Elora wouldn't hear of anyone else carrying it. She bore it bravely, holding it so that Percy's stony eyes could look out like the figurehead of a sinking ship.

The real Percy, the one with cold skin and a million dead memories, was lying in a white sheet. Senna, Emrys, and Nare stood at the cardinal points of the fabric pall, bearing its weight and carrying Percy's body to an open carriage at the end of the line.

According to Emrys, Senna had made several decisions he didn't recall deciding. He'd pointed at the clothes he'd wanted Percy to wear—white and long, to cover the sun sickness wounds that would never heal. He'd written down the titles of the music he wanted the quartet to play. He'd even chosen the flowers that would fill the empty space of Percy's fabric coffin—wildflowers, the same Percy had stood among when they'd first left the Dam.

"We'll take care of the rest," Emrys had said with a sad smile. *"You've made a lot of decisions."*

All of those choices meant nothing now, because Senna wasn't admiring Percy's fine clothes, listening to the musicians play their mournful requiem, or breathing in the earthy scent of wildflowers.

He was looking at Percy's pale face, trying to memorize every line, every faded freckle, before he'd never have the chance to again.

The procession had been marching along so slowly, Senna almost didn't realize they'd made it to the carriage. Stairs had been placed at the carriage's base, allowing Senna and the other pallbearers to ascend into the carriage's flat bed and lay Percy among even more flowers and soft pillows.

Percy's closest friends exchanged a single look. Then, with delicate reverence, they lowered his body onto the padded carriage in tandem and stepped back to the ground.

Lilting music from the quartet's instruments filled the agora, a changing song to signify the procession's end. It was time for Elora to mount Percy's bust onto the carriage. Only, instead of emplacing it at Percy's head, she approached Senna and laid it gingerly in his arms. Neither of them said a word. He set it in its rightful place, but he could not look in the statue's eyes.

Queen Casta arose from her front bench to approach the dais, but Emrys held up a hand. He, instead, mounted the dais with two strong steps, gesturing for the musicians to cease playing.

"My friends," bellowed the voice of Prince Emrys of Redwind. "Thank you for joining me and my loved ones in mourning Prince Percy of Talsura. There is none among us who is a stranger to the way the wind quickly shifts. What begins as a clear breeze can easily blow red, thick with blood. We Redwindans know all too well that this tragedy strikes down those we want to keep most. Maybe we will never know why it does. But we do know we wanted to keep Percy, a beloved ally, friend—"

He looked at Senna.

"And brother. Yet, we keep the most beautiful thing Percy gave us. He whole-heartedly pursued a future many of us can only dream of—one of peace, one of community, and one of love. Although it looks different than we planned, Percy's future *will* be one of peace, and he is surrounded by community and love today."

Emrys' voice wavered. Senna tore his gaze from Percy's body to look at his lover—who hadn't cried once, despite having to wash Percy's blood off of his own hands. Emrys, who had been so ceaselessly strong for Senna and his sister, holding them together so that they could fall apart without losing themselves entirely.

"When Percy and I first met," Emrys continued, "I made the mistake of believing him to be naive and ignorant of the ways of this continent. I thought, here is this boy who has not lived through the sun sickness or the exile, come to Redwind to fix what had been irreparably broken. But I was the naive one among us. Percy showed me that it is not only okay to dream about a better future, but fearsomely necessary. He may be gone from us, but that doesn't mean that that dream is too. We honor and keep that dream today.

"I know so many of you heard the circumstances of Percy's death—rumors about how he unknowingly hosted a canon and how that canon has threatened all that we hold dear."

He chuckled, shaking his head.

"I admit, I myself have found what has happened confusing and daunting. But please rest assured we have not taken those threats lightly. The Redwindan throne will do what it takes to ensure that this is the last tragedy suffered under Jasrath, outcast canon of thieves. For today, we mourn our fallen, who, despite all feuds and animosity between our lands, loved us. And whom we have loved fiercely." The sincerity of Emrys' words burned Senna's eyes, spilling down over his cheeks. "I yield now to Votary Ciaran Lynwood, Head Votary of Mount Livia and friend of Percy."

The young man who took the dais did not look like a votary. His hair was frenzied, sticking in all directions, and his face was a terrible shade of white. If Senna didn't know any better, he thought that lad would be sick. Ciaran scanned the crowd, hands trembling, but when he looked at Senna, his jaw went slack. He looked—pitying? Shocked? . . . Guilty?

Then, as soon as the unreadable emotion had arrived, it was gone, replaced with the dignity and decorum Senna expected from the votary. He began his prayer with chanted, ancient words Senna didn't recognize.

Then, in the common tongue, Ciaran said, "We call upon Oesyth's favor and ask that Percy's rest is free from strife and disturbance. We ask that she soothe the suffering of those he leaves behind, especially Percy's guard, Goldheart Senna Kane, his betrothed, Elora, and his dear friends, Princess Acathea, Captain Calloway, and Nare. We thank the canons for the gift of Percy's life, despite the—" His voice choked, but he swallowed and continued. "—unfair circumstances of his death."

Senna blinked.

A hand pulled the horses' reins out of his grip. When his vision cleared, he found himself in the front seat of the carriage riding out of the agora while a somber song rang out on the violins. Around him, the onlookers wept, extending their hands in blessing at Percy's body.

"Maybe I should drive the carriage," Emrys said softly.

Senna sank into his seat. He'd lost more time. He didn't remember grabbing the reins, much less attempting to drive.

It's over already? his gaze asked Emrys.

"It's over. Now all that's left is to drive to the Dam and the Talsurans will help you take it from there."

Emrys made it sound so easy. But without his voice, there was no way for Senna to explain that *this* was the easy part—letting Emrys do the talking and the driving. If Senna looked broken and lifeless among the Redwindans, they would understand. In Talsura, though, things were different. He would have to be the strong guard they'd chosen, even if underneath his skin, he didn't want to be alive anymore.

The carriage broke out into the open air. Yesterday's sun that had stripped Percy's life away was now covered by a blanket of clouds.

"This is all so surreal," Emrys said into the silence. "You know that I would give *anything* to stay with you in Talsura. I hate that I have to send you inside the Dam without me, and I hate that it's because if fucking Phaedra sees me, it blows our cover." He fixed a pleading look on Senna. "Can we turn around? I'll see if Nare will follow you in. She doesn't usually keep too much inflorescence on her person, and she's strong. She can—"

Senna squeezed the hand that held the reins. Very, very carefully, he controlled his breathing. His face. His pulse.

Because Emrys didn't know. He'd never attended the royal lessons like Thea had. He didn't know enough about Talsuran politics to understand what would happen next. He certainly wouldn't be driving Senna to the Dam and the trade channels if he did.

Even if Senna could speak now to tell Emrys that he was driving him to his death—which he couldn't—he wasn't sure he wanted to. There would be no avoiding it. Why put Emrys through more pain than he had to? When it was all over, Emrys would see he was better off without Senna.

"*It's okay,*" he mouthed. He was glad it was only the words—his tone would have betrayed the lie. He drew a sigil into his hand and laid it flat on the reins. Could he perform these sigils so easily because of the magic he'd been storing inside of him?

The taste of magic made the horses push the carriage harder. Soon, they appeared over a cresting hill and in view of the Dam.

This was it.

Senna knew what he had to do now. He'd dismount and carry Percy's body to the castle, where he would tell Phaedra a watered-down version of the truth. And then . . .

"You won't tire carrying him for so long?" Emrys asked nervously. Senna shook his head gently. He would carry Percy forever if he had to. Emrys spared an agonized glance at Percy's resting form still sleeping among the flowers. "I really do hate this. But the sooner we get it over with, the sooner you can return to Redwind."

Senna pressed his lips together. It didn't have to be a lie if Emrys was the one who said it.

Emrys moved to step into the bed of the carriage, but Senna stopped him, leaned across the open space, and kissed him.

As a boy, Senna had wondered about what his first kiss would be like. He hadn't thought to wonder about his last. But it was everything he supposed it should be—warm and intimate, with a familiar taste. He was loath to pull away, wanting the sweetness to last forever. It couldn't, he knew that. But with Emrys' lips on his, Senna felt a little like the last few days were a dream and he was still wrapped in Emrys' arms in a Mount Livian guesthouse.

Emrys was the first to pull back. His smile was suspicious and sad. "Are you sure you'll be alright, my heart?"

If this was the last moment he'd ever spend with Emrys, he needed to command the broken machine of his voice one last time.

"Thank you," Senna managed in a whisper. "I love you."

Emrys' face was as bright as it was sad. "You sweet man," Emrys murmured, combing his fingers through Senna's hair. "I'll say it back when you return to Redwind. How's that for a fair trade?"

Senna swallowed, urging the tears in the back of his throat to stay hidden. He nodded, kissed Emrys' cheek, then hurled himself into the back of the carriage before he could do something disastrous like tell Emrys the truth. Careful not to crush any of the wildflowers, Senna knelt, covered Percy with the excess sheet, and drew him into his arms.

Percy bore the dead weight of a man, but he was still the same baby they'd laid in his arms when he'd been only a boy himself. *Guard this child with your life.* Senna leaned Percy's head on his shoulder.

He deserved every bit of what was coming to him.

Senna stepped onto the ground, allowing Emrys to turn the carriage around, facing his home.

"Be safe, and write if you need me," Emrys insisted. "I mean it, Sen. I'm not above risking our kingdoms' fragile peace to come for you. I would burn down the moorlands if you asked me to."

He reached down and cupped Senna's jaw. Senna turned his head to kiss the knuckles. His throat burned, and burned, and burned.

Senna stepped back.

Emrys heaved a deep breath.

With the last of this strength, Senna drew a sigil on the carriage's wood. It disappeared, blinking out of sight as if it had never been there, taking Emrys with it.

Senna would never see him again.

Senna blinked.

He hadn't lost any time. His face was still warm where Emrys had touched him and his palm still vibrated from the travel sigil.

He knew what he had to do, but he—he just needed a minute. A minute to pretend.

Here stood Goldheart Senna Kane. Percy was merely asleep, and in the morning, they'd go back to Redwind and pick up where they'd left off as if nothing had happened. This would not be the last time Senna saw the daylight.

The clouds above parted, spilling a birthmark of sun onto the ground. Senna moved over to it and peeled the white sheet back from Percy's face. The sun offered warmth and color that Percy did not have himself.

Once Senna carried him through the Dam, Percy would never touch the sunlight again. Though Senna still did not understand how, it was his fault that neither of them would know the sun's rays again.

Percy would never touch the sunlight again.

Percy would *never*—

Senna's knees gave out. He crumpled to the ground, careful to hold tight his grip on Percy. His restraints fell loose, and he began to shake violently. He'd been numb enough to make it this far, but reality was now finally falling over him.

There was no air to breathe. No blood in his veins to keep him alive and warm. Every strand of his existence began to unravel.

"Percy," he whispered, unblinking eyes so wide they burned. "It's time to wake up."

He waited, thumbing over Percy's freckles.

Percy did not wake.

Senna did not recognize the sound that came out of his mouth, nor the tears. When he wept, it was a lamentation that he'd not been allowed to have as a child—loud, messy, hysterical. His body heaved, trying to gasp in as much air as it could, but it fell out of him in broken sobs.

Senna laid Percy on the ground, covered the dead boy's ears, and *howled*—long enough that the back of his throat tasted like blood. Thunderous enough to rattle the ground on which the canons stood, but not enough to wake the dead.

With the sharp ends of his nails, Senna clawed his face, the ground on which Percy laid, and the white sheets covering his body. The smooth ivory came away crimson and muddy and tearstained. Tears and blood wove together on his face.

The cacophony of a dozen running men echoed up the hollow expanse of the trade channel, but Senna didn't hear the sound—at least, not until the stampede skidded to a halt at the edge of the trade channel.

"You! Who are you and what are you—?"

Senna didn't process anything about the timbre of the voice—only the words themselves, which his mind could not help but understand. He lifted his gaze, but only enough to make out a group of silver boots. In turn, he revealed his face to the onlookers. It uncapped a flurry of proclamations.

"*Goldheart Kane?*"

"Who is that he's holding?"

"That isn't—that can't be the *prince* is it?"

"He's—dead. The prince is *dead*."

"Goldheart Kane, what happened!?"

"He won't answer, he's delirious."

"He's *grieving*."

"What do we do?"

At this, they all fell quiet. They knew what came next.

Finally, one brave soul spoke up. "I don't have any love for the goldheart, but—but we *can't*, can we?"

"We don't have a choice. You know the law," this came from the head silverheart, a woman who Senna knew well, but could not remember the name of at the moment. A protest came from behind her, but she made a silencing noise. "The decision is already made."

"Will he put up a fight?" This question was not meant for Senna's ears, but he heard it nonetheless.

He drew his gaze up to the lot of them, frenzied and wild. They were a blur before him, silhouettes of bodies and armor.

"Let us see," said the silverheart captain. She marched on heavy steps forward, only to be stopped by one of her men.

"Captain—the sun hasn't set."

She shook him off with a hard shrug. "It's cloudy, you fool," she said. Then, she turned to Senna and crossed into the open air.

Senna watched her carefully—a readied beast poised to protect. He knew the captain's movements well. He'd been the one to train her. To test her skills. If this had been a typical day, he would have been able to predict her movements down to the breaths she took. But this was not a typical day.

"You know the law, Goldheart," she told him firmly.

Although Senna's throat burned, he found he could speak. "Let me carry him home."

"I'm afraid I can't allow that. The prince's body must be taken to our healers to be prepared for burial. You will have an audience with Her Majesty the Queen."

Senna's grip on Percy tightened.

"No," he gritted out. "Let me carry him. That's an order."

"Your orders lost their legitimacy the second His Highness died." She squatted before him, the way people approach foxes trapped in a cage. "He will be safe in my care. You have my word."

This reasoning would have worked on the goldheart she knew. But she was right. Percy was dead—therefore so was the goldheart. Her promises were as powerless as his commands.

The captain offered an open hand. Senna struck. He pulled the knife stashed in his boot and lunged, tackling the captain to the ground.

Yells erupted from the tunnel—a moment's hesitation as the knights decided whether or not they were brave enough to risk the open air. Only one mustered the petty courage. Fingers tangled in his hair, yanking him away from the captain. The pull was hard enough to tear a yelp of pain out of Senna's mouth.

In the end, it didn't matter how much strength he'd put into the arm around Percy's waist, the prince went rolling onto the ground. The captain seized him before Senna could get to him first. She kicked Senna hard enough to keep him down.

"You should have protected him when it mattered," she spat.

Senna wasn't sure quite what happened next—what he said, what hopeless measures he took to break free and take Percy back. But he guessed he yelled some more. Maybe he cried. Maybe he spit blood on the faces of his captors.

But what he would never forget was the sun. The way it snuffed out as the guards dragged him further into the trade channels. The way he would miss it, somehow, even though it still lived inside him.

His hands were empty. He was going to die.

EMRYS

T HE CASTLE WAS TOO quiet after Percy's funeral. They'd spent more time without Percy than they had with him, yet his absence left the castle feeling like an unlit lantern—still firmly standing, but lacking its warmth and brightness. Emrys could feel the pitying gazes of the waitstaff as he trudged up to his room.

He was the last person who deserved any pity. Percy had been his friend, surely, and a good one at that. But he would never feel the loss as profoundly as Thea and Senna did.

Emrys sighed, glancing out a nearby window. Senna couldn't return soon enough. He'd gotten used to waiting around for Senna, but this was different. This time he knew Senna needed him. He wouldn't feel settled until Senna was back within his borders—his protection.

In the meantime, he would prepare his room for Senna's arrival. He'd clear some room in his wardrobe for Senna's things and give the space a proper cleaning. But there was something he needed to do first.

Thea had left her door unlocked, something she only did when she was too troubled to let the servants in and out. Emrys found her curled up on a padded bench by her window, bleary eyes fixed blankly to the mountains on the horizon. Her hair was loose and unbraided. An empty journal lay on her lap, nothing written on the pages.

Emrys approached, laying a gentle hand on her shoulder.

"I'm back, sister. Would you like something to eat?"

Thea startled as if waking, then peered confusedly back at him. She wore the face of someone who'd spent the last hour in another reality entirely.

"Thea," Emrys pressed gently. "Are you hungry, darling?"

Thea sniffled, wiping her dry, red eyes. "No, I'm afraid I'd be sick if I tried to eat now." She glanced behind him. "Where's Senna? Resting?"

"No, I drove him back to Talsura after the funeral," Emrys explained. "Believe me, I'm counting down the minutes until his return. I can't imagine how bitterly long Talsuran burials are."

Something strange came over Thea's face then. It was a perplexing mix of incredulity, horror, and despair.

"You . . ." she said brokenly. "You did what?"

Emrys tried not to bristle, but he did straighten his back. "I took him home. He has to attend the burial."

"Oh, *Emrys*." Thea dropped her hands at her sides, helpless. "Emrys, *no*. What have you *done*?"

Even though Emrys didn't know what she was talking about, it felt like his body did. Nausea slammed into him, adrenaline lighting up his nerves so fast his hands shook. All the air in his lungs vanished under the weight of his beating heart.

"What—What do you mean?" he stammered, dread rising.

Thea threw herself at him. She slammed her hands on his chest hard, then again, messier. She was *furious*. Hysterical. Emrys felt like he was going to be sick.

"*What do I mean?* Emrys, this is *exactly* why you should've been listening to Mother all this time about attending your goddamn political lessons. How *could* you?!" She fell to her knees, a hand pressed over her chest. "How could you?"

Emrys dropped down and seized Thea by the shoulders, wild gaze meeting hers.

"Tell me," he demanded.

More tears spilled over her swollen eyes. "Do you know what happens to goldhearts when their royal dies? The crown *kills them*, Emrys." She slammed his chest again, dissolving into weeping. "They *die*."

"*No.*"

"You delivered him to her!"

"I—I didn't know. I swear! He said—" Now tears gathered on his own lashes. "He *knew*? And he let me—" He doubled over, face crumpling as he pressed his forehead to the floor and swore. Then he was rushing to his feet and sprinting toward the door.

"Where are you going?"

Emrys spun around, eyes fierce.

"Where do you think? To save him. If that fucking harpy has any kindness in her, she'll wait until after the burial. And executions take planning, don't they? That means there's still time."

"What if she's as cruel as we know she is?"

Emrys squeezed his eyes shut, not wanting to utter the words.

"Then she'll draw it out," he said, sick. "He has to hang on long enough for us to make it to him."

A tear slid off of Thea's chin onto the floor. "What if he doesn't?"

Emrys wrapped his fingers tightly around his blade, digging his fingernails into the meat of his palm.

"Then the Talsuran bloodline ends today."

T HEA WOULDN'T LET EMRYS go alone, despite his best efforts to keep her at home.

"Ready four horses," she had instructed, fashioning her hair into a high bun.

"Four?" Emrys deadpanned.

"Of course. You, me, Nare, and Elora."

Emrys had tried to argue, but Thea had wisely pointed out that every second wasted arguing was another second Senna could be fighting for his life.

That left him in the royal stables, arguing with the head groom about needing four of the royal horses.

"These same horses have survived a days' long trek to Mount Livia. They're not going to be daunted by a stroll to Talsura," Emrys exclaimed.

"Aye, Captain. And it was these same horses that just made the journey two days ago. They'll suffer irreparable damage if you push them."

"They're the royal horses. They've sustained greater strain than this."

"I'm afraid I have to disappoint you, Captain."

"I don't think you're comprehending the full conflict properly, so allow me to demystify you," Emrys hissed, stepping into the man's face. "I have known these horses all my life. I know them better than you know the backs of your own eyelids. They will sustain the journey. If you continue to argue, know that you are going against a direct order from your captain and your princess."

"What about the direct order from the queen?" came a voice behind them.

Emrys ground his teeth together and spun around.

"Mother," he seethed.

Casta's jaw clenched. She wasn't expecting him to acknowledge their familial bond in front of the servants. Emrys was too distracted to care. With a flick of her hand, she waved the stablemaster to the side.

"Someone told me there was an altercation happening that I might want to see. I thought I instructed you to speak to our staff with respect," she said evenly.

Emrys ignored this.

"I'm going to Talsura to save Senna. Tell the stable master to sign out the horses."

Casta made a pitying *tsk* noise.

"Oh, sweetheart." She took a few steps in, offering a hand out for Emrys to take. Emrys merely stared down at it like it might bite him. "Who told you? It wasn't one of the servants, was it? I had asked them to stay quiet for a few days, but I could tell some of them felt awful keeping something from you."

Emrys cocked his head, ears ringing.

"You—You *knew*."

Casta sighed. "Of course I knew, darling. It's my responsibility to know all about our neighbor's laws and regulations."

Emrys threw his hands out. "Why didn't you tell me?"

"He didn't want me to."

"Why would he? His hope is dead. He just lost the only person who loved him for his entire life."

"*You* love him."

Emrys paced in a small circle, urging his heartbeat to slow. His anger was barely leashed and the lead was slipping from his hands. He pressed his lips together and looked away.

"You know I do," he said, devastated. "So it begs the question why my own mother wouldn't do everything she could to protect someone I love with all I am. Why would you let me suffer? Let Senna suffer?"

The queen folded her hands over her dress, taking too long to gather her thoughts for Emrys' liking.

"I liked Senna," she started.

"Don't talk about him like he's already dead."

"Fine. I like Senna. I know that he is compassionate and respectful. Those are rare qualities in a knight, much less a friend and ally. I will miss his visits, just as I will miss seeing Percy." Her smile was sad. Emrys couldn't stand to look at it. "Senna knew that this was the best course of action. If we harbored him after Percy's death, Phaedra would have every right to invade our kingdom and take what she believes is rightfully hers. She isn't foolish. She knows Senna has connections here."

"I can't believe this," Emrys moaned.

"Even if you manage to rescue Senna, you can't bring him back here. Not with a bounty on his head."

"But you said—"

"I lied."

Emrys dropped onto a hay bale, his face falling into his hands.

"It doesn't matter," he stated. "I'm going. I'll walk to the outer limit stables. The stablemaster knows Senna there. He'll help me even if you won't. We'll be gone as long as it takes."

"We?"

"Thea and our friends."

Casta shook her head bitterly. "Son, I don't think you understand. I cannot allow you to bring a fugitive into this kingdom. Not only would it endanger our people, everything that we've worked so hard to build, but this family."

"This *family*?" Emrys cried. "We barely have a family."

She recoiled as if he'd slapped her. "Surely you don't mean that."

"I don't know, *Your Majesty*. I have served my queen for many years, but it's been some time since I've seen my mother. Your highest priority is this kingdom. I understand the weight and pressure that comes with leading and founding a kingdom. I have been right at your side this whole time. But that was your decision. I didn't get to choose to bear all the responsibility. I didn't choose to sacrifice the relationship I should've had with you to the good of our people."

"That's not fair—"

"Do you know who the real person supporting me and caring for me all this time was? Thea—my sister, even though you told her she was a loyal employee to your cause. What a cruel thing. You know all she wants is your love and approval. *Why* would you tell her she wasn't a member of this family?" he cried, wild down to his core now. "It's despicable. I'm ashamed of you. I'm ashamed you won't do what's right and let her be the true heir to the throne."

A gasp from behind.

It was Thea. She stood stunned, a packed bag slung over her shoulder and staff at her shoulder. Casta pretended she wasn't there.

"Listen to me, Emrys. You don't have to agree with my choices. But you cannot bring Senna to Redwind. You want to rescue a Talsuran criminal? Fine. I'm not foolish enough to think I can stop you. But know this, you're making a decision. If you decide to start a life with your Talsuran goldheart, then you forfeit your life as a captain. That includes your allowance and all the privileges it affords you."

"You'd disown me?" Emrys breathed, stunned.

"Not forever," Casta said. "You'll return home when you've learned your lesson. Frankly, I don't think you'll be able to make it a week on your own."

"He won't be on his own," Thea said, stepping forward. "I'll be with him. I've survived on the streets before."

Finally, Casta was surprised.

"No, you won't. You must remain here as the princess."

"Don't you remember? I'm only a fallow employee. Due to a family emergency, I resign," Thea said. To prove her point, she took the signet ring from her finger and threw it in a pile of horse dung.

"Acathea!" Casta gasped, but Thea did not back down. She held her chin up high and strong.

"I've made my choice too," Emrys announced devoutly. "I won't let Senna die. I won't leave him alone."

Queen Casta had survived an exile and the founding of her fledgling kingdom—she knew when her efforts were wasted. Her shoulders sank, and for a flashing moment, she looked like the mother Emrys remembered. But if Emrys waited for her to change her mind now, he'd be disappointed.

He retrieved the ledger from the stable's post and handed it to the stablemaster, who was trying to appear busy nearby.

"We're taking the horses. Four of them," Emrys reiterated plainly.

The stablemaster did indeed take the ledger, but he made no move to mark off the horses or remove them from their stalls. He peered up at the queen, waiting. Casta crossed her arms over her chest, watching Thea and Emrys with a cutting gaze.

"Do as he says. But remove the horses from your ledgers," the queen snapped. "They won't be coming back."

E MRYS WAS GETTING BLOODY sick of the moorlands. If he'd been thinking about it, he would've committed the memory of Redwind more firmly to his mind—the way it looked when he crossed his borders for what might've been the last time. The moorlands might've been the one place his scarred mind wouldn't forget.

He'd at least made it to the outer limits before he began to cry. He'd urged his horse ahead so the others wouldn't notice.

What madness this all was. Percy was dead. Senna was probably being tortured this very second. He'd been banished from his home—*again*. It all was too much. It was *too much*.

One of the other riders fell into pace beside him, but Emrys didn't look up. Thea grabbed his wrist.

"He's going to be okay," Thea swore. "We're going to get to him in time. And then we're going to figure all of this out, okay?"

Emrys kept his gaze steady ahead, but he squeezed his sister's hand, afraid of the noise he'd make if he opened his mouth.

"I should thank you—for standing up for me," Thea continued, retaking her reins. "It meant a lot to hear what you said. Thank you, Emrys."

"No don't, please," Emrys murmured, pained. "It was long overdue. I should've done it right when she made her true feelings known. I couldn't believe she meant it. But now I do. You don't owe me thanks for saying what was true."

"I'm only glad Nare and Elora weren't there," he said with a sniffle. "They'll be able to return to their jobs once we get Senna to safety."

Thea tossed a glance over her shoulder. "Knowing these two, we won't be able to send them home. We'll have to find somewhere big enough for all of us."

"We'll figure it out." Emrys didn't have any idea how, though. Then, "Nare! What do you know of Talsuran executions? Specifically of the goldheart? As much as you can recall, please."

Nare raced ahead, face sterner than it had been at Percy's funeral.

"You sure you want to hear it?"

"No. Tell me anyway."

Nare heaved a deep breath, shaking her head.

"Talsura has been performing executions since its creation," she explained easily. "For a time, it even hosted executions for neighboring kingdoms that didn't have preestablished systems of punishment. Talsura eventually merged with those kingdoms, which led to its massive size."

"Guess that makes sense why Mount Livia was the only one that remained," Elora chipped in. "It'd be difficult to conquer a mountain."

Nare nodded in agreement. "Traditionally, all punishment was conducted in the Agora of Alpedis, where we held Percy's funeral. The type of punishment varied depending on the crime, but executions tended to be decreed for those that we'd consider, by today's standards, not worthy of the crime. I imagine now the executions are conducted somewhere in the castle, somewhere the court wouldn't be able to hear the—the noises."

"Talsura is all about its underground areas," Thea suggested. "Does the castle have a crypt or catacombs?"

Elora perked up. "It does. When I worked in the palace, I was assigned to dust some of the older underground memorials. If we can get to the agora's entrance to the channels, I think I could sneak us into the castle and find them."

"It's a good start at least. A way into the castle without being noticed," Emrys pointed out. "What are we walking into?"

"We can make assumptions about the level of security based on the structure of the execution," Nare explained. "For the goldheart, it always seemed to me less about punishment and more about balance. A trade—power and authority second only to the royal family in exchange for death for a job poorly done."

"Senna was unparalleled in his job," Emrys said defensively.

"I agree," Nare promised. "The fact remains that Talsuran law demands that a goldheart dies when their royal does—even in the case of unavoidable factors like sickness. The punishment is . . ." She threw Emrys an apologetic look. "Up to a hundred lashes, issued by the surviving crown. In this case, that's the queen herself. The number of lashes depends on the severity of the failure."

Emrys shrank. "Sun slay me."

"There is a bright side. Because it's a royal execution, it means that the knighthearts won't be anywhere nearby. It's considered a last respect to the goldheart to allow their subordinates to remain ignorant to their suffering."

"What does that mean for Senna?" Elora asked. "How bad will his sentence be?"

"It's hard to say," Nare said. "Really, it depends on how much the queen knows. Obviously, she knows that Senna took Percy out of the kingdom at least once. But if she knows he's a siphon, then she could accuse him of engaging in activities that nullified it and endangered Percy. That would be—less than ideal."

"I can't imagine what he did to nullify his siphon. He didn't seem to know he had it in the first place," Emrys said exasperatedly.

"It's possible that it was an accident, like he stumbled upon a new method of magic I'm not acquainted with. The field is ever-evolving."

"But if it's the magic you *are* acquainted with . . ." Thea pressed.

Nare shifted uncomfortably on her horse. "Then I think he was poisoned. I think that poison uncapped his siphon."

"Who would poison Senna?" Elora wondered, frowning.

"Someone who wanted him and Percy dead," Nare said.

It seemed to hit them all at once. Emrys could've smacked himself, it was so obvious.

"Jasrath," he said. "He summoned a herd of dre'malors to Mount Livia. Why couldn't he poison Senna?"

"The only question is *how*," Nare pointed out. "If Percy was his host, then he and his magic had to exist on a level of stasis. Or, I don't know, dormancy. He would've needed an extra pair of hands to create and administer the poison. *And* summon the dre'malors, for that matter."

Elora set her jaw, as if talking about this pressed too hard on her grief. "Who would help an outcast canon kill Percy?"

"Another outcast?" Nare guessed.

"Right now, our priority is getting to Senna before he—" Emrys cut off, drawing in a heavy breath. "We can worry about the details later. I think the horses have walked long enough. Let's get a move on."

PERCY

ERCY LAURENT'S STORY ENDED the way all legends do. With the death of royals and canons. With pestilence, power-hungry men, and the orphan boy with the heart of gold and blood-soaked hands. It was a violent death, one that did not lend itself to what was fair, nor what was right.

Yet, in the morning, Percy woke.

At least, he supposed it was morning. He was lying in a curled heap in the middle of the floor of a room he didn't recognize from the ground. Blue light bled in through a single window on the far side of the room, giving everything a sort of melancholy air. Pushing himself onto his elbows, Percy squinted into the dark indigo space. There was a crib pushed against the wall, a shelf overflowing with pristine, expensive toys—

"Hello, Percy."

—and a man sitting politely in a reading chair.

He must've been a tall, lanky sort of person, judging from the way his legs stuck out before him. Long waves of pale hair spilled over his shoulders, not a strand out of place. Percy couldn't tell the real color, because every inch of the man was glassy, blue, and translucent. He glowed around the edges in a way that reminded Percy of the artistic depictions he'd seen of spirit visits in his books.

On a whim, he looked down and found that he was made of the same intangible sapphire light.

"Oh, silly me," he stated blankly. "I'm dead."

The man in the chair offered an empathetic smile. "Yes."

Percy pulled his legs up from underneath him, letting the implications of his fate seep in. He was dead. Which, on a factual level, meant that he would never be king. He would never see his friends again. He would never marry Elora. And Senna—

Oh. *Senna.*

The sadness floated around his mind on an intellectual level. He waited for it to sicken his heart, to draw tears to his eyes, but it never came.

"I don't—I don't feel dead. I should probably feel *sad* to some extent, shouldn't I? I feel rather numb."

"Ah, well, there's a reason we say *death puts us out of our misery.* You'll be able to feel the things that make you feel good. All your negative emotions will be harder to access, though not impossible."

Percy blinked, then realized he probably didn't *need* to blink.

"I apologize if I seem out of sorts," he said. "I don't know where I am and I'm afraid I haven't a clue who you are either."

The man stood, his long mage's robes sweeping over the carpet. Every part of him that was visible dissolved into the air. Percy gaped at the tiny sparkling fragments sizzling in his wake. They lingered for a moment, then drew together, reforming into a different shape: a glowing antlered deer.

Transfixed, Percy reached out and caressed the back of its head. It peered up at Percy with the same eyes he'd been looking into only seconds ago.

"*You,*" he said raptly. "You were the deer on the mountain. You told me to command the dre'malors to die. You saved my life. You saved us all."

The light dissolved once more under Percy's touch, taking proper form again as the tall man.

"My name is Laurentine Saville. I am the canon of rare and unknown magics."

"I *know* you," said Percy slowly. "It was your journal we spent months trying to open. We had no idea you were a canon. All this time, we thought we were dealing with Alpedis." He glanced around. "Can you tell me where we are?"

"This is Caenia, home of the canons and of spirits passing through. It was originally in the spirit hills of Mount Livia, but now it lies overtop of the entire living world. As for this room specifically, I believe it is your childhood nursery."

"That can't be. My mother had my nursery turned into her closet."

"Time is strange here. You may see your nursery, and a living human standing in the same spot would see your mother's overly exorbitant collection of mourning rags. The reason we see the nursery is because it was the most important place to you."

"How can that possibly be if I don't remember it?"

Laurentine hummed. "Let the canon of rare magics show you a trick. Stand still and close your eyes."

Percy obeyed. He felt a tiny gust of wind, and it wasn't until he snuck a peek out of his cracked eyes that he realized Laurentine had laid three fingers against his forehead. Then, a vision flooded over him.

This same room, bright and vibrant with childlike colors and the smell of baby soap. A young boy with choppy hair and red-rimmed eyes beside the bassinet rocking a baby swaddled in a fine blanket.

"Guard this child with your life," said a voice behind them. The boy turned around and—

And it was Senna—nine years old, terrified, and sickly. He looked down at the newborn child in his arms and tentatively pressed a kiss to his forehead.

"I swear. I swear."

The vision vanished, leaving Percy rubbing over his chest. Laurentine was right, the pain was harder to access. But it was there, only deeper somehow.

Percy cleared his throat. "Are you some sort of afterlife escort?"

Laurentine barked out a laugh. "Sadly not. I've been waiting to meet you for quite some time. I'd only hoped it would be much later in your life. It's because you're here early that I owe you an explanation—one I should have come into your dreams and given you a long time ago."

"An explanation. For what?"

Laurentine gave a pained smile and replied, "Oh, the very complicated web of foolishness and depravity that affected every moment of your life. Starting before your birth and ending with my husband stealing your life." Laurentine helped Percy to his feet. "Believe me, the story is rather convoluted and if I'd known where all my choices would lead, I'd have done it all differently. But I can't, and the consequences aren't yet finished. There isn't much time. I'll explain on the way. We must get to the catacombs."

"I forgot the castle even *had* catacombs. What's the hurry?"

"It's best if you see for yourself." Laurentine took Percy's hand and tore off down the hallway. Underneath Caenia's blue hue, Percy could see the real castle. They passed right through his familiar servants, all bustling about to complete their daily tasks.

"I am your distant, but illegitimate cousin," Laurentine explained. "Your father and I grew up together as boys. We were inseparable, but we matured into different men and drifted apart. Your father, Mathis, was being groomed for his role as king, but I had no claim to my royal blood, so I took to magical studies instead. Mathis always bore resentment toward my passions, because his tutors had expected *him* to be a prodigy. But despite his jealousy, I loved your father, so I offered him my greatest possession—my knowledge. In his early days as king, I provided counsel on all things magical, giving him access to what I'd learned as a member of the Academes. Your friend, Nare, joined our ranks as a child."

"I remember."

"The trouble was, your father received counsel from other sources, as well."

"My mother," Percy guessed.

"Precisely. I accidentally hinted to your father about the most powerful magic that exists. He put the pieces together for himself, discovered the truth on his own. I should have ensured that your father could bear the responsibility it took to wield such powerful knowledge, but he made a wrong step at every turn."

"What did you tell him?" Percy asked, though he wasn't sure he wanted to know.

At this, Laurentine looked pained. He stopped in the middle of the hallway and grabbed Percy by the shoulders.

"The canons can be killed. Their power can be stolen right from them, given to someone new, who takes over that role as canon. *Anyone* can steal a canon's power, not just another canon, but also spirits and living people."

He released Percy and continued their path.

"I should've expected he'd tell your mother, but when he did, she put this lie in his head. She told him that I would spread this secret around to the regular Talsuran people and create a war of power. He believed her, because I had always been a strong proponent of empowering everyday people to use magic to build meaningful and happy lives. Sometimes, that entailed removing barriers like education costs and magical class requirements. But I never wanted the world to know how to kill a canon."

"But he did kill a canon, didn't he?" Percy said nervously. "I saw it in a dream once. He went out to the moorlands and called on Jasrath to steal his power."

"I'm afraid it's more complicated than that. Because of your mother, Mathis thought that I was planning treason. He tried to control me by stationing me as the royal mage, but I refused. In response to my refusal, he sent Goldheart Ilias to my home and had me killed." He drew in a shaky breath, which was strange since Percy didn't think they were breathing. "My husband found me tied to a pole in the streets, the ground soaked in my blood. He went mad with grief. He immediately sought revenge, but it required more power than he had as the canon of thieves. But he was the only other person who knew how to kill a canon, so he killed Alpedis, stole her power, and became the canon of the sun and sky. The first thing he did with his new power was raze my village to the ground. In a stroke of impeccably terrible timing, only *then* was he summoned to the Talsuran moorlands."

"Why would he answer a summons like that?"

"He was summoned *magically*. He had no choice. Mathis called upon the canon of the sun, thinking he could do to Alpedis what Jasrath had already done. He wanted the sun's magic for himself to end the famine that had plagued Talsura for nearly a decade. When Jasrath appeared, it was a bitter confrontation. Jasrath wanted to kill your father for what he'd done to me. He wasn't quick enough. Mathis had already begun the rite to strip Jasrath of his power. But here's the rub—"

"*You* were the magical prodigy. Not Mathis," Percy realized.

Laurentine smiled sadly. "Yes, exactly. He didn't do the spell right. When he tried to consume Jasrath's power, he consumed *Jasrath* himself instead. Hosting a canon in his body took an immediate toll and he became deathly sick. Jasrath tried to get out, and despite having some power, could not perform his duties as canon of the sun. Its magic was left unchecked."

"That's where the sun sickness came from," Percy said.

"It got worse when your father finally died. I expect Jasrath hoped to be free once Mathis was dead, but the spell your father miscast wasn't for just a singular body, it was for his lineage. He died and Jasrath's spirit, his canon's body, had to go to his next host."

Percy halted at the top of a long stairwell.

"Me."

Laurentine looked straight up at him, unwavering. "You unknowingly hosted Jasrath in your body for your entire life. It's why you were able to command away the dre'malors. They'd been summoned by Jasrath, and in a way, you *were* him. Because you were the end of your lineage, Jasrath planned to have you killed so he could at last be free. I believe your intentions for marriage hastened him."

"If he couldn't control the sun sickness, then how was he able to—to kill me?"

"Here is the last thing you don't know. Perhaps the most important." He waved a hand. Percy teleported down to him. Carefully, delicately, he continued.

"Your mother knew that Jasrath would target you. When she finally discovered how and why people were dying of the sun sickness, she knew she had to protect you from it or else she'd have to face Jasrath's revenge. Before she raised the Dam, she sought out a child whom she perceived was immune to the sun sickness."

"Wait—"

"She took this child from his home and had her mages perform an extremely powerful and dangerous spell on him. He would be a siphon. All the raw magic around him would siphon into his body and be stored there, where it could not hurt anybody. Then, she stationed this boy next to you, so that even if the sun's power found you, it would store in the siphon and you would never die of sun sickness."

"*No,*" Percy spat out.

"Perhaps it would be easier if I showed you."

Percy stumbled a step back, but Laurentine was quicker. He touched the center of Percy's head, tossing a dizzying image into his mind.

Nine-year-old Senna Kane, laid out on a stone table. His pallid arms and legs restrained by leather bands. Magicians in rich, dark robes spilling ancient words over his struggling body. A raw scream tearing out of Senna's mouth in agony as something inside of him was permanently torn open. The childlike cries for a mother who was already years gone.

Percy squeezed his eyes against the vision, only for the vision to shift.

Phaedra holding Senna by the shoulders minutes after his ritual, making him promise he would never ever leave Percy's side. Senna's bloodshot eyes as he agreed.

When the vision shifted again, it was decades instead of minutes that passed. Some of the moments Percy remembered.

Senna remaining at Percy's side, his resentment slowly waning. Flickers of a boy Percy knew—Ciaran, the votary from Mount Livia. Ciaran starving, shunned for stealing. Jasrath offering freedom at an impossible price. A recipe for poison to nullify even the most powerful siphon magic. Ciaran grinding mountain crystals together and pouring them into the steaming brew. Ciaran pipetting exactly five drops into Senna's wine, spilling more tears into the chalice besides.

"Ciaran tried to tell me," Percy said strangely. "He tried to tell me that if I didn't seek Jasrath's favor, I would die. He was right."

Laurentine's hand found his shoulder.

"There was nothing you could have done. Jasrath would've kept trying until he succeeded."

Percy sank onto the stairs, holding his shaking head. His pain was still distant, but even the edge of it was enough to gut him.

"Then it's over. I'm dead. Jasrath is free."

"Do not underestimate a canon's grief. Until Jasrath is satisfied with his revenge, it won't be over," Laurentine warned. "He's the canon of thieves. He is *never* satisfied." He offered a hand. "Take heart, Percy. You must be brave and our timing must be just right."

"Our timing?"

Laurentine's head snapped up, like something in the air had called to him. He took another one of those breathless inhales, and Percy felt the air around them spark with magic.

Percy latched on to Laurentine's sleeve. "What are you—"

Laurentine sliced his hand through the air. The space before them fractured, creating a thin portal pulsing and shimmering. Laurentine stepped through the fissure, gesturing for Percy to follow him. A rush of the magic shoved Percy forward, hurling him through the portal and onto the ground. He pushed himself up onto his elbows, the earth beneath him cold and damp. If he were alive, his arms might've stung with friction burns, but the sensations didn't affect him. Above him, the ceiling was tall and vaulted. At its middle, a lamp burned with ice-white fire, spilling cold light over the echoing chamber.

Another breeze of magic swept underneath him, lifting him upright. It forced him to look at what was in the center of the room.

Percy's spirit flickered.

Because there was Senna, on his knees, hands chained to the floor. His skin was coated in a thin layer of blood-tinged sweat. Bloody spittle dripped down the side of his mouth, chin hanging low on his chest. Even his hair was tinged in crimson. The wretched cause seemed to be Senna's back, which was torn open with gaping lashes from a violent flogging.

The hand holding the switch was his mother's.

Percy lurched forward on instinct, but Laurentine held him back.

"Let me go. I have to help him. She'll kill him."

"Spirit visits are all about timing, Percy," Laurentine warned him in his ear. "When Senna's siphon was unsealed, your spirit did collect some of its power. You will be able to touch and speak in a way that other spirits can't during their visits. But that magic is finite. Don't squander your chance."

"So, what, you expect me to just stand here and *watch*?"

Laurentine nodded firmly. "You will know what to do. When you act, I will help."

Percy didn't want to watch, but he could not let himself look away. Dread pooled in him as he watched his own mother drag her long, dirtied switch through the dust and damp of the ground. It trailed behind her like a leashed beast, circling Senna as she did. She stopped at Senna's back. Senna's face hardened when she was out of view, as if he were steeling himself for the next blow.

"You insolent wretch," she hissed bitterly. "Fifteen lashes and you won't even make a sound. Do you know what you've *done*?"

Senna's face cracked, like the reminder was worse than a hundred lashes.

"You knew what I was," Senna whispered. "But you didn't tell me. You didn't tell me I was a siphon. I never would've let him leave. I would've been more careful."

She snatched Senna by his hair, hauling his face back. "You dare turn the blame on me?"

"No," Senna said so quietly, Percy had to take a few steps forward to hear him. "The blame is mine."

"No," Percy whispered fiercely. "Does he really believe that?"

"Of course the blame is yours." Phaedra released Senna's hair, and he lurched forward, taking panting breaths. "This kingdom will burn to the ground and it will be all your fault. Do you know what the canon of thieves will do now that he's been unleashed?" Senna's brows knit together, but Phaedra was raging on. "Everything I've worked so hard for—the *years* I've spent conniving for the authority I now possess—you've ruined it all. When Talsura falls, the people will cast condemnation on *me*. All because you've freed Jasrath."

Senna's face tilted up to look at her, damp hair sticking to his cheeks.

"Is that what angers you?" he asked lightly, like he could not believe it. "Not that your son is dead, but that he can't host your greatest threat anymore?"

"What other use would I have had for him?"

Anger flared in Senna's eyes. "He was your *child*."

"He was an impudent, spoiled, naive *wretch* that could not do the one thing he was meant to."

Senna roared in fury, pulling against his own chains to grab for Phaedra. The chains had to be rubbing his wrists raw, but he didn't stop. He wrapped one of the chains around Phaedra's throat and pulled with all of his strength.

"He wasn't a wretch. He was *mine*," Senna said with so much hatred, Percy felt the air go cold. "When Jasrath comes for you—and he *will* come for you—not even the Dam will be able to hide you."

Phaedra's rage was only contained by her inability to breathe. A sickly bluish red crept up her throat, and she clawed at Senna's wrists, sharp nails digging into his skin. Then, seeming to realize it was futile, she clutched the hilt of the switch and rammed it into Senna's stomach. He fell back with a wheeze, landing hard on the ground.

Phaedra heaved so hard her breaths nearly sounded like growling. She raised the switch above her head.

"Be brave, Percy. This will be difficult," Laurentine whispered in Percy's ear. "But it is not yet time."

The first lash echoed throughout the chamber like a crack of lightning.

Blood splashed along the bridge of Phaedra's nose, spraying along her teeth as she grinned. "Sixteen." Another strike. "Seventeen."

Percy stood struck with horror so profound, he could feel the coldness of his own body lying somewhere in this blasted castle. His own lifelessness and uselessness plagued him now in equal measure, leaving him completely pathetic, unable to save Senna from enduring this pain.

One lash after another, the switch tore apart the bleeding flesh of Senna's back. At last, Senna screamed. The sound was wild, deafening, but not loud enough to drown out the sound of the switch striking him.

Eventually, Senna's cries waned into pained whimpers. He floated around consciousness with fluttery eyes, the pain growing too much. But Percy knew the laws of his land. This would soon be over. He only needed Senna to endure it long enough.

"Twenty-seven, twenty-eight, twenty-nine," Percy counted under his breath.

"*Thirty!*" Phaedra howled.

She tossed the switch aside, sending it rolling at Percy's feet. Thick red drops stained her clothes, as if she'd gone out of her way to fling Senna's blood all onto every inch of her being. Percy knew she could be cruel—had been the subject of that cruelty for his entire life—but this was depravity manifest.

It would go on no longer.

Phaedra freed a ceremonial knife from her belt and brandished it in the air, waving it about the air like a war-won trophy.

The chamber door burst open, thrust off its hinges by vines the size of tree trunks. Through the gaping mouth poured four familiar faces. Thea, Nare, and Elora stood at the front of the room just long enough to take in the scene before them.

Emrys did not stop. He stumbled on his own feet, arm outstretched to unleash another inflorescent attack. *"Get away from him!"* he bellowed. But when he spread open his palm, all that came out were a few red leaves. Percy guessed he'd used all his magical reserves to get here, but now was left powerless under the cover of the Dam.

Phaedra watched the few twiggy leaves float to the ground, then began to *laugh*—cracking cackles that reminded Percy of the hags he'd read about in his old storybooks.

"*Pathetic* Redwindan lambs come to join the slaughter. Oblivion finds us all, even diseased vermin."

A long look passed between Emrys and Senna. Percy wasn't sure what was said in that look, but he knew that Emrys would choke on thorns in this torture chamber before leaving Senna alone to die.

"We aren't the ones who scutter around the darkness like rats in the sewer," he hissed, raging.

With a snap of her fingers, fire engulfed Phaedra's hands, forming into a boulder of flames. She hurled it forward into the dry vines. The fire consumed the inflorescence like a starved man at a banquet. Nare yanked Thea away before she could get caught in the heat.

Then Phaedra turned to Senna, looked into his eyes, and said in a sneering voice, "Long live Senna Kane, Goldheart of Talsura."

She raised the blade. Emrys would not get to him fast enough.

Without conscious thought, Percy inhaled the magic around him, centering it in his spirit. The power was both near and far, and when he exhaled, it propelled him with it. He disappeared, not by the strength of his own intangible legs, but by magic.

Percy was not—and then he was. Right in the empty space between Senna and Phaedra, in line with the lowering knife. He caught it above his head, staring deep into his mother's gaze. Her eyes widened, the uncanny sky-blue giving way to the terrified, gaping darkness of her pupils.

"You will not harm my goldheart," he said. His own voice sounded dangerous, as if it were multiplied on itself—its own sort of weapon for his command. He wielded it again. *"You will not harm Senna."*

Phaedra's eyes narrowed.

"What makes you so sure I won't?"

"Because he is favored by the canons. And because he is armed."

"Yes," said Laurentine's voice, although Percy could not see him. "Follow your intuition. It's Caenia's magic guiding you. Feel it in your chest. All magic wants something and yours wants to help you. Let it."

"Armed?" Phaedra spat. "He is chained to the ground, soiled in his own blood."

Percy stepped back so that his body floated through Senna's. He could not see Senna's face, but he could feel the hurricane of the sun's power still swirling inside of him. Even though it had been uncapped for long enough to take Percy's life, there were still years worth of sun magic churning within Senna. Dormant, waiting to be unleashed again.

"Don't you remember, Mother? He's a siphon." The words were directed to Phaedra, but the intention of them, the unspoken command, went right to the seal of Senna's power. It caressed it, uncapped it ever so slightly.

But, oh, even the pittance of Senna's power was enough to remind Percy what it felt like to be *alive* and remind his mother what it was like to suffer.

"What have you *done*?" Phaedra shrieked. Thorns had begun to tear through her arm, mixing her wet blood with Senna's drying.

Percy did not waver. *"You'd better back away."*

Phaedra remained in place, tearing the growth out of her arm and widening the cuts. No matter how much she pulled away, it continued to spill out.

"It's not pleasant, is it? Dying this way. I only had minutes," Percy deadpanned. *"We'll have that in common if you don't relent. You, me, and all of the exiles you failed—all victims of your own making."*

"No—"

Again, Percy centered Caenia's magic, this time behind his mouth. *"Desist."*

Several things happened in short succession.

Phaedra flew back away from Senna, landing in a heap on the ground. Senna's chains clanged against the floor as they fell free. The fire burning away the trunk roots dissipated like a candle with no wick. Empowered by the thick sun magic, Emrys emerged from the smoke, throwing his arm out toward Phaedra's prone form. Thick roots cracked through the ground, entrapping her. She pushed and struggled, but could not squeeze her way out. All she managed was the start of a yell before a mouthful of moss silenced the rest of the sound.

Percy stood in the center of the room, his Redwindan friends gaping up at him, Senna's gaze heavy on his back. He owed them too many goodbyes, with not nearly enough energy to utter them. He smiled at Thea, his best friend. At Elora, the woman he loved more than anything. They'd know the truth in his heart—they'd have to.

"Your time grows short," warned Laurentine's voice from somewhere unseen. "The goldheart is waning."

His friends must have heard the words too, because they all turned to look behind him where Senna was kneeling in his own blood. Emrys had an awful look on his face, like he wanted terribly to run up to Senna, haul him over his shoulder, and get him the hell out of danger. He didn't budge, yielding to Percy's next move.

"Hear me, Emrys Rosecroft," Percy said sternly. Emrys straightened. *"Protect him with everything you are."*

Emrys gasped, but clasped his fist over his heart.

"I swear."

It was time to say goodbye to Senna.

Be brave, Laurentine had said.

Percy turned around.

Senna was alive. He was pale, shaking from pain and blood loss. But Senna's eyes were wide, wide, wide, staring up at Percy with the sort of awe he'd had when he'd first beheld the world outside the Dam.

"Hullo, Sen," Percy said fondly.

Senna's face crumpled on itself, terribly. Fat tears streamed down his cheeks, leaving clean streaks through the blood and dirt.

"I'm sorry," he wept. "I'm so sorry. I'm so sorry, Percy. It's all my fault. I'm so sorry. It's because of me."

"No, Sen. It wasn't."

"It was! It was! I killed you."

Percy smiled softly. He placed his thumbs over Senna's eyelids and soothed the tears away, just as Senna had done when he was a baby. Just as Senna had done when he'd died. The gesture seemed to soothe him enough to let him breathe, but Percy knew the grief would return the moment the contact broke. He needed a way to prove to Senna in a lasting way that he didn't blame him.

Perhaps the same magic that had shown him the truth could give Senna the same clarity. He wasn't the canon of rare spells like Laurentine was, but knowledge and power felt so different here—like he didn't need to *learn* the spell. It'd been shared with him, and so, too, was it his to share.

He laid his hand over Senna's face and thought about the memory leaving him through his fingertips, dripping out like water from a leaky faucet, into the siphon inside Senna's body. There were a hundred drops, one for every memory Laurentine had given him—the violent history neither of them had caused. The way they'd been forced to suffer the ignorance of it. Now Senna knew all of it.

When he pulled away, Senna's expression was still devastated, but the rage at its edges was no longer directed at himself.

"Do you see now?" Percy said gently. *"It wasn't your fault."*

Senna shook his head. "You're still gone."

"But you aren't. You're still here," Percy said with a small smile. *"And really, that's what I wanted for you all along, wasn't it? The opportunity to find out who Senna Kane really is. Now you can. Perhaps it's not the way we thought it'd happen, but I'm grateful just the same."* He held Senna's face and placed a soft kiss on his forehead. *"You will always be my brother. I love you."*

Senna's lip trembled, lungs low on breath when he whispered, "I love you."

Percy brushed Senna's tears aside one last time, then stepped back with a shuddering breath. He felt the magic holding his spirit visible start to unravel, pulling away from him, dandelion crowns lost in a strong wind.

His vision blurred. When it focused, he was back in the nursery where everything was blue and immaterial.

For a moment, all Percy could do was stare at the floor. He felt Laurentine's presence waiting in the same chair, watching him.

"How do you feel?" asked the canon finally.

Percy turned his gaze inward, letting whatever he was feeling surface.

"Incomplete," he answered finally.

Laurentine's thin lips lifted. "Good."

"Good?"

Laurentine folded his hands across his lap, his smile growing.

"It means you have a choice to make."

SENNA

P ERCY DISAPPEARED, AND WITH it, a piece of Senna's heart.

The unspoken meaning of his visit was clear: succumbing to his injuries in the middle of this torture chamber was not an option. He had to do the thing that went against all his instincts. He had to live. He had to *survive*.

With some effort, he lifted his head. His attention snagged someone racing toward him—a familiar face with loyal, violet eyes. All at once, Senna remembered that living would not be all terrible.

Senna summoned enough energy to propel himself forward directly into Emrys' arms. He murmured Emrys' name again and again, clinging with all his strength.

"Thank the canons," Emrys breathed shakily. Senna felt the warmth of Emrys' hands hovering over his back, as if he wanted to hug back, but wasn't sure where to put them. "I can't believe you, Senna Kane. Honestly, I can't believe you." He settled with burying his fingers into Senna's hair. "I thought I'd be too late."

Senna nuzzled into Emrys' shoulder. "You came."

"Of course I bloody came. I love you. I'll always come for you." He held Senna's face, looking into his eyes. "You—your safety, your happiness. *That's* what I protect."

Shame flooded Senna. "I almost—I didn't tell you—"

"I know, my heart. It's alright. Believe me, I know how easy it is to let grief drag you under. But you're not alone. Did you really think all of us could stand to lose both of you?" Emrys kissed his forehead. "We have to get you out of here."

Thea approached his side, eyeing his back with a sick expression. "Can he walk?"

The thought made Senna feel like he'd be sick.

Nare knelt at Senna's back. "Not without a little help." Then, to Senna, "Sorry, friend. This'll sting." She drew a featherlight sigil on his back with the soft pad of her finger. A strange mix of tingling and pain tore up his spine. Senna gritted his teeth. "Doin' great, Sen. It bites for a moment, but then it'll feel smooth like silk. Most importantly, you'll be able to walk for a while."

True to her word, the pain's gnawing edge subsided, replaced by numbness. Senna sagged even further into Emrys' arms in sheer relief. Emrys seized the opportunity to grow something along the worst of the wounds—needle yarrow, judging by the way his skin was stitching himself together. Senna winced when he felt the long strands from the base of his back all the way to his neck. It was a miracle there was anything left of him at all.

"The magic will only be able to delay the inevitable until we can tend to his wounds for real. Even with the needle yarrow, he won't make the trip back to Redwind," Nare continued.

"What about somewhere halfway?" Thea offered, somewhat distractedly. She rubbed her heart, eyeing the spot Percy had appeared.

"It would need to be somewhere outside the Dam where the Talsuran guard can't find us," Emrys thought out loud. "Could he make it to Sascha?"

Nare shook her head. "Mount Livia is too far."

Through the open door issued the sound of approaching guards.

"Guess we weren't as discreet as we thought." Elora shuddered.

Thea tossed a wary glance at Phaedra and Senna didn't have to guess what she was thinking. The knighthearts would only have to take one look at their queen trapped under inflorescence before attacking.

"I think we should get the hell out of here before we decide anything," Thea murmured.

Nare nodded to the queen. "What about her? Is she going to die?"

"One can only hope," Emrys growled. "I suppose we'll hear about it if she does, but it's not our problem. Now how do we get out of here?"

Tiredly, Senna nodded toward the side of the room where a metal grate was embedded into the floor.

"The hatch," he grunted. "There are steps to the trade channels."

"Understood," Thea said, wiping sweat from Senna's brow. "Elora, you and I will help Senna walk. Emrys and Nare will stand at our head and tail in case anyone finds us. And you, brother mine—" She kissed Senna's hair. "You have to live long enough to help lead us out. You *must* stay awake. Is that clear?"

Senna smiled tiredly. "Yes, Your Highness."

They disappeared into the trade channels like shadows. Pain muddied the clarity of Senna's awareness, but he managed to collect some moments of the journey—Elora's steady hand pressing gauze to his back as they lowered him into the tunnels, Emrys locking the grate with violently sharp thorns, Thea and Nare bickering over where they should go once they made it past the Dam. He supposed he must've stayed awake long enough for muscle memory to direct them out of the trade channels. He'd memorized these channels in hopes the knowledge would save Percy's life. He'd never expected it to save his own.

It wasn't until they crossed the Dam and the first breeze of fresh air grazed Senna's face that his strength gave out. Distantly, he heard Emrys' voice—*Don't worry, I've got you. I've got you. Go ahead and rest a moment. Promise me you'll stay awake. Just a little longer.*

There were other voices too. *Do you hear anything? Have they followed us?* And, *No, there are too many exits to these trade channels. Even if they were trying to follow us, they'd have to pick the right one.* And, *It all seems a little too easy, doesn't it? Us getting out?* And, *Easy?! Are you joking? We need to find somewhere safe.* And, *How? Senna can't go on.*

"I'll carry him," came Emrys' voice, clear and close. "Help him onto my back."

There was some maneuvering, like they were trying to lift a very bulky and deadweighted doll. Once he was draped over Emrys, he felt . . . safe. As if he were in the one place in the entire world where nothing bad could happen.

It was impossible to stay awake after that. His friends talking to him was enough to keep him teetering above the cusp of consciousness, but barely so. Through his hazy, fluttering eyes, Senna saw a sky full of treetops. Hints of the stars broke through their leafy crowns, mixed in with cloud-filtered moonlight.

"When they built the Dam, they left the outskirts of Talsura out of the borders," Elora said. "In theory we should be stumbling across abandoned houses any second. Then it's just a matter of getting supplies."

In the thickest part of the woods, a figure blurred by the trees.

"Wha—?" Senna murmured, but no one heard him.

"Food won't be an issue," Nare pointed out. "And neither will drinking water if I can get the conjuration spell right. Haven't needed it in a while."

"Then we're short on the few things we need most: sutures, clean dressings, and medicine," said Emrys.

"We left our horses outside the Dam somewhere around the perimeter," Thea added. "If they haven't returned home, then they might be able to carry one of us to get what we need. Let's just hope we didn't leave them too far away."

In the woods, another flash, another figure, maybe a second. Then, in the moonlight, a familiar tattoo—two snake eyes blinking. Watching.

"Em," Senna murmured, weakly tapping Emrys' chest. "Em, watch out."

But the warning came too late.

A flash of bright, *wrong* sunlight beamed in the path, blinding and explosive. Emrys struggled to keep his footing, but the force of the light propelled him back, sending them both rolling through the dirt. The plummet was hell on Senna's back, fallen twigs and stones tearing at the needle yarrow holding his flesh together.

Senna's eyes protested with the effort it took to look up. The flare had disappeared as quickly as it had come, but the heat of the burst still lingered along his skin. He squinted into the road, stomach dropping.

There, in the middle of the path, was a horde of Grit Fingers. They were cloaked in the nighttime shade, the forest's shadows indistinguishable from their dark clothes. Each was armed with lavish weapons that gleamed in the moonlight.

Senna could not see his lover, but he heard Emrys draw his blade, coaxing a spiky root from the ground with the free hand.

Emrys was going to fight his way through, Senna realized sickly. What other option was there? Thea and Elora had proven they could hold their own, but Emrys and Nare were the only ones with any sort of battle training. Against a dozen thieves in the dark, they were outnumbered.

Snake-Eyes traipsed to the front of the group, swinging his dagger in circles around his finger.

"It seems you've arrived at a toll bridge," Snake-Eyes said mockingly. "I've come to collect."

"Didn't we already embarrass you enough in Mount Livia?" Emrys taunted. "You just had to escape and beg for more?"

"Don't wag your tongue at me. *You* stumbled into *our* territory. It's so convenient when the prey meanders into a trap on their own without any shooing. Jasrath must've answered my prayers." He held his hands in an exaggerated prayer motion and looked longingly at the sky. Then he snapped his hands back and growled. "Pay your toll, pay your toll! The cost is low. Deposit the goldheart into our hands and my thieves won't demand your lives—only what's in your pockets."

"Uncap the siphon," Senna groaned, hoping Nare could hear him.

"I can't," she said through clenched teeth. "Your magic is what's keeping you alive. If I uncap the siphon, you'll be dead in a second."

What good would his magic be if they were *all* dead? His fingers dug into the ground, and he tried to push himself up. Fire-hot pain erupted up his back and radiated to the scars in his chest, throbbing harder with his gasp. He dropped back to the ground, Emrys catching him before he could crash again. The numbing magic in his back was losing its potency every second.

He cursed. A lifetime's worth of training, a decade's worth of wielding his blade, and he still couldn't protect anyone.

"I'm waiting," Snake-Eyes crooned, howling the words up into the sky wolfishly. "Unless you'd like to make this fun!" He tossed the dagger into the air. It spun three times above their heads, before descending as a full-length sword. Snake-Eyes caught it, brandishing it this way and that, a magician showing off his trick. "Do you need a little—*nudge*?"

Elora chirped in surprise. One of the Grit Fingers was breathing down her throat, a curved blade prodded into her back.

But it wasn't only Elora—Thea and Nare each had two thieves at their sides, with even more behind them. They lifted their hands, faces pale.

"Emrys," Thea whispered.

"I know," he hissed. "I'm—I'm thinking. There's some sunlight on the moon, but . . ." But it wasn't strong enough to take on this many thieves. They were so densely surrounded, Senna doubted they could find a breakthrough point either.

Senna drilled his nails into Emrys' wrist. "Open the siphon."

"*No,*" Emrys growled. Desperate, he stuck his hand to the ground, fingers buried into the forest's underbrush, the way he always did when he was about to seize inflorescent control.

The second he touched the grass, though, ivory moonlight spilled over his hands. The roar of a thousand thunderous hooves echoed everywhere all at once, quaking the ground underneath Senna. The prickling of the hairs on the back of his neck was the only warning before a beast leapt over his head and landed between the goldheart and the thieves.

It was the deer of molten light. The same that had appeared to Senna and Emrys on their first journey to Mount Livia. The same creature that had appeared to Percy, instructing him to kill the dre'malors. And the first time it had appeared to Senna, it'd spoken: ***You are the one with the heart of gold who has my favor. You must be my blade.***

The deer stamped around the clearing, commanding the attention of all who beheld it. Then it stopped, and looked at Snake-Eyes. There was no fear in its body language, nor in its eyes.

"Let them pass," it said.

Snake-Eyes sputtered in surprise before devolving into loud, crazed laughter. "You're just a trick. An illusion."

"*Then you may tell Jasrath he has made an enemy of his own husband.*"

Emrys gasped, tightening his grip on Senna. The grass underneath them wilted, its bright color draining like blood from an open wound. Strands of the grass wove together, tangling among the fallen twigs and dry leaves, until a body formed from the dead thicket. Vines grew from its head, blowing in the sharp breeze all around it. The twigs of its mouth broke as it spoke.

"Laurentine," Jasrath breathed. "My love."

Three simple words. Yet, they were the final piece in a long, complicated story—one that Percy had tried to tell in visions and memories. One that, only now, Senna understood. All this time, Jasrath had been plotting against them—to free himself, to steal Senna's power, to gain revenge over Talsura. And all this time, Laurentine, the man whom the anger was for, had been with them, protecting them. They'd thought it was Alpedis, but Jasrath had killed Alpedis and stolen her power. Laurentine was their true savior.

"*Jasrath,*" Laurentine uttered. His gaze was his weapon and it brought the exiled canon to his knees. **"*End this plot of yours.*"**

"Laurie, y-you've been in Caenia all this time?"

Hatred as hot as flames alighted in Senna's chest. The strength of it blasted his pulse through his veins, overpowering the tiredness that threatened to keep him powerless on the ground. How easily the canon of thieves stood in the road, as if *he* were one who deserved to grieve. As if his hands weren't soaked in Percy's blood.

"*You,*" Senna gnarled weakly.

Jasrath's eyeless gaze drifted back to Senna. A low growl rumbled in the back of his throat, eyes narrowing. This was a choice of his own making—protect the favor of the man he loved most, or seize the power he desperately craved. Senna hoped he got neither.

"*Let them pass,*" Laurentine said. **"*End this plot of yours.*"**

"I can't. I need the goldheart's power. I need it to avenge you."

Jasrath tilted his face at Senna and took one terrible step forward. His arm stretched out to Senna, branchy and unnaturally long.

Laurentine stabbed his antler through the hand. The tips tore through the twigs and brown vines all along the arm, wrenching the limb apart with a dozen sickly *CRACKS*. Jasrath yelped, but Laurentine was quicker. White flames consumed the dry wood, eating up his arms. With all his strength, he dragged his head in a circle, forcing Jasrath to collapse into a heap on the dirt road. Laurentine rammed a hoof into his husband's wooden gut, sending him hurling back into the rabble of his thieves. The flames on his arms extinguished, but the embers dropped to the ground, bright orange, blinking out one by one.

"You have chosen," Laurentine said. *"Our marriage is voided."*

"No," Jasrath groaned bitterly.

"When the goldheart comes for you, I will not interfere. Know this: he is my blade. Today was a warning. You'll not be afforded another."

Jasrath dug his thorny hands into the ground, clawing through dirt and stones like a tiller cutting through the earth. He wailed in frustration, the black circles of his eyes boring into Laurentine's. He dropped his head, pounding his fist to the ground, yelling as his hands splintered off and broke into pieces. Burned, viny hair fell over his face as he snapped his head up.

"This isn't over," he snarled, then disappeared.

Realizing that their leader had abandoned them, the thieves scrambled back. Laurentine plunged his antlers at them, waving the white flames in an unspoken threat. Snake-Eyes grumbled, then vanished off into the shadows of the forest. The rest of the thieves followed, evaporating like snuffed candles.

Laurentine turned his head to them, eyes sparkling opals.

"There is somewhere the Talsuran guard and the guild thieves will not find you. Will you allow me to take you there?"

"Is it somewhere we can care for him?" Emrys cut in, wrapping an arm around Senna's waist. "With medicine and supplies?"

"Better. There is a healer who will mend him if you tell her I sent you. There you will find one final gift—an apology for Jasrath's behavior."

Laurentine began to glow blindingly bright. ***"Everyone, come now. Place your hands on the goldheart's shoulder."*** Then, ***"Until next time, Senna Kane."***

Laurentine pressed his damp deer's nose to Senna's forehead. Darkness swept over them, and they were gone.

EPILOGUE

I F THEA HADN'T BEEN taken from the streets to be a princess, she imagined her life would have looked something like this. Six people packed into a humble house—*Laurentine's* house—all trying not to get in each other's way. All trying not to grieve in each other's spaces. The house looked different than when she and Nare had first visited. It was cleaner, with signs that people actually lived in it. There were dirty dishes, more shoes by the door, and more sounds coming from rooms that had once lain quiet.

Thea could agree it wasn't the most ideal arrangement. When Nare had told Lane, the Academe scholar still living in the home, that Laurentine had sent them there for shelter, Lane had almost packed her things and left. But then she'd taken one look at Senna—his pale and pain-furrowed brow, his weeping back—and decided to stay to oversee his recovery. Even now, a month and a half later, Lane and Nare could barely stand to be in the same room together.

Then there was the matter of the missing presence in the house. If Thea thought for too long about how much she missed Percy, it stripped her of all motivation to do anything more but lie down and sleep. She kept herself busy by replicating all she could remember of Laurentine's journal into a new leather notebook.

Senna was not so lucky. After Lane had cleaned out his wounds and stitched them together with proper sutures, Senna had taken to sleeping. For the first few days, Emrys stayed by his side, napping with him, keeping him company. Eventually, Elora suggested that Emrys give him some space. Some time alone.

After a while, Senna did get out of bed. He still didn't talk to anyone much, though his friends kept an eye on him while he labored in the garden along the sunny side of the house.

That was the last of Laurentine's gifts. When they'd arrived at the house, impossibly, Percy's body and ceramic bust had been waiting for them. Percy had still been wrapped in his fine Talsuran burial silks, but there had been a glowing white rose keeping the fabric closed.

They'd buried him a distance from the side of the house. The grave was opposite of the yard where Senna kept his garden. But from it, Senna could tend to his plants and still look at the bust sculpture that Elora had made. She'd carefully carved the inscription on the base. It was Percy's title, the years of his life, and an epitaph, the lyrics Emrys had written as a child:

> *"I love him so I'll let him go.*
> *Farewells are hard, I know he knows.*
> *But I'd give anything to say*
> *please fly home to me one day."*

Emrys told Thea that gardening was the first hobby Senna had ever had.

"Thea, would you go tell Senna it's time to change his dressings, please?" Lane asked as she came down the stairs. "I need to get the healing tinctures on the stove."

That was another thing that Thea was still getting used to. For weeks, everyone only called her *Thea*. Never *Your Highness*. Actually, no one had called anyone anything except for their names—no trace of the goldheart, captain, or princess.

"Of course," Thea replied. She pushed away from her desk and closed her half-filled journal. Today, she was scribing down the details of Laurentine's spirit visit. It wouldn't be taking so long, except her proofreader (one infuriating librarian) had told her she needed to write slower so her handwriting was legible.

Thea crossed through the house, past Elora, where she was sitting in the bay window sketching. Her dress brushed against Nare sitting on the floor amidst a mess of books. Her personal project had been to go through the rest of Laurentine's books to see which ones she wanted to add to Redwind's library, and so far, the *keep* pile was mountainous.

"See anything you like?" Thea asked, nudging one of the piles with her toe.

Nare winked. "Eh, I don't mind the current view too much."

Thea scurried by, ignoring the heat blooming in her cheeks.

She found Senna kneeling in a fresh bed of soil, thumbing tiny seeds into the ground one by one, then sprinkling them with water. The sleeves of his loose white shirt were rolled up to his elbows and his hair was tied in a messy knot with one of Elora's purple ribbons. He wore a gardening apron, the front of which had several dirt handprints. Under his breath, Senna was humming a song Emrys had been writing when he thought no one was listening.

Thea squatted down across the flower bed and pointed at a row of tiny green sprouts. "Whatever these are, they seem to be popping up quite nicely."

Senna didn't startle. He looked up and smiled softly.

"They're cucumbers. I thought they'd be nice since we can eat them so many different ways. We could pickle them, if someone snuck into town for vinegar."

Thea crossed her arms over her bent knees. Wisely, she didn't mention that they might not be staying here long enough to see his harvest come in. It'd been the unspoken understanding between all of them that they would take some time to regain their footing and let Senna heal. No one had spoken about what would come after, but then, they'd never finished what they'd set out to do.

"Cucumbers were Percy's favorite, no?" Thea said, instead.

Senna pressed his lips together and nodded.

"Something to do with royal tea sandwiches all having cucumber slices on the inside, I think," he murmured with a sad smile. "They were the only thing he could make himself."

"I'd like to hear more about what Percy was like growing up sometime. If you ever have the heart to talk about it."

Senna drew his hand aimlessly through the dirt, expression complicated.

"Alright," was all he said, but it sounded genuine.

"I look forward to it. For now, think you could use a break? Lane says it's time to change your dressing."

Senna wiped his hands on his apron and rose. Thea leapt to his side, supporting him so he could stand as quickly as he needed. For once, he didn't argue at being helped. He merely let Thea act as his crutch, even though they both knew he didn't really need it. The worst of his injuries had healed over and now they just needed to keep the dressings clean enough to stave off infection.

When they got inside, Lane pointed an affronted finger at Senna's hands.

"Wash those filthy things before you soil all my sterilized dressings!" she said.

Senna washed his hands and took a seat on the bench, eyes glinting with a small smile.

"Canons, it's like I never left my ma's home," Elora griped. "Careful, Sen. Next thing you know, she'll be yelling at you for tracking mud across her floors. It's all downhill from there."

"We're on a hill right now. Literally everything is downhill from here," Nare called out.

"Not your healing though, Sen," Lane commented, pulling up the back of Senna's shirt. "Everything is closing up nicely. You seem to have kicked last week's infection. Likely thanks to that cream Sascha sent to us. What did you say they put in all their healing supplies?"

"Crystals," Senna answered politely.

Lane hummed. "I'm not one for jewels, but those I can get behind. Alright, you know the score by now. Let me know if this stings."

Without warning, the front door burst open. Emrys flounced in with supplies balanced precariously in crates and bags wherever they'd fit on his body. He let them all drop unceremoniously on the ground, forgotten. In two long strides, he captured Senna's face, kissed him soundly, and said, "Hello, my heart."

"There are four other people in the room, you know," Thea grumbled.

"Apologies, sister! I didn't realize you wanted a kiss too!" Emrys cried, throwing his arms around her and smacking his wet lips to her cheek.

She swatted him. "Ugh, that is vile. Get off."

"Happily," he said, plopping down next to Senna, draping his legs over his lover's lap. Senna leaned his nose into Emrys' cheeks, eyes falling shut. Thea couldn't help but wonder what it must be like for someone's presence to bring such comfort.

"I take it no one in Redwind came for your hide," Nare asked, filling herself a glass of water at the sink.

"If anyone recognized me, they've done me the great service of pretending I am as furtive and cunning as I think I am. None of the guards stopped to interrogate me. I even heard whispers that the townsfolk have continued on with the exchange without me."

"That's wonderful," Senna said.

"The markets had everything on Thea's—lengthy and expensive—list. Everything except the cucumbers."

Senna's face lit like it was a struck match.

"That's what I planted in the garden."

"They won't be ready for another two months yet," Thea warned gently.

"They'd be ready sooner if you'd let me give them a little tender loving affection," Emrys crooned against Senna's cheek.

The smile on Senna's face dimmed. "No inflorescence."

"Come now, you've got direct experience with my tender love. Is it really so bad?" The frown lines on Senna's face remained steady. Emrys sighed. "Oh alright. I'm sure two months will fly by."

"Are . . ." Elora started, then she looked at Senna and hesitated. "Are we still going to be here in two months?"

Thea folded her hands across her lap. "You're welcome to return back to your studio at any time, Elora. You weren't banished like Emrys and I were. But we'll probably remain here for the time being."

"Oh, to hell with that. Percy died for this—this crusade you've all embarked on. Do you really think I can go back to carving and pretending I wasn't a part of it?" Elora closed her sketchbook. "I just find it hard to believe that you've all lost sight of our own cause enough to think we'll still be living here like a commune of outcasts in two months' time."

"No one said we've forgotten the cause," Emrys said defensively. "Is it so bad to take our time? Anytime we've been at risk in the past, it's because we haven't thought things through."

"What happens when you've waited too long and all your options disappear?" Elora said. "What happens if you have to start fresh all over again?"

"Look, El. I know losing Percy was—" Thea's throat closed. She swallowed and tried again. "It was a reminder that we're not invincible. We're messing with forces that affect real people with real lives, including our own."

"I don't think a little time is a bad idea," Nare offered with a shrug. "Look at it this way, Emrys is going to have to go groveling to his mother eventually if he wants her support. The anger won't feel so fresh after some separation. Not to mention, it'll prove that we're not imminently at risk of going to war with Talsura or Jasrath." She held up a finger. "And, for the record, I still think it's absolutely unfair that of all the people to have survived the sun sickness, it's *Queen Phaedra*."

Lane propped her elbows on the kitchen island. "Why *do* you think the queen of Talsura hasn't come looking for you?"

"Probably because she thinks I died," Senna said. "Or maybe she *is* looking for me, but none of the knighthearts are brave enough to leave the Dam. But I agree that we have to finish what we started. Only now, we have to kill a canon."

"I thought you said Jasrath agreed to let you go? That's why you came here. He'd never hurt you in Laurentine's home," Lane cut in.

"It's not only about what he did to Percy. It's about what he did to Islevaria—to all of us." Senna tangled his fingers in Emrys'. "There's something I need to tell you all about. I didn't say anything before because . . ."

His gaze dropped to the floor.

Emrys kissed his hand. "You don't have to explain, sweetheart. We realize it's been hard."

"But you deserve to know. When Percy made his spirit visit, he shared—memories, I think. Broken, confusing memories, but they tell our history. The reason for the exile, the reason I was made goldheart, and the reason Jasrath wanted my power for himself. It's long and complicated, but it's important."

Thea opened her journal to a new entry. "Then by all means, go ahead."

So he told them what he had seen. He spoke and spoke until Emrys got up to get him a glass of water. He shared the memories in vivid detail until the sun sank under the valley and they had to light all the candles.

"Well," Thea began. She flipped a few pages to the beginning. "If we're going to stop Jasrath, I ought to tell you how it's done. First, what do you all know of a place called Caenia?"

I N A HOUSE WHERE they were around each other all the time, Thea prized the moments when she could be alone in her room. She could sit on her bed, look out over the dilapidated village, and no one would probe her for her thoughts. It was the one place she didn't have to pretend, even to her own friends.

Thea lay in her bed, eyes locked to a painting across the room. She wasn't really looking at it though. Her mind was too full with images of what Senna had shared.

"Knock knock."

Thea leaned up onto her elbow. Nare was standing in the doorway, silhouetted in her candlelight.

"Wasn't sure if you wanted more quiet time to yourself before I turned in."

"It's your room too," Thea said immediately. "You don't have to ask."

It wasn't Nare's presence that disquieted Thea. It was how comfortable she was around Nare that disquieted her. How she craved alone time and silence, but was unaffected by her roommate's loud footsteps and boisterous personality. If it had been anyone else snoring in the bed across from hers, she would have slept in the garden. But lately, if Nare *wasn't* snoring nearby, sleep was harder to wrangle.

They'd learned so much about each other while sharing this space. Thea had seen Nare undressed enough to know that she had a snaking string of moles on her back. Nare had seen Thea's skincare routine enough times to recount all the steps with perfect accuracy. It was natural, being near each other this way.

Nare sat on the edge of Thea's bed.

"Seems like there's a lot on your mind. Are you thinking about your mother?"

Thea flipped over so she could look at Nare fully.

"Somewhat. I've been considering my place in the world—where it actually is compared to where I thought it might be."

"Where's that?"

"I still don't know. But I think I've made peace with the fact that I might never live in the castle again. That I might never be princess again. Before it was all I wanted, but this has proven to me that I can feel worthwhile outside of my mother's approval."

"You *are* worthwhile outside of your mother's approval."

Thea pressed her lips together in a tight smile. "It's hard to remember sometimes."

Nare shifted uncomfortable. "I wish you could see . . ." She closed her eyes and started over. "I wanted to talk to you about something. I *have* wanted to talk to you about something. For a while now. I think it might help you see how worthy you are, but I don't want to tell you at a bad time."

Thea sat up. "Is it a bad thing?"

"No, I don't think so at all. It's—a different thing. It might upset our routine. Maybe the way things are. Between us."

At this, Thea sat all the way up, placing a hand on Nare's thigh.

"I appreciate the warning. It's true I don't like change, but you and I understand each other. I think it would take a lot to change our friendship."

"Well, that's just it. I—" Nare slid her hand underneath Thea's. "I'd like to change our friendship. Maybe I shouldn't be bringing this up when we share a room, in case it goes poorly. But surely, you've *noticed*—I mean, you're so smart—"

"I'm sorry," Thea interrupted. "I'm not sure I'm following."

Nare drew in a shaky breath, taking her time letting it out.

"You are one of the most spectacular people I have ever met. I truly mean I have never encountered someone so willing to seize their own happiness, to chase it with abandon. You know exactly what you want, and you swallowed your well-earned pride and asked for help from a stranger. You trusted me with one of your most dangerous secrets, and the honor of that gift is not lost on me. I admire you, Thea."

"That's really—but, I still don't—"

"Do you know what it is like to see a woman who is so brave-hearted and beautiful?"

"I have some idea," Thea said, still a little confused.

"Do you know what it does to *me*? I want to be around you all the time. I *care* for you. So much. As more than a friend."

To her credit, Thea did not pull her hand back. She did not want to. But she didn't want to be having this conversation either. She wanted to be near Nare, but she did not want to look at her right now.

Patiently, Nare waited for her to say something. Thea wanted to, she wanted to say whatever perfect thing could preserve what they had. Yet all of her words were ruin. She could taste the damage on her own tongue.

"I—" Thea stammered. "Nare . . ."

Nare drew back and Thea missed the warmth immediately.

"Wow, um, I really made a pig's ear out of this one, didn't I?" Nare said. "Now you have to sleep in the bed across from mine, which is just—a really shitty move on my part. Well done, Nare! I should just sleep in the hall, shouldn't I? I'll just grab my pillow and be on my pathetic, useless way—"

Thea snatched her hand before she could flee and pulled her back down.

"Sit," she said finally. "Please."

Nare sat. Thea wet her lips.

"You and I have talked about practically all there is to talk about, but never about—about this. About me." Thea drew Nare's hand into her lap and petted it, the motion somehow calming. "You know my inclination is toward women. What you don't know is that I am not quick to romantic affection. It comes, but rarely. But it only comes when I know someone's soul intimately. The connection required has to be profound. I cannot do casual affection, emotionally or physically." Thea released a breath. "I don't say this to discourage you. Quite the opposite. I think I'm halfway there—with you. But I need more time. I want to get to know you better."

"Great, I've got all the time in the world. The canons know I don't shut up," Nare said immediately.

"The only way this works is if you don't pressure me to go any faster than I can," Thea warned. "You can't change the way you interact with me. No flirting. No moony eyes."

"I always flirt with you," Nare scoffed lightheartedly. At Thea's glare, she lifted her hands in surrender. "Things will be so normal when you wake up, you may mistake this conversation for a dream."

"Good. Thank you."

Nare stood and shook out her hands. "If it's alright with you, I think I'll take a ramble around the village. I'm all adrenaline just now. I don't want to toss and turn all night and keep you awake."

Thea nodded. "Be safe."

Nare took two anxious steps toward the door, looked at Thea, and crumbled. "Okay. Okay I have to go. You better be asleep when I get back."

A fond smile lifted Thea's lips. "I'll try."

That night, Thea dreamt of their cottage. She felt weightless traveling through the dream space, walking up her imaginary porch and into the house. Her heels clicked on the hardwood floor. It was empty, just as it had been when she had first visited.

"Nare?" Thea called out. No reply. "Emrys? Senna?"

"Hullo, Thea."

Thea gasped, spinning around.

There, at Laurentine's desk, was Percy.

"I apologize for entering your dreams without permission, but I'm afraid I need your help," Percy said calmly. "I need you to get a message to Senna."

Thea blinked, still uncertain if this was real. "O-oh, of course. What is it?"

"That he needs to get some goddamn sleep," he said with a tired chuckle. "Because Percy, the canon of command, would like a word with him."

Thanks for reading!

I hope you've enjoyed *Goldheart*! If you liked this novel, the best way you can help out is by rating it and reviewing it on its Goodreads page.

You can also find me on Instagram or visit TessCarletta.com to sign up for my monthly newsletter to stay up-to-date on bookish news.

Writing this book was an undertaking like nothing I've ever completed before. It wouldn't have happened without the amazing support I received. I want to give a huge thank you to the following:

Erie Arts & Culture for supporting this project through the Lydia McCain Unrestricted Fund of the Erie Arts Endowment.

My editors Sam Willow of Scrollwork Edits and Rhiannon Martinucci. Thanks also to as my accuracy reader, Jaida McDonald and all the other incredible accuracy volunteers who offered their insights and voices, even though they didn't have to.

My dear friends from the Right Here, Write Queer podcast. Y'all are my lifeline and I love you so dearly.

My beta readers: Hannah D., Nina, Becca, Bronwyn, Grace M., Abby, Will Forrest, Deborah H., Kait, Toby Ennis, Laura Bear, Lu, Myra Limme, Heidi H, Bekah, Rachel Green, and others.

Those who supported this project on Kickstarter: Abi, Cecilie Knudsen, Aleks Michael, Ryan C., Chris Monceaux, Sierra Nicholes, Phoenix K., Kay M. Weston, Dimetri, Laura Bear, Pip, Stephanie Weigle, Lily Bui, Grace Montgomery, Briar Kingsley, Rosie Pregler, Marybeth Floyd, Victoria P., Lotti Dart, Becky, Ripley M., Elijah Cowles, Caroline Schroer, DK Kirik, June T Adria, KatieOlive, Tess B., Sunnie Shelstad, Luna Daye, Alana Savchuk, Heidi Hoffmann, Melita K., Guzbourine, Jen B, Hearting_NoOne, Heather Cash, Emm Walsh, EverAfterPrint, Myra Limme, Elizabeth Rathburn, Zen Sayer, Rachel S., Naomi Moramarco, Rachiel R., Becca, Julianne B., Liberty, Harlowe Savage, Vesta, Faith Dam, Thedion, Adriana Loughridge, Daunell Jean Barton, C Manning, Albert Cua,

Cherry Fox, Phoenix B., Ashley M., Lisa C-G, Rachel Emily, Alison Haas, Jessica Collins, Noelle, Joey Evergreen, Alistor H., Lauren Rose, Kupo, Fennigan R., Kaitlyn L., Wilbe, Shaelei, Manuel Q., Marine L., Jaida McDonald, Laora, Marzi, Kayden Persephone, Nicole Hoefs, Abigail W., Tim Sauke

...and readers like you! Thank you!